Scott Wellinger

Bestselling Author

CHRONO

Deni: Vol. 1

CHRONO

Deni: Volume 1

by scott wellinger

For my hometown.

Aspirations, hard work, and determination are not geographically specific.

Dream big Yellowjackets.

scott wellinger

the author of **CRASH** and Venom

Sinn

a warren dennihan prequel

Sinn

A warren dennihan prequel
By Scott Wellinger

PROLOGUE

TRAFFIC WAS A NIGHTMARE ON STORROW DRIVE. The Big Dig project had ensured that the entire city of Boston was a metropolis parking lot. It had been for years before and would continue to be for the foreseeable future. The colossal construction project had begun in 1991, after two decades of planning, to alleviate the very traffic it was causing. The undertaking was supposed to be finished in 1998, but six years after the due-date there was still no end in sight.

The two lanes headed west on Storrow were just as congested as the eastbound lanes. While those that were aimed west, away from the Interstate 93 ramp towards Harvard and MIT had the Charles River and the Esplanade to view on their right, those headed toward it had only the tall buildings of BackBay to study. The luxurious apartment buildings with back terraces overlooking the Charles were admired and fantasized over by everyone including the eastbound traffic, further taunted by the signage stating '*If you lived here you would already be home*'.

Along the Charles River was the jogging path, the Hatch Shell at the Esplanade where the outdoor movie and concert season had recently begun, and the crew teams rowing their way past the onlookers stuck in traffic. The early May weather was in the mid-to-upper sixties, though lightly raining as it had all spring. The joggers were plentiful in the sun-showers as their faith in the activity was rekindled by the annual Marathon that had taken place just a few weeks prior. The Boston Pops had just played the opening weekend for the Hatch Shell, and the U2 cover band *The Joshua Tree* was supposed to play the upcoming Saturday night. The eight-oared sweep racing shells were moving in the water past the four-wheeled deadlock like they were standing still. Because they were.

The pedestrian bridges that passed over the four lanes of halted traffic had graffiti reminding all who were trapped below of the Bambino Curse. While the city did long to reverse the curse, they wanted to reverse the traffic situation more. Little did anyone know that one of those two wishes would be granted later that year.

When traffic is halted to such an extent, virtually any motor vehicle violation is ignored by the Massachusetts State Police which patrol Storrow Drive. It was an unwritten rule for all of the arteries, not just Storrow. Pullovers in heavy traffic are hazardous to all parties involved. One can't speed, nor weave in and out of traffic when snails are moving past you. Derelict vehicles that overheat or cease to run are met with hand gestures and shouting, versus AAA or a tow truck because help simply can't get there. In truth, most troopers just sit on the side of the road or avoid the congestion all together during peak times. Nothing will make the already unbearable gridlock worse save for the flashing lights of a cruiser pulling over some poor slob.

The Probationary Trooper William LaDue did not receive the unwritten memo or message regarding discretion during traffic jams. He sat in his 2002 Ford *Crown Vic* patrol unit bored out of his mind.   His cruiser parked off of the curb under one of the graffitied footbridges, staring ahead at the park and the General George Patton statue that stood in it. There are only so many jog-bras and swinging ponytails one can stare at to pass the time. The occasional flick of the wipers to clear the rivulets off of the windshield in order to see said jog-bras. He couldn't leave, there was no place to go. The young go-getter had only been out of the academy for slightly more than ten months, had just gotten out on his own in-fact. He sat there alone wanting more than to babysit traffic. He decided to punch in the tag numbers of the vehicles that were not passing him. One such license plate caught his fancy.

The red, white and blue MA commercial plate had a DEC 04 expiration date. That was not the problem, the end of December was about eight months yet to come. What set off bells and whistles was the fact that the tag was registered for a dark, 1999, tourmaline metallic *Econoline E350*, yet it was attached to a brand new, white, 2004 Chevy *Express Cargo* van. Against conventional wisdom, Trooper LaDue decided to ring him up.

William turned on his lights and gave a long yelp from the siren on his cruiser to alert the squatters. Nobody moved, nobody could move. All hoped the new development didn't include them.

The cruiser continued up on the lawn, pulling next to the white van being sought in the right lane. There were two passengers, definitively, one in each of the bucket seats in the front. There were possibly more in the back, though there were no side windows in the utility vehicle to discern for certain. LaDue was alone in his cruiser, which meant he needed to call a backup cruiser. The situation was already a problem and getting worse.

The Trooper pointed to the passenger, then pointed to the lawn in front of his patrol vehicle. He then reversed his Crown Vic, allowing the van to jump the curb ahead of him. Only it didn't. The van didn't move. William engaged his loudspeaker.

"Pull up onto the curb and turn off your vehicle."

The hesitation was notable, but the request was eventually adhered to. The van slowly rode up the curb and onto the newly green park lawn from the combination of wet spring rain and sporadic sun. The gap the van created in the traffic was absorbed by vehicles who were all too eager to move the few short feet forward. The pullover was garnering attention from the pedestrians on the overpasses as well as the runners along the path. Something to occupy those who were stuck in traffic. But not too much. Just another day in the city.

Dispatch was giving the young trooper grief about the backup he was requesting, reminding him of the hour and traffic. As if he was unaware. LaDue was informed that a two-man cruiser was on route but to hang tight. In the meantime, he called out the tag number over the radio to dispatch in an effort to learn more information than what he could obtain from the screen in his vehicle.

"Dispatch, this is Romeo-two again. I've got a Mass tag November-7-8 4-5-Echo. Reads here as belonging to a dark blue 99 Ford, but I got it on a brand new white Chevy. What have you got?"

"Romeo-two, that tag is coming back stolen, along with the vehicle. Take caution, hold off. Backup is on route. Over."

"Roger-that."

Probationary Trooper LaDue was officially excited. Not only did he now have something to do for the remainder of his shift, a large portion of it at least, he now had a situation that was likely to be more involved than a mere traffic citation. He was told to wait for backup but he couldn't. Excitement got the better of him.

He exited his patrol vehicle and walked up the driver side of the van. He did so cautiously, looking into the large side mirror to get a visual on the driver while unsnapping the flap over his service weapon. LaDue was sure to stay tight to the van, making it that much more difficult for the driver to fire a shot of his own at a six o'clock angle versus a seven or eight. The Trooper would have told him to roll down his window, but it was already down. He called out to the driver from just behind his driver-side door.

"Reach both hands out of your window, and open your door from the outside. Slowly. Then step out of the vehicle."

"What is this about Officer? I couldn't have been speeding, we were at a stand-still," said the driver. He stuck out his hands but did not as yet pull on the black handle to his door.

"Just step out of your vehicle and we will get to that. How many passengers are in there with you?"

"One. And me." He pulled the outer handle and the door began to open slowly as instructed. "Don't you have to have a reason to pull me over?"

"And I do. Just tell your passenger to stay calm, you do as your instructed, and we will all get through this as calmly as possible."

The driver was about the same age as Trooper Ladue. Maybe not quite as old, which is to say that they were both barely old enough to rent a car. They weren't still using acne cream but they were still about half a decade from thirty. Once out of the van, the driver was pushed against it; his right cheek pressed into the white, metal side.

The trooper then quickly dodged to his left, looked into the van and came back out of view of the passenger. LaDue was right-handed so using his weapon would not be a possibility without exposing his torso, opening himself up for taking a bullet. He again called into the vehicle while putting handcuffs on the driver.

"Inside …. I need you to put your hands forward so I can see them and slowly climb over to the driver side toward me. Do just like your friend here did and this will go nice and smooth."

"Eat a dick!" The passenger then called out to his friend, "Hey Danny. I think this pig is alone. No backup."

The cuffed driver called back, "Little late for that now. We're smoked. Backup just pulled up." Another two-toned blue cruiser pulled up behind Ladue's. This one contained two State Troopers.

"Fuck!" The shout came from inside the van.

"Listen to your friend here and just come out nice and easy."

"Why'd you pull us over?" The passenger was still not over onto the driver's side, and LaDue was in the process of getting the driver to move to the back of van and sat down on the lawn by the road. He was not yet there when he heard it.

LaDue heard the passenger door to the van open and the word "GUN!" shouted. One of his backups had tried to apprehended the other occupant. Before the passenger could be pulled from the vehicle, he fired at the backup trooper. The return fire hit the passenger. Twice. The passenger fell out of the vehicle, his weapon kicked away, relieving him of it and sending him face-down onto the lawn in the process. Then, "Clear." An ambulance needed to called. The passenger was alive but bleeding badly. The process happened in the time it took for LaDue to get to the back of the van.

Once the situation was completely under police control and a short debriefing had occurred, LaDue then moved the driver next to his accomplice and were both told that they were pulled over because the tags did not match the vehicle. The passenger while bleeding and in pain had already been read his Miranda rights as he was picking up a weapons charge along with an attempt on an Officer. For now. That gave them probable cause to search each of them and their vehicle. The troopers started with the suspect's pockets, asking if they stuck their hands in their pockets were they going to get stuck with anything? Knife? Syringe? The driver was the only one who responded, answering 'no', so both of their pockets were emptied. The writhing passenger had no ID. He was pulled further away and was trying to be stabilized by one of the backup troopers. The Driver had a license that identified him as Daniel McKennie.

"What are we gonna find in the van, Daniel?" The protocol was that LaDue would handle this suspect. His stop, his collar, his show. Rookie or not, this was his bust.

"Nothin'. I wanna talk to Warren Dennihan. He is one-ah-you. Statie. Goes by Deni. You know him?"

"Mr. McKennie, are you calling in a get-outta-jail-free-card already? What are you afraid of? You can talk to me. You *should* talk to me. What's in the van?"

"I ain't sayin' nothin' else unless it's to Deni. Nothin'."

"Have it your way, son." Nobody pointed out the fact that the man-child trooper had just called his like-aged suspect 'son'.

The second backup trooper stood watch over Daniel and helped LaDue. The other backup was still questioning the as-yet unidentified passenger, while he tried to get the bleeding under control. His only responses were the repeated insults to the trooper on top of him. "Cocksucka" being the theme while he spit up blood. LaDue opened the back double-doors to the van. It was filled from the back doors up to the front seats with crates.

"I'm willing to bet that whatever is in these crates is not good for you Daniel."

LaDue used the lever end of a tire-iron from the back of the van, after getting help pulling one of the large crates out of it. When he opened it, he was both elated and astonished. The crate was filled with shredded paper as packing and modified Heckler & Koch *G3 Assault-4* rifles. The second backup was over his shoulder, just as stunned.

"Holy shit boys! It's redneck Christmas. Mother-load."

Part One

Metro Trailer Park
May 2004

1

I WAS RELATIVELY NEW TO THE TROOP H DETECTIVE UNIT of the Massachusetts State Police Department. It had been almost ten months, ten months exactly May 15th, when I was promoted from patrol. I was still responsible for Boston and Metrowest, but instead of sitting on the Mass Pike ticketing people trying to get to and from work I was doing something important. I conducted investigations for serious crimes against persons within a certain area of greater Boston. Those areas were well-defined, though sometimes in the course of an investigation there were pissing contests with either the Springfield or Worcester units.

Within the various troops, there were ranks that everyone sought to climb. The writing was on the wall for me, I was not going to climb any ladder. I was a Detective Junior Grade, purely by attrition, and that is how I would retire. The politics were obscene, the bullsh more than I could stomach. To be honest, rules aren't really my thing to begin with. Odd, I know, but sometimes what stands between me and the objective is a rule. I like to look at the big picture, the pencil pushers like to scrutinize over whether that picture is on Polaroid or Kodak paper.

So you could say that while I liked my work, I absolutely hated my job. You could say that because it was absolutely true.

I hated my boss, I hated my partner, and I hated the back-stabbing assholes that wanted my job. One would think that in law enforcement the job should be about justice. Justice for the people who were wronged, for the people of the City of Boston. But if you think that, you would be absolutely wrong.

What it was actually about, was politics. Who owed whom what favor, who knew which of their colleagues was dirty and what that damage could do if anyone were to find out. Those little tidbits of information won you chips in a big game that I wanted no part of.

So it was customary for cops to consult with other cops on cases. Information traded in exchange for get-out-of-jail-free cards. A collar wasn't a collar until someone from the DA's office was involved. Then other deals were made. Somehow the prisons and county lock-ups were full, but don't ask me how.

What wasn't customary was for me to be called in on one of these deals, which is exactly what happened on Tuesday May11th, 2004. I remember the exact day because the Tribe was at Fenway, and Pedro was scheduled on the mound. I had tickets, but of course I didn't get to go because of this nonsense that I am about to tell you.

It was 6:15 PM and I was at The House, ready to check out for the day and get over to Fenway for the seven-oh-five start-time. That's when the kid called my name, Warren Dennihan. Only everyone calls me Deni, so I could tell right off the jump that I probably didn't know who was calling me.

"Dennihan!" The Trooper calling me looked like he was fifteen years old.

"That's Detective Dennihan, who are you?"

"William LaDue. Trooper LaDue. I got a situation from a routine stop that went sideways, guys callin' for you."

"Oooooooh, you're Billy. The new kid. Billy the Kid, I heard about you. Real go-getter that went to Brown."

Normally I would never have heard of a new trooper, even in my own building which this kid was not. But LaDue was the talk of the Staties. He was from Rhode Island, really smart, and had gone to Brown University. You don't get too many smart guys who want to be a glorified meter-maid for the Commonwealth of Massachusetts State Police. So people talked. The rumor was that he was one of those do-gooder action junkies that thought this was a noble career and he would make a difference. I gave him a year, two at the most before he figured it out. Meanwhile his mom was probably real proud to pay top-dollar for an Ivy League education for a job that pays $35k a year if he is lucky enough to get overtime. But the Massachusetts State Police is the largest police force in New England, so if he had to be a cop at least he was in the Ivy League of shit jobs.

The kid tried to fit in because he was different. Most of the guys in the department were either ex-military or ex-crooks. Either way, none of us had gone to Brown so our options were far more limited than his. This kid could be anything he wanted to be, yet he took the job away from guys and girls who needed the opportunity. Nobody liked him because he was supposedly a silver-spooner, so he tried all the harder. He even put on the fake Boston accent, which was invented to be a strong as mine. He dropped his R's, making them sound like ah's, like 'ah' instead of 'are'. He added them when they didn't exist, like 'sar' instead of 'saw'. My accent, unfortunately, is real.

"Uh, yeah. That's me. Anyway, I got one Daniel McKennie that is in a real fix and all he wants is you. After we Miranda'd him, he didn't say he wanted a lawyer or nothin'. Fuckin' punk just wants you, guy."

"Enough with the accent before you hurt yourself. Did you say McKennie? As in little Danny Mick?"

"I didn't say 'Danny Mick', but yes. He is down in room six waiting to speak with you." Thankfully LaDue dropped the accent, but now he sounded like a preppy douche.

I knew Danny Mick from the neighborhood. I grew up and still lived in Southie. For those that don't know Boston, Southie is South Boston. It is a rough and tumble Irish neighborhood, full of projects and three-deckers, where you are a criminal or you don't have hair on your nuts yet. I dated his older sister, Roxy for a while. By date, I mean we wrestled naked in bed quite a bit back in the day. She was a hot-mess back then and rumor had it that she still was.

"Do you know why he wants to talk to me? What'd he do?"

"Van full of assault rifles. His partner pulled a piece on us. He died on the way to Mass General. My backup called it in so Detective Hobbs is already in the loop. His case now, so you'll have to get with him." The trooper's accent was back. I could see why he rubbed people the wrong way. He definitely pissed me off.

"Hobbs is already down there?"

"Yeah. He told me to find you, but I was gonna anyway cuz the kid's been askin' for you," LaDue said.

"You wouldn't know shit if it was in yer hand would ya? I thought you were supposed to be smart? Hobbs is already my partner. So my case now."

"Whatever. I told him I would find you, and I did. Good luck. Who lets me know where to show up for the trial? You?"

"Just get outta here, Billy."

"William."

The kid had the balls to stare me down. Standing your ground is something I admire. To a point.

"Hey Billy? Kick rocks will ya?"

16

When I had finally gotten rid of the eager beaver, I made my way to Interview Room Six. Outside the room on the bench was my partner, Detective Sergeant Rick Hobbs, the partner that outranked me that I couldn't stand.

Rick Hobbs was the kind of guy that after being with him for twenty minutes, you would actually be so irritated that choking a baby was deemed a plausible outlet for your anger, though obviously not appropriate. Only I had to spend way more than twenty minutes with the bag o'douche, I had to spend a minimum of five days a week with him attached to my hip. He was the know-it-all, holier-than-thou type that never made a mistake. Arrogance is fine, except that he screwed up all of the time and blamed everyone else for his fuck-ups. He was so self-absorbed that he probably liked the smell of his own shit. Other than that he was okay.

"There he is. Where ya been, Deni?"

"I was gonna file my fives before goin' to the game. Pedro is pitchin' tonight."

"Why bother? The Sox do great every year until the All-star break, then they suck their way out of the division. Yankees will be in the World Series again this year, mark my words. Sox will be lucky to get the Wild Card."

"Yeah well, it's a marathon not a race and it woulda been really nice to catch the game. Whatta we got?"

"Spiv by the name of Daniel McKennie. Only twenty-four and he's got a sheet as long as my fuckin' arm. Got caught with his dick in a pig. Ten cases of assault rifles in a brand new stolen van with stolen plates from yet another stolen van. Address puts him in Southie, probably in a triple-decker. You know that neighborhood, it's a metro trailer park. They infest the area like cockroaches. Anyways, he says he knows you and I assume he wants a walk. I don't see it happen'n partner."

"We've been workin' together, what? Ten months right? How is it you don't know I come from Southie? What am I now? Trailer trash?"

"I remember you live there. I make it that's how you know this mutt."

"I used to date his sister, that's how I know him. And just watch your mouth. If things woulda gone different aways back, maybe I woulda been with him. Maybe drivin' the van."

"Whatever. He could be your kid for all I give a shit. But there's no way he walks on this, no matter who you're bangin'."

"I'm not gonna get into it with ya, Rick. Just gimme some time with tha kid, huh? No microphone, no video, just me and him. We good?"

"Knock yourself out. He's snagged, confession or not."

I went into room six and the kid was sitting in his chair, stoic and handcuffed. I removed my sport-jacket and placed it on top of the microphone in the center of the table and took my seat across from him. I knew what Rick agreed to and I also knew what he was capable of. Not a big trust factor between us.

"Got yourself all jammed up here Danny."

"Are we alone or are they watchin' on tha other side a tha mirror?" His accent was a bad as mine. Maybe worse. You tend to run into that in Southie. Get two of us together with an outsider as a bystander and they will tell you that we are speaking a different language, because what comes out of our mouths doesn't sound like english. I probably didn't have to cover up the microphone in retrospect.

"Yeah, just us. But I'm not sure what I can do for ya, kid. You're pretty fucked."

"What am I gonna do, Deni? Slopes is gonna shit a cow, man."

"Aaaah, Danny. Slopes? What did he get you into? Guns?"

He nodded his head. "G3s."

In the thirty-seconds I had spoken to Danny, I had already sized up what was going on. Everybody from Southie has a nickname. When you live twelve to twenty people in one three-family three-decker, you get a neighborhood with a ton of people with the same name. It's called a three-decker, or triple-decker as the non-locals called it, for the complicated reason that there is an entire community of houses with three ascending decks. The houses are practically attached to each other, side by side, the style exactly the same. A basement with three floors built up on top, each floor a different apartment, all having decks both front and back.

The Irish-Catholic community in Southie isn't devout by any means, but they follow the 'no form of birth control' rule. Nicknames were the only way to tell us all apart. Even if you were the one and only, like Warren Dennihan, you still got a nickname. Sean Teague was the given name to Slopes.

In Southie, there are probably fifty Sean Teagues. Slopes got his name because he is one of the rare cases where the disease Bell's Palsy became permanent. Either it wasn't diagnosed quickly enough or an antibiotic wasn't given soon enough, or he didn't take it. In any case the side of his face drooped like it was sliding off his face. He was very sensitive about it, but that didn't stop the nickname. Slopes was a boss for the Irish mob.

Back in the 70s, former IRA 'Volunteer' Patrick Nee came to the US and became a leader with the Mullen Gang. They then went to war against the Killeen Brothers gang over Boston turf. James J. Bulger was the boss of the KB crew back then, he got a nickname too - Whitey. When it was all said and done, the Mullens and Killeens joined the Howie Winter gang, because their war depleted the two gangs to a point where they couldn't survive. When Howie Winter went to jail in '79 for rigging horse races over at Suffolk Downs, Bulger took over the whole shah-bang. The Winter Hill Gang became the biggest confederation of organized crime in the east after the Irish Gang War. In '94 Whitey Bulger went into hiding because he turned FBI informant, but his crew was still doing business without him. They were still bookmaking and loansharking, which were some of the least horrible things they did. The Winter Hill Gang had made the papers recently because they held a bunch of no-show jobs on the Big Dig. They had formed a dummy corporation called the C. Dáil Corp., which James Kerasiotes of the Mass Turnpike Authority awarded a contract without a bid. They got paid for literally nothing. No wonder the Big Dig project was long over the deadline and over budget.

Danny telling me that he had a cargo van full of Heckler & Koch *G3A4s* meant that they were still smuggling guns for the IRA. Those guns were one of the types of the signature weapons used by the IRA in any cause they engaged in. It also meant Slopes had a come-up and was now Mr. Big in Boston. Bottom line was that those guns were going to be paid for in one way or another, which ultimately meant that Danny Mick was fucked in the permanent sense. Prison was the least of his worries. Danny didn't want me to get him out of the hoosegow, he wanted me to get him square with Slopes.

All of the information came to me in just a few sentences, and it took me almost no time at all to connect the dots. I felt for the kid a little bit. As the gentrification had begun in Southie, yuppies taking over our neighborhoods, increasingly fewer legitimate opportunities were available to make a living. I caught a break when I was kid which allowed me to extricate myself from that life without leaving the neighborhood. I was one of the few lucky ones. Danny was on a different path. With more affluent kids like young Billy buying houses, taking over the neighborhoods, and taking the decent jobs, there would be more like Danny getting classed out.

"Jesus Danny. How many G3s?"

"Two hundred."

"And your boy tried to shoot a cop? Why didn't you just take off? Try and dust the rookie who pulled you over?"

"Ya tellin' me? Gridlock on Storrow. Nowhere to run."

"I hate to add insult, but which of you two geniuses decided to move it all during peak traffic? On Storrow of all fuckin' things?"

"Big Dig redirected us. Slopes told us the pickup and drop times."

"Well then he's the idiot. No reason to move that much hardware during broad daylight in rush hour. What's really going on here?"

"No clue, man. I just did what I was told. We got fucked cuz of tha tags. Cops don't usually do pullovers in traffic. Nobody was more shocked than me to see tha fuckin' cruisa flick his lights."

19

"Fair enough. You were unlucky enough to get the one go-getter with a badge. But still …."

"So what do I do? I'm a dead man. If I PC, they'll think I ratted. If I don't I'll be on the business end of stabbing. You gotta talk to him for me, Deni. He knows you."

PC meant Protective Custody while he was awaiting trial. And he was right. It would actually be easier to kill him while incarcerated than it would out on the streets.

"I'll see what I can do, but I'm not makin' any promises. If Slopes is runnin' the mob crew here which runs guns for the IRA, I might not even get the chance to talk to him. I'm a cop and everyone within 30 blocks of the neighborhood knows it. He's gonna be pretty insulated. I don't even know where he is these days."

"He never sits anywhere for more than a minute. Go see my sister. She'll get you to him. Please Deni. You gotta help me."

"No I don't. I told you I would have a chat, but it ends there. How does your sister know where he is?"

"Just you and me talkin' here? She gets her junk direct."

"You know the shit I'm gonna take if my partner or my boss hears that I'm runnin' around trying to save your ass? Where were these guns goin' anyway?"

"In the end? I got no idea. I just go from point A to point B when I'm told. Somebody else was gonna move'em later. I'm not exactly high up the food chain ya know."

"My point."

"What's your point, Deni?"

"I shoulda gone to the game, that's the point."

2

GETTING RID OF MY PARTNER, RICK HOBBS, WAS QUITE THE CHORE. He was nothing but questions once I was finished chatting with young Danny Mick. I didn't know if he had watched the conversation through the glass in the observation room or not, but he seemed to not know what was said. He was all about if Danny confessed, where the guns were going, where they had come from, and the like.

Everywhere I turned he would be there asking me another question, practically dry-humping me up one hall and down the next one. I didn't like the guy anyway, but at that point I was ready to strangle him. I was already in a bad mood for missing the Sox game. The situation was made worse by the fact that I had to see a girl I used to sleep with back in the day, in order to find a mobster who was probably going to kill the guy I had just spoken to, because he had lost two hundred assault rifles. I really didn't need my partner nagging at me as a topper.

Hobbs knew that I knew all of these hoods and racketeers. I grew up with them. Hell I still lived near them. The entire department knew that I had a relationship with these hooligans, I had been hired specifically for the intel. When I wouldn't go undercover after completing the academy, for what I thought were obvious reasons, they sent me to watch traffic on the Pike. That was the main reason I would never get any further in the department. The higher-ups had long memories and I didn't play politics, so my fate was sealed.

At the age of thirty-two, I was younger than my partner who was a decade my senior. I was in exponentially better physical condition as well but age had nothing to do with it. The old cliché about cops eating donuts was brought to life with Rick Hobbs. But not just donuts. If the foodstuff involved massive amounts of preservatives and fat, he loved it in mass quantities. It is my personal feeling that clogged arteries also clog up blood-flow to the brain. Does that mean that all fat people are stupid, of course not. What I'm saying is that if you are a guy who is not working with a ton of brain power, lack of blood to the noggin is an added hurdle that is ill-afforded. I'm no genius by any stretch, but I would bet the ranch that I would beat him in anything from arm-wrestling to a spelling bee.

"Hobbs! Enough already. I just want to finish my shit and maybe catch the back end of the game, okay?"

"I'm your goddamned senior partner and you never treat me like we're a team. What did he say? Where were the guns goin'?"

"What are you, a broken record? 'What did he say? .... What did he do? .... Where were the guns goin'? .... Why do I have a small penis?' It gets old. I told you I was going in there alone to talk to tha kid. We talked. Case closed. He wasn't lookin' for a walk, he just wanted to talk about the neighborhood. He knows he is goin' away for a long time, and we didn't need a confession. So for the last time, back .... the .... fuck .... off. Any of this gettin' through?"

"I still outrank you last I checked, but have it your way. We're gonna be boxed out anyway. With that kind of hardware, the ATF will be down here first thing."

"They have all the fun don't they? Alcohol, Tobacco *and* Firearms is like the trifecta. Booze, guns and stogies sounds like a good time to me. So you think they will show up in the morning to haul away the lot?" I played stupid. I didn't care either way, to be honest. But he was right. The ATF would want the case especially because it was a lay-up. Maybe the FBI would want in also.

"Guns and the van are already down at ballistics in Maynard, they will probably let us analyze and run them through the database, but they will take over the investigation."

The crime lab for Massachusetts was located in the western part of the state, about an hour away off of route 62 in the town of Maynard. They investigate; blood work, for DNA and toxicology; hair fibers and skin; weapons and ballistics. It was our CSI lab. In this case they would completely strip down the van for fibers or trace evidence that could lead to other suspects involved in the gun trafficking. They will also examine every weapon to determine its origin, who has used it, and if the weapon had been used in any other documented crime. Fingerprints and ballistics would take some time and since Maynard was the only lab in the state, there was a back-log.

"Well good for them. Tie it up with a bow and get it off our case load," I said. Hobbs was following me back to my desk. Our desks.

"They are gonna want to trade him in for a bigger fish, Deni."

"I'm sure."

"Sooooo .... "

"So what?"

"Who is your little friend working for? You want me to put a bow on it? Give me the ribbon."

"Do you ever sing a different tune?" I faked sign language and enunciated extremely slowly in the hopes that he would finally get the fact that I was not going to give him Slopes. "I .... don't .... know .... who .... he .... is .... working .... for. He knows he's going away for a long time and I used to bang his sister. He wanted me to talk to her, say goodbye and that he is sorry. Do you honestly think he would tell a cop who he is working for? Surest way to get clipped is to give up his boss. He's well-trained. He'll do his time like a man and shut his cock-holster."

"You must know who he runs with. He is from your neighborhood. Winter Hill Gang? Gotta be, right?"

Exasperated, I sat on my desk dropping my fives in my to-do pile and focused on the pain in the ass partner standing before me.

"You're not my boss. You're my senior partner and I don't know how to say it any different. You keep askin', I keep tellin', but nothin' sticks to that meat between your ears. I don't know. But let's say that you are right, he is workin' for the Winters. What in the holy fuck are you gonna do about it? They been doin' business in this city for a long-ass time. They survived the gang-wars, Federal RICO Task Force .... but you? You think that you are gonna rid the city of them when you can't understand the simple concept of 'I don't know anything more than you do'. How does that play?"

"Why do you always protect them?"

"What are you talkin' about now, Hobbs?"

"You know that metro trailer park like the back of your hand. You know who is doing what five steps before they do it. You could be a goddamned hero. Just go down there and scoop up the whole crew. But instead you let them do whatever they want and you cover for them."

"Let me ask you somethin'. Is that what you think this is? Me covering for a kid in the neighborhood? Covering for 'my people'? You've got some set on you, Hobbs. There have been probably a million man-hours spent tryin' to bring these guys down, and while they get a couple of the dregs, the mob keeps truckin' along. But let me spell somethin' out for you. Where do all of those nickel and dime crooks go if the overlords go down? Disorganized chaos. You think all of those guys are gonna just go out and get a job? No fuckin' way. They go into business for themselves and crime actually gets worse. Those bodegas that are currently under protection are fair game. Pawn shops sprout up all over to take place of the loan sharking. Drugs are on every corner instead of specific ones through the Winters. Or worse? New York and Rhode Island guinea crews move in and pick up the slack. There is no eliminating them, Hobbs. You just try and control it the best way you can."

"So you cover for the kid?"

"I'm done. I got nothin' more to say to you. It's not our case anymore anyway, you just said. You don't get to be a hero on this one. Just give it to the ATF or FBI or whatever and move on."

"I'm gonna request a new partner."

"I've heard that before too. Let me know how it goes."

Hobbs stormed away from me, away from our desks which unfortunately faced each other. The desk farm that was the Troop H Detective Unit was set up in one large room with desks that were like a Tetris puzzle. There were no partitions or cubicles, that was deemed as counterproductive and obstructed teamwork. All partners had desks that were facing one another, not just Hobbs and me. I was thankful that he had decided to walk away instead of having to face him while I finished the work that should have been completed hours prior.

I removed the fives that I had to finish from my to-do pile. Fives are what detectives call the DD-5 form that must be submitted on active cases. My boss, Lieutenant Manny Titanitaukis (who we call Lieu to his face and Tits behind his back), is little more than a case manager. He has to manage our share of the 2,000 homicide cases, 9,000 rape allegations, 75,000 armed robberies, 125,000 reported assaults, 130,000 auto thefts involving a carjacking, and countless other felonies that get called-in every single year. Troop H handles most of the cases since we are responsible for crimes against persons in greater Boston, but the local stations and other departments handle a good many as well. Tits needs to file his own paperwork to keep his bosses apprised of which cases are solved and which are pending. We have to submit a form, the DD-5, for each development on each case that we handle.

I was behind on my paperwork. I was originally going to just submit the fives that Tits was having a fit over and head to the game, but it was now after 9:00 PM which meant that by the time I got over to Yawkey Way the game would be over. So I decided to hunker down and finish all of my outstanding paperwork. Tickets wasted.

The realization that the date that I was supposed to bring to the game, the one that I didn't go to, hit me like a ton of bricks. I pulled out my new Motorola *V3 RAZR* flip-top cell phone and saw what I already knew. Fifteen missed calls and twenty-two unread text messages. My ass was grass.

3

I WOKE UP ON WEDNESDAY MORNING ALONE, which was not what I had been planning when I bought the very hard to come by tickets to Fenway. I had been planning my personal opening day game for the 2004 season for a couple of weeks. I had been seeing this girl, Jill, for a while and had promised her we would go. I say promised because we had been down this road before, just not with tickets to the Red Sox. She made me say over and over again that we would definitely go see Pedro throw filth at the Indians. But in fairness, maybe not in those exact words.

She had not answered any of my phone calls last night when I realized that I was more than two hours late in picking her up. I decided against calling her again that morning. For one, I get up at 5:00 AM to go work out and then to The House and, two, she was likely still really pissed and/or sleeping with someone else. I decided instead to listen to the voicemails from the night before telling me what a shit-bag I am while I made coffee. I would have read the stored texts also but I had no idea how to on the new phone. I don't even know why she sent them because she knows my feelings about them, and I definitely never send texts because I have a bitch of a time using the numbers to type in one of the three letters on each button I want for each and every word.

By the time the Dunkin' Donuts coffee was brewed, I had been thoroughly dressed down as the calls went from concern to tears to vulgarities and anger. Needless to say I deleted them. Maybe there would be a forthcoming conversation, maybe not.

I grabbed The Globe. It said that it was going to be sixty-five and sunny. Finally a nice day. I then pulled out the sports section. The Sox won, 5-3 to an always sold-out stadium and now had a 20-13 record. *Dammit.*

The gun bust didn't make the front page, above or below the fold. Didn't even make the police log buried in the small print. I thought that odd. Instead, the front cover was a follow-up about the US bodies that were hung by Iraqis off the bridge in the Sunni Triangle the previous March. They were apologizing for the controversy surrounding the graphic pictures they had used on a story printed in late April. To be honest, I hate that newspaper. It's a rag owned by the New York Times, and I hate Nuevo York. But the Herald is worse.

After the morning shower and putting on the off-the-rack suit from Filene's Basement in Downtown Crossing, I went out to the street to find what was left of my car. My two-door silver Pontiac *Grand Am* a-la 2001 was, for lack of a better term, fucked up.

I had bought the car new in silver because silver tends to hide scratches. When you live in the city, parking is a nightmare. If you are lucky enough or rich enough to park in a lot, the cars are so tight that you need a can opener to get it out. The doors get dinged super-easily and daily. Mostly, you have to park on the street which means that you get love-tapped on both bumpers pretty much daily as well.

The car that was left for me was not love-tapped or dinged. The tires were slashed, all of them, and the only remaining glass was in shards on the inside of the car. Upon closer inspection, my Blaupunkt car stereo with no-skip CD player was gone. It was supposed to have had an anti-theft system also but that had obviously failed. I knew better when I bought the damned thing. When I was a kid, stealing car stereos was my bread and butter. There was no such thing as anti-theft. The manufacturers use the term to charge more for them.

I didn't realize Jill was *that* pissed. So I missed a few dates, welshed on a few promises. She was a hundred and fifteen pounds soaking wet, there was no way she did that on her own. Maybe my stereo was payment for the job. Maybe she was the payment.

The car was a piece of shit anyway but it meant that I wouldn't be going to spar and I would need to take the train into work. I would also have to rec out an unmarked from the motor pool which was going to be a royal pain in the ass. All in all not a great way to start my day.

After the 'HELLOMOTO' was gone from the screen after flipping open my cellphone, I called my partner to tell him what had happened and that I was going to be late. He actually sounded relieved to not have to deal with me for a couple of extra hours and I can't say that I was distraught about that part of it either. He didn't offer to come pick me up, let's put it that way.

With the extra time to kill before I could catch the Silver line to the Red Line on the MBTA Ⓣ system, I thought it a good time to go see Roxy. Danny Mick's sister. It was early and she was probably still drunk and partying, but why not? Last I knew she didn't work nor did she have any plans to.

Roxanne McKennie, or Roxy, still lived in the same three-decker that she grew up in. Only she now lived on a different floor. Like almost everyone in that neighborhood, you either moved out to a different floor of the same building, or you moved in with someone else who was on a different floor of their same building. Roxy had moved out and back in so many times that her parents weren't able to rent out the top floor in the likelihood that she would be back. This was one of those 'she was back' times.

The rickety wooden stairs that went up to the third floor to Roxy's place sounded and felt like I was going to fall through them. It was a good thing she didn't weigh much if she had to negotiate these stairs every day. I was a lot younger when Roxy and I had dated, so I was going in the front door on the first floor back then. The creaking and whining of the stairs must have alerted her to my presence because she was waiting for me at the landing at the top of the third floor.

"Warren Dennihan. To what do I owe the honor of your fuckin' presence?"

It was a bad split and she was obviously still not a fan. But looking at her, I was validated in my decision to break it off because she looked terrible. She was thirty and looked like every single one of those years was hard. She was once very pretty, or at least I thought she was back then.

"Hey Roxy. You look, eh, good?" I said it more like a question, which she registered.

"Go fuck ya self." She said it in a way that only Boston women can say it. A way that strips a man of everything he is, down to his bones. Emasculating just doesn't quite say it.

"C'mon Rox. Take the high road. I gotta talk to you about Danny Mick."

I reached the top of the stairs by then but she wasn't letting me onto the landing where she was standing, which put her waist by my face. I was looking up to her pleading my case.

"Seriously, let me in so we don't have to do this in public."

"What? You afraid that somebody might see you slummin'?"

"I still live down here, Rox. I don't wanna do this the hard way, just let me in. Your brother said that you would talk to me."

"My brother don't know shit about shit. What did he do now? If you're looking to bust him, he don't live here. Try downstairs."

"He's in lock-up, so I'm not lookin' for him. He sent me to talk to you. Are you gonna let me in or what?"

"You're a cop, ya cocksucka. Go get a warrant."

"I don't need a warrant. I'm not backdoorin' ya here, Rox. I'm tryin' to help the poor prick. He's in a lotta shit, hun."

"So whatever you find in here you can't use against me?"

"Are you gonna shoot at me? Stick me with somethin'? No? Then I think we're good."

She let me inside and it was a complete dumpster-fire. To say that she wasn't much of a housekeeper would be the understatement of all understatements. I don't think the place was rentable if she did move out for good. If the lower two floors were in the same condition, the best thing to do would be to watch it burn and collect the insurance.

"I love what you've done with the place. Jesus, what is that smell? Open a window or somethin' would ya?"

"The king has spoken. You gonna pay my heat bill? Open a window he says."

"It's sixty-five degrees outside and not raining for once. It might actually be warmer outside."

"You come up here to give me decorating tips Martha Stewart, or you gonna tell me what my brother did?"

"Enough with the attitude, smart-ass. I mean it. I'm in no fuckin' mood. He got busted yesterday moving half an arsenal for Slopes. ATF is gonna be all over the kid today or tomorrow to give up the goods. If he went over or was plannin' on goin' over state lines the FBI might want to get a foot in. Wherever those guns were going, they ain't gettin' there. Slopes is gonna be none to happy as it is, so he gets word that Danny Mick spoke with cops? It's gonna get a damn-sight worse."

"So what are you gonna do for him mister hot-shit?"

"You're gonna tell me where to find Slopes so I can try and reason with the guy. Maybe keep a shiv outta your brother's belly. He does his time and keeps his trap shut, he lives to be an old man. With a little luck, someday a free old man."

"And what do you get? You doin' this outta the kindness of your heart or do I gotta suck you off or somethin'?"

"You're a real class-act, Rox. Top shelf kinda girl. Tha fuck happened to you?"

"You, ya piece of shit. You chewed me up and spit me out. You don't like what you see? Look in a mirror."

"Don't put your shit on me. We were like a million years ago. I boosted shit, which made you get all hot and bothered. We rolled around and had a few laughs but that was pretty much it. I put that crap behind me, but I never forgot where I came from. I might not have been man of the year with you, Rox, but whatever you became ain't on me. You were never an angel but this goin' the extra mile. Just tell me where to find Slopes and I'll leave you to get junked up or whatever it is you do."

Quips and snappy digs at me were over. She was a sobbing mess. It might have been what I said, but more likely I was a reminder of what could have been for her. She had a choice when I broke it off with her forever ago. That choice was to get out of the life if not the neighborhood, or get sucked down into it. At thirty years old it was not too late. But she thought so, and that realization was painful.

I felt bad, but not bad enough to console her. Not bad enough to give her a hug and lie to her, tell her everything would turn out aces. Not bad enough to even sit down in that mess. I stood in front of her like an idiot waiting for her to get a grip. It seemed to take a while.

"Rox? Where do I find Slopes?"

28

Her midnight makeup from the night before was running off of her face. She looked through me not at me. "Abandoned warehouse down on Wash. I don't give a shit what happens to you, but don't go down there like a storm troopa. For Danny's sake."

"Yeah sure. I know. Try to take better care of yourself, Rox."

"Don't come back here Deni. Ever."

4

THE CALL TO DETECTIVE HOBBS INFORMING HIM that I was going to be later than I had expected went over without much fuss. Which was a shocker because he always wanted to be attached to my hip. If he had an inkling of what I was doing, he didn't say it. I couldn't perceive even the slightest of notes that he cared one way or the other what I was doing. Maybe he was requesting a new partner, but we had been down that road a few times in ten months. I was still his partner so we know how that played out.

I hadn't initially planned on going to see Slopes that morning. I hadn't planned on seeing Roxy that morning either, but there was no time like the present. If, in fact, the ATF was going to talk to Danny Mick that day or the next, I thought it best to discuss the situation with Slopes before hand. Better to be proactive than reactive, sorta thing. The ball was rolling, so this last errand would hopefully end my to-do list with this project.

The abandoned warehouse on Washington Avenue looked like it was a squatter's paradise. The realtor sign said that it was going to be converted into lofts but it didn't say when. That sign was covered in graffiti so either the development was postponed, out of business, or it was just wishful thinking. The windows were boarded up but there was no door preventing an easy access.

I walked right in like I owned the place. But I was glad I didn't own it. Rats were having their way with the first floor. It was difficult to see with everything being boarded up, but I assumed they were rats given the sounds. The sun outside was shining bright for a change, but not enough to provide light inside the derelict building. The sound of the movement of the critters alluded to the fact that they were many and enormous.

The Big Dig was displacing all of the rats in Boston. Tunnels and bridges were being built to send traffic under or over the city to alleviate surface road traffic. Those tunnels were where the rodents lived and had been forced out among the two legged infestation. It got to a point where restaurants in the city were having to buy cats to roam their establishments at night. Exterminators could not keep up with the number of sightings and were ineffective when they did treat. This Chinese restaurant that I frequent has three enormous cats that they let roam the restaurant at night when the place is closed. They are the biggest domesticated cats that you have ever seen in your life outside of the jungle cats you see at the zoo. The owners never feed them.

Making my way in the dark as my eyes adjusted, I was halted by a man carrying a sawed-off shotgun. He didn't have to pump it for me to know that I was in trouble. I wouldn't be able to get to my holster and retrieve my weapon before being filled with holes.

"Wrong way cop."

I raised my hands in surrender. "No need to get all cranked up. I came alone."

"Maybe yes, maybe no. Either way you need to turn around and be on your merry way, for you get tuned up."

"I need to talk to Slopes. It's urgent."

"He ain't takin' calls at the moment."

"Even if I were to say that it's about the 200 G3s that are about to be turned over to the ATF?"

There was a pause. The only sounds were the rustling of the rats and the gears in the man's brain grinding, working on a thought. I could barely see him but I wanted to get a read. I didn't get one. Nor could I tell if he was the only person in front me.

"I'm listenin'," he finally said.

"I'm sure that I have your attention, but I need to talk to Slopes. He knows me."

"Everyone knows you. Like I said, he ain't takin' calls. You could be Jesus himself and he wouldn't see you right now."

"I'm going to reach into my jacket pocket for a business card, my cell number is on it. Will you give it to him? It's extremely important that I talk with him."

"Wicked slow muthafucka."

I slowly pulled out one of cards that were loosely strewn about the inside pocket of my suit jacket. They were always in there. I sent my suits to the cleaners after every third time I wore them and always forgot to take them out. I have no idea what dry cleaning is, but those cards never get damaged.

The card was extended out in front of me between my index and middle fingers. The armed security man moved through the dark building toward me and took the card. He didn't say another word, nor did I. The awkward silence was palpable and I read the situation like that was the end of the meeting, so I turned and left.

Outside of the building I flipped open my phone, dialing my partner after my eyes adjusted back to the bright sunlight.

31

"Hobbs, Deni here."

"I know, I can see that it's you on my caller ID. What's up? Are you coming in at all today?"

"Yeah, I'm not too far away. I'm — "

" — you're on Wash, yeah I know. I see you. I'm parked up on the corner."

I was stunned and speechless. I turned to my right and then left to discern where my ambusher was lurking.

He flashed the headlights on the unmarked 2003 Dodge *Intrepid* that he had obviously pulled from the motor pool. We normally use my *Grand Am* to get around as it is less conspicuous. The *Intrepid* was dark blue and although not a Crown Vic, it still screamed police car. I looked behind me to make sure that the thug whom had just received my business card didn't see that I had police company, or Hobbs and I would both be dead men.

I hightailed it down the block toward my partner. Seventy-five yards later I was seated in the passenger seat.

"Were you following me?"

"I thought we were partners. But I guess after your conversation with your buddy last night, you decided to take this case over on your own."

"You're kind of a one-trick-pony aren't ya Hobbs? Same thing all the time. We don't have a case to take over. I told you last night, he wasn't askin' for a walk or for any favors other than to talk with his sister. Did you follow me over to her place this morning?"

"The crack-den? Yeah I saw it. Cozy."

"How long have you been staking me out? Did you see who fucked up my car last night?"

"No. That wasn't a lie to buy time this morning?"

"Forget it. Just get us outta here before we get killed."

"And this morning's conversation with one Roxanne McKennie led you to an abandoned warehouse down here on Wash?" He pulled out from his pseudo-parallel parking job and continued up Washington Street. We were headed toward the Theatre District and Chinatown.

"That conversation produced the concern that whomever her brother was involved with might be just a tad-bit upset that the guns are now under the control of the police. That her brother might be in danger. I wanted to see if I could try and protect him."

"Jesus H. Christ Deni. Who's side are you on? This is textbook interference with an ongoing investigation. The only way to protect him is to keep him quiet. Keeping Daniel McKennie quiet keeps Sean Teague and the mob in business and is completely against what we are trying to do here. You know as well as I do that the only play here is to put your friend into protective custody in exchange for his flippin' Mr. Big."

32

Hobbs had just slipped up. He already knew that Danny Mick was working for Sean Teague, A.K.A. Slopes. He had just said so. What I didn't know was if he had already known that because he listened in to the conversation I had in room six, or if he knew that the abandoned warehouse on Wash was where Slopes was temporarily headquartered.

"First of all, the suspect is not my friend. Second, how long have you known that this was an Irish thing? "

"How stupid do you think I am? We're in the South End, just on the other side of the Channel from Southie. G3A4s are like the Irish calling-card. Your metro trailer park is to the mob what Pawtucket is to the Red Sox. Nothing happens in Boston involving the Irish without Sean Teague knowing or planning it. The question is what are *you* doing?"

"I'm getting out of the way while, according to you, the ATF takes over. Danny Mick getting stabbed in prison does nobody any good. He's not gonna flip on his crew, whoever it is he works for."

"Don't bullshit me Deni. You and I both know who you just saw in there. Is he 'not your friend' too?"

"As usual I don't know what you're talkin' about and I didn't see anyone in there. Pull a bitch and go see if there's anyone in there if ya don't believe me."

"I'm not turning around, we're almost outta Chinatown."

"Where are we headed?"

"Temple. We caught another case."

I tuned the car stereo into 100.7 WZLX, the classic rock station. Hobbs protested but I turned up the volume so I couldn't hear him. Queen's *Another One Bites the Dust* blared out of the tinny speakers. I hoped Freddie Mercury was wrong.

5

WITH THE THOUSANDS OF CASES THAT COME INTO TROOP H every year, Detectives have dozens of cases going simultaneously. Real life isn't like *Law & Order* where you see cops going from place to place talking with witnesses or tracking down leads on one case at a time. In the real world, Boston anyway, we have to plan our day so we aren't jumping all over the city all day.

Traffic is always bad, with the city-wide construction it's that much worse. The Big Dig will have you re-routed one way on this day, and then you are forced onto a completely different route the next. You could never plan on how long it would take you to get from place to place. If you were going to be in one borough of Boston, you tended to stay there for the day.

If we were on one side of the city, say Dorchester, we took care of all of our cases and made all of our stops that needed to be made in Dorchester. It saved on time and it saved on gas. With the conflict in the Middle-east that was making the headlines every day, oil prices were always on the rise. Gas was getting to be a concern for everyone, especially the pencil-pushers in the Staties.

The general public gets crazy when they read in the paper or see in the news that an error by the police has led to the release of an accused criminal. I'm actually surprised it doesn't happen more. Juggling statements from several different witnesses on several different cases in the same day; investigating leads simultaneously, sometimes we mix stuff up. Or lose them all together.

It was almost the middle of May and my partner and I had already caught over three hundred cases so far that year. Some of them were closed, most were not. You have to prioritize. It sounds horrible but some things just never get investigated. Murders and rapes are top priority while others just don't ever see the top of the pile.

Take what happened to my car for example. I'm a cop and nobody cares what happened to the *Grand Am*. What do you think happens when Cindy Citizen calls in to her local precinct? That one incident involved multiple crimes. Vandalism 1 and Larceny over. Which meant that the value of the thing that was destroyed, my car, was of a value where if there was a conviction up to ten years could be sentenced. Then the civil case which may or may not be taken up by my insurance company. Then there was Larceny over, which means that the stereo/security system that was stolen was valued at *over* $500. That was yet another punishment of up to five years. Up to fifteen years is a long time and would be a righteous bust for someone. But consider yourself lucky if you get a flat-foot to even go out and take a statement. That's what insurance adjusters are for.

The case that we caught out on Temple Place was a woman who had already complained of being stalked and threatened. She had filed a restraining order and been to court to have the temporary order upheld. But that didn't make her stalker go away.

Her apartment was allegedly broken into and her personal garments had been gone through the night before. That was yet another call that this poor woman had called into the local precinct, another case to add to the thousands. She somehow managed to go to sleep after the violation. I had to give her credit for being strong. Going to sleep would have been difficult for anyone without serious medication. But she managed, medication or no.

She woke up that morning to find her stalker in her apartment staring at her through the slats of a closet door. He had apparently never left the apartment the night before and watched her all night. The police hadn't gone out to look at her apartment yet, so she left things they way she had found them as best she could. When she found the pervert in her apartment masterbating while she showered for work, there was an altercation. She managed to get in a few good licks but took many of her own. Crimes against persons, the Staties were now involved.

The victim was in pretty bad shape but she was a fighter. She was coherent enough to give a statement of what happened before heading off to the hospital. She would live another day but she was going to have permanent scars both physically and emotionally.

This case was easy enough for us to close. Hobbs and I didn't have to wait for the Maynard lab to do the blood work. The victim had drawn blood in her struggle with the attacker, both having two different blood-types. The lab could DNA match the suspect, but the victim had told us who it was and the backlog would take forever. With the previous paper on him, his address known, and the injuries we would see when we found the asshole, this was an easy one.

We didn't have any other business on that end of the city, so we headed back to my neighborhood. The guy that was causing the victim years of therapy was from Southie. You normally stick up for your own, but not this guy. It is embarrassing that the perv lived among the people I grew up with. We might be a lot of things, but we aren't skinners.

The suspect came home after we sat on his house for about an hour and a half. The victim got more than a few good swings on her aggressor. We were twenty yards off his front stoop and we could see his wounds.

The toughest part about how that went down was that I had to go all the way back to The House to process the paperwork on that prick, then come all the way back to my neighborhood because that was the end of my shift. It would have been nicer to just go home after we collared him, I was nine blocks away. He confessed in the car ride on the way in. I wish they were all that easy.

I was still thinking about the pervert and how much he bothered me when I got home to my three-decker that night. Also rattling around my brain was the fact that Danny Mick was no longer in holding. Nobody would tell me where he was either. I went down to check on him when we got back to The House after dealing with the skinner. Tell him how things were progressing. He was gone and off the books. ATF pick him up? Shipped over to South Bay awaiting arraignment? Nobody knew.

I grabbed a bottle of cheap Irish Whiskey off of the counter as I walked into my house and turned on the TV to NESN. I wanted to forget about Hobbs, Danny Mick, Roxy, and the perv. The Indians were at Fenway again and my beloved Red Sox were not fairing as well. Kind of a shit day all-around.

But it got worse. I took off my jacket, draped it off the back of my recliner, reacquired my bottle of booze, and made my way to the kitchen for a glass when I saw that someone was already waiting for me in there.

I reached for to my armpit for my service weapon. My hand never made it to the Glock. He had me dead-to-rights. His Smith & Wesson *Model 500* hand cannon was pointed straight at my chest. The revolver didn't hold but six shots, but he wouldn't need that many. A fifty caliber projectile through my chest at that range would leave a big enough hole to stick a hand through, let alone necessitate six rounds. Even if I had my nine millimeter in my hand I was grossly out-gunned.

I could scream. My tenants above me would hear me most likely. But would they do anything? In my neighborhood screaming and gunshots were not uncommon. People only paid attention when it got really quiet.

"You're slipping Deni. Never would have been able to get the drop on you back in the day."

"Age. It's a bitch. Nice to see ya Slopes. Maybe you shoulda called first."

"You were lookin' for me?"

"Yeah but I guess you were wicked busy and couldn't talk. Danny Mick. You seen him lately?"

"I heard he got snagged."

"Doin' your work, Sean."

"What ever do you mean, Officer?"

"If we were playin' cops and bad-guys we could do games, dance for days. But I reached out today as a guy from the neighborhood. That used to mean somethin'."

Whether that six pound cannon that he had trained on me was getting too heavy or if he felt like things were maybe getting more comfortable, I don't know. But he lowered his gun, keeping it at his side in case he needed it. He stared at me with his one sharp eye while mulling over the situation.

"Care for a Whiskey?" I raised the bottle from my hand to show him it wasn't top-shelf.

"One."

"Then be a sweetheart and hand me two glasses out of the cupboard behind you." 'Sweetheart' sounded like 'sweet-hot' from a Bostonian and it's meant to sound sarcastic. I'm not sure if I said it to throw him off or piss him off, but in any event Slopes didn't bite.

"Fuck that. Take a pull from the bottle."

"Fair enough."

I unscrewed the top, took a pull and handed him the bottle. He took it with his left hand, his right still on his gun. I didn't really want to share a bottle with him. His Bell's Palsy made him a drooler. There was always a small pool of saliva on the right side of his mouth that sagged with the entire right side of his face. His eye and cheek sloped downward like it was about to slide off of his skull. Thus his nickname.

He took a generous pull himself on the left side of his mouth, all the while keeping his eye fixed on me. The first sip of the cheap crap that I could afford always made me wince. Not so with Slopes. I don't know what he normally drinks but the burn I felt going down was absent from his chest. Irish boys can drink, but I think that Sean Teague could bury me. He wiped his mouth with his sleeve before he continued.

"So did you come to see me because you have information for me, or did you want some from me?" He kept the bottle.

"Let's cut the bullsh. You and I both know that Danny Mick and his boy were pickin' up and delivering a shit-ton of assault rifles for you. I don't know what you were going to do with them or where they came from, all I know is that he had them. That many guns with everything but a four-leaf clover stamped to the side of 'em means that he is a big-dog now. No state case anymore. They are gonna wanna trade up. I talked to Danny Mick last night off the record. He's scared."

"He fuckin' should be."

"Not of the time. Of you."

"Like I said."

"He says he will do the time like a man, but he wants to maybe get out someday. Whoever you got on him, have them protect him in there not kill him."

"Deni I ain't sayin' that them guns was mine. But *if* they were, they had a purpose." He took another long pull of the bottle. Apparently 'one' meant one bottle, not one drink.

"I think everyone gets that. From what I can tell we had an eager rookie who was bored. You got unlucky. In your business you win some, lose some. No need for the kid to earn a shiv."

"It is what it is. Why do you care, Deni?"

"He asked me. And I knew him since back when he was still on the tit. I used to go out with his sister, Roxy."

"Shit, Deni. Everyone used to go out with Roxy. She been rode more than the nags at Suffolk Downs, man."

"Like I said, we look out for our own."

"Irregardless, big risk for you," he said.

"No shit English professor. This is unofficial. My partner knows that it's probably you who orchestrated this thing. But without Danny Mick, nothing gets back to you. The other guy died on the way to the hospital, but I'm sure you know that. The guns will be gone through at ballistics, but if there is nothing there …. Not our case anymore anyway, like I said. I am curious as to where he is though."

"Who? Danny Mick? Fuck should I know. You got him. You just talked to him."

"Had him. He was pulled out of holding sometime today. But no record and nobody knows where he is. Which is wicked fucked up. I figured you know more about where he is than me."

"And why is that? He's at your house."

"Because you have a much more vested interest in where he is than I do. I am just curious, you should be worried."

"Rumor is that ATF has him. I'll find him. You know I will."

"Yeah I'm sure. Listen, he's a sweet kid deep down. Just let him do his time. But lemme ask you a question. Just between you and me slopes, why did you have the kid go on this one? And why in broad daylight? With stolen tags? Somethin' that big — "

" — what are we friends now or somethin'? You give me a swig of your shit booze and you get to ask me things that are outta left field? Not my guns. How many times I gotta tell you?"

"Okay guy. I guess not."

"As far as your request goes? He keeps quiet, he lives. That's my guess anyways, since it ain't my thing. It's how things work in prison. You snitch, you die. Thanks for the hospitality."

He put the open bottle down on the counter behind him and walked past me, out of my kitchen, out of my house.

The visit from Slopes was a bad way to end my day. If that was how it ended. But it wasn't. I was pondering if Bell's Palsy was contagious and if whatever lived in Sean's spit was killed off by alcohol and whether I needed to go to the liquor store, when I heard the locks on my front door rattling.

I was in no mood for company. My car was totaled, my partner was the same douche-bag he was every day, I risked sanctions by sticking my neck out for the kid brother of the girl I used to bang when I was a hood-rat, I had to deal with a poor woman who had begged for help and didn't get any until she was almost killed by the asshole who was tormenting her from my neighborhood, and I had received an unwelcome visit at gunpoint from none other than Sean Teague himself. I was kinda done for the day.

At some drunken point in our brief relationship I had made the mistake of giving Jill a spare key to my place. You had to unlock both deadbolts and the lock in the door knob to get inside, a process that she was having difficulty with.

When she finally did gain entrance, I was standing there with the second to the last glass remaining in the bottle of Whiskey in hand. She had been drinking. I had been drinking. One of us was swaying.

"Come right in. Please."

"I've come to tell you how much I hate you Deni."

"Take a number. Hey, couldn't you have called to tell me that?"

"I wanted to see your face when I told you that you're a piece of shit."

"Ah. How do I look? The same?"

"Why can't you be a good guy, Deni? You always make promises, and you always break'em. I'm a good girl. A catch. Why do I put up with your shit?"

"Good question. Come have a drink and we can talk about it for days."

"I shouldn't drink anymore. Besides I am very mad at you. I don't drink with people I'm mad at."

"I'm pretty pissed at you to, but a drink seems appropriate. Why did you have to trash my car?"

"What are you talking about?"

"Are you going to deny having someone kill my car? You seen it? Go look at it."

"You're drunk," she said as she held herself up with the help from the wall in my parlor.

"No shit, so are you."

"I'm giving you back your keys. I need to date someone more like me."

"Ha. Rich from Connecticut? Good luck finding one of those in this neighborhood."

"Educated with a real job, asshole."

"Yeah that makes sense. A business guy? Somebody with money is more your speed?"

"Fuckin-A. But I'm not shallow. I don't need rich, Deni. I just need the guy to be decent."

"That's nice. Keep in touch."

She left and soon after I blacked out.

6

THERE AREN'T ANY FEDERAL HOLDING FACILITIES OR PRISONS in Massachusetts. How Governor Mitt Romney or any other before him had managed to keep the Federal Bureau of Prisons out of the state was anyone's guess. Instead, what the US Marshals, FBI, and ATF were forced to do with any of their federal persons of interest, was to incrementally pay through the teeth.

The state of Massachusetts, like any other state, have criminals who's acts elevate them to a federal level. If you could call those acts elevated. Most states have at least one federally funded property for super-max, max, medium or minimum-security work camps to house their felons. But those from the commonwealth state need to either be shipped to another state or federal dollars are spent to house them in county facilities.

The closest federal lock-up to Boston was in Berlin, New Hampshire. Unfortunately that facility was only medium security, with only two rows of chain-link fence topped with razor wire. Most men who were either waiting for such elevated trials or had already been convicted necessitated much more aggressive restraints and protocols. So the state charged the government, and therefore every taxpayer in the country, to house them in with the Massachusetts locals.

The Middlesex County jail in Cambridge sits atop the no longer used Superior Courthouse. It is one of the only high-rise maximum security prisons in the country. The courthouse is no longer used because the building was constructed when lead paint and Asbestos were used. The jail above was used with the same materials but when you get your hand caught in the cookie-jar, a little Mesothelioma is deemed part of the punishment. The jail was supposed to be abandoned as well for the same public health reasons, but with overcrowding there was no place to relocate those that call the jail their temporary home.

The high-rise was originally designed to house 160 inmates, though the building that was certified too great a health risk to hold that many routinely holds between 340-400. The cells therein that once held one inmate, possibly two, now had three and sometimes four.

This facility is where they had moved Daniel McKennie to be detained pre-trial. The ATF and the federal prosecutor wanted to move him away from his possible cohorts and put him into protective federal custody. There were a few very real problems with this design. There was no federal facility for him in the general vicinity, which meant he would need to be moved up to Berlin, NH or out to the Super-Max state facility in Walpole. Also the suspect refused to cooperate in giving up his crew. The federal prosecutor assigned to the case couldn't justify the added expense of protective custody in Walpole, nor move him north to Berlin when the person he wanted to protect wouldn't flip and wouldn't ask to be PC'd. So the prosecutor stuck him close by in Middlesex County.

Danny Mick was housed in gen-pop at Cambridge, where he shared a cell with two other inmates. This was not his first time he had been incarcerated, though it was the first time at Cambridge. Danny Mick had been in a juvenile detention center, police lock-ups, even other county facilities in his young past. Consequently he had run into many of the inmates he was currently housed with from the commission of his past misdeeds or during the punishment he received from doing them.

He seemed to be getting on well with those he had come in contact with, both old acquaintances and new. The block was set up in such a way where he felt cautiously optimistic about his new living arrangement, even if temporary.

General Population on E was a long corridor with a polished-concrete floor and light blue, painted, metal caged doors to the cells on both right and left sides. Some metal picnic style tables were bolted to the floor up the middle of the corridor for when one side or the other was let out for rec or chow. There were very few times, at most once per week, when both sides of E block were let out of their cells at the same time for assembly.

Danny Mick had been in Cambridge for roughly three weeks, was getting fairly comfortable with his situation and surroundings, when all hell broke loose.

Memorial Day assembly on Monday, May 31, 2004, was scheduled to be the same as every Memorial Day of years past. Barbecued burger-like substance and hot dogs on stale white bread were served along with a movie projected onto a white, prison, bedding sheet. The same movie was shown every year, Oliver Stone's *Born on the Fourth of July*. Despite the violence in the movie, none had broken out in the jail since it was first shown in the early 90s. It was, therefore, green-lighted for every year henceforth. The prison population seemed to enjoy mixing company with those whom they were not normally allowed social contact, whether they actually watched the movie or not.

Until 2004.

The festivities were cut short because one of the best and brightest housed there decided to clog the all-in-one sink-toilet. The building was old, the plumbing just as vintage. The miscreant stuffed the toilet and continued to flush repeatedly, flooding just his cell at first then backing up the entire line on E. Others began to join in on the fun, stuffing and continually flushing their cells as well. Though the jail is a twenty-four-seven facility, the jail didn't have a maintenance presence on the holiday weekend. The flooding escalated past the point of no return. The building was already more than double past the intended capacity and therefore there was no place to move the inmates. The water flowing out of the toilets and exploding out of the sinks disallowed use of the cells and bunks for sleep. There was also no longer anyplace for evacuating bladders or bowels.

Emotions and tensions ran high while the COs that had the least tenure and couldn't get out of working Memorial Day tried to figure out what to do. Mini fights broke out, which brought out the lug teams, but there was so much chaos it was impossible to squash every skirmish.

Other floors began to flood as well as the entire plumbing system became clogged. Cracks and holes from E egressed water onto floors below but not so much water as to keep the water from rising rapidly. The same such cracks and crevices were depositing water from floors above, down into E.

The toilet-water had risen to a foot above the concrete floor and was still rising. The entire block was wading around as lockdown was thought to cause more problems than allowing them to find higher ground either in the cells or the rec area.

The opportunity was seized. Danny Mick had been up on a top bunk in a cell that was not his own. He was visiting a new-found friend while he waited out the flood. The friend was pulled out of his own cell by a couple of inmates and in all of an instant, Danny Mick was cornered in a cell with three others that were not his cellmates nor belonged in that one. Two others positioned themselves outside the cell to stand watch. Not that anyone would be looking at what was transpiring, there was too much else going sideways to worry about individual cells.

"What's going on boys?" Danny Mick knew what was happening, nervous jokes not withstanding.

The leader smiled, then shrugged his shoulders. "It is what it is, kid."

He was about to ask what his attacker meant, when the three pulled him off the high bunk he was using to stay dry. He didn't have time to scream or call for help. His face was shoved to the floor under the rising water that was geysering out of the toilet. The drowning was not a painful enough way to die, so the plastic cutlery that was given for the makeshift barbecue meal had been fashioned to a very sharp point, and then used to stab him too many times to count.

Danny Mick tried to fight back, but with three men holding him under water and his inability to acquire air, the fight was all but impossible. His lungs burned, desperately trying to tell him that they were in need of oxygen. That burning only being surpassed by the burning from each thrust that was being driven into his body, each stab adding to the agony. The jagged edge of the molded and flimsy plastic tearing his flesh both on the way in and out

43

of his body. The water around him was turning pink from the blood and shredded meat escaping this thrashing body. Danny looked more and more like chum being submerged into shark-infested waters. The more he flailed, the more his heart pumped blood out of the increasing number of holes in his torso.

The thrashing and splashing was doing nothing to get him on the other side of the mortal danger he was in. He pulled at prison jumpsuits, dug his fingernails into what ever skin he could find purchase on. To no avail. The walls began to close in on the small room around him. His flailing waned. Only his bleeding increased.

When Danny Mick's body had gone slack, his head was pulled out of the water. As if by miracle he still had a very slight pulse. The lead aggressor dug the utensil into the jugular as far as the makeshift shiv would go and sawed the skin from jaw hinge to jaw hinge. The neck opened and the tongue was pulled out through the new hole to cover his adam's apple.

The grisly body was then pushed back into the crimson water. Hands were rinsed in the water's tide and the weapon was hidden as the attackers left the confines of the cell.

The group of assassins then receded into the crowd and commotion in the corridor. With their mission accomplished, they were free to wade through the water and wreak more havoc with the rest of the inhabitants on E.

7

MY MEMORIAL DAY WEEKEND THAT YEAR WAS PRETTY BORING. Lonely and boring. I was no longer dating anyone and I didn't have any plans with friends because I don't have many friends. The department was looking for volunteers to work because nobody wanted to work the holiday. Barbecues and such. Whether the detectives requesting the day off had someone to remember was a question I didn't care to ask, but I did volunteer.

What I mean by volunteer is that I agreed to work the holiday. They were going to pay me, and they were going to pay me big-time. The Massachusetts State Police have holidays, floating holidays, sick and personal days besides the vacation days that they give their employees. Memorial Day was a paid holiday for Monday. I worked the weekend and Monday which meant that I got twenty hours of overtime and double-dipped on Monday's pay. Time and a half each weekend day and on Monday, on top of a day that I was already getting paid ten hours for.

I needed the money. I still needed a new car. Three weeks and my insurance still hadn't come through with a check for a new one. I was thinking of upgrading anyway. The two-door sport coupe was way too small for me. Trucks and large vehicles are impractical in the city but they are roomy and good in the snow. I had my eye on the Cadillac *Escalade*.

The weekend was a washout anyway. It rained or was overcast every day. Temperatures never reached sixty. Why not get paid to be wet and miserable?

Saturday the twenty-ninth I spent a good chunk at the MMA gym in Brookline. When you grow up in Southie you learn how to fight early in life. Period. Even the dorks and homos fought. Call it a Darwin thing or whatever you want, but in Southie you either learn how to defend yourself or you don't make it out of puberty. I had picked up Mixed Martial Arts at a fairly young age, added to my street fighting abilities made me a pretty good fighter. I took several amateur bouts, a few semi-pro fights, and two UFC fill-ins as an undercard. That is where I met Kenny Florian.

Kenny was a Dover boy who was a natural athlete. He did the soccer thing and got a scholarship for it, Boston College I think. He had come up to MMA a few years back and made his debut the year prior. He was a black-belt in Brazilian Jiu-Jitsu like myself, so we sparred regularly. He was training for the Drew Ficket fight in July and I was training because I had a lesser known fight coming up as well. We were both light or welterweights, depending on the fight. He was a true lightweight, 5'10" and 145 pounds. He would gain weight to go up to welters. I was a true middleweight, 6' and 170 pounds but cut weight to make the fights. It was a good arrangement. We weren't friends so much as we worked out together.

MMA was just one of the ways that I made extra money on the side. When I got promoted to Detective in Troop H, they gave a lousy $5k bump. That amounts to two bucks more an hour, before taxes. Since I was never going to get promoted again, that meant that I was stuck at that pay scale ad infinitum. The only thing I had to look forward to was my yearly cost of living increase, which everybody knows doesn't cover the rate of inflation. Meaning that over the course of my career, I would progressively make less money. They wonder why cops go dirty.

My tenants on the floor above me and on the top floor of my three-decker paid my mortgage, which was kind of another way to supplement my meager income. Though I had to set money aside like I still paid a mortgage for when stuff needed to be fixed. When you live in a building that was built in the early 1900s, things tend to go bump in the night pretty regularly, and my tenants aren't exactly gentle on my stuff.

And yet another way to add a little coin to my pockets was to take on some PI work. Private Investigators sometimes get a bad wrap; but with the caseload that cops have, citizens often have to get someone who is a bit more committed to their cause. I had run into a couple of PI's and lawyers on some of my cases, and had taken on a couple of side jobs through them which paid very well. This was completely against Mass State Police rules and if I was caught, not only would I be sanctioned and probably fired, but I could face criminal charges as well. I never took a side job on one of my own cases so I figured criminal charges were a stretch. Also I knew specifically of many cops who were on the take in one way or another, so my secret was safe as long as I kept theirs. Of course my partner didn't know. I hoped he didn't at least.

I wasn't getting rich by any stretch, but I wasn't struggling like others within the department. I had to piece-meal a living as best I could with whatever talents I have, which made free-time and friends a pipe dream. Living in the city, or any major city I would imagine, isn't inexpensive. In Boston, houses were going to the yuppies. Southie has a ton of old buildings that get bought up because they are run-down. The buyers and flippers sell to those who can pay. Nobody can make it in the city on forty grand unless they are on the government tit.

I took Sunday off from the gym, but only because it was closed. Many things in the city were closed down for the holiday weekend. But not the bars.

Boston has a proud tradition of drinking, be it holiday or no. We are a proud heritage of both social and binge drinking. Add to that culture fifty-eight colleges and universities scattered about the city and you have yourself a time. If you throw something over your shoulder in Boston, it will hit a bar or a liquor store. On holiday weekends, the population as a whole hits the sauce pretty hard.

With alcohol comes drunken fights and nonsense. But otherwise crime is pretty low during long weekends. Major crime. The local cops handle all of the drunk and disorderlies, noise complaints, fake IDs, and the other petty bullsh. So while they are busy filling up their paddy wagons, detectives like me are bored. I had very little to detect.

One of the drunken assaults was pretty bad and the college chick who's college boyfriend got beaten-up was encouraging her lover to press charges. That is how I got involved. The city cops aren't allowed to handle major crimes. The guy who was roughed-up was in need of hospitalization. The crime actually fit the guidelines for attempted murder, so I went to the hospital to take statements. The boyfriend was embarrassed that he lost the fray and wanted to just lick his wounds and call it a weekend. Man-up. I kinda respected that. But the girlfriend was having none of the man-code and wanted to press charges. Only she can't, it has to be the person who was assaulted or else the charges won't stick. So around and around we went trying to figure out if I had a case to pick up or not. Technically, the state, meaning me or an Assistant District Attorney, could just make a call to investigate without the victim but let's face it — who adds work when they are already overworked and underpaid?

Investigating other cases that I had ongoing was an exercise in futility. Nobody wants their long weekend ruined by scheduling appointments with cops, so those were on hold. My partner had opted for the holiday off, so that was another hindrance on focusing on our open cases.

So that was my Sunday.

Monday was much of the same. Hangovers and late starts meant that even the phone calls into the station were sparse. I putzed around after going to the gym but that was about it. I should have felt a little guilty for taking the equivalent of double-time and a half for doing nothing but I didn't. Even Tits didn't come in on Monday, not that I complained.

I was waiting for the dial-up internet modem to finish connecting and squawking static at me when the call was patched through to my desk. I lifted the receiver to my phone, the receptionist told me I had a call on line 4. I was surprised that there were enough calls coming into the station to extend to the fourth line and thankful for something to do that didn't require the internet. I was no good at it.

"Detective Dennihan speaking."

"Your buddy didn't keep his end." The voice was low and muffled like they were trying to disguise it with something over the phone.

"My buddy huh? Who is this?"

"He wasn't gonna keep his mouth shut. Now it's shut for good."

"Who? What are you talking about?"

"He woulda squealed and begged if he hadn't drowned."

"I've got no time for pranks, guy. Either tell me who this is and what this is about or I'm gonna hang up."

"You should have taken better care of him Deni. Hiding him at Cambridge isn't hiding him."

"For the last time, what in the hell are you talking about?"

"Danny Mick didn't leave me a lotta room. Had to be done."

The caller had my attention. I had completely forgotten about Danny Mick, to be honest. Out of sight, out of mind. After my talk with Slopes, the subject never crossed my mind again. I had other cases, other things going on. I didn't even know where he was. I figured the ATF had hidden him somewhere.

"Who is this? What did you do?"
Click.

Thoughts ran through my head at about a million miles an hour. *What happened to Danny Mick? Why didn't the ATF move him out of state? Why wasn't he better protected? Who just called me? Was it Sean Teague that went after him? Why? The caller was right, Cambridge was no place to hide him if that's what the plan was. He shoulda been up in Berlin or Walpole. Why was he in Cambridge? Was he really there? Probably a prank call.*

I got on the phone and called the Middlesex County jail in Cambridge. The phone rang unanswered for what seemed like forever. When someone finally did pick up, I learned that it was absolute pandemonium over there. I had to give my name, rank and badge number several times to several different people before someone was finally allowed to tell me anything at all.

" …. these guys flood the place all the time but never this bad. The plumbing wasn't designed for this many — "

48

" — I'm not callin' for an architectural lesson, chief. I got an anonymous call that said a possible inmate there, Daniel McKennie, is in danger or has already been killed. First, can you tell me if he *is* there?"

There was some fumbling and rustling of papers that I could hear on my end of the phone.

"C'mon guy. Yes or no? Simple question, simple answer."

"It's very chaotic here right now. Give me a min …. uh, yeah. Here he is. Daniel McKennie. E block."

" 'Uh, yeah here he is' like you see him or 'uh, yeah here he is' on some piece of paper or on a computer screen?"

"Screen."

"Get him out of E block."

"You don't have any authority to demand that we move an inmate."

"Do you want the death of an inmate under your care tied to you? I am officially notifying you that there has been a threat against an inmate that you just confirmed is incarcerated there. If something happens to him because you didn't respond to that threat, both you and the Middlesex County are in for some serious shit."

"If we moved an inmate every time someone was threatened, we — "

" — I'm on my way down there. So help me if anything has happened to him, I will make it my mission in life to make you pay for it." I might have broken the phone when I hung up.

8

WHEN I ARRIVED AT THE MIDDLESEX COUNTY JAIL IN CAMBRIDGE, the place was on total lock-down. Mine was not the only Memorial Day that was ruined. Higher ups had been called to come in as there had been massive flooding and riots were beginning to form on some of the various floors. Nobody had time for me until things were settled down.

I sat in the visitor's waiting area for hours as I watched modified school buses pull up and get filled with shackled prisoners. They were being moved to other facilities within the counties. Suffolk County at both South Bay and Shattuck, Middlesex County at Billerica, and even the minimum security at Roslindale were all going to be filled up with the three hundred ninety-four inmates that were housed at Cambridge. These facilities, like Cambridge, were already beyond capacity but the new prisoners would all be put in the hole if necessary. The solitary confinements of those other facilities were not going to be so solitary by the end of the day. Two and three inmates in a tiny cell designed to be just big enough for one. Those facilities would also now go on lock-down as they had to ensure that inmates couldn't commingle.

So I waited. And I sat. Then I waited some more. I scrutinized every inmate that was led onto a bus to see if I could spot Danny Mick. I did not. All of their jumpsuits were saturated and although it was raining I thought it unlikely that the light precipitation was the reason.

Three hours after my arrival, Deputy Sheriff Dominguez finally came to get me from the waiting area. Personally.

"I'm sorry to have kept you waiting Detective Dennihan. As you can imagine we have had quite a time of it."

"I see that. When I called they said there was a flood, everyone and their brother is soaked." Everyone except him. The Deputy was as starched as the ironing board his clothes

50

were pressed on. His tanned skin looked darker in the white uniform. He looked Latin, of course. Puerto Rican maybe. His accent didn't give any hint of Spanish or Boston.

"It has gone beyond that, I'm afraid."

"How so?"

"We will have to investigate, but it seems that the flood was a diversion."

"Was my guy the cause of the diversion?"

"Come into the office over here so we can speak in private." We were already speaking privately but I followed him.

Deputy Dominguez led me to an office that was behind the empty reception window. There was no need to staff it, there was not going to be any visitors today. Once the door was closed I was offered a seat in front of a desk, the Deputy sat behind it. Whether it was his desk or not I didn't know nor do I know now.

"The plumbing is bad here, Detective. The inmates often flood the blocks to mix up the tedium of — "

" — yeah, I don't mean to interrupt but I already got the plumber's guide to the galaxy. What does that have to do with my guy? Where is he, and is he safe?"

"'Your guy' huh?"

"Deputy. You've had me waiting for an eternity and I'm sure that you know why. I called to ask about inmate Daniel McKennie, because I received a call sayin' that he was either going to die or already had. He's *my guy* because it was put on my plate. I'm sure you know all of this, so why are we having to go through the charade?"

"Who did you receive the call from?"

"I have no idea. His voice may have been disguised. Definitely unidentified."

"Do you have a guess?"

"No not really. My *guess* would be that Danny Mi .... inmate McKennie, decided to fess up who he was working for to the ATF, and whoever that was decided they didn't want to be implicated."

"You are not the detective working his case? Because you are listed as one of the two arresting detectives on his paperwork."

The pullover was a traffic misdemeanor, so LaDue would get credit for that but didn't for the felony arrest. He gets credit for the ticket issued for driving an unregistered vehicle. He might even share credit for finding a stolen vehicle. When the guns were found, however; the questioning and therefore the case was turned over to detectives. Hobbs and I were still listed as the cops linked to the case. When we turned it over to the ATF, they should have had their own investigators question McKennie and those investigators should have been the people listed. The fact that I was still on his paperwork was confusing.

51

"Wait. I'm still on his paperwork? So he really is still *my guy*. Didn't the ATF bring him here to hide him for pre-trial? We turned this case over to the ATF like three weeks ago."

"Yes but he refused to speak with anyone but you. The federal prosecutor tried to put him in protective custody but he wouldn't go. He refused to cooperate."

"That's wicked strange. I'm still on his paperwork even though my partner and I turned him over to ATF is odd to say the least, but whatever. Where is he now?"

"He is dead. Brutally attacked and killed."

He let that sink in and I was thankful for the moment of time. My mind raced as to how a suspect this big had fallen through the cracks. Jurisdictional Purgatory.

"Shit. I'm too late. What happened?"

"Either the flood was used as a diversion, like I said, or whoever did it seized the flood as an opportunity. He was stabbed more times than we had time to count so far. We will have to send him out for an autopsy, but at first glance he was drowned while he was being stabbed so nobody would hear him scream. Have you ever heard of a Colombian Necktie?"

"Ah Jesus. Yeah. Slice from ear to ear and pull out his tongue through like a necktie."

"Correct. That is how they treat snitches."

"That is how who treats snitches? I thought they normally get a buck-fifty."

A buck-fifty is referred to a large slice across a rat's face. The ensuing stitches to sew up the person's face requires a minimum of hundred fifty. When another felon sees the facial scar, they know not to trust the person because of the buck-fifty. That is why the slicing is done to the face.

"There are several ways to deal with a rat, Detective. Testifying in open court earns you more than a buck-fifty."

"So he *was* going to testify."

"That's just it. We don't have any record that he was. In fact, that is why he didn't get PC'd. He refused to testify. We still don't have a record of who he was working for. If we had known, at the very least we would have mandated stay-aways."

A stay-away is exactly that. It is a list of inmates and visitors that are to stay away from one another. Sometimes it is because they just don't get along. Other times it might be that they are witnesses against each other in the same case. There are all sorts of reasons to keep two or more inmates away from one another. Working in the same crew suspected of gun trafficking on an outstanding case definitely qualified. The trouble being that they had no idea from whom to keep Danny Mick away from.

52

"Then why the necktie? Why kill him? That's what the person on the phone said to me. He 'wasn't gonna keep his mouth shut'. That it 'had to be done'. Why would somebody think that? If he wasn't going to testify, according to you, who thought that he was?"

"We will investigate. But in all probability, with the chaos and rookies that we had on E? We are not hopeful in finding out, let's put it that way."

"So the kid is dead and nobody is ever going to pay for it? Have you questioned the Block? It had to be someone on E. We can look at known associates of everyone on his floor. Probably won't be long before we make a connection."

" You aren't listening. We've had a massive flood. Mini riots. We had all we could do to lock down the place, we certainly haven't questioned anyone yet."

"So the guy gets away with it?"

"I didn't say that. What I am saying is that it will be difficult if not impossible. We will do our best. We'll start questioning inmates in the morning, look at all the camera footage. But the hard truth?" He didn't finish his question. He didn't have to.

"I'm sure his sister will thank you," I mumbled.

"What was that Detective?"

"Nothing. Which Morgue is he going to?"

Three hundred ninety-four were being transferred out of Cambridge that night. Three hundred ninety-three to other cells, one was headed for the slab at Shattuck.

9

OUR CASE INVOLVING DANIEL McKENNIE had been over for weeks. I had forgotten about it, truthfully, and there wasn't any outstanding paperwork for me to sign that reminded me of it. Three weeks had gone by and neither my partner nor I had mentioned it or, as far as I'm concerned, gave it another thought. We were busy with other cases and he was the ATF's problem, supposedly. I never transferred him, but I assumed that Hobbs did. He was my senior after all.

Only Danny Mick, the poor prick, had never made it that far. I desperately wanted to go down to the Boston office of the Bureau of Alcohol Tobacco and Firearms and find out what in the hell was going on down there. How had they botched up a witness so badly that he was slaughtered in prison?

That is what I wanted to do. I had already stuck my neck out for the kid, beyond what was reasonable in the eyes of the law and my police department. I wasn't in any trouble, yet. But if I made a huge fuss over a dead witness from my neighborhood, that could very well change. What good would it do anyway? Danny Mick got himself involved with the Irish mob, Sean Teague A.K.A Slopes, and was now dead. My getting more involved was not going to change that situation. So what I actually did was nothing. I ain't proud of it, but the truth is the truth.

So I let it go with the exception of going to see his sister, Roxy. The County lock-ups don't send a Correctional Officer or anybody else to the homes of those that are survived by the deceased inmate. They send a kite, a form letter, to those that are on the inmate's contact sheet. They will also reach out by telephone to those on said sheet. If those provide no response, they may go so far as to look up the phone numbers of those that visited the inmate at the prison from the visitor sign-in sheets.

They do this not for humanity reasons, not because they want to notify next of kin. Not at all. They do this for budgetary reasons. They want somebody to claim the body so that the funeral costs could be deferred to the families that created the societal rejects. The hope was that the family member or loved ones would want better arrangements than what the county would provide. Cemetery space, or any land near the city, came at a premium. Plots were expensive. So the bodies were unceremoniously thrown into an incinerator. The ashes were then disposed of along with the other biohazardous material from the medical wing. More often than not, the bodies were not claimed, either the families couldn't afford better or they didn't care. So ziplock bags of human ashes were disposed of with used syringes, bandages, and other medical waste.

I know what Roxanne said the last time we spoke. I know she didn't want to see me. I didn't want to see her either. But I knew what would happen to Danny Mick if she was not properly notified. If the state could get through to her on a phone, which was a big if, it was a tough way to learn of his death. If she opened her mail, another big if as I had seen Roxy's apartment, it would be an even tougher way to find out. 'We regret to inform you' …. and 'hey by the way come pick you your corpse so we don't incur any further expenses for the taxpayer'.

Boston can be a hard city, with hard citizens. None more so than those who reside in Southie. But nobody deserves to hear that their brother was a human pincushion by form letter, no matter what the guy did. So I took it upon myself to go see her.

Tuesday, June first, I took some personal time and headed over to Roxy's place. I waited until later in the morning because I knew that she was not an early riser. Actually that's bullsh. The real reason was that starting off your day with that kind of news is almost as bad as reading it in a letter. But what time of the day is the best time to learn of a sibling's death? I was just avoiding it for as long as possible. In any case, I went to the gym, beat the shit out of some kid that wanted to spar with me, and headed over.

I was still without a car, so I was forced to use a Dodge *Intrepid* from the motor pool. It was unmarked but a five year old could have told you it was a cop car. Traffic parted for me like I was Moses, and those that were contemplating something illegal waited until I was out of view. There were some people in my neighborhood that worked, because there were plenty of places to park on the street.

The stairs leading up to Roxy's dump creaked and groaned as they had the last time, as I'm sure they did every time someone used them. But unlike the last time, she was not waiting for me on the landing at the top of the stairs.

I don't remember how many times I knocked on the door. Nor do I remember how many sets of knocks. I know that it was a lot. I know I waited for a long time in between, waiting for her to wake up out of her hangover or drug-induced coma or whatever. I remember that the inside of the windows to her front door were so dirty that she could have been on the other side of it and I wouldn't have been able to see her.

55

Through all of it, there was no answer. I was trying to decide whether I should wait out in the car for her to come home, or if I should just come back later. Those two choices were oscillating back and forth in my head long enough for me to take out the pins that I always keep in my wallet.

I might have mentioned that I used to do some shady things when I was a kid. Steal car radios, the occasional car. A few B and E's. When it comes to picking locks, I have a gift.

For those that have called a locksmith in the past, you know that they have a wrench and some specialized pins for lifting the tumblers inside the lock. I don't need those. I have titanium pins that easily fit into my wallet. I have a few in there as backups but I only use two of them at a time. One to turn the bottom of the lock, the other to lift each tumbler one-by-one. This is what takes most people the longest amount of time. There are a minimum of five tumblers inside the key hole, which is what the high points of a key hit to lift them. Each one has to be lifted and stay disengaged in order for the lock to turn. Getting each one to lift before being able to turn the lock open can be exasperating. You then have to do this for each lock on the door. In Southie, the front doors always have a minimum of two and a deadbolt can have as many as ten tumblers.

I was inside of Roxy's apartment in under forty-seconds. She had two deadbolts plus her door handle. The stink that wafted at me when the door opened was nauseating. It was the olfactory equivalent to a punch to the face. I guess that is what you deserve when you break into someone's home.

The kitchen was to my right as I entered the front door. Against every signal by body was sending to my brain, every signal that my brain was communicating back to my muscles, I continued inside. I was forced to bury my nose into the outside of my right elbow, my eyes were watering like I had been sprayed by a skunk.

It was unlikely that she had any dishes or glassware in her cupboards. They were all in her sink. Food had been left out on the counter. What it was would require a biology degree and a microscope. She wasn't in the kitchen, which is all I needed to know for the moment so I didn't enter any further than that into the doorway.

I turned around, heading into the apartment. The TV was on in the parlor but it was static. She either didn't have cable or it was shut off. The mess was the same as the day that I had gone there. The same exact piles of detritus that prevented me from taking a seat on my visit three weeks prior, had I had a notion to, were still where they had been at that time.

I moved my way down the hall toward what I assumed would be a bedroom. The first doorway I came upon to my left was the bathroom. I am unsure how one would call that a bathroom, except that there was a toilet and bathtub. I wondered how one could get clean in a place that was dirtier than the human that needed cleansing. Mold was growing in the grout between the tiles. Mold that was at a point of taking on a life of its own. There was no decorative shower curtain, just the liner that hung open as if to invite one into the sad excuse for a shower. That liner was also covered in mold. The toilet paper roll contained none, and every cosmetic belonging in a cupboard or medicine cabinet was strewn about.

Completely repulsed, and not wanting to touch anything, I continued down the hallway. My eyes burned like they had bleach in them. Bleach that the apartment desperately needed. Or a fire. I was going to need a shot of antibiotics when I got out of there. I made a mental note of it.

The bedroom door was open. The small bedroom was dark, the shades drawn to close out the already dark and rainy fifty-one degree day outside. The room was situated in such a way where you entered on the left side of the room, the bed and furnishings would have been feng shui'd to the right if the person occupying it cared about such things. The only furnishing in the room was a mattress without a box spring set onto the floor.

Roxy was on her back, on the bed, naked on top of the covers. It was cold outside and just as cold in the apartment. She was as pale blue-gray as the blanket that she laid on top of. The color of steamed bluefish. Her face turned away from the arm that had a needle sticking out of it.

I knew the answer before I had confirmed it, but I felt for a pulse on her neck anyway. She was dead and coming out of full rigor.

It had been in the fifties for more than a week, cold for this time of year but no freezing temperatures. Temperature affects rigor mortis, I didn't need the M.E. to tell me that. I also didn't need a Medical Examiner to tell me that she had been dead for at least twenty-four hours. Before her brother.

I didn't know if that was a blessing or not. But I mulled it over.

By the time the Medical Examiner and his team arrived, I had already gotten used to the smell. The team wrestled with the detectives who were assigned to the case about opening windows, spraying anything that would make the noxious smells more tolerable for the people who had to work in the apartment. The argument was based on whether the opening of windows or the addition of a fragrance or both would contaminate the crime scene. It should give you some idea of just how bad the smell in that place was. People who were accustomed to the smells of death were overpowered by that particular fetor.

Case assignments for Troop H are based upon case load and who is available. For lack of a better term, it is a macabre lottery. The fact that I knew the victim or that Hobbs and I had been originally assigned to the case involving her brother didn't even come up. If I was eliminated from investigating crimes involving people that I knew in the city, I wouldn't be investigating much. Hobbs and I were full, so our names were not up on the board. When I called it in, two other detectives from Troop H were assigned.

It was a case worthy of assignment only because of my insistence. By all accounts, it looked like a junky-whore overdose. She had track marks old and new, she lived in squalor, had a history of prostitution and drug use. Everyone was busy, why investigate something that doesn't need investigating?

I didn't need a gut feeling to know that she wasn't likely to have overdosed prior to learning of her brother's murder. And there were a number of signs that I looked for, that were lacking. For example, where was her stash? Junkies have a stash-box with all of their paraphernalia and their drugs. None. So where did the needle and the drugs come from? Another thing that bothered me was why she was naked. It was very cold for this time of year and her heat had been turned off or shut off from what I could tell. Why get naked before juicing up?

Once the team started doing a prelim on Roxy, taking pictures and getting her ready for the move to the slab, the M.E. was starting to see things my way. Mark Bowman was the examiner who had been called out on the case.

"Deni I thought you were crazy on this one. Another junkie death, why waste time and resources? But I think you might be right."

"Ain't I usually? What brought you over to my side of things?"

"First, experienced heroine users know how much to juice up. When you are completely addicted, you don't want to use it all up in one dose. You want enough to get high, but there is always the next fix. Where ODs tend to happen is when they are forced to quit then start back up, or take time off for some reason and then start back up at the dosage they used prior to quitting. The point is that there is almost always a downtime prior to an OD. They do a short bid in jail, rehab or they try to quit …. so they go back to the same dosage that they were using before they stopped using. The other explanation for an overdose is if they get a bad batch."

"So assuming she uses the same dealer, you're sayin' she was probably clean for a while and went back to it?"

"I didn't say that. I won't know for certain until we do a tox screen, but judging from the track marks and needle holes I would say that it is unlikely that she had a recent break. What makes it strange is that she used enough to kill a horse."

"Suicide? How can you tell?"

"I can tell how much she used by the stains inside the syringe where the plunger drew in the fluid. Unless you can afford very good heroine, it usually leaves a coloration on the inside of the syringe."

"So suicide? You just said — "

" — unlikely. I know what I said. Again, experienced drug users know how to hit a vein. This one missed. She wasn't even close. There was enough in the syringe, I'm guessing, to do the trick without hitting one. If you wanted to off yourself you would make sure to hit a vein so you didn't wake up."

"Cry for help?"

"Possibly Deni. But added to the fact that you said her brother was killed in prison yesterday, and that he was possibly involved with the Winter Hills .... I tend to take your side in that she was murdered. At least helped along. I'll do a tox screen of course, but I'm guessing that what she was injected with was pretty horrible shit. Between the amount and the color of the juice .... "

"How long has she been dead, Mark? She's not stiff as a board anymore. I guessed at a day."

"Oh at least. I'll let you know for sure once she is on the table but I would say a day at a minimum. It takes three to four hours to start the chemical process, full rigor at twelve hours. The body gradually comes out of it, dissipating in another twenty-four hours. Give or take. Add it all up? I'd estimate it at about forty hours."

"So she was dead, probably killed, before her brother. Like I thought."

"I would say that it is a fact that she died before Memorial Day Weekend went into full swing. Saturday evening at the latest. When did her brother get killed?"

"Yesterday. Tough weekend for the McKennie clan," I said.

"I would say so."

"But why?"

"Not my department, Detective."

"Not mine either, I guess."

Part Two

The Old Men in the Mountains
July 2004

10

THE SECOND SESSION OF THE WAYLAND COUNTY SUPERIOR COURT, in Wayland, New Hampshire, was packed to the gills. It always was following a Fourth of July weekend. Independence Day was a time when people got drunk, and usually had or were around fireworks. Sometimes a bad combination however fun. Lots of arraignments and first appearances to get to. But that was not why the courtroom was full on Monday, July 5, 2004.

The courtroom was packed because of the press. Over the long weekend, there had been a murder. Murders didn't happen in New Hampshire very often, even in the southern part of the state just north of the Massachusetts border. The usual crime-beat reporters from the Wayland Courant would be there of course. The local FOX affiliate certainly in the majority Republican state. However there were CBS, NBC, ABC affiliates, and others that had traveled north from Boston also in attendance as well.

Sadly, the victim of the case was not what made the story newsworthy. The presence of the crowd trying to gain the scoop was there to follow the suspected ring of crime that surrounded and were believed to have perpetrated the murder. The headline was about the private compound up in the White Mountains that had been the target of many investigations over the years; rumored to have been involved in any number of crimes, but nothing that had ever stuck. They were older, gun-toting, 'Live Free or Die' types that secluded themselves against visitors with both man-made barriers as well as the natural mountains. They were referred to as 'The Old Men in the Mountains', though what they actually called themselves was anyone's guess. They rarely spoke to anyone.

On Saturday the third, just two days prior, a known member of this group was standing over the body of a man that he had shot in the face. Seven times. The victim was being monitored by the New Hampshire State Police for distribution of methamphetamines. Liam Breen was seen entering the building, gun shots were heard. Breen was arrested and brought to an interview room for questioning. They questioned him for several hours but garnered no confession. They wouldn't need one. He was caught virtually in the act.

The search of Breen's vehicle, which was allegedly used to drive down from the hidden compound in the mountains, resulted in the discovery of trace amounts of methamphetamine, heroine, cocaine, and an assault rifle with the serial number filed off. That weapon, along with the one used to kill the victim, were sent to the New Hampshire ballistics lab for testing. Breen's vehicle was registered to a P.O. Box not associated with the plot of land in the White Mountains.

The proceeds of the search of the vehicle were then used as probable cause in an application for a search warrant. That application was approved by a judge, the warrant issued for the entire property as it was purportedly linked to Liam Breen based on his comings and goings. That address was a gated property of over five hundred mountainous acres with one gated dirt road access.

It was a logistical and operational nightmare. Approach of the gate was met with gunfire. Backups were brought in, helicopters and all-terrain vehicles were used to secure the perimeter. There was a six hour standoff before heavy artillery was used to gain access and bring down the group.

The siege, a-la Waco, Texas, was plastered all over the news. Many different law enforcement agencies were brought in to help subdue the outlaws, but ultimately the ATF took the lead over the case. But not before two local police personnel were killed and seven law enforcement personnel were severely injured in the process. Tens of thousands of dollars were used and/or damaged in the name of justice.

Fourteen men over the age of fifty were apprehended and taken into federal custody. Several labs were discovered on the property. The men in the mountains were financing their enterprise with the manufacturing of massive quantities of drugs. They were a well armed enterprise as well. Assault rifles were a mere tip of the iceberg. Cases of weapons were opened including; HawkEngineering *MM-1 40 mm* revolver grenade launchers, Saab *AT4* rocket launchers, Russian *AN-94s* and *RPG-7s*, *TAC-50* McMillan tactical rifles, Heckler & Koch *G3A4s* and Armalite *AR-18* assault rifles, and hundreds of cases of ammunition. World War 3 could have started in New Hampshire. The war on drugs was not the only victory that day assuredly.

There were territorial pissing matches going on. The state of New Hampshire had seven vehicles that were either swiss cheese or had been blown up. They wanted a stake in the game or financial remuneration. The ATF wanted the case as it was a huge weapons boon. The FBI wanted the case because it was an unprecedented drug seizure on US soil.

Meanwhile, Liam Breen wasn't talking and had not been present during the raid. Neither federal government agency nor the federal prosecutor for the district needed Breen.

They wanted him, but gave the lowly locals their low hanging fruit. The ATF took jurisdiction over the seized assets and criminals with the help of a federal prosecutor.

The Honorable Judge Grace McCaglia had a circus before her. This was only the first appearance for Breen and she already had a headache. This case was going to put Wayland, New Hampshire in the spotlight. And not in a good way.

Most preliminary hearings, such as the first appearance, are handled by lowly prosecutors or an Assistant District Attorney in a high-profile case. The DA, Timothy Cromwell himself, was present to handle the hearing.

"Mr. Cromwell. How nice to see you today. We normally don't have the honor of seeing you down here in the trenches." Grace McCaglia was a brand new Judge, had just sworn onto the bench that year in fact. She had worked in the District Attorney's office for several years, but at forty-one she had accomplished more and at a younger age than Cromwell. The two had worked together then, and the fact that Cromwell was jealous of her success was no mystery.

"This is very important case, your honor." He felt odd calling her 'your honor'.

She stared almost through him with her mystic blue eyes. Her black hair matched her black robe. She sat confidently at her post, if she was at all hesitant about her role, she didn't show it.

"It is. So let's get on with it, shall we? State of New Hampshire v. Liam Breen, yes?"

She turned away from Cromwell, taking in the well dressed defense attorney, Dan W. Forde Esquire. The dark gray, designer, Jones New York suit with light blue pin-striping screamed money.

"Mr. Forde, you are the attorney of record for this case?"

"Yes and no, your honor. I have two motions in front of you that I would like to address."

"This is first appearance, counselor. Motions already?"

"I have a conflict, Judge. I am the attorney for the enterprise that Mr. Breen works for. You may have heard of the case pending before the — "

" — save it counselor. I am aware of who Mr. Breen allegedly works for. I will dismiss you when a new attorney is assigned. Is he naming another attorney or is he seeking a public defender?"

"We have not yet gotten that far, your honor. We would need some time to assess that and get back to you."

"Fine but that will not delay this case. We move forward with you as the attorney of record until that is finalized. Next issue, or should I say the first issue .... "

"Yes your honor. With all due respect, I am asking that you recuse yourself from the rotation in the pool. That would eliminate any chance of this case being heard before you."

Wayland County had four judges on rotation with others that could be pulled from other courthouses in other counties if need be. Cases were heard before judges on a 'lottery' basis. This was deemed another way for the woman with scales to be blind. Forde had just asked her to be taken out of the rotation, meaning that there would be no way for her to hear this case.

"Pardon me?"

"There are several reasons listed in the brief your honor."

She took a moment to look over the document that the clerk placed in front of her. Lawyers can read lengthy documents at lightning speed, Judge McCaglia was no different.

"None of them good counselor."

"This is a very high-profile case and you are a freshman judge. Second is that the accused is Irish and will be using a defense that — "

" — stop right there sir. Are you saying that an Irish defendant cannot get a fair trial in the whitest state in this country? You must be joking."

"You are Irish, Judge."

"Are you referring to my last name? I think that I have heard enough — "

" — there are other reasons listed, your honor."

"Motion denied."

"It's an appealable issue your honor."

"One which the next attorney will take up I'm sure. Since the cart is before the horse, lets correct that shall we? Mr. Cromwell, the charges please."

"Murder one, your honor," he said. "Multiple counts of felony possession of a firearm, unlawful modification of a banned firearm, multiple counts of possession of an illegal firearm, three counts of possession of narcotics, and felony possession with the intent to distribute. We reserve the right to amend the charges."

"So noted."

"Your honor, I would like to address that this was a murder for hire," Cromwell added.

"One thing at a time, Mr. Cromwell. Next item up for bid is how the accused pleads."

Forde turned and whispered into Breen's ear. Then Liam Breen spoke.

"Not guilty on all charges."

"Very well. There is no need to discuss the issue of bail. Denied. I assume that is where you were going with explaining the murder for hire stipulation, sir?"

"Yes judge," Cromwell said.

She looked to her clerk. "We are going to set a date on *my schedule* for discovery and motions for sixty days out. I want to hear this case." She then turned back to the District Attorney. "Any dates off-limits Mr. Cromwell?"

"None your honor. I will free myself up on any date the court wishes." He said it directed more toward the press than McCaglia.

"First of all, you cannot hand pick cases Judge," Forde spat out. "If you are not going to take your name out of the pool, that is one thing, but hand picking the case for your docket? With all due respect, that is beyond your scope." He said 'with all due respect' like there wasn't any.

"Be very careful Mr. Forde. You are dangerously close to contempt. What is your second of all, counselor?"

"So we aren't going to discuss that you just slated yourself for this case?"

"No. Did you have anything else before we set a date?"

"I have some dates that might conflict," Forde said.

"Since you are dumping this case I don't need to hear them." She then turned back to her clerk, looking for the calendar date.

"We are looking at Monday, September 6, Judge," the efficient clerk said.

"Very well. First thing on September sixth in Session Four. I'll take a short recess before we get to the rest of first appearances so the courtroom can be cleared of the media circus. That is all." She then slammed the gavel onto the sounding block. Everybody rose as she stepped down and left the courtroom for her chambers.

11

IN THE BACK OF THE COURTROOM, amidst the press and other onlookers, were attorneys Jacob Grantes and Ryan Wells. The two partners had been watching the show intently, watching Forde bury himself before Judge McCaglia.

The two gentlemen were in their early thirties, having met in law school in Boston. They had become fast friends and practically inseparable since. Jacob Grantes, or JG as everyone called him, was an extremely talented defense lawyer. He was a hard worker, raised in northern Vermont by parents who had to toil for every nickel. He was the only child, the first generation in his family to get a college education. His friend and partner was not the only lifelong friend he met in college, he had also met his wife Anna.

Anna was also an only child, but her upbringing could not have been more different from JG's. Anna's parents didn't struggle to make ends meet. Their ends met and then some. Her father, Norman Craig, was an investment tycoon. He had started his own international conglomerate, responsible for other businesses and personal finances in the hundreds of millions of dollars. He provided financial stability but was rarely home. Anna's mother, Olivia stayed home and along with a staff, provided Anna with any and every day-to-day need.

It was the Craig's, JG's in-laws, that provided the seed money for the law firm just a few short years prior. They saw how talented Jacob was, how great he was to their daughter and what a life he could provide if given a solid foundation.

Ryan Wells could have been the brother that JG never had. They were alike in so many ways and yet so different. He also grew up hand to mouth. He too had to work while in college. Only he didn't have in-laws to pay off his student loans or give him money to start his own law firm. JG had asked Ryan to partner with him in his burgeoning practice and he was happily along for the ride. Ryan met his wife, Angie, when they opened the law firm. What started as an interview for a receptionist turned into a job and a recent marriage.

Grantes, Wells & Associates was formed after both had graduated law school, passed the bar exam, and a brief stint as public defenders. Both attorneys had left those jobs behind, as they were making no money, and became immersed in the new enterprise. Wells had no financial investment but was determined to provide as many billable hours as possible. Grantes took the big cases that were winners. Wells took the flyers. He was the 'hippie liberal' who was more interested in the spirit of the law than the black letter.

The two attorneys had been at the Wayland County Superior Court for other cases in other courtrooms at the Superior Court building. JG had the final criminal court hearing in a car accident, which would then begin the civil court phase of the defense. Ryan had to defend a violation of a restraining order. Once they were finished with their business, they rushed over to the Second Session out of morbid curiosity.

Neither of the two lawyers were getting rich because of the new venture, and the coffers of Grantes, Wells & Associates were all but bare. They would often hang around the courthouse to see if they could pick up a client. There was always someone without a lawyer. Public defenders were the last resort, they told their potential clients. They knew because they had each been one right out of college. Once it was determined that the client could pay, they were off to the races. JG was more selective, Ryan took everything with a bank account.

"What do you think?" Ryan whispered to JG as the Breen first appearance was about to close. Judge McCaglia was officially irritated. They had both been in front of her earlier that year and knew that once she started interrupting people, speeding things along, she was fed up and moving on.

JG lifted up his newspaper displaying a defiant Saddam Hussein in court to cover up the fact that he was speaking while there were ongoing proceeds in this courtroom. "I think Forde is digging himself a hole he might not get out of. McCaglia is fair but she has a long memory."

"No, I mean about the case."

"That's what I meant. She is going to make sure that she sits on the bench for …. whoa. You mean you want this case?" JG was shaking his head like he couldn't believe his ears.

"Yeah. You just heard him say that he has a COI and can't be his lawyer. They don't have one, at least not on record or they would be here."

"Ry, do you realize what kind of publicity this case is going to get? Hell, we are sitting here. This is going to take a bundle of cash to defend. Experts, subpoenas, investigators …. money the firm doesn't have. I'm not even going to get into the fact that if what is being covered in the news is accurate, this case is unwinable. The jury pool is officially polluted."

"Forde doesn't work for free, JG. He's getting big bucks from someone. He hasn't done pro bono work in years I'll wager."

"Why do you think he is dumping this case? No money in it. The feds have probably seized all the assets. I wouldn't touch this with a ten-foot cattle prod."

67

The entire courtroom rose, as instructed by the bailiff. The judge was stepping down from her perch and headed into her chambers. Breen was being taken away by the Correctional Officers for the holding cells in the basement of the courthouse. Forde was packing up his briefcase.

"But you're not me."

Before JG could protest, Ryan had already left the bench seating in the back row and was scurrying his way to the defendant's table. Grantes had never told his partner which cases he could or couldn't take, as long as he was bringing in money. Billable hours. The firm needed every dime to stay solvent. G, W &A were beginning to make a name for themselves in the area, but they were not Dan W. Forde Esquire. If Ryan did get this case, it was going to be a ton of work. If there wasn't any money coming in from it, that limited the number of other paying clients he could take. JG didn't need the personal income, he was rich through marriage, but Ryan did. If no money was coming into the firm, Ryan didn't get paid. Nor did Angie. JG and his wife Angie could continue to live their lifestyle without generating an income. Ryan and Angie were new to these social circles and might not continue to be in them.

JG told himself to reserve judgement until he had heard all of the facts. Maybe Forde wouldn't give Ryan the case. Maybe Breen didn't want the hippie lawyer in the linen suit. Maybe he had a nest-egg hidden someplace. Maybe this case *could* be won.

Yeah right.

"Mr. Forde. Hello. Do you or Breen have a lawyer in mind to take over the case?"

"And you are?"

"Oh, yes, of course. How silly of me. Ryan Wells. I am a partner in the law firm — "

" — ah yes. The boutique shop around the corner, across the street from Sully's Tavern."

"Right. We aren't directly across the street from them, but yes. McCaglia is a ball-buster huh?"

"She made a grave error, one that is reparable by appeal. By whomever takes over the case, that is."

"So you haven't got another lawyer lined up yet? I might be interested."

"Do you think your little shop can handle this case? I'm sure that other lawyers might be better suited. No pun intended." Forde ran his eyes up and down Wells.

"I don't follow. The pun I mean."

"You seem very nice, Mr. Wells, but this is a large case. A murder case tied to guns and drugs. The only thing that you are missing is the long hair and a 'peace, love & harmony' tie-dye shirt. This is not a good case for you. Breen is going to take one look at you in your wrinkled linen suit and send you packing. Save yourself the embarrassment."

"He should be the one embarrassed. He was caught standing over the body that he shot seven times in the face. Allegedly. Can he pay?"

"He says so."

"Then let me worry about whether he says yes or no. Will you support it? Put in a good word for me?"

"Sure. We can go down there together before they truck him back if you want. Why isn't your partner, Grantes, here with you?"

"Oh he is. He is sitting in the gallery." He looked over to where he had been sitting with this business partner. He was no longer there, nor anywhere in the courtroom. He turned back to Forde. "You know JG?"

"We've met at the club."

"I'm a member of the Wayland County Country Club also. I am surprised we've never met before."

"It's a big club. Maybe we can correct that at some point."

"Great. Will you give me ten minutes or so? I want to go find JG and chat with him for a moment. I'll meet you down in holding?"

"Sure. I'll set it up with the COs. Just prepare yourself for Breen to toss you on your ass."

"I'll keep it in mind. Thanks. Hey by the way, why are you dumping this case?"

"Didn't you hear me with the judge? COI. Conflict of Interest."

"I heard, but really why? Trying to separate him from the heard? That can be a double-edged sword. He tries to clear himself of the huge stand-off and the cop killers, but they could get the itch to make sure he doesn't testify. Is there any danger of that?"

"That is all confidential information with my actual clients, and you know as well as I do that I cannot be privy to, participate in, or assist in the cover-up of any planned criminal activity."

"Understood. If you want to punt this case you had better give me a glowing recommendation downstairs then."

"I stand corrected, Wells. You might be just the lawyer for this case."

12

LIAM BREEN WAS SITTING ON THE SAME SIDE OF THE TABLE as Dan Forde when Ryan Wells entered the conference room. They both looked about the same age, in the low fifties, though Forde obviously took better care of himself. They were in conversation when the door opened.

Breen's hair was disheveled and mostly white. His large body was covered in tattoos, including his neck and the back of his hands. He looked worse up close, Ryan thought, than he had from far away in the back of Session Two. Ryan made a mental note that if he were to lock down his client that costume makeup would need to be applied to cover up the visible body art.

"Mr. Wells. We've just been discussing you."

"Excellent. All good things I hope." Ryan said this looking at Forde. He sat in the chair opposite the two other men, setting his leather briefcase down on the floor beside him.

"I got some concerns, " Breen said. He was cuffed and chained to an eye-hook that was bolted into the concrete floor.

"So do I Mr. Breen." JG had told Ryan that if he really wanted this case he was going to have to take charge. This group that had allegedly done all of this damage, been involved in so many criminal activities, were a hardened group. He was going to have to grow a pair, put Breen and probably Forde in their place if he was garner any respect.

"My first concern is that I get paid," he continued. "This is going to be a long trial and an expensive one, unless you want to take a plea. I'm not even sure what kind of time we could get everything reduced to, so at least for now we plan to take this to the hoop. $75,000 now and another $75,000 if this goes to trial. If we run out of dough before trial, we will need to fill the piggy bank. That is my concern, Mr. Breen. Money. Is my concern warranted?"

"I don't have it on me but I can get it. If I decide to go with you."

71

"Well it's time to make that decision big-boy. Mr. Forde here just told the judge that he isn't your lawyer anymore. Anything that you told him so far is still privileged, but just the same once we decide to go forward together we are going to part company with your former attorney."

"How do I know that you are any fuckin' good?"

"I guess you don't. You have to rely on your former attorney to set you straight. But you need to find a lawyer before you head back to the tombs, Liam. Can I call you Liam?"

He nodded.

"Good. So Liam, you have been down this path before I'm sure. What will happen is that you will have to meet with people at the Wayland County House of Corrections to determine if you qualify for a public defender. You will have to fill out financial forms, which you probably don't want to do. If you can afford my fees, then you probably don't qualify anyway. Meanwhile things are going to be happening with your case that you will be unaware of. Mr. Forde here will also be unaware of any progress because the prosecution will not keep him in the loop because he is no longer your attorney of record. The Honorable Judge McCaglia is a tough jurist. She made herself your judge. She likes to keep things moving. So while you are wasting away your days at county, without a lawyer, your case is still moving forward without you. Finally, when and if you do get somebody else that will take your case, they are going to have to play catch-up with very little time to prepare because she only gave you sixty days. What do you think that will mean for your chances of ever seeing daylight again?"

"I won't sell my boys down the river. You gotta know that goin' in."

Ryan looked at Forde and nodded like he understood.

"The so-called Old Men in the Mountains? We can talk about that when we sign some paperwork and free ourselves from the company of their attorney. Any other concerns?"

"Are you gonna look like a hippie when we go to court?"

"I don't see that as a legitimate concern of yours, but I'll address it. I am a defense lawyer with my own style. I like to be comfortable. I am not going to dress or pretend to be something I'm not. The jury will see right through it. My job is to make sure you look the part though. You could use a little peace and love on your side right now. Peace and love is good. Tree-hugging is good. Guns, drugs, and murder are bad."

"Ok. I'll do it."

"Good. Now, Mr. Forde. Thank you for your time and services but I would like to spend some time with my client please."

Dan W. Forde Esquire stood up with his briefcase. He patted Breen on the back with his free hand, gave a wink out of view of Breen. "Good Luck and remember what we talked about," he said. "And Mr. Wells, I will send the necessary documents that you will need to your office. Call if I can be of further assistance."

"Thank you again," Ryan said as Forde left the conference room.

"With that out of the way, Liam, we have to talk about logistical matters before I have you sign a form stating that I am your lawyer."

"What the fuck? You just sent him outta here sayin' that you *are* my lawyer."

"And I will be once I get the first seventy-five grand. I'd like to say that I trust you, Liam but we just met. You gotta earn my trust. How am I going to get the money from you when you are in jail?"

"The boys will send you — "

" — uh, uh, uh. No can do. First, that money has probably been seized. Second, they have their own case, in which they are probably going to separate themselves from you. That separation is good for us by the way. They can't be paying your bills and be separate. And last but not least, I represent you. The money has to come from you. Where you get the money doesn't mean a thing to me."

"Ok. Well that makes things a little more complicated. I gotta a girl on the outside. She can go get it. I can call her from lockup tonight maybe."

"Or you can call her now. Use my cell."

Ryan pulled out his Samsung S300 clam-shell flip phone, handing it to his client.

"But be quick, if they see you with it we are both in trouble."

"Can I make another call after?"

"Don't press your luck. Just call this girl of yours."

Breen started to dial as best he could with his hands cuffed. He then brought his head down to his hands so he could hear.

The person he called must have answered at that moment because he started talking into the phone. Breen was speaking in some type of code to her. He was saying it quickly, Ryan hoped that she was either a very good listener or was writing what he was saying down. And as quickly as the call was made, the phone was flipped shut and slid on the table back to Ryan.

"Is she going to give me the money in cash or what?"

"Yeah cash. You take cash right?"

"Cash and I are best friends."

"My ol' lady can meet you with the money later on tonight. Forde told me that your office is by Sully's tavern?"

"Yes, it is down the street and on the opposite side."

"Ok. Well she don't know where that is, but she knows Sully's. She will meet you there at five or so."

"Very good." Ryan retrieved an Attorney of Record form from his briefcase. " I am going to post-date this for Wednesday the seventh. Go ahead and sign it. If she doesn't show, Liam, I am going to shred this. But as long as she pays me, you have yourself a lawyer. I will give her a receipt for the money and put in escrow. As of Wednesday, if all goes to plan you will have a new lawyer."

"You better get me outta this, hippie. I done my part."

"Oh your part is just starting Liam. That was just the finances. We will meet later this week or early next and we are going to go over every bit of this thing. You are going to tell me where all the bodies are buried."

"I told you that I won't give up the boys."

"You've said. But in order to do my job, I need to know every detail of every illegal activity you have committed or know about."

"That's gonna be a long conversation."

"I'm sure."

13

SULLY'S TAVERN WAS A DIVE BAR. It was not a charming dive bar that was trendy or kitschy. It was a pit. Ryan and JG went there because it was close to their practice, discussing repeatedly how much the establishment needed a makeover. Post work or post trial cocktails were consumed there often. The community went there as well because it was located on a main thoroughfare and the drinks were cheap. That thoroughfare was just three blocks away from Barstone, New Hampshire.

Wayland and Barstone shared a border, one that was delineated by a set of railroad tracks. The cliché was made real, clichés come from someplace. While the affluent of Wayland lived their lives, commuting on those tracks in and out of Boston for their daily work commute, the Barstonians lived on the other end of the spectrum. The Sheriff's department made sure that the debauchery of Barstone stayed on the appropriate side of the commuter rail.

Barstone shared the same county with the same name as the town that it was the stepchild to. Which made the Wayland County Courthouse abustle with Barstonians despite being located in the town of Wayland.

Grantes, Wells & Associates was specifically located in Wayland for its proximity to the courthouse, on the edge of Barstone which gave them the vast majority of their business. Ryan had picked up a few clients from Sully's. Defendants would tell of their woes to their friends over drinks, stories overheard by an eager attorney. Ryan's current case was the first time he had been hired by a client who frequented Sully's prior to meeting them there.

Ryan picked out his usual barstool, one that afforded him the best vantage point in the noisy bar. He could see those that were playing, or on the chalkboard waiting to play, pool. He could watch those that preferred darts hurl their projectiles toward the green and red wagon wheel. But that day he was most interested in the entrance.

He had a picture in his head of the woman he would be meeting. Liam Breen was in his fifties, covered in tattoos, had a long history as an outlaw, and was currently in a real fix for being involved with a tribe of men of the same relative age who ran guns and cooked drugs. Lest we forget that he had committed a violent murder. Allegedly. The woman that Ryan was envisioning to walk through the front door to Sully's Tavern could be summed up as a haggard, middle-aged biker chick.

How he would pick out that particular hardened woman who had spent a lifetime with hardened men was going to be the trick. The drinking establishment usually had its fair share of rough and tumbles. His linen suit stuck out like a toucan in the Sahara.

Ryan had been distracted by the fight that was about to break out between the pool players, both men wielding their respective cues as weapons, when he received a tap on his shoulder.

He turned around to a gaunt woman in her late twenties, dirty-blonde hair, and large loop earrings. She wore a brazen amount of make-up, especially around her eyes which glowed the color of jade. The young woman's scant clothing was designed and cut to show off her tattoo-daubed endowments. Some of the artwork was inked onto her breasts, which were mostly available for view as well. Her stiletto heals were like stilts, how she could walk in the contraptions was a mystery to him. As was the person.

"You must be the lawyer," she said.

"For Breen? Yes. I'm Ryan Wells. And you are?"

"Maddy." She had an orange sling backpack draped over her shoulder, the strap ran down between her artistically decorated and propped-up breasts. She removed the pack and tossed it to him, which was unnecessary as they were but two feet apart. "Here's your money."

"Thank you. Let me sign this receipt." Ryan slung the bag over his shoulder and removed the folded, prepared carbon two-ply receipt from his inside suit coat pocket and signed his autograph. He handed it to her and said, "You don't want to give somebody that kind of money without a receipt. For future reference."

"And you should generally count the money you're given before handing someone a receipt for it. For future reference. So it looks like we both got shit to work on."

Ryan laughed while she turned to leave, but he stopped her by grabbing her wrist.

"Hey! You don't grab on me! Never." This gained the attention of several men in the bar.

"I'm sorry," he said with his hands up in surrender. "Let's go get a cup of coffee someplace and chat for a minute. This was not the best place to meet."

"What like a date? I ain't a coffee and muffins kinda girl."

"Not a date, Maddy. I need to go through this bag, and I also need to take a statement from you. It would be nice to get it out of the way now so we don't have to reschedule."

"Fine. But you put your hands on me again and I'll cut your throat."

"Understood."

The diner down the street was open but empty. The hour was too early for most people to eat supper, and happy hours were usually spent elsewhere. Even on a Monday following a booze-filled weekend. Ryan led Maddy to the back corner booth though the desire for added privacy of being in the back of the establishment was unwarranted.

Ryan tossed his briefcase and the backpack into the booth on his side and sat himself, taking up the end. He was retrieving a yellow legal notepad when the disinterested waitress came by to collect an order. He ordered coffee, and since the diner didn't serve booze Maddy didn't order anything. The woman rolled her eyes as the tip on a cup of coffee was not worth the time for her to pour it.

"Listen, we may have gotten off on the wrong foot here. I am going to do my best to minimize the punishment for your .... boyfriend?"

"Don't put a label on it, lawyer. I let him climb on top of me and he pays my bills."

"Sugar Daddy?"

"Why cuz he is older than me?"

"If I need a character witness, the nature of your relationship is going to come out."

"I ain't gonna be taken any stand or testifyin'."

"Why?"

"I wouldn't even make it inside the courthouse. I got outstanding warrants."

"Yeah, that wouldn't be good. What are they for?"

"Prostitution and larceny. It was from a ways back."

"How far back? You aren't very old. Mid-twenties?"

"It was before I met Liam. He told me to tell you whatever you want to know except about what goes on up in the mountains."

"We can work on your legal situation afterward if you like, but for now that is exactly what I want to know. What goes on up in the mountains?"

"Not a chance. I tell you and I'm dead. 'Sides, you don't wanna know or you're a dead man too."

"I already know what I've seen in the news or read in the paper. They are into guns and drugs. They provided him with the work and the weapon. This man that was killed, he did something to the men in the mountains and they sent Liam to kill him right? Those guys have their own trials to worry about. They are out of business. We need to focus on your …. daddy or whatever. Murder for hire is, among other things, a life sentence at best."

Maddy looked at him with pity. She shook her head while she spoke. "Why is Liam hitchin' up to your wagon? You don't even know what you got into." She paused, trying to decide whether to walk away from the table and the situation forever.

"Look, mister hippie lawyer. They ain't never outta business. They got eyes and ears everywhere. You think they don't know about that seventy-five grand in your bag? Liam is nothin' to them. And there will be a dozen more men to pick up where the others left off. Business is business and you stumbled into somethin' here that you ain't equipped to carry."

"Like what?"

"I've already said too much."

"You haven't said anything."

"Then that's the way I wanna leave it."

She got up and left the diner.

Ryan dug out his cell phone, saving the phone number that Breen dialed from the conference room into his contacts. He typed M-A-D-D-Y into his phone, though he didn't know if it was a 'Y' or and 'IE' at the end. She was going to be a tough nut to crack.

14

IMMEDIATELY AFTER LEAVING THE BRIEF MEETING WITH MADDY, leaving the diner, Ryan called the firm's primary investigator. Cole Renner was a PI out of Boston but would work anywhere within a two-hour radius. Ryan told him what had transpired that day. How he had grabbed a high-profile case in court. He gave him Liam Breen's name and his connection to the recent news event in the mountains of New Hampshire.

He told Renner about Maddy. How she had put up a tough façade but was obviously scared. Ryan wanted to find out more about her, about Breen. About the entire situation. Maddy had told him that he was now involved in defending a man caught in a situation that was bigger than a murder-for-hire conviction. Which meant huge.

Cole said that he had heard of the case, as anybody who was up on current affairs would have, but didn't know more than anyone else at that time. He said that he would get started on Breen, the compound, and this girl Maddy in the morning. He congratulated him on acquiring this big case and hung up.

On Ryan's way home to his wife Angie, Stephen Still's *Treetop Flyer* came on the car stereo. He liked the song but had never really listened to the lyrics. As Ryan listened, trying to clear his head, the words registered with him. *"Then some old boy walks up, and he says "Hey son" wanna make some fast cash?"* ....

He began to feel that it was a bad omen. He wanted to change the station but decided to listen on. The song continued, *"Well there's things I am, and there's things I'm not .... I am a smuggler and I could get shot .... I ain't going to die, I ain't goin' to get caught"* ....

The rain washed down on his windshield and he was suddenly filled with a chill. He turned up the temperature of his Jetta but neither the sixty-eight degree rain nor the internal temperature of the car was the issue .... *"I'm a treetop flyer"* ....

A bad feeling. He shut off the radio and tried to shake it off. Maybe this case was a mistake. The rest of the drive home was done in silence.

The next day, after his morning routine with Angie, they both took their own vehicles in to work. They both worked in the same place, Angie was the receptionist for JG and her boss/husband at the firm. Angie liked to go in early to get things arranged for the day. And each day would often lead to Ryan heading off to court or in one direction or another, leaving Angie without transportation. She left the office daily at exactly 5:00 PM unless infrequently needed longer. Ryan's hours were less regimented. So two vehicles were taken every day despite their desire to be more green.

Halfway through his fourth cup of fair trade Arabica coffee, Ryan's office phone squawked with Angie telling him that Cole was on the line for him. He put down his coffee mug on his desk and picked up line one.

"I have to see you today. I'm in the area. I'll stop by the office."

"Hello to you too. What's going on Cole?"

"I'm on my way. I'll speak to you in a bit."

Ryan had other things that he had planned for the day but he agreed. Within an hour of that phone call, Cole was in his office. Resigning.

"You're just going to leave without notice? We have cases that are ongoing that we are depending on you for. I was depending on you for the Breen thing specifically."

"Yeah, and that's what I want to talk to you about too. You should quit that case."

"I can't just quit the case, Cole. Have you spoken with JG about this yet?"

"You've got other investigators."

80

Ryan got on his office phone and asked for JG to be sent in to Ryan's office. Angie relayed the message and a minute later JG entered the office wondering what the emergency was.

"Cole is leaving without notice."

"What?" JG looked stunned and pale. "Is this about pay?"

"Guys, this isn't about pay. Some things have come to light, and I just want to get away for a bit."

"Now? It's not a great time, Cole," JG said with an agitated tone.

"Why don't you use one of your other investigators?"

JG responded, "They do background checks. Criminal history. They aren't equipped for this type of .... "

There was a brief moment of silence while all three of them composed themselves. Ryan remained seated behind his desk, JG and Cole also sat on the other side of the desk but facing on another. Cole began again.

"I'm gonna level with you, Ryan. This latest thing that you have me on is not good. I poked around a little bit last night and this morning and you should quit the case."

"I've already committed to it. I've been paid. Paperwork has been filed with the court. I'm the AOR. I can't just walk away. Is that what this is about? This Breen case? What has you scared? The guys in the mountains? They are all locked up in federal custody."

Cole looked at JG, then back at Ryan.

"That's the tip of the iceberg. They run guns and drugs in and out of Boston and points west."

"So? That has nothing to do with my case. Just because he belongs to the same organization? He is being charged separately for murder one, among other charges."

"Ryan don't be stupid. The Old Men in the Mountains are Irish. They have been around a long time, not because they spread cheer and goodwill. They do business in Boston. Connect the dots."

"You're saying that the group that Breen works for makes drugs for the Irish mob to distribute?"

"They also house the guns that are brought in for distribution. And that is just the beginning."

"There's more?"

"Yeah. A lot more. The Winter Hill crew doesn't just run numbers and fix races anymore. Those Mc's are tied in with the real Mc's across the pond. I've already been told, in not so many words to back off."

"Who came to talk with you?"

"Like I said, in not so many words. My girlfriend's Pomeranian was stabbed and stuck into her purse. The dog was running around when we got up. I left to look into this Breen thing on the bright, like you asked, and she took a shower. She gets dressed and finds the dog. She calls me screaming saying that the dog was wrapped in a bloody resignation letter to GW & A. Meaning someone was inside my house, while she was showering. She didn't hear the dog bark, and it was stabbed to death and stuffed into her purse. They got in and out of a locked house and stabbed a fuckin' dog without a sound. She's freakin' out. I'm freakin' out. So here I am. She's been wantin' me to do somethin' else with my life for a while now anyways. I've been tryin' to fight it off, but now with this? I ain't gotta leg to stand on. She said it was either you guys or her." He placed the dried blood stained resignation letter on Ryan's desk. "I didn't type that blood-soaked letter, but I'll sign it if you need somethin' in writing."

There was another long pause as everyone in the room processed the information. They all stared at the soiled document in horror. Cole was again the first to break the silence.

"I've got a guy that I can call to help you out on the side," Cole said. "Maybe it can work into a full-time thing. He's fearless and he's not happy with his current work situation. I've used him to help me out on jobs in the past. I can call him if you want."

JG was finally out of shock and was regaining his color. He had a yellow lab and the thought of it being stabbed didn't sit well with him. "If you trust him Cole, set up an interview for all us to meet. You should be there too."

"I'm really sorry guys. I can't risk my life for this job. Or my girlfriend for that matter. I signed up to do background checks and stuff like that. I didn't sign up for death threats and mob investigations. This new guy is from South Boston, he knows all the players. I'm not saying that he will take the job, but he has been real good at heavy lifting for me in the past."

"It's ok Cole," JG said. "We understand. Thank you for your past work and good luck to you. Be careful."

Ryan added, "If you could set this interview up with him sooner rather than later, I would appreciate it."

"You're still movin' forward?"

"Yes. Will you set up the interview?"

"Uh. Yeah. Of course. Will-do." Renner shook his head in disbelief. "I will bring him up to speed on the other little things I have going for you both as well. It's been a pleasure. I'm really sorry. Hey, I'm just gonna say this one more time so you can't say I didn't warn you. You should get outta this, and like …. now. You really should quit."

82

After cole had left the office, JG had remained to discuss the latest development with his partner.

"So this case is already haunting us. I told you this wasn't a good idea."

"We now have $75,000 in escrow for this case. We needed the money, JG. I need it. This is a murder case that Breen is going to insist we take to trial, meaning another $75,000."

"At what price? I don't want to put my family or Angie or you in any danger with this. We just lost Cole. Do you know what your are doing? Get out. Give the money back. We don't need the money that bad."

"It will be relatively quick cash. Breen has already said that he isn't going to flip on the other guys. The feds don't want him, they have plenty already. I am pretty sure that Cromwell isn't going to be cutting any deals since Breen was caught standing over the body. He might be willing to drop some of the ancillary charges to avoid the cost of a trial, but this is a high profile case. The gun that was in his hand is probably going to confirm that it was the weapon used to make swiss cheese out of the victim's face. Breen is in all likelihood going to prison for the rest of his life and we will get a great payday out of it. I'll do the best I can but unless there is a major screwup …."

"Just be careful. And let me know if you get any threatening correspondence. And by the way, are you going to tell Angie what you've done or should I?"

15

THE CONFERENCE ROOM AT THE WAYLAND COUNTY HOUSE OF CORRECTIONS was booked for the lawyer and client to speak, but they were only given a half-hour. Other lawyers needed the room and the time as well. More than a week had gone by since the last time Ryan had seen Liam at the courthouse. Eight days was the soonest Ryan could get in to the prison to see his latest client. Between his other cases and the available times for the conference room, time was getting away from them. With everything that had happened, eight days seemed like an eternity.

Ryan had been led to the conference room and was waiting for quite some time. He was hoping that his half-hour time-slot hadn't already begun. While he waited for his client to be brought to the room, he organized all of his thoughts into bullet-points on a legal pad. The meeting was going to have to be concise.

Breen was eventually brought into the conference room looking no worse for wear. More often than not, incarceration took its toll on the prisoner. The volume of noise and shouting, the close proximity to your cellmate, the horrible food, lack of contact with the outside world, all have an adverse affect on the inmate's psyche which manifests into physical disfigurement.

Sunken eyes, a hunched back, and pallor were but a few of the tell-tale signs of depreciating physical and mental well-being. Ryan had seen it a number of times, the client that he had started the case with was not the same person by the end of the trial. But not Breen. Breen didn't normally look great, nor did he in the conference room. But he didn't look like incarceration was having any affect on him at all. Just another day in paradise.

The CO who brought in Breen, apologized for the delay while locking the prisoner into the chair. "Sorry for the delay counselor. It's a zoo in here today. You're time will start when I get out of here. Just hit the panic button if you need us." He nodded his head toward the large red button housed in a clear plastic, flip-top box by the door. It looked like the big button that they showed in the 80s cold war movies. The button that would send off nuclear missiles toward the Soviet Union and would then destroy the entire world as we knew it.

"That won't be necessary, I'm sure, but thank you."

When the CO left, Ryan got right to it. "How are you doing, Liam? We don't have very much time and I have a ton of questions. It's already the thirteenth and time is moving pretty quick — "

" — it ain't for me."

"Nevertheless, I need you to be straight with me and don't beat around the bush so we can get through all of this. Good?"

"Yeah, sure."

"The compound where the big seizure happened, up in the mountains …. that's where you worked, correct?"

"You already know that."

"So what did you do for them?"

"Let's not go there, ok? We should focus on what I got charged for."

"We will, believe me. I'm getting there. I need to know all about the background of why you allegedly killed that man. The District Attorney is going to come up with anything and everything they can to hang you. They will turn over what they have to me, and I don't want to get ambushed by it. It's called discovery. But I'd like to be prepared before then."

"I know what it is. Allegedly? I thought you said that I could be honest with you. We both know I killed that motherfucker."

"I think you are focused on the wrong thing here Liam. And now taking the stand is officially off the table. I can't put you up on the stand to testify that you are innocent, which is what you have pled, knowing that you will perjure yourself.

"But let's get back to the compound," he continued. "Those men that are in federal custody lived there, yes?"

"Off and on. We all did," Breen said.

"And they found labs where you guys were making cocaine and methamphetamine and such. That was the main business, yes?"

"No comment."

"C'mon Liam. You've got to lay it out straight for me. My investigator quit because he has been intimidated. Someone doesn't want us snooping around to find out the truth."

"And I don't want to tell you either. I've told you over and over again that I won't roll on the boys."

"I won't have you testify about it. But it goes to supporting facts. If the guy that you shot in the face seven times was into your …. organization …. for money, or if he had stolen something from them, he has a very different expectation of surviving the act. It's the

85

difference between a horrific homicide for hire on a random or specific victim versus mutual fray."

"Stop speaking lawyer and get back to English."

"It's like when two people get into a fist-fight. If you just walk up to someone and cold-cock them, you are guilty to a higher degree than if you and the other fellow decide mutually to take it outside and settle your differences like men. Obviously murder is murder, and much different than a fist fight. Especially if you were hired to do so. But the concept is somewhat similar. The victim didn't agree to let you use his face as target practice, but if he created the circumstance where violence to his person was inevitable, then that is mitigating. It's called the inciting event."

"So you could get me out of this?"

"No. I'm not saying that. Not at all. What I am saying is that I need all of the facts and time is wasting. So tell me if drugs are what you guys were doing up there in the mountains."

"That's some of it."

"And the arsenal that you boys had up there, that was to protect your enterprise? Protect the compound?"

"Yes and no."

"Liam?"

"You don't know what you are askin' dude. Seriously. Leave it alone."

"Liam …. why does everyone keep saying that? Maddy. You. My former investigator."

The struggle of how to proceed was visible on his face. The torture within Breen was displayed on his person as though the torture was physical. The silence was deafening.

"We used them for protection, but we moved guns too."

"Moved them where?"

"We were the housing and distribution for another group. We were like the middle men."

"For whom?"

"How does this help you get me out of here? This is like opening up that box that you can't shut. Whatever it's called. You know what I mean?"

"Pandora? Pandora's box?"

"Right. If I tell you what you're askin', you can't unknow it. There's no need to know it in the first place."

"Then just nod your head if I get it right. Irish mob?"

Breen did nothing.

"Boston?"

He looked at the ceiling and nodded his head. "Boston is who we work for. They have bosses too."

"Irish .... Ireland?"

He nodded again.

"Now we are getting somewhere. So what did your victim do to get himself killed?"

"He did something for us and couldn't keep his mouth shut about it. You see what I'm telling you? This thing is better if you just keep the reason he got himself dead out of the picture."

"I don't think that is going to be an option. Cromwell is going to want to prove motive as part of his case. They are going to look into it, and he may get evidence from the federal prosecutor to do it. Without your side of things, I don't really know what you expect me to do here, Liam. Why take this to trial if I can't tell the facts of the story?"

"Forde told me to plead not guilty. So I did. We go to trial to find a loophole, right? Isn't that what you lawyers do? That judge made a mistake, right? So she pays for it by lettin' me go."

"It doesn't work like that. This isn't the movies. She really didn't do anything completely wrong. It's in a gray area. Best-case is that we argue for a new judge. But you are still going to lose a trial."

"I can take a pinch. What kinda time can you get me down to?"

"There is nothing to bargain for. A federal prosecutor is dealing with your comrades in arms, they don't need you. That is why you are here and not with them. The D.A. can't get at them because they are being prosecuted federally, so you giving him information about other, bigger fish is pointless."

"So what did I give you $75k for then?"

"Because if you ever want to get out of here you are going to have to tell a jury that you were under their thumb. It's called coercion. Meaning that getting out was not an option. You feared for your life and so you had to take another life. That you did their bidding because you were forced to and under duress. That gets things down to the remote possibility of someday breathing free air. You are in your fifties and you have been a criminal, in and out of jail, your entire life. You've never been convicted of killing anyone before, which is really the only thing you have in your favor right now. Explaining your situation within the grand scheme of things is the only way you don't spend the rest of your life in prison."

"You don't know what you are askin'."

"I'm not asking you to do anything. I'm giving you your options. That's what you paid me for."

There was a loud knock on the conference room door. The CO on the other side of it was letting the two men know that their time was up.

87

"You think about it Liam. Let me know what you want to do. I'll be in touch."

16

SATURDAY, JULY SEVENTEENTH, was the first time that all parties were able to meet. Cole had arranged for his replacement to accompany him up to Wayland, New Hampshire, from Boston. Grantes and Wells were at their practice without their one and only associate, Angie. Weekends were sometimes necessary to catch up on work, however both attorneys had decided to minimize the extra workdays for their receptionist. It was deemed good for both moral and finances.

The two attorneys were amidst other work when the two investigators entered the firm. Cole knew that walk-ins were not being accepted on this particular Saturday, so he locked the door behind them. He knocked on each of the partner's office doors and led his replacement into the only tiny meeting room that doubled as a lunchroom. They had all jokingly referred to it as 'conference room one'.

Cole was obviously very comfortable with his surroundings as he was making a pot of coffee while waiting for his former employers.

"Hey Cole," Ryan said as he entered the room.

"I'm sorry for having to ruin your Saturday," JG said to Cole behind Ryan. Grantes closed the door out of habit more than necessity.

"No problem. It's the least I can do. This is Warren Dennihan. The man I recommended to take my position."

The tall thin man stepped toward them, pumping each of the attorney's hands with a firm handshake. He was ruggedly good looking, in his early thirties with dark blonde hair and bluish eyes. He looked a little more rugged than usual as he had a black eye, swollen cheek, and a fattened/split lip. Both attorneys looked at each other and then Cole.

"Call me Deni," he said to both of them.

"Ryan Wells. Uh …. are you alright?"

"Yeah. Sorry. I normally don't look like this. I had an MMA fight last night. Amateur bout. It went a little longer than I expected."

JG and Ryan exchanged nodds. The explanation seemed to appease them.

"I'm Jacob Grantes. With a name like Jacob I have several nicknames, but most people call me JG." With introductions out of the way, he continued taking the lead. "Why don't we all have a seat so we can discuss if this is going to be a good match."

Warren removed his sport coat, filling the shoulders of it with the corners of the back of the chair, then took his seat. The loose-fiber white tshirt that he was wearing did little to veil the tapestry of tattoos that covered his torso. Had the shirt been darker, none of his body art would have been detected. JG gave his partner another look of concern before continuing. The bad-boy look was complete.

"So tell us a little about yourself, Deni," JG continued. "You come with a recommendation from Cole which we value but know little else about you. Other than you participate in Mixed Martial Arts. Very brutal hobby."

"I get paid for it, so it's more than a hobby. But you're right, it can get interesting. I'm currently a Massachusetts State Police Detective for my day job, but I hate it. I been doin' side jobs for Cole here and there for a while now on top of everything else."

"Your accent is thick, Boston born and bred?"

"Southie."

"Should I be concerned that you are still in the employ of the state of Massachusetts and working as a private investigator on the side?"

"If you wanna be concerned, go ahead. I gotta make sure I can make a living doing the PI thing before I quit. I don't make much with them, but I can't just leave either. So for now, I'm gonna have to juggle whatever you throw at me and my regular job. If this works out."

Ryan jumped in because he was fixated on the fact that this Warren Dennihan was from South Boston. "If you are from South Boston you must know your fair share of criminals. That is a rough part of the city."

"Yeah. I know a few. Why?"

"I'm not sure what, if anything, Cole has told you about the reason he is leaving us. But we …. I …. have a case involving some people who have made it quite clear that they aren't interested in being implicated."

"From South Boston?"

"I believe so. My client has stated that his bosses work for an organization based out of Boston. That organization is well known for being in and around South Boston."

JG interjected. "Before we get into specifics, we need to make sure this is going to work out. This is an interview not a briefing. Confidentiality agreements need to take place once we decide to move forward. I am still concerned that what you know about our defendants is fundamentally at odds with your job in prosecuting these defendants."

"I can see that. Maybe this isn't going to work. I'm not gonna beg. All I can tell ya is that I have had my run-ins with the Irish mob down there. That's what we are talkin' about right? I just dealt with them again not to long ago as a matter of fact. If you want to hire me for this one thing, then see where it goes …. I think I have some knowledge to bare."

It was Cole's turn to jump in. "I suggested Deni because he has done work for me in the past, off the books. He can't officially have a PI license until he leaves his current job. But because of that job he has a conceal and carry permit, and he knows how to handle himself. You did win that MMA fight last night, right Deni?"

"Yeah but you don't need to sell me like I ain't in the room." He turned to the attorneys. "If you don't want to work with me, no hard feelings fellas."

"We're not saying that," Ryan said. "We aren't saying that are we JG?"

"No. But I would like my concerns noted. If we decide to move forward you are going to have to sign some documents stating that anything that you learn about a client cannot be repeated. Criminal charges can be brought against you if you violate that confidentiality. We run the risk of disbarment, so we will cut ties with you and worse if that ever happened."

"I get it. No need to beat an already dead horse. Should we talk fees before I sign my life away?"

"Cole, would you give us a few minutes please?" JG wanted to talk about the financial arrangements without their previous investigator. He had served his purpose, it was time to move forward without him.

Once Cole had left the room, they discussed fees. It was a good thing for Warren that JG had begun the bidding. Warren was used to getting paid by Cole, which means that he had been taking a bath. Used and abused. The opening number was almost one and a half times what Deni was going to start with. But he wasn't dumb. He threw out much higher numbers and they finally agreed to double what he was expecting per hour, in addition to expenses.

For Warren, this was going to be a good deal. Even if it turned out to be just the one job, he was going to make more money per hour than he would for a full day of pay as a cop. In his mind he had already left the state police.

17

THE WAYLAND COUNTY HOUSE OF CORRECTIONS was a zoo again on Sunday, July eighteenth. Every Sunday was a non-contact visitation day, which meant everyone in the prison who was cared about by anyone on the outside of the razor-wire was corralled at various times of the day for visits. The visitation room was the size of a school gym. That room was then divided into two areas like two interlocking capital E's. The two long hallways which ran up the spine of each E had smaller hallways veering off of them lined with seats and phones. The prisoner would then sit in the non-private seat and speak to the visitor or visitors that were on the other side of the bulletproof glass in their corresponding E chamber.

Fights would always break out, which would set off the Ellis alarm and lug teams would interrupt visiting time. The fights were over anything and everything. It could be; another inmate listening in on a conversation, or checking out another inmate's scantily clad girl, not enough time to visit, a visitor wasn't allowed in because they were a felon, a phone doesn't work because it is broken and they cannot hear their visitor, or any number of other reasons. When somebody is confined in close quarters twenty-four-seven, it doesn't take much to set that somebody off.

There were a few brawls early that morning because the temperature of the prison was freezing. The Sheriff had mandated that the heat be turned off during the summer months. It was also deemed unnecessary for air conditioning to be operating as it had been an unusually cool summer thus far. It was not quite sixty-three degrees outside, not even sixty inside the prison. The coolness of the prison didn't seem to cool tempers.

Because of the number of inmates that get visits, on all of the pods within the prison, they have to be corralled off from their prison block by Correctional Officers. They are moved in a single-file line down to an enormous anti-room. That room has four cages inside it, with a hallway through the middle leading to the visitation room. The inmates are held in a cage with others from their pod within the anti-room until there is an available seat and phone in the visitation area. They are held there again once they are finished with a visit until a good number of inmates from the same block are ready to be corralled back into their pod.

On that Sunday, Liam Breen was brought down to the cage to await his visit. He was hoping that it was Maddy. He was hoping also that she was going to show off some flesh. Liam had been incarcerated for nearly two weeks at that point and had been without sex. He had not gone that long without it since the last time he had been jammed up. Maddy knew the drill. She would wear something that would barely cover her body, but just enough clothing where the guards would not turn her away. He would use the mental picture of her to jerk off in his cell, tiding him over until the next visit.

Other inmates he had come down with had already had their visits and were waiting to go back up. Liam had still not had his visit. The group that he had come down with were collected and brought back up to his pod, and Liam still waited. He asked any and every officer that went by, or who opened one of the other cages to fetch an inmate, or to bring one back, what the hell was going on. He was ignored. Another group came down and were deposited into his cage without any indication as to why he was not allowed to see his visitor.

The new group, one by one, went out for their visit. They discussed who had come to see them with others when they returned. They would exchange stories with others who were in the same cage, or with inmates from other pods in the other cages. Back and forth, back and forth, inmate by inmate, until all of those prisoners had finished their visits.

And yet another group came down. Yet Liam remained. This group was not from his pod. They were of a different block completely, wore different color Bob Barker jumpsuits. This group remained quiet while the COs deposited them into the cage. Remained quiet while they waited to go for their visit. Liam continued to ask whomever passed in a uniform what was going on. Shouted it in fact. And each time he was again ignored.

Breen realized something was wrong when as one of the third set of inmates was removed from the cage to be led to the visitation room, he winked at him. The corner of his mouth turned up when he did so. Breen looked behind him while he held on to the bars of the cage to ascertain if the wink was for him. The others in the cage silently chuckled, looking down at their bobos. Something was up and Breen was nervous.

Within a minute of the wink, the Ellis alarm went off. This brought the lug team. Two or more inmates were going to spend some time in the hole. This kept the COs in the immediate area busy while they regained complete control over the situation. Various visitors would be asked to leave, inmates lugged. The distraction was set.

Two of the inmates in Breen's cage, one on each arm, grabbed him from behind. His legs were kicked out from underneath him, sending him onto his back. The two inmates on his arms, pinned his shoulders to the concrete floor with their knees while a third pinned his feet.

"Can't take any chances Breen. It's just business," a large white man said to him. He stood over Liam with his arms out like there was nothing he could do.

"Oh fuck."

The man who spoke to him, that was standing over him, lifted his leg and stomped on Breen's throat. His wide foot covered the entire neck from hyoid bone to trachea. There was an audible snapping sound before the onlookers cheered on the attack.

The stomp, or shot-foot as it is called, was powerful. The first shot snapped the thyroid cartilage. That cartilage is what forms the laryngeal prominence, or the Adam's apple. With that crushed, Liam would have a difficult time, at best, speaking as it houses the vocal folds. It also houses the air passageway leading to the lungs. That one stomp would have done the job if given enough time.

But the attacker didn't stop at one. The two hundred forty pound man came down with all of his strength and weight on Breen's neck again and again and again. The man stomped and smashed like he was trying to kick a hole in the white floor with the heal of his foot.

He smashed the larynx over and over again, collapsing the hollow passageway to both the stomach, and more importantly the lungs.

Shards of cartilage and bone and blood were forced into Breen's lungs. With his vocal cords destroyed and his air passageway collapsed, there was no fight left in him. The men who had been holding down Breen now had a very easy job. Liam's muscles were no longer getting oxygen as none were allowed into his lungs. No oxygen was getting into his blood. What began as a struggle to free himself, was now a resistance-free bag of bones. His heart stopped pumping. His brain ceased to function.

With the larynx crushed, the stomps then started to destroy the spine. The first cervical vertebra of the spine is the atlas, or C1. Stomp after stomp, the atlas was pulverized as well. The snapping and crunching after each thrust under the blood-soaked bobo could be heard over the cheers of the audience. The atlanto-occipital joint, the skeletal device that allows the head to pivot on top of the neck, was next to be destroyed and ceased to do its job. The head rolled off of what was left of Breen's neck in the most horrific and unnatural of ways. Not much more than nerve chords and skin held the skull onto the rest of his body. Liam Breen lay dead on the linoleum floor staring at the feet that destroyed him. His lifeless eyes clouding.

The men in the other cages around them continued to cheer on the attack. It was the prison version of a UFC cage match. Only this fight was not sanctioned, all of the participants were not willingly so. Blood had spattered the concrete walls and was pooling under the dead inmate.

It took less than thirty-seconds to kill Breen. Twenty or so stomps. With all of the commotion in the visitation room due to the arranged distraction, the murder could have taken three times as long and nobody would have been able to stop them. The lug team dealt with the visitation room fight, hauled the inmates involved down to the hole and yet the Ellis alarm still whined and yelled. Radios relaying information and the teams then made their way to the anti-room.

By the time the lug and medical teams had arrived at the cage in the anti-room, Breen's body had already been kicked into the corner and his attackers having a laugh over it. They were carrying on, covered in blood, like they had not just collaborated in committing a gruesome crime. Like they had not just murdered a man in the most heinous of ways. In the coldest of blood.

18

THE SUMMER HAD FINALLY PROVIDED WEATHER that lived up to the bill. Summers are supposed to be warm, sunny, and spent on a beach if at all possible. The summer of 2004 in New England didn't provide much sunshine, nor many days on Hampton Beach or Cape Cod. That year there was an unusual amount of rain and oscillating temperatures. One day it would be sixty degrees and rain, the next it would be eighty-one and rain. Tuesday, July 20th, was a gorgeous day: seventy-five and sunny.

The people of New Hampshire, like everywhere else in New England, are used to weather fluctuations. The old saying, "If you don't like the weather, wait ten minutes" was true more often than not. Moods change with the weather. Sun brings out the best in people, rain not so much.

Nobody would have welcomed a change that day. Moods were lighter, people were happier. Southern New Hampshire had acquired the same tough exterior as the locals of the major city to their south. In Boston they would just as soon spit on your face as look at you, at least outwardly. But not on that particular day.

Ryan Wells was having a great day. He woke up and had his morning routine with Angie. Their lovemaking was almost always in the morning. Ryan was physically ready for the task at that time of day and Angie preferred it. That day, however, it wasn't just business as usual. Needs weren't just met, bodily needs weren't merely satiated, the experience was special. The sun is an amazing thing.

His coffee tasted better. It was the same fair trade Arabica coffee, from the same faux stainless steel Cuisinart coffee maker, but it was more delicious than usual. Ryan had a spring to his step. The perma-smile on his face would normally have attracted attention as he passed others, but they too seemed to be having the same stellar day.

At the office, JG was less frantic and demanding. Angie had the glow of a woman who was as content as any person on the planet. Ryan gave her a sly wink as he entered his office and closed the door.

There's not a whole lot on my plate today, maybe I can take Ang and sneak out early, He thought. *Maybe we can get over to the beach for the first time this year. This is going to be a great day.*

Until the phone call.

"Ry, honey, District Attorney Cromwell is on line two," Angie called out through the intercom on the phone. The green light next the 2 button was blinking. The two never mixed business at the office and home familiarity. But the day had gotten the better of Angie. 'Honey' was a slip that went by Ryan.

This really is going to be a great day, Ryan Thought. *He wants to put a deal on the table already?*

"Great Ang. Thanks. Hey what does your day look like? How about a half-day? Maybe we can enjoy some of this rare sunshine. Maybe the beach?"

"Sounds great. I'll see what I can put off until tomorrow." Her enthusiasm was palpable.

Ryan pressed the intercom button which ended the call with his wife slash receptionist, then lifted the receiver to speak with Cromwell. He sat back in his office chair and propped his feet up on the corner of the desk.

"Mr. Cromwell, I wasn't expecting to hear from you today. When can I expect discovery files on the Breen case? If you are calling to wheel and deal already, I'm afraid I cannot do that until I know what you know."

"The discovery package for that case was given to the courier yesterday, you should have it by noon today. But that isn't why I'm calling."

"I didn't realize that we had another case together. I have another case with your office, but to hear from the D.A. personally on them is a little — "

" — unusual, yes. I *am* calling about the Breen case, but not about where the state sits. There isn't going to be a deal, Mr. Wells."

"You're calling to play hardball? It's a little early for that."

"I'm afraid it is just the opposite. Breen is dead."

"*WHAT?*" Ryan put his feet on the floor and sat upright. "Is this some kind of joke?"

"Who would joke about something like that?"

"When did this happen?"

"Sunday."

"Are you kidding me? Two days? It took you two days to tell me?"

"I just found out myself. I sent out the discovery package yesterday, you will see the date and time when it arrives. Why would I have sent it out if the trial was moot?"

"How?"

"It's under investigation, but so far it looks like somebody doctored a visit. He sat in a holding cage waiting to see a nonexistent visitor. The right crew revolved into his cage and they crushed his throat. There is video surveillance of it. It is one of the most brutal killings I have ever seen, and I have been at this a long time."

"How do you doctor a visit?"

"Somebody shows up and says that they want to visit the prisoner. Their name goes on a list, the inmate is then brought down to a holding cell and waits for an available spot. Only the visitor doesn't stick around for the visit."

"Is there a record of who the visitor was?"

"Yeah, It's right here." Ryan waited while he heard Cromwell rustle some papers on the other end of the line. "A woman. Madeleine Truss. We are looking into her but we can't find her as of this moment."

"Maddy."

"Excuse me counselor?"

"The woman Maddy. She's his girlfriend."

"We figured. Some girlfriend. I'm not even sure how she was let into the facility. She has outstanding warrants. The correctional officers would make a phone call to the locals and snag her when she showed up for the visit. Somebody screwed up."

"Huh."

"For what it's worth I'm sorry. I heard you really wanted this case. Just disregard that package, I'll send the paperwork to McCaglia's clerk."

"This has never happened to me before. Do I need to be there for a hearing?"

"No. I send the NAP paperwork to the clerk, like I said. Then the charges are set aside."

NAP meant Not Able to Prosecute. This is rare. Usually the state either decides to prosecute the case or not. Sometimes they will hold off on moving forward until there is enough evidence to sustain an indictment and then possibly a guilty verdict. To NAP a case meant that there was sufficient evidence but for reasons such as dead witnesses, destroyed evidence, or in this case a dead defendant, there would never be a trial.

"Could you do me a favor?"

"Sure, Mr. Wells. If I can."

"Keep me posted on the girl."

"Will do. I was kind of hoping you could help *us* with that."

"I don't know much. I met her one time to arrange the payment of my fees."

"Where did you meet?"

"Sully's Tavern. That's where she wanted to meet. Well, that is where Breen said that she wanted to meet."

"I'll see if I can get someone in the Sheriff's office to stake it out. If she's a regular she will go back."

"Did you try her home?"

"We didn't think of that. You're so smart, Ryan. I'm the District Attorney for Wayland County, of course we did. Empty. We checked Breen's house too. The compound is locked down so she didn't go there. I don't really have too many man hours to spend on this. Whether she set it up or not, the doers are already in custody so I can't justify the expense on a conspiracy to commit charge. Just between you and me? If I was her I would put New England in my rearview and break it off. Never look back."

"That's probably what she did. Thanks for the call."

"I would say that it's my pleasure, but it's not."

"I get it. Thanks again." Ryan hung up the phone.

Thanks for ruining my day.

Ryan was lost in thought for quite some time after Cromwell's call. Nobody disturbed him. Angie was rushing around, trying to finish every bit of immediate work that had to be completed that day, and organizing how she would catch up on Wednesday. JG was busy with his own work, his own cases.

The courier package from the District Attorney's office arrived at 11:06 AM. Angie walked into Ryan's office after a quick knock. She had signed for the documents at the reception desk and was delivering them like she had done countless times prior. Documents would often come by courier from somebody in the D.A.'s office, another attorney, or sometimes the client. She noticed her husband lost in his own world. His face and demeanor indicated that something was wrong. A one hundred eighty degree change from earlier. It was an aura that only a wife could perceive. Anybody else may have simply dropped the package and left the room.

"What's wrong?"

"My client was murdered in prison. This was the big case that I took from Dan Forde."

"Oh no. I'm so sorry."

"I think it's fairly obvious who did it, who had it done. But I'm trying to figure out why. He kept saying that he wouldn't flip on them. I kept urging him to tell me about those men at the compound. I kept saying that it would be the only thing that could help him."

"You can't think that this is your fault."

"I don't. Well I didn't until you just said it. But what has me befuddled is who knew that I was trying to persuade him to talk about that criminal activity. I'm certain that he wouldn't tell anyone, he knew what would happen which is why he didn't want to talk to me about it in the first place. And I didn't tell anyone, of course. So who could have known? And why kill him?"

"I don't mean to sound callous, honey, but is it your job to find out? You're a defense attorney."

"I realize that Ang. Thanks for the reminder," he snapped. "But this guy paid me seventy-five thousand dollars for a defense that's now unnecessary. His girlfriend actually gave me the money when she knew what was going to happen. Why pay me the money if she knew about the plan set in motion? And it's also bothering me that somehow I might have played a role in it."

She went around the desk and hugged him from behind his chair. Another familial act that was deemed inappropriate in the work place. Another act that wouldn't be highlighted. But like the sunshine, today was different.

"It's not your fault, honey. You were doing the best you could for your client."

"Which is why I owe it to him to finish the job. I think doing the best for my client at this point is finding out what in the hell happened. And by whom."

19

ANGIE DISGUISED HER DISAPPOINTMENT THAT THE SHORT DAY OF WORK was cancelled. She realized that it was a bit selfish to want to get out with her husband in the middle of the week. But how many weekends had he spent at the firm? And the ones where he didn't work, the weather had been uncooperative. The client was dead and without some serious smelling-salts that was not going to change. But she understood, forgave him for snapping at her. She went back to work, leaving her husband in his office.

Ryan had told her to hold all of his calls. He wanted to delve into the discovery package that the District Attorney had sent over. It was probably pointless, but he wanted to look it over anyway. Maybe there was more to this case than he knew. His former client was not a fountain of information that gushed forth. Ryan had to pry every tidbit.

Before he opened the package, he flipped open his cell. He scrolled down to the name Maddy, pressed the button with a green phone on it. The three-toned message from the operator said that the number was no longer in service.

She's gone, he thought.

He went back to the package, opened it and spilled the contents out onto his desk. The majority of the file contained crime scene photographs. They were very difficult to look at. There was a ton of blood and pieces of flesh strewn about with little plastic tents with numbers on them.

The state contended that Breen had not wasted any time when entering the residence of the victim. He went in blasting. The first shot, according to CSU, was to the victims chest. He had been standing in his doorway, the shot sent him back ten feet, where he fell onto his parquet floor. The victim then held his chest, probably in pain and maybe had the presence of mind to try and contain the immense amount of blood that spewed out so close to his heart.

CSU then determined that Breen fully entered the residence, walked up to the victim and stood over his body. The blood from the first shot was pooling around the body after being jettisoned from the wound, splashing the boots and pants of Breen. This was discovered by the splash pattern of blood on the clothing as well as how the blood formed under Breen's boots.

Standing over the body, Breen then fired seven .45 caliber mars short case projectiles into the victims face. These are rare, coming from an atypical weapon that is no longer manufactured. The Webley-Mars automatic pistol was fabricated in the UK but discontinued due to the large recoil and muzzle flash. This didn't stop Breen from making gunpowder and skull laced hamburger out of the victims face.

Pictures of the weapon were shown, footnoted and referenced to the ballistics report. The pistol, casings, and remaining ammunition was sent to Nashua to be studied and logged into the national database. Other weapons and munitions were discovered and logged from Breen's vehicle. Those too were sent to the lab.

The report that followed tied all of the weapons to Boston. It was a brief report that listed the history of the weapon. It mattered not that the serial numbers were etched off, the science of ballistics is unwavering. Ballistics is the scientific study of the mechanics of launching and flight behavior of a projectile. That projectile, once fired, has been marked with a fingerprint of sorts which tells the scientist which exact weapon it was fired from.

The weapons were used in various crimes throughout the years, all of which took place in Boston. This was the first that they were documented in New Hampshire. While Boston is a big city, and many weapons are bought and sold there, the information made the connection to organized crime that much more plausible.

The report was vague. It simply stated when the items were being examined, where and from what crime/case numbers they had been attributed to, and the serial number of the weapon if known before they had been filed off.

Ryan knew just the person he could ask to ferret out more information regarding these weapons.

"Hello?"

"Warren, er …. Deni?"

"Yeah?"

"This is Ryan Wells. Can you talk now?"

"I'm at work. Gimme a sec." The background noise changed for Ryan over the phone. Deni was taking the call on his cell phone and was audibly moving to a more private location to speak.

"I'm sorry to bother you at work, but that is why I'm calling."

"I'm at my desk, so I can give you a few minutes but I might not be able to say too much, if ya know what I mean."

"I get it. First I have to tell you that the case we hired you for, the trial run case, is finished. The defendant is dead. He was murdered in prison."

"Oh shit. There is a lotta that goin' around lately."

"What?"

"Never mind."

"Anyway, I am kinda thinking that he was killed so he wouldn't divulge any information about the combine in New Hampshire. But he did tell me that those good ol' boys were making drugs and housing guns for the Irish crime syndicate down there."

"Yeah I know, we kinda talked about that the other day."

"Right. So I received the discovery documents from the District Attorney. He sent them over before he knew that Breen, the client, had been murdered. See, discovery is when the prosecutor — "

" — I know what it means. I'm kinda in a crunch here. No offense but get to the point."

"Sorry. In that package is the ballistics report from the Nashua lab. They ran tests and entered all of the Breen weapons into the national database. They came from Boston."

"Stop the presses. A gun used in a southern New Hampshire crime came out of Boston? What are the chances?"

"I sense some sarcasm."

"I should hope so. I'm layin' it on pretty thick, guy. Listen, I'm really busy. If we don't have any more business together and I ain't gettin' paid, then I got work to do at the place where I am gettin' paid."

"You're on the clock. If I were to give you the data on this report from the weapons, can you get more information from the Boston ballistics team?"

"Not legally. But give me the information and I'll do it on the sly."

"I'll email you the report."

"Just tell me. I'm really not good with all that."

"You're not good with emails?"

"If it's a file I have to upload or download or whatever, then no. And I can't exactly ask someone on my end for help. Just read me the damned information."

"First is a Mars auto." Ryan read the serial number that was attributed to the weapon. "It's an old pistol and it has a long history of use, but most recently was five years ago."

Deni had hunt-and-pecked the data into his computer while Ryan relayed the information. "Yeah I see it here on my end. Used in a masked armed robbery on the North End. Bodega worker took a round in his shoulder for the trouble."

"Did they ever catch the suspect?"

"No."

"Hmmm. This might all be a dead end like you said. Another weapon was an assault rifle that they found in his SUV. H&K G3A4." Ryan again read the serial number from the report though the numbers had been filed off prior to the police discovering it at the scene.

There was a long pause. All Ryan could hear from his end of the phone was the muffled hustle and bustle of the police station in the background.

"Deni? You still there?"

"Yeah. I'll be damned."

"What's up?"

"Oddest thing. The last case number on this weapon, before yours, was my case. You definitely got your connection to Winter Hill down here."

"Winter Hill?"

"Irish mob. In this day and age, Irish mob in Boston and Winter Hill Gang are one and the same."

"That's great. Why is it odd?"

"Because it was part of a cache of weapons that were seized in a road-side bust a couple of months ago. That weapon is supposed to be held after testing at our ballistics lab in Maynard Mass."

"I don't understand."

"I don't either. You said this is the weapon this Breen guy had in his SUV?"

"Yes."

"The same Breen that was your client and killed in prison?"

"Yes, Deni. Why?"

"Because my case was the one where this rifle was seized. That guy was killed in prison too."

"That's quite a coincidence."

"I don't believe in coincidence. Especially when I know the crew my guy worked for. We've got a serious problem here."

"So let me see if I can connect the dots here, Deni. Breen worked for these red-neck yankees up here in the mountains that were into drugs and guns. The assault rifle that was taken out of his vehicle at his arrest was tied to the Irish mob down there in Boston. The same organization that my client didn't want to roll on. The same organization that is facing federal charges by the Department of Justice. My client from that group was killed a couple of days ago in prison. That assault weapon was supposed to be locked in a lab as part of a larger seizure from said mob. The suspect in that crime was also murdered in prison, presumably before going to trial since it just happened recently. Do I have this right?"

"Yeah. First in a long line of questions is how the fuck did that gun leave a secure state facility in Mass and end up in the mountains of New Hampshire within a couple of months?"

"I'm sure I don't know."

"And *I'm* sure as shit gonna find out."

20

WHEN I GOT OFF THE PHONE WITH RYAN WELLS, I was hot under the collar and dropped everything that I was doing. A not-so-old case that had been bothering me was just thrown back at me like a punch to the face. Danny Mick was murdered in prison, thus ending that case. His sister, a good-time girl that I used to have good times with when I was a teenager was also killed. Probably by the same people. Though that wasn't ever my case, they were linked by more than just family blood.

Those two murders were, in my mind, tied to Slopes. I had known that piece of shit almost my entire life and could have been in his crew back in the day. That crew being the Irish crime syndicate, or the Winter Hill Gang. They had been and were still the biggest of the gangsters in New England. And they were rumored to be doing the bidding of the real puppet masters in Ireland.

I had been hired to do a side job, some private investigative work, for these lawyers in New Hampshire. Their client was now dead as well, murdered in prison. They had at least one gun that was supposed to be under lock and key in a secure facility in western Massachusetts. It was supposed to be there because it had been tagged and put there pending examination in the Daniel McKennie case. I wanted to find out how that was possible, and I wanted to find out in that exact minute.

I got up and grabbed my jacket off of the back of my chair.

"Where's Hobbs?" I shouted it out to the general public, figuring somebody would respond but nobody did.

A runner was going by. I moved in front of her to stop her. She came to a quick halt, looked up at me with obvious annoyance.

"Sexual harassment is frowned upon in the workplace, Detective."

"Believe me, there would never be anything sexual between you and me. Look in a mirror. Have you seen my partner? Ricky Hobbs?"

106

"You're right. I'd go dyke before your dick."

"Funny. Have you seen him or not?"

"Yeah, he's in one of the observation rooms. Interview four I think. He's helping somebody out. And you should be careful with that Ricky thing, he hates being called Ricky."

"I know that't why I call him that. Thanks," I said as I moved out of her way.

She moved past me. "Don't mention it."

"Good luck with that lesbian thing."

I rushed down to the observation room and walked right in. Troop H records all of the interviews so it is customary to knock softly first so as not to disrupt the interviews. But I didn't really follow all the rules because sometimes they don't apply. Often they don't apply to me. Hobbs was standing there watching through the one-way glass while another detective was playing bad cop with somebody in the actual interview room. He held up his forefinger to his lips, the international call sign for be quiet. I didn't follow that either.

"C'mon we gotta go. It's almost one o'clock and we gotta get over to Maynard."

Hobbs looked annoyed with me, which was fine. He was my partner so technically wherever I went while on the clock, he was supposed to go too. He always wanted to adhere to that rule, but I never did. With the caseloads that we have, you sometimes have to divide and conquer if you want to get anything accomplished. Which is why he was in the observation room monitoring an interview while I was at my desk. In Hobb's mind we were still in the same place.

"What do you mean Maynard? I didn't know we had to head out there today."

"We need to check on the ballistics for the Daniel McKennie case."

"Oh. I forgot about that." The truth is he didn't remember the Danny Mick case but didn't want to admit that he had forgotten about an ongoing case. We didn't have an ongoing case involving Daniel McKennie. Not anymore. But the joke was on him even though he didn't know it. "I kinda told Foster that I would help him sweat this guy out."

"I can head down there solo. Gonna spend more time in traffic than at the lab anyway. You good with that?"

"Well no. Just gimme an hour and I'll go with you."

"Ricky. Just clear this up and I'll go out to Maynard. You forgot. It's no big deal. I'll watch your back you watch mine. Are we straight?"

"We really should go together," Hobbs insisted.

"Just relax and do ya thing here. We straight?"

"Uh. Yeah. Sure. We're straight. I'll tell Tits your in the bathroom or something if he asks."

Titanitaukis was a very hands-off supervisor as long as you closed cases. We didn't have the highest closure rate, mostly because of Hobbs, but we weren't on his radar either. He wouldn't ask.

"Good. I'll keep you posted," I said as I closed the door to the interview surveillance room. I wondered if Hobbs knew that in all likelihood our conversation was recorded in the background of whatever interview was being conducted in the adjoining interview room.

I wasn't lying when I said that I was going to be stuck in traffic. Storrow Drive both out and back would be enough to piss off The Pope. Route 2 west was going to be a parking lot. Not going there, most likely, but on the return because Route 2 was a heavy commuter route. I settled in for the long ride in my new *Escalade*. Traffic didn't bother me as much when I drove my new ride. The novelty would wear off, but it hadn't yet.

The twenty-five minute drive took me the better part of an hour. Goddamned rerouting at the end of Storrow messed everybody up. I wished, daily mind you, that they would make a public service announcement as to what they were going to destroy each day, so people could avoid that area. But they didn't. Not even to the police and rescue vehicles that needed the quickest routes.

When I arrived in Maynard and had gone down to the ballistics department, it was Willow who was working. Willow was a hot twenty-something that I flirt with every time I saw her or called her. She wasn't conventionally hot, she was librarian hot. She had this long spirally hair that was pulled up as not to interfere with her experiments or what not. Willow had pouty lips and wore glasses which added to her scholarly look. She had once told me that she was from Vermont and that her parents were hippies, thus the name. People used to call her pussy-willow behind her back. I won't lie I did it a time or two also.

Nothing had ever happened between Willow and I, but that didn't keep me from flirting with her each and every time we spoke. I think that she secretly enjoyed the attention, knowing that it was harmless and not going anywhere.

I was in no mood that day, however. I realized, of course, that she was the nerd and that she had nothing to do with security. She was not the reason that the guns that had been taken off of the street were back on them. There was no way that at a hundred and twenty pounds, and at five foot something that she would be able to stop someone in arming their own personal war. But guns had walked out of her building either before or after she had run tests on them and I wanted answers as to how.

"Just the person I wanted to see. What the fuck is going on down here?"

"Wow. No quips? No innuendo or double entendres? I was looking forward to a little rapier whit."

"I don't know what you just said but I'm not a rapist. I'm in no mood."

"All business today. What is it?"

"I've got some questions for you." I handed her a piece of paper with the list of serial numbers for the guns that were confiscated when Danny Mick had been arrested. I gave her a brief second to look them over.

"These were guns that were sent here for testing. What happened to them? Have you tested them yet? Where do they go after you test them?" I rattled off the questions and the questions seemed to rattle her.

"I - I - I - I send them over to be catalogued." She stuttered and typed a number or something into her computer. "See? Right here. I ran my tests, entered all of the data, and sent them to cataloging."

"And they get stored there?"

"I believe so yes. But I have nothing to do with them after I do my thing. What is this all about?"

"Lets go over to wherever they get stored, shall we?"

"I'm really busy here Deni. Just tell me what's going on if you want my help."

"At least one of these guns walked out of here and was involved in an another crime, in another state. How does that happen?"

"Uh, well, wow. Yeah?" Willow looked genuinely confused. "I have no idea. That doesn't make any sense. Are you sure?"

"No. I just wanted to spend my day in traffic to come down here and punk you. I was bored and Ashton was available. Of course I'm sure."

"Ashton is here?" She started to primp, looking for the hidden cameras, playing along with the sarcasm. Seeing that I was still in no mood for our usual banter, she stopped. "Fine. Let's go see what's up."

She led me down to the gigantic underground warehouse. It reminded me of Costco, only it was all below the frost level. Willow flashed her ID to several people, asked several others for the person in charge. I held back and my tongue which was unusual but necessary.

The highest ranking person down in the basement was this kid named Bryce. I hated him the second I heard his name. Bryce? Who names their kid Bryce? Yuppies who want their kid to get regular beatings from the normal kids with fewer options. These were the kind of people who were taking over Southie. What he was doing down there and where his career had taken a left turn into a toilet, I never found out.

Willow handed him the long list of serial numbers and yuppie-boy went to work on his computer. They were all stored together, because they had all come in and were tested together. So we left the front desk, got into this golf-cart type thing and went behind the floor-to-ceiling chain-link fence to find the lot number.

Bryce turned down one aisle and put the cart in park. Willow and I got out with him but he told us to stay where we were for a minute. He went to get a forklift. As I leaned up against the cart staring at the massive shelves in a long line, I knew what we were going to find. Or not find. There was a huge gaping hole where a skid was supposed to be up near the ceiling. I had the feeling that was where our lot used to be. I pointed the empty space out to Willow who understood what I was saying without having to say it.

I should have been a psychic. Bryce came back with the forklift, went to HH47, which was the shelving and catalogue code assigned to our lot, which wasn't there. He was confused, we weren't. He had just caught up to where we were.

"I gotta call my supervisor," Bryce said.
"You do that."

21

THAT WAS THE FIRST NIGHT THAT WILLOW AND I SLEPT TOGETHER. Or not slept. But not in the way that you think. We stayed at the lab in Maynard all night waiting for people with more responsibility to arrive. Supervisors then had to validate what everybody else already knew. They made excuses like they were probably just mismarked and in another part of the warehouse. So another team of people came in to investigate, which took most of the night.

By early morning my neck and back were killing me from sitting in a chair all night. I was overtired and the coffee that was in the area where we were waiting was terrible. It was from an old percolator machine and was the consistency of applesauce. In other words undrinkable.

I had been on my cell phone for a good chunk of the night, and it was dying. Willow had been on hers as well and it was dying. At least she had her phone charger which she had procured from her office.

Hobbs had offered to come out there. Insisted on it in fact. But I told him not to bother. I would let him know when I knew something. Which was kind of a lie. Either way I wouldn't be going to the station that day, which was fine with me. Hobbs would eventually have a shit-fit.

I told Ryan what was going on and he wanted to come down also, but I thought that was counterproductive. If a defense attorney was down there spouting off about misplaced evidence and the like, the searching would slow or halt. I wondered if he could get ahold of the federal prosecutor that was handling the old men case. I thought that he would have some considerable weight to bare and I wanted to rattle a saber that was bigger than little ol' me. He said he would try.

Ryan called back a short time later and said that the federal prosecutor was already aware and incensed. That was his word, because I thought incense was the stuff hippies like Willow used to make their house not smell like marajuana.

The federal prosecutor was so mad that he was going to be there, was on his way in fact. I knew his pants were going to be in a twist over the fact the missing guns from my case were the weapons seized in his. Ryan said that he didn't know that he was going to get that pissed or he would have waited until later in the morning to call him. He was getting in his car in the middle of the night and going to be in the little town of Maynard in the very near future. I thanked Ryan and asked if he was going to be down here also, to which he replied that he wouldn't miss it. He actually sounded excited.

When I informed the scurrying troops in the warehouse that a federal prosecutor was on his way down here to get to the bottom of what happened, people started to shit themselves. I may have ruined the element of surprise, but it was fun to see reflex-like finger-pointing and frantic calls to government officials.

It was absolute pandemonium. Willow was upset with me for making the issue so colossal, that there was a simple explanation that didn't require this level of exposure. She insisted that she knew the people that she worked with. There was no way that I had uncovered some horrible conspiracy. Because of me people were going to lose their jobs, she said.

I just wanted to know how guns that were under the watchful eye of the state of Massachusetts could be involved in another crime, in another state within a few short months. It's not like we were talking about one gun. We are talking about two hundred guns. You can't just throw them in a back pocket and sneak out the door.

There was planning and stealth involved. There was somebody on the inside that had helped in the execution of that plan, or at a minimum turned their head while the deed was done. In my mind, this event couldn't have been isolated. If it could be done once, it could be done again. So how many guns had walked out the door? How many times had various cops like myself taken guns off the street just to have them go right back out again?

For these reasons I didn't care if someone lost their job. The very least that will happen to them will be losing their job. With the federal prosecutor for the district on his way, and Massachusetts State officials notified, there was going to be hand-wringing. Whomever was responsible was going to be publicly crucified.

With the fiasco that happened in New Hampshire making national news and guns being on the front page almost daily and in the front of the collective public's mind, the public was going to be wanting someone's head on a spike. Two more school shootings had just taken place in February. One in Washington, DC, the other in East GreenBush New York. The public was tired of gun violence. News of this was bound to make it into the press. And at the worse possible time for those involved. Since this scandal would be made public, so too must the punishment.

The fact that these guns had left Maynard only to end up in the New Hampshire storyline was about to be a debacle of the highest order. There were four deaths in Massachusetts related to these guns, which was bad enough. Then confiscated and supposedly secured. Now there were the dead and injured in the New Hampshire seizure with these weapons as well. I was relishing the implosion.

Walter Glibczieck, the federal prosecutor for the district Boston was in, a title in which there are only about ninety in the entire United States under the Department of Justice, and Ryan Wells were just two of the people in the massive influx that had come onto the scene. Walter had brought a team with him to assist in the investigation presumably. Other teams were called in by the state to cover their asses. Walter, Ryan, and I holed up in a corner to discuss what had happened and what was going to happen. Once introductions were made, and fortified with the applesauce-coffee that none of us took more than one regretful sip of, we convened.

"Mr. Wells tells me that you are a Massachusetts State Police Detective. You were assigned the Daniel McKennie case, yes?" Walter was a large, John Goodman type character.

113

His presence in a room didn't go unnoticed. His physique and his title had everyone within view watching him, which is why we conducted our meeting in whispers.

"That's right Walt."

"It's Walter."

"Whatever. I had Ry call you because I wanted you to throw your weight around …. eh, bad choice of words, but you get it."

"I think what Deni is trying to say, Walter, is that things are getting a bit out of control. In the cases involving these guns, the suspects were both killed in prison and — "

" — yes Mr. Wells. As I told you on the phone, I'm aware. I know more about that case than you might imagine. Having access to federal databases, the ATF, DOJ, FBI, and US Marshals gives me a perspective on just about everything."

I freaked out and my voice rose above the whispers we had an unspoken agreement to use. "How long have you been following this? Suspects and potential witnesses are getting snuffed out left and right while you sit in some ivory tower doing nothin'? I'm not impressed, Walt."

"Mr. Dennihan — "

" — Deni."

"Turnabout is fair play. Just because I have unfettered access to information doesn't mean that I get that information as timely as I would like. Had we figured out all of the connections sooner, maybe we could have prevented some deaths. But we must look forward. We now know the connections to the Boston mob are real. The Winter Hills have a multi-faceted relationship with the group of men at the New Hampshire combine that were recently apprehended and now facing prosecution. We are also aware of the hierarchy of these groups. New Hampshire reports to Boston, Boston reports to the IRA who report to Sinn Féin."

"Who's this Sin Fine guy?" I asked for both Ryan and I. I could see that he didn't know who it was either by the look on his face.

"Simply put? Sinn Féin is to Ireland what Conservative Republicans are to the US Government. They are a major political party and the IRA won't wipe their own asses unless they are given the green light by them."

"So this Sinn Féin is a group that makes money from illegal activity here? That doesn't make sense," Ryan said.

"Why doesn't it make sense?"

"If the Republican party was making money by sponsoring illegal activities, the country would be up in arms," Ryan defended.

"There are differences in what is considered legal. Have either of you ever heard of The Troubles? Mr. Dennihan?"

"I seem to stir up a lot of trouble wherever I go. Can you be more specific?"

"You might want to brush up on Irish History. You are Irish and from Boston, yes?"

114

"I am Irish, yes. Is that why you are so pissed? This Sinn connection?"

"The reason I am here, the reason that I am so pissed, as you put it, is because with these guns missing from this facility — my case against the New Hampshire arm of this organized crime ring is out the window."

"I don't follow. They're the same guns. You have them now from the New Hampshire raid," Ryan said.

"My only leverage against them is the shootout at the O.K. Corral with those guns. The deaths, injuries and damage sustained from the raid. The fruits of the search once we eventually gained access to the compound are going to be null and void. Liam Breen is dead and he isn't going to be talking to anyone anytime soon, but his conviction and testimony could have been used to help our case.

The warrant to search the compound is likely going to be thrown out of court. Breen was suspected of being a member of that group, but nothing has ever officially tied him to the group, and the warrant was predicated on that connection. The compound was not his official residence. A warrant for his place would have been appropriate, but not the compound. The judge who signed the warrant was overzealous. Everything seized from that warrant is forbidden fruit. So the only thing I have tying guns from Boston to New Hampshire was Liam Breen. Without him the entire proceeds from the seizure are ill-gotten gains from an illegal search."

"So you were waiting to see the Breen testimony before making a motion to reinstate the proceeds from the compound warrant," Ryan said.

"Let's just say that I was watching your case very closely."

"Not closely enough, Walt. You didn't know that they were the same guns."

"Unfortunately no. You're right. I was focused on getting the weapons seized on the record and use them to nail the group. I was focused on the future not the past. Clearly I should have been more interested in if the weapons had a history. Once he was convicted of murder using the weapons that he did, they would be marked, exhibited, and on the record. The transcripts could then be used in federal court against the group. The weapons could be back-doored in when they deny having illegal weapons when they take the stand. If need be we could have reduced Breen's sentence once he was convicted by getting his sworn testimony. Now that I do know that these guns are from organized crime in Boston, I want to investigate how they walked out of this building."

"When were you going to fill me in on this plan?" Ryan was shocked by the now moot revelation.

"That's not the point. The point is that none of that matters now. I only mention it to show that I have a vested interest in finding out how these weapons left the custody of this secure state building and ended up in New Hampshire. That information could get the weapons back on the record and secure a conviction for the Men in the Mountains or whatever the press is calling them."

"Look at this place? It had to be an inside job," I said. "How many people know this place exists, and even if they did which crates have which thing that they want? Then gettin' past security?"

"Deni, what made you think to have Mr. Wells give me a call?"

"Once I found out they were the same guns, and knew for sure that they were taken from here, that it wasn't a mistake? I wanted to call down the thunder. Plus I thought you would wanna know."

He nodded his head.   "Suffice to say that this is not a shining moment for law enforcement."

22

THE GUNS WERE GONE OF COURSE. Teams of people were still searching the underground warehouse that was supposedly secure, and the official spokesman said publicly that the investigation was still ongoing, but everyone knew that the G3s weren't in the facility. They were missing from one secure lock-up and housed in another the hard way. The National Guard was brought in to secure the sight, and assist in the search within the Maynard lab. They were going to comb through the entire building looking for them, which was going to take weeks. Each crate would be pulled off of the shelves, inspected and matched to the catalogue. It would be like going into Costco, taking each item out of each enormous case on all of the massive shelves and matching the SKU numbers to the store's database. It takes time and manpower.

If anyone on planet earth thought that those weapons were still in that warehouse, they were kidding themselves. The teams were going to go through the motions, however. Even that large of a cache was like trying to find a particular set of needles inside a needle factory.

I was now the personal pet of a federal prosecutor. Walter Glibczieck called my boss, Tits, requisitioning me to use my knowledge of South Boston for the good of his investigation. Walter used the justification that if he was able to amputate a huge revenue source for the Winter Hill crew, by securing a conviction for the New Hampshire combine, a huge portion of organized crime in Boston would be crippled. What he was really doing was looking at a bigger picture; and bringing down the IRA foothold in the United States, his district anyway, which would be a big boon for his career. The plan was not lost on me.

Titanitaukis saw the big picture for himself also. Politics drives me crazy. He knew that his helping Walter would give him a chip in the big game. He also knew that if he played a part in taking down the Irish mob in Boston, even if it was only financially, that it wouldn't look horrible on his resume. The Captain signed off on it as well. What he got out of this arrangement was anyone's guess. Another deal was made I'm sure.

So they had me do their bidding, like the minion that I was. If shit went south they were going to roll the whole thing up on me and choke me with it. I was told to go around Roxbury, Dorchester, Jamaica Plains, Mattapan, Charlestown, and of course Southie rustling up every known hoodlum in the hoods of Boston. The shakedown wasn't without precedent.

Tits reinstated Operation Ceasefire for this scheme. The project was first enacted in 1996 to curb the gun violence and gang activity. The police would hit all the hot spots in the city, shaking down all known criminals with relation to gun violations. Everyone and anyone with a gun infraction on their record was fair game. These raids produced results in two ways; by seizure of any and all guns that a felon possessed, and then the felon would roll on others who had weapons in exchange for leniency. Wash, rinse, repeat.

Technically Operation Ceasefire was still in use and had an annual budget, but it was rarely used. The budget was pilfered for other initiatives every year, thereby making the shakedowns nonexistent. As long as there were guns coming off the streets year after year; there weren't any questions, the program considered a success, and tax dollars continued to be earmarked for an operating budget.

Whether the program was successful or not is debatable. There are as many strategies for eliminating gun violence as there are politicians with those strategies. Police the ammunition not the guns, ban assault weapons, enforce and make more strict gun sale laws, much harsher penalties for gun-related infractions, are but a few. Operation Ceasefire was just another strategy in a long line of programs utilized as much for political capital as they were for the root-goal. Numbers were skewed to make each and every pet project deemed successful, and therefore funded.

The new evidence was indicating that no matter how many guns were confiscated off of the streets, no matter which program was utilized to do so, those guns were finding their way right back out onto the streets from whence they came. This fact was going to put a great many of those politicians with strategies on the hot seat.

So off we went. My current cases were re-tasked, my focus was on the shakedown. Hobbs was partnered with other cops to collaborate on their cases and to gain help with his (formerly ours). I took the lead in the attempt to scavenge for every scrub in every borough until we had a bigger cache of weapons than the one that was lost. I was also attempting to glean as much information as I could about how the lot that was stolen had been accomplished.

In other words, I was trying to create a bigger headline than the one that was currently filling the media. Turn the negative into a positive. Spinning information to ensure that the people who were supposedly running things still had a job the next election. Did I mention that politics drives me crazy?

I didn't mind creating a stir in Roxbury or the other boroughs. I knew a lot of those people but I didn't live in their neighborhood. I didn't arrest as many as I was probably supposed to. I just took what I had to for weapons or information and had the uniforms go in with a paddy-wagon.

Where I treaded lightly was in my territory. Southie. I poked around more than anything else. I kept my ears open and my mouth closed. No big waves. The rumors had gone around about what I was up to. But nobody could prove it so the rumors stayed as such.

This went on for a couple of weeks before I was told, not too subtly mind you, that my footsteps were too heavy. I was stirring up things and people that need not be dredged up. Nobody said anything, but the message was received loud and clear.

I got up early on the last Friday in July so I could go to the gym. It was going to be a beautiful day weather-wise. Seventy-seven degrees with the sun shining. The only drawback to the day was that I had my usual detail of roaming the streets in search of someone with a gun in their possession scheduled for after my workout. I was able to find a phenomenal parking spot on the street in front of my place the night before. When I opened my front door to leave for the day I spied that the premium parking space had come at a price.

My new *Escalade* had a smashed driver-side door window. I had lived in that neighborhood my entire life and never did I have so much trouble with my vehicles being vandalized as I had that summer. People in my neighborhood knew what I drove. They knew I was a cop. Fucking with me was like asking for trouble. Live and let live kinda thing.

I approached the door and looked inside to see that nothing had been touched inside, but a few pictures were thrown on the driver seat on top of the shards of glass. I carefully reached in, retrieving the photos to see what the chicken-shit vagrant wanted to say but not to my face.

The first two pictures were of my old *Grand Am*. Smashed, beaten, and broken for my viewing pleasure. I had originally thought that it was my old girlfriend Jill who had been pissed off enough at me to have someone destroy it for her. I had stood her up, ignored her, and made her feel like a second-class citizen one too many times.

But the photos that followed made me realize that Jill had nothing to do with my car. The pictures that followed were of Roxanne McKennie at her worst. She lay there the way she was found in her apartment. Dead with a needle in her arm. One can only assume that the photos were taken before the police arrived. Before I arrived. Which means that the person who took them was likely there when she died. One can infer all sorts of things from that, none of it good.

The only reason to include those photographs in with the pictures of my car all fucked-up was to tell me a story. Bad things happen when I get involved with anyone who is even remotely associated with Sean Teague. Slopes. I had been asking around over the last couple

119

of weeks, asking if anyone knew where I could get a good assault weapon for hunting game in the city. Asking if anyone knew how the Winter Hill crew took the guns out of a state holding facility. I was more subtle than that, and not in Southie, but the questions were asked. Those questions had gotten back to him. He was sending me a message telling me that inquiring minds get dead.

I had my *Escalade* towed to a garage to be fixed and got an *Intrepid* out of the motor pool. I told the guys who were going to fix it to take their sweet time. Everyone in the world could spot an unmarked police car. The curly pig-tail antennae off the back was a sure sign. Anyone who messed with that car, even in Southie, was foolish. And even if they did I could not have cared less about a car from the motor pool. My *Escalade* was safer in a garage for the time being.

Later that day, I received a call on my cell saying that the person had information about the Winter Hill crew. They wanted to meet. I did too, only I wanted the meeting to be in a very public place, and not in Southie. The informant agreed, so we met at a Starbucks in BackBay.

There were endless numbers of Starbucks in the BackBay area of Boston. Even with Dunkin Donuts being the majority favorite coffee by New Englanders in 2004, there was a Starbucks on almost every corner. This particular one was near Copley. I sat by the window waiting, watching for some sign that this was a set-up, but I saw none. I spied the thousands of pedestrians walking under the tall buildings of the Prudential Center and the John Hancock Tower. The Westin Hotel and Copley Place Mall. The Boston Public Library and Trinity Church. As Dave Matthews said, 'Ants Marching'. None of them gave me a second glance.

"You're Deni, right?"

I turned to look over my shoulder at the tall man who was standing behind me. He was dressed in a Red Sox cap, t-shirt, and nondescript jeans. "Yeah. You wanted to meet me? You're Nate?"

"It's not my real name, but let's go with that. I'm only here because they did Danny Mick wrong." The green-eyed youngster moved in closer, uncomfortably close to the person occupying the seat next to me.

"What do you know about it?"

"We did some work together. I guess we were friends. Either way, I liked the kid."

"I get it. He wasn't half bad."

He took a seat next to me once the person that was occupying the stool got uncomfortable enough to leave.

"You're from the neighborhood. He said you aren't bad for cop."

"Great. So we are all good guys. What do you want, Nate?"

"I want Slopes, that slippery fuck, to pay for what he did."

120

"Slippery Slopes? Ha. That's a new one," I said.

He was not amused. "Business is business but this was excessive. He kept Roxy under his thumb so he could keep Danny Mick on the hook. Then when shit goes sideways he makes him out to be a rat. Has him killed like that."

"I know all of this. Well not the Roxy part, but most of this I know. Roxy was a junk-box for almost as long as I knew her. If she didn't get it from Sean, she woulda got it from some other shit-bag."

"Do you know that as big as Slopes is, he is nothing in the big scheme?"

"Irish?"

"As in *THE* Irish. Those Mc's across the pond have their hands into everybody and everything. That's how those guns got out of a secure state warehouse."

"And you can give me proof on that?"

"Fuck no. Course not. Slopes may be middle management, but he ain't stupid."

"Then what are we doin' here guy?"

"Slopes had to replace the guns from the pullover which were going to New Hampshire. Or get them back. Now that the whole shah-bang is gone from New Hampshire after the big raid? He's fucked. Those guns ain't in no state facility. They are in federal fucking lock-up. IRA may have their hands in a lotta pockets, but they haven't figured out how to get them guns back yet. So it's easier to just send over another shipment of 'em. At least until they can figure out how to get those others back, which rest assured they will do."

"So how exactly did the two hundred or so walk out of Maynard?"

"Don't know exactly. Somebody was paid off to get them out. My guess is that if you were to go into the guns that were seized from New Hampshire, you are gonna see those guns in there."

"Yeah. I know that too. The guns that were pulled off of Liam Breen were the same as from the lot that was supposed to be in Maynard. So obviously they were part of the same seizure in New Hampshire. You're not exactly sharin' the knowledge here kid."

"You don't see what I'm sayin'? That was just the tip of the iceberg anyway. One more small shipment to add to stock. That war chest up in New Hampshire was saved over time for one end user."

"Who?"

"New York, Chicago, West Coast."

"I thought you said one end user?"

"Same organization, but that ain't what you should be focused on."

"Oh really? What do you think I should be focused on?"

"The here and now. Those guns ain't there, not available. Because they got taken back again and put into federal custody. They gotta be replaced and all-of-a-sudden like."

"Where's the here and there? New Hampshire?"

"Try to keep up will ya? I'll make it simple. All of the guns were supposed to end up in New Hampshire so they could go elsewhere. Now they are in federal custody."

"You keep sayin' that. So fuckin' what? So they are going to bring in and move one large shipment to replace it?"

"Now you're startin' to see things."

"When? Where?"

"Don't know. But I know they are comin' in the same way they have been, only this time in bulk."

"How?"

"Ain't you payin' attention?"

"I know you better stop talkin' in riddles kid, or I'll beat that latte back outta ya."

"Irish guns are comin' in for Irish crews."

"Ireland? They come here from Ireland?"

"Fuck Yeah. Dublin to Boston Harbor."

Part Three

The Troubles are Féin

August 2004

23

I RAN OUT OF STARBUCKS ENERGIZED and ready to bring down the whole house of cards. Sean Teague was playing chess and it wasn't until I had received a little help that I understood the entire board. I needed to start making some moves of my own. I couldn't do much about New York, Chicago, and wherever else those assault weapons were supposed to eventually end up. Much less Ireland. The only thing that I could do was take care of my own. My own city. I needed to find Slopes.

The rest of Friday and all of the weekend and the following week was spent trying to find him. Search as I might, he was nowhere to be found. Nobody knew where he was. It didn't matter which felon I confiscated guns and drugs from, nobody knew where he was. Arrests were made but nobody was flipping no matter what they faced. Slopes was either in hiding or he was out of town. Operation ceasefire was creating quite the stir.

Monday, August ninth, ten days after my anonymous tip, another message was sent. This one suggested that I didn't understand the first one. The *Escalade* and photos hadn't achieved the desired affect. I was still investigating and Slopes didn't like it. I admittedly don't like to follow rules or instructions and I was never overly keen on school. I guess I do learn a bit slower than some.

I went home exhausted from the weekend search. My superiors were happy with the number of arrests, but they weren't too excited about having authorized all of the weekend overtime to come up relatively empty. It was late and I was beat, both with fatigue and in Sean's game. So far. I collapsed into my recliner with three fingers of cheap Irish Whiskey. And I passed out.

A couple of hours later I awoke after I heard a window break. Immediately I was breathing in heavy smoke. The smoke alarms were going off, piercing my eardrums. Flames were climbing up the walls and licking the ceiling almost immediately. The place was going up like a tinderbox.

I rolled out of my recliner and crawled along the floor. I was concerned about myself, but I was worried about my two tenants above me more. The flames were lining the ceiling, burning up. If they were trying to leave their beds on the second floor, they would burn their feet in the process. I needed to get out of my apartment and up to theirs and get them out.

Crawling toward the front door, I opened it and tried to get out of my burning powder keg of a three-decker. The moment I stood up outside after opening the front door, a blanket of automatic gunfire sprayed at me. Holes were being pierced into the siding on the front of my house by the dozens. If the bullets flying at me weren't enough, splinters of wood washed over me like hot shrapnel. I dove back into the fire. The front door was not an option. This was not an accidental fire, this was intentional. And if both sets of tenants upstairs didn't get help, it was going to be a mass murder.

Burning things were falling toward me from above, making my route to the back exit slow and winding. The building was old and going up quickly. I reached the back door off of my kitchen and slowly opened the door to escape while remaining low. Gun fire sounded off like taps on a snare drum. My service weapon was still attached to me in the shoulder holster, I fired a few shots of my own from my Glock-9. The breadbox on the counter housed my Sig Sauer P227, which I reached up for. A .45 caliber was better than a 9 mm but they continued their volley of automatic gunfire. I rolled back into my kitchen after I traded shots from my Glock with my left hand and shots from the Sig with my right for their sea of projectiles. I was trapped inside the fire. My lungs felt like they were already on fire.

Still in the kitchen I grabbed a dish towel and wet it from the faucet without raising myself high enough to be seen through the back window over the sink. Using the wet towel to somewhat cover my nose and mouth, I fashioned it around my neck and held it to my face by biting down on it. I sat on the floor to collect my breath and some quick thoughts.

I had to get out of there. This was obvious. But the way out was not as clear. All New England houses have a basement. The plumbing has to be beneath the frost-line or the pipes would freeze during the cold winter months. But going down there was only getting myself further under the blaze. The entire building would burn and collapse on top of me. But I felt it was my only shot.

Crawling on the hot floor, I made my way to the basement door. It felt like my skin was already burning. The towel covering my nose and mouth was heated and began to steam, burning my face and eyes. I half-slid down the unfinished wooden stairs to the basement. I only used it for storage and odds and ends. The boiler was down there.

Think Deni. Think.

Parts of the ceiling to the basement were on fire. I had bought myself a little time by being downstairs, but that time was fleeting. The bulkhead doors leading up to the small backyard wouldn't work. The shots fired toward my kitchen door proved that I would be going right into the lion's den.

I was turning in circles trying to find an answer. The east side of the house was covered with shrubs. There were basement windows on that side of the house, covered by the shrubs in order to hide an easy access for thieves trying to enter my house. The windows were very small, almost to the ceiling from inside the basement and just above ground level outside. I ran over to one of the windows, climbing on top of storage boxes to get at it. If there was a way to open the damned thing, I didn't know what it was. I used the wet, steaming towel to break the window as quietly as possible.

It was a tight fit, even for me. I was in good shape, the only fat on my body was from my booze habit. Slithering out of the basement and onto the ground above, I could finally breath. The shrubs were scratching me as I repositioned myself in them trying to assess where to go from there.

I could hear the screams of my tenants above, though for the moment I could do nothing for them. From the outside of the building, my house looked completely engulfed. The masked men ran from the back yard and into the front to join their accomplices. Satisfied that the job had been completed, they double-timed it right past me as I hid in the bushes. Once they were past, I darted into the back yard and up the back set of stairs to the apartment just above mine.

My upstairs tenants had obviously tried to get out of the burning building from the back exit as well. The deck, siding, windows, and back door were all peppered with the same gun fire as my place below. I kicked in the back door only to find what I had already feared.

Their bodies were cooking and blistering like a pig on a barbecue in their own living room. One or more of them were shot, because blood had been pouring out of them and onto the hardwood floor. The blood was bubbling as it boiled and steamed off the oak flooring. The crackling of burned and blood-soaked wood added to the horrible smell of burnt flesh.

There was no time to lament, I hurried up the second set of stairs to the top apartment. The same bullet holes lined their exterior as well but from a different angle. The shooters had shot from the ground level, sending bullets through the pressure-treated deck and into the siding. There was hope that the nice young couple hadn't been shot. As I did with the apartment below, I kicked the door in. The fire was working in this apartment but it was not quite as aflame as below. Yet.

The apartment was also boiling hot and it was all but impossible to breath. I made my way back into the recesses of the apartment calling to them. The young couple had lived in my apartment for a few years and had just been married that year. They were working on beginning a family. They didn't answer. I continued to move through the apartment, as quickly yet as thoroughly as I could. The top floor was now really starting to burn. *Please don't be home,* I thought. The floor was very hot and the rubber soles of my cheap dress shoes were beginning to melt and stick to the floor. The deeper into the place I went, the worse the flames got. The building seemed to burning from the outside in. I needed to get them out before there was no longer an exit.

When I got to the back bedroom, their door was closed. I reached for the knob but the heat was radiating off of it. I decided to kick the door in, which was a horrible mistake. The second the door opened an explosion like that of a grenade went off. Some sort of backdraft blew me back down the hallway, sliding down the hot, steaming floor. My skin continued to burn on the hot floor. I knew what was waiting for me inside that bedroom. But I had to go look. I tamped the flames that were on my clothes and went back into the room. They were curled up together, on fire while they lay in each other's arms on the burning bed.

One could only assume that they burned up instantly. There didn't seem to be any writhing in pain. Burning to death is the most horrible way to go. Maybe they incinerated when I kicked in the door. *Had I killed them instead of save them?* I hoped that they died from smoke inhalation before the blast but I didn't think about it very long. There was no time. No time to go toward them. No time to feel a pulse. For their sake I hoped there was no longer a pulse. They burned and blistered and charred in each others arms. The clothing they were wearing was singed and melted into the fiber of their seared bodies. There would be no family.

I was able to get out of the top apartment and down to the ground in my backyard before the building finally succumbed to the flames. I was hacking up creosote from my lungs and taking a physical inventory of my burns while I watched my life go up in flames. The things that I accrued in my life. For the moment I was still alive and able to accrue more bobbles and trinkets. I could not say the same for my tenants.

Their lives literally went up in flames.

24

TUESDAY WAS MOSTLY A BLUR. I had spent the rest of Monday night in the hospital. My burns needed to be treated, X-rays and things took place to make sure that the smoke inhalation didn't do more damage than indicated by the phlegmy soot that I was coughing up. I looked a wreck. The cuts, abrasions, burns, and singeing made me look like I had gone through a war. It felt like I was in the middle of one.

I'm not easily scared, but this ordeal had me rattled. I had been warned and I didn't listen. I was determined to take on Slopes for what he had done, and ultimately it wasn't me who had paid the price for it. But the battle wasn't over yet.

I had looked for Sean Teague all weekend after being tipped off as to his next plan. Those assault weapons were nothing but trouble. I had lost a car, had to replace a window on the second, and now my house. But it was nothing compared to what others had paid. They were dead. Danny Mick, Roxy, this Breen guy that the New Hampshire lawyers were pissed about, the dead and wounded from the compound raid, and now the six people who lived in the two apartments above me were all dead. I should have heeded the warning.

When I was allowed to leave the hospital mid-morning, I was taken to the station for questioning. I was upset and hopped up on meds so exactly how it went down is hazy at best. But I can tell you that after my statements to both police and fire investigators about the fire, I was handed over to Tits and Walter. This conversation was more clear because I was getting a lot of heat for wanting out. I wanted justice but I needed a break. I needed things to cool down. My skin for starters.

I was brought into Lieutenant Titanitaukis's office to have a chat. Walter was there and sat silently at first while things started off apologetic and cordial.

128

" …. Detective Dennihan, I am so sorry for what you have gone through," Tits finished after questioning how I was feeling.

"So you're alright? The hospital released you, so you must be cleared for duty. You probably look worse than it really is," Walter offered.

"Easy for you to say, huh Walt? I was burned and shot at in my own home. I saw the people that depended on me for a place to live burned alive. Cleared for duty? I'm taking a fuckin' vacation."

"Now?" Walter was having none of it. "Obviously you pulled at an important thread. That was an awfully big risk they took by burning down a State Police Detective's house and then having target practice on it. You can't give up now."

"Fuck you. I am."

Tits asked if I had any vacation time coming. He indicated that he might not approve the request if I had them to spare.

"I've got three weeks lined up. I'm takin' 'em. End of story."

"Why do you think they took a big risk at trying to kill you?"

"Because they know I was looking for them. Because somehow they know that I was tipped about the next shipment."

Walter looked perplexed by this. He was looking around the room, at both of us trying to determine where he had been left behind. I then realized that I hadn't reported this fact to Tits, so it was never sent up the food chain. My lieutenant was a hands-off kind of boss, and I didn't offer anything up until I had to. There wasn't a DD-5 for Operation Ceasefire.

"The next shipment? When? Why was I not told about this?" Walter seemed almost frantic.

"Because I don't know when, exactly. I got a tip last Friday, which I was going to report to Tit …. eh, my direct supervisor, if and when I could corroborate it. The tip is anonymous but seems reliable, but who knows? The person is pissed off about the way Slopes just kills with impunity. Friend of one of his victims, you might say. Guns come in to Boston Harbor directly out of Dublin. Slated for all points west from Boston now that New Hampshire is under wraps. God only knows how many stay here in the city. I know those assholes were using automatic rifles to trap me in my house."

"FRIDAY? It's tuesday. Why didn't anyone share this information with me?"

I didn't have the heart to tell Walter that I had received the information eleven days prior not four like he obviously thought. Tits already looked like a one-legged cat trying to scratch on a frozen pond. He was as white as a ghost trying to figure out if his career just hit the skids because of me.

"Because I felt that there was more information to gain before I reported on a wild goose chase. It was an anonymous tip. If I kept you apprised of all of the tips I get, we would all be

129

running in circles. I have been scrounging up every cocksucker with a bottle rocket in every corner of Boston. What do you think I was doin' all week .... er .... weekend? Sean Teague, A.K.A Slopes, is in the wind. I can neither confirm nor dismiss this information about a big shipment."

"But you said that you think it's reliable. It's reliable enough to send you all over hell all weekend long. Reliable enough for them to take a big chance at killing you."

"Walt, it could be a trap. They lure us down to the docks and have open season on the police. Besides, how do I know that they know about this tip?"

"Then why try to kill you in your own home?"

"I guess I don't follow you there Walt."

"If the goal was to get a slew of cops down to Boston Harbor, then why try to kill him in his home?" Walter said to Tits like I wasn't the one who asked him the question. "There would be no need. Just kill him when he gets at the ambush. And for that matter, why not give him the date and time if it was a true ambush? Lieutenant, you have withheld some valuable intel on this project."

"I haven't withheld anything," he said. Backpedaling and distancing. I really hate politics.

"So you are saying that you have no control over your own personnel? That you don't mandate that information come through the chain of command?"

Tits was flummoxed. Between old Scylla and Charybdis. Any way you slice it, he didn't look good.

"Sorry to interrupt you two. But it seems like you two got a lot to discuss. So I'll just submit my vaca slip and be on my way," I said.

"I haven't approved your vacation time, detective." He was going to take his embarrassment out on me.

"Then call it medical, call it leave of absence, call it I quit. Call it whatever you want, I'm not going to be into work for a while. If I take this to the Captain, I'm not too sure you have a leg to stand on. I was almost killed for Chrissake."

I got up to leave gingerly. My medicine had officially worn off. It was early afternoon and I was in the mood for copious amounts of alcohol.

"Deni. Could you wait for me outside the office for a minute while I finish here with your Lieutenant? I'd like to have a private chat with you if that is all right with you."

"Yeah, I guess. Don't take too long. I need my meds."

I have no idea what the two talked about in Tits's office. I just know that it took a hot minute and I was ready to bail. I sat on the bench outside the office and every person that walked by gave me the stare. I looked horrible. I get that. Those that I knew would try to find out from me what they probably already knew from rumors. Troop H was like a high school. You couldn't have a hangnail without everybody knowing about it and giving advice as to how to avoid them in the future.

I was about to leave without speaking with Walter when he came out of the office. He asked me if I wanted to get out of there, which of course I did. We got into his car and we went to Parish Café, the one in the South End. I had been in there a few times. Swanky joint with high end comfort food. They make amazing drinks there as well, which is what I wanted.

We found a spot right at the bar. I normally don't go for elaborate concoctions, but when you go to Parish, it's kinda what you do. But nothing on the hand-crafted menu contained whiskey, it was all vodka or some such thing so I went with Jameson. Neat. Walter had some Belgian beer called Delirium Tremens. Food was not on my agenda, but he ordered two elaborate sandwiches called the Zuni Roll.

The conversation was going nowhere, but I didn't push it. I was on vacation and I wanted to drink. I couldn't drive the car from the motor pool while on vacation, and the *Escalade* wasn't ready yet because I had told them to take their time. Walter was someone to drink with and chauffeur me around, so I was going to milk it for all it was worth.

The sandwiches arrived and so did the moment to bring up the secret agenda and the reason that I was taken out on the town.

"What's wrong with a Sam or a Harpoon? You too good for local beer?"

"Belgian beer has more alcohol."

"Looks expensive for so little."

"So …. how well do you know these assholes that tried to kill you?" Subtle.

"I grew up with the prick. He's been in my house. We don't take windy walks on tha beach if that's what your askin'."

"I didn't say that you were in their pocket. I just mean that you think like them, right?"

131

"I wouldn't say that. I know how they think. Somewhat. If I really knew then I probably wouldn't be in this fix and I woulda found Slopes by now."

"Fair enough. I want you to stay on this case."

"You've only had one beer, slow down. Did you not hear that I'm on vacation?"

"And I'm asking you to not be on vacation."

"Look, guy. People are dead because I didn't know when to walk away. Every time I turn around I get further involved. Fucked deeper in the ass. I'm out."

"Where will you go?"

"What part of 'on vacation' is throwin' you for a loop? Two words, Walt. Look 'em up."

"Yes, Deni. I understand the concept of vacation. Where will you go?"

"I don't know, but it's going to be outta town. Maybe New Hampshire. I can pick up a couple of bucks pickin' up side jobs. Maybe go house hunting. You might have heard I'm in the market. Maybe my time in Southie has come to an abrupt end for good."

"What about Ireland?"

"I really don't like traveling too far. I don't like planes, I'm not much on …. " The meds mixed with whiskey had slowed me down. " …. wait …. you want me to go see if I can find out when the guns are comin' in. Go fuck ya-self."

"Do it for all the people who have been killed. Do it for the people that died in that fire. You owe it to them to get justice. You are a cop, Deni."

"I'm no federal agent. Get the ATF to do it. Or the FBI. Not me in other words. You seem to have everybody under your thumb, get some other slob. What am I gonna accomplish in Ireland anyway? I'm a Massachusetts State Police Detective. And I'm barely that."

"The ATF or FBI would have to be brought up to speed. I believe that they also have a leak. I don't want you to do anything more than just track them. Don't stop it, just get a vessel number and a crate number and come home. You don't have a place to live, and you need a vacation. Why not get paid to see the sights? You are Irish."

"Who's gonna talk to me?"

"You'd be surprised. Act like a tourist."

"A tourist with an inquiring mind about the IRA and this Sinn party?"

"Sinn Féin. And yes."

"Sure. That'll work. I don't know my way around to even know who to ask. This whole thing is fucked up. Did you come up with this? You been drinkin' more than those fancy beers?"

"I'll set you up with someone who has worked with our office before on investigations. You will be fine."

"And what if I come up with nothin'? What then?"

"Then you come up with nothing. But we both know that when you get on a scent, you're like a blood hound. A relentless blood hound in heat."

"Thanks for the imagery, Walt."

"And if you aren't properly motivated already, I'll sweeten the deal. While you are collecting your vacation pay, any information that you come up with that leads us to that gun shipment earns you a bonus, courtesy of Uncle Sam."

"What kind of bonus? A pat on the back?"

"Money. A bonus like I said. A sizable one. And I'll pay your freight. How can you say no to an all-expense paid vacation with a bonus?"

"Tits …. er …. Titanitaukis is never going to agree to this."

"You will be working for me. Under the direction and protection of the Department of Justice and the Attorney General's Office. One case, one goal. Find the new shipment of guns. Leave Tits to me."

25

I MUST HAVE BEEN DRUNK. Or the mix of booze and meds. Or Walter had caught me at a weak moment. Whatever the case, three days later, on Friday, August 13, I was on a plane. Friday the thirteenth. Talk about tempting fate.

I was trying to look at it as a free vacation. A good vacation for me was to head down to Fort Meyers to see Sox spring training, not go across the big pond. Spring training was long over and the Red Sox were having a decent year at 21-15 so far. I would have loved to take a week or two off and see Schilling, Lowe, or Wake on the mound. Pedro throw filth. I definitely needed a vacation.

But every time I would think about how great a free vacation to my ethnic homeland sounded, I dismissed the idea that I was getting myself in way beyond my depth. The thought of the fire and gunfire at my house and the increasing number of deaths would pull me back to the reality of it. This wasn't a vacation. This was leaving the proverbial pot for the fire. An even bigger one.

I wasn't scared. We'll call it concerned. Nervous maybe. Full-on uncertainty, certainly.

Walter had fortified me with a coach seat on American Airlines, compliments of the Department of Justice. He also gave me some traveller's checks and said that he would have a contact from the Garda Síochána meet me at the airport. The Garda detective was also a member of the anti-terrorist police task force, very familiar with the IRA, and had just been instrumental in the seizure of a trove of explosives and detonators in February of 2004. He would point me in the right direction, off the record, and help me to get situated. His reward for hospitality and clandestine support was going to be the accolades from any arrest he was able to sustain from the leads I was investigating on the Ireland side of things. Politics at work yet again on an international level.

While waiting to get on the plane in Logan airport, I had called Ryan Wells to let him know what I was up to. We had spoken after the fire, and he said that if there was anything that I needed to let he or JG know. They seemed like real nice guys.

"So I won't be around for a bit, Ry. But I was only on a trial basis for the one job anyway right?"

"Right. But this helps us with the Breen case anyway. If we can further prove the connection to the Irish mob via the IRA through the guns coming over from Dublin, we can prove conspiracy."

"Okay but we don't have a case anymore, right? He's dead."

"I found his girlfriend, Maddy. Actually she found me. She went into hiding and wanted to see about hiring us to look after her interests. Seems Liam had a hidden stash of money."

"So .... "

"So she is definitely not the sentimental type. Money and security is what makes this girl tick. So if we can prove that Liam was murdered because of this large conspiracy, we have a civil case. We can sue the entities with deep pockets down the line. She put down another retainer for a civil suit, for a shot at really big money down the line. She also can't be on the run with so much cash, so she gave us money for us to set aside for her. She's on the run and scared."

"You're hiding money for her? Isn't that money from illegal activity, Ry?"

"Nobody can prove that. Besides, it came from her not him."

"So what are you sayin'? Cut to the chase. Am I on the clock for you too?"

"If we can get proof that Breen was murdered to shut him up, then yes. Money for time and a bonus on the back end if we win a civil suit."

"Deal."

"Good luck, Deni. Keep me posted."

Almost seven hours of being sandwiched between two other passengers without enough alcohol was about all I could take. My skin still burned from the fire and I was continually being touched by the people in the seats to the left and right of me. We landed safely in Dublin, but the pilot could have crashed the damned plane and I would have welcomed it.

I had a freakish feeling at the terminal because the building was held up with a suspension tower that looked exactly like the Zaxim Bridge they were in the process of constructing in Boston as part of the Big Dig.

The sign in the terminal for the baggage claim said *Bailiú Bagáiste Agus Slí Amach*, which I assumed was Gaelic, with English printed underneath it. I sincerely hoped that there weren't going to be any communication issues. I am Irish, but only to a point.

135

After claiming my bags and walking out the main exit, I stood on the concrete and brick kerb in front, watching the double-decker buses pickup and drop off. I again wondered how in the hell I had gotten myself into the mess. I was standing by the pick-up area like an idiot waiting for someone who may or may not show up. I started digging into my carry-on for the name of the hotel I was staying at when a tall, thin man with freckles and ginger hair called out to me. Don't ask me what he said because I don't think it was English. He introduced himself, Detective Garda Cian Daly, but I'm glad I knew it in advance because I never would have understood it otherwise.

He was nice enough to help me with my bags, speaking in tongues to me while we walked to his car. The only word that I could clearly make out was 'kerb'.

The white, elongated, rectangular license plate number K SF 2837 in black lettering was attached to a Ford sedan. It was a model I had never seen or heard of before. It was a *Mondeo Titanium V6*. I guess Ford has the market on police vehicles the world over.

We left the airport on Swords Road, through two rotaries and onto the M1, or Motorway 1. I wondered if Cian thought I was a mute, because he kept yapping away while I watched us negotiate another rotary on the left side of the streets from M1 to M50 in silence. It is an odd feeling being on the driver's side of the car without a steering wheel.

" .... bit whisht ain ya lad?" He looked at me to his left while he was driving on the right side of the *Mondeo* so I knew I was going to need to give him a response.

"I'm sorry but I don't understand a word of what you're sayin'."

"Ah. Taught you were a cod, der. Eh, touched. Not a bright one."

Not a bright one. Got it. He thought I was an idiot because I didn't speak. "I'm just going to need you to slow down a little, so I can understand you. Is that English or Gaelic?"

Cian spoke much more slowly which was still quite fast. He spoke to me the way people speak to retarded people. Loudly but not slowly. Like I was deaf instead of not understanding. Like no matter how slow he spoke, I was going to be a bit slower.

"English is the primary, everyone speaks Gaelic though. I'm told that yer the gurrier, but don't put a spanner in the works. Just make you're enquiries and turn it to me. If I you, I wouldn't touch Sinn Féin with a bargepole, I wouldn't."

I needed a secret decoder ring. But the gist was to not make waves. Just let him know what I found out. I didn't like the bosses I had, and I had just inherited another. This one didn't speak English though he insisted that it was.

"I understand. I'm just here to find out when the shipment of guns is going out, hopefully get a vessel and a crate number. That's it. Technically I'm on vacation. Any help you can give is appreciated."

"Consider this a home from home. Put your oar in but don't get nicked, I can't help ya from that scrap," he said.

"Are you going to be with me every day? I could use a lay of the land. Walter said that you would point me in the right direction. Like I said, I could use the help."

"Aye. Though I've got me own urns in the fire. I'm a bit known here, so you mightn't want a sight with me. You'll be banjaxed and in the shore but quick."

The Garda Station was located about twenty kilometers from the airport near Pheonix Park. Cian introduced me around and took me to his work space. What I gathered from his explanation at his desk was that he had introduced me as one of his many distant relatives visiting from America, of which the native Irish all have large families and can relate, because we were going to be seen together on occasion for as long as I was in Dublin.

Cian opened up a few binders once we were alone and in a more private area, taking me through a show and tell session that was very much like Charades or Pictionary. I was able to learn a lot about Ireland and the IRA. He put various photos and mug shots out for me to put a face with the modern incarnations of Sinn Féin and the Irish Republican Army.

Two of the myriad photos were shadows. Pictures without any definition. They could have been Colin Powell or Colin Farrell. Cian Daly explained to me that these were important people within the organisation, but no clear photos had ever been taken of them. He said that they knew the two names and rank, that they knew they existed, but no witness had ever seen the men with their own eyes or had lived to describe them.

I began to ask a number of questions about these mystery men, but Daly said that he would get to that. First he needed inform me about a great many things that I was obviously unaware of. It is embarrassing, to say the least, of how little I had known about my own heritage. How little I knew of any european history, let alone the struggles of my own ancestral homeland.

The history lesson would begin.

In the 1920s the Irish Republican Army was utilised by a governmental elected assembly called Dáil Éireann after Easter Rising. The army was used to wage a guerrilla war against

British rule in Ireland during the Irish War of Independence. The army was successful in that it held off the British enough to encite the Anglo-Irish Treaty.

The treaty allowed the Irish to police themselves but recognised England as the governing body. This is when the IRA split into two factions, those that supported the treaty and the majority of whom did not. Civil War ensued.

During World War 1 the unrest was still unresolved. Unionists illegally imported guns as the reliability of British forces were uncertain due to their use in the war effort. The unsupportive majority became yet more popular when public executions occurred by the British as a result of the rebels boycotting fighting for the British in the war. Because of the overwhelming rebel popularity, a new Irish Nationalist Party was formed, Sinn Féin, with the IRA at its beck and call.

Sinn Féin, who would best be assimilated to the staunch Conservative Republicans in the United States, after electing Éamon De Valera as their president, then created their own parliament after winning the forthcoming election. The now officially named IRA was the only army. The Sinns have been in and out of majority political power since, however they have never relinquished their power over the IRA despite having been sidelined as the official army of the Republic. The IRA was supposed to have been disbanded.

Once the IRA had been 'officially' set aside in the 1930s, they began their long history of doing what they must as a means to an end. From the 'Christmas Raid', where they pilfered virtually every last bit of ammunition from Pheonix Park, to attaining German weapons from the Nazis in WW2, to 'Operation Harvest', to the 'Long War', the IRA has done what it must under the direction of the Sinn Féin political party.

Even throughout 'The Troubles', the sectarianism between the Northern Ireland Protestants and the Southern Catholics, the Sinns have, " …. refused to criminalise those who break the law in pursuit of legitimate political objectives". Those objectives could be simplified into one phrase, "The vision of one true Irish Catholic Republic under an Irish Príomh Aire (Prime Minister)".

The vision not withstanding in 2004, the gun trafficking continued from Libya, the Middle East, and wherever else they could obtain assault weapons like the H&K G3A4s stolen from the Norwegian Police for the purpose of rearming under 'Operation Harvest'. The IRA continued to be engaged in paramilitary activity and were on the World Terrorist Watch list. Sinn Féin communicated their voted will to the IRA Army Council General, who then communicated to the vast number of illegal secret cells. The takings from their illegal activity, either from their own ventures or that of a myriad minion enterprises, went back to funding the political party that indirectly directed them. The Irish organised crime syndicate in Boston, Massachusetts was one of any number of enterprises sending money up to their puppet masters.

The faces of the top players in the hierarchy were on display in front of Deni. Finn Rourke, or Fin, was the IRA Army Council General and a high ranking member of Sinn Féin. He was headquartered in Dublin and was virtually untouchable. No crime could ever be linked to either him nor his immediate neighbours on the council. His number one and number two 'Volunteers' were Darragh Kane and Aiden Dunne respectively. They had been tied to a number of small crimes but because of Sinn Féin had never spent one full day in prison. Never even arrested or pictures would have been taken.

Darragh Kane and Aiden Dunn were insulated from prosecution in Dublin, or anywhere else in southern Ireland for that matter. The vast number of secret cells spread out all over the world actually executed the dirty work. Any illegal activity that could be traced back to Kane and Dunn would then be handled by Sinn Féin, according to Daly. Evidence and people went missing. Every investigation was frustrated by this arrangement.

The number one Volunteer under Fin, Darragh Kane, was the first shadow-picture. He was essentially the direct report to the IRA Army Council General, and was an all-around mystery. This Kane was at the top of this illegal pyramid, and didn't have a face.

The number two Volunteer, Aiden Dunn, was the second nondescript picture. He was second in command under Kane, the second mystery man. Both of these men were responsible for directing the IRA secret cells. Whether their leadership overlapped was anyone's guess.

Cian Daley was excited that this was the opportunity to change that. Daley had been informed by Walter that this would be the devastation of an illegal network of unprecedented proportions. While the world was focused on Saddam and Bin Laden, other wars were secretly being waged. And the end was near.

Warren Dennihan was realising that he was up to his knickers in shit and he didn't have the shoes for it.

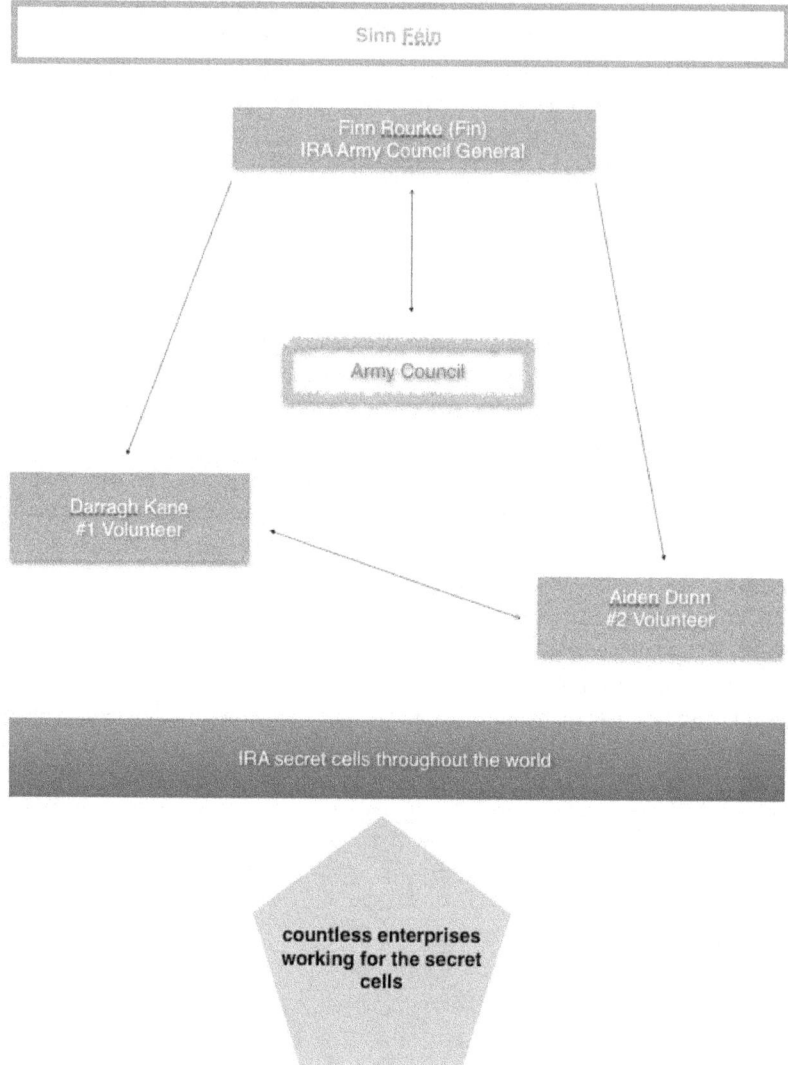

Sinn Féin

Finn Rourke (Fin)
IRA Army Council General

Army Council

Darragh Kane
#1 Volunteer

Aiden Dunn
#2 Volunteer

IRA secret cells throughout the world

countless enterprises
working for the secret
cells

26

AFTER THE PICTURE SHOW AND TELL, Cian said that it was time for a 'rake of pints'. I'll translate. He meant it was time to get shit-faced. I checked into my hotel and met him at the public house which was close to both the Pheonix Park Garda station and my hotel. It was packed to the gills at half six san oíche. Happy hour was happy hour everywhere in the world.

I was starving and knew that food was essential with the amount of alcohol that was about to be consumed. He ordered me a 'Boxty' and a pint of piss-warm beer. I explained that I wasn't much of a beer drinker after tasting the pint. It was true that I am not a beer drinker, but I could have dealt with the Guinness if it had been cold. Cian made some comment about Americans and their beer having to be ice-cold because it had no flavor before he called to the 'landlord' to pour me a Redbreast 12 yr Irish Whiskey. His exact wording I can't recall, but that is what I received. The stuff was magical. I had never tasted anything so delicious in my life. It has become my favourite.

The food was another story. The plate that was put in front of me wasn't what I had been served every year on Ste. Patty's day. No cabbage on the plate as far as I could tell. It was a pancake-like thing made of potatoes wrapped around mystery meat and gravy on top. It was inedible, which I suffered tremendously the next day for not eating.

When I woke up on Saturday morning in my hotel room, it felt like I had been spit out of meat grinder. The Arlington Hotel O'Connell Bridge was centrally located in Dublin, but that is not why I was thankful to be staying there. I was thankful because Arlington is a popular street name in Boston and was easy enough to remember even in my drunken stupor. The three star hotel had either seen enough Americans go through their establishment or had seen me stumble in at whatever ungodly time I had returned; because travel packets of acetaminophen, vitamins, and a bottle of mineral water were waiting on the hotel room dresser on Saturday morning. They had just moved up to five stars in my book. The conversion from USD to Irish Euro was 1.2. At €70,50 per night, I thought the place was worth every penny. Especially since I wasn't paying for it.

Their coffee was shit though. I was forced to drink tea. I wasn't sure if tea had more or less caffeine than coffee, so I drank it like whatever I didn't consume was going to be dumped into the harbour back home. In any event, it worked to cure my Irish Flu. I pissed out the poison from the previous night and slept it off.

I met Cian in the lobby at 'half 'til noon' on Monday as was prearranged. Or meán lae. He drove north and east on M50 toward Dublin Port and the ferries to such places like the Isle of Man. We were going to do a little snooping and enquire how one would circumvent customs if they were moving cargo in and out of Dublin. Given that the IRA was considered a terrorist group and that both the US and Europe had experienced recent devastation as a result of terrorism, I wasn't the only one who was curious. Cian found it confounding albeit not surprising.

Cian had music playing in the *Mondeo* which saved me from having to understand what he was saying but was still an assault on my ears. I asked him what the music was.

"What are we listening to?"

"The Corrs. *Runaway*. Ye know them?"

"No, I don't *know dem*," I said emphasising his pronounciation. "It's horrible. It's like Enya trying to be The Cranberries."

"Easy lad. National treasures they are. They can't all be U2."

"Fair enough I guess." I turned the music down which didn't seem to make Cian happy. "How much do you think we are really going to be able to find out down at the port?"

"I'm on the anti-terrorist police task force, they see me a kilo 'til, but they won't be so cod as to mitch me or they'll be gettin' it in the neck."

"Was that English?"

"We'll be fine is all."

"Why couldn't you have just said that?"

We paid the toll through the Dublin Port Tunnel and drove in silence. I was glad he was driving. Not only is everything confusing with the bi-lingual signage, but traveling on the opposite side of the road was more daunting than I cared to admit. The car resurfaced above ground and we continued to Promenade Road, Tolka Quay Road, Bóthar Ché Na Tulchann, and then very slowly down Terminal Road South toward the water.

Dublin Terminal One holds ferries setting to sea for the Isle of Man, Liverpool, UK, as well as others on the southern face of the port. Along the northern side of port is a different type of sea. This sea houses storage units and a long line of enormous crates waiting for one of the I-beam cranes to hoist them onto the enormous cargo vessels. Each one of the crates was the size of an 18-wheel semi trailer or larger. Some of the containers were transported from the docks by those large diesel trucks.

The docks were beyond any word for huge. Cian used the word Brobdingnagian. I had to look it up, but even that word doesn't describe it. The number of crates would be like trying to count stars. If I had a map to the specific cargo container that was filled with weapons earmarked for my country, I still wouldn't have been able to find it.

Cian parked the car and we began to walk toward the end of the dock along the water's edge toward the end of the pier. When I say toward it, I mean it in the same way as if I were telling you that I had parked the car in the most satellite parking lot of Disneyland and was walking to the deepest part of the amusement park. It was going to be a fair hike. As he put it, I was lucky that I had my 'runners' on because we were in for a 'feckin stroll'. I was lucky that my Doc Martens were comfortable even though they weren't sneakers.

The water was rough and the tall Atlantic Ocean waves chopped at the sturdy support structure of the dock. The white-caps came nowhere near the top of the thirty foot high dock on which we were walking. The dock was nowhere near the decks of the cargo ships parked near it waiting to be loaded. The waves would have sent the breakfast of the novice seaman of a smaller vessel back from whence it came. Rocking even a moderate vessel into seasickness. But the titanic cargo vessels didn't move. They were as steadfast in the water as a skyscraper is on land.

As we walked along the edge of the dock, I had a strange feeling because the work area far ahead of us was busy, but nobody was paying us any attention as of yet. In my mind there was no way that we were not being watched. Not with the number of containers and being right on the port. But nobody revealed themselves. We continued to walk for what seemed like kilometers. Why we were walking instead of driving the rest of the way was a question I asked myself regularly as the trek progressed. We passed forklifts and other vehicles for conveyance that were obviously used on the paved pier. Cian was mumbling to me from ahead as he led the voyage. Even if he was next to me I'm not sure I would have understood him. I was slowly getting the hang of what he called English, but I still had a long way to go. It wasn't a horrible day for a walk, it was 21°c but the wind off of the Atlantic was cutting right through me.

I-beam cranes, forklifts and other heavy machinery were being operated all around the end of the docks. Monstrous cargo containers were being moved around like they were matchbox cars. Workers were everywhere but not making a bid to greet us or find out why we were intruding the area.

143

Cian was finally stopped at the Customs Security Building by the man that we had spent the better part of an hour to see. At least that was the man that we questioned. He was a short and thin man who looked to be in his late fifties or early sixties. The older gentleman was the equivalent of a Dock Supervisor and Customs Officer for the Dublin shipping hub. He wore a firearm at his side but it was difficult for me to determine which flavor because it was concealed by his holster.

Daly and the man were familiar with one another because they got on with smiles and jokes whilst I stood like the third wheel that I was. After all the playful banter was exhausted, I was finally introduced, again as his distant relative from America.

"Niall McCourt," he said as he stuck out his hand. His accent was as thick or thicker than Cian's. This was going to be slow and deliberate communication on my part.

I reciprocated with, "Warren Dennihan. Deni. Are you in charge around here?"

"I'm no Guv. You're the bobby ain't cha lad?"

"The bobby?" I looked to Cian for an explanation.

"He knows you're a policeman. You must have the fug about ye. It's ok, no need to yammer on the tale." Cian gave the nod to proceed.

"I am, yes. From Boston, Massachusetts. We're having some trouble with a group of criminals over there that seem to be getting stocked with supplies from here in Dublin. I was hoping you could help me find out how that's possible." I looked back at Cian to see if I had said too much and eloquently enough, said it slow enough to be understood, and that his nod meant what I thought that it meant.

"Anything's possible lad. Not as likely though. If I knew, I'd put the size twelve on 'em. You've go some neck on ye. Arrivin' at accusations. Any proof to go along with those jewels?"

"Definitive proof? No. But we have someone on the inside of the Irish mob over there that gave us the tip. There have been small shipments over time, but some of them have been seized. So there's supposed to be a big shipment coming our way in the near future. If it were to come off of this dock, how would they do it?"

"What's the meanin' behind 'they'?" Niall had a stern face and a cocked head.

I looked to Cian again for help, but none would come. "IRA," I said.

McCourt changed the position of his head from a cocked position to a nod. "If the army was movin' supplies through here boy-o, they'd have to have a ticket on the inside. I been here since I was wee. Seen a jumble or two. If you've gone down a trove from this lot, has to be a lad to slick the gears."

Inside. Slick the gears. Got it. "And how would you do that?"

"Wouldn't be me man." The stern face was back.

"I know that it's not you, but if it were. How would you do it? You've been around a long time, 'seen a jumble or two', as you put it. How would you do it? It seems like it would be more difficult in light of recent events."

"Easy is a state in yer mind. But it me? Army doesn't trade like that without feelin' worse for it. Not without the Sinns havin' a word in. Sinn Féin has a power in the government son. If it me, the container'd have the consulate seal. Container can't be touched and is put through."

Niall walked us between some cargo containers to his office. The office was essentially a container that was modified into a permanent office space. In that office, he explained after having to repeat himself several times so I could understand, that every container was locked and sealed. The containers were deposited onto the docks or filled there via what they called a 'juggernaut', which took some time for me to figure out that he meant a tractor trailer truck. Once the cargo was verified, the container was locked and a thin metal tag was looped and contact-welded on the door. That metal tag had a series of numbers pre-stamped into it. There was no way to re-open the container without cutting through the seal. If the seal was broken, it was automatically seized. Since the stamped tags were randomly assigned at the time of welding, there was no way for a smuggler to know what tag number would be assigned to their cargo container with a proprietary serial number. The tag assigned would then be linked to the specific container number associated with shipper and receiver.

McCourt did admit that it was impossible for every single container that was to be shipped be thoroughly inspected prior to being sealed. Many times instead of the cargo being inspected prior to closing the doors, the container was sealed without the doors ever being opened for an official review. Containers to be thoroughly inspected prior to assigning and welding a seal were picked at random, by a randomly selected customs agent. It would be too risky or impossible to deliver contraband onto the docks with hope of slipping through without inspection, knowing which seal number would be randomly picked for which numbered container, and having the randomly selected agent in your pocket. The probability of not getting caught was astronomically slim, even if someone was paid off.

The only way to safely deposit cargo for shipment without risk of inspection was to have a governmental seal. If that seal was stamped onto the shipping manifest associated with that cargo, there would be no inspection and a tag would be welded on without delay. Those cargoes were immediately craned onto the vessel as they were deemed too important to risk tampering. But those governmental seals would have to go to another government agency on the receiving end.

Because containers with a welded seal that were attached to a governmental seal were protected with diplomatic immunity, there could be no inspection. This did, however, present another problem for the smuggler. Diplomatic 'pouches' were shipped from government

145

entity to government entity only. Meaning that somebody on the Boston end would have to be blessed with some government credential or another to be allowed to open said container. The containers full of weapons going to the US were clearly not ending up in the hands of the government, so there was a shell game occurring somewhere en route.

If this was, in fact, how they were doing it.

When Niall was finished with his explanation he looked to both of us with obvious pity. "Cian's been at the task for more than a tick a' the clock. You might be frettin' over the thuggery on your side a things, but my say is yer too light to be puttin' your weight about. Let be done what's to be done if ye care for yer health lad."

My take on Niall's laissez-faire approach to Sinn Féin and the IRA was that he was either a sensible older man who wanted a retirement, or he had inside knowledge and was protecting someone. The fact that he was saying anything at all to me swayed me toward the former.

"I'm just over here to find out what I can, Niall. I'm not planning on taking down an army by myself."

"Best not son. They're thick as thieves and yer a drunk lamb at a wolf party."

27

THE RIDE BACK INTO THE CITY OF DUBLIN PROPER was a bit more comfortable than the trip out to the docks. Comfortable in the sense that I was happy to be seated after an eight kilometer walk, out of the wind, a bit less unnerved by the roads and traffic, and the music was better. A song called *Sometimes* by My Bloody Valentine was played on the car stereo that I would have sworn was the Smashing Pumpkins if Cian hadn't informed me otherwise.

My only unease was in the fact that I was dealing with an organisation that had roots that were getting on a hundred years old. This army had been at the beck and call of a major political party and had committed countless violent acts for their benefactors. They hadn't been stopped or slowed to a near crawl in the entire existence of the institution. Cian had been seeking out those roots for years and hadn't made a dent. I was meddling with an entity that seemingly could not be killed but that most definitely could get me killed. All I wanted was some information. But at what cost?

While the music was better and the ride comfortable, my thoughts wandered through the deaths that had already occurred because of the designs set forth by Sinn Féin. I had no illusions that this Finn Rourke had pointed to the Bostonians like a God and commanded his wrath upon them. Like any major organisation, the lofty figureheads have little knowledge of the trenches. The day to day. Or maybe he did and didn't care. But in my mind he was still just as responsible. He ordered his will be done full-stop. He needed to pay. I hoped this partnership with Cian would see to that.

This Darragh Kane and Aiden Dunn, according to Cian, passed down that will to the various sects of the IRA. The message had to be simple enough not to be misinterpreted or altered like the telephone game we played as kids. The story started on one end and barely resembled the same message on the other. That prime directive was then passed down to the likes of Slopes in Boston from one of these countless factions without waiver. Then he passed it on to his minions in the Winter Hill Gang and the geriatrics in New Hampshire.

This was a well-oiled machine that I was dealing with. The communications and networking ran deep enough where all parties knew their role, and all parties executed with a precision that had kept them in business for generations. Documents were forged. People manipulated. Salaries paid. Bribes divvied. And the collateral damage continued.

Danny Mick. Roxy. Breen. All Dead. Guns were stolen from the Maynard Ballistics facility. Guns and drugs were the business within the business in New Hampshire. All of these things were affecting my city because of the will of this organisation. How many other cities were also affected?

I knew that tracking those guns was not going to bring any of the dead back to life. Nor would it stop Sinn Féin. Nor the IRA. Nor the Irish mob. Nor all crime in Boston. But they had tried to burn me out. Bullets and fire had me scared at first. And while I might have been ill at ease riding in that car back into the heart of Dublin, I was becoming invigorated at the thought of some justice. No matter how small.

The conversation in the car was light. All of our conversations were light because I had difficulty understanding Cian. He had been yammering on while I was listening to the music and lost in thoughts of retribution. When I had come around, determined to move forward with the next phase of the investigation, I enquired as to what exactly that next avenue would be. I was ready to run through a wall, I just needed to be pointed at it.

"So where now Cian?"

"Little else for today. Near impossible to get a formal word with a Sinn at the hour."

"It's still pretty early. Are you calling it a day?"

"Whattaya have me for? We go to the pub for a pint of the black stuff now."

"We just left the docks where Niall just told us that the only way he could see where the weapons that are plaguing my city can leave this one undetected is with governmental help, and you want to stall investigating that information? I'm not sure how things get done in Dublin, but in Boston we call that a lead and we follow that trail as quickly as possible."

"Easy lad. No need to be daft, now. All talks happen in pubs. Socialise and be merry. Get on with every toerag. Pay better attention without yer blood up. You'll be stunned with the handiwork. You lot seem to scrap yer way to stardom, we wet the tea and let it steep."

"Getting drunk seems to be the national pastime. Normally I'd be right there with ya. Our pastime is baseball which I am missing more and more the longer I have to be here. Why can't we put pressure on one of your informants or something and get to the bottom of the lead? We know that Sinn Féin is behind every move the IRA makes. Surely they can get around the red tape. We need to find out how. If you don't want to help me, then I can snoop around by myself."

"Yer takin' a piss, Deni. You'll get nowhere with that talk and disposition. No need to be two sheets or spit drunken venom. Take heart. Spend the quid and filch your answers."

"I just walk up to some random guy in the bar and ask if he knows of any government official who might know about illegal shipments under the protection of diplomatic immunity? I know what daft means, and that sounds like it."

"No such random in this pub, sir."

"We're going to a Sinn Féin bar? Is that it?"

"Aye. Don't get yourself slain in the effort, boy-oh."

The Public House, O'Neill's, was the pub frequented by the political party and legal partners of Sinn Féin. It was packed from dark wooden, old-world wall to wall. It was early afternoon, not even prevening and the place was abustle. In the States it wouldn't have even been happy-hour yet and the occupants were many and merry. It was Monday mind you, and these boys weren't working. But the tarts were. My entrepreneurial spirit had designs on owning such a pub as it seemed to be a no-risk investment opportunity in Ireland.

The beer and whiskey soaked flooring gave off a sour odor that represented decades of consumption along with the fighting and merriment that accompanied such activity. The walls were covered with old paintings of aged men of whom I had no knowledge. The establishment was like stepping into a time machine that could also transport you to a different place on the planet. The culture was oozing from the porous wood with the same mystery and supply as the stale alcohol. Each barstool and glass seemed to have an ancient story that I had not been privied to. The whiskey tasted better and the drunken stories seemed more rich. I felt as out of place as a karaoke machine would have been in that pub.

I was introduced to many people. Names became a blur. My coherence became a blur. I tried to remain quiet and take in the people, interactions, and surroundings. Cian seemed to get on well with the crowd. I was Irish and yet this tribe was a mystery. Detective Garda

Síochána Cian Daly of the Anti-terrorism division was mingling with both men and tarts that he said were linked to or members of Sinn Féin. When it comes to drinking in Ireland, I guessed, love the ones your with.

As the delicious whiskey took hold of me, the more removed I had become from any and all conversation, the more agitated I became. We were getting nowhere and we were getting there as quickly as I was becoming inebriated. The trip to the pub was justified to me as part of an investigative tactic. The only things we were investigating as far as I could tell were the bottom of our glasses and the strength of our livers.

The decision to take the investigation to the next level was not mine. The whiskey was doing the deciding and it was not soliciting any outside input. If my sense of reason was putting up a fight, it had lost like so many drunken battles that had taken place in that establishment before me. I got off my stool, left my relatively empty corner of the crowded pub, and conducted my uninhibited interviews.

I don't know what was more reckless, my questions and accusations or the fact that I had no idea of the names and ranks of the men I was interrogating. I was bounced around from one boisterous clique of men to another, making my enquiries with drunken abandon. I was most definitely getting noticed and not in a good way.

The boozy trip around the pub had left me with no answers, no leads, and thirsty. I looked for Cian to see if he needed another Guinness but he was nowhere to be seen. The pub was not that big and as crowded as it was, it took no time at all for me to give up on looking for him. He was either in the toilet or was taking a breath outside. I shrugged it off and headed to the barman to grab my next libation, but I never made it there.

A group of men encircled me before I could get to the bartop. Drunken Irish gibberish was thrown at me like a monkey throws his feces to articulate his unhappiness. They only word that I understood, 'cunt', came at me with venomous frequency. Then the shoving began. I sought sobriety and clarity as the situation dictated the necessity, but it would not come. They were corralling me toward the back door. Where that door led was a mystery to me at the time, but wherever it was, I was fine to let that mystery go unsolved.

Once they had me in the hallway leading to the back door, I was trapped. They were forcing me toward the back door from the pub end of hallway. The rage and volume intensified in the small space as I backed toward my doom. Any thoughts of trying to push my way back into the pub through the six or eight men that composed the angry mob was thwarted when the glassware was thrown at me. One such glass struck me on the side of the head, shattering and sending me to one knee.

As the alcohol-thinned blood began to flow from my head, flowing onto the sticky floor, a side door in the hallway opened up and I was helped through it. Blood and booze from the broken glass was stinging my eyes.

"Find yer own American! I want this one fer meself," said a female voice.

I searched my surroundings with my good eye. One of the tarts from the pub had gone to the ladies' room. In my sluggish stupor I had forgotten that the gents and ladies' toilets were located in the hallway that I had been pushed down. The ladies' was the last door before the back door that would have likely led to a beating or worse. The toilet was a one-holer, meaning that only one woman could perform a bodily function at a time. This particular woman who had helped me into the small space, entered behind me after calling off my aggressors and locked the door.

"Fine mess you've carved yerself," she said. "Let's see if we can clean it up."

She pushed my head into the filthy sink, turned the faucet on, cupped water into her hands, pouring it onto my wound. It stung at me while the crimson water cascaded down to the sink and into the drain.

"Thank you. Who are you?"

"A Catholic girl not wishin' to stand idly by while you get murdered."

"Well thank you Catholic girl."

"Let's not extend gratitudes yet. Yer not outta the furnace. Those lads are plottin' outside the door 'bout now, they are."

"So what's our plan fine Catholic girl?"

"We leave together. You'll be my prize for the evenin'."

"Listen if you're a whore, I'm not buying. You put yourself in harms way for me with thanks, but if you think getting me out of this jam gets you a john, you've misread the situation."

"I'm not bringin' you to a vice den for a slap n' tickle. I'm savin' yer life, lad. I'll bring ye to me flat. Yer gonna need a sew. I can't stop the bleedin' just now."

"I've got a hotel room."

"And they'll kill ye in the bed it's in."

"I'll argue with you later Catholic girl. First we need to get outta here."

"Best call me Rowena."

"Deni."

"I'd say it's a pleasure but I mightn't until it's certain neither of us is die'n today."

151

28

"IT'S NOT SQUALID YET BY NO IMAGINATION A PALACE," Rowena said as we walked up to her first floor flat. Which is a bit confusing because in Ireland the first floor is really the second floor. They call the first floor the ground floor. I was never the math whiz, but I think that would mean that if her apartment was on the sixth floor, it would really be the seventh.

She was right. Her flat was neither a palace nor palatial. But it was cozy and minimally decorated as though she cared about the limited space that was available. It was tasteful. Not kitschy or robust with knick-knacks that would make the confining space more so. There were just enough things in place to make one feel comfortable, to give a sense of personality without overcrowding or filling every bit of space.

The flat was clean and well maintained. If she was a prostitute, my immediate thought was that she must have been a clean one. The hardwood flooring was shiny, the area rug was clean and free of debris. The furniture in the parlour was tidy like it could be shown for an open house. Turning into the kitchenette, the tiny space was also clean and uncluttered.

Her apartment was a structural representation of her. She herself was very compact. She had the build of a skinny fifteen year old boy. She stood about 1.7 meters, or 5 foot 7 inches. She was the definition of lanky, the very picture of heroine chic without the dark circles under her eyes. She was not beautiful in the traditional sense, yet not ugly. What shape her body did have was angular. Her johns would be interested in purchasing time with her for her compactness. For the probability that her orifices were as tight as her body. For the male-ego fantasy of breaking her with their members.

Rowena grabbed my head and again shoved it into a sink, this time the basin in her kitchen. 'Bleed in there, not on me floors,' she said in a huff as she left the small kitchen space and entered another small room.

While she grabbed her sewing paraphernalia, I thought about how she had handled getting us out of the Sinn Féin pub alive. The back door led to an alley where other Irish men were waiting. Instead of them completing the job their comrades had started in the pub, they were told by Rowena that they were going to have to pay her to hand me over. I was money for her. In prostitution, money is everything. For Irish men looking to beat the life out of an American, money is everything also. They didn't want to part with one Irish Euro.

Rowena was allowed to take her foreign customer to whatever vice den the alley-men thought she worked in. She told me that the lads would either sleep off the drunken venom; or more probable, they would finish their handiwork on a later date. I was hoping for option one.

When she came back to the small space with her skin and clothing repair kit, she leaned into me as if she were trying to morph from two people into one. The space was small and claustrophobic, her adherence to me made it more so.

She poured some sort of alcohol on my head and it would not surprise me if the wound hissed, making a sound that would assault one's ears as much as it did my nerve endings. I must have pulled away or moaned but she was not having any of it.

"Quit bein' the mot?"

"What? Speak English. You all say you speak the language but none of you do."

"Girl. Quit bein' a feckin' girl."

"Is this why you got me out of that mess? You wanted to torture me yourself?" She started sewing my head, the numbing properties of the Redbreast whiskey I had consumed at the pub were gone.

"An American missin' er dead would make the dailies but it'd done nothin' for me cover."

"You're a cop? er, Garda or whatever?"

"I'm no Bobby," she said. "I'm no brasser either. I'm a pressmen. You lot say 'reporter' ye know."

"You work the Sinn Féin pub as an undercover repor – ow! Jesus Christ take it easy .... as a reporter?" She was stitching my head like it was attached to a torn teddy bear. "You sleep with these guys to prime them for inside knowledge? Kinda dangerous for a small girl like you."

"I'm in the wick! Nothin' of the sort, ye wanker. The lads get loose-tongued when their bolloxed on the black stuff. Their aims and ambitions get put in the dailies without a notion as to how. I lay with none of them, ye sap. Ye put quite the spanner in when you got a fifty and necked in. If I hadn't put me own diddies in, you'd be missin' and never heard of again. Those are officials, fella. Have a way of doin' evil works without spoil."

"Sorry to get you involved. Your diddies or whatever. " She rinsed off my head with more booze and stepped away. Which is to say that we were still very close.

153

"Jest an expression. Means tits."

"You don't have any of those do you?"

"Whisht! Shet yer gob!" She slapped my wounded head and I immediately regretted joking with her. "There's a towel in the press. Dry yourself ye ingrate." She pointed to the cupboard, which I opened to get a towel. She exited the kitchenette for the other small room. My skin was tender and swollen away from my skull. I opened another small door to find a bottle of Poitin. I pulled the top off and guzzled as much of the harsh poison as I could stomach. Alcohol at any cost.

When I followed her to the parlour she had a towel on the floor and pointed for me to sit on it and told me to strip. I must have had a confused look on my face because she explained that I was a mess and she wanted none of my filth on her furniture. The order to strip was so that she could put my clothes through the wash.

Once I was as naked as the day I was born, she tossed me another towel to 'cover my bits and body art'. Any man hates their genitals to be referred to as bits. It's emasculating. We prefer other terms that don't infer size; or if necessary, to aire on the larger size. As far as the body art, there was no covering that up. I was covered front and back, shoulders to thighs with the exception of my forearms and 'bits'.

I wrapped the towel around my waist and sat on the towel she had placed on the floor, but my tackle was still showing because she wanted me to cross my legs before her interrogation began.

"Quite the daft booze-hound to be strollin' into that pub for a pint. Have ya lost yer mind? Or are you eejit?"

After a quick moment of hemming and hawing, after deciding that she had a cover that needed protecting same as me, I decided to tell her my story. I felt that the reward would outweigh the risk. "If I tell you why I was in that bar, you cannot repeat it or print it."

"A fair prop. Go on."

I explained that I was a Massachusetts State Police Trooper from H, in the city of Boston. I explained that while I handled a portion of all major crimes against persons in the city, my specific area of expertise was in South Boston because of my background there. She learned about Sean Teague, and about how he was running an organised crime syndicate in Boston. After some interruptions for clarification, she also became aware of the gun and drug trade that Slopes ran into and out of the city via the compound in the mountains of New Hampshire. That the seizure of those guns and drugs was going to cause quite the headache for Slopes unless he was able to restock. I told her about the informant that linked the Winter Hill crew to a satellite sect of the IRA, which she already knew was run by the Army Council of Sinn Féin. She didn't know about Darragh Kane or Aiden Dunn specifically, only that there had to be top people to communicate messages from the untouchable Finn Rourke to the secret cells of

Volunteers. I further explained that I was sent to Ireland to uncover information about the when and the where of the large replacement shipment that was to be sent via Dublin. I told her that Detective Garda Síochána Cian Daly was my contact here. That he was the one who brought me into the pub.

She said that she had covered many a story about the secret cells, as they are the ones who publicly 'claim responsibility' when an atrocity they execute needs a message tied to it. Rowena spoke about how the IRA always uses the name P. O'Neill when they communicate those messages through the press. How she had suspected that there was no such person which is why they continue to use the name. She continues to report on the political party and their agenda from the inside of a pub. She reinforced Cian's correlation of Sinn Féin to the Republican party in America. She said that Sinns bleed for the cause, hold their politicians in the highest regard. The mourning of a lost member was like the death of Ronald Reagan to Conservatives, which had just happened in June. She showed me a piece that she had written to ensure I got the point.

She portrays herself to be in the 'bugger trade' so she can uncover the mysteries and inner workings without suspicion. She has on occasion had to accompany an interested gentleman to a hotel room where she would 'give him a crack'. He would wake up the next day with a lump on his head thinking he got proper fucked, when in fact he had just been 'made hames of'. He had given the goods and his money without a release.

Rowena said that her stories were the scandal. Her reports were like no other pressmen in Ireland and many sought to find out who she was. She had a fake name on her column, with a fake photo. She sent her columns to the paper by a courier who didn't know what he was carrying. Very cloak and dagger. If something was urgent she would contact her editor at the paper, her boss, but did so as rarely as possible.

When we both finished explaining why and how we were in the pub, she said that it was 'amadán' to have gone in there, and even more foolish for Cian to have left me there alone.

"I don't know if he left me there. He just wasn't there when I was looking for him. He might have stepped out. He might have been embarrassed or trying not to get killed himself."

"Aye. likely," she said. "On the toilet or no, he might have been a bit more cop-on."

"Cop-on? Like help me question people?"

"No. Cop-on. Eh .... have more brains in the way of things."

"Streetwise."

"Aye. That's it."

"If you all speak English, why is this so difficult?"

"It's less English as Gaelic, garsún. Gaelic used to be first language, English taught as a second in the south of Ireland. Now Gaelic is second, more the pity. Most of the Gaelic sticks though, so it's English in name only."

155

"That's what Cian said. It's damn near indecipherable if you ask me."

"I didn't."

"Fair enough. As a reporter, do you write the way you speak?"

"It's the accent most like. You'd be able to read better'n listen."

"A lot of words are different, so I don't know about that. Anyway …. so now what? Where do we go from here?"

"You keep me on the ticket, I'll let you settle here."

"You want me to stay here? What does 'on the ticket' mean? You want the story?"

"Aye. I help you. You help me."

"I don't know. This is supposed to be hush-hush. Low key. There's a big dog federal prosecutor at home that wants this under the table. I find out what I need and go home."

"Fine job of silence. 'pass the pitcher of mild, and while your at it do you know of any gobeen men?' About as subtle as an advert, that. All rights ye should be dead."

"Not my finest moment, but I don't want to be here forever and a day, Row."

"Rowena," she said. "Like most you have great grá for the whiskey. Let yer mouth run riot. Settlin' here in me flat will help with the death, but not if ye keep at it."

"Any suggestions?"

"If I you? I'd set an appointment with Finn Rourke himself, I would. He won't touch ye personally. Won't nothin' happen to ye on or after seein' him. Much the risk. His hands stay clean, you stay alive."

"You honestly think that he will tell me anything at all about his illegal maneuvers? He'll laugh me out of his office."

"Aye. But you'll have the sense of him. He'll know to take care and less like somethin' will happen to ye. A word with him means there's a link. A death tied to Fin would need an explanation. It's the politics of it." She left the room as she spoke, taking the bottle of Poitín with her. Returning a few moments later with a bottle of whiskey and two glasses.

"That might work. Cian will never go for it though. He has already told me he wants his involvement to be as silent as possible. Daly is on the anti-terrorist task force. He has been introducing me as his cousin or somethin'."

She poured the brownish liquor into the two glasses. "Then he'll not know. You go on like yer still in yer hotel, still takin' his cues. We'll confer when you come here."

We both shot our whiskeys back, set the glasses down on the table between us, and she poured another round.

"If I'm not to be touched after I meet with Fin, why would I need to stay here?"

"Amn't sayin' no harm will befall ye. I mean to say less like. And they know you're here and why, fella. The less predictable you are, the quicker you'll get what you desire. This is a story and I mean to help. You get yer guns, I get me story."

"How do I know that I can trust you?"

"I'm no slíbhín. I've me secrets and you yours. We keep what we must between us or the devil take us both."

She raised her glass to toast, I did likewise.

"Sláinte," she said. She was about to down her glass but she stopped. I must have a had a puzzled look on my face because she explained before slinging it back. "It means to our health."

29

FOR THE SECOND TIME IN UNDER A WEEK I WOKE UP from a night of alcohol poisoning. Drinking or drunk would be bad enough, but this was not just having too much to drink. This was poisoning. It took me a few minutes to gather myself, remember where I was. I was still drunk truth be told. I had been nearly piss-myself drunk in the Sinn Féin pub. I had almost gotten myself killed then finished polluting myself by getting hammered with the woman who had saved my sorry ass.

My head was excruciating. Whether it was the hangover that had not yet gone into full swing or the sutured wound from the glass that was shattered on my head was anyone's guess. Maybe both. I felt the tender stitching and winced as I did so. The thought that there might still be glass in there was fleeting. It had certainly felt like the woman was thorough in her cleaning at the time, even in my inebriation.

Further personal inventory led me to the realisation that I was naked under my sheet. The question of how I had gotten naked was another in a series of notions flooding through my sluggish brain. My clothes were being washed. I had a towel. The towel was now gone. Rowena.

I turned to the other pillow, the other side of the bed. Speak of the devil. She was sleeping next to me. A slight lift and a peak under the covers revealed her naked body as well. She lay on her side, back to me. Her long slender body was motionless with the exception of the slow rise and fall of her midsection from her breathing. Rowena's body really had no shape other than where bone hinted through skin. The curve of her spine was the only undulation. She had been wearing a wig the night before, as the head laying on the pillow next to me had very short hair.

Rowena was already awake and pretending to be asleep, or the draft from the lifted sheet woke her.

158

"Don't have a blarney. I don't sleep in pyjamas or knickers."

"I got bombed last night. Did we …. "

"Feck no," she said. She slid her legs and feet off of the bed and headed toward a chair with clothes draped over the back of it. "I'll get us a fry-up."

There was no explanation as why we were both in her bed and naked, other than she doesn't wear clothes to bed and that we didn't have sex. When I sat upright to leave the bed, a massive bout of vertigo took over. I struggled with keeping what little that was already in my stomach settled where it was. With my feet on the floor to the side of the bed and my tender head in my hands, elbows on knees, I waited out the storm of spins and nausea.

I looked around the room once the sheet was pulled off of me and I was able to stand without fear of losing my balance. A mirror and a dresser. A long necklace hung from the corner of the mirror. The medallion looked like it was a religious token. Ste. Christopher. I remembered from catechism that he was the patron sainte of lost things and causes. I continued to look around, no clothes. None that belonged to me I should say. The waft of grease and food came into the small room from the small kitchenette. My stomach went into cartwheels but I was forced to go closer to the smell of breakfast to determine the whereabouts of my clothes. The flat wasn't big by anyone's standards, there were only so many places that they could be.

"Have you seen my clothes?" I stood in the doorway to the kitchenette, naked in want of garments.

"Aye. In the cupboard 'round the way." She stood over the pan on the two burner stovetop, pointing ahead of her with a spatula. I assumed correctly that on the other side of the wall against which the stove was situated was some sort of laundry closet.

Around the corner was a tall, narrow door which hid the tiny, front-load, convenience sized washer and dryer that stood vertically one over the other. "Should be done," she yelled from around the corner. I picked a door, the bottom one, and saw my dried clothes laying in the bottom of the circular bin.

My balance was still not back to normal so I sat on the floor to get dressed. I needed to go to a gym. These nights of drunken debauchery with no exercise was not good. I am a drinker, no question, but this was an entirely different level. I felt as though I was a little leaguer trying out for the majors. The fast ball had gone by me and I was waiting for the pitch.

Dressed, I reentered the kitchenette to see breakfast was being plated. It was unrecognizable. She handed me the plate and commented on what must have been an obvious look of apprehension.

"It's meat hash. Jest put in yer gob."

No wonder I don't play poker.

159

In truth I was starving. Liters of alcohol consumed with virtually no food. And no exercise. My body was freaking out.

The 'meat hash' was eggy mystery meat. The best way to describe it by looks would be Spam in an egg mixture and heated in grease. The best way to describe the taste and texture would be fucking gross. But I ate it. I needed the food, needed the grease, no matter what the flavor.

Over breakfast I asked Rowena what had happened and why we were in the same bed and if that was going to be the arrangement every night that I came back to her flat. She replied that she grew up one of eleven kids, that sleeping in the same bed was not just for married people. I thought it morally questionable to have siblings sleeping naked with one another, but I knew nothing of her upbringing and I knew that I was no sainte. Maybe she had the moral high-ground.

She also said that she would give me what she had and work her contacts to get me further background information on the current mainstays of Sinn Féin, and schedule an appointment for me to meet with Finn Rourke. She told me not to go back to my hotel under any circumstances, that she would go there later in the day to collect anything that I might need. 'Jest go to Pheonix Park like it's any other labour day.' Which meant just go see Cian and pretend that Rowena doesn't exist. I could do that.

I just wish I had a better poker face. With her at least. She was one of the few people whom I have ever met that could read me like the dailies.

"Wait. Row, isn't today Tuesday?"

"Aye."

"So is Cian going to pick me up at my hotel today? We didn't really talk about it. Maybe I should go to the hotel to see if he calls."

"Jest go to the Garda station. If he's not present, wait a bit."

Rowena gave me directions to a corner where I could grab a taxi to the Garda station. She said that it was not smart to grab one off of the street in front of her flat. This investigation and arrangement was likely going to take a few more days at the very least, and me getting into a cab every day would create a predictable pattern. I obviously knew that patterns were bad.

So I followed her directions and went to the corner of Paráid Lósaif and Plás Bhaile Coimín. The old stone buildings set on old narrow kerbs amidst old narrow roads between them gave me the odd feeling. And it wasn't the fact that I was still a bit hungover.

Boston has old buildings. These structures were ancient by comparison. Weather and years had warped and stained every surface. At night, I could have been in the North End of Boston. During the day, the history and age of the area hits you in a way that makes you feel small and insignificant. So much of the world has happened decades and centuries before and in other parts of it. If the structures could talk, I would have been there a while to hear the stories.

The cab rolled to me and stopped within a few short minutes of my waiting. The day was another 21°c and the sun was trying unsuccessfully to peak through the clouds. I didn't mind the wait. I was still lost in thoughts of old when the cab pulled up. It took a few extra seconds for the address to which I was headed spark in my brain and leave my mouth to the driver.

Cian was sitting at his work station, at his desk when I arrived. He hadn't looked up to notice me and seemed genuinely surprised to see me when I sat in the chair next to his desk as I had before.

"There he is. The bold boy of the minute."

"You seem surprised to see me. Wasn't I supposed to meet you here? Was I supposed to see you at the hotel?"

"Aye. But you had the piss in ye, lad. Thought you'd be sleepin' off the trouble you've caused. Are ye better now?"

"What trouble?" As if I didn't know. "You disappeared. I looked for you, but I couldn't find you."

"Stepped out for a fag. You the talk when I came back, ye were."

"Yeah. I might have ruined the element of surprise. I was asking questions I shouldn't have. I just got tired of sitting there and waiting to hear something that was never going to be discussed. Did you honestly think that I was going to stumble upon a conversation about a shipment of guns to America?"

"Naw man. But you mightn't let the world know you were searchin'. You could have met someone to point you straight. You could have heard a name."

"So now what?"

"Now I see if there's construction in the damage. Go phone yer mates."

"So you're going to call your Sinn Féin friends? Isn't that a little odd that you are tasked with stopping the IRA from committing acts of terrorism yet you are buddy-buddy with the group that tells them what to do?"

"Watch yourself bucklepper. Don't get yer parties muttled up lad. I keep enemies close. And not all of those lads are mixed up in the troubles. Some surely, not all. I let you here as a courtesy and you spit on me hand. I'll do my best to keep air in yer lungs, you mightn't want to continue workin' against me efforts."

I apologised and told him that I did appreciate his efforts to keep me alive. On the inside I wondered just what type of effort he was making. I could have died in that pub the night before and he was out having a smoke. But insulting him or his obvious political preference was no way to keep the peace.

Cian was right in that all members of a political party are not prone to evil designs. Even from what little I knew about the hierarchy, I had the sense that there was one man at or near the top, Finn Rourke. He was the Army Council General. The rest of the party was over and around him, and the army council was likely unaware of maneuvers he sent down to his number one and number two Volunteers. The arrangement likely left the majority of the nationalists in the dark. While they might agree with the philosophy behind his actions, the deeds might not be what they had signed up for. Or maybe they had. Either way politics was not my business. In fact I hated it. The guns going into Boston were my business and I needed to stay focused.

I called Walter Glibczieck, the federal prosecutor, just to check in. Which was a giant pain in the ass. My mobile phone was not set up for international calling. 'Hellomoto' from my phone was useless other than fortifying me with the cell numbers that I needed to call. I then had to get the international code to dial the US and use the land line at the Garda Station. All just to make a phone call to an answering machine because he was otherwise occupied five hours behind Dublin time. He would be informed when he heard the message that there was nothing to report. I was no closer to attaining the shipment information a week in than I had been back in Boston.

While I had the phone handy I called Ryan Wells at his office in New Hampshire. I wanted to inform him that there was still no progress and see if there was any new information about Breen's murder, his old lady Maddy, or the other old men. Also forced to leave a message. I expected nothing less as it was still early morning there.

My last call was to Troop H. Tits and Hobbs had not been into the station yet, according to the receptionist/operator. Did I want to leave a message? No thanks, I was just checking in.

I was hungover and friendless. Kind of a thing with me.

30

AFTER MAKING ALL OF MY FRUITLESS PHONE CALLS and after Cian had made his, we decided to take to the streets. He said that he had someone that I should talk to. The informant was someone that Cian used back in February when he had made the big weapons and ammunition bust. He was located up in Belturbet, which was inland and near the border between northern and southern Ireland. The UK - Ireland border. The trip would be just shy of one hundred thirty kilometers and take about an hour and a half. One way. In other words the trip would eat up the rest of the day.

I sat in what would normally be the driver's side seat of the Ford *Mondeo*. We took Motorway 3 most of the way, then onto N3, or Navan Road. Cian inserted a compact disc blaring the music of Stiff Little Fingers. The music wasn't bad but at the high volume it didn't help the hangover. The disc was repeated over again when it was finished the first pass through. The only track that I remember off of that CD, and still listen to on occasion to this day, is *Alternative Ulster*.

We took the right onto Upper Bridge Street and parked in Fitzpatricks Flats. The area reminded me of Lowell, Massachusetts. In other words it was beat up, mostly one way streets with lots of pedestrians, and of course public houses. The buildings were converted from townhouses of various styles and shapes, juxtapositioned side by side on both sides of the streets, into small businesses. The roundabouts and one-way streets were confusing and tightly spaced. The kerbs were only wide enough for one person and were not elevated off of the road. Traffic moved quickly despite the confinement, though both vehicles and pedestrians seemed to be used to it. I was happy to be inside the building where we were to meet the informant.

The ground floor was 'to let'. The space was empty and looking for a business to start paying the freight. This may or may not have been a cover to make the building look less desirable, but what I do know is that we were on the third floor walk-up which was called the second floor. The red door was cracked open and upon entry the flat looked like a crack den. The only living space that I had seen in that poor condition was Roxy's a short time back.

A gangly, spotted kid stood in the center of the room unfased by our entrance. Cian made the introductions.

"Oisin, this is Deni. Deni, Oisin Hanamy." We both nodded, neither of us making a bid to shake hands.

"American then?"

I hadn't even said a word yet.

"Yes I am. Cian told you about me?"

"You have the look about you. Shall we head to Duffy's then?"

"Duffy's?" I looked at Cian to see if he knew who this Duffy was. The look of confusion was obvious to both men.

"The pub across the way. We can use the back room over pints of the black stuff," Oisin said.

"Does anything happen here without alcohol in hand?" I had startled myself with that comment. Coming from me that is quite the statement.

"The day ye come into this world and the day ye leave." They both had a laugh at the younger man's witty response. I shook my head but followed them down the narrow back stairs anyway. We left through what could have been a kitchen and down a set of stairs attached to the outside of the building. Oisin was exaggerating how far away Duffy's was. Across the way meant the green building across the back alleyway that was no wider than a sub-compact car.

Pints of Guinness were being poured as we entered the pub. They took a minute to pour as the nitrogen gas creates what initially seems like more foam than beer. The foam cascaded into dark brown and then black liquid on the bottom of the glass, creating the elixir that these Irishmen craved. We didn't wait for the pints to be completed, we continued into a back room that stood empty until we arrived.

I didn't have the heart to tell them that I didn't want a pint of beer. I wasn't a fan of warm beer. Cold beer was a struggle depending upon the type, warm was like broken glass and turpentine. But I was still reminiscing about my lack of whiskey-soaked discretion the night prior and I didn't want a whiskey more than I didn't want a warm beer. So I shut my mouth, had a seat, and waited for my Guinness.

The pints didn't sit on the table long when they were delivered by the barman. They were hoisted into the air and what sounded like 'jeers' was said under their breath to one another. I was still grabbing my beer off of the table by the time they had already slugged a quarter of their ales as if it were milk. They had the white foamy mustaches to complete the simile.

164

Cian began the meeting. "Oisin here is what's dubbed a fountain. Seems to know a great many things about a many people."

"A supergrass," I said. "So what's the trick? How do you stay alive?"

"A super — what now?" The two native Irishmen looked to one another for the meaning of the term.

"Means you have a lot of people to tell on, Oisin."

"Aye. I'm a trusted lot," he said. "I pass on what I can when I can slide it through without suspicion." His accent was as thick as the beer he drank. No matter how many words he used that I was familiar with, I still strained to understand him.

"And this thing in February? That was a big deal. You were able to slide that by?"

Cian broke in. "That was a grand bit indeed. Made my year, it did."

"It was a rare bit but there were many who knew 'bout it. Not solely me," Oisin said.

"So are you Garda?"

"Naw. I get free of my indiscretions with a turn of word from Cian."

"So what turn of words could you give me about a large shipment of assault weapons headed for the States?" I looked around the table like I was finally glad to be talking with someone who could help me.

He had a look of mixed confusion and shock which he fixed on Cian. The young man was stunned into silence which he filled with the consumption of Guinness. Oisin drained his glass and continued his apparent look for help from Cian. It was also apparent how often he frequented that establishment because three more pints arrived virtually the moment he finished his adult milk. Cian also gunned his back and received his replacement. Mine was still full with a new one delivered as backup.

"I know nothin' of guns marked for the new world," Oisin said.

"What is this colonial times? New world?"

"Phrasin' matters not, fella. I don't know 'bout those guns." He looked scared. I had enough street smarts and had interrogated enough people in my short time in Troop H to know that I was being shined.

"Let me put it to you this way, guy. I've got a network of felons back home that have now been caught twice with their hands in the cookie jar. H & K G3A4s a plenty, among many others. They are an Irish network. Not Irish like you, but Irish just the same. Anybody who might have known about the guns they got caught with is now dead. I also have information that those suedo-Irish are runnin' guns around my city and beyond to make money for your Irish. G3s are the assault weapon of choice for the Irish. The IRA. Especially after stealing so many in the Norway incident a while back. See what I'm gettin' at? Do you see where the dots connect? Now you, being the 'trusted lot', must know about when and where a new shipment is being sent over to replace all the weapons that are currently in a federal holding facility."

"Are ye mental?" Oisin's eyes were wild and crazy looking.

"I've been told that I'm insane a time or two, yes."

"If what yer sayin' is true, lad, that's a tall order to be filled. Trusted or no, they'll use only top people for that work. I'm not top people."

"I think Cian here can probably incentivise you to make more of an effort. I want to know the when and how. Those guns get through customs somehow," I said.

"Ye understand your not just putting me neck in, but me arse as well. Enquirin' minds tend to turn up missin'."

"They're going down, Oisin. How do you say? Nicked? You can be with them or not. Your call."

"And how does one live through such a plan?" He looked at Cian when asking the last. He knew any promise I made at freedom and sanctuary were wasted words. Another round of drinks were brought to the table. All of us were falling behind, me more so.

I told him how he could steer clear of the troubles with my unsolicited, sage advise. "The same way you have been. Don't get caught."

"Of course. I'm the only garsún breathin' free air. Couldn't be me who told tales," Oisin said.

"How did you do it in the past?"

Oisin again looked at Cian for help. "This lad is funny as rubber crutches, Cian. Where'd ye find him?"

Cian didn't answer. Instead the two swallowed the rest of the pints of black and began on the queued round. I was struggling to finish my first, two waiting behind it. I had a feeling there was going to be a third if I didn't man-up.

Oisin told me of the February affair, albeit with reluctance. The IRA had a warehouse in Newtowncunningham, near the border of northern and southern Ireland, near Londonderry. Just south of the United Kingdom. That warehouse stored hundreds of kilos of explosive material, bomb making hardware, Russian rocket launchers, and shoulder-fire missiles. He had been sent that far north on 4 February of 2004, with a band of other Volunteers to caravan out a small portion of the vast supply on lorries, namely the launchers and missiles. The trip back to Dublin with the large withdrawal was a success, only Oisin had spent the money he had been paid to execute the transaction poorly. He had been caught trying to turn those Irish Euros into more by investing and turning over large quantities of heroine. He was busted by Garda Detective Cian Daly on 8 February.

Oisin fessed up to both the Dublin withdrawal of weapons, which was long gone, and the Newtowncunnigham trove. By the time the anti-terrorism crew arrived at the Dublin location on 13 February, the safe house was empty. Cian and his group within the anti-terrorism division went north and succeeded in commandeering the warehouse there. The simultaneous raids had very different outcomes.

Much of the Newtowncunningham trove was outdated and in danger of accidental detonation. The seizure was deemed a success, however. Accolades abound for Cian Daly and his crew. 13 February, 2004 was a big day in Cian's career.

Not so much for the Dublin attempt. They had come up empty. Literally. The abandoned building had not so much as a trace of gunpowder or explosive material. It didn't even make the dailies as not to spoil the glory of the Newtowncunningham raid.

Oisin didn't spend a single day in detention. Cian let Hanamy go after the fess-up and Oisin watched in pretend astonishment when the raids went down. He said that he was able to get away with informing back then because there were many people who knew about it.

I was still nursing my second Guinness at the completion of the story. The queue of beverages was getting lengthy and I was receiving help on them from the other two gents who had caught up and were finishing theirs, and now mine, with ease. They weren't drunk, not even close. Not that I could tell either way. But they were feeling more affects of alcohol than I was for sure. Something wasn't sitting right with me, and I was sure it had nothing to do with the beer.

31

THE TRIP BACK TO DUBLIN WAS LACKLUSTER. Same roads, same Stiff Little Fingers CD. Cian told me that he wanted to go to the pub when we got back, which I had to spend the hour and change declining the invitation. He also wanted to drop me off at the Arlington Hotel, which Rowena specifically told me not to go near. I'm not usually one to follow rules or instructions, but she knew the city and this lot better than I did so I declined that offer as well. He dropped me off in front of the Garda station near Pheonix Park, where I walked several blocks zig-zagging to ensure I wasn't followed. Once I was sure, I hailed a taxi.

My failure to remember the address where I had hailed the cab to the Garda station that morning made the ride longer and more expensive than it had to be. I finally sorted it out, recognising some of the old buildings and got out of the vehicle €35 lighter.

Rowena was waiting for me in her flat, already tarted up in her uniform. She was 'dressed to be buggered' as she put it. But she didn't want to leave without hearing what had happened to me. I told her it was a long story, asking how her day had gone. She pointed to the corner of the small flat, where my luggage was resting.

She had gone to the hotel in disguise with my room key that she had pilfered when doing my laundry. She was a clever monkey. She said that she wasted no time in the room, threw everything that was possibly mine into the bag and got out of there within a few short minutes. She also said that if she had forgotten anything to let her know and she would go back, but only if it was worth the risk. Rowena had brought another disguise and changed into it prior to leaving my hotel room with my luggage. Essentially she had entered the Arlington one woman, and left a different one towing luggage.

I have to say, I was impressed.

She begged me to tell her what happened when I told her of the trip to Belturbet. I simply mentioned that I went, not who we met or what was learned. She desperately wanted to know but agreed that she should go to 'work' for appearances sake. I promised to tell her the entire story when she returned later that night.

I had no idea that later that night would only be three hours later. She had picked up a 'thick bockety' man as quickly as she could in order to get back to her flat. The drunk man had little whits about him, she said, and her low-ball offer was too good to refuse. He took her to a squalid kip of ill-repute where she 'fit him up' by knocking him out, stealing his money, and taking an indirect route back here.

When I asked her with a chuckle how that behaviour fits with her being a Catholic girl, she said that the money pays for all the drinks she has to buy on the many nights that nobody is interested in her pretend services. Stepping out on their missus was a sin and they should feel lucky for only a lump on the head and a few quid short. *Lucky for them,* I thought.

I explained to her what had happened at Duffy's earlier that day while she stripped out of her nearly non-existent outfit right in front of me. Only three garments and a wig. Row had no need for a bra. She might be Catholic but she was not modest. I'm a recovering Catholic but I didn't think immodesty was part of the ten commandments, apparently she didn't think so either. It didn't take her long to take off the three things she was wearing that could have been sized for an infant, and I was having difficulty focusing on the story while she stood in front of me in the nip.

"Focus on your dealin's and not on me gee," she said bending over to catch my eyes with hers.

"Can you get dressed? You don't have much to look at, but the part that makes you a woman is hard to ignore when your naked."

"Got a colleen back home?"

"Huh?"

"A girl. Do you have a girl waitin' for ye back home?"

"No. Not really. Why?"

"I'm the colour curious, ye cheeky devil." She left the parlour to go put something on. It was a normal sized tshirt, which means it was oversized for her. She was back in all of ten-seconds without her wig. "You look at me like you've not seen a woman in some time."

"I don't think we treat being naked quite the same way you do here. Or maybe it's just you."

"Oisin is the lad that feeds your Cian Garda Fella. Yeah?"

"Yeah. And as far as I can tell, he hasn't fed him anything since February. Meanwhile, he hangs out in the safe house and goes to work for the IRA when called upon. He also stays out of prison or jail or whatever you call it here. He's got quite the deal for himself."

169

"And you believe he'll fess up what yer lookin' for?"

"I'm not sure. Something doesn't seem right. He kept looking at Cian for the go ahead. Like he wasn't sure it was a good idea to talk with me. The February bust didn't seem to phase him, it was when I started asking about the new shipment."

"He's lookin' to his handler is all."

"Maybe Row. Maybe .... "

"You in your Row. My name is Rowena ye fugue. Deni is short isn't it?"

"Yes."

"Fer what now?"

"Short for Deni. Can we move on?"

She stared at me for a few moments before speaking.

"Cian gets recognised for the watered down lot, whilst the Garda in Dublin are left with bell in hand, yeah?"

I sat up straight from the slouched seated position on the small love-seat. "Yeah. That was lucky that he got that location huh? It could have been him in Dublin with the short straw."

"Inside deal within inside deals, seems to me."

"Wicked Pissah, Row. Nailed it on the head, I think. That's what's not right — what's been buggin' me. He and Oisin have it worked out where he gets the .... wait you called it a 'watered down lot'."

"Wicked Pissah?" She looked lost.

"Focus Row. 'Watered down lot'?"

"The old stuff that's like to accidentally detonate or is shite."

"Yeah Oisin pulled the real stuff out of the warehouse on the convoy, which then disappeared sometime before the raid," I confirmed.

"The business near Londonderry was a put up. Made to look flash."

"Right. Oisin gives up the fake goods, so they can hide the real ones. Cian got doped and he doesn't even know it."

"So if I'm straight, Deni, Cian is a fiddle. Oisin gives him little or nothin'. You'll get nowhere 'til you strike yer own petrol."

"I'm attached to him at the hip. He says where we go and who we talk to."

"You'll see him in the mornin' then?"

"I think I'm supposed to go over there. I bailed on him to go to the pub tonight, but didn't make an official time to meet. Did you see him there? At the Sinn bar, eh .... "

"O'Neills."

"Right. He was there when you went over?"

"Naw. Cian wasn't there."

"Hmm. I wonder where he went? I'll find out tomorrow I guess."

"Don't see him. Go to the consulate."

"You mean customs?"

"Naw. The American Consulate. The Embassy."

"You think I should just go home? I don't know anything yet."

"Naw, ye cunt. Ye go and see about shipments," she looked at me like I was half retarded. I could see the pity in her eyes. "If they hand pick the ports, how do they mean to get the guns out?" She said it slow like she was spoon-feeding me.

"But if I tip my hand, we'll never find the guns. They'll just find another way out."

"Aye. Force their hand, man. Think cheeky like. Tell them they come out the north. Dundalk, Belfast, Derry …. all searched high and low. Raise a fuss. The army gets word that ports are bein' sacked and it'll force their hand."

"You should have been a cop, Row. Fuckin' genius. They'll move quick and they might make a mistake. We know they plan to move them out of Dublin."

"More like they're stored here as well, Deni."

"Right. But where?"

"They'll not want to move them far. Near the port if I had guesses," she said.

It was at that very moment that I decided to hitch my wagon to Rowena. She was smart and had an investigative mind. Cian was lazy and foolish to wait for evidence to fall into his lap. She was keeping me alive both in the literal sense and in the mission. This partnership could work.

32

THE SURGE IN ENERGY IN THE INVESTIGATION called for a celebration. Rowena obtained another bottle of whiskey out of her press, which I continually called the cupboard but the cupboard was the closet which was confusing to me for some reason. She returned from the kitchenette with the bottle along with two glasses. I didn't ask where the old bottle went, I was afraid I already knew. I didn't get as shattered as I had the night before, but I still had some fuzzy spots in my recollection of the events after our successful meeting.

Again I woke up on Wednesday, 18 August, in a fog. Again I woke up naked in bed along side of Rowena who only sleeps in the nip. Again I snuck a peak to ascertain what I already knew as she lay facing away from me.

"You can stop starin' at me arse now." She didn't move or open her eyes as far as I could tell.

"Why are we always naked? I know you always sleep naked, but why am I? I could just sleep on the floor or something."

"You had designs of a sexual nature, but yer whiskey dick let you down."

"Now I know your full of shit. My whiskey dick has never let me down." I had a number of drunken one night stands on a number of occasions, and while the sex may not have always been earth shattering, there was never an equipment failure.

"Suit yourself. I'll get us fixed for breakfast."

I would have to have been more drunk than I thought to have tried any advances on Rowena. There was nothing sexual about her. Not unless I was a Catholic priest and she played the role of the preteen alter boy. She could win an oscar for the role.

By the time I had taken a shower in the undersized standup and changed into an alternate set of clothes that I had packed for the trip, she had challah toast with jam waiting for

172

me. It was then her turn to shower, only she didn't close the door to the tiny bathroom. Instead she called out to me from behind the slender flap that made for a shower curtain.

"I'll come with ye to the consulate." The announcement wasn't an offer or question.

"Don't you have work today?"

"Nothin' to report. The story is with you."

"Is that really a good idea to be seen walking around with me? You said that it was dangerous."

"Consulate will be safe. 'Sides, word will get 'round that you've a meeting with Finn Rourke the start of next week. You'll live that long I expect."

"I have a meeting with Fin next week? When were you going to tell me that you set that up?"

"I told ye last night, Deni. Can't ye remember? Have ye always had trouble with memory? I didn' think ye was that pissed."

"No. And I wasn't 'that pissed'. I just don't remember everything from last night is all. I definitely don't remember you sayin' that. Anyway, you don't think he'll try to have me killed by then? What's to stop him from sending Kane or Dunn to take care of me before then?"

"He'll be interested in what ye know. Dead men don't tell tales, but they can't fess up what they've shared and with who neither. They'll keep tabs on ye, but you'll be alive 'til the 16th at least, I reckon."

"You reckon? Well that's comforting."

The American Embassy is located on Pembroke Road or R118, which is about ten kilometers away. We packed ourselves into Rowena's subcompact 2002 Renault *Clio* for the trip. There were four doors plus the rear hatchback but only two side doors were needed. My knees were in my stomach in the passenger seat and I wished that I could rip it out, sit the back seat for the added leg room. I am not a large man, Rowena was tiny. There is no way that the two of us should have had to logistically sort out where our arms and shoulders would cohabit. The twenty minute ride was an unhumorous two person clown car skit.

She punched a button on her car stereo and U2 came out of the surprisingly large speakers for the tiny car. I could tell it was Bono's voice as it's unmistakeable, but the song I hadn't heard before. The recording was from a live performance. The cheering crowd in the background was also unmistakeable. Row explained that it was a bootleg of *Sometimes You Can't Make It On Your Own*. They performed the song in a recent concert before it was scheduled to be released in a few months on the forthcoming album called *How To Dismantle An Atomic Bomb*. 'I never miss a show' she said. She also said that she 'wanted to have Edge's babies' and that U2 was 'The best feckin' rock band on the planet'. I just thought the music was good.

The round building looked more like an isolated hotel than an official embassy to the United States. The iron fence surrounding it looked more like the bars of a prison cell, only the vertical bars had spear-like ornaments on the top of each one meter column. There was a gate for cars, but ours wasn't allowed in. Maybe because the heavily armed security team didn't think that the conveyance we were in was actually a car. I had my doubts as well.

We parked on the street and were asked for identification prior to being let into the secure building. My passport was still being held at the Arlington, but I was let through with my Massachusetts driver's license. The guard may or may not have seen my badge.

Rowena had a more difficult time getting in despite having all of the documents one would possibly need to get in. Passport, Driving Licence, press documents, public health card, and the like. Everything but her birth certificate. She was eventually let in and we were escorted to someone at a director level, as per our request.

I was met with a cold stare upon my first request to speak with the Consulate General or some sort of Ambassador, but when I said it was an issue of national security to the United States we were led to a waiting area. Eleven September was still fairly present on the minds of those whose job it was to protect our citizens, even abroad.

Director Humphrey listened intently to my entire spiel after we were made to wait over an hour to speak with somebody high on the food chain. He was uncomfortable with the press being on hand for the telling of the story, but I made it clear that she would be present for the meeting or there wouldn't be one. That if there was no meeting and a catastrophic event happened, she would make sure that the world knew that he refused the meeting that could have prevented it.

I played it straight for the most part. I told of the circumstances that led to the deaths of Danny and Roxy. Of Breen. I explained that I was working with a member of the Anti-terrorist task force within the Garda Síochána to track the guns, but that detective wished to remain anonymous for reasons of cover. That the IRA was about to move an armament by boat to Boston. I left out any mention of Sinn Féin as Rowena pointed out that the supporters of the party were vast and hidden. I also made Humphrey believe that the trafficking was going to come from an as yet unidentified port in Northern Ireland. In truth, I said that to him outright. Which was a big fat fucking lie.

Humphrey seemed to have his political appetites whet by the information. Enough facts were thrown in along with conjecture. I gave him the names of my US handlers. Walter. Glibczieck, federal prosecutor. Lieutenant Manny Titanitaukis, my boss. Even the New Hampshire lawyer, Ryan Wells so Humphrey could fact-check the Breen story. I urged him to check the names but quietly as this was a quiet mission. He was willing to trade favors for the opportunity to advance whatever agenda he had rolling around his large, salt and peppered head.

Our favors were simple because we knew that they were not likely to find the weapons that we had told them they would find. Not in the wrong ports and cities. I wanted the crate number and cargo ship identification in order to have my bosses seize them when they arrived in Boston. Humphrey agreed. Rowena wanted to have exclusive rights to the information and interviews that was to be forwarded to the press. She would be the first if only pressmen to have the story. He again happily agreed. He wanted to be the one to liaise with the United Kingdom and quarterback the search.

Only there would be no story. In the words of Row, they would be left with 'fuck-all'. While he liaised and quarterbacked, while the authorities were turning over every rock and searching every crevice in Northern Ireland, the weapons would be set to move in the South.

We left the meeting after declining protection or sanctuary. I told Humphrey that I needed to contact my Garda connection and re-acquire my passport from my hotel. I assured him that I would be fine and back on a plane to Boston as soon as I knew the information that he agreed to provide. He gave me a direct phone number to call him and I was to do so at a minimum of once per day. The 'information highway went both ways,' he said.

Rowena and I were pleased with ourselves.

So far, our ruse had worked.

33

OUR SMUG SATISFACTION WAS SHORT LIVED, however. The meeting with Director Humphrey had gone to plan, and we had another plan lined up for how to go about attaining my passport from the Arlington Hotel O'Connell Bridge.

Row drove us back to her flat to don disguises in order for the plan to work. Because of her various undercover reporting assignments in her eight years in the field, thirty on the planet, she had a wide array of costuming in her tiny home. She made herself into women of various sizes and shapes, sometimes even men.

The plan was to sneak into the hotel in costume, go up to the room and run through it one last time to ensure that there was nothing in it that I had left behind. I found it unnecessary since I hadn't spent but much time in there other than to sleep off hangovers since I had checked in, and Row had already been there, but I went along to get along. Rowena insisted that the hotel was at a minimum being watched, probably from the lobby, if for no other reason than to track my movements. I would then call down to the desk, informing them that I would be checking out. I would then politely request that the concierge bring my passport up to the room in exchange for the room key while she exchanged her original costume for another. We would then leave from an emergency exit on the side of the building unseen, an exit she had noticed when she had retrieved my luggage.

I didn't like my disguise. Row wanted to exploit the fact that I choose to have no body hair, save for my head. To put it bluntly, I made a muscular and ugly woman. The wig, hat and oversized sunglasses could only hide so much of my face. She said that they would be looking for me, a man. Women would garner little attention unless she was an attractive woman. There was no fear that I would get a second look.

She, on the other hand, did want to attract attention. Mostly to take it off of me as I insisted that nobody would think that I was actually a woman. Transvestite maybe. But not a woman. Row donned a blonde wig, large stuffed bra, and god only knows what to accentuate hips and buttocks which didn't exist. Rowena looked stunning, I have to admit. She could have picked up any man that she wanted, only to be disappointed if the evening crescendoed into sharing a bed. The hour glass figure was an elaborate hoax that would have fooled even me. She had the dimensions of Barbie. The fact that a bust, waist, hip proportion like Barbie was biologically impossible didn't diminish the unreasonable desire for it.

That night we called two cars to pick us up four blocks from Rowena's flat, as there was no possible way we could take her *Clio*. Her shapely disguise made it unlikely that she would be able to drive, nor would I be able to fit next to her with my new bust and big hat. Add to the logistical nightmare in the risk of someone getting the plate number off of her car and arguments 'pro Renault' were null and void.

Row and I arrived separately. Her car dropped her off at the front entrance first. She attracted all sorts of attention, which made my exit from my separate cab and entrance into the lobby completely unseen. She took the large formal stairs out of the lobby while I took the lift. There was no way that I would be able to negotiate stairs in heels. I could barely pull off walking in them on a flat surface.

I had to wait for the lift to arrive down on the ground floor, so we arrived on the top floor, which would be called the fourth in America, at the same time. We could not have planned it better.

The hallway was empty with the exception us. She was nonchalant as she searched her purse for a room key that didn't exist while I fumbled for the actual key from mine. I stopped short of inserting the key when I noticed the 'Do Not Disturb' sign hanging from the door knob. I looked both ways down the hall as I removed the hangar, showing it to Row. She gave a shrug of her shoulders which told me that neither of us had utilised the sign prior to or in the process of leaving the hotel room.

I used the key to gain access as quickly and as quietly as I could. Whomever was on the other side of the door needed to be surprised. In the police academy they teach you to enter low when gunfire is suspected. Armed suspects who don't want to be questioned or apprehended tend to aim high for the chest or face.

Turning the unlocked knob ever so gently, I crouched down leaning into the door with my side. The narrower the target the more difficult to hit, even low. With the door ajar, I slowly opened it while listening for any noise. I could hear none.

Upon the door opening wide enough to peer in, I knew why the sign was hung. Room service or any other hotel employee would have most definitely caused a commotion when seeing the room.

At a near crawl on the floor, I entered the bathroom which was the immediate left inside the hotel room. It gave me the opportunity to listen for any movement, get out of immediate gun range, and inspect the bathroom for occupants. No other human in the bathroom. I kicked off my heels, and charged left down the hall but nobody else was there either.

"It's clear."

Row entered the room and gasped. My hotel room, for lack of a better term, was fucked up. Somebody had lost weight destroying the place. This kind of damage takes energy and determination. What they were looking for was anyone's guess. Or maybe they were sending a message.

"Jesus, Mary. We've got to get out. Sharpish like."

"I'm with you. Let me call the desk." Only the phone was destroyed. Shit. "Can you call the desk from your cell?"

She dug into her purse and retrieved her mobile. She fiddled with the phone for a few seconds and handed it to me. It was ringing. The woman at the front desk announced the name of the hotel and stated that she was very eager to help. I believed her and told her what I wanted and that I was in a bit of a hurry. I had an imaginary flight to catch.

"Be right up sir," she said.

"Row, get changed and quick." But she was already on it. Unabashed, she stripped down to the alternate costume that was already underneath the Barbie disguise. I looked around the room amased. Full-on stunned. Even the wallpaper was shredded off of the walls. Curtains torn down. Mattress was knifed, pillows disemboweled. Desk and dressers were destroyed. Whomever had been in the room didn't like the program on the tele one bit.

"How'd they get in the room and do all of this damage without being heard, Row?"

"You've taken a piss in someone's shak shuka."

"I have no idea what that means, but if you're telling me that I've made an enemy I'd have to agree."

The knock on the door gave both us a start.

"Be the wife," I whispered.

"Aye. Let's get on with it."

"Who is it?" I quickly made my way to the toilet.

"Hotel Concierge sir."

I handed Row the key and jumped into the bathroom. With that door closed, she opened the main door to the room.

"Husbands on the toilet," she said in her least Irish accent and with the door opened only a crack. "Here is the room key. Are there any incidentals?"

"Eh, no. I'm only allowed to give the passport back to the holder, miss. Obvious reasons I'm sure."

I heard the concierge making trouble. I yelled out to him, nearly deafening myself with the hollow echo of the bathroom. "It's ok. I'm just going to finish my business in here, and then we will be on our way. We have a flight to catch immediately. Can you give my passport to my wife please?"

"I'm really not allow — "

" — and if you could call us a taxi and have them out front, that would be great. We are running very late and don't want to chance missing the flight."

After a mental wrestling match, the concierge agreed. "Of course. Thank you very much for staying with us." He handed my passport to Rowena and made his way toward the lift.

She closed the main door, opened the bathroom door and said, "Let's get the feck outta here. Now like."

We hauled ass down the stairs that Rowena had taken up. I was carrying heels, purse and trying to hold my skirt up so I didn't fall. One floor up, on the first floor, there was a large and open landing. One could see the entire lobby from that vantage point and either finish walking down the main staircase to it, or take the smaller side stairs to the emergency exit.

Rowena hesitated at the landing, looking around the lobby while I caught up to her down the stairs. She spotted what she wanted to see within a few seconds and guided me down the side stairs with a bit too much force. I nearly fell down the remaining twenty stairs to the base. The only thing that stopped me was the open railing on the right side of the stairs jammed into my armpit. I held myself from catapulting down the rest of the way like a gymnast falling onto one of the parallel bars.

"Hurry," she said. "They're charmin' up the lobby."

"Who's they?" I regained my balance and took the remaining stairs two at a time down to the exit.

"Sinns. Keepin' an eye on ye, they are," she said.

"Yeah? Charmin' the paint off walls I'm sure."

"Aye. I'd know them lads anywhere. From the pub. See them every night."

"Tonight would have been the last time."

"Aye. Means we're takin' the right path."

"I hope you're right."

34

THE IMMEDIATE THREAT WAS OFF OF US by the time that we had returned to Rowena's flat. We made sure that we hadn't been followed. We ran from the Arlington Hotel O'Connell Bridge as fast as possible, Row taking the lead with a novice transvestite in tow, running seven blocks where we shared a taxi back to another corner that was yet another six or seven blocks away from her flat. I was in great physical shape save for the past several nights of damage to my liver and the escape was exhausting.

We barely spoke during the trip back to the flat. Both of us were more concerned with the possibility of being followed. Watching every vehicle that followed our taxi. Scrutinising every pedestrian that noticed our harried travel. Once we felt safe, which wasn't until we entered the flat, the conversation came in the form of bouncing theories off of one another.

"The Sinns had to have followed me to the hotel," I said.

"When? Ye haven't been back to the hotel, have ye? Ye've been with me. Somebody knows who ye are, Deni."

"What is the possibility that it's random? American in the hotel .... "

"Naw. You're graspin'."

"Maybe somebody at the hotel is a member of party."

"Then the concierge wouldn't have come alone and without a fuss, hey? Who'd ye mention the hotel to?"

"I might have mentioned it to the dock superintendent. I'm not sure."

"We'll go see him tomorrow," Row said. It didn't sound like a suggestion.

"Why? Why go there if he was the rat?"

"See if he mighn't know somethin' or found information. We'll know by the look of him if there's a plot. Who else?" Row was waving to me like she was a traffic guard motioning me to move forward.

"Nobody. Cian may have told Oisin, but why?"

"To what end ye mean? To kill ye. Seems clear."

"Why would Cian want to kill me? He is working with a United States Federal Prosecutor. If I die, he'll have some explaining to do."

"He mightn't have been deliberate. Just in passin'. This Oisin'd get a chuff up if he gave ye to the IRA."

"Maybe. We should check him out too. Hey Row? Did you mention it to anyone you work with?"

"Me editor. But I doubt he gave your room a goin' through."

"No but he could have told someone else who could have done it. Like you said, nothin' deliberate."

"Naw. Graspin' again."

I paused to strip out my alter ego and think the situation through. The pile of large women's clothing next to the sofa was getting high. Row, ever the tidy one in her small space, picked the garments up off of the floor. She returned with a random selection of clothes from my luggage.

"Put some trousers on. We're not like to solve the mystery tonight. Might take care of yourself, however. Common theme is someone wants to make a hell on earth for ye. In the end, seems clear that neither IRA nor Sinns care for yer help."

"Yeah. Seems clear. They aren't really hinting, Row and I'm unarmed. I came over to this side of the pond to find out some information and get back on a plane. I can't go up against the IRA. That would be insane. Besides, that's Cian's job. I'll let him know what happened in the morning. I'll poke around a little more with you and Cian, but either way I need to get home. I'll meet Fin next week and see about gettin' outta here the next day."

"Sure that's wise?" She sat down next to me on her sofa. I was still undressed, the pile of clothes she gave me on my lap. The only cloak of any kind was the tapestry of tattoos under the cold sweat from the run on my skin. Her voice remained calm.

"Sure what's wise, Row? Going home empty handed or poking around?" My voice was not calm.

"If they are holdin' court in the Arlington lobby, Deni, they'll be holding court at the airport as well, I don't mind tellin' ye."

"So I can't leave and I can't investigate this without being chopped up and dumped in the Atlantic. Great. I'm all about busting some heads, but I'm defenseless. One on one I'll take on whoever they wanna throw at me. But a fuckin' army in another country? Fuck that. That's suicide and I ain't no martyr."

"We may be able to sneak ye out to Scotland or England. Fly home from there, hey?"

"In truth Row? I've got no home to go back to. Those assholes burned down my house with two other families in it. I watched them suffocate from breathing in all of that smoke and carbon, then roast like a fuckin' Christmas ham. I think I came here partly for payback and partly to get away from it all."

"A man without a country." She moved yet closer to me, put her skinny arm around me. She slowly massaged my shoulder with one hand and pulled me toward her with the other. My head rest on her bony shoulder. "We can sort this out."

Some time passed in silence, then she confided. "I've covered some bombings. Seen the devastation. Ye never get that smell outta yer nose. The burnt flesh. The sight of it. Haunts ye 'til death I imagine."

She kissed my temple, then pressed my head into her neck below her chin. She just held me in silence. I was thankful for it. It was a touch that I didn't know that I needed. Some time had passed that way, it could have been a year for all I know. I was lost in the moment. Lost in thought.

Rowena held on to me, kissing the top of my head every so often. The tiny woman was strong. Not so much in the physical sense, but in the spiritual. She was made of tough stock. Of strong fiber. Of durable faith and morals. But all of us have a breaking point, and that embrace was hers. That vulnerability.

She lifted my face from below her chin, raising it to hers. She stared into my eyes without competition. Row looked into my eyes as if to see if the feelings she had at that moment would be found in me. At least that is what I read in her pale brown eyes. Maybe I was trying to figure out why I was attracted to this woman. Maybe she was trying to figure out why she was attracted to me.

I don't have the same faith as she. I am a Catholic, same as Row. But the resolute knowledge of the difference between good and evil is not the same. Between sinner and sainte. Who determines what is right and wrong? Like between two lovers? We had not exchanged vows. But for that moment we both knew what was right.

The communication between us that followed was from touch and feel. No words were spoken, none were needed. Our mouths met, soft and gentle at first. Tongues caressed. Her hands moved from my jawline to the back of my neck. Mine tucking the wisps of her short hair behind her ear. The pile of clothes on my lap was no more, falling onto the floor between us. We kissed long at length, enjoying the feel and taste of the other.

A rush of adrenaline came back. This time not because I felt like I was in danger, but in a wanton desire. Our pulses were raised. I gently and steadily moved closer to her, on top of her. Row slid back on her side of the small sofa, head resting on the pillowy arm. Her slim body lay nestled under me and between my legs. She warmed her hands on my waist, back and buttocks. I didn't mind. In fact I craved her touch.

Rowena's appetites and juices also began to flow. Realising that she was fully clothed, and obviously wanting to correct that, she pushed me up but not completely away from her. I went to my knees while she sat upright. She removed her blouse, then continued to kiss me. Row grabbed my hand and pulled me to follow her down the short hallway and into the bedroom that we had slept in but had not yet truly shared. She adeptly began removing what clothing she could along that short journey with her free hand.

She pushed me down onto the bed. It was her turn to be on top. To take charge. The remainder of her garments were removed, no longer necessary for the pleasurable task at hand. I lay there, watching her. Not because she was graceful. Not because she was putting on an alluring show. Quite the opposite in fact. The nimble woman was on a mission. That mission was me.

Her mouth was used for more than her gentle and passionate kisses. She tasted, caressed and pecked whatever she wanted. Row moved about my entire body, siphoning me with her lips and tongue from head to toe.

The lovemaking was gentle at times, animalistic at others. Rowena's spry body moved on mine or with mine as the positions changed. I didn't think about anything other than pleasing her, not even my own pleasure as it built to a geysering release.

I have been wrong about a great many things in my life. Stealing cars as a cocky preteen. Wrong to want to spend my career as Massachusetts State Police Detective. Wrong about what I thought made for an attractive woman. There was nothing immediately striking about Rowena. Nothing that conjured sexual thoughts or desires. I was never more wrong about this woman, though. She was gorgeous. A sexual Jedi.

35

NEITHER OF US SLEPT THAT NIGHT. Or the next. I could tell you that we spent the two days in torrid love. That we used each other to fulfill each and every sexual whim. But that would be a lie. We did spend some time doing that. Afterwards exchanging in post coitus dialogue with same fervor as we had the physical acts during it. The talk wasn't of our acts of love though. These passionate talks were of the mission. The mission to bring the illicit activities to light. To strategise. To find the cargo hold. It was as if each of our carnal releases had shed any and all of our apprehension or fear as well.

Rowena suggested that we go down to the docks. It was half 'til three on Friday morning. She knew from other investigations, other reporting, that the dock workers start their first shifts early. If this supervisor that I spoke with, Niall, was working, he would be present earlier than the rest of the workers to direct them once they arrived.

The drive to the docks seemed longer than it had when Cian and I went though it took a quarter of the time. For one, the tiny car was claustrophobic. All of the U2 in the world couldn't make the car bigger. Every turn in the road pushed me either to my right against Row or against the tiny passenger door. Second, Rowena was driving like a fucking maniac. *Bullet The Blue Sky* was blaring while we bulleted down Promenade Road. I don't know why she was in such a hurry, but she was.

Because of the size of her Renault, we were able to drive along the pier where Cian and I had walked. I was thankful for not having to walk on the north side of the Dublin port, but there were some tight spots that we encountered that I was sure Row was going to get us killed. At an early point we passed the small shuttle bus loading the dock workers in order to carry them to the same location we were traveling to, nearly sending us into one of the enormous containers. The tiny bus packed and carried the workers from the main gate along the north side of the port to their work area. It was the commuter equivalent of Row's Renault. We dodged in front of the parked lorry and left it in our dust.

The sun would soon illuminate the horizon of the ocean in the distance as far as the naked eye could see. Sunrise was just two hours or so away. It would become increasingly less dark, obstacles which were narrowly avoiding would become more visible. I had mixed feeling as to whether I wanted to see the near misses or live in the dark.

Row parked her go-cart sized car between two large containers. The doors were able to open just wide enough for both of us to exit the vehicle. I explained where I had met Niall McCourt the first time I had gone out there. On foot. The converted container that had been modified into an office was dark. The one window cut high into the container was too high to peer in, but it was obvious that no light was turned on. In the dark of the early morning, that meant that nobody was in the office or Ray Charles was now in charge of the Dublin cargo dockworkers.

I turned the knob and tugged on the office door, but it was as we assumed. Locked.

"I guess we wait for the bus that you passed to arrive," I said.

"Odd that."

"Odd what, Row?"

"Not a soul here to manage the workers. I've been here before, Deni. Someone's here to make work for the lads. Punch-ins. Give direction. Turn the feckin' lights on."

"So what are you saying?"

"I've already said what I'm sayin'. It's feckin' odd."

"Don't let the fact that we've slept together cloud your judgment, Row. No need to get snippy with me."

"How quickly you change from scared boy to bucklepper. I'm not causin' a stir, fella. I'm just pointin' at facts."

"I don't know what a bucklepper is, but I wasn't scared. I was just caught up in the moment. That's all. Don't get things twisted."

"Ah. Right then." She said that she understood, but the shaking of her head and staring out at the rising sun indicated that she didn't. I let it go.

"Maybe Niall is on the bus. Maybe he's runnin' late today."

After a long breath she turned and looked at me. "Help me stack a pile. I'll go into the office through the window."

"They'll be here in a few minutes. It'll take that long to pile up the crates and barrels. If the window is even unlocked." I went into my wallet and pulled out my pins as I went up the decking outside the office door."

185

Row was protesting, telling me it would take too long to try and pick the lock but she wasn't able to finish her argument. The door was unlocked and opened by the time she had closed the gap between us.

"Quite good with that kind of mischief, aren't ye?"

"In fairness this was an easy lock. I hope whatever they store in here isn't important."

"Let's not stand on ceremony. Carry on now," she said.

I entered the container/office first. The door opened outward swinging out and to my right. Rowena was on the stairs behind me waiting for the door to open past her, while I felt around the left side of the door for the light switch. The light came on, the fluorescents flicking their way to life. It took a brief second or two for my eyes to adjust to the harsh lighting. It took another moment for me to interpret what was before me.

"Don't come in here, Row."

"What's the crack, now?"

"Nothing good. Wipe down the door knob!"

"With what?"

"Your fuckin' shirt! Anything. We gotta get outta here. Now." I used my shirtsleeve to wipe down the light switch. She used the bottom of her cotton shirt to polish the knob out on the stairs. I tried to move down the stairs, past Row but I couldn't. "Is it wiped?"

"Aye. As best I can."

"Then let's get the fuck out of here."

I jumped over the wooden railing off the steps and onto the dock. Moving quickly back toward the car. I turned to realise that she wasn't following me. She couldn't help herself. She looked in before closing the door behind us. Row muttered a prayer while giving herself the sign of the cross, never completing either task. I should have turned the lights off when I wiped down the switch. Some things you just can't un-see.

Turning back toward the office, I raced back to her. I closed the office door with my elbow and tossed Row who was now catatonic over my shoulder. She put up no struggle nor said a word as I ran with her back to the car.

The dockworkers were always quiet during the morning lorry ride to the daily punch-in. Many of them would attempt, no matter how feeble, to get the extra winks their bodies required before the start of their shift. The first shift started early on the Dublin docks. In the winters, the sun wouldn't yet be awake until well into their shifts. Today the sun would be slowly making its way to the horizon when the time-clock would punch the all too early hour onto their manilla-stock cards. Hangovers abound most days. This day was no different in that regard.

The driver had cursed under his breath as the speeding Renault *Clio* weaved in front of the bus, nearly clipping the front as he was trying to load his lethargic workers. His day had just started and it was already terrible. Traffic was unusual on the docks at that hour. Especially going toward it. He continued to pronounce devilish outcomes upon the reckless driver under his breath as he made his way to the destination to avoid a stir with his slumbering cargo.

He was still spitting and sputtering about the incident when the tiny vehicle sped back toward him a short time later. The morning commute was nearly over, about to arrive at the destination, when the same vehicle raced toward him in a game of 'chicken'. The lives of the dockworkers were at stake, a head-on collision with the much smaller vehicle mightn't kill anyone but the occupant of the small auto but he couldn't take the chance. He immediately stuck the manual down, grinding the gearbox while simultaneously braking hard. The undersized bus quickly came to an abrupt stop, causing a small uprising with the men in the back.

The *Clio* dodged around the bus appearing to gain speed rather than slow down. The driver was too busy ensuring that his cargo was unscathed, the occupants of the bus too unaware to identify either the driver or a registration. In a matter of seconds, the offending vehicle had again disappeared.

The first dockworker to get off of the bus was the first to open the door to the office. As per usual, the light was on inside for the crew to claim their timecards to begin their day. Unusually, Niall the old sod was not out by the bus greeting everyone shouting demands. The lethargic docksman opened the door to the office, looking right to find his timecard in its usual home. The slotted holder held the usual contents which he removed, slid his card into the clock, stamped and replaced it in its proper spot. As he turned to exit, giving way to the next to start his day, he glanced left. His knees weakened. Bile from his stomach was rising and burning like lava spilling toward the top of a volcano.

"Jesus, Mary and Jos - " The vomit spewed forth despite his desperation to keep it down. The putrid liquid projected out onto the stairs toward his coworkers. He tried to regain his faculties after the first push. " — uuuuuuuuuuuuuuuuuuhhhhhhh. Don't come up here, lads." He braced himself against the door-jam, looking out at the mess he created instead of the mess that was inside the office. Deep breaths.

What was left of Niall McCourt was spread out inside the office. The gruesome scene didn't illustrate exactly how he was killed, only that he was dead and in the most horrific of fashions. One could plainly see that he was tortured, pieces of him cut and torn off. But not how or in what succession. Not that anyone but the Garda detectives would want to know.

Blood was splashed about the inside of the converted container like a crimson paint can had exploded onto the files and binders and desk. Bloody bits of flesh clung to walls while the congealing liquid pooled on the floor.

Niall's severed head rest in the basket for outgoing post. His eyes plucked from their sockets. A knife had been used to cut them out. The same knife appeared to be used to cut open his face, enough to hurt him badly but not so much as to disfigure him to the point where he was unidentifiable. The torn flesh hung off the cheeks and jawline. The knife was stabbed into Niall's right ear as if there was no other place to hold it.

The older man's torso was tied to his office chair. His body had also been carved with entrails exposed to the fluorescent lighting. The freshly torn innards were pulled out of his abdomen, still hanging and dripping down onto the floor. His penis and testicles were removed and on the bloodred floor in front of where he sat.

Fingers and toes were strewn about the floor of the office. Niall's bloody nuggets snipped from the appropriate appendage. They lay under the desk and on shelves and on the floor waiting to be bagged for further identification. A toe rested next to a removed and cloudy eyeball.

The handle of a screwdriver was protruding out from the side of Niall's left knee. The business end of it wedged underneath the kneecap and had been used to pry it out. The right knee was not immediately present. Nor the leg from the knee down that it was supposed to be attached to. It was likely to be inside that death chamber somewhere, just as likely removed as part of Niall's horrific infliction of pain.

"Get the Gardaí. Feck. Phone everyone."

36

IT WAS MY TURN TO GIVE COMFORT TO ROWENA. She said nothing in the Renault on the way back to her flat. She said nothing when we nearly were in a head-on collision with the lorry that carried the labourers to work. Row didn't make a move when I covered her face, and turned mine, in an effort to conceal our faces from the driver and passengers of the tiny bus as we passed them by. What I had originally thought was catatonic turned out to be reticent silence. She turned off the sound system in her car, no U2. The tears flowed as she looked out the left window, the passenger side of the *Clio*.

Row didn't comment or flinch when we were nearly involved in two other accidents on the trip back into Dublin proper. They would have been my fault, driving on the opposite side of the road on streets that are all but unmarked is not easy.

She got out of the car when we arrived back at the flat in the early morning. Row said nothing as we walked in, she just plopped herself on the sofa in the same spot where I had been sitting and in need of some comfort.

I am not a caretaker, nor a good caregiver. Like the typical male, I presume, it is not that I don't want to provide solace for those in need. It's just that I seem to be incapable. I never say the right thing or do the right thing or at the right time. When I get sick, I want to be pampered and soothed until the illness leaves my system. In the times where I had a girlfriend, Jill or any of the other transient partners, they had always expected the same in return but I could never give it. Not in the way they wanted. Not in the way that they had expected.

So was the case this time. I offered tea. No response. I sat down next to her and put my hand on her knee. She pushed it away. I tried to kiss her, touched her small breast in an effort to be intimate. She pushed me off like I was a rapist.

190

Rowena had seen, she said in our previous days, a great number of horrific things in her time as an investigative reporter. Bombings and murders, terrifying all. I understood the difference this time. I knew what made the sight at the docks so different from what she had seen in the past. A bombing happens in an instant. The poor prick that blows up has his brains and body spread out all over east Jesus before he knows what happened. People being shot sometimes suffer for minutes before either receiving medical care or die. A murder is more terrifying, more painful, but the dirty business happens in a relatively short time in order not to be caught in the act.

Niall McCourt was tortured. Torn limb from limb. He was cut, disemboweled, castrated, stabbed, and chopped. His demise took time. He suffered plenty. You didn't need to be a medical examiner or see the first three seasons of CSI to determine that. All it took was one look, one quick peek at the train wreck that you were told not to look at, peak through the fingers covering your face at a horror film, to take in the gruesome scene. If the smell of torched flesh from bombings was stuck into Row's brain, Niall's torture would haunt her for the rest of her days.

Since Row was inconsolable, had gone into her room with the door closed and locked, I decided that it was high time to contact my people back home. They were five hours behind, which meant that they were all sleeping at almost midnight their time, but I didn't care.

Tits was not in the precinct of course. He wouldn't arrive at Troop H for six or seven hours yet. He was the least important call anyway. I was working for the feds in conjunction with a local crime. I had already decided that I was going to leave the Staties anyway.

Walter Glibczieck, the federal prosecutor, was my second call. He didn't seem happy to be disturbed at that hour but he said that he was used to it and expected it with the time difference. He said that he received my message, that he had tried to call my hotel room a number of times but I was never there.

I told Walter what was going on. I told him that Cian was of little help. He was more interested in pubs than justice. Whatever the Department of Justice was paying him for support, it was too much. He had led me to two possible sources, one of which was just brutally tortured and killed that morning. I also informed him that I might need legal help if a witness placed me at the scene.

Walter seemed concerned when I told him that I was no longer at the hotel, that the room was destroyed and likely I would have been also if I had been in the room at the time of the breach. Again, I might need legal help if the Arlington Hotel went after me for the damage.

The fact that I was staying with Rowena, and investigating the whereabouts of the gun shipment with an investigative reporter sent Glibczieck over the fucking edge. "The mission was supposed to be clandestine," he said. "Your head is getting fucked up because of a piece of Irish trim," he also said. I lied and told him that there was nothing sexual going on, that she was plugged in and had engaged the very people that I was investigating. I knew what I was doing.

I told him about Oisin Hanamy, the informant Cian used up in Belturbet, and the fact that I didn't like the guy. There was something about him that was off. I asked Walter if he had access to Irish crime files as a United States Federal Prosecutor. "On a limited basis, and only if it's important in a crime within my jurisdiction," he said. It would also tip our hand he pointed out.

In talking with Row, the idea that the February bust was a hoax had percolated in my brain. It seemed about right. I wanted Walter to see what he could dig up. He promised nothing and in truth I didn't expect much. If nothing else I just wanted another set of ears to hear what I was thinking, tell me if any of it made sense.

He seemed disappointed that I hadn't been able to uncover any information about the gun container as of yet. I reminded him that my only real source for information, Niall McCourt, was tortured and killed. That I had only been there about a week and clearly it was dangerous. I hadn't even met Finn Rourke yet, but when I did in a few days I would be sure to ask him nicely if he would give me the manifest information. I was sure he would tell me. Walter said that the sarcasm was noted.

Just as long as he didn't fuck me out of my bonus.

My final phone call was to Ryan Wells. The phone call with Walter had chewed up over an hour. Ryan was 'just headed to bed anyway' when I phoned him. I informed him of what was going on as well and that I was interested in being with Grantes, Wells & Associates on a full time basis. That I wanted to be an associate. This side job was partially for him. For Breen. That I wanted out of the Massachusetts State Police Department. He said that he understood, that he would talk it over with JG but that I was proving myself with this case. He reminded me that if they could prove collusion and conspiracy with a guard or guards through the Winter Hill Gang through the IRA connection, a civil lawsuit would be in order. That I needed to attain that information in order to get additional money from the firm as a result of winning a civil suit on the back end.

I said that I understood completely, and we hung up. I had added pressure in getting information that was proving impossible to attain. But I was going to need every dime when I got back to the states. I hoped that I lived long enough spend it.

Row was still crying or sleeping or whatever when I finished speaking with Ryan. I'm sure that I had rung up a significant international phone bill, but I would sort it out with her later. She was not answering and I needed to go.

I did my zig-zag for a few blocks and picked up a taxi to go to the Garda station near Pheonix Park. I wanted to catch up with Cian. I stopped the taxi a few blocks shy of the station, walking the rest of the way. The Niall murder hadn't just spooked Rowena. It had pissed me off as well.

"Detective Garda Daly is away on an investigation," the reception lady told me when I arrived and asked for Cian. "If ye'd like to wait I'd find out when he might be expected back. Yer name?"

I told her my name and I waited while she did whatever she did to get an answer. Pass it along to someone else? Call him on his mobile? Who knows? I just know that a few minutes passed before another, younger, prettier woman walked me back to Cian's desk. She told me that he was on his way back from an incident on the Dublin docks. I pretended like I wondered what that could be.

Nearly an hour I waited. But in that time I was able to nonchalantly snoop around his desk and work space. I didn't at first, but curiosity had gotten the better of me. A half-full bottle of Redbreast 12 Year Whiskey was in his locked file cabinet. They don't make very good locks in Ireland in my experience. It was too early in the day or I would have put another dent in the bottle. But that wasn't the best thing that I found in the cabinet. A copy of what I assumed was the complete file for the 13 February, 2004 Anti-terrorism police raid was the treasure. And I struck gold.

I didn't know when Cian would be back, and I didn't want to get caught with the file. I tucked it into my pants along the small of my back and headed toward the door. I let the lady at the reception know that I wanted to go grab a quick mid-morning bite whilst I waited. She nodded like she understood, too busy to deal with an American I presume.

The café around the corner was busy and it had only one table left available. I didn't know how much time I had so I didn't want to go searching further away from the station. I quickly grabbed the last table, much to the dismay of the young gay couple that were looking to occupy it. I knew I was going to have to buy something in order to justify my being alone and taking up a two-top table. The couple already had purchases in hand, I had skipped a step.

From my position at the table I could see the sad looking things they were passing off as pastries in the case. Not interested. The bilingual menu, Gaelic and sort-of English, had only one thing on it that I recognised. One *Sweet American* coming up. I pulled out the thick file from my back, thankfully none of the contents had fallen out. Opening it on the table, I felt the weight of the two homosexual men staring me down. I think one was trying to convince the other to say something to me about stealing the table. I kind of wondered how uppity they would get now that their Irish was up. Hell hath no fury ....

"I'm sorry. I need the table, it's important," I said like I actually gave a fuck. I come from a city where people are not in the least concerned with their fellow citizens. The only people we are remotely kind to are tourists. I was a tourist, so they could fuck off — gay or straight.

The server brought me over an enormous concoction which she explained was a Nutella milkshake. It had mini-marshmallows on top. The *Sweet American* was called such, I can only assume, because of its over-indulgence. But I ain't gonna lie, it was really damn good.

Most of the thick file was a pictorial documentation of the weapons seized. There were many. All were outdated even to the naked eye. The explosives and detonators had been manufactured by Germans for World War II. Although the bust was large, it was not much of a loss for the IRA. You could have offered any of the seized material to a six year old from my neighbourhood and they would have told you that they were good; they could get better, newer, and more reliable stuff on the streets of Southie.

I read the reports that led up to the bust. The call came in to Cian directly. Detective Garda Síochána Cian Daly reported to his superiors on the Anti-terrorism Task Force that the call came in from a known and reliable source. The source, Tadhg O'Carolan, was said to be on the informant payroll. A subsequent investigation to find Tadhg indicated that no such person could be reached. Cian later testified that the informant had gone missing, probably dead after informing the Garda about the trove of weapons in Newtowncunningham. Cian had also been the one to pay Tadhg in cash.

Hmm. Why would the IRA kill an informant that gave the Garda almost nothing? The thought went through my head quickly, then I was on to the next document in the file.

The next set of documents were the records that stated that there were no records. The simultaneous bust in Dublin was just that, a bust. They found nothing. Same informant.

How could this missing Tadhg guy, a 'known and reliable source', be right about one thing and completely out in left field about the other?

I read on. An expense report for the housing and safekeeping of Tadhg O'Carolan. Dated after the seizure. He was being held in a Dublin safe house according to the expense report.

Who were they keeping? He was supposedly already missing by then. Is Cian the one that is making him 'missing'? Why is Cian hiding him from Garda? They are still paying expenses to house this guy.

Another document, listing all known informants and a schedule of payments, when monies were paid and received. No Oisin Hanamy listed.

Wasn't Oisin supposed to be the one who tipped Cian off? Both Cian and Oisin told me in Belturbet, in Duffy's, that he was the 'trusted lot' who informed on the troves. Yet there was no record of him. Cian just happened to go up to Newtowncunningham and become a hero based on the tip from a nonexistent informant? And the guy that is being kept in Belturbet as the real informant is off the books? Something is seriously fucked.

Four documents later, I thought I knew just what it was. As it turned out, I had half of it right. I was in real trouble. Rowena was in real trouble. And trouble was upon us.

I didn't go back to the station. I bolted out of the cafe, running like my life depended on it. It did. Mine and Rowena's.

37

ROWENA DIDN'T WANT TO COME OUT OF HER ROOM. I ran most of the way back to her flat, getting into a taxi only when I was almost run over by it. I crossed Sráid an Teampaill and failed to look for oncoming traffic. Failed in that I looked in the wrong direction. The taxi stopped in time for me to be on the hood, which the driver called a bonnet. At least that is what I think he kept yelling. He definitely lost his bonnet. It was dented where my right hip and elbow made contact. He thought his Irish was up, but mine was in fighting position. And not in the old-school fighting position like the Notre Dame mascot.

Before it came to him getting a beating, the taxi driver said he would take me to Row's flat. She had told me that pickups and drop-offs in front of her flat were a bad idea. It was unsafe. We were beyond that now.

I didn't want to alarm her, make her any more scared than she already was. She was likely still in some level of shock from what we will call the Niall incident earlier the same day. But I did want her to come out of her room and I wanted it in all of an instant.

My gentle knocks were not getting the job done. My exaggerated calmness in getting her to open the fucking door wasn't either. I heard no answer, no rustling or movement. I didn't have time for her bullsh, so I picked the lock and entered. I wanted to kick the door in but thought better of it, as that would not do in keeping her calm. As calm as possible anyway.

She was sitting upright on the bed but she was passed out. Her chin was to her chest, drool had formed a line to her lap, forming a puddle there. She had an empty bottle of whiskey in her left hand, the top turned over onto her divan and what she didn't consume had been spilled, soaking through to the mattress.

"Shit. Row, you gotta wake up." I gently nudged her. Shook her. Felt her pulse. Her pulse was there but weak. She was beyond drunk. Hammered didn't quite say it either. After tapping her cheeks, her eyes opened but didn't focus on me.

196

Harder taps to the face. "Wake up. Up and at 'em. You picked the worst time to get fucked up." I lifted her up, attempting to get her to her feet. Her jeans were soaked. The Divan, sheets and mattress were as well. What I originally had thought was spilled whiskey was actually a combination of spilled bottle and spilled bladder. As much urine as booze.

Alcohol poisoning. I had seen it enough times with college kids. Boston is loaded with colleges and universities. Regardless of how accustomed to drinking Rowena was, the body can only process so much alcohol at one time.

The consumption and processing of alcohol by the human body is the exact same for every person, regardless of size. Bigger people can handle more, as are the bodies that are used to the presence of alcohol in their system, but the time it takes to handle the toxin is the same. Whiskey, in this case, starts soaking into the bloodstream right from the mouth through the lining. Without food to mix and aid in digesting, thereby slowing down the immediate uptake into the small intestine, it goes immediately there and into the bloodstream. Once the molecules are in the bloodstream, it takes about 5 minutes to reach the brain, act as a depressant, and slow down all body functions. The whiskey is then transformed into sugars, for simplicity sake, in the liver. It takes about 20 minutes for the molecules to reach the liver. Once there, the liver can then only handle the breaking down of alcohol at a rate of approximately 8 milliliters per hour.

I don't know how many of the 750 milliliters Row drank, but even if she had only a quarter of the bottle, she was going to be drunk for about 23 hours too many.

The dead-weight of a hundred pound woman seemed like ten times that. I positioned her in front of the toilet and stuck my fingers down her throat. Bodily functions may have been slow, but eventually the gag reflex kicked in and the whiskey-soaked bile came up. But not enough. Three more times we repeated the process. Finally the dry-heaving began.

Satisfied that there was no more booze in her belly, I now had to deal with the poison that was already in her bloodstream. I turned on the shower, using only the cold water. I peeled of her urine-steeped jeans and held her under the water. She could kick and scream all she wanted, this was happening.

We didn't have the time for this nonsense. We needed for her to at least get her thinned blood moving. Row went from one set of wet clothes to another, as the process of holding her up while I tried to dry her off after the cold shower were several steps we could ill-afford. The new outfit clung to her like she had been caught in a mid-morning rain. In a way, she had.

I finally got her into her tiny car after throwing her over my shoulder. I was able to quickly throw a couple of changes of clothes for her into my luggage along with the file that I had taken from Cian. The bag took up what was supposed to be a back seat and the hatchback part of the vehicle, which I later figured out was called a boot. I thought she kept telling me that she *had* to boot, meaning puke, but I digress. Stepping on the petrol pedal of the *Clio* was like begging a dead horse for another mile. But it went. The small car wasn't peppy enough for my taste or immediate needs.

Rowena was conscious but speaking in tongues. She was of no use so I had to stop at a petrol station to buy a map. I had forgotten the way to Belturbet.

Oisin Hanamy's safe house was all but impossible for me to find. But miraculously I was able to find Duffy's. Stumbled upon it really. I parked the car to get my bearings and low and behold I was across the carriageway from the pub. The hour was late by the time that I found the place, so we slept in the cramped car until morning. It was not even noon on that Friday and Duffy's seemed busy from the outside. It was Tráthnóna somewhere in the world.

"Stay," I whispered. A bit like you would a dog. Not like Row was going to go anywhere anyway. She was snoring and sleeping.

After retrieving the file from my luggage, and realising that I had no weapon, I hustled quickly but carefully the back way toward Oisin's. I used the back stairs, same way that we had gone when the three of us went to the pub, only in reverse. My ears trained on every sound.

The closer I got, moving up the back stairs, the more sounds I heard. It sounded like someone was getting a beating. Muffled moans with thumps and undistinguishable commands. The outside staircase was giving audible moans and squeaks of its own. I was hoping to be undetected, every strain of the old wood sounded to me like a cannon. Much like the teenager who comes home past curfew, thinking that every step could be heard two houses down. In the case of the teenager, the parents probably did know. In my case, I hoped that the sound of the apparent beating would mask my unstealth approach.

I've never heard anyone definitively say whether the slow squeaks over time attracted more or less attention than if the predator moved more quickly, or with one, louder, audible sound and closed the gap in less time. But I chose the former. By the time that I had reached the top landing, there were no more moans from the victim. Just the voice of the attacker, soliciting information that would not seem to come.

There was just a wood-framed screen door separating me from the kitchen, from the torture room that was as disgusting as I had remembered it. I popped my head above the bottom of the torn screen, at waist level, to take in as much of the situation as possible in the shortest amount of time.

A large kitchen and dining area. Devoid of furnishings save for the chair the victim was tied to. Center of the room. Bloody victim, unidentified. Large unidentified male standing before victim, back to me, handle of a pistol sticking out of his waistband. Mold, mildew, garbage bags.

I took it all in, exposed for less than two-seconds. I would have to cover 6 meters before the tormentor realised he was about to be attacked and reacted with his weapon. I hadn't trained in Brazilian jiu-jitsu in over a week; since I had been in Ireland, and I normally would train almost every day. Not that it would make any difference against a gun. I reached for the screen door handle, turning it as slowly as I could yet still turning it. It wasn't locked.

The door cracked open without a sound. I stood crouched and ready to pounce once the door was open enough for me to go through it. Looking through the crack, I noticed the large coil spring that was fastened in place to automatically close the door. It was rusted in the same manner of disrepair as the rest of the flat. Opening the screen door any further would not only let the occupants know I was entering, but possibly the neighbourhood as well.

If I thought about it too long, I would run the same risk of exposure as if I just did it. Rip off the goddamned plaster already. The ear-piercing screech of the coil could have awakened the dead. It may need to be put to the test.

The large, blond man turned and reacted quicker than I would have expected. It wasn't Oisin. He had no look of shock or confusion. He didn't assess the situation and call a meeting. He turned toward me, buried a large knife into the carotid artery at the base of the victim's neck, and reached for his weapon in a fluid motion. He was right-handed, that was his knife hand, and that was the hand he used to reach behind him to draw his pistol. He moved toward me, closing the gap.

I bolted through the door like a track star leaving the line. Only I had not yet heard the gun go off to start the race, nor did I want to. If a full second went by, that was long. His arm had not yet come around from behind him, which I needed to ensure stayed that way. By way of greeting, I raised my left knee into his abdomen, the momentum from my journey from the door and my strike taking the wind out of him. While making contact with my knee, I used both of my arms to hold his right arm behind him. The arm bar would only work if he was unable to spin out of it, which I tried to discourage with repeated blows to his body with my knee.

The mystery man was strong. As much as I tried to pin his arm behind his back, the more he struggled for the opposite. The gun went off, the victim in the chair was hit on his right side. I moved behind the man, which was a calculated risk. He would be able to spin out of the precarious hold if I didn't act quickly. I stomped on his foot and tripped him forward, tugging on his arm and wrist the entire way down. He broke his fall with his left hand. When he made contact with the floor, I heard the snap and felt the arm in my hands weaken. I had broken his right wrist and arm by putting pressure on his wrist and elbow, hyperextending them both. The gun fell to the linoleum floor. I kicked it away from the fray toward the screen door.

I tried to hold him on the floor, but he was able to spin. I had lost my grip on his broken arm. He was down on the ground facing me, ready to continue the fight with one hand. And two feet. He kicked me away from him, sending me into a pile of garbage. The man made his way toward the door, toward his weapon but I reacted and stopped him. He had managed to get to his knees, crawling toward the door when I was able to get a football kick to his ribs.

Without a cry, he rolled away from me and back toward the victim strapped to the chair. He had time to get up draw the knife out of his prey, who's bloody head sagged to his chest. There was no reaction from any of us when blood gushed out of the knife wound. The knife was wielded at me with a fully functioning yet obviously awkward left hand.

The thick file was still nestled in my waistband in the small of my back. I withdrew it and tried to roll it up as best I could. It was like trying to roll up a thick phone book. It can be done but not easily.

The knife came at me. I batted it away with the rolled file, sending an elbow to the striker's face for the trouble, then stepped back again. I could not let him circle me, could not allow him to get close to the door. Each time I tried to get close to the door to retrieve the gun, he would attack me with the knife. Again he didn't react like a person who was hurt and again he attacked. The knife deflected off of the file, slicing my outer bicep while I buried my left fist into his throat.

He stepped back but came at me again before I could assess the damage to my right arm. Before I could get the gun. I again batted the knife away from me with the file, this time it opened slightly as I was losing grip on it. He had lost grip of the knife and it was gone from his hand. This was my chance to end it. I used the thick file on his face, using it to shield his face. Pounding one side of it, the other side slamming into his face. He backed up into the refrigerator, trapped there. I worked his face with my upper body and elbows, smashing into the thick file which was compressing his face. I worked his legs by sending my bony knees into his thighs. Left, right, left, right. He tried to reach for me, reach for anything with his left hand, but the damage was being done and quickly.

The man fell, his tired and beaten legs gave way, no longer able to support him. He fell to the base of the refrigerator, I moved down on top of him. Adrenaline took over. Anger. I continued to beat him as I kneeled on his chest. The weight and strength of my entire body coming down onto his face. Smashing the folder into his broken nose. His broken cheekbones.

He tried to move his head to one side or the other for air. For something else for me to pulverise. I regained my composure too late. Too late for the large blonde man.

A near death experience gets the blood racing. Fight or flight. I had been in many of them. Southie. In the cage. When you get into a situation where it is kill or be killed, thinking goes out the window. Instinct takes over or you are the one who gets dead. It's primal. That is why they have someone presiding over the MMA fights in the cage. Inevitably, all fights go to the ground, the pounding and beating won't end until too late. Someone needs to have their head about them to stop the fight, or one of the two men who voluntarily enter the fight will die.

My instincts took over in that safe house. It wasn't a safe house for me, and my life was in danger. And there wasn't a ref in there to call the fight. Kill or be killed. The man was dead. I beat the life out of him. I'd like to say that I am sorry about that, and the truth is that I am. But not for the reason you think. I'm sorry because I could no longer question him.

The man that was strapped to the chair was Oisin. I sat there trying to take an inventory of the situation, on the linoleum floor. His face and body was beaten so badly, so bloody, that it wasn't until further scrutiny that I was able to determine who my victim's victim was. Dead.

Oisin had been beaten within an inch of his life, that last inch taken by the knife wound. The bullet hole to his side was unnecessary and after-the-fact.

I wiped the outside of the bloody file on my victim's shirt while I searched him for a clue as to who he was. Why he wanted Oisin dead.

Mobile phone.

The message on the inside of the Hutchinson flip-top mobile phone said:

86 dunn

86 dunn? My mind raced.

The blonde man killed Oisin. *Did Oisin know where Dunn is?* I had gone there because he and Cian had a cocked-up story. I wanted to confirm what I had suspected. And what I suspected put both Rowena and me at great risk.

The term '86' originally came from the Irish. It was then carried over to the New World and then used in the Old West when settlers pushed westward across the country. The term has survived for use in restaurants. Every restaurant and public house in the world. Why? Because that is where the term was first used. 86 originally meant proof. As in whiskey. Whiskey was aged in barrels. The longer it aged, the higher the alcohol content. When a pub, or later a saloon, ran out of 122 proof — you were 86'd. In reference to the lower proof, the under developed stuff. Now, chefs yell to the waitstaff to '86 meatloaf', meaning take it off the menu. It is no longer available.

Somebody ordered to 86 Dunn, and I'll bet it wasn't a chef. Dunn. As in Aiden fucking Dunn, the number two Volunteer under Finn Rourke. Take him out. Make him no longer available.

Oisin wasn't on the books as an informant. He said the other day with Cian that nobody knew he was a rat, except Cian. That he was a 'trusted lot'. He kept looking at Cian for direction. Every word came with an approval.

I looked on the phone for the number the message was sent from. No number, just the contact marker 'K'. The situation was worse than I thought. The Sinns were ordering an IRA fire-sale.

Moving down the stairs, two and three at a time, grabbing the Hekler & Koch *Mark 23 9 mm* pistol formerly owned by the dead blonde guy on the way down. I raced back to the car. Row and I officially needed to be off the grid. My mind was still racing. I was going to be walking into the lion's den. The meeting with Finn Rourke.

Am I really going to take the meeting? If I do, will I leave the meeting alive? I have nobody to back me up.

When I got back to the car, I realised just how alone I was. Rowena was gone.

38

I AM USED TO BEING ALONE. I don't have many friends. Girls seem to come and go, sometimes with the seasons. No family to speak of. My partner, Hobbs, probably hates me. I know I hate him. I'm alone at home, alone in the cage, I was alone in Ireland. I could only rely on myself. My brain.

But my brain was playing tricks on me. Questions and answers were being shouted at me like a schizophrenic. *They are following you. Who are 'they'? Everyone is dead. You're next. Danny. Roxy. Breen. You're tenants. Niall. Now they have Rowena. Forget her she's dead. Get out of Ireland. How? You're being watched. Get out of there. Now. Find a hotel* ....

The passenger door opened to my left. I pulled the *Mark 23* from between my legs and pointed it across my body at the intruder. Rowena.

"Feck! Point that elsewhere, ye cunt."

"Jesus Christ, Row. You scared the shit outta me. Where'd you go?"

"I needed a toilet."

"Where'd you go?" I looked around to see if she was followed or watched.

"Duffy's."

"You look like you're still drunk. Get in the fuckin' car."

"I am indeed. And added to it."

"Great. Listen Row. I need you to get in the fuckin' car. Now."

She complied but not without warning. "You'll watch yer tone."

"Row, I swear to Christ I will knock you back out. We are in some serious shit."

"Yer bleedin'. Y'all right?"

I hadn't had the opportunity to check my sliced arm as of yet. Adrenaline working over time. It was a scratch. A deep scratch that needed stitching, but they wouldn't get any. One of my tattoos was pretty fucked up.

"I'm fuckin' aces, Row. Are you listening to me? You can't just run off like that. And sobriety starts now. We are gonna need our whits."

"Can't just go into a pub and use the toilet. Patrons only. I had a quick bite of whiskey and returned."

"Who saw you?"

"Everyone in the pub. We're in no immediate harm, Deni. I've told you a thing or two about secrets. Where'd ye run off to anyway?"

I started the car and drove. Where to I wasn't sure. But I knew that we needed to get moving.

"Remember the informant Oisin Hanamy that I told you about?"

"That's his flat, hey?"

"How'd you know that, Row?"

"We're in Belturbet. The only garsún ye know here is him."

"Oh. Yeah. Right. Well that's not his name anyway and he's dead."

"Ye killed him?"

"No, I killed the guy that was sent to murder him."

"Who's that?"

"There are a lot of who's involved, Row. Let's just get to a hotel and I will explain the whole thing to you. What I know anyway. I've got to call Walter back home. I'd rather just explain it all once."

"No hotels," she said.

"We can't go back to your flat, Row. We need to lay low and think about the next move. We are literally going to be hunted, if we aren't already." I was flying around corners, driving aimlessly, being cursed as the devil from every direction.

"You'll need a passport for a hotel. Passports are faxed to the local Garda stations in Ireland."

"Yeah, no cops."

"I'll call me editor. He'll sort us out. Where's me mobile?"

I pulled over into a petrol station. Dug into my luggage, retrieving her mobile phone from the boot. She called her editor, told him we were near Northern Ireland but not where specifically. She was definitely still drunk, she would have failed a field sobriety test with her wobbling alone. But she was handling speech and communicating with her editor quite well considering. I was impressed.

While Rowena was checking in with her boss and getting us a place to lay low for the night, I was searching around to see if we were being followed. I did not believe that we were. She was taking forever, but I gave her the space she needed.

"We've a spot. We'll need to be tidy and brief. Only for the week-end."
"Whatever. Is it close?"
"Naw. But I know where. I'll drive."
"Yeah, fuck that. You're hammered. Just give me directions from the passenger seat."
"Sadly, I'll be better at the helm than you."

There was no arguing with her. She wouldn't move, wouldn't get in the car unless she had the keys. And I wouldn't have a place to stay without her. We were causing a scene, so I gave her the keys.

Once we were back on the road, she said something other than, "gimme the feckin' keys."

"If your caught with that gun they'll put ye ta death. American with a weapon? They'll proper feck ya," she said.

"I'm dead without it. So either way. I'm pretty good at staying alive, Row. I mean to keep that streak alive."

"Pun intended? I've been lucky as well. Maybe you tell me what scrap you've got me in."

"I told you I will. When we get to wherever we're going."
"We'll not be there right quick."
"The way you're driving, I doubt that."

Evening was upon us, but it was not yet full-dark outside. The house was a rural one very close to the UK/Northern Ireland border, off of L1506. The cottage was quaint and owned by an out of town relative of Row's editor. The spare key was placed under the potted plant by the back entrance. I unloaded my bag out of the *Clio*, grabbed a blanket from one of the cupboards and covered the car.

Row must have been hungry because she immediately started to cook something on the stove.

"Fess up. What's going on now? I'm not about to wait any longer. Call yer man after."
I put the file on the kitchen table while she stood above the pan. I emptied the contents of the folder, but threw the blood-stained folder itself away in the bin.

"I went to the Garda station by Pheonix Park to see Cian. To check in. After what we had seen at the docks, I wanted to report our side of things to Cian. We might have been seen by any number of people on that bus. He would know that we were there."

"Aye. And?"

"So they said at the station that he was still there investigating it. He was there for quite a while. I didn't know when he would be back, but I got to thinking. Why kill the old man? Why kill Niall? The authorities are aware of what I'm looking for, but they think it's up in the north."

"Only the IRA would know where the cargo is really bein' sent from," she interjected.

"Right. So how? Why? There are only two possibilities, Row. Somebody is plugged in at the embassy, or Cian."

"Aye. Cian brought ye to the docks. He knows who said what and who has eyes open."

"Exactly. So I start going through his file cabinet, and what do I find?" I pointed to the file on the table. "Cian is Anti-terrorism. He has a file on the whole shah-bang. Informants, who's alive, who's dead. Who got paid what and when...."

"And Oisin is listed."

"No. That's just it Row. He's not. Cian took me all the way up here to point out that he had a guy on the inside. Oisin was the one who ratted out the Newtowncunningham and Dublin stockpiles. Dublin was a bust, not literally, and Newtowncunningham was just old shit. Nothin'. But who got all of the accolades? Cian, in case you weren't paying attention."

"I don't follow."

"You will. Stay with me. So I'm digging through this entire file, Oisin isn't listed anywhere. Payouts made, list of all the tips and by whom. The biggest seizure so far this year and not one mention of Oisin. Not one Irish Euro spent to keep him in that safe house. The tip came from some other guy .... uh, it's right here .... Tadhg O'Carolan."

"Who the feck is he now?"

"He's fuckin' nobody Row."

"Maybe I'm still too drunk for this."

"Tadhg is Oisin. So why keep that a secret? An informant is an informant, right?"

"Aye?"

"Then I found this .... " I turned over a document, flipping it so she could see. Row took the pan off of the burner, moved over to the table. " .... look at the date of that document. Tuesday, 3 August, 2004. The day that I arrived in Ireland. It's a facsimile saying that this message was intercepted from DK to AD. Only look at the date of the fax on the top-right corner. It was post dated. I am named as a top-tier IRA secret cell operative. You are my accomplice. That you're my contact here. Your address is listed below."

"This is rubbish, Deni. I don't understand."

"You go to the Sinn Féin pub every night. That is no longer a secret. This document suggests that I work with the Sinns through you."

"Aye, but — "

" — aye, but nothin', Row. There are only two people who could possibly set me up for a fall. Only two people at the date of that document besides Walter back home and you."

"Cian and Oisin."

"Cian was the only one who knew that I was here, why I was here and that I was pulled out of O'Neill's by you. This is his file."

"Cian was settin' ye up for a fall, seems like."

"Right. So I know we need to get the fuck out of Dublin. We made our way here to see Oisin. He doesn't exist on paper, yet the two people who knew why I am here and what I am looking for, and who are top people in the Sinn Féin party under Finn Rourke do know. That document says 'DK and AD'."

"Darragh Kane and Aiden Dunn. But we just said that Cian and Oisin were the only ...."

"And Oisin was killed." I pulled out Oisin's killer's mobile, flipped it open. I handed it to Rowena.

86 dunn

She looked at the phone, then back at me. I continued with an explanation that probably wasn't needed. "DK sent somebody to kill Dunn. He couldn't do it himself because he was investigating a murder on Dublin Port from earlier. You should have seen Oisin looking to Cian every time he spoke when we came up here."

"Oisin Hanamy is Aiden Dunn."

"Also known as Tadhg O'Carolan. I was onto the only person that could give up Darragh Kane. He had to get rid of Oisin or Aiden or whatever the fuck you wanna call him."

"But Deni. Cian was the lad who introduced you to Oisin. Eh, Aiden."

"I think the plan was to kill me. And You. Only explanation. You said that Cian wasn't in the pub that night that you went back. But we were supposed to go there after meeting Oisin. I bailed but Oisin slash Aiden could now put a face with a name because we had met. You were supposed to be there too."

Rowena was transfixed. Staring into my eyes. "Detective Garda Síochána, Cian Daly, of the Anti-terrorism Task Force in Ireland is Darragh Kane. The top Volunteer in the IRA .... "

"And when the mission failed, he needed to take Dunn out."

"What do you propose we do now, Deni?"

"Now I have to keep my appointment and see his boss, Finn Rourke."

"Ye can't still be thinkin' of takin' the meeting. You've lost the plot."

"You're not the first girl to think that I'm crazy."

207

39

NEITHER OF US SLEPT. Again. The first night crawled, every sound a call to arms. Rowena's hangover became so bad, her head pounded so brutally, she wouldn't have been able to sleep if her life wasn't in peril. The demise of Niall and Aiden Dunn were still locked into my mind. That was my future.

I am a recovering Catholic. Meaning that I haven't been to church since the last wedding for funeral. Which just so happened to be a mass for Daniel and Roxanne McKennie. But I prayed to Jesus that night. Then I thought about Jesus. He allegedly knew the night before his torture what he was in for. I bet he didn't sleep a wink either.

The attempt at sex to occupy the time was rejected like Row was a goalkeeper. I was batted away and reminded of her headache. I offered to find some sort of medicine in the cottage, find her enough water to supply a camel, but those too were rejected. Her heart wasn't in it, she said. I very much enjoyed it when she was in the mood, and I desperately tried to get her there. I failed.

We were told, meaning I was told by Rowena, that we were to leave the place as we had found it. We didn't really dirty anything, but we cleaned anyway. Wiping and undoing everything that we had done. Retracing our steps. The bloody folder was removed from the bin and taken with us. I asked how she would explain the missing food we ate over the course of the weekend, she didn't like my sense of humor. I didn't tell her that I was serious.

The appointment to meet Finn Rourke, the Army Council General, was scheduled for 10:00 AM sharp on Tuesday, 24 August. We came up with a game plan on the way back to Dublin. I don't know who was more nervous, Row or me. When I get nervous, I get quiet. When she gets nervous, she won't shut up. She chattered the entire way while Bono and Edge did their work in the background.

Row stopped at a postal annex on the way back. She made 2 copies of the file, one for her and one for me. Over €100. Like I said, the file was thick. I would eventually take the bloody originals, but not into the meeting with Rourke. If anything was to be confiscated, we wanted them to be the copies. And we wanted him to know that they were copies.

When we arrived around the corner from his office, we got out and split up. I had only the clothes on my back, her mobile phone with Dunn's murderer's mobile programmed into it, and a copy of the file. Row had the gun, both the original and her copy of the file, Dunn's murderer's phone, and my passport. If things went to shit, which I had every belief that they would, she had detailed instructions on what to do.

Rourke's office was more secure than the US Embassy building. I was patted and re-patted. Told I would not be allowed in without identification. The Council General, Rourke, was called to approve my entrance into the building.

I was led up to his office, where I didn't have to wait. His office door opened and closed behind me. The office was CEO-sized. Rourke's desk was larger than the car we drove there in. The man was slight, but I made no mistake of his power. He wore thinning, white hair. His hunter green eyes were almost an implausible colour. When he smiled I almost expected bloody fangs, instead his teeth were yellowed and crooked.

"Please have a seat Mr. Dennihan." He had a most definite Irish accent, but his English was perfect. "This is an impromptu meeting, and it was fit in. I do not have a great deal of time." We both sat down.

"Deni. Call me Deni. And I don't know how last minute this meeting is. It took me more than a week for you see me. How busy could you possibly be? Or you just thought that I'd be dead by now. Right Fin? Can I call you Fin?"

"No, you may not. Sir will do."

"Ok, there Fin. We have a big problem you and me." I decided to go on the offensive. I am not timid or meek when I'm nervous. Especially when I'm nervous. "We both know that you are the puppet master and the minions went rogue on you."

"I have no idea what you are talking about. This is going to be a short meeting if you think you are going to come in here and spout off with ridiculous accusations."

"Let's start from the beginning then, shall we?" I waved the thick, photocopied file like I was hot and I was in a Baptist church. You are a member of the political party Sinn Féin, yes?"

"Yes."

"You are the Army Council General, yes?"

"Also correct. Everyone knows this."

"I know a lotta things most don't there, guy. I'm here lettin' you know that I know."

He sat back in his chair, rolled his eyes and shook his head as if to say 'very well' but actually said nothing.

"You are the guy who tells the army what to do, the guy that takes the council vote and communicates that vote with the actual army."

"That is what a Council General does. Yes."

"You also control the IRA on behalf of Sinn Féin, yes?"

"No. That is not correct. The Irish Republican Army has been disbanded."

"We both know that's bullsh, Fin. You fucks have been documented as active, publicly, as late as February of this year. You are on the same terrorist watch list as those Al-Qaeda assholes."

"I am one of the top politicians in — "

" — and we just went through all that. I know. You have Darragh Kane, AKA Cian Daly doin' your bidding. You had Aiden Dunn, AKA Oisin Hanamy, AKA Tadhg O'Carolan as his backup until very recently. I was there. I got the motherfucker's phone who was sent to do it. Did that news make it up the flagpole yet?" I took the phone out of my pocket and showed it like it was a badge as way of proof. It was Row's mobile not the murderer's but he didn't know that. The phone went back into my pocket.

"Why are you here, Mr. Dennihan? You have no jurisdiction here. And I am too busy to listen to your rantings. I entertained this meeting as a courtesy to the press."

"And since then, you know that I'm not a member of the press."

"Correct."

"And you took the meeting anyway." It was a question, but I didn't project it as one.

"I was curious, and my curiosity has been exhausted." He rose from behind his giant desk.

"I wouldn't get up if I were you," I said. I opened the file in one of the clear spots near me on the outside of his monster desk. "I know about your gun shipment. I know that you are into a ton of illegal shit all over the world to pay for your political party and this big-ass desk. You had Niall McCourt killed. The guy you sent to kill him just so happens to be investigating the case. I'll bet that one doesn't get solved. I've got it all here in this file, Fin. These are photocopies of Kane's originals by the way. Kane being Cian the dirty cop or Garda or whatever you call him. I've got phone communications from Kane to Dunn, Dunn to Kane. Now that Dunn is dead, how long do you think it is going to take for Kane to cut a deal? He'll bury you in a heartbeat to save his sorry ass."

"Americans and their Hollywood."

"You don't wanna come clean, Fin? If what you do is so noble, why not own up to it?"

"I think that I've heard just about enough. Will you leave of your own accord, or shall I have you thrown out of the building?"

"I'm leaving." I got up to leave but turned to him as I opened his office door. "This is going to the press. This is an international incident you've got on your hands. 911 is comin' up on its three year anniversary, fuckface. We don't like terrorists, you are about to see just how much."

I played a heavy hand. I had no idea what, if anything, the US government would do. Officially. We were at war with the middle east, not Ireland. Walter Glibczieck wanted the guns to prove that he could get guns off the streets of America. I was here for that purpose only. There was nothing I could do to Finn Rourke other than make his life miserable. Titanitaukis would get his win. The state of Massachusetts would get their win also, a much needed win after the big Maynard Ballistics Lab fiasco.

Everything hinged upon what Rourke would do. Other than to have me killed, which I had seen enough in the short time that I had been there to know he would most certainly do. I wanted him to make a mistake. I wanted him to move the gun shipment quickly. I wanted the manifest information. I wanted to go home. Hell, I wanted a home to go to.

All eyes seemed to be on me as I left Rourke's office building. Call it paranoia, call it whatever you want, I was keeping my head on a swivel. Once I hit the kerb, Rowena came from around the corner. We met and walked toward her car without losing our stride. She nonchalantly slipped me my newly acquired gun and my passport.

"How did you make out?"

I shrugged my shoulders. Row had a grin on her face as I asked, indicating that she had made some progress. Progress was crucial.

"I think we know when and where, Deni."

"Nice! .... Well?"

"I'll tell ye in the car. Less ears." She looked around as we made for the car at a brisk pace. We were almost at the tiny Renault *Clio.*

"Toss me the keys, Row. I want to drive down to the docks again. We will have to walk it this time, I don't want anyone to recognise the car."

"Amn't a fan of your drivin'."

"I'm not askin', Row."

She tossed them, but tossed them like a girl. Or should I say not on target. The keys skidded across the kerb on the left side of the car. The keys fell off the edge and rested between the shoulder and the driver's side tire.

"Nice throw. You should play for the Yankees."

"Feck off."

I reached down to snatch the keys, when it caught my eye. A small, red, flashing light reflecting off of the pavement from under the car. It looked like a reflected, blinking, laser pointer. Paranoia? I went down to all fours, looking under the car. Black box with a blinking light under the driver's seat.

"Fuck! Run Row! Ruuu ....."

Everything went in slow motion. Her eyes widened to the size of an Irish Euro coin. Deer in the headlights. I went from all fours to like a runner off the starting blocks to full sprint. Hands and arms pumping. Legs propelling me as they moved. Knees to waist. Heels to buttocks. Slow motion like in the night terrors. The evil thing is upon us, and we cannot move fast enough.

Rowena didn't seem to move. Panic had rendered her immobile. She was on the other side of the car, in the road, and behind me now. *Should I go back to help her?*

The explosion was large enough to destroy a Humvee, let alone a subcompact car. The device took out the vehicles both in front of and behind the intended target. Metal shrapnel sliced through everything surrounding it like an infinite number of Ginsu knives, toward an infinite number of points from the center.

I was able to travel nearly ten meters prior to the explosion and was catapulted another ten plus meters. I was covered in cuts and scrapes. Sound was replaced by ringing in my ears. Clouds of smoke from the fire replaced sight. Debris falling like hail. Fiery balls falling like sparklers. What was left of the car and the surrounding area was more like a meteor crater.

When last I saw Rowena, she was no more than one meter away from the car. From the explosion. She was a petite woman. She wasn't as durable as any one of the structures that were now damaged or destroyed. She was human. She was tender flesh over tiny bones. And there was no way that she could have survived.

40

RYAN WELL'S OFFICE PHONE AT GRANTES, WELLS & ASSOCIATES rang after being directed from Angie the receptionist. The attorney was drafting a final summation for a trial the following day, Friday, involving a woman who had beaten her own child to death. The mother of three had lost her job, along with the third in the line of fathers of her brood, and didn't qualify for benefits. She snapped. Temporary Insanity was the defense Wells was going with at any rate. Nobody won TI defenses anymore. This one was the long shot of all long shots. New Hampshire juries are filled with mothers and fathers who have had tough lives. They may beat their children, but they don't beat their children to death.

Lost in thought on how best to spin the facts of the case, how to pull on enough heartstrings to attain a 'not guilty' verdict on murder two, nullify a jury, hope for probation on the reckless endangerment of the two other minors, while the phone continued to ring. His wife, Angie, knew he was in his office. She knocked on the door, pulling Ryan out of his deep focus, hearing the incessant ringing. He answered the phone without his wife having to enter his office.

"Ryan Wells."

"Ryan. This is Walter Glibczieck. The federal - "

" - I know who you are, I remember you. It hasn't been that long. How are you? What's going on?"

"Do you have a few minutes?"

"I'm sort of in the middle of something, but I can spare a few minutes."

"I'm calling with regard to our mutual friend. Warren Dennihan?"

"Deni. Is everything alright? Last I knew he was in Ireland for you." He omitted that Deni's efforts would help him in a potential civil suit as well. That he was there for the firm as much as for the federal government.

"Yes, well it helps you too, yes?"

"With the Breen case?" *Time to downplay it*, he thought. "It helps once we solidify all of the connections. Triangle trade all over again. Guns, drugs, and money. Once we can prove the conspiracy, we may have a civil case against several parties. Including the prison. But that is a long way off. A long shot at best."

"And bring criminal charges against his murderers."

"Prosecutions aren't my department, Walter. That's your gig. I just defend or sue the people you prosecute. So what is this about? Like I said, a civil case is a long way off."

"Have you heard from Deni lately?"

"A couple of phone calls, but it's been a while. I'd have to check on the dates to give you an exact amount of time. Why? Has something happened?"

"I'm not entirely sure, to be honest. I haven't heard from him. But he did mention a reporter the last time we spoke. I was against it, but he had already worked out a deal with the woman and he seemed to be getting further with her."

"And?"

"And her editor faxed me documents from her, at Deni's behest, indicating that the contact that I had Deni working with over there, the Detective Garda on the Anti-terrorism task force, is duplicitous."

"That's not good, Walter. You should get somebody over there who you can trust to get him out. I told you this was going to be too dangerous. You and Titanitaukis cooked this — "

" — save your righteous indignation, Ryan. There's more."

"More? Great."

"CSPAN is reporting a car bomb that went off in Dublin near the Sinn Féin and headquarters last Tuesday. Have you seen the report?"

"Nobody watches CSPAN, Walter. The people that produce CSPAN don't watch it. But let's not get crazy. So he hasn't checked in …. car bombs happen over there all time. Don't they?"

"The car belonged to the reporter that Deni was partnering with. The IRA has denied responsibility, but the experts say it is of the same type that is commonly used by them."

"Could be a coincidence."

"Ryan, the statement from the IRA came within the same hour of the bombing. They denied their involvement before the investigation. Before the authorities knew what type of device it was. Which is an admission of sorts. Sinns, IRA, the reporter that he was working with, the fax outing an insider …. those are a ton of coincidences."

"So you think that Deni is dead?"

"I'm not sure, that's why I'm calling you. I want to see if you have had contact with him since this happened."

"Since Tuesday? No."

"It's Thursday, Mr. Wells. We have to assume at this point .... "

"I'm not willing to concede that yet. Why are you so quick to cut and run?"

"Because this was supposed to be a clandestine operation. Just information. This is turning into a complete cluster-fuck of the highest order."

"So are you going to send someone over to collect him? Investigate? Help him? The embassy should be notified."

"I can't. This was off the grid. This is about burying it at this point. We need to cut him loose. Cut ties."

"You are just going to leave him over there? Why are you telling me this Walter? You know that I can't just walk away from this. What you are suggesting is immoral, not to mention — "

" — I'm telling you this as a courtesy, Ryan. You might want to get yourself a new investigator. If you hear from him let me know. I certainly hope that you do. I hope that I hear from him. I'll of course let you know if I do. But if not, we have to assume the worst. This would be an international incident with a country in which the United States is an ally. I'm calling to tell you that if this goes anymore sideways, I am going to need you to be a friend. A friend that can be a very powerful one for you. Do you understand what I'm saying?"

"I do but I can't believe it. I am disgusted with you, Walter, but I know exactly what you are saying. What if I have enough friends? I wonder if someone above you would make a better friend?"

"I wouldn't do that if I were you."

"Are you threatening me, Walter?"

"Of course not. I'm merely saying that you can get further ahead with sugar than you can with spice."

"Well, I think that I have heard enough of what you think about how I make and keep friends. One of my new friends is in trouble, so you say."

"What I'm saying to you, counselor, is that you can never have too many friends. But you can have too many enemies."

41

SIRENS ECHOED THROUGHOUT THE STREETS OF DUBLIN. Only I couldn't hear them. I had a different sort of ringing in my ears, the kind from tinnitus, or ear drum damage. I imagined they sounded like European sirens. High, low, high, low, high, low. Pitch change after pitch change. Ambulances, fire brigade, and numerous other emergency vehicles cordoned off the area. One kilometer block by one kilometer block.

I tried to get up but failed. I tried to discern what was happening, but it only came in pieces. A slow strobe light if you will. Snapshots in time. Time that I was losing. All I can remember were all of the lights and all of the sounds that must have accompanied them. The gurney. The blood. Oxygen mask. Tubes. The ambulance. All of it coming in flashes.

The day I woke up, the day I really became aware of my surroundings, I will never forget. 31 August, 2004. It was a Tuesday. I rose in my bed into a semi-upright position. The hospital bed. Hoses and things were sticking out of me. Agitated would be the understatement of my state. Bits of the explosion came back to me. So too did the pain.

How long have I been out? Which hospital am I in? Rowena.

I started pressing buttons and yelling for someone to pay attention to me. I wanted attention. I wanted answers. Two security personnel of some sort were standing outside the private hospital room. They looked in, saw that I was awake and proceeded to flag some people down.

The doctor came in first, followed by a nurse who did little more than tidy up. The doctor was a short, rotund sort of woman. Glasses. Very librariany. She checked my chart and asked how I was feeling. I was able to hear her British accent. Her voice was muffled but I still thought it a minor miracle.

"I'm fine. How long have I been here?"

"A few days. A week actually. You had lost quite a bit of blood and you were very weak. You are lucky to be alive."

"Yeah, Yeah. I need to get outta here. Wait. Where is here?"

"Mater Misericordiae University Hospital. One of the finest in Dublin, I should think. Do you remember why you are here?"

"Car bomb."

"Yes. Precisely. Please don't remove your intravenous lines. You have had several pieces of metal removed from your body, many lacerations, two fractured ribs, and you were concussed quite badly. Not your first from the looks of things and I assure you that removing your medication is not in your best interest. The pain alone will be quite debilitating. Please do try and relax."

"I have to get outta here, doc. The motherfuckers that did this to me will be back to finish the job."

"That is why we have you under protective watch," she said. "Those hospital security men stationed outside have been there since you came out of surgery. I believe there will be a Garda presence imminently. Your friend has the same level of protection outside the critical care unit."

"Friend? Rowena? She's alive? I want to see her right now." I tried to get out of the bed, but a surge of pain hit me, and one of the guards entered into the room in case I succeeded.

"She is hanging on. I can't say for certain for how long, or if she will ever recover. She sustained a great many injuries, some of which are to vital organs. The blast literally chucked her quite a distance, I am told, where she landed on her spine. She has undergone two operations to remove fragments in vital areas. More surgeries have been scheduled. She is unconscious and machines are helping her to remain stable."

"The blast .... I don't know how she made it this long. It's just .... she was so close ...."

"About that. The Gardaí would like to have a word. They have been clambering all week to see you. Should I tell them that you are ready to receive?"

"No! Fuck no! I won't make it past the end of the day if you let them in here. Tell them I died. Tell them whatever you want, just don't tell them that I'm conscious."

"They are conducting an investigation and are arranging a more long-term security arrangement for you. I cannot impede that or I shall face criminal charges."

"How long can you give me?"

"I should think an hour or two would be reasonable to collect your thoughts."

"Fine. Where did you put my stuff? My belongings? And Rowena's?"

"They are in property. I cannot give those to you until you are discharged."

217

"I have evidence in there. I want to go through it, collect my thoughts like you said. Then I will hand it over to them for their investigation. Then and only then will I be ready to have a chat. But I need Rowena's stuff also."

She gave me an inquisitive look before committing to a response. "I'll see what I can do." She nodded to the nurse who was still pretending to tidy up.

"Thanks doc."

Within a half-hour the nurse came back with the bagged items. The bags were large and sealed. I had to sign for them. I dug through them once she left me alone. The guards outside the door didn't seem to be interested in looking in through the large, narrow, vertical window that ran parallel to the door to the room. I was in the room. I was safe. Their job well done.

No clothes. They must have torn them off of us when we got here. Or the shrapnel did the work for them. My wallet was there, my badge and all of the euros present as far as I could tell. The files were strewn all over the inside of the bags. Some of it burned or bloody. I was trying to piece it all back together as best I could from all of the copies, who knows what was missing. Keys to the now non-existent car. My passport. Both mobile phones. No gun.

They either didn't want to give the *Mark 23* to me, which was understandable, or they didn't have it in the first place. Either way I didn't have it. Either way I needed it to protect myself. Probably the first reason. Row said that it wouldn't be good to be caught with it. Add that to the fact that the body in Belturbet housed a bullet from it. Another reason for the Gardaí to want to speak with me.

I had about another half-hour left before the Irish version of the cavalry would be coming through my hospital room door. I didn't want to be there for it. The machine that was keeping track of my pulse, attached to my forefinger, was plugged into the wall. Was. No alarms seemed to be going off, so I continued to disconnect things. I left the I.V. port in my arm but removed the lines to the bags that were hung on the rack. I put the medicine bags in my property bags. If I really did need the pain killers and whatever else they had me on, I would have it, but the doc probably just told me that to keep me dependent upon her.

With bags packed, all I needed were clothes. A hospital gown over my wrapped torso with my ass in the wind was not going to do. I needed clothes and a way out of the room. The two guards at the door were going to be a problem. I hoped that they were stupid. I opened the door to find out.

"The doc said that you guys were going to bring me to some sort of interview room? I have the evidence that I need to hand over to the investigators here in these bags. Care to lead the way?"

They looked at me like I had sprouted four heads.

218

"She didn't say anything to you? Go check it out if you want," I said.

The guard on the left side of the door nodded to the other and took off in search of the doc. One down one to go.

"Make sure he gets me some clothes too will ya? My ass is hangin' out. It's embarrassing. In the meantime, do you wanna just bring me there? I know what she said."

"Amn't bringin' you anyplace without proper authority. Go back in yer bed now."

"I gotta use the shitter anyway. This one is clogged. We can stop at a toilet on the way."

"Jest hold it a bit. He'll be right back. We'll sort ye out then."

"You want to pick up the mess? You'll have to when I tell the orderlies that you knew I had to go and you wouldn't let me. What's the harm in letting me use a working toilet?"

"Bollucks. Make it quick."

He walked me down the hall. "Why do you need yer bags?"

"I have evidence in here. I can't just leave it layin' around." He seemed satisfied with the explanation.

As I began to move for the first time since the bombing, the soreness took over. My body ached all over. The medicine was wearing off or my head and torso were in bad shape. Maybe all of the above. We took a left around the doctor and nurse station. Behind the counter there were several people talking in front of a large dry-erase board. I kept my head down and tried to keep the guard between the gathering and me. It seemed to work.

Further down the hall on the right was the individual restroom that the guards themselves used, he told me as we approached it. It was a large room with an oversized door for handicapped access. He opened his arm and pointed to it. It was at the end of the hall and across from the stairs.

"Quick like," he said.

As I turned the handle to open the door, I pretended it was locked and occupied. "Someone's in there."

"We'll go on to another then," he said.

I finished turning the knob. "Oh maybe not. Maybe it was just stuck."

"The guard gave me a concerned look, like I was playing games. Which of course I was. "Do you want to check it out first?" I opened the door a crack and let him come around me to look inside the one room.

He popped his head in just far enough for me to shove him against the door jam and slam the oversized, heavy door on the back of his head and neck. I looked back toward the nurse station, fifteen meters or so back, thankfully nobody noticed me. I slammed the door one more time for good measure. The guard began to slump when I reopened the door again, pushing him inside.

219

With the door locked, I was able to quickly change into the uniform that I removed from the unconscious guard. I swam in it, but it would have to work. Club and mace. No gun. That would have to work as well.

42

I FELT BAD FOR LEAVING ROWENA at the hospital. I didn't even get a chance to see her. But the window of opportunity for me to escape was small. There was no time. Mater Misericordiae would be on lockdown in a matter of minutes. Once the first guard came back to the second guard who was not at his post and missing, it would be all bells and whistles. Full tilt.

After descending one flight of stairs, I entered onto the second floor. I quickly meandered around that level looking for a lounge or a locker room. I needed another change of clothes. They would be looking for a man in a stolen guard uniform as soon as they realised what I had done. I had no other clothes, they had blown up with the bomb. I needed a change of clothes and I needed it before the hospital was completely sealed.

Nothing doing on that floor. Another staircase down, one more flight.

A group of doctors were headed into an area that said 'fostaithe amháin'. I assumed it meant employees only. Hoped. I followed the group in and there was a lounge on the left, to the right were two sets of locker rooms. I was met with odd stares as to my presence. Thinking quickly, I put on my best Irish accent. Mixed with my harsh Boston accent, it must have sounded odd to say the least. The stares didn't end after I spoke.

"Beg pardon. We have a patient thats gone missin'. He's a bit of a handful so ye mightn't want to be here for the moment." I looked around the area, all eyes on me. In keeping with the lingo, I might have been buggered. Nobody moved.

"Everyone out now!" I shouted. They all poured out. The club that was part of the guards uniform I then used to rattle on the men's lockers, those that had business in there quickly exited. I searched for any and all clothing that would fit, shoved it into a backpack that I took out of a locker. The evidence bags went into it as well. I thought about changing then

221

and there but didn't have time upon further review. The call to remove the employees had created a stir outside in the hall.

Keeping my back to the wall in the hallway, trying to hide the backpack, I called to them.

"It's clear." I held the door open for the first few to re-enter then made a dash for the stairs again.

Out the front door, I turned to my right to see the car park. I ran as fast as I could toward it. My body weary and beaten, sore and protesting my every move. I wasn't yet to the structure when I heard the emergency alarm from the hospital sounding.

Once in the parking structure, I found a car that looked easier to steal than the BMWs and other luxury cars in the assigned spots on the ground floor. I settled on a silver Peugot *206*. I didn't know what year it was, I didn't even know the car existed before that day. It just looked like a four door piece of shit that I could steal.

Which I did. No car alarm thankfully. I had never stolen a car where everything was on the right side as a kid in Southie. Certainly not as an adult. An adult police officer. But …. desperate times and all.

Car manufacturers think that they are slick by installing steering immobilisers in the column so if the car was to be stolen the thief wouldn't be able to steer it. The locking system is from the key ignition switch. But virtually every manufacturer as of 2004 had a very simple cylinder on the steering column. They made this so that locksmiths and local dealers could fix a problem if there was a lost key or the locking system malfunctioned. Pulling the wires down from underneath the steering column, connecting the 12-volt lead to the four other wires, and a lock-picking pin from my wallet jammed into the ignition and I was on my way. It took me longer to get into the car using my pins than to drive the car away once I was in it.

I pulled out under a flyover once I had left the hospital grounds so I could change. Again the clothes from the men's locker room didn't fit quite right, but close enough. Next stop, back to the docks.

It took me a hot minute to figure out how to get down to Dublin Port from the hospital. At first I went the completely wrong direction. I realised my error when I went by Boston College Ireland and Sainte Stephen's Green. Talk about weird. The fact that I had to drive by another hospital, the children's hospital, made me think that I was driving in circles in the wrong direction. I lost track at four times I went by that goddamned place. Or maybe it was a third hospital all together. At any rate, Seville Road empties out onto North Dock. From there I found my way.

On foot. I parked the stolen silver Peugot 206 like it was waiting for the Holyhead, UK ferry on the south side of the port and walked. And walked. To the other side of the port, where shipping is the industry not ferries to Isle of Man, Liverpool, or the like. Then along the docks to the containers.

The docks were shutdown until the investigation was to be completed. The doc said that I was down for a week and it was still on lock-down. I don't know what other evidence they aimed to collect but security was tight and no vessels were allowed in or out of Dublin Port. I found out from one of the underlings on the outside of the cordon that shipments in were either re-routed to another Irish port, or were anchored in queue out in Muir Éireann by the Poolbeg Lighthouse.

It was like a gigantic raft party like the college kids form on spring break. Only these were cargo ocean liners instead of rented Bayliners. Freighters are massive. They have to be in order for shipping internationally to be cost-effective. They range in size and scope depending upon what they carry; tankers, general, dry-bulk, reefer, etc., but can be 350-400 meters long. Another measurement used is TEU, or twenty foot equivalency unit, for measuring length. You know the thing is big when you use 20-foot increments to measure them. To put it in perspective, a Nimitz-class aircraft carrier is 330 meters long, or 4.5 acres. The aircraft carrier is 20 meters shorter than the smallest vessel in the bay. Weight is yet another category for measuring size. DWTs, or Dead Weight Tons. Each of the vessels in the water waiting to be loaded and unloaded could carry up to 400,000 DWTs on top of the vessel's empty weight. Now imagine about a dozen of them in one spot. It was a floating city.

I had to wait until dark to get further onto the docks. There was a small detail of security that night but nothing compared to when I arrived earlier in the day. There was lighting but not so much as to be spotted ten meters away like during daylight hours. The sun had been mild yet baking my skin. I didn't want to go anywhere else while I waited for the sun to go down. I wanted to monitor who was let inside the cordoned area and who was made to leave. I sat in Irishtown Park for the rest of the day. I watched and I waited for night to come in order to make a move. And finally, it did.

43

NIGHTFALL CAME LATE, AS IT DOES EVERY NIGHT in the almost-autumn summer months. Of course it felt even later because I had been waiting and baking in the sun all day. Sneaking past the cordon and security was easy. I spent the first hour with my neck and skin against the cold steel trying in vain to cool it. Moving from crate to crate with as much stealth as I could muster down the long pier toward the office where Niall was carved up like an Easter ham.

I actually thought an hour was quite good considering. Sliced, bruised, broken, and then burned, I moved as fast as I could and as quietly. There were a few random guards meandering around the dock yard. They didn't look like they were looking for anything in particular, which suited me just fine. The office was where they had concentrated the majority of their numbers. The office and the cordon at the entrance to the pier.

And the office was going to be a bitch to get into if it was locked. I am good at picking locks. A fucking magician actually. But I'm not invisible. If it took 10-seconds to get in, which it could possibly take a few seconds longer than that, it would be 10-seconds too long. I studied the men that were watching the perimeter of the converted office space for a weakness, some way to get to the door unseen. There wasn't a way. Locked or not, I was not getting into the modified container through the door without being seen or taking some people out. There was no back egress. The normal two-door latch on the end of all 40-foot long containers was welded closed when it was converted into an office. The only door was the door that had been cut into the side, with a small deck and stairs leading up to it.

I climbed up on top of a nearby container to reconnoiter the surrounding area. I had been circling the docks, counting and ascertaining the best way to breach. If I had to take out some of the guards, I wanted to have to deal with the fewest number. They moved around with purpose. They were well trained. And they weren't wearing Garda uniforms. In my mind, that meant that without anything other than a club and mace, I needed to avoid engaging this particular enemy.

There weren't any lights on in the office. Meaning if I was able to get inside, I would be alone. As long as I kept the lights out or blocked the one high window and kept quiet, I would be uninterrupted for as long as I needed. I just needed to get in there.

The closest surrounding container was ten meters from the office. I thought if I could get on top of the converted container, I could jump down from it getting behind those that were guarding it. I couldn't jump that far. Olympians can't jump that far.

A crane had a line dropped above the closest container like a fishing rod into the sea. The heavy hook rested slightly more than a meter above my head, too high to jump. Delays delays. The obstacles were growing more aggravating. But it was not a time to get my Irish up. It was a time to assert my dogged determination. Affect my stubborn will.

The crane seemed far away. Especially since I had to avoid several guards, remain quiet while covering ground. This took more time. Climbing onto the top of the operator's cabin in my condition, then onto the long arm of the crane. Moving up and out on my tender ribs and belly using hands and feet in the rungs. All the way to the top. Moving up and out over the container. Dropping down onto the 9 cm wide, braided, wire rope cable from the jib. Taking breaks on the descent as the cable was cutting into my hands. All of this took time.

What began as mission just after dusk, was now close to one in the morning by the time I had lowered myself, hand below hand, down to the hook. My feet rested on the weld connecting the hook to the cable. My arms burned. My hands were bleeding. The cable was already swaying from my journey to the bottom of it. Back and forth like a pendulum. Moving me closer to the top of the office. The heavy hook now slightly heavier with me on it. Gaining momentum back and forth, slowly but surely.

Next was a crucial part of the mission. Silence. Dropping down onto the roof of the container could be noisy. *Would it echo? Would this adventure be finished before it began?* I was thinking and pondering these and other questions while fixing my gaze on my target. The roof. There was something sticking up from the top of the container. It was difficult to see what in the dark.

Do or die. Time to get off of the cable. Timing was key. Back and forth. Silently swinging in the night. I was separated from the hook and cable. Falling in the air like I was tire-swinging over Fresh Pond and jumping in off of the quarry ledge back home. Only this landing would not be so soft. Not by a long shot. The containers were built to stack on top of one another. For storage. For transport. The roofs were ribbed and welded in a grid fashion for support. While the landing was silent, it was hard and extremely painful.

After taking a physical inventory to ascertain if I had broken anything else on the fall; determining that other than my ribs and my head continuing to pound, my bleeding hands added to the rest of the dried blood and scabs on my body, my scraped knees and tender ankles, I was no worse for wear. The object that I could not make out on the roof was an open window. A skylight you could call it. It must have been opened to help with the smell of death. Wide open. I couldn't tell what it was because the lights had been extinguished. Another drop through the opening and I was in. Finally.

My eyes were already used to the dark from being out in it for hours. But this was Stevie Wonder dark. I felt my way around. A hard hat. Clothing of some kind. A light switch would be out of the question at least for the moment. The smell inside the office could have gagged a maggot. A poorly ventilated morgue. Somehow it had gotten worse since I had last been in the modified container, even vented.

Whatever clothing or piece of cloth I had felt hanging on the wall, it was big enough to cover the small window. The window was high above the desk. I slid a lamp and something else that was tall over to the edge of the desk and used them to keep the cloth in place. In that blind search, I had knocked something on the desk over. I froze in place until I determined that only I had heard it. Fortunately nobody came to the door to inspect a noise, if they had even heard one. The clumsy error was serendipitous. The turned over object was a flashlight.

Nobody seemed to have made an attempt to clean the office. The walls and floor still looked and smelled like a crime scene a week after the event. They had gathered up all the evidence, all the bits of human remains that was once Niall McCourt. All but the blood stains and the smell was left to putrefy the office.

I searched every file. Every piece of paper in that office. It took all night. Every document. There had once been a computer, but it was gone. The chords lingered where the machine once lived. Every business that had anything stored there had a file in the cabinet I presumed. Every company that shipped something off of that port. Every boat that was parked out in the floating car park. Nothing pointed to Sinn Féin or the IRA. To the destination. The answer would be in the destination. File cabinet after file cabinet. Drawer after drawer. It was narrowed down to one of three vessels that would be carrying the shipment. Only three vessels from what I could tell would be headed into Boston Harbor in the foreseeable future. Which means it wasn't narrowed down at all. It might as well have been twenty. Each vessel had the capacity, depending on weight of each container, of roughly 1,500 containers. The three possible vessels meant having to search 4,500 plus, forty-foot containers for crates inside those containers holding weapons. Not gonna happen. If, which was a big question, they were still going move forward with shipping them out of Dublin.

Maddening. I felt like I was getting nowhere and time was running out. I wrote down the names of the three freighters that would be headed into Boston Harbor, and other related pertinent information on a piece of paper before deciding that I needed to get out of there. Dawn was coming.

I rose out of the top of the converted office no wiser than when I went in. Not realistically. Three vessel names. The light began to outline the shape of the horizon off to the east on the back side of the container. The top of the sun would soon peak out of the Atlantic Ocean.

Getting out of there was much easier than getting in. The back side of the office faced the water, to the left was the way I had swung in. To the right was a sea of containers. I would jump down from the office roof and disappear in those containers, making my way back to the park. From there I could leave the Dublin Port.

But go where? What now?

I decided that it was time to call Walter Glibczieck again. And once I got off the docks, that is exactly what I did.

44

"THREE VESSEL NAMES. THAT'S ALL I CAN COME UP WITH," I blurted from the confines of the stolen Peugot. It was a little past midnight on the east coast of the states. I had called four times from Aiden Dunn's killer's mobile phone. Walter let it go to voicemail each time, his voice requesting that I leave a message with a name and number, which I refused to leave. I just ended the call and dialed it again. He picked up the final time

"Who is this? It's the middle of the night." He sounded odd to me. Not pulled out of sleep. Just odd.

"It's Deni. I'm calling from a stolen cell. I've got vessel names. But that means close to five thousand containers. It's just about as far as I can go here, guy."

"Deni? I thought …. How do I know it's you?"

"It's fuckin' me. I've had some close calls but I'm alive."

"Prove that this is you."

"I'll tell ya what. When I do get back stateside, I'll beat the life outta ya with this cell phone. What the fuck do you want from me, Walter? Focus on the prize here."

"Okay, it's you. Uh, so …. three freighters?"

"That might be the best we got. Three ULCVs. Big suckers. The Annika Mærsk, The Cecil Mærsk, and the Giddeon Mærsk. All waylaid in the ocean just off Dublin Port. Those are the only ships headed to Boston."

"They all have the same last name? Mærsk?"

"Yeah I assume that this company, this A.P Moller-Mærsk Group out of Denmark names all their vessels with the last name. Is that important?"

"Remember the Heckler & Koch G3A4s that were stolen?"

"Norway. Norwegian Police. I'm not too up on world geography, Walt, but Norway and Denmark ain't the same country last I checked."

"No but there is a plant in Denmark. The *G3A4*s were designed and are manufactured there."

"I don't believe in coincidences, but I'm not seeing how that fits."

"Me neither. Did you say that all three of those vessels are parked in the ocean?"

"Yeah, it's very heated over here. The embassy knows I'm here and why, the Sinns know …. the contact that you sent me to …. he's like the IRA's number one fucking guy."

"Cian Daly?"

"Ya Mean Darragh Kane? They are one and the same. People are dying left and right, and I'm next."

"You said as much in the fax that you had sent over by the fucking editor of a major Dublin newspaper. You were supposed to keep this quiet, Deni. The US Embassy has been notified? You have this reporter on this. Car bombs? Not exactly going to plan, is it?"

"What do you want from me? I'm doin' the best I can."

"All this noise and we are still going to have to narrow the shipment down, Deni. I can't issue warrants to search those vessels with what you've told me so far."

"Let me spell it out for you chapter and verse, chief. They took out Aiden Dunn, the number two guy. They tried to blow me to the fuckin' moon, and that reporter that I was working with? She's probably gonna die or is already dead. I questioned this poor old guy, Niall, on the docks down here and they filleted him. Cut him limb from limb. Literally. These boys over here don't fuck around. If you piss in their Guinness, you wind up dead. You and everybody ya know. And in a very painful, very public way. I got in a tussle with one of these fucks up in Belturbet and he's dead. If I don't get the fuck out of Ireland soon, I might not ever leave. I'll be in the ground or worse, in a prison. Does that spell it out for you? Get me the fuck outta here, Walt."

"They killed somebody on the docks? The Dublin Port?"

"Everything I said, and that's what you picked up on? Yes. They tortured the poor prick."

"In Dublin."

"Walter. I know it's late over there but if you could fuckin' focus for — "

" — Deni. Why would they kill someone on the very shipping port that they mean to move their illegal guns out of?"

"Because they're sick fucks? Who knows?"

"Those vessels are waylaid because of the investigation. Correct?"

"Yeah Dublin is on lockdown. You think they aren't coming out of Dublin now? I was thinkin' the same thing."

"But they are the ones that killed this old guy, Niall, that you spoke with. You're sure?"

"I didn't watch them do it, but it seems real clear. Yes."

"I think that means that they are *definitely* moving the weapons out of Dublin."

229

"I didn't sleep all night. Walk me through that logic, Walt."

"They would normally have to go through customs to move their shipments, right?"

"I'm with ya. That was my guess, yeah. Well, Niall's guess in fairness, but we see how that worked out."

"So maybe they had some arrangement with this Niall, or maybe they didn't. But now that the port is closed, they won't need customs forms. No vessels in or out. So they are going to sneak them out of the closed port."

"That makes sense, Walt. The focus will be on every other shipping lane outta Ireland. They are gonna move the guns out right under their noses. They were probably going to create some sort of distraction to close this thing down all along. A shipment like that is too large to slip through customs like they have been doing in smaller loads, so they create a diversion. But that was a big splash. They cut this guy up really bad. Why go that big unless they were pumping him for information?"

"You tell me. You are the one over there. But if I had to guess? From what you've told me? They planned to shut down Dublin anyway. Niall talked to you, so they wanted to find out what he said. Like I was saying, maybe they had an arrangement with him and they wanted to find out if he had mentioned that to you. They killed two birds with one stone by creating the necessary shutdown with a murder, and pumped him for information at the same time."

"I guess. So how do they sneak a boat the size of Brighton outta Dublin?"

"Are all three of those vessels on their way in?"

"I don't know. There was a computer but it's gone. Those are the names of the freighters that are parked in Muir Éireann. They were listed on a random piece of paper. Looked like a loading and unloading schedule. I wrote down what I could."

"Were there departure or arrival dates on the ships?"

"Uh, I don't know. Let me see .... " I took out the piece of paper that I had written the vessel names and information onto.

"Which is the first to arrive in Boston, if you have it," Walter asked.

"The Annika Mærsk. Today is what, the first? So like two and a half weeks. Nineteen days. Says here 20 September. If I'm reading this right."

"Two weeks. That is about how long it takes to for the vessel to make the trip. It takes time to load those ships. Days. That's the ship. It's already loaded. It's already loaded and on it's way out."

"So once the port is cleared, the boat will float out with the guns. Still. That's like almost two thousand containers. What now?"

"Now I get with the DOJ and go through that cargo manifest with a fine tooth comb. We narrow it down and get the search warrants. Now we get you home."

"Good. How? And what about Rourke and Kane?"

230

"We can't do anything about that until we seize the weapons on this end. Then we pass along the information to the Irish government and move on. We deal with our guys on this end, they deal with theirs."

"The Sinns are the government here. The majority anyway. They don't really prosecute the way we do. It's complicated," I said.

"Our focus isn't on the supply of guns Deni. There will always be guns. There will probably always be an IRA, officially or not. But if we stop the demand side of things on our end, we've done our job. Rourke and Kane will be out of business in my district one way or another. Good Job. I'll call the embassy and get you out of Ireland."

"They are watching the airports. Row - uh, the reporter here, said that best way was out of Scotland or England."

"Fine. I'll contact someone to help you get to a safe spot and let me know where to get you a flight. Is this the number where I can reach you?"

"No. Don't call me, I'll call you."

"Deni, you need help. You can't just be out there on your own. Let me get you some help."

"I'm good. The last time you set me up with help, he turned out to be the fuckin' enemy in all this."

"I had no way of knowing that Cian was Kane. Or that Oisin was Dunn. But you are going to need help. You destroyed a hotel room, killed an Irish citizen — IRA or not — and beat up a hospital security guard. You're already a suspected IRA secret cell operative, there was a car bomb …. Listen, by now there isn't a Garda station in Ireland that doesn't have your photo. Let me help you Deni."

Huh. How the fuck does he know all that?

"Deni? Deni, you there?"
"Yeah. Yeah. I'm here. I gotta go."
"Just tell me where you are."
"I'm on my way home, Walt."
"Stay put. Tell me where you are so this doesn't get anymore out of hand."
"I'll call you when I get to a safe spot."
"Let me find one for you. What else do you need?"
"Just make sure my bonus is ready when I get home."
"Goddammit Deni! Deni?"

231

45

I SPENT THE REST OF WEDNESDAY, 1 SEPTEMBER getting back to Rowena's place and sleeping. I'm not sure if that was the wisest place to be, considering that either Finn Rourke, Darragh Kane, or one of the minions car bombed us. They put a device on Row's car hoping to kill me, Row, or both of us. Rowena had an unknown name and was in a hidden flat. Yet they managed to find her and me. But nothing in her flat seemed to have been touched. Not yet. So I stayed.

In truth, it was difficult for me to sleep at first. I made myself an American meal as best I could with what Row had on hand. Then a hot shower. My ears keen on every noise while I was wet. The hot water felt good on my beaten and broken body, but I was too skittish to stay in there for long. A dry-off with a thirsty towel but with nothing to wear. I raided Row's cupboard for something to be clothed in. Her space was entirely too small for the clothes and costumes that were packed and piled together. Knowing her there was a system to it, but I didn't know what it was. I settled for remaining in the towel, draped around my waist. Laying in Row's bed didn't rest my mind. It wandered and wondered. *Is she alive or dead? It was just a matter of time, even the doctor said so. Did her involvement with me get her killed?* There was no mention of it on the TV for the time that I had it turned on. I put on one of Row's many U2 CDs. I would have put on something else, but there weren't any other CDs as far as I could tell. The signature twang in Edge's guitar in the song *Bad* echoed in the small bedroom. Bono seemed to speak to me " …. Let it go …. and so fade away …. I'm wide awake …. "

I took a fresh bottle of whiskey from the press. " …. I'm not sleepin' …. " He kept singing, still speaking to me. Haunting me. It took almost a quarter of a bottle of the whiskey and the medicine from the I.V. bags to do the trick.

And sleep I did. Fuck you Bono.

I lost a few days. I woke up long enough to piss and hydrate. I was completely and utterly drained.

232

I woke up on Saturday, 4 September, feeling somewhat refreshed. It was evening and I was alive and well. Ish. Sleep didn't repair my fractured ribs. Nor did a fairy sprinkle magic dust on me in the middle of the night or morning to heal my stitched head and countless cuts and scrapes and burns. But I had survived so far.

Rourke and Kane had either thought the job had been accomplished or they thought that it was beyond comprehension that I would go back to Rowena's flat. I'm just stupid enough to be smart sometimes. Whatever the case may be, my enemies had let me be for the moment.

Several phone calls to Director Humphrey at the embassy went unanswered. 'Call me' he had said. I left messages to call me back at Rowena's flat, but he never did. Each time I stressed how important and urgent it was and that I desperately needed to speak with him. His help in getting out of Ireland would be crucial and urgent. But he never called back. And I didn't dare to go back there, I was certain that the embassy would be watched. I wouldn't make it to the gate.

The next morning I took another hot shower. This one was a long one. The I.V. port had to go. So did the stitches that were pulling on my head and body with every move I made. The wounds bled but they hurt less once I was finished fussing with them. Once I was out of the water, I wrapped my torso up with a new roll of tape. Partially to help clot all of the bleeding, partially to hold my ribs in place. Why Row had bandage rolls on hand was mystery. A pleasant one. Maybe she used them for some of her costumes. She had nothing to wrap up, nothing to hold in place. I missed her.

Thoughts of her and her well-being consumed me while I tried to find suitable clothes. There were none. I would have to don one of her myriad disguises. When I looked at the mirror in her bedroom, I was struck with an idea that I could not shake.

For laughs, I checked the washer/dryer to see if there were clothes in there. Rowena, ever used to having to remain neat in her tiny living space, had washed some of my clothes. They were wrinkled but dry.

I wish I could thank you in person, Row.

That thought added to the idea that I couldn't shake.

I put on the wrinkled jeans and Nirvana tshirt before grabbing the costume. Said goodbye to Row's flat for the last time. I'm just stupid enough to be smart sometimes.

The Mater Misericordiae University Hospital was no longer on lockdown. I learned in the police academy, and repeated many times to those I had partnered with, that criminals will often return to the scene of the crime because they can't help themselves. Often times that's how they get caught. It is ridiculously stupid. When I was boosting stuff as a kid, I did it outside of Southie. Mostly because the syndicates would beat the life out of me if I fucked up their gig, but it made sense to not be seen anywhere near the crime. I had just escaped from captivity and possibly being murdered, assaulting a guard and stealing a car in the process, and now I was going back.

I needed to check on Rowena. It was a need that I could feel in my bones. I would never be able to live with myself, always wonder what happened to her. She had helped to keep me alive, gave me shelter. The least I could do was see if she was still alive.

The taxi ride over to the hospital cost me nearly €20,00 but it was worth it not get caught in the stolen Peugot. I was finished with that car. In the unlikely event that I needed to drive again in Ireland, I could always acquire another one.

The trick to entering or leaving a secure building is to act like you belong there. If you look like you are trying to get away with something, then everyone assumes that you *are* trying to get away with something.

"Your badge sir," the security man said as I entered the employee entrance with the various second shift crews.

"Oh. Right. Let me dig into my pack ...." I don't know if my accent was Irish or British or what. I took the back pack with my costume in it off of my shoulder, pretending to dig for an ID badge that didn't exist inside the accessory. ".... well this is a bit embarrassing. Surely you remember me." I looked him in the eye. "I'm here every day."

"Right. Name?"

Think, Deni, think. I blurted out the first name I could come up with. I didn't want there to be a pause. Who pauses when asked their name? "Smith." Definitely not an Irish name. Stupid.

The security man typed on the computer resting on the desk inside the employee entrance. He looked at me, then back at his screen, then back at me, before finally nodding his head. He handed me a green temporary badge with a clip on it. "Do see personnel about a replacement. This is acceptable for today only. You'll need them to make you a proper one for tomorrow, ye will."

"Thanks very much," I said. "Reckon I just left mine at home." *Reckon? Where'd you come up with reckon?* I walked away from the desk, looking at the temporary badge I was given. *Smythe.* The accent must have worked. Dr. Brannish Smythe. What a horrible name. But it would fit my costume. Better to be lucky than good.

I changed into the scrubs from Row's backpack, covering up with a long doctor's coat that I found in the familiar employee locker area. I didn't have a stethoscope or any other scope for that matter, just the green badge which I clipped to my left front pocket on the coat.

The lift was crowded so I utilised the stairs to the top floor. The critical care unit was located to the left, at the end of the hallway where I had escaped. I took the left at the top of the stairs, passed the restroom where I had knocked out the guard, walked slowly past the doctor and nurse station. Names were written on the dry-erase board, but I didn't want to linger in front of it or be seen staring at the board. The short, round, British doctor lady might have been there. I didn't want a chance encounter, costume or no.

Another hallway to the right would have taken me down to where my hospital bed had been located, the left would lead me to Rowena. Assuming she was still in there. She may have been moved to another part of the hospital. Maybe she was recovering. Maybe she was dead and in the morgue. I really didn't want to take a trip to the morgue.

The long hallway had rooms that were occupied on both sides. The critical care unit was down at the very end of that long corridor. Since I wasn't able to really study the dry-erase board for fear of being recognised, I flew by the seat of my pants and resolved to look in on a number of patients until I found Row. But I could see which room was hers from the end of the hall by the two guards stationed outside the room. Hospital or Garda I was not sure, nor am I to this day.

At least she is alive. A flicker of hope.

The guards stopped me only to write down the name off of my badge. They didn't know what kind of doctor Smythe was, nor did I. When asked why I had not been there as of yet, why the name Smythe didn't appear on any of Row's other visits on their list, I simply told them that I was a specialist.

She looked terrible. She was always skinny and frail looking. She's Irish, so she's always pale. But her pallor was of skim milk. Grey-blue. Her breathing sounded like Darth Vader, more machine than anything organic. I imagined that NASA had less equipment than what was hooked up to Rowena. I don't know what I was looking for, but I looked at her chart anyway. It was all medical terminology for the fact that she was fucked-up and in a bad way.

235

The closer I got to the top of the bed, to her head, the less I wanted to see. The large neck brace holding her head facing the ceiling. The clear, plastic, fighter pilot breathing apparatus attached to her nose and mouth. The tubes tied together going into her arms were almost the diameter of her arms. She was somehow skinnier than she had been when I met her. One of the machines looked like an accordion was inside it, it moved up and down with the audible sound of her breathing.

Another machine had a digital spike and valley illuminated on the screen like the lines on a lie detector reading. The clear intravenous bags hung from the two racks like water balloons. Row was strapped down to the bed, probably to ensure that she didn't cause further spine damage by moving. Like she could or would move. It was horrible to watch.

I touched her hand, but there was no response. No movement. You see in the movies, hear people tell their miraculous stories, that they knew everything would be okay because of the blinking of the eyes or a squeeze of the hand. There was no blinking of the eyes. There was no hand squeeze.

"If I did this to you, Row, I'm sorry. I don't know if you can hear me, but if you can I want you to know that I never meant for this to happen to you. You're a good girl. I should have warned you that I always destroy good girls. I just came to say goodbye I guess. I'll see ya in the next life. Say a good word for me up there will ya? Not that I deserve it."

I reached into my pocket and took out her Sainte Christopher Medallion I had taken from her bedroom mirror. The patron sainte of lost causes would have his work cut out for him on this one. I put it in her hand, closing it around medal, and bent down to kiss her hand goodbye.

Just outside the room, as I was leaving, a man and another doctor were making their way toward Rowena. They stopped me, enquiries began.

"Who are you?" The doctor asked.

"Doctor Smythe. Specialist." I kept it short and sweet. I figured the less detailed I got, the less I could get hung up on.

"Right. The nerve specialist? How is she?"

I looked at the gentleman in tow with the other doctor, then pulled the physician off to the side.

"It's all right," the doctor said. "He is her editor and emergency contact. She is a donor, so we are keeping her alive with machines until it becomes necessary to turn them off. We hope for the best, but this is very bad. The Chaplin is coming up shortly to give last rights. I think it is a waste of resources to move forward with the other surgeries, don't you?"

"No. I don't." I said it a bit angrily. The tone didn't go unnoticed.

"She won't survive the surgeries. You must know that."

"We won't know that until we know it. If she doesn't survive, you can still harvest her organs. There is no downside to trying."

"As you know our resources are — "

" — what does the gentleman say?" I pointed to Row's editor.

"He says to do whatever we can to help her recover."

"Then we had better get to it."

The doctor left me for Row's room. I left the hospital, never to return.

46

THE FERRY TO LIVERPOOL WAS A LONG ONE. And expensive. While the north side of the Dublin Port was closed for investigation, the south side was doing business as usual. There were several ferry lines doing business. With destinations to Isle of Man, Liverpool, Holyhead, and others; I could have taken a less direct route to England had I cared to part with more Euros. The Irish Ferries Company, P&O Irish Sea, DFDS, Moby, and a slew of others were all in the business of transporting people out of Dublin. I had a choice of who I wanted to give my money, compliments of the US Department of Justice and Joe and Jane taxpayer. But the various lines must have had an agreement, because they all fleece their patrons for the same fares.

The Stena Line was the last booth inside the Dublin Port South Terminal that I price-shopped, so that is the Ferry Operator that took my €49,50. It was also the soonest departure time on a Sunday. I was forced to wait as many hours as the trip would take once it left Dublin.

Over the three hour wait in the terminal, and as we cruised by the Poolbeg Generating Station and the lighthouse, after we made way, I watched the freighters in Muir Éireann. They didn't move. They were all at anchor awaiting the lift of the temporary embargo. From the terminal I could not see The Annika Mærsk. Nor could I when we weigh anchor, nor as we set sail for Liverpool, United Kingdom. The large ferry sluggishly gained speed as we moved out of the harbour, floating past the parked vessels, slowly gaining speed to the 20 knots per hour that we would travel over the whitecaps. The freighter carrying the arsenal headed for Boston had already made way.

The powers that be of Stena Line had decided to turn a profit from the sale of alcohol on the ferries. Why I was shocked is beyond me, it was Europe after all. Nothing seemed to be accomplished in Ireland without being plied with alcohol. Why I was taken aback was because most people who take the ferry drive their cars onto it. I was one of the few people who didn't have a vehicle of some sort. Cars, scooters, even bicycles. The three hour ferry ride, with booze at the ready, was long enough to get a good buzz. Long enough to get drunk if one so chose. Then you arrived on the other side and were allowed to drive said vehicle off the boat and onto the streets of Liverpool. The logic is as dizzying as the heads of the consumers.

But who am I to judge? That's what I did. After I called Ryan Wells. Minus the driving of course. I used the mobile phone that came as proceeds from the scuffle in Belturbet.

"Ryan. Deni. How are things in New Hampshire?"

"Holy Shit you're alive. Worrisome. It's good to hear from you. I got a call from Walter Glibczieck saying that you were probably dead. Are you okay?"

"For the moment. I'm sneaking back to Boston. I haven't booked a flight yet but I'll figure it out."

"Be careful. You might not have as many friends as you think."

"I don't have many friends in the first place, Ry. Whattaya mean?"

"It might have just been political maneuvering, but when Walter thought you were dead he called me to let me know that he was cutting ties. He was trying to get as far away from you as possible."

"I spoke to him already. He knows I'm coming back. There is a ship already on the way to Boston with the load of weapons," I said.

"When was that? He called last Thursday, when he learned about a car bomb that you might have been involved in on that Tuesday. I guess he saw it on CSPAN. What's going on?"

"Yeah. These assholes tried to kill me. I was knocked out for a bit. So what? He said that if I was dead, that you guys know nothing about it?"

"Exactly. He has your boss Titani — "

" — Tits. What about him?"

"Well he has him on a leash, I think. And he was basically threatening me. Telling me that he was a bad enemy to have. You just might want to be careful. Does he know of your whereabouts? I'm getting a bad vibe about him. I don't like that you have hitched up to his star."

"No. I don't think he knows exactly where I am. I told him I would find my own way back. I was kinda getting the same feeling when I was talkin' to him. He knew stuff that I'm not sure how he'd know. I got a good knock on the head, and I'm pretty paranoid these days, but all I got are my instincts."

"Good. I think your instincts are good on this one. You might want to keep him in the dark for the moment," Ryan said.

"Thanks for the tip. He's probably just being a political douchebag, but you can never be too careful. He probably didn't want to have to explain shit going sideways. He wouldn't

239

have sent me over here if there was something else going on. But with everything that has happened, it's better to be safe than sorry." I don't know if I was defending him or trying to allay my own fears.

"Do you still have my cell number? Call me day or night. I'll pick you up from the airport."

"Thanks. Will do. I am gonna need a place to stay also."

"We can figure that out once you get back. Day or night. I feel partly responsible that you are in this mess."

"It's not your fault, Ry. You didn't start it. I'll see you on your side of the pond."

When we hung up, I rested my elbows on the side of the ferry. I thought for few moments about what Ryan had said, and looked at the mobile phone. I looked around the vessel, nobody was paying me any mind. One last look at the device, then a toss over the side. If they wanted it back they could search the bottom of the Atlantic.

By the time we had made way into the sound in Liverpool, under the A59 flyover and moored onto the pier, I was more than buzzed. As a pedestrian, I was allowed off of the ferry first. I had thought that I would hail a taxi, which I did but not before taking the BusyBus over the River Mersey to the terminal. The terminal sits next to the Titanic Memorial and I was glad not to have surrendered to the same fate.

The taxi stand had a line of them waiting for fares. I chose the first one in line, just like I would in Boston, although I was unsure if the etiquette was international. I said, "The airport." I thought that meant that we were going to Heathrow. When you think of airports in England, do you think of any other airports? I didn't. I might have actually thought it was the only one.

Instead, we took Strand Street to A562, to A561. The roads had other names like Parliament and things like that, changing every few hundred feet but the numbers remained the same. Three roundabouts and thirty minutes later I was parting with another €40,00. I was going to need to cash in some more traveler's checks because I was running out of Euros.

John Lennon Airport. I shit you not. Those Brits are sentimental. And there were no direct flights to Boston. And none would get me there until Monday, 6 September. I thought the nice lady at the terminal asked me for cunnilingus. She seemed cute enough and I was still buzzed so I agreed. A few awkward moments later I realised that she was asking me if the airline Aer Lingus would be ok. The Irish airline. Meaning fly back into Dublin.

"No! Fuck no. Anything else. I'll go by carrier pigeon if I have to."

240

Icelandair it was. So I spent the night in Reykjavik, Iceland. But only in the airport. It cost me over €2000,00 for the privilege of sleeping in an uncomfortable position on a chair. Another country, another airport that thankfully had bilingual signs. Brottfarir and Hlið. I mean …. how would one even pronounce them, let alone interpret them? Phonics is not always fun.

The bank of uncomfortable chairs was next to a bank of ATMs or flight kiosks or some other popular machines. So even if I was able to contort my body a-la Cirque du Soleil into a comfortable position, the traffic to those machines would have made it impossible. They made these god-awful digital noises when they spit out the tickets or money or whatever. The machines were as popular as Vegas slots. Maybe they were spitting out money. I really should have checked instead of trying to get sleep, since it didn't come anyway.

The flight out of Reykjavik couldn't have come quick enough. The night crept along like an Icelandic Banana Slug. Which in case you didn't know is about as slow as slow gets. I didn't know it either until I read it on one of the illuminated walls littered with nonsensical indigenous animal facts in the terminal.

They called out the flight number at 5:05 AM on 6 September. But then we were made to wait before boarding. The magazine and book store employee lifted the garage style door and began placing racks for the daily newspapers out while we waited to venture on to the jetway and out of that frozen hellhole. The Guardian, a major newspaper out of London, was one such paper being put out on display. We were all forced to stand right in front of the kiosk and a headline caught my eye. The one just below 'US Death Toll in Iraq Passes 1,000'. The headline was above the fold, the actual story below.

Suspected IRA Leader and Garda Detective Slain in Dublin

I threw money for the paper at the poor lady that was setting up shop for the day. I had no idea how much The Guardian cost, but I knew I gave her way too much. The boarding began and I walked onto the plane reading the front page article. It continued inside the front section, on page four while I found my seat and plopped into it. But to sum it up, Darragh Kane was dead. Rowena and I weren't the only ones who figured out that Cian Daly was also head of the IRA network of secret cells. What they presumably didn't know, because it wasn't printed, was that Finn Rourke was his overlord and was likely the reason he was dead.

Rowena was about to follow Kane into the afterlife if she wasn't already dead. I hoped they would end up in very different places if there was such a thing as an afterlife. Being a recovering Catholic, and in some cases simple logic, dictates that I have doubts. But I held out hope.

The only three people alive that I knew that had specific knowledge of Finn Rourke's nefarious deeds were now me, Ryan Wells, and Walter Glibczieck. And according to Ryan, Walt was a shady shit.

You're not out of the woods yet, Deni. Once Rourke knows for sure that I am alive, it won't take his new minions long to correct the mistakes of their predecessors. They have secret cells in their network all over the world. Slopes and the Winter Hill crew were brutal killers but very low on the international criminal food chain, though they were always looking to move up. Maybe they were looking to make the terrorist watch list. The Winter Hills tried to kill me by killing my home. They had already done so much damage, taken so many lives. Danny and Rox. Breen. My tenants. Imagine what they would do when Slopes was properly incentivised. Let alone if Rourke sent an actual crew over the pond to supervise the task. I might see Row in time for orientation at the pearly gate.

Part Four

Sometimes Life is an American Story
September 2004

47

HOME SWEET HOME. Logan airport, Boston, Massachusetts. Home of baked beans, clam chowder, and my beloved Red Sox. I wanted to kiss the fuckin' ground. But first customs and a pay phone. Ryan said that he would be a couple of hours, but he would be there. What else did he have to do in the middle of a Monday? So I had some time to kill. Thankfully I didn't have any luggage to cart around.

Speaking of clam chowder, I hadn't eaten anything resembling good food since I had left Boston. So I spent a couple of hours at the counter of Legal Sea Foods over in Terminal C. They didn't have Redbreast 12 yr Whiskey, but the food made up for it. Clam chowder, then the sashimi tuna, then the jasmine special. I pigged out. I drew the line at Boston cream pie. I was too full.

Ryan picked me up a couple of hours after I called him, just like we agreed. I met him out in front, we made small talk while he drove me over to pick up my *Escalade* from the garage that had fixed my window. He was nice enough to pay for my replacement window and storage before I followed him north to New Hampshire. The ride up was uneventful save for the U2 song that came on WZLX, the classic rock channel. *With Or Without You.* It reminded me of Row, and I was definitely without. It never would have worked out between us, but I didn't want her dead.

The hippie drives slow. If I didn't know any better I would have thought that Ryan was stoned and paranoid driving. I drive fast, partly because I think that the speed limit is more a suggestion than anything else. But also I was a cop. So being forced to do the speed limit or less meant that I had plenty of time to decompress.

Ryan and Ang were nice enough to offer me a room at their place. He and his wife Angie had already settled it, I found out when we pulled into his driveway. Ryan informed me as we exited our vehicles and were walking toward his front door. There was no thankfully declining. If I wanted a dime from him for my work, or the possibility of any future work, this was going to happen.

Angie was at their house in Wayland, New Hampshire, waiting for us to arrive. She was a nice lady. She was the efficient receptionist of Grantes, Wells & Associates by day, loving wife by night. She was very pretty and I had thought that Ryan had himself a catch. She was already home from work for the day and welcomed me in, showed me upstairs to the room that I could "have as long as I needed." She said supper would be ready in an hour, so I would have time to shower and change if I wanted. I didn't tell her that I was still full from Legal's and that I had no clothes to change into if I did take a shower.

She and Ryan caught up downstairs. The walls were thin so I couldn't help but overhear that there were a great many things that she had to reschedule in order for him to have blown off the entire day fetching me. She wasn't nasty about it. Didn't even seem irritated. Just the facts mister.

While listening but not listening to them, I made a list of all of the shit that I needed to do. Check with my bank. See how much money I had to my name and cash the few remaining traveler's checks I had. Call my insurance company. See if they had a check for me to rebuild my three-decker. Call Tits. My boss was probably wondering what was going on with me. Buy new clothes. New cell phone. New life. All would cost a fortune.

Supper came and went. Some sort of chicken and polenta thing. They were health nuts. I picked at it but was really not interested in eating. I had to be polite. So I did what all of the anorexic girls that I have taken out to dinner had done; pushed food around my plate to make a mess, take a bite every now and then to make it seem like I was eating. If Angie was offended, she didn't let on.

The three of us had drinks in their parlor. Angie with some sort of French white wine. The bottle said 'sincere' or some damn thing. Ryan had some sort of special dark beer. They had whiskey for me. The bottle was brand new so Ang must have bought it at the State Liquor Store on the way home. They really were very nice people.

"So Deni," Ryan said once drinks were poured and we were all seated comfortably. "All of your work is immensely helpful in the Breen civil case. "I've heard some or all of it, but I would like to hear about the case in full. Keep in mind that we will need to provide proof. Tell me everything, fact and theory. We can work on how to prove it all later. It might be a year or two before it ever sees civil court."

245

"You just want the stuff that relates to Breen? That's pretty simple and you know most of it. Breen was part of the old man combine up here in New Hampshire. They held guns and made drugs to make money for the Irish mob syndicate. The mob in Boston, works and distributes guns and money all over the country. All over the world." He nodded and listened to me, Ang also. But this was not what he wanted me to explain.

"So those guns that were confiscated here, and misplaced down in Maynard, are all part of the same supply chain that is coming over from Ireland," I said between sips of whiskey. "Those weapons are slated for distribution out of Boston to all points west. A safe guess is that they are for other enterprises that feed money through Winter Hill up to the IRA secret cells. Now they have to be replaced. Anybody that knew anything about the operation was killed so they wouldn't fess .... er, I was in Ireland too long .... rat on what was going on. My guy, Danny Mick. His sister, Roxanne. Breen. And of course they tried to kill me.

"Sean Teague, AKA Slopes, was protecting his Boston crew. The Winter Hill Gang. They are directed by the IRA because the army is supplying guns in exchange for money that they pay up to the Irish Republican Army Council, headed by none other than Finn Rourke, the Army Council General. Finn Rourke is also one of the leaders in Sinn Féin, a political group that is all about a pure Ireland. While they might have pure ideals, their deeds are not so much. Whether the Sinns as a whole know it or not is unknown, because the entire organization is so compartmentalized and this Rourke treats the supposedly disbanded IRA like his own personal security force. He *had* two guys named Darragh Kane and Aiden Dunn doing his bidding. Passing down orders to the secret IRA cells within the network to keep the money coming in. Funding the Sinn Féin party."

I let that sink in for a second while I refilled my drink. I told them I would be right back, went up the stairs to my room, returning with the copy of the The Guardian.

When I returned to the parlor, I put the newspaper on the coffee table between us. "Slopes was using the Finn Rourke playbook when he decided to take out anyone and everyone that stood in the way of moving product for cash. Even me. Those *lads* in Dublin decided to have a fire sale.

"I'm not sure if Ry told you this Ang, but Darragh Kane was also Cian Daly." I pointed to the newspaper. "Cian was the guy that Walter sent me over to consult. He was supposed to help me figure stuff out. Instead Daly was playing me for information and tried to kill me. He wanted to know how badly the Boston shipment was fucked before they did the job. When it all went south, Rourke decided to kill everyone. I met this informant, Oisin Hanamy. He had a couple of names but he was really Aiden Dunn. He reported to Kane and Rourke. He's also dead. Kane outlived his usefulness." I was still pointing at the newspaper. "And now he is dead."

This too was given a moment to breath. To marinate. Ryan broke the silence.

"So how do we prove this connection to Breen?"

"When the guns get here. They are due into Boston Harbor on the twentieth. That delivery will tie up all the loose ends. According to Walter, he can't touch the Sinns or the IRA. But we can dry up their funding by cutting off the gun demand. By busting everyone who collects that shipment, we establish the connection."

"Connection is collusion. It's not a long leap from collusion to an elaborate conspiracy to commit murder. There's plenty of motive," Ryan said.

Angie leaned forward on the couch. "Maybe I'm missing something but from what Ryan has told me, why don't we think that this Federal Prosecutor, this Walter person, isn't involved? He sent you into the hands of this IRA guy. They tried to kill you. The mob here and the IRA over there. Why do we trust this guy? He thought you were dead and threatened Ryan to keep his mouth shut about sending you over there. Right Honey?"

"He did." Ryan was looking into his drink, nodding his head.

"Does he know that I'm back Ry?"

"I haven't told him."

"Fine. So he stays in the dark. You said that he has my boss, Tits, on a leash?"

Angie laughed. "Tits on a leash," she mumbled. "That's funny for some reason. I'm sorry." She tried to compose herself. Her laugh was infectious and we all joined her in the laugh.

I continued after the moment of levity subsided. "As soon as I check in at Troop H, they'll know I'm back and then it's going to be open season. I'll have to be careful. You both seem like nice people, I don't want you to end up like my tenants. I probably shouldn't stay here."

"And go where?" Angie looked concerned but determined. "You'll stay right here. We will all be careful."

"At Grantes and Wells, we protect our employees," Ryan said. "I spoke with JG and we want to hire you on full-time. If you still want that. You can work other cases or what have you, but we want to get first priority on our investigations. You said that you wanted out of the Staties, are you still interested?"

Ryan handed me a check with a fair number of zeros on it. "For your work so far on the Breen case. There is more down the line when we get our cut of the settlement. Breen's girl wants justice. By justice she means money. Just make sure that we nail this shipment coming in on the twentieth."

I was stunned to get a check that large. I knew what I was charging them an hour, but the check was much more than what I was figuring to bill them. This was a great start to getting out of the Massachusetts State Police Department. My days as a cop were officially numbered. With the pile of shit I was in, maybe all of my days were numbered.

48

I PUT OFF THE PHONE CALL TO LIEUTENANT TITANITAUKIS for as long as I could. It took me a couple of days just to get my own shit together, never mind taking on another helping of it. Tuesday and Wednesday were spent getting my own house in order, even though I didn't have one.

The bank was happy to see me. With the deposit of the business check from Grantes, Wells & Associates, of which I was now considered a part of, my account was looking pretty good. I went to the post office to find out what was happening with my mail. The mailbox that was attached to the three-decker was no longer in existence, so they just held onto my mail at the South Boston Post Office. My insurance check had come through. Along with my notice of cancellation. They had paid out for a replacement car and a home in the same year. They were done with me. I put the check into an escrow account with same bank, Citizens Bank & Trust. The new house could wait until this case was over. With my luck, it would just get burned down again.

New clothes, check. New cell phone, check. Down the list I went in an attempt to get back to normal. All of these errands were done with the pedal to the floor and a thorough look in my rearview. As far as I knew, only Mr. and Mrs. Wells, and probably JG, knew that I was back in New England, alive and somewhat well. I wanted to make sure I kept them as safe a possible. They were kind, I hated to think of them of being in any danger of dying a horrible death. I hoped that they would break my current streak.

Each night I went back to their place in Wayland like it was my new home. Suppers were a time to catch up. Chat about everything. And nothing. I missed having someone to talk with. But how can you miss something that you've never had? Ryan and I would follow up after supper with drinks and NESN. The Red Sox crushed the A's both nights. They had a record of 84-54 and were still behind the goddamned Yankees.

I had called Tits after supper on Wednesday night. I was told to meet him the following morning in his office. Nine o'clock would be perfect. Perfect for him. Traffic out of New Hampshire into Boston at that hour was going to be an absolute goat-screw. The big dig would have shit torn up and diverted so horribly that it would take the normal bumper to bumper traffic and make it exponentially worse. I would have to leave at oh-dark-thirty to make the appointment.

Thursday, September 9th was already a terrible day by the time I rolled into Troop H in Downtown Boston. Three hours of traffic followed by detectives pestering me the second I walked into the station. "Where have you been?" seemed to be repeated over and over and over again. I wouldn't miss that. Eyes on your own paper.

I was surprised to see Walter Glibczieck in my Lieutenant's office as I entered it humming Warren Zevon's *Lawyers, Guns and Money*. It had come on the car stereo on the trip over, I had blasted it and it was stuck in my head. I wasn't worried per se, but seeing him made me stop humming rather abruptly. I expected Walter to be salty that I had not been in contact with him. And I expected that if Tits was going to sack me, getting fired would save me the trouble of quitting. It just surprised me is all. Less than twenty-four hours after I let Tits know that I was back, and Walter was sitting in his office awaiting my arrival.

"Walt. I wasn't planning on seeing you today." He stood and shook my hand, then sat back down. I repeated the ritual of pumping hands with my lieutenant before the entire room took a chair.

"I was wondering if you were ever going to call me," Walter said.

"Of course I was. I want to get my bonus check. I just needed time to get situated. In case you've forgotten, I don't have a house anymore."

"None of us have forgotten your sacrifice, have we Lieutenant?"

"No. Of course not. But we do have some concerns."

"I have some of my own, guys. Like what are we gonna do about Slopes? Ya know, Sean Teague and company?"

Walter appeared like he was trying to find the correct words. He was struggling. "The Mass State Police aren't going to pursue this any further. The ATF will take it from here."

"So I'm off this case? Just like that? I do all the grunt work, take a few attempts at killing me in stride? Just move on?"

Walter handed me an envelope. "Your bonus as we agreed. You've more than earned it. Thank you for your services."

"Lieutenant this fucking bullsh and you know it. The Winter Hill crew has been operating with impunity for how long? We get a shot and closing it down, after busting my ass, and we have to walk away?"

"Unfortunately it's a jurisdictional thing, Deni." Tits said my name like he was reminding me of my place in the world. Which he clearly thought amounted to the shit that is between the tread on the bottom of a hobo's shoe. "Hobbs is out in the field. You can catch up with him tomorrow after you've cooled down. You two can get caught up on his open cases. That's it for now."

"No. That's not 'all for now'." Eyebrows were raised. "Two weeks. I'm giving you my two weeks. I'm done with this shit."

Tits nodded like he wasn't surprised. He might have even been relieved. Maybe it was the goal. "Put it in writing."

"Fine. I'll give it to you tomorrow."

Walter's turn. "Deni? Keep in mind that if you go anywhere near this investigation, I will personally throw the book at you. Obstruction, interfering with a government investigation, misconduct …. you will be my personal pet project. There is an unsolved murder in Ireland that the Garda would love to close the book on. We can add that to the pile. And these are just off the top of my head. Imagine if I were to get creative?"

"I read you loud and clear. Are we done?"

Silence.

When I left the Lieutenant's office, I slammed the door loud enough for the suspects sitting on the bench on the other side of the precinct to jump like they had heard a gunshot.

"Ry, it's me. Almost exactly as planned. Although Walt was there."

"In the office? At the same time? Deni, did he give you your bonus check?" Ryan was somewhere noisy, he had to shout into his cell phone.

"Cash not a check. But it's all here."

"Deposit it. Right now. And don't lose that track of that deposit slip. Get a notarized statement from the bank that it was cash, and the numbers on the bills."

"How am I going to find a notary public that quick?"

"Your bank will have one on duty. They all do. At least one. Get them to count it, note the bills, make a statement and put a seal on it. Very important. Did they fire you?"

"No. I had to quit, but other than that it went perfectly. I was just a little surprised to see Walt there."

"Your Lieutenant might just be a pawn, but treat him like he's in on it."

"Will do. Walt made the threats. He wants me off of this. I'm supposed to check in with my old partner tomorrow. Not a lot of wiggle room."

"Can he be trusted to cover for you?"

"No. He's the king of all douchebags. If I go to the bathroom he's gonna want to hold it for me. But I'll figure somethin' out."

"Great. We'll talk tonight. I'm in court right now, and Judge McCaglia is in a mood. I gotta go."

"Knock'em dead. See ya later."

49

FRIDAY MORNING WAS A GIANT HEADACHE FOR ME. Rick Hobbs, my partner, was attached to me like a conjoined twin. I had to listen to him give me the rundown on what he hadn't accomplished in my absence. He was successful in that he had accomplished nothing. He had not solved one case. He had only taken more on. The guy was about as useful as tits on a bull. It takes talent to do so little and still have a job. I truly felt for his next partner. Poor prick.

Hobbs might have been a nice guy. Who knows? But I could never get past his uselessness. And how annoying he is. I had the constant desire to do the world a favor and choke the life out of him. His wife must be a saint.

He had requisitioned a *Crown Vic*, so he felt that he had the right to drive it. I preferred to drive in the *Intrepids* that were in the motor pool, but word had spread of my imminent departure so I had no say in the matter. He also got to pick the traveling music. Fucking Chick Corea. *Hound of Heaven.* Jazz.

"Jazz is very intellectual," he said as way of counterargument.

"Then turn it up. You need all the help you can get."

"I never complain about what music you put on."

"That's because I listen to good music, not a cross between elevator Muzak and eighties porn."

"You don't have much longer to put up with it do you?"

"No, I don't. By the way, I was hoping to meet someone for a long lunch today. You can drop me off down by the Seaport District if you want."

"Where are you going? Barking Crab? Jimmy's?"

"Jesus, Hobbs. I'm not inviting you, so really it's none of your business."

253

"We're partners, so it does concern me."

"We're not married partners. We are investigative partners. Detectives. Though you haven't detected much while I was away have you?"

"Funny. We have leads we need to investigate today. Are you going to milk out the rest of your time? Cuz that is gonna suck for me."

"Because your clearance rate has been so high without me? Get over ya-self."

"I'm glad I'm getting a new partner. I've been asking for someone else since you and I were assigned together."

"Good things come to those who wait, Hobbs."

The rest of the morning was spent talking to two different people who were supposedly the last two people to see a woman who had disappeared. Neither of them knew where she was, only that she seemed in good spirits the last night that they had seen her. In other words, they were of no help. Wasted time and energy instead of doing what I wanted to be doing, which was namely to find Slopes.

Hobbs dropped me off on Congress Street on the western side of the Seaport Hotel and Conference Center at a quarter past noon. "Will an hour be enough time?"

"Better make it two."

"C'mon Deni. Really?"

"Tell ya what. I'll call you when I'm ready. You can pick me up right here." I didn't wait for a response. Instead, I slammed the car door and ran east on Seaport Lane, between the two buildings of the hotel. Halfway down the tiny street, past the cabs waiting for fares, I quickly entered the lobby. A right past the lounge, around to the left, past the bakery, and right out onto Northern Avenue. Congress and Northern run parallel, connected by Seaport Lane and others. I wanted to make sure that I had lost Hobbs. There was no place in my mind that I didn't think that he wasn't going to follow me and report me to Tits. He could just pull a bitch at the next one-way and watch me. When I crossed Northern Avenue, I looked both ways for the *Crown Vic.* Hobbs was nowhere to be seen.

On the other side of Northern Avenue is the Boston Seaport World Trade Center and on the other side of that was the Atlantic Ocean. Inside that building, among other entities are the Massachusetts Port Authority (MASS PORT) and Seaport Transportation Management. Those two entities report to the Bureau of Customs & Border Protection (renamed CBP after 9/11) and to the Department of Homeland Security all of the information about every vessel that comes in and out of Boston Harbor. Whether the boat carries people or cargo, these organizations know about them or other large boats with very large weapons get involved.

It was a beautiful day to be down by the water, sixty-nine degrees and sunny. I would have loved to spend the afternoon sitting on the docks and sipping beverages at the Barking Crab. But I wanted to solve this case more.

I circled the building from within, up flights of stairs and down. I wasn't followed. The MASS PORT office was on the eastern-most side of the building on the first floor. The actual first floor, not the ground floor like I had to deal with in Ireland. It took no time at all after the flashing of the badge to get cooperation.

"I want to see the shipping manifest for a vessel that is scheduled to dock on September 20th. The Annika Mærsk." I said to the gentleman in his early fifties behind a desk.

"Of course. If we have it. They are supposed to submit prior to arrival since 68 FR 68140 was amended. But this is only the 10th. We might not have it yet." He stood up instead of immediately typing the name of the ship into his computer terminal. He moved closer to me, his back to the ocean, Coast Guard boats and the bay behind him.

"68 …. FR …. whatever? What's that?"

"FR means Final Rule." He leafed through a folder, putting a piece of paper in front of me on top of the half-wall that separated us. Then quoted it verbatim while I read along. "Right there. 'The cargo information required is that which is reasonably necessary to enable high-risk shipments to be identified for purposes of ensuring cargo safety and security and preventing smuggling pursuant to the laws enforced and administered by CBP. These regulations are specifically intended to effectuate the provisions of section 343(a) of the Trade Act of 2002, as amended by the Maritime Transportation Security Act of 2002.' In other words, the information doesn't have to be listed on the Automated Manifest System until twenty-four hours prior to arrival. We are talking Bulk Cargo, yes?"

"Yes. But I don't understand. Somebody on the shipping end enters the manifest data in to this system — "

" — AMS, yes. A computer system."

"And it ends up on this end. But it can be well on it's way before having to be declared before it gets here?" I immediately remembered that there was a missing computer from Niall's modified office on Dublin Port.

"Very good. Yes. It is a very political and jurisdictional thing. Once it is at sea it is considered to be in international 'no man's land'. It is up to the nearest country's Coast Guard or Military to protect those waters. Once it is in port, then CBP or MASS PORT or other agencies get involved."

"So who has access to this computer transmission? It can be altered prior to reaching the destination, am I right?"

"Theoretically. But only a bonded transporter or a third-party AMS service provider would have access to the specific manifest entry."

255

"Explain. I'm not good with computers. So use small words."

He laughed and slowed his speech like I was mentally challenged instead of technologically challenged. "For example China. Believe it or not, even here in 2004, there are still some bulk shipping companies that still only use paper manifests. Since 9/11 the AMS, the computer system, has been mandated. No more loose paper manifests. So these companies that are behind the technological times utilize a third-party to transfer their paper manifests onto the AMS."

"Seems very risky. Some random company can mess up or completely omit cargo from a freighter that sails on into a port. After everything that has happened that seems very dangerous."

"Again, they have to be bonded by the CBP. They would have to be a vetted and trusted enterprise or they are not allowed onto the system or into the port. But you are correct. It isn't perfect, but when we are dealing with international organizations it's the best we can do at the moment. If it weren't for these ships, virtually no international commerce would take place. Imagine the number of planes it would take to move the amount of cargo that these vessels move. Airports would be at a standstill."

"So do you have the manifest or not?"

He moved back behind his desk and typed into his computer. "It's here yes. The Annika Mærsk. What do you want to know?"

I went around the half-wall that we had been speaking over, through the saloon style half-door and stood over the gentleman's shoulder. His computer screen was blurry. The dark blue border with the yellow background was harsh on the eyes. Only a government agency would make something that needed to be studied at length so difficult to look at.

"How do you read this ..... er ..... I'm sorry I don't even know your name?"

"Glen. And they can be hard to read. Unless you know what you are looking for it's like trying to drink water from a fire-hose. So what are you looking for?"

The vessel ID, vessel name, time and date of both departure and arrival, house bill, ocean bill, and voyage number were all in white boxes lined up on the yellow field. And that was just the information at the very top portion of the window. One could scroll down at all of the information, every container, for seemingly days. Container number, cargo type, both port codes, U/B, Dec, status. All columns with endless numbers and letters underneath them.

"How can I tell who sent what to whom off of this, Glen?"

"That would take some investigating, sir. There has be over a thousand containers on this manifest."

"More like fifteen hundred. And even if we found the container or containers I'm curious about, who is to say that what is inside is what is listed? Right?"

"Sort of. Theoretically all containers are inspected and have a seal on them."

"Yeah well I know for a fact that they aren't all inspected on the shipping side of this equation. Are they inspected on this end?"

"Not unless they are suspicious. I see warrants for containers all of the time. But, no offense, you seem to be fishing."

"I know what is in at least one of those containers. I just don't know which. Can you look into this? Give me a list of the companies that shipped the containers, how many, and who they shipped it to?"

"I'm kinda busy, here officer."

"Detective. And I'll make it worth your effort. Can you do it?"

"It's not coming in until the 20th. How long do I have?"

"As quick as you can. The sooner I get it, the more worth your effort it will be. Do we have an understanding?"

Glen smiled. His entrepreneurial spirit had been kindled. "I think we do detective."

There were more things that I wanted to do in my allotted two hours. Find Slopes. Find some lunch. But I didn't have the time. Other than getting Glen on the case, I went through an old cell phone bill I had collected from the South Boston Post Office to determine the phone number of the informant that I had met at Starbucks in Backbay near Copley. He had proven very helpful thus far. I wanted to thank him and see if he had any other bits of useful information. Like maybe if he found out more information about the shipment that could help me isolate the container or containers. Maybe he knew where Sean Teague was. But I would never find out. The number was disconnected. Something told me it wasn't because he had failed to pay his bill.

50

LUCKILY IT WASN'T OUR WEEKEND TO PULL OVERTIME. I had only been back working with Hobbs for one day and I already needed the break. And some space. I heard nothing but the third degree on Friday when he picked me up where he had dropped me off at the Seaport Hotel. I didn't share any information about my 'lunch date', nor did he share any information about how he had spent the time. Suffice to say that in terms of our mutual caseload, about as much got accomplished at the end of the shift as in the beginning of it.

Saturday was spent scouring Southie for Slopes or any of the Winter Hill crew. I combed the streets all day. I went to the abandoned warehouse on Washington. It was under construction, nobody other than some Shawmut workers were in or around the building. So I continued to scour, turning over every rock, questioning every kid that was playing stickball in the streets or was in the process of mischief until they spotted me. They all knew the drill. They all knew me, and they knew who Slopes was and what he was capable of. If they had any information, they knew to keep it to themselves.

I hit every seedy dive bar in my neighborhood that night. And there are many. Too many to hit in one night, so I concentrated on the non-gentrified watering holes. Like Croke Park, Whitey's old hangout. The Corner Pub. The Blackhorn. The L Street Tavern. And my actual hang out, Murphy's Law.

I questioned no one. I just drank and listened. I did learn something from my time in Ireland. People came over to catch up. Find out how I was doing since the fire. Where I had been. Whether I was going to rebuild. Only one guy that I knew well from Murphy's had the balls to ask me what they all really wanted to ask me, which was — who did I piss off bad enough to warrant being burned out and about a thousand bullet casings out in front of the fire on the street? Like they didn't know.

258

Slopes was laying low. Nobody was talking about him. I didn't recognize anyone from his crew in any of the dives. Except The L. Of course it was the last place I had hit for the night. It was the last place that I would think to look for a mob guy. The L Street Tavern was one of the bars *Good Will Hunting* was filmed in. Pictures of Matt and Ben and Robin were everywhere. The place was cheap and divey, but in a hipster kind of way. The new folks in the area who were gentrifying the neighborhood love it because of the recent history and prices. Tourists love it like they love Cheers.

Of course I was half-buzzed by the time I saw him. Shey Brenner. Mindless kid who was way down on the Winter Hill hierarchy. An idiot who was faded in the back. Swaying like a Weeble. He weebled, he wobbled, but he wouldn't fall down. He was yelling at one of the many TVs while the Red Sox killed the Mariners. Nobody had the heart to tell him that it was a west-coast day game and NESN was replaying it 'in two'.

I waited until he stumbled his way outside in front of the bar for a smoke to corner him.

"Shey Fuckin' Brenner! Slummin' with the yuppies and tourists tonight, huh chief?"

His eyes tried to focus. His mind tried to focus. Then bingo. "Deni? Tha fuck are you doin' down here?" If you think my Boston accent is bad — try this drunken idiot's on for size. If I wasn't from Southie I wouldn't have understood him.

"Lookin' for the big kid. Where you been, Shey?"

"I been around. Everyone wants to know where you been though."

"I've been around too."

"Why you lookin' for me?"

"I wanna know if you were the one who peppered my house and burned it?" I helped him over to the 8th Street side of the bar. Leaned him up against the wall so he wouldn't fall, though he probably wouldn't. He might have been in his early twenties, but he had been drinking for years longer than he was legally allowed to.

"Don't start shit again, Deni. You know tha drill down here. Live and let live. Until you don't."

"So it was you? Are you still lookin' for me? I'm right here."

"If it was the crew, you know they wouldn't put me on somethin' that big." He lit another cigarette off of the first. Only he lit the filter instead.

"So who was it?"

"No fuckin' clue. Lemme buy ya a beer. Stop askin' stupid questions."

"I help you out Shey, and you help me out. It's deal time."

"Yeah you don't seem to be helpin' out the neighborhood so much these days. You tryin' ta make captain or some shit?"

"I'm done as a cop. But big shit is coming down. And it's comin' your way. You don't have many beers left, Shey. It's gonna be Walpole for you. So whattaya gonna do?"

"Are you fuckin' with me?"

"Nope. Why would I fuck with you Shey? You burn down my house? Fuck it, I got my insurance. Like you said — 'Live and let live'."

"What do you want from me?"

"The guns."

"Fuck you, Deni. You don't even know what you're askin'." He lit a third cigarette properly this time.

"I know things are about to get real bad for Sean and the crew. Raids. Details. I don't give a shit about my house, Shey. I'll rebuild. But my tenants were killed. Murdered. Those murders are still on the books. Investigation is still open. I start pointing the finger at you guys?"

"Everybody already knows who did it. But nobody can prove it."

"You boys peppered the house from the middle of the fuckin' street, Shey. People saw you assholes. Those guns that you used were the same ones from New Hampshire. Same ones that went out of Maynard Ballistics lab as quick as they went in. Same types that are on their way over here from Ireland right now."

"Nobody is talkin'."

"Not yet. But like I said, shit is going down. You have time to get out."

"And do what Deni? Last I checked the fire department ain't hirin'."

"You only set fires anyway. You have a choice here fuck-tard. You can spend the rest of your life in Walpole, or you can be a free man."

"You can't make deals anyways. You ain't a cop anymore you said."

"Two weeks left. Little under. I file you as a CI, give you immunity and you skate."

"Fuck that. I ain't no rat. You know that."

"Rats are survivors. You wanna survive? All I want to know about are the guns. I already know when they are comin' in. I just want a container number."

"Fuck that. We got a system. We're straight. It's a lock. 'Sides. I don't know what you're talkin' about."

"That's what you're goin' with? Down with the ship?"

"Whatever you say, Deni. We done?" He flicked his butt onto the empty 8th Street.

"I guess so. You realize I'm gonna make you pay right? This was a one time offer. All of those deaths. Danny Mick, his sister, Breen, my tenants .... You had a chance to make it right, but you wanna play games. So now I'm gonna make you pay. You and the whole crew."

"My advice for you Deni is to disappear. Go back to wherever you was hidin'. People who fuck with Slopes tend to have accidents. You get the bagpipes and a parade if you're a former cop who has an untimely demise?"

I wanted to kill him right then and there. With my bare hands. He had more than my Irish up. The motherfucker was egging me on. He knew that I knew what he had done and was going to do. And he was basically laughing in my face. Killing him didn't get me the

260

result I needed. Killing him wouldn't put Sean Teague or his crew in a panic. Wouldn't make them come out of hiding and make a mistake. I wanted Slopes to know that I knew that the guns were coming into Boston Harbor, and that I knew when. I wanted him to think that he was fucked. Not delivering those weapons meant certain death. The syndicates would see to it. Getting caught with them was a slower and more painful death. Prison and out of business, then the Irish would get to him on the inside.

"I don't think I'll have to worry about it. Go back in and have your beer. By the way the Sox win 9-0 asshole." I wondered if he would ever know how I knew that, and what else I possibly knew.

51

SEPTEMBER 11, 2004 WAS UPON US. CNN ran an all-day remembrance. All 2,749 names of the deceased from the towers were read aloud at Ground Zero. The lights of the Empire State Building were extinguished at 9:11 PM. George W. Bush made his appearances and speeches. Iraqi interim Prime Minister Ayad Allawi also issued a statement of condolence not only for the victims of the September 11 attacks but also for all victims of terrorism.

"Three years ago, the hand of terrorism claimed the lives of thousands of innocent people at the World Trade Center in New York," Allawi said. "Terrorism did not stop at its mean act but further wreaked havoc in several spots of the world, with no discrimination between one religion and another and one people and another."

US Embassy officials all over the world also laid wreaths in honor of the global victims of the attacks. British citizens were conducting business in both New York and Washington, DC. The Irish. The Swedish. While most of the devastation was suffered by Americans, on American Soil, the world over joined us in our continued mourning.

But while Americans paused to remember fallen loved ones and where they were when the towers fell, life went on. Businesses were open. American Airlines still had flights by the thousands taking off and landing. The Red Sox still had a game at Safeco Field, albeit with a different result than games one and two of the three-game stretch.

I had been out all night trying to learn more about the logistics of the container or containers that were coming off of The Annika Mærsk. They were going to need more than an *Econoline* van to move them out of Boston Harbor. Shey was of no help. It took until the wee hours of the morning to come to that truth. Then the drive back up to New Hampshire. I took a very circuitous route to Wayland to ensure that I wasn't being followed. Shey was drunk, but not too drunk to make a phone call.

My morning start was a late one. Meaning it was late afternoon by the time that I got my ass out of bed. Neither Ryan or Angie said a word about the time when I descended the stairs.

"Good Afternoon" didn't even seem sarcastic. I wondered how many September elevenths would go by before people went back to being who they really were the rest of the days of the year save for Christmas.

Angie said that she had errands to run. A grocery run was one such errand. She asked me if there was anything in particular that I wanted. She also said that she would be doing some cleaning, asked if there was any laundry that I needed done. Sweet woman. Although this was a new-age couple, she still seemed to take on the more domestic roles. I wondered if Ryan mowed the lawn and the like, or if he got out of his chores because of his workload. Ryan was in his office, presumably tackling his pile of work, when my cell phone rang. It was Glen from MASS PORT.

"Working the weekend Glen?"

"When else was I going to get this project of yours done?"

"It's done? Pissah. What'd you find?"

"I don't know. Probably nothing. But I put together a list of businesses sending and receiving cargo on The Annika Mærsk."

"That was fast."

"You said you would make it worth my effort. I worked through the night after my shift and all weekend so far to get it done. Do you have a fax number I can send it to?"

"Hold on." I went into Ryan's office. "Hey Ry, do you have a fax machine here?" He was sitting behind his desk doing something when I interrupted him.

"Of course." Ryan gave me the fax number in the 603 area code.

"Thanks. Glen? You still there?"

"Waiting."

I repeated the number and he said that he was punching in the number on his fax machine as we spoke. "You should have it in a few minutes. It's six pages, so it might take a second."

"Thanks Glen. Lemme know if you come up with anything else. I'll take care of you Monday. Tuesday at the latest."

"What was that about, if you don't mind me asking," Ryan said after I flipped my cell closed.

"Guy at MASS PORT is faxing over a list of the parties that are shipping and receiving on the incoming freighter. I'm hoping that I can narrow down the search to specific containers by picking out the sender or receiver."

The fax machine was making its hums and noises, indicating that it was deciphering the incoming message in order to spit it out onto paper.

263

"Deni, do you think that they are going to be stupid enough to list Sinn Féin or Winter Hill on the shipping manifest? These people have been conducting illegal business for generations. They haven't been doing business this long because they make those kinds of stupid mistakes."

"Well according to Glen they have to put something down on the manifest. They have this computer system called the AMS, or something like — "

" — yeah I know. I get it. Unless they just get the cargo on the freighter without the paperwork. Or have a legitimate business list the items they mean to ship then switch the cargo before the ship takes off. Or have diplomatic seals on it."

"I didn't take you for a glass is half-empty kinda guy. From what I understood, not having paperwork or the seal on the cargo raises more eyebrows than just providing false information. They can't switch it without breaking the seal. And they can't have a diplomatic seal unless a government official is on the receiving end. They aren't sending to the embassy, cuz the US Embassy in Ireland is aware of what's going on. So my guess is that at least one of the entities on that list coming out of the machine right now is phony. I have to give the guy money, so we might as well look it over."

"I'm on board. But I hope that you aren't spending too much money, because I think that you are going to pay this guy for nothing."

The facsimile was finished. The beep at the end announced the fact. We each took three pages of the list of shippers and receivers. Ryan seemed to scan through his three sheets very quickly at his desk. Lawyers have the ability to take in large quantities of information very quickly. They have to read through piles of legal documents and statements of various types on a daily basis. Statutes and briefs which are never brief. Speed reading comes with the job description.

I was taking longer sitting comfortably with my feet propped up in the corner of his office. Much longer. I scanned each name, let it rattle around my skull. When nothing in that name rang a bell, I moved on to the next. It took me an hour to go through my three sheets. I think Ryan went back to whatever he was doing before I stormed into his office asking for his fax number. I came up with nothing.

"Lets switch," I said. Ryan just shrugged, handed me his list after I made the journey from my seat to him. I could see by the look in his eyes that he thought this was a big waste of our time. Definitely his. "I don't want to hear it. You might have missed somethin', or I might have," I said. "You went through your list pretty quick. You probably did miss somethin'."

"Because I can read fast? You think I missed something because I can read fast?"

"No. I think you might have missed somethin' because you skimmed it lookin' for somethin' obvious. You didn't appear to be puttin' any thought to it. Like you said, they haven't been able to get away with this for as long as they have by bein' obvious."

We reviewed each of the other's list. I returned to my chair, settled in for another lengthy and fruitless search. Halfway down the second page, about thirty minutes later, about when I started to lose hope, I saw it.

"P. O'Neill Inc! What did I tell ya?" I shouted it across the office.

Ryan was already finished reviewing my list and was onto something else. He looked over at me stunned as my shout had scared the shit out of him.

"You found something?"

"P. O'Neill Inc. That's it. That's them. To and from."

"I must have missed something."

"You sure did. You missed it big time."

"Enough Deni. Who works for whom here? I missed it because I don't understand how P. O'Neill has anything to do with our guns."

"The IRA, Irish Republican Army, they always use the name P. O'Neill on every thing. They have for the past 40 years. Public Statements, Public Houses, you name it. I'm not sure who this guy was or is, but they use the name for everything. Some people think that it's the nick name of the committee of seven on the Army Council. Whatever the case may be, we got 'em."

"So you think that they are moving guns under a dummy company that has the same name as the one they use as a signature for all of their misdeeds?"

"They don't see them as misdeeds, Ry. They see it as a means to an end. They avoid prosecuting illegal acts if they are done in the name of the Republic, for the good of Ireland."

"Isn't it a little obvious?"

"You're a lawyer and you missed it."

"Let me see that list, would you?"

I handed him the list. The contact information for P. O'Neill Inc. on both sides of the pond was listed. +353 1 803 2215 for Ireland. 617-703-2215 for Boston.

"Hmm," Ryan said while rubbing his chin.

"What?"

"Look at the cargo container number." He handed the paper back to me.

"PONU0322155. So What?"

"Do you know anything about international cargo shipments, Deni?"

"I went to the Dublin Port and Boston Harbor. I know about as much as what I've told you. What are you getting at?"

"I happen to know a decent amount because I had to defend a client once that was in business as an importer-exporter." He took back the piece of paper and motioned me over to his desk.

"Good for you, what's the point?"

265

He ignored the jab and went into his explanation. "The first part — 'PON' is the owner code. Makes sense. P. O'Neill .... PON? Then the next letter is the category identifier. In this case 'U'. Which means that it's a 40 ft. container instead of a reefer or trailer. Then the next six letters are the serial number, '032215'. The last '5' is just a check digit. Look at the serial number and then look at the two phone numbers."

Ryan slid the paper on his desk to his right, giving me a better view.

"Both phone numbers have the last six digits of 03-2215, which matches the cargo container serial number," I said.

"They wanted to make it idiot-proof. But that isn't the best part."

"That's pretty fuckin' good, Ry. What's the best part?"

"Do you recognize the Boston phone number? It's a cell number. Who's cell is that?"

My eyes lit up like a Christmas tree. I looked at Ryan who was already nodding, already steps ahead of where I was. We both said the name at the same time.

"Walter Glibczieck."

52

THERE WAS AN EMERGENCY, ALL-STAFF MEETING Monday morning at Grantes, Wells & Associates. When a law firm has an emergency, all-staff meeting it sounds like there was a great many people, hunkered down in a room for serious business. While there were only four people in the small conference room, the discussion was serious. Jacob Grantes, Ryan Wells were the fountainheads, and Angie Wells and I as associates were all hunkered down to discuss recent revelations.

I had taken a personal day, calling Troop H and leaving Lieutenant Titanitaukis a message. He called back later which I let go to voicemail. He called again, which I also didn't pick up. Neither of the messages were happy in nature or tone. He wanted me to know that calling out for the remainder of my days would jeopardize the money in my pension account. I didn't see how that was possible but I wasn't going to call him back to argue the point either. Nor did I choose to speak with Hobbs when he called and left three messages.

Ryan filled in JG on what was going on with the investigation, and how it related to Breen. They had received a $75,000 retainer for a defense that he no longer needed, and another retainer for a forthcoming civil suit once we proved collusion. Finding the weapons in container number PONU0322155 was a key piece in that case. The rest of the information was given to JG in waves as he walked around the conference room table digesting the information. I would fill in some of the gaps as I saw fit, Angie was silent as she took the minutes.

"So let me see if I have this right," JG said when we completed the briefing. "The federal prosecutor, Walter Glibczieck, is in bed with either Sinn Féin, the IRA, the Winter Hill organized crime network including the enterprise on the compound here in New Hampshire, or all of the above? The missing guns out of the Maynard Ballistics Lab? All him?"

"*All* him?" I looked around the table. JG sat down in the only remaining empty chair. "I don't know for sure if it is all him, but he has to be involved."

"Walk me through it."

Ryan spoke up. "The Irish move guns into the United States as one of the many illegal activities the army conducts with their secret cells. That is fact. They do this in order to supply their countless enterprises like the Winter Hill crew and Men in the Mountains with hardware and salable merchandise for all of their enterprises west. Proceeds from the drugs and other illegal activities fund the various groups and are used to buy guns which feeds the IRA with money which then feeds the Sinn Féin political party. And the cycle continues."

"How do we know that to be fact, Ryan?" JG was playing devil's advocate.

"That cargo container ends up in the hands of …. what's his name, Deni?"

"Sean Teague, or better known as Slopes."

"Right. So when they get busted with those weapons, that proves that connection. As you know, parties who are participants in an illegal activity have an implied collusion under Title — "

" — yes, Ryan. I know the law. But that only proves the IRA — Winter Hill connection."

"JG, when the ATF goes in for the kill, grabs up all the weapons and remaining evidence, how much do you want to bet that those weapons will match the type that were stored in Maynard and New Hampshire? The weapons seized from the New Hampshire compound have already been proven to be the same as those missing from the Maynard Lab, from Breen. Thus proving the IRA — Winter Hill — New Hampshire connections."

"All of the members of the IRA secret cells are called Volunteers. They lead a meager existence in order to send money up the chain, " I said.

"Good. Go on," JG said. He was thoroughly engrossed and writing on his yellow legal pad.

"Deni going over to the other side of the pond created quite a stir, everyone and anyone that could possibly testify against this …. "

My turn again. "Finn Rourke …. "

"Rourke …. is now dead. And there is really nothing we can do about them anyway, that is for a federal prosecutor to sort out. They would need to make a deal with Ireland for extradition. Which Walter won't do if he is involved."

"Which you still haven't proven, guys. Why would the federal prosecutor send Deni over there to solve the case if he was involved in the enterprise? That's counterproductive."

Ryan had not yet told JG how we connected him to the weapons distribution, only that he was connected. He slid the list from the fax machine over to JG, along with an itemized phone log for both his cell and his office phone compliments of Angie. He then walked him through the connection that he had made the day prior.

" .... and as far as sending Deni over there? We think to kill him. They tried. He sent Deni right into the hands of the number one and number two Volunteers and when they failed they were killed." Ryan slid The Guardian newspaper that I had given to him across the table.

"Wow. This is unbelievable." JG was shaking his head, trying to make room in there I guess.

"So what do we do?" I asked the room, but really I wanted to JG to say it. Ryan, Angie and I had discussed it at length in his home office on Sunday.

"We are not prosecutors. We are defense attorneys. We don't help the prosecution. But we need this container seized in order to prove conspiracy and collusion, which gets us a prima facie civil case for our deceased client Breen." He stood back up and paced around the small lunchroom/conference room. He paused to think, I broke the silence.

"Which means we need to out Walter. When what I really want to do is kill him."

"You can't kill him Deni," JG said.

"Obviously. So then what do we do?"

"We get the ATF involved."

"We don't know how deep this goes," I said. "What if we report it to someone who is working with Walter?"

"There has to be a record of people who he has worked with in past cases. We *don't* notify any of those people. We go around his inner circle."

"Great. So how do we find that information out without tipping him off that we are snooping around?"

The two attorneys looked at each other, knowing the answer. But Ryan answered me. "All court filings, even federal court, are a matter of public record. As an attorney, I can have that expedited through a clerk. Within a couple of days we can have transcripts of his last few federal cases with regard to gun trafficking in the area. We make a thorough list of all names in those cases and avoid them like the plague. Then we set up a meeting with anybody but those people from the ATF."

"All this goes down on the twentieth, don't forget," I said. Today is the thirteenth, so that leaves us a week to get ready. At the most."

Everyone knew what we had to do when we left the table. Unfortunately I would have to do double duty. Go into the precinct each day to work with Hobbs, and try to find Slopes by night. Then drive all the way back up to New Hampshire to report any news and get some sleep. It wasn't so much the distance, it was the traffic. People from Wayland commuted into the city every day, they just usually did it by commuter train. It was going to be a long week.

JG and Ryan didn't have it any easier. They had other cases, other demands on their time, while trying to get copies of all transcripts and evidence to their office as quickly and quietly as possible. They would then have to go through all of the data and make comprehensive lists of all persons whom had crossed paths with Walter Glibczieck. I had a hunch that much of the tedious work was going to be passed onto Angie. But she was a sweetheart, she probably wouldn't mind it one bit. And she was also very efficient.

On the way out of the office after the meeting, a very attractive woman was waiting in the reception area of the law firm. She screamed money from a mile away. She wore a pink tennis shirt that had an alligator on it, a short white skirt that didn't have a single wrinkle nor did it leave much of her legs to the imagination. She had a tennis bracelet on as well that looked like it was worth more than my *Escalade*. Why they linked those bracelets to tennis I had no idea, who plays tennis with something that expensive? Whether she was about to play or not, she looked like she participated in a regular exercise regimen of some sort. Her thin body was hugged nicely by her expensive clothing.

I couldn't help but notice her, I doubt she could walk into any room and not be noticed. She was staring back at me as much I was staring at her. I wondered if I had met her before when I realized that JG was behind me, she was staring at him.

"Deni," JG said. "This is my wife Anna. Anna, this is Warren Dennihan. He is our new investigator."

"Pleasure," she said.

"Yeah. Pleasure is mine," I said. "Ya did okay for yourself there Guy." Everyone in the room laughed but I didn't know why. I thought I was stating the obvious. I wanted to be a lawyer, apparently they get all the girls.

She recovered from her demure giggle and said, "We both did okay for ourselves. Babe, are we still on for lunch at the club?" She looked at her husband and pointed to the clock on the wall of the reception area.

"I'm sorry, no. Something has come up and I am going to be busy. Raincheck?"

The look of disappointment on her face was short-lived. "No worries. I'll call Chamille and see if she is free."

I walked out of the law firm thinking about Rowena. She would not be categorized in the same class as Anna, but I didn't know why. She might not be as attractive or as rich, but she was a beautiful person. I was lucky to have known her.

53

ISOLATING AND VETTING COLLEAGUES AND WITNESSES for a federal prosecutor under the radar is tricky. And time consuming. The documents were requested and sent over in a cardboard file box that was the size of a case of copy paper. There are only about 90 federal prosecutors in the United States, each covering a specific district. So they have a lot of work and a great many contacts.

The documents weren't sent to Grantes, Wells & Associates. One phone call and the jig would be up. They were sent to the Wayland County Superior Courthouse, then brought over to the firm. An intern in the records department of the court was the daughter of country club friends of JG and Anna. She loaded the heavy documents into her newer VW *Beetle* and carted them over.

Names were then highlighted from over 3,000 pages of court documents. Those highlighted names were every witness, suspect, ATF agent, prosecutor, court clerk, DOJ employee, and judge that had been involved with Walter Glibczieck. The highlighted names were then compiled onto a list, categorized and prioritized in order to then move onto the next step. Vetting.

That is where I came in. When I wasn't combing the streets of Boston every day with Rick Hobbs the one trick pony, I was investigating the names that had been compiled onto lists. Angie would give me a fresh set of names every morning, I would do my best to get as much information as I could by the time I rolled back to the house late in the night. Looking up jackets, parking tickets, registrations, and such of the names and family members on the lists was difficult. Made more so by the fact that Hobbs was always attached at the hip. When I stayed late, he wanted to join me. I was running out of excuses to shake him.

All of it took time. Days.

Slopes and his crew had gone into hiding. Boston is my city. I know it like the back of my hand. They had obviously moved out of Southie. Other than my encounter with Shey,

271

nobody had seen or heard from the Winter Hill crew in what seemed like ages. Normally that would be a good thing, but I wanted to set up more permanent surveillance. In order to surveil, I needed to find them. Allston, BackBay, Bay Village, Beacon Hill, Brighton, Charlestown, Chinatown/Leather District, Dorchester, Downtown, East Boston, Fenway Kenmore, Hyde Park, Jamaica Plain, Mattapan, Mid Dorchester, Mission Hill, North End, Roslindale, Roxbury, South End (different from Southie), West End, and West Roxbury. Vanished. Nowhere to be found. Even Shey was gone. They had taken laying low to a new level.

On Friday the 17th of September, JG and Ryan decided that we had to set up a meeting with the ATF. With only three days left before The Annika Mærsk came floating in, the authorities needed to be notified. An eager young agent was chosen as he was not on any of the lists of names associated with Walter and he was vetted by me.

Jamaar Dennard made the trip from Philadelphia. He was working on another case when JG made the call. Grantes had chosen him because he was the hot hand, had made his bones the hard way, and conducted himself like he always had something to prove. He grew up an African-American from a single mother in the projects of Mattapan, so he knew Boston. Jamaar had to fight all odds at every age. At thirty-two he was still fighting to be taken seriously, fighting to get what was due. He took a train from Phili to Boston, then the purple train up to Wayland where I picked him up in the *Escalade* and drove him to the firm.

"Thank you for making the trip Mr. Dennard," JG said.

"Jamaar. And you seemed to leave me little choice." All of us were there and pumping hands, making introductions. Angie had set an extra chair for him at the conference table, we made our way in to begin the meeting.

Once we were all seated, JG took the lead. "It may seem odd to you, Jamaar, that defense attorneys are contacting you with regard to an illegal gun shipment coming into Boston. But this situation is complicated and those weapons being seized are very important to a pending case that we have as well. It is in our mutual interest to see that this is dealt with swiftly and publicly."

"You said something about corruption in the ATF, the DOJ specifically in the Attorney General's office? I would ask that you provide proof of that before we proceed." Jamaar had either been educated or he had taught himself to lose the typical ebonic accent that is commonly found in Mattapan. His diction was overly perfect. He said "ask" instead of "axe" for example. "I made this trip on good faith, but I assure you that I cannot nor will not move forward without something more tangible."

"We will get to that. And it's one federal prosecutor for certain, not the Attorney General's office on the whole. But first I have a document which I would like you to sign. It clearly states that all of the information that you are about to receive is off-the-record,

272

confidential, and any admission to a crime or crimes will be granted immunity from prosecution." JG was taking the lead and being very lawyerly while he was protecting me.

Jamaar skimmed through the document and signed it. He too was a fast reader.

The next hour and a half was spent going over the entire case. We all took turns telling our portion of the events leading us to that very meeting. Jamaar would interject for points of clarity, questions or requesting some shred of proof to what he was hearing.

I spoke of the stolen van driven by Danny Mick that was pulled over on Storrow Drive. The confiscated weapons sent to the Maynard Lab for testing that were stolen allegedly by Walter or his associates, which we couldn't prove, but somehow made it out of the facility and into the hands of a group of men nestled in the White Mountains of New Hampshire. I told of how Danny Mick was killed in prison, his sister Roxy taken out with a staged overdose of the poison that plagued her for most of her life. Ryan told him the details about the Men in the Mountains, the manufacturing of drugs, and the trove of assault weapons originally from the Maynard facility, which Jamaar was already familiar with. How those weapons had matched the type if not the exact weapons from Danny Mick pullover. How his client, Breen, was one of those men and who was also killed in prison. I told of my trip to Ireland after being burned from my home at the request of the federal prosecutor, Walter Glibczieck. How my tenants were burned alive. Of how Walter had sent me into the arms of Sinn Féin and the IRA for the only logical purpose of finishing what Slopes and company could not. How Rourke had ordered the killing of anyone and everyone that I had talked to over there, including an investigative reporter that had been looking into them with me. Agents and double agents. Moles. The phony seizures of weapons. Niall, the dock foreman. The entire story, everything, was laid out before him. Documents, newspapers, phone numbers, and other evidence was set on the table before him as the facts were divulged.

"The Annika Mærsk comes in on Monday. PONU0322155 is going to be a forty-foot cargo container filled with assault weapons that will wreak havoc on not only Boston, but cities all over the US," I said, finishing my portion.

"I'm going to need time to look into this," Jamaar said.

"You don't have time. We are into double-digit murders on this and it will get much worse once those weapons are distributed. Walter was handling this, but as we have pointed out, he is complicit in how they have gotten away with this for as long as they have," Ryan said.

"My boss will need to verify — "

" — we came to you because there are very few people who can be trusted. We checked you out. You need to act," JG interrupted before Jamaar could finish.

"Why didn't you come to me with this sooner?"

273

"Because this story has a lot of twists and turns. It's fantastic. Without proof, you wouldn't have even gotten on the train," JG said.

"I'm going to need a team down there on Boston Harbor. I have to get clearance to move a team. That could take days."

"Do what you have to do, Jamaar. But keep in mind that they have moles everywhere. A leak and this all goes sideways. And you don't have days," Ryan was emphatic.

I added my two-cents. "And the Winter Hill crew is on lock-down. You won't see them coming until they pick up the goods. A tip-off and they could stay hidden."

Jamaar scratched his chin. "So we sit on the container until they show up to empty it? They could wait days, weeks to empty it."

"They won't," I said. "They need to get these things off the pier and in distribution. Especially since everything that has happened. But I say we let them do all the work."

"I don't follow."

"You will. We just need some help."

"*We* Mr. Dennihan? Thank you for your offer but we will take it from here."

"All that I have been through with this and you are going to shut me out?"

"It's a jurisdictional issue now. As well as one of liability. I can't have an outgoing Mass State Trooper getting killed during an ATF raid. My ass would be in a sling," Jamaar said.

"I'm gonna be there one way or another. I'll sign a waiver or whatever."

Jamaar stared into his hands which rested on the table. "I hope I don't regret getting on that train."

54

THE NIGHT WAS BLACK. Not Jamaar black, blacker. There wasn't a moon on Monday night and the clouds were thick. It was only fifty-eight degrees and the wind was gusting. While the wind helped the balls leaving Fenway Park for the Orioles, it did nothing to help us in our reconnaissance. We couldn't see shit, nor could we hear anything more than wind, ocean, buoys and bumpers rattling off the docks.

We had been there all day. The Annika Mærsk docked very early in the morning, the cranes began unloading it a few hours after that. An ATF presence and I watched from a distance, using binoculars. They stayed hidden throughout the day shift on their post, into second shift, and I stayed in mine.

Glen was happy to have gotten paid handsomely for his previous help. So much so that he gave us information on how the docks are unloaded, how they sort through the containers in the hopes of getting more. With thousands of containers from that and other ships, there was an elaborate system as to how they are unloaded so the receivers can find their shipment. The cargo is unloaded by container type. The forty-foot containers that are not subsequently loaded onto large trucks for further transport are unloaded into a specific holding area. Within that area on Boston Harbor, the containers are then divided by alphabetized serial numbers. PONU0322155 was dropped by a Super-Post Panamax into the 'L-Q' storage area. We watched and waited all day but nobody came to open it.

Until that night. The docks were closed after seven at night unless you were one of the unionized crew on second shift working the docks. The Big Dig had taught us that unions can be bought. Somebody was paid to let the white International *Workstar* truck through the gate. They were nice enough to use a white truck. Had it been a darker model we might not have been able to see it as well in the darkest of nights. A horde of men came out of the back when the two men from the cab opened it. The back of the truck was parked but a few feet from the double-doors of cargo container.

"He we go boys," someone from the ATF said over the radio. We all had earpieces so the transmitters wouldn't make noise, but with the wind it wouldn't have mattered if we were shouting into the radios and the volume was turned up to ten.

"Let them load it like we planned," I said over the line. "We will just take the truck once it's loaded, let them do all the work."

"Roger" came over the radio, one by one.

The horde of men in the enclosed back of the truck was actually eight men. Ten total. They snapped the thin, metal seal off the container and began to load the *Workstar*. Large wooden crates were hoisted from the cargo container into the truck systematically. They appeared to have a rhythm, like they had executed the task before. The twenty-foot bed of the truck was nowhere near the length or height of the cargo container. From my angle I could not see if another trip was going to be necessary, or if the forty-foot shipment container had been filled in the first place.

It took almost an hour for the ten men to load the truck. When they were finished, the double-doors of the cargo container were shut and latched. Even with the wind, we could hear the metal-on-metal.

"Now," came over the radio. Then, "Deni stay put."

Fuck, I thought to myself. I may have even said it out loud.

From their posts came more than a dozen ATF agents as flood lights were turned on. My eyes were blinded as they had become accustomed to the pitch black. Someone over a bullhorn announced that they were from the ATF and for everyone to put up their hands. I blocked the blinding light with my left hand, looking away. I heard gunfire. And more shouting. And screaming. People were being shot, I hoped it was the bad-guys from the Winter Hill crew.

As I looked in the opposite direction, away from the blinding light, hidden at my post. I saw movement in the darkness twenty yards behind us. Then more movement. It wasn't one person, there were several.

My mind raced as instincts took over. I ducked down and yelled into the radio, "It's an ambush! Behind us!"

I moved around containers heading back to where Slopes's back up was moving in. More gunfire came from them. The ATF was caught in the middle. The detail from the truck and the backup were firing automatic weapons toward the middle. Shouts of "man down" and "I'm hit" were shouted over the radio into my earpiece. I continued to move back, trying to get behind the backup team. My Sig at the ready. I was thankful for my presence of mind to bring a step up from my 9 mm mandated Glock service weapon.

As I rounded the corner of one container, a man with an Israeli Tavor Tar-21 turned toward me. Two shots landed on him. One through his neck, one through his left cheek on his face. Blood spouted as he fell, firing dozens of rounds into the air as the gas-operated rotating bolt was activated by the reflexive finger on the trigger. When the man fell, the rifle was dislodged from his hand. I moved toward him, my eyes oscillating between the wounded man and my surroundings. I thought of picking up the weapon, as it would have been a marked upgrade, but decided against it so not to be confused as one of them by the ATF.

He had virtually no pulse. Blood covered my left hand as I pulled my fingers from his carotid. No idea how many there were. I popped my head to my right, looking to see if another assassin was lurking around the next container. None. I stood crouched, thinking, listening.

A sound of gravel behind me. How I heard it over the wind is a mystery. I turned in time to see another man backing up slowly. He didn't see me, as his back was to me, his weapon aimed in the other direction. Slowly he backed toward me. I returned my Sig to its holster, stood up and with one swift motion braced the rifle toward the ground with my left hand and choked him with my right arm. His Adam's apple was pressed against my right antecubital fossa, or elbow pit, my right hand clutching my left shoulder to choke him out. Pulling upward and arching my back, he had no leverage, his body weight adding more pressure to his throat and cutting off his oxygen. I continued to look around for more aggressors until he passed out.

Gunfire and screams near the truck could still be heard faintly over the wind, frantic yelling through my earpiece.

And voices behind me. I grabbed my gun from the holster, turned behind me. Two men running right at me. Six shots. Knees, thighs, and groin were hit between the two men. I dove behind a short crate as they fired back at me from the ground. After trading clips, I popped up and fired four more shots. They didn't return fire. Slowly moving toward them, gun trained, and looking through the pitch black night to determine if I was hunting or being hunted.

The two men were alive but hit and struggling. I kicked both of their Heckler & Koch G3A4s further away from them. I squatted to question them.

"How many of you?"

Neither answered me. They just stared at me as I looked down at them.

"Where's Slopes?"

Again they stared at me with pained looks, remaining silent.

"I'm right here."

I stood up but didn't recognize him in time. Slopes moved toward me. I raised my gun, but also not in time. It felt like a shotgun blast to my chest. It must have been instinctual, but I emptied my clip as I fell to the ground.

The rest comes in waves. It was difficult to see in the dark. I couldn't breath. Air, anything for air. The pain in my torso cannot be described. I lay there, eyes toward where Slopes was. He was gone. Still no air. Gun shots, somewhere in the distance. More screams. Can't move. Somebody crawling toward me. Out of bullets. Slopes. Gurgling and bleeding. Face and chest covered in blood. Then total darkness.

55

THE ENTIRE FRONT PAGE OF BOTH THE HERALD AND THE GLOBE were dedicated to the colossal event. The city had dubbed it the 'Boston Harbor Bust'. The headlines were many, several writers with their various takes on the many angles.

Irish Mob Forever Silenced. The Department of Alcohol, Tobacco & Firearms have been long collaborating with Boston Police following a lead about a major arms shipment.

Federal Prosecutor Arrested In Scarsdale Home. The article went on to say that he had alleged ties to the recent political catastrophe in Maynard, and in the mountains of Wayland County New Hampshire.

IRA Has Not Yet Claimed Responsibility For Arms Shipment. Despite evidence and statements, the Irish Republican Army has refused to issue a statement regarding their involvement with the arsenal of assault weapons seized in Boston Harbor.

Organized Crime from New York, New Jersey and Providence Move In On Whitey's Old Turf. The Winter Hill Gang, named and successful since Whitey Bulger's days, has left an open market ripe for the picking. Other Area's crime syndicates have already staked their claim not twenty-four hours after the famed Boston Harbor Bust.

Will Whitey Come Out Of Hiding? The article was complete speculation that Whitey Bulger would come out of hiding to reclaim his thrown and his territory.

Sean Teague, A.K.A. Slopes, Shot And Killed. Famed leader of Boston's Irish Mafia, The Winter Hill Gang, was shot and killed during arrest. A mug shot from a previous arrest provided.

ATF Agent, Jamaar Dennard, Receives Commendations. Governor Mitt Romney and other officials will be holding a public news conference to recognize the ATF agent for his role in taking assault weapons off the streets.

Undercover State Trooper Shot During Boston Harbor Bust. *A* Massachusetts State Trooper out of Boston, who was working closely with the ATF, was shot during the apprehension of the suspects. He was in his final days as a detective, and is listed as in critical condition in an undisclosed hospital.

The famed Boston Harbor Bust concluded with 9 dead and 7 wounded, other articles went on to say. The mix of dead and wounded were on both sides of the skirmish. The seizure was considered a success, however, as an arsenal was taken out of distribution. HawkEngineering *MM-1 40 mm* revolver grenade launchers, Saab *AT4* rocket launchers, Russian *AN-94* and *RPG-7s*, *TAC-50*, McMillan tactical rifles, Heckler & Koch *G3A4s*, older Armalite *AR-18* assault rifles, and hundreds of cases of ammunition were reported to have been taken into custody. The Irish Republican Army could have started another army with the hardware shipped.

Other major news from around the country and the world were relegated to other pages, other sections. **Democrats Say GOP Playing to Terror Fears** was buried. Though world news did beat out local headlines in the sports section. **Europe Roars to Another Ryder Win** beat out the story that although the Orioles had beaten the Red Sox at Fenway Monday night, at 89-60 Red Sox Nation would likely claim the Wild Card Spot.

As usual, the newspapers had some of the facts wrong. I was shot in the chest, that was true. The Tar-21 felt like a shotgun blast to the chest because of the number of rounds that hit me. But I had been wearing a Kevlar vest at Jamaar's insistence, so I had more broken ribs but thankfully nothing had gotten through. And just as thankfully the recoil from the automatic weapon didn't pull the barrel up far enough, or quickly enough to send a dozen rounds into my face. I had lost consciousness because I had hit my head on the side of a container when I had fallen backward after being shot. The bust was late and the papers wanted to get the stories in before the competing rag covered it first. So while I was being treated, I was not in critical care. In fact I was released before noon on Tuesday, broken ribs and concussion-like symptoms not withstanding.

In the cab from Beth Israel to Troop H, my phone rang. That wasn't a big deal, since the bust which occurred just hours prior, my phone had been ringing incessantly. Everyone in Boston wanted a word from me. But the number struck me. It was a longer sequence starting with +353.

"Yeah."

"You've gone an made yerself famous now, haven't ye lad?"

I couldn't believe my ears. "I never thought I would hear from you again. How did you find me?"

"T'wasn't difficult. Especially since you've made quite the splash. I wanted to thank you for the gift?"

"What gift?"

"Had to be you that left it."

"How do you figure?"

"I'm an investigative reporter, it's my job to figure. I didn't reckon you were the true Catholic."

"I'm not Row. But I hoped it would help. How are you doin'? You sound different."

"Aye. And I believe that it did help. They say I'll live. What will you do now that you're no longer a Bobby?"

"I've got work lined up. What are you gonna do? Still gonna dress up like a whore?"

"I might. Someone's gotta do it."

"Just take care of yourself, Row. I'm glad you made it, but you can't cheat death more than once."

There was a long pause, music was playing the background. I couldn't tell what it was but it didn't sound like Bono.

"Is that the new U2 album, Row?"

"Naw. Tears for Fears. *Everybody Loves A Happy Ending.*"

"We both know that it's almost never a happy ending."

"Don't carry a worry about me, Deni. Sometimes life is an American Story."

EPILOGUE

NOBODY WOULD HAVE NORMALLY GIVEN TWO SHITS about Tuesday, September 21st being my last day. But when I arrived to turn in my badge and Glock, my desk was swarming with people. Not because I was now semi-famous or had gone out in blaze of glory or some other such nonsense. Boston isn't as big as New York City, but it is a city nonetheless. Famous one day and a nameless loser douche the next. The reason why I was popular was because Jamaar had used his newly found influence to send me a row of tickets to the Red Sox game Tuesday night. He sent them to Tits for me and whomever I wanted to take with me as part thank you for standing by the 'working with Boston Police' story. Part gift for me on the job well done and part congrats on getting the fuck out of civil service. Jamaar had called me on my cell while I was on it with Row. He wanted to make sure that I went to claim them. Why I listened to that message instead of the countless other messages left by the countless other people wanting to hear my side of things is beyond me, but I did. The people in the precinct were loitering around my desk waiting for me and wanting a seat to the game.

In a stadium that seats only 35,000 people, Red Sox tickets are nearly impossible to come by. They sell out every game although they never win when it counts. But whether a good season, when we just miss the ALCS; or a bad one, when the lowly Blue Jays and Orioles have better records, you can't get a seat.

I moved around slowly with my broken ribs and fuzzy brain, clearing out my desk while trying to clear out my twenty-five new best friends. All things considered I was in a great mood. I was no longer going to be a political pawn. I had ended my career as a Statie with a bang. Row was alive and well for the moment. And I was about to tell Hobbs he could go fuck himself.

Hobbs approached my desk, hand out. Whether we wanted a shake or a ticket I have no idea. But he got neither. Not from me anyway.

"Listen Hobbs, I want you to take this very personally when I tell you to kick rocks. Okay?"

"Why are you always an asshole? I just wanted to say good luck."

"I want to say go fuck ya-self. I feel bad for your next partner. Do you know who it is yet?"

"Yeah. Sheed."

"A girl? Ugh. That poor woman."

From deep into the crowd around my desk I heard her say, "I know right?"

The crowd moved around me as I moved toward her. "Take two tickets, go have fun. I feel bad for ya. Tits has 'em."

People started clambering for their seats both physically and verbally as they followed me on to Lieutenant Titanitaukis' office. The door was open. I set my badge and 9 mm on his desk.

"Sheed gets two tickets. She is gonna need some fun after getting the horrible news."

"You have any other thoughts on who you would like to go?"

"Nope. I'm done. Give 'em to whomever you want."

"You're not going to go? After all of this?" He pointed to the newspapers on his desk.

"I don't want to hang out with any of these people."

"What do you have against them, Deni? You think you're better than them?"

"I just don't like them. I don't like politics, and I really don't like office politics. You got yourself out of this pretty clean, by the way. How'd you swing it?"

"I don't know what you mean."

"You and Walter were pretty tight. He's arrested and you aren't. Lemme guess, you're saving your ass by testifying against him."

"I'm not at liberty to say."

I shook my head, walking toward the door to his office. "And they let you keep the badge. I won't miss a fuckin' day of it." With that, I left Troop H as an employee forever.

Over the course of the next few months, more about case came to light in the press. Bringing the story back to the front of the minds of those that cared to know about it. Walter Glibczieck was responsible for the guns disappearing from the Maynard Ballistics Lab, just as we suspected. The FBI had jurisdiction and originally wanted both the Massachusetts and New Hampshire cases, but the ATF took control thanks to Walter. He made sure the ATF handled all of his cases as a federal prosecutor, as he had several agents in his pocket.

He was the person who organized which prison Daniel McKennie would go to, and the block he would be housed in. The inmates therein had carte blanche as to how he was to go away after being given a false 'rat' story. There were pictures of Walter confessing in court, the John Goodman look-alike on the front of every paper. But he would never be heard from again. Probably because he ratted on the Winter Hills to save his own ass, but that is pure conjecture.

Everybody knew what happened to Roxanne McKennie. She was a junkie. A junkie from Southie. It could never be proven and Walter didn't confess to it, so it was never solved. Her file is still sitting among the cold cases in Troop H.

Maddy went on to win her civil case, almost two years later. She wanted Walter to pay. She wanted the guards and inmates who were on Walter's arm to pay. Breen was her man. She learned how to be sentimental. There were a great many 0's to lose if she wasn't. Who ultimately paid the punitive damages was the state of New Hampshire. The department of corrections therein would never be the same.

She told on the stand that she had received a phone call saying that Liam Breen was requesting that she visit. When she saw the ATF hanging around, which turned out be Walter's cronies in the visitor's lounge, she fled in fear of being arrested herself. That was what had gotten Breen out of his cell and made vulnerable for his murder. Whether it was true or not, the proof was that Liam Breen was dead. Maddy left the area a very rich woman and was never heard from again.

The IRA didn't make any more or less headlines than usual that year in the United States. The occasional car bomb. An assassination attempt. De rigueur. Not until 2005 did they officially announce the end of their campaign. But that story had been told and heard before. The press release was signed by P. O'Neill.

But not Sinn Féin. They continue to be a strong political force in Ireland to this day.

Drunk one night I tried to call Director Humphrey at the embassy to inquire about what if anything happened on that side of the pond. He never returned my call. Nor did Rowena.

Everyone had moved on. So I did as well.

I went down to the game that Tuesday night after leaving the precinct, but I didn't sit in the stands with my so-called friends. I sat practically in the belly of Fenway Park, at Cask 'n Flagon. The bar sits on the corner of Landsdowne and Brookline. Anybody who has been to Boston or Fenway knows where it is. The owner owed me a favor or two. So I sat there that night, watched the Orioles lose 3-2. I was there on Sunday the 26th too, final home game of the regular season. We beat the shit out of the Evil Empire 11-4. I was there again when we swept the Angels, the only game of that series in Fenway, on October 3rd.

But on Sunday the 17th, when the Sox came back to win their first game of the series, 6-4 in twelve innings in game 4, it was fucking amazing. I sat there drinking Redbreast thinking we were out of it. Crying into my drink, though I had been used to it. This is it. Done. Then we weren't.

Then we won again. And then again on the 19th in the forty-eight degree rain. And one more time on the 20th to send the goddamned Yankees home for the year. Four in a row with their backs against the wall.

A flicker of hope. Sweeping the Cardinals, Schilling's bloody sock, and winning the World Series for the first time in 86 years confirmed why Bostonians believe even in their dying breath. When their heads tell them one thing, their hearts something else.

Past sins had been forgotten. Trading Babe. Penance was the curse of no Pennants. But the curse was lifted and sins forgiven. The slate was clean.

285

Although I never heard from her again, Row was right. Sometimes life is an American Story.

Scott Wellinger

CRASH

A NOVEL

CRASH

A warren dennihan novel

By Scott Wellinger

PROLOGUE

THE NIGHT HAD DRAWN DOWN like a blanket over the small New England town, tucked in the mountains of southern New Hampshire. A cloudless, late summer sky made the bright stars the only form of illumination, which were little more than pinholes of light off in a distant universe. The pine forest that shot up from the fertile ground gave off a rich perfume reminiscent of Christmas, which was less than half a year to come. Above the tree-line, the natural rock formation known as *The Old Man on the Mountain* was a slight, silhouetted backdrop bidding the tourists a final goodnight whilst he slept. The narrow, windy roads meandering through the hills below that watchful cliff north of Boston, Massachusetts, were fortified with guardrails and graveled pulloffs to accommodate the looky-loo tourist vehicles. The fall foliage leaf-peepers were still a month or so away, but the hiking and camping season was still in full swing. The heavy traffic from the visitors trying to get a last trip in before the arrival of colder nights, was nonexistent in the hours after dusk. The hikers, campers, and naturalists had long since ventured home for the night or abandoned their parked vehicles on one of the pulloffs on the side of the road, as they made camp somewhere in the darkened forest.

The *Old Man* was the sentry for several communities below his perch on the White Mountains; the county and township of Wayland, New Hampshire was by far the most affluent. The old and new money was drawn from the financial hub of Boston in the form of large salaries. The town flourished as the commuters preferred to spend their ample earnings in the sanctity and "tax-free" state of New Hampshire over the Metropolis of Boston which fed them to the South. Another form of income for Wayland was the tourism, but the affluent of the community was torn in that while the outsiders boosted the economy, they trampled over their turf. The people of money from Wayland did appreciate the financial relief from tourism, which was their dilemma in refraining from ousting their numerous intruders. The visitors should be felt yet not seen.

The winters were the most difficult for the citizens to avoid the onslaught of outsiders. The skiers would come from the flatlands to trample the towns and, in their opinion, the face of their great State. Throughout the rest of the year, they spent their time and income away from the flatlanders at the Wayland Country Club. Golf was just one activity taken in there, and in truth many claimed to play more often than they had a tee-time for. The sanctuary was more for camaraderie and companionship than the activities the club promoted. A place for the wealthy to rub elbows with others of their kind in the same area.

This particular night, those with money were keen to show off just how much they had and were willing to part with. The Gala and Charity event that was taking place in the pavilion was under way, all of the who's-who in place and opening wallets for the silent auction, though whom or what charity would be receiving these sums was anybody's guess. While the sprinklers were misting water over the lush back-nine of the manicured golf course, which could be seen out of the large windows, elegant gowns and tuxedos flattered the bodies of the occupants in the club. Live, light jazz music and the mumbled conversations of the local power couples mingling under the giant chandelier could be heard faintly in the distance, while the rest of the community went about their Saturday night. The well-to-do's had their evening festivities, freeing their assistants and staffers to have theirs.

Arelia Diaz had made her plans weeks prior, when she learned that she would have a rare night off. She was a live-in maid for one of the rich and beautiful, though she called herself a caretaker, and was looking forward to blowing off some built-up steam with a night of dancing with her girlfriends. The initial response from her friends at her invitation for a night out on the town was a jealous decline, until they too were informed that they would have the night off. Her friends in the area were also in the employ of other event attendees and would also have the night free from; babysitting, nannying, serving, cleaning, maintaining, cooking, or the myriad other tasks their employers were too important to perform. A night of dinner; gossiping over the comings and goings of their respective power families, and certainly dancing would be just the cure for the tedium that ailed them. Only one friend, Marina could not make it. She was told that she would have to take care of a child, though her employer didn't have any children.

Arelia was a mid-thirties Brazilian woman who had left her own family back in Recife. Other than her gaggle of female friends, she was alone in the United States. She had no spouse or children, which was the mainspring for many nights of tear-soaked cheeks and a saturated pillow. The oldest of four daughters, she saw limited opportunities in her native village and networked into an immigrant sub-community tucked into the American Northeast almost ten years prior. Alone but not alone, she was content in managing a dream household, though it was not her own.

Ms. Diaz did not consider herself to be what the Americans called a *cougar*, she was too young to be considered for the part, but she was going to be on the prowl this night. All women had needs, this was a rare opportunity, and she was going to make the most of it. She painted on a pair of the most expensive jeans she could afford, her ample bosom bursted out of the front of her new, sparkling, black-yet-shear blouse, exposing her black push-up bra, and donned a pair of high heels which lifted her four inches higher than her usual five-foot-three inch frame. With her raven hair done (in what was coincidentally called a Brazilian Blowout), and her makeup accentuating her big, beautiful brown eyes, she would be turning some heads. She still had what it took to bag any man she wanted, despite her lack of practice.

She would not be bringing anyone back to her suite at her employer's palatial home, this was not allowed, nor did she have any intention of staying with an interested gentleman. Her duties would resume bright and early in the morning. Her employers would likely be as moody as usual, as demanding as usual. Maybe they would even be a little hungover, though they would never in a million years admit that to the help. The agenda for the night would be dinner, *Forró* dancing, and a copious amount of flirting. Unfortunately the line would have to be drawn at flirting.

She was given an older, red, Honda *Civic* to use in her daily errands, which she was using while on her way downtown to meet her girlfriends. It was a small yet able car, in spite of the age, much like Arelia believed herself to be. She had plenty of life left, this was just a means to an end. A way to go back to Brazil with enough money saved to provide for a family she would make, and their family after she was gone.

Diaz was used to the car and all of the idiosyncrasies that came along with it. She loved the limited freedom that the car provided her, but she loved the stereo system the most. In the ten years of being the caretaker, she was never allowed to listen to her music loud enough to be heard by anyone in any part of the house. Nor was she allowed to use headphones as she was always on call. Always. Failure to hear, much less respond to a call from the main house would mean an immediate end to the life she had built here. Relegated to vehicular sonic therapy, she would blast her beats as loud as the car stereo and tiny speakers could muster.

She had the windows down, feeling the night air through her already blown locks of hair. The outside sounds were competing between the crickets, the sounds of the Country Club in the distance, and Arelia belting out the Portuguese lyrics over the loud music of her favorite band *Falamansa*. She was blissfully unaware that this would be her final concert.

As she rounded a sweeping blind turn on Wayland Country Club Road, the singing and car-dancing was immediately interrupted by the harsh LED, high-beam headlamps glaring into her eyes from seemingly nowhere, yet everywhere. She knew nothing of candlepower light measurements, but the retina-burning headlamps blinding her surely could have illuminated Fenway Park. Diaz could not see anything, much less navigate the rolling left turn. She could not see the lever protruding off of the steering column to flash her own high-beams at the offensive driver coming towards her. Could not see her bearings on the road. She was desperate to see a yellow line. A white one. Anything to pinpoint if she was in a lane. There were no vibrations from the warning grating on the side of the road, because there wasn't any grating on the side of the road. No reflectors, not that she would have been able to see anything being reflected in the already blinding light. She would have welcomed the grazing of a guardrail, just so she could sort out where she was. Everything was happening so fast. Brakes were unused. The stereo remained at full, deafening decibels. There was no time to turn it down. No time to think. No time to sweat. Was there somewhere she could pull off? But that question did not register in the time it took her to sail off the road.

The little-Civic-that-could missed the end of a guardrail, grabbed the bit of gravel just off of the pavement, bulleted her through the small pulloff. The car continued, severing a maple tree that was contemplating the changing leaf colors soon, continuing on to impact the base of a large rock formation. The car came to an immediate halt from the forty-plus miles per hour it was traveling just seconds prior. The rear of the car was the last to learn of the immediate stop being insisted upon by the fixed and rooted boulder. It had no choice but to follow the rest of the cars' lead and jetted into the air, rear tire spinning as it tried to continue beyond the mess. It failed.

The sound of the dance music halted, replaced by the sound of mangling of metal and the pulverizing of bone. The jagged metal sliced through flesh which added to the cacophony of horrific sounds. The macabre series of sounds lasted but a beat, but the devastation would be permanent.

Nothing would be continuing beyond the crash. Not the maple tree, not poor Arelia Diaz formerly of Recife, Brazil and more recently of Wayland, New Hampshire. Where her body existed in the cab, where she was car-dancing to her favorite band, singing as loud as her beautiful lungs could project, was a sick sculpture of metal, plastic, glass, rubber and human organs. The front of the car no longer existed. It was impossible to discern car from body, where the red paint from the Honda started, through all the blood, and the end of the former occupant. Her lifeless face rested, burning on part of the steaming engine; searing what was left of her beautiful features, her head and neck was now where the backseat should have been.

The offending headlights stared onto the wreckage for a time, determining what was already known. The lights crept slowly toward the destruction, attached to the black vehicle that was camouflaged by the dark of the night. They would abandon the devastation they had caused. The upbeat, accordion-based dance music and singing, followed by the horrifying reverberations of the crash were no more. The sounds were replaced by the ticking of the cooling, destroyed engine; the sizzling of flesh; the acceleration of the fleeing murderous vehicle. And crickets.

1

UGLY. THE IMAGE APPEARING back at him in the makeshift mirror was ugly. No other word could summarize the reflection and the atmosphere surrounding it; his every thought and emotion. The stainless steel metal above the all-in-one, Willoughby sink-toilet reflected pure ugliness. The image itself superimposed upon the backdrop of the institutional beige walls, the florescent lighting, the grey concrete floor.

Jacob Grantes had never been considered a hunk, nor an Adonis, he was not a physical specimen for which to lust. He had never been compared to the likes of George Clooney but he had been somewhat attractive, smart, confident. His six foot one inch frame, his square jaw, his sea-green eyes were some of the features that admirers had named when defending him as 'a catch'. The image that had once stared back at him, however, had disappeared, morphing into the figure that was reflected back at him in the polished steel. He was splashing water on his face, one push button at a time, but no matter how much water he applied, how much he washed, and how much he scrubbed his face, he could not cleanse the ugliness inside or out.

Grantes, inmate #437261, had been a guest at the Wayland County House of Corrections for the past six months, having been denied bail. He had not been in trouble with the law prior to the events leading him to this very moment, which made the denial pending trial quite unusual. Jacob was accustomed to living in a large home, family, and the picket fence; which made the current accommodations all the more intolerable. His cell was an eight by twelve foot concrete room with a double bunk, a small desk and a sink-toilet which he had to share with his celly. The space was tight and the nerves were stretched even tighter. Twenty hours per day were spent in this tiny space. Best friends could be put together in such a way and it would not take long to become mortal enemies. To make matters worse, the door to the cells lacked bars, it was a solid door, which allowed little air flow, with a narrow, horizontal slot at waist-high for food trays to be passed through, or to be handcuffed prior to exiting. The small, vertical window was convenient only for the Correctional Officers who had to execute head counts. This solid metal door was manufactured to make the most loud, God-awful clanks and noises when opened and closed. Studies had been done on this; millions spent, to craft an audible assault on inmates in an effort to make them uncomfortable, on edge, and contemplating the actions that had led them to their current place of residence.

The CO had awoken Grantes with a loud, mechanical unlatching, the grinding of metal as his cell door was sliding open at 5:30 AM.

"Grantes. You got 15 minutes to shit, shower 'n shave. Court. You'll get chow on the ride over."

"Yeah," he said between splashes of water on his face.

His grumbled reply indicated his malcontent, as this was to be a real shit day. It was to be a different kind of shit day, but a shit day all the same. All other days had the exact same schedule; filled with misery, meetings with so-called counselors, and a myriad of conversations with fellow inmates all of whom proclaim to be innocent or screwed by their lawyer. This day would be a shit day of a different color but a shade he knew quite well. Jacob Grantes had previously spent most of his adult life immersed in the muck and mire of the legal system, but on the other side of it. As an attorney, he knew exactly what this day would entail. The splashing of water on his face would make none of it go away.

"Jesus Christ, can you shut the fuck up? What time is it, bro?"

The shout came from a lump in the sheets, covering the body laying on the top bunk in his cell. Grantes's celly had a very low tolerance for anything beyond sleeping away his bid. This is known in prison as a bed-bid, and he is not the only one trying desperately to dream away the time.

"It's early. Sorry. I have court today. But it looks like you'll have the cell to yourself for the day."

"Goody." He said this without removing the covers which made him appear as though he was levitating five feet above a filthy concrete floor.

"You'll be able to shit in peace at least. I wish you'd spent a little time out of the cell so I could crap without an audience."

"You really gonna shower?"

"Yeah, I'm getting my shower bag ready now."

"That means that the door is gonna open and close a couple more times. Why you gonna shower anyways? Gonna be front and center with a jumpsuit and shackles anyway, clean ain't gonna matter."

"They'll let me change into a suit."

"Ha - you're funny. You're an idiot, but you're funny. Where are you gonna get a suit asshole?"

"I came here in a suit. My lawyer will have another one if they won't let me have that one out of property."

"You're gonna be in a holding tank, good luck getting one of the courthouse COs to let you change. Lazy assholes might have to do extra work," he said. "Whats today anyway?"

"February fif—"

"— the case moron. What part of the case is it?"

"Oh. Discovery and motions. It's when — "

" — I know what it is. Fifteen minutes tops bro. They're not lettin' you change into a fuckin' suit. Two bus rides and a day in the tank for fifteen minutes. Have fun."

"Shithouse lawyers."

It amazed him how much legal knowledge inmates had. Especially those with high recidivism. Grantes's cellmate had a very vast and intimate knowledge of the law from a certain prospective. He was, therefore, known throughout the prison as a good shithouse lawyer. His celly was of course aware that Jacob was a real lawyer, which only caused that many more passionate discussions.

"We'll see."

2

JACOB GRANTES AND HIS BEST FRIEND, Ryan Wells, had started a law practice together fifteen years prior. They had, over time, cornered the bustling criminal and legal market of nowhereville. The small southern New Hampshire town of Barstone, in Wayland County, was considered to be the other side of the tracks by the more affluent locals. Those elevated locals being the residents of the affluent town of Wayland, which was literally just across the tracks of the commuter rail into Boston, Massachusetts. The clichéd delineation was real. The constituents of Wayland Township made it quite clear to all of the inhabitants of Barstone, and really anywhere else for that matter but less vocally, that they were not welcome. The elected Sheriff of Wayland County, his office located in the town of Wayland by design, was well aware of what would happen if the petty crimes and riff-raff of Barstone were to bleed into the backyards of the wealthy community. And so the two towns within the same county coexisted; the town with the same name of the county reaped all the rewards, while the slums went about being the outcasts.

The law office of Grantes, Wells & Associates was strategically located in Barstone, on the border of the two towns. They needed the criminal element, and therefore the business from the Barstonians, and they wanted the much more civilized legal filings of Wayland. The two townships utilized the same courthouse as they were in the same county. Life was never boring for the two attorneys. Defending the proprietors of a Meth Lab one day; filing an uncontested, fourth divorce on behalf of the scorned trophy-wife on the next.

The *Associates* in the name of the firm was a mistruth. JG, as he was called, and Ryan were the only partners, the only lawyers, and there were no others seeking partnership. None would be sought out either as they were not seeking any new blood for such an arrangement. The associates consisted of their part-time private investigator, Warren Dennihan; and their full-time secretary in Ryan's wife, Angie. Warren had his own thriving business, with his own partner, and was subcontracted by the law firm whenever a top investigator was needed. He was rarely, if ever, in the office. Angie was in the office every business day, much to Ryan's chagrin, and she had almost no legal knowledge. What she lacked in legal prowess, she made up for in organization and efficiency. She was invaluable and JG had said in the past, in plain language to Ryan, that whatever problem he had with the arrangement, to get over it.

296

The arrangement had been Ryan's doing in the first place. He had hired Angie Grummond, as was her name at the time, without consulting JG on the spot at the first interview. Rather than ask the prospective employee out on a date upon their first meeting, which was ultimately what Ryan wanted to do, he decided to hire her instead. The would-be sexual harassment suit in waiting didn't last long, as they were officially an item by the time she was finished her training. JG didn't mind as much as he had initially let on, not even annoyed if truth be told. The headache of starting a firm was a larger migraine than that of an office romance. Besides, Ryan had been JG's best friend since law school, almost for as long as he could remember, and he had never seen his friend so happy.

The startup capital for the small firm came from the money bestowed to Jacob via his surrogate family. His in-laws had been more than good to him, they had filled a hole left in him by the passing of his natural parents. His wife, Anna, had come from money and while she had married for love, her parents could think of no reason for them to struggle financially. They had made the idle threats to rescind the money once they learned that Ryan was to be made full partner from the outset, but all concerned knew the threats were empty. Their apprehension came from genuine concern as they saw their son-in-law, Jacob, as the much more talented of the partnership. With Jacob viewed as having a much higher potential than his friend, especially since he had no money invested in the venture, they felt Ryan was there for the ride instead of the build.

Ryan was not a bad lawyer. He was no Shapiro either. He was talented but he was also a free-spirit. Wells would get caught up in the spirit of the law rather than the black letter. He took flyers. Rather than take on more legitimate claims, he often went to the hoop with little on evidence and heavy on the liberal sentiment. He would often take on the lost cause that was rejected by JG; acknowledging that he might win some, but he would lose more. Ryan was an idealist. He was interested in the law for the good it could do. He actually thought the lady with the scales was indeed blind. He still does to this day.

JG had depended on Ryan to bring in fees not necessarily wins. Winning of course would draw the big cases, but with a location in Barstone, New Hampshire, who was he kidding? JG had the wins, Ryan had the passion. But that was all in the past. What JG needed from his friend and partner now was a win. A big win. He needed him to win the case of his life. For Jacob's life.

3

"All RISE. PLEASE COME TO ORDER, court is now in session. The honorable Judge McCaglia presiding." The bailiff shouted with much too much in the way of volume. There were few people in the fourth session of the Wayland County Superior courtroom. It was entirely unnecessary to shout at that level, but Grantes decided that the loud volume coordinated nicely with the loud color of the neon, hazard-orange prison jumpsuit he was wearing.

He had asked the Correctional Officer, politely mind you, if he could change into a suit that his lawyer had brought for him to wear to court. He even bargained to leave on the shackles, but the request didn't warrant any response. He repeated the question in case the officer didn't hear him. The CO had heard the request because he gave the sternest of looks upon hearing it a second time, though he still gave no response. Ryan had then gotten involved when he arrived but the plea to the Deputy Sheriff was in vain. The officer didn't like the hippie lawyer in the linen suit, and never liked any inmate ever. He was appointed to rid the county of these unwanteds, and this nonconformist was working to free them. Chalk one up for the political right, getting one over on the liberal left.

"You may be seated," said the judge. She was the moderately attractive Judge Grace McCaglia. Wearing the usual black robe, matching black hair that may have been colored to do so, and mystic blue eyes that could virtually see through a person. She confidently presided with a no-nonsense efficiency.

In her late forties, she had accomplished more than most attorneys had in the course of their entire career, in a fraction of the time. In the *Live Free or Die* State of New Hampshire; there were rumors of political favoritism, affirmative action, and sleeping her way into a judgeship. Any explanation was more plausible than that she had earned her position. These whispers did not go unnoticed which is why she once prosecuted and now presided strictly but fairly. There would not be any second-guessing her rulings. She would not allow anyone to be justified in criticizing her for not being the right person for the bench.

"Where are we in the matter of the State of New Hampshire v Grantes?"

"Where are Anna and Brady is the better question." JG whispered into Ryan's ear as they sat in their seats at the defendant's table. He looked around the room but with few people in it, it was quite clear that his wife and son were not present.

"No idea. Three messages without a response this morning. Maybe they are giving her a hard time about a four year old in the courtroom?"

Ryan finished whispering the response as he stood to address the judge.

"We would like to request a continuance, your honor."

"On what grounds? This has been ongoing for six months, time is ticking here sir."

"We are still in discovery, judge. Both theirs and ours."

"Theirs? A Grand Jury was convened and subsequent to Rule 8, they found probable cause to sustain an indictment. The 90-day threshold was met. Do you want to weigh in here counselor?"

She swiveled her chair to her right so she could face the prosecuting Assistant District Attorney. 'Weigh in' was a poor choice of words and she immediately realized it.

Pierce La Fontagne was an enormous man. Fat. He was an unhealthy glutton that could blame whatever or whomever he wanted to regarding his obesity, but it was a fact that he tipped the scales at over four hundred-fifty pounds. He was always disheveled and just as disorganized. How he had lasted as an ADA was a mystery, but his nickname was not so mysterious. They called him Jabba, after the enormous creature in *Star Wars*, behind his back. And he knew it. He spoke with as slow a purpose as his metabolism.

"We have. Ah. Given the defense and have enough to provide the state to move. Ah. Forward with the case, Judge. We. Ah. Don't need much, but we do need a little more time." The fat on his neck jiggled when he spoke. He never looked up to face the judge when he spoke to her, as he was still shuffling papers in the disorganized mess he had created at the prosecution table. Besides his disorganization, not making eye contact with her infuriated her. She felt it was a sign of disrespect.

"Does that mean you are ready or not? Kind of late in the game aren't we, counselor? You had enough to sustain the charges, do you have what you need to move forward or don't you?"

"Ah. We feel confident that the current evidence will prove our case beyond the threshold of reasonable doubt."

"I can tell." She had to pause to control her anger. She was a professional to her very core. She swiveled back toward the defendant.

"Mr. Wells. Have you received all of this said evidence? If so, then I'm confused. Speedy trial gentlemen. The defendant has the right to one, he is remanded and sitting in prison awaiting the disposition of this trial. So I would think his lawyer would be more adamant about moving this forward. He pleaded not guilty. ADA La Fontagne and the state requires a speedy trial, and frankly I demand it so I don't get backlogged. Six months gentlemen. This has been going long enough, wouldn't you both agree? We move ahead forthwith." Efficiency experts could learn a thing or two from Judge McCaglia.

"I agree that six months is a long time, your honor. Especially for my client, who was only remanded due to an imminent threat justification, which we will get to in a minute with the other motion you have before you."

Ryan had filed to have the issue of bail revisited. Jabba had used a justification that argued that Jacob Grantes was an immediate danger to society and should be remanded as to allay any danger to the community. She was already disgruntled with the prosecutor, he was hoping to use that to his and therefore his client's advantage.

"But with all due respect, judge, I do not agree with the a forthwith," Ryan continued. "In order to provide a proper defense against the charges, I need to ensure that the burden of proof and all pertaining evidence is met and provided to me by the prosecution. The ADA has just told you and I, after some equivocating I might add, that they now have all the evidence they plan to use when and if this goes to trial. I need time to assemble all the counter-evidence supporting our claim against the charges, and that proving that my client is innocent."

JG nodded his approval. His friend and partner was doing well. Unlike television and movies in Hollywood, the State cannot come out of nowhere in the last minute of the trial with a damning piece of evidence. It was now time for the prosecution to put up or shut up and Ryan had just spoken legalese saying so.

"OK. So we are moving forward to trial with this, correct gentlemen?"

The two opposing men nodded in agreement instead of stating it aloud for the court stenographer. The judge didn't make them, she continued instead.

"I don't see a green sheet with any deals on the table as of yet. So Mr. Wells, how long do you need?"

"We request ninety days your honor."

"Three months for discovery and prep for trial? You are joking right? Nice try. ADA La Fontagne, is there anything else you would like to state before I rule on this?"

"Ah. No your honor. I would just like to reiterate that — "

" - No need to reiterate anything, I heard you the first time. You've got thirty days." She turned toward the clerk to dictate. "Let's set a date for pretrial and jury selection at or about one month from today."

"Your Honor with that being settled, I would like to revisit the issue of bail. The motion should be before you," Ryan said.

He was hoping that since things had not exactly gone his way thus far, Judge McCaglia would throw him, and more importantly JG, a bone on the motion to revisit the issue of bail.

"That has already been denied. I denied it six months ago. Is there anything new to bring forth where I would reconsider?"

"He is a prominent attorney in the area, Judge. He has a family, is a husband, and father. He is the sole breadwinner. This has created an enormous hardship. His driver's license has been reinstated at this point, but we would surrender it again in lieu of incarceration if the State is still concerned that he is an imminent threat. But if we are now talking another thirty days before a trial is to even begin, I see no reason or threat to continue to remand him. He has been a model inmate, never been in trouble with the law prior to this case, and he has — "

"Save it Mr. Wells. You have nothing new here. A woman is dead. The allegation is that she is dead because of your client. Drinking and Driving is serious and a blight on our society. When a child is in the car on top of this, allegedly, it is reprehensible. I continue to believe that he may be an imminent threat. The fact that he is a prominent figure in this community; and that he is an attorney; that has been before me and this court in the past; is not a reason for him to benefit. He cannot garner favor from a court that is supposed to judge his alleged crimes. Any defendant before me with these same allegations would get remanded, remain alcohol-free, surrender their license to drive a motor vehicle, and pending the outcome of the trial matriculate a Substance Abuse Program. I'm sorry Mr. Grantes, but you are to stay at the Wayland County House of Corrections pending trial. Stay in the Substance Abuse Program or there will be consequences, sir. As Mr. Wells just stated it is only thirty more days."

She paused only for a moment while she briefly looked over the rest of the documents regarding this case in front of her.

" So unless there are any other motions, we will resume these proceedings in thirty days. No more delays gentlemen, either one of you. Court is adjourned."

The gavel was only tapped onto the sound block but it sounded as though it was slammed through to the other side by a sledgehammer.

301

4

THE TRUTH WAS that the hardship the Grantes family was facing was not at all financial. It was Jacob who was suffering the most, but they were all unaccustomed to this torment. Not being able to see his wife and four year old child was all but killing him. Brady was not supposed to be without his father. He hadn't been in his life up to that point. Anna had been distant in recent months but they had dealt with serious difficulty in the past. They would get through it. Their college romance had started blissfully and had some serious downs despite their intense love for one another. Their eventual vows to take each other through good times and bad had taken significant meaning.

Norman and Olivia Craig had done whatever they could to encourage the college romance of their only daughter, Anna. Jacob, not Jake or JG as others called him (his natural parents had taken the time and effort to pick a name for him, and it was rude to bastardize that effort they had said repeatedly), was decidedly the perfect match for their Anna. Especially with the boys she had brought home in previous courtships. True, Jacob's family didn't come from wealth, nor had they built any. They had faith that this legacy would change with Jacob. He had work ethic, was smart, and pre-law. Yes, this is what they had in mind for their girl and they would do whatever they could, financially or otherwise, to support Jacob's goals. As long as Anna was included in the equation.

Jacob was always humbly appreciative, respectful in declining the offers of money or the "just because" expensive gifts, but would relent over time. Anna joined in on the pressure to accept these material tokens of affection for they were deemed as simple manifestations of parental approval. She viewed the entire subject as "only money". Of course it was only money to her, she had been privied to these same gestures and more over the course of her entire life. These were just an extension of her expectations from her wealthy parents.

"You should just get used to it honey, they won't let up. They love you and they just want to show you how much. Besides, you deserve to live a certain lifestyle even if you don't know it yet," she said in one of their more memorable spats on the subject. There had been more discussions regarding this very subject, all of which she won with some version of the same statement.

302

Jacob's fight for financial independence with her was a broken alliance, however. He would say things like, "I'm used to doing things for myself, babe. It's not that I am unappreciative of it, but there is something honorable in building a life for ourselves, by ourselves. I feel like I am forever indebted to them."

These declarations would fall on deaf ears and would either reluctantly fade or would be the impetus for a battle royale, depending on the value of the gesture and how much Jacob really wanted to press the issue. Eventually Jacob acquiesced, as he did every time. As the relationship developed, the lifestyle became de rigueur. He had lost every battle and the war as well. In truth, he had built up enormous debt and was very thankful for the financial help. Boston University was not cheap, Boston University School of Law even less so. The money, cars, apartments, the ability to go to Law School (only 11% of those applying to BU School of Law get accepted. The competition is stiff, but Mr. Craig was friends with someone on the Board of Trustees, or so he said).

"It's not bribery," Norman Craig had said. "I love Anna," he also said. It was to ensure that they had a strong foundation on which to build their life together. Of that, Jacob was sure.

Jacob's biological parents loved him with all of their hearts, albeit with fewer trinkets to show for it. Actually, there weren't any trinkets. Reginald and Elizabeth Grantes had to work and toil for every nickel of property or possession they owned, and even then the nickels didn't add up to anything of worth. They doled out hugs and kisses the way Norman Craig doled out money. Before the Craigs, Jacob had been a wealthy man. His parents attended or coached every athletic endeavor their only son struggled to perform. Neither parent had attended college but made it a priority for their son to get the education they did't have. They would not, could not, contribute financially. But they were motivating and supportive.

Young Grantes left upstate Vermont to attend Boston University and achieve his and his parent's goals for him. His parents remained there, driving south for visits or sending care packages of sweets to their starving student. They were pleased to learn that as of his sophomore year, their son would no longer struggle financially. The ends would more than meet. Unfortunately, in the end, they would never meet Anna.

✳✳✳✳✳

It was the start of Jacob's second semester, of his second year at BU that Reggie and Liz would drive down to Boston to visit their son for the last time. He had been home for Christmas break and every other sentence was, "Anna this" or "Anna that".

303

He had been a social mingler in high school, never the most popular kid but was a welcome addition to any clique. He was better than averagely attractive. He was polite, and was familiar with many a female as well, in large part because of his standing in a plethora of social circles. He had many dates, with a few sporadically retained as official girlfriends over the years. He certainly didn't have any that he had prattled on about for days on end.

His freshman year had been new and exciting, but also the most difficult endeavor he had undertaken in his life up to then. There were precious few stories regarding the fairer sex as he said there was no time. That was only half true. The other half was that going to University was not about settling down but about exploring, both academically and socially. It was novel that this Anna would commandeer so much of a conversation, which made necessary the trip to Boston.

Interstate 89 is a long, windy, treacherous highway running north-south over and around the Green Mountains, crisscrossing Vermont and into New Hampshire. This is one of two major highways in Vermont, and is the quickest way south to Boston, Massachusetts. The two lanes of patchy, frost-heaved road are tricky to negotiate any time of year; soft shoulders, ice, elevation changes, with notorious fog make it more so during bad weather.

January brings major snow storms almost every year, often dropping several feet of snow in a relatively few number of hours. This particular *Noreaster* should have postponed the trek south to Boston, the storm well-tracked and advised in advance. But in the Northeast, weather personnel and meteorologists, were wrong as often as correct. Though every weather girl, on every channel, was forecasting the same snow advisory. But the days had been requested off, cashing in vacation and/or personal time, so the show must go on. And so on that January afternoon, Reg and Liz Grantes of Burlington, Vermont embarked on their journey south.

Jacob found it odd that his parents had not called him once they had arrived in Boston. They had a reservation with a late check-in scheduled at the Buckingham Hotel on Commonwealth Avenue, as was customary when they visited. When he had not heard from them, the thought of the big storm resonated in the back of his mind. He almost immediately disregarded it, however; his father had driven in the snow his entire life, had taught him how to drive in the stuff. He called the prepaid cellphone they used only when traveling, as cell phones were not the rage with the senior Granteses back then. He could not get through. Their voicemail was not set up, of course. It was not until he called the hotel and been informed that they had not checked in that he began to worry. More phone calls to their friends and to their places of work without a definitive answer to their whereabouts led to panic.

By 10:00 AM the following morning, panic became horrified shock. The Vermont State Police informed him by telephone that neither had survived a severe car crash. Neither had been alive when authorities had arrived at the scene.

"We hate to inform you over the phone," they said. "How very sorry we are," they also said. "Please come to Montpelier, Vermont to identify your parents."

304

They had not made it out of their own state. The reports showed that the snowy weather conditions inhibited sight; mixed with the unplowed snow on top of black ice, with an unfamiliar rental vehicle that was not equipped with all-wheel drive, were some of the elements contributing to the disastrous formula. The guard rail was ill-placed, meaning that there wasn't one in place. A guard rail would have at a minimum kept the vehicle on the road. The lack of this safety measure did the opposite and did not keep them on the road. The rental vehicle launched off the elevated highway into the icy ravine below. The final element in their premature demise.

The aftershock of the catastrophe had left Jacob scarred both emotionally and financially. Anna and her parents were there to reassemble the pieces as best they could. The financial piece was easy. Norman took care of the massive debt in one phone call. Anna was there for the emotional part. This was not as easy. But they dealt with it.

Reginald and Elizabeth Grantes, formerly of Burlington, Vermont, had loved life. They cared not for money but for the happiness it could provide from joyous memories. They loved each other and they loved their son, and in that they were rich. Realistically, they were not. They lived paycheck to paycheck and didn't manage those very well at all. There were always events deemed too important to pass up, spending money earmarked for bills; spending in lieu of life insurance, savings, or a 401k. They were upside down on their mortgage in part because of the market, but primarily because of the repeated refinancing and remortgaging.

Without life insurance, in their terrible financial condition, and most recently with the cost of their final expenses, they had left their only son with an enormous financial burden. He was already in debt because of his educational loans and the catastrophe would make him more so without a house or substantial property to sell. And so at the ages of 58 and 56, Reggie and Liz respectively, had left their son broken and broke. Had it not been for the Craigs, he would have been broke for the rest of his life.

5

JG WAS ANXIOUSLY AWAITING the arrival of his lawyer at the table in one of the courthouse conference rooms. He was immediately escorted there after his brief legal fray in the fourth session upstairs. Ryan had worked it out to conduct a meeting with his client before he was bussed back to prison, should he not make bail. Which to his misfortune is exactly what happened. Ryan seemed to be taking a long time doing whatever he was doing in the eyes of JG; leaving him alone in the dark, windowless conference room with a court officer standing watch in the corner. It was an awkward silence which made Ryan's absence seem even longer. He was not in any hurry to get back to his cell, nor his celly, but he was overwrought with how his case was progressing thus far. Or not progressing, which consumed his thoughts every minute of every day in prison.

The large wooden door opened with a start, ending the tension that had been building in the small room, adding a different sort of unease. Ryan moved quickly to a chair opposite his client, setting his leather briefcase down on the oversized table between them.

"I'd like to be alone with my client please," he said over his left shoulder to the officer.

"Sure thing. I'll be outside the door when you're finished."

Once the babysitter had left, the lawyer-client pretense was abandoned. "Well, that didn't go very well." The hearing had not gone well, they both knew it, and neither one would sugarcoat it to say that it had.

"Ya think?"

"Look pal, we have them on the ropes, right where we want them," Ryan said.

"Rope a dope, huh? Who's the dope? They're kicking our asses, Ry."

"Well I don't know what I could have done differently in retrospect. Thoughts? I mean what would the Great Jacob Grantes have done?"

JG's elbows were on the table, head in hands. He needed a lifeline. The sarcasm and mucking it up with his friend needed to cease. He was on the verge of breaking down.

"You did what you did, Ry. I mean you did what I would have done. That woman is a ball-buster."

"McCaglia has always been brutal, you knew that going in. You've been in front of her before. Hell, she was as an ADA, she is now on the bench. She has something to prove, always has, and she doesn't cut breaks unless she absolutely has to. And she doesn't have to here. We don't have anything going for us, and Jabba isn't chomping at the bit to cut a deal either."

"Exactly. So what do we have we going for us?"

"I was just speaking with tons-of-fun upstairs after our hearing. That's what took so long. I've got the 'one and only green sheet' right here. This is the only deal he is offering, or is ever going to offer, he says. It's not a good one, I'll warn you."

He reached into his briefcase on the table, removed the green court document the La Fontagne had given Ryan a few moments prior. It was conveniently on top and quickly slid directly in front of his jumpsuit-clad friend. A green sheet is a bargaining document with legalese and three vertical columns in the middle horizontal third. The form is on No Carbon Required (NCR) paper with three sheets; one for the ADA, one for the defense, and one for the judge. The first column is for the prosecutor, which offers a sentencing recommendation if the defense forgoes the expense of a trial. The middle column is the defense counter offer, which typically chips away at what the State wants. The final column on the right, is the deal formed between the two and goes to the judge. He or she reads the statutory minimums to ensure nobody is ponying up the courthouse, then usually rubber-stamps the deal. When all is said and done, all the judge wants is to clear their docket, keep justice moving just like everyone else. This is called a green sheet for the complicated reason in that the color of the document is a light green. Though it must be signed by all parties, it is only legally binding when and if a formal hearing takes place and agreed to on the record.

"He likes where he is," Ryan continued.   "As you can see, the offer is Vehicular Manslaughter, OUI 1 with injury, leaving the scene. He drops the child endangerment, and puts a recommend of eight to ten on the VM, concurrent. Loss of licenses, two years after release on the drivers, law for life because we are talking felonies."

"Not much of a deal."

"You would get fifteen years on the VM alone at trial. Add in the OUI-with, leaving the scene, and indifference would get you another ten-plus separately. Add the child endangerment back into the charges if we go to the hoop, and you would not be able to see your kid without someone watching over your shoulder until he is legally an adult. Eight to ten, to run concurrent means with good time, two years off the minimum. You've been in for six months already, so you would be out in five and half. No child supervision, no probation. It's not good but it is the best we're gonna get I'm afraid."

The drivers license didn't make that much difference to JG. The loss of his ability to practice law could also be dealt with, he had money and he could always find something to occupy his days. Maybe he could teach. The five and a half years away from his family was intolerable. He could not lose his family for any longer than he already had. Supervised visits

307

with Brady was unacceptable also but at least he would be able to see him other than through glass. These thoughts were going through his mind but he wasn't vocal about them, which caused a long pause. He continued to stare at the offer, lost in the ramifications if he agreed to what was written.

"What's going through your mind? Talk to me. There is nothing saying that you can't be behind the scenes at the firm, you just wouldn't be able to take cases when you get out."

"You think that is what's bothering me, Ry? How long have you known me? You really think that is what's hanging me up?"

"No, I don't. I'm just trying to help. But Jabba isn't going to budge. It's this or we go to the hoop. But you have given me nothing to work with on defense. We go to trial? I think unless we come up with something really damned compelling, you're going to go away for a long time."

"Have you been in touch with Anna yet? I'd like to discuss this with her."

"She isn't, nor was she, here today. No answer either. Voicemail is full. I'm really not sure where she is, but I'll keep trying." He pulled out some other documents from the briefcase, spreading out the pile on his side of the table. "What I would like to discuss is all of this circumstantial evidence and see if anything jogs your memory. Anything we can hammer away at. If we weaken anything he has, maybe the deal gets better."

"We've been through this, I don't remember anything about that night. Well, other than Sully's anyway."

"Yeah well we are going to go through it again. You admitted to quote, 'being hammered' when they picked you up at your house. You were passed out by the way. Again, Brady was upstairs asleep but unsupervised."

"I can't believe I drove in that condition, much less with Brady in the car. Then left him on his own like that in the house. I just can't believe it."

"Thats what they're going with. I have a statement from the bartender, Jenna, that you left Sully's between 8:00 and 8:15 PM. You also admitted to being at the bar in the back of the cruiser, which means you had to be really banged up. You, of all people, know better than to say anything to the police after you've been arrested. But anyway, you left and picked up Brady at the Destriers at 8:20 PM; the servant that was watching him told Chamille Destrier that she put him in his carseat in the back of the running car, that you never spoke or left the driver's seat. She said she found it odd behavior, but this is all third hand through Chamille because the servant doesn't speak English, apparently. The police never spoke to her directly to confirm or deny anything. Chamille was at the charity event next to your wife, so we strike the kid being in the car as hearsay. I think that is why the big-boy is dropping child endangerment, the kind soul."

"Yeah, what a sweetheart."

"Right. So you drove away and must have bounced off a tree, veering into the opposite lane where this poor woman happened to be coming right at you. She goes off the road and plays chicken with a big tree and an even bigger rock. She lost and you went home to sleep it off."

308

"It's not funny, Ry. Please don't make light of the fact that this woman was decapitated by a smoking-hot engine. I feel awful."

"Sorry, just trying to add some levity. Anyway, they have matching paint from the tree, black sapphire pearl, and the scrape on your Volvo has wood and bark all through it. Exact. No real credible argument there, I'm afraid. Furthermore the rubber zig-zagging on Wayland Country Club Road matches the Michelin 235/60R18s on your ride. Cops investigated your tires, they've got you dead to rights there too."

"Match? *Cops* are matching this all up? Can we get experts to refute them? Volvos are a dime a dozen in New England, hell I have two of them."

"Lab techs. This isn't *CSI*, they didn't stop everything they were doing and get top experts from all over the country to fly in on the state's dime, no. But you don't have to be an expert to see that all of this doesn't look good. Picking apart their lab technicians with our expensive ones is not going to win over a jury, if that's what you're thinking."

"That is exactly what I am thinking. The techs are overworked, underpaid, they make mistakes — "

" — this is New Hampshire, JG. They are neither overworked, nor are they underpaid. These aren't MIT grads by any stretch but they don't have a whole lot to investigate, trust me. Just between you and me, I looked at your car, the road, the tree. You killed this poor woman. If you were anybody else — "

" - So what are we doing here then?"

"You're my best friend. I'm trying to mitigate your responsibility here. I'm trying to help. I don't know, find a technicality. What we're doing here is trying to get the best deal we can."

"Great. Just great. You think five and half is the best I can do?"

"We haven't discussed the 911 call yet. Anonymous, but that is how they nailed you. How they knew to go to your house to grab you."

"What is there to discuss? You've already told me to take the deal, right?

Ryan paused. He shuffled the stack of papers containing all the condemning evidence. He really wasn't sure why he was against taking the deal but he was. He knew his friend, knew him better than any other male on the planet, and something was not right. Endangering the life of his only son, the one they had so much trouble conceiving, was not scanning. True, he had been drinking more in the months before the accident, but to get that blackout drunk was not something he would expect from his friend. He was mister safety. People disappointed. But not JG. Not Jacob Grantes. He had never disappointed. Not until now.

"Look, I'm not telling you to take the deal. At least not yet. We finally have all the evidence that fat-body has compiled; so we put Deni on it and see what he comes up with. I mean, the cops didn't pick you up at your house until 9:45 PM, which gives you a huge window to get shattered in the comfort of your own home. If everything comes back the way it looks here, which admittedly is really fucking bad, then we pick away at the bartender and the illegal lady."

"Please leave the vic alone. Arelia, right? Jenna too."

"Look. Jenna is a sweet girl, we go there and knock a few back and she is always good to us, but she over-served you. She claims not, but obviously she screwed up and is covering her ass. As far as the victim, she is dead. Which is unfortunate. But she shouldn't have been in this country to be dead. She was illegal. I feel for her just like you do, but when it comes to my friend or someone who may or may not even pay taxes? I might be a 'hippie' but I look out for my own. We've kinda got a role reversal here, huh? You're usually the cutthroat."

"Prison changes people I guess. Usually for the worse, not more sympathetic. But it is what it is."

"Maybe. But if shit goes south, all the cards lead to what we have before us, then we go after the ladies. The bartender has some responsibility here, and so does the vic. This *is* New Hampshire. We don't like drunk drivers but we don't like illegal aliens more."

"Not very Politically Correct of us, is it?"

"Unfortunately, like you said, it is what it is. Peace, love, and get a green card."

"Well lets hope it doesn't come to that. Just get Deni going because we don't have much time."

"I'm on it. I'm not going anywhere. You need anything?"

"Actually, yes."

"Name it."

"Find Anna."

6

RYAN WELLS WAS JG's longest and closest personal friend. They had both grown up poor but not impovered, had been instilled with a strong work ethic, and were the first in their respective families to go to college. They had met at BU during freshman orientation and were all but inseparable since. Grantes had been a loyal friend in pulling Wells into the fold of the partnership and Ryan had been loyal in many other ways, including during the death of Jacob's parents. They were each the brother to the other.

The two were so alike in so many ways that they could have been biological brothers. Ryan was good looking, tall and had what was once an athletic build. They would both be forty this year and had previously made plans for both families to go on vacation together to celebrate. Until the incarceration, all had looked forward to the time away. The only major difference between them was professionally. They were both strong advocates, but the hippie would live in the shadow of his more talented, leaning to the right, brother.

As Ryan left the courthouse, he pulled his iPhone out of his long winter overcoat to call Warren Dennihan, the firm investigator.

"Deni, how are you?" He immediately regretted not using his bluetooth ear device to make the call as he juggled his briefcase, the phone, and his car keys to open his parked car.

"Same shit, different pile. What's up?" Warren Dennihan was a *Southie*, or from the district of South Boston and had the severe accent to prove it. Bad. Or 'wicked bad, guy'. It was almost like he spoke a different language as *pahk tha cah in hah-vid yahd*, just doesn't quite describe how broken his English really was. He didn't pronounce *r's*, unless of course they were not in the word like *drawr* instead of draw. It was work to hold a conversation with him unless you were familiar with him or his kind.

"I just finished up with JG's hearing. It didn't go well."

"I figured. I got my partner workin' my other shit, so how much time do I gotta clear up?"

"Ah shit," Ryan said. He had dropped his phone while opening his car to get it started and warmed up. He had to retrieve it out of the snow but fortunately it still worked. With the new synthetic oils and the fact that he drove an Audi A6, he didn't need to get the car warmed up for performance reasons, but he couldn't get the winter-fighter to work on his cold body until the engine was pumping warm air at him.

"You ok?"

"Yeah, Yeah. I'm here. Just dropped something. So everything we talked about? That's what they've got. The whole shah-bang. We've gotta work on it."

"By we, ya mean me."

"It's been a tough morning, are you really gonna give me a hard time right now?"

"Always. Hey listen. I've been callin' WHOC, I know a few guys over there. Not much I can do to look after him in there. Its all political. He's a lawyer, so nobody trusts him, and he can't gang up. At least he knew not to PC, just take a beat'n like a man if thats what they wanna do."

"If it was going to happen, it would have happened by now."

"Not necessarily, but we can hope. How much longer?"

"That depends on you, Deni. Thirty days if this goes to the hoop. Trial will be probably about two weeks or so, after that depends on what we get. I was hoping we could get enough to kill a trial, maybe enough to get a deal. They are offering eight to ten, which means five and half when all is said and done."

"All depends on me? No pressure. Who's breakin' balls now?"

Ryan was still sitting in his car, which was starting to kick out the warm seventy-four degree air that was set on his in-dash computer. He still couldn't drive, however; the car had not yet picked up the signal for the phone and you cannot drive and talk on the phone in New Hampshire unless handsfree. "Hey where are you?"

"Around the corner from you, I'll be there in thirty secs or less."

"Good. This might be easier face to face. I have a ton of documents you should look at."

"Do you still drive the silver Audi?"

"Yes, of course. I love this — "

" — I'm behind ya."

"Holy crap. That was fast."

Deni parked his blacked-out Escalade and relocated to the passenger seat of Ryan's vehicle. This was the part that took the thirty-seconds. "Let's see it all," he said without explanation of how or why he was in the immediate area.

"So this is everything." He handed Warren the stack of evidential material from his briefcase, then continued. "I know we discussed it when this thing happened, and since, but something just isn't sitting right about this case. You think I'm nuts though don't you?"

"I don't think you're nuts, per se, but would you really go through all this bullsh for anybody but JG? I agree that somethin' isn't stirrin' the kool-aid, but you and I both know he did it. He was drinkin' like a fish for months before this all happened. I was thinkin' family trouble at the time, but who knows? That kid is his life, so I can't see him throwing that away. But we all fuck up, doesn't have to be on purpose for it to do damage."

"So does that mean that you are on board? I gotta know that you are on this."

"Loyal as lab, huh? Yeah, me too. I'm in, and you know it. I just need somethin' to work with here, guy."

"Look I never ask how you do what you do, because I'm not sure I want to know, but we are going to need all you've got on this. We need to dig into; Jenna, the bartender we know from Sully's Tavern, the Destrier servant or au pair or whatever she is, the 911 call is a bit wonky, and if all else fails — we make the vic the most despicable person who has ever illegally entered the borders of this country," Ryan said before pausing. "I was kind of hoping for a sliding scale on this one. I know you have to clear your calendar and this is going to take some time, but with me taking this case, I have all of his cases I have to work, and mine, and of course he isn't in the office taking cases so the firm is really financially tight right now and — "

" — hey relax, buddy. I can't dig up what ain't there, but I'm on it. As legit as possible anyway. As for the fee, don't worry about it. I owe tha kid. He's been good to me over the years."

"So what are you thinking?"

"I've got a couple of ideas. Mostly hunches, but I know people."

"I know you know people, that's why you are so good at what you do. Anyone I know?"

"Stop kissin' my ass Ry. I wanna check out the bar first. Jenna."

"Business or pleasure?"

"Both."

"I've got another project that's just as important."

"I'm listenin'."

"Find Anna and Brady. They didn't show up at court today and she is not answering phones. It's weirding me out, and JG is really freaking out."

"Huh. Lets go over to the house. You drive."

"Right now? Deni, I've got — "

" — you said it's important. Was that fact or bullsh?"

"Fact."

"Then start driving."

7

"HE'S BACK. ALL DAY BRO, just like I said. How did it go?" Loder, inmate #437254 was Grantes's cellmate. A dichotomous character, Loder had an IQ in the basement and a temperament in the attic. He has also spent well-nigh his entire adult life in one prison or another, and therefore looked the part. He was large with crudely drawn tattoos, cocaine fingernails, and eyes that were continually moving when he was awake. He didn't look for trouble, but he seemed to find it, and knew what to do when those moving eyes found some. Fighting was in his wheelhouse and everyone including his cellmate knew it.

Grantes didn't want to get into any conversation, let alone one with his celly. After his long day; his fruitless motion to get out of prison; the fact that he was right back in his drab, concrete cell; that he had not been able to see his wife and kid were all working to tune his last nerve guitar-string tight. It looked like Loder was in a fighting mood to top it all off, which meant that any dialogue with the Neanderthal was going to end in high-order violence. A situation he wanted to avoid all the way around.

"Yeah well, you know how it goes. Long ride over, longer wait in the tank just to come right back." Grantes was by design vague with his fellow inmates, just as they were with him.

"Just like I said. So how did it go?" Loder asked again.

"I thought it was bad form to keep asking someone about court?"

"Then let me see your paperwork."

"Not gonna happen. I'm back here so chances are, you can take a stab at how it went."

"I'll take a stab at you, you fuckin' bug. I got no problem with the hole for a week if you wanna go to HSU."

"Calm down, Loder. It's been a long day, a longer six months, and I just want some piece and quiet. If that means I have to go to the Hospital Services Unit to get it, then so be it."

"Then let me see your paperwork so you can think."

"You know I'm not a skinner, so why do wanna see my paperwork?"

"Prove it."

"Look Loder, I'm not a skinner, I'm not a rat, and I'm here, so you know I'm not PC. What do you say you just lay off?"

"You're a fuckin' lawyer, same as a rat to me fuck-stick."

"That's a hell of a stereotype."

"It's only a stereotype if it's wrong. Don't you lawyers call it profiling if I'm right?"

"You're quite the philosopher."

"And a rat is a rat, asshole."

"Lawyers can't rat," he said. He really wanted to finish that last statement with — "you moron" — but he didn't. Instead he said, "we have an obligation to keep quiet, which you know."

"Not if you can prevent a crime. And I ain't your fuckin' client."

"You're right about that. But if I were your attorney, I would be an even richer man." *Shit.* He said it.

"I'm going to bleed every dollar outta you, asshole — "

" — I'm sorry. Sorry, sorry, sorry. It slipped out, I'm sorry. I just need to think. You don't really want to get lugged do you?"

"No cameras in here, bro."

"You liked your day alone that much, huh? A week in the hole for you; and I get hospitalized, and stuck with someone worse than you in another pod when I get out. Spare us both would you?"

"I liked it here alone. Got to rub one out. Took a shit in peace too, it was nice." He was calming down, and Grantes was thankful.

"Masterbation and defecation, what more could you ask for? I'm glad to hear you had a good time."

"I got parenting class tonight, so you got the cell to yourself after chow. You can think all ya want then. My mags are inside my Temperpedic if ya wanna crank one out." By Temperpedic he meant the paper-thin mattress that wouldn't provide cushion to an overweight molecule. Skin mags were contraband, playboy and soft stuff was tolerated but Loder had the hard stuff. Why he wanted to look at women being penetrated was a mystery to Grantes. Why anyone who was facing the number of years his celly was, without having access to an actual female, would want to look at females in coitus he thought was torturous. But this was an olive branch and Grantes accepted it though he wasn't going to use it.

"I'll keep it in mind, thanks."

The knowledge that Loder was a parent frightened Grantes. Somewhere, sometime between his many bids with the Department of Corrections, he had managed to impregnate someone. *That poor woman*, he thought. It was either against her will or she had some serious self esteem issues to agree to getting onto a bed with Loder. Maybe it wasn't a bed. Either way it was repulsive to Grantes. Teaching Loder to be a parent may have been an idea best suited for the garbage. It wasn't even a good idea on paper. Loder would never see this child, at least that is what any decent person would hope. He hoped more vehemently that he could hold his own son. To see his wife. *Why had they not been at court today? Did she forget? That was very unlike her. Why couldn't Ryan reach her? She was never without her phone, ever.* All of these thoughts and questions were consuming him. And they began to drive him crazy.

Loder was still jawing about something, but Grantes wasn't listening. He was cracking up and any interaction with the shitbag standing just a few inches away from him would only succeed in eliminating his good time; ensuring he went to the infirmary, then solitary confinement, and finally onto a different pod where anger management would surely be on the agenda. Being lugged was not going to solve anything, it would only make matters worse. He was earning ten days off his eventual sentence per month in good time while he was on his current pod, designated for drug and alcohol related offenders.

Grantes had been down to the hole in his first week of incarceration, when he was on the new-man block. Everyone goes there when first arriving at WCHOC, regardless of the offense. Murderers, check. Wife beaters, check. Masked armed robbery, check. Even those who simply violated probation. All blended together in a testosterone-infused concoction.

On Grantes's fourth day on new-man, a GD, or a Gangster Disciple, had approached him about offering protection. He politely declined the offer and thought the matter closed. Later that day, he knew better when a rival gang-member from the AB, or Arian Brotherhood, approached him with the same offer of services. It turned out that he knew the second thug who had approached him. He had defended him once a while prior on a drug trafficking charge, which he had successfully reduced down to a simple possession. The AB knew this, which was why they had sent that particular thug with that particular offer. He again declined after reminiscing a bit, but thanked him. The conference had not gone unnoticed, creating further discourse between the two gangs, out of the many factions that were on the pod. The discourse went from foul language to high-order violence the likes of which he had not seen even in a movie or a video game. He was caught in the middle and was lucky to get out of it with just a broken rib, which in relative terms meant that he went untouched. But the pain was just as agonizing as the twenty-three and a half hours a day he had to spend in the hole after the four days he spent in HSU. He never wished to return.

By good fortune he had avoided it for the night. Tomorrow would be another story, that would be yet another struggle, for yet another day. But he would get the chance to look over the legal documents that Ryan had copied for him, documents every inmate had the right to have in their possession. While his celly was learning how to refrain from kicking the ever-loving shit out of his next of kin, he would strategize on the best way to get the hell out of this hell. Thus far, he was coming up with blanks in his recollection of the events leading him to this dark place, and this dark time.

316

8

RYAN DID FINALLY UTILIZE HIS Audi's bluetooth technology to call Anna's cell again. This time Warren was in the passenger seat, listening. They left the courthouse parking lot while they listened to the phone ringing over and over again through all ten speakers in the luxury automobile. The automated voice was telling them that the voicemail box was full in surround sound.

"Where is she?" Ryan asked Deni. Though he knew that his investigator had as much knowledge of her whereabouts as he did.

"Did you try the house line?"

"Duh. I didn't think of that Deni. Of course I did. No answer."

"Listen, guy, don't give me attitude or I'll give you a beat'n. I'm just askin'."

"I'll try again, if you'd like."

"If it's not too much trouble."

He didn't respond to the jab, he just dialed. Rather, the car dialed. Again, there was no answer in audiophonic clarity. They continued for the rest of the short trip in silence, after some time turning right into the driveway which had not been cleared of the latest dusting of February snow.

"Who do they pay to plow the drive, Ry?"

"I don't know but I can find out."

"It didn't snow last night. It's been a couple days. I'm not lookin' forward to whats inside that house, I ain't gonna lie."

The all-wheel drive handled the rest of the driveway without an issue, and Ryan put the car in park. He had to admit, though he didn't want to, that it appeared that there was something very wrong about the home. He left the car running, to keep it warm, as this was likely to be a short trip to the front door and back. He got out of the car and lost his balance as he slipped in the snow. His loafers were buried along with his butt and elbows.

"Shit. Ahhhhhh, fuck me."

Deni was belly laughing so hard he nearly fell over himself, as he came around the front of the car.

"Oh man, thanks. I needed that. I don't know what we are gonna find in there, kid. My stomach is in knots — "

" — ya know, you could help me up you donkey, instead of standing there laughing."

317

"Oh yeah. Sorry."

Warren helped up his soaked friend, pulling him up with one arm. Ryan tried to drag him down but it didn't work. He was wiry but he was ridiculously strong. He also had better shoes in order to find purchase on the slick drive. Once Ryan was on his feet, Deni looked up as if he was studying the sky for a bit, then moved toward the garage doors.

"Where are you going? You've been here before, front door is this way."

"Nothing is comin' outta the chimney. No heat either means nobody is home or whoever is in there, doesn't need heat."

"Come on, Deni. Don't say stuff like that. I've already got a bad feeling, you don't need to say that."

"Both cars are in the garage. Wait. It's the same car. They have two of the same car?"

"Yeah, XC90s. His and hers. You know JG, mister safety. Volvo makes the safest car, so he got one for each of them."

"I knew he had a Volvo, I didn't know they had two identical his and hers. Little weird, no?"

Ryan didn't reply as he made his way toward the front door like a hockey coach without his skates. Once he arrived, he knocked and rang the bell while he looked into the vertical window just to the right of the huge front door. Nothing. The house was dark and without movement.

"You got a spare key, Ry?" Deni approached the door, standing behind his friend.

"Yes, but not on me."

"Is it in your car?"

"No, it's at my house. Should we go get it? What do you think?"

"I woulda thought you would have it on you. It's not like we were comin' over here or anything."

"I wasn't expecting to come over here. But in retrospect — "

" — is there any mail in their mailbox?" The mailbox was to the left of the door instead of by the road like most other houses in New Hampshire. Ryan opened the lid to look in. By the time he had removed the contents, Deni was opening the front door.

"Yeah, they have mail. Hey, was the door unlocked?

"Sure. We'll go with that. The door was unlocked."

"Deni, breaking and entering is a crime. You used to be a Massachusetts State Police Detective. You know that picking that lock is a crime."

"Did you see me pick a lock? You comin' in or what?"

"This is not my day," Ryan said. He followed his friend inside carrying the mail. "Hello? Anybody home?"

"Stop yellin'. You know as well as I do that there's nobody home. But stamp the snow off your feet just in case. You know how Anna is."

"Yeah yeah. Loafers are ruined anyway, I think. And there could be somebody home, think positive."

"Who wears loafers in the winter?"

"A lawyer who has a court appearance. I wasn't expecting this side trip."

"House is wicked cold and the dog ain't humpin' my leg. I'll bet your shiny car out there, nobody's here."

"So what does that mean? She forgot? Chances are she had some appointment today and she forgot. That's why she isn't home."

"She forgot her husband's court date and went to an appointment with the dog? Who you trying to convince, kid? Besides, the thermostat says sixty-two degrees. That sound like Anna to you? This is what a three million dollar home? They ain't worried about a heat bill. It's set so the pipes won't freeze, not so people don't freeze. I'm not sure what it means except that nobody is home."

They made their way through the living room toward the kitchen. Ryan deposited the mail on the countertop. Warren opened the stainless steel fridge. Nothing. It was empty like it was new off the showroom floor.

"Maybe she went grocery shopping." Deni was ever the smart-ass.

"No, no, no, no, no, no. This is not good. This is really, really not good."

"Lets go upstairs and see what we can see. But you're right, this is not good. She's leavin' him. At the worse possible time, she's leavin' him."

"We don't know that, Deni. There could be another possibility."

"Like she's dead? Is that what you are hoping for?"

"No, of course not. I mean another, less dramatic possibility."

"What color is the sky in your world, Ry? I know you're a hippie and all, but you must smoke some incredible weed. Do you grow your own or do you have a dealer? You don't take the dog and clean out the fridge if your comin' back. And if you kill someone, do you help yourself to the cold-cuts before takin' off?"

"Stop yelling at me. And why now? Six months this has been going on, why now? There has to be another explanation. Maybe they sold the house and moved."

Deni was walking toward the stairs to head up them toward the bedrooms. "Seems like JG woulda mentioned it though. I didn't see a 'FOR SALE' sign or 'SALE PENDING' out by the road. And it's probably just a coincidence that she isn't answering her phone. Or any phone, for that matter."

Ryan went through Brady's bedroom door like he was charging through it. Not a single toy. Deni squatted down as a catcher would in the middle of the room. The bed was there, and a bureau but that was it. He looked to his left and right. The left wall was painted to look like Fenway Park's Green Monster, the right wall was an enormous aerial photo/painting of Gillette Stadium.

319

He was starting to lose his cool. He went into the bathroom attached to Brady's room and started going through the child's drawers and cabinets.

"The drawers and medicine cabinet are empty in the bathroom, Deni. Thats it, I'm calling her cell again."

"Go ahead. I'm sure she'll answer this time." He was shouting from the master bedroom.

Ryan broke out his phone and touched the redial button on his screen. "It's ringing now."

"It sure is." He made his way back to his friend in the child's bathroom. The ringing phone was in Deni's hand. "Should I answer it?"

"What?" Ryan said. He turned to see the ringing phone and his investigator when he entered. Ryan's iPhone was still up to his ear.

"She left it on the dresser in the walk-in closet."

"Oh dear God no." Ryan looked at his touchscreen again to shut it off, realizing that the phone was wet. He felt his cheek and it was soaked as well. Tears were rolling down his face and dripped off of his chin. "What am I going to tell JG?"

"I don't know. Nothin' to tell him yet, for sure. According to you anyway."

He sat down on the toilet without a look. Fortunately the lid was already down.

"Not now, Deni. Please don't fuck with me right now."

"Sorry pal. It took you a while to get here, but you're with me now, right?"

"What are we gonna do?"

"First we need a drink, and I know just the place. Get it together, you're driving."

9

SULLY'S TAVERN WAS A SWANKY JOINT that attracted a mixed crowd. It was located in the downtown area of Barstone, New Hampshire, just off of interstate 93. It was also convenient; in particular for those employed at Grantes, Wells & Associates, which was across the street. The appointments were as expensive looking as the hand-crafted drink concoctions served there. The dark interior still had traces from the previous incarnation as a dive, Irish bar. The stainless steel and plush, artsy booths and lighting were added to the pre-existing dark wood to give it a unique design of Old World pub meets trendy meat-market. The employees were all attractive women, save for a few of the hired muscle and kitchen help. These females were encouraged to be scantily clad, whatever clothing they did choose to wear needed to be black. The concept worked, the place was always busy no matter the time of day.

Warren arrived alone after being dropped off by Ryan, who was too distraught to be seen in public. He had been here countless times before to meet or celebrate with the lawyers he worked with on the other side of the street. A break in any case or the conclusion of one, good or bad, would inevitably end up at 'the office' as they had nicknamed it. He had been in more recurrently in the months before JG's arrest, which is why Deni had a hard time bringing himself in there since.

The place was always busy. It was the unofficial happy hour, however, so the place was an absolute zoo. Technically in New Hampshire, a bar can't advertise a happy hour without being fined or closed. Discounted prices, however, or getting one free after buying one was business as usual after 5:00 PM at Sully's. Deni was recognized at the door through the masses, being allowed through, and made his way toward the front bar.

"Hey handsome, what's your pleasure?" the buxom bartender said. As with all the staff, she was very affable. Another reason for the consistent level of business.

"I need to see Jenna."

"Don't they all. I can make you feel just as good, hun. Whiskey drinker if I remember right. Right?" If she was frustrated that this transaction was taking too long with a full bar, she didn't show it.

"Right. Irish Whiskey. Make it a double, but I still need to see Jenna."

"Coming up. But she's pretty busy right now, sweetie."

"I didn't ask ya if my timing was spot-on, I asked for you to get me the Whiskey and Jenna."

"Easy tiger." She handed him his drink. "The bar in the back, but you gotta pay me first." She eyed him up and down as he overtipped in cash and walked toward the large room in the back with a second bar. She was staring a little too long for the next customer in line who was belligerently ordering his libations to deaf ears.

Deni walked back toward the ancillary bar, having to gumby his way through the loitering crowds of people which were shouting to one another over the music. Once he arrived, he spotted his target busily making elaborate cocktails at a packed bar. All the barstools were taken, plus three and four deep in places, where patrons were vying for her attention. Other female servers were buzzing to and from the bar delivering trays full of drinks to the high tables and booths. He stopped one of the young ladies abruptly but before he could utter a word, like lightning she said, "I'll be right with you luv. As you can see I'm a busy girl, but I'll be back. I promise."

Before she could leave, he gently but firmly grabbed her bare arm. "I just need to speak with Jenna, it's important. Can anyone relieve her for a few?"

She wasn't shocked by the physical contact, but it was quite apparent that she was annoyed by it. This happened many times because the staff was both friendly and provocatively dressed. There was a protocol for handling the countless gropers. A massive bouncer had arrived at the scene as if by magic, leaping into action like an angered panther. He grabbed Warren's shoulder with his monstrous paw, covering it in its entirety.

"Hands off — "

Deni, all in one motion; put his drink down on the offended server's tray, removed the hand off of his shoulder by twisting it, contorting the monster so the limb wouldn't be snapped off his large body. The man was down on his knees before the Whiskey had time to slosh back and forth in the glass. He did not let go of the bouncer when he addressed him, recollecting his drink.

"I was just askin' if I could have a word with Jenna. No harm, no foul. If I let go of your arm, are you gonna be calm, or are you gonna be hurt for-real?"

The bouncer's ego was more damaged than his wrist. So far. The question was whether his bruised ego was going to affect any more of his appendages. He took only a moment to decide.

"If you let me up, I can cover for her for a couple minutes. You can use the office, but can you make it quick? We're really busy here man."

He was let go. Right away he was rubbing his wrist and wincing. "What is that? Karate or something?"

"Or something."

The bustling bar went silent as patrons and staff alike took in the show. The bouncer went behind the bar to relieve her. When she came around to him, she didn't look happy. The bar was slowly returning to normal. Which meant really damned busy.

"Why did you hurt him? You're half his size."

"He started it." He finished his drink and put the empty glass on another tray that was passing them.

"Lets make this quick," she said as she headed toward the office.

"It'll take as long as it takes."

"You know the poor bastard is going to want to know what you did to him. The least you could do is show him sometime. I'm sure he's embarrassed. He was just trying to protect us."

"Boyfriend?"

"No. But it doesn't mean you need to use that MMA stuff on him." They arrived at the office. She looked better in the bright office light than she did in the dim lighting, which was strategically set to pick up mates in the bar. Which is to say that she was a stunning woman. Her flaxen hair was pulled back to reveal jade eyes that weakened knees. She was wearing a black bustier, which looked more like an expensive lingerie top, pushing her ample breasts up to her neck. The very short black skirt accentuated her firm buttocks and hips. The knee-high boots lifted her small body, ensuring that patrons could see her when she was behind the bar.

"So what's up tough-guy? You could have just sat at the bar like a normal person instead of beating people up. It's hard to believe you used to be a cop." She had waited on him many times, been the recipient of his flirtations just as many times. They had met.

"The bar is kinda loud, and we need to have a serious talk."

"You're supposed to be some kind of a sleuth, you can't tell its not a good time?" She sat in an office chair, crossing her legs. The ornate piping at the top of her thigh-high, black stocking was revealed.

"I like the garter belt."

"You brought me in here to flirt? Jesus, you almost ripped Chris's arm off so you could have a go at me in private? You're unbelievable."

"Sorry, force of habit. I came to talk to you about JG. Jacob. What do you call him, Jay? He has so many nicknames."

"Oh my God, Jake. I call him Jake. Is he okay?"

"Yeah, no change. He is in the same spot. You look wicked good by the way."

"Deni. Focus. Stop leering and get it together. I wear this crap because I have to. I'm nice to you because I have to. So now please tell me what is this about?"

"Hey, calm down. I'm a guy. When a girl who looks like you is in front of me? Its like a reflex. I genuinely am here to talk about the night of the charity event. That night. The night Jake was here."

"You already know the cops came and talked to me. I only poured the guy two Stone IPAs. That's it. I gave them a copy of the receipt and everything. You've seen him sling those things back. He loves them. He gets a phone call, he goes to the bathroom, and bails. I would never have let him leave here as bombed as they say he was. I would do anything for Jake, so believe me, I had no idea he was that shattered."

"You would do anything for him? Is that part of the job too?"

"Go fuck yourself. You know what I mean. I didn't over-serve him and I can prove it. I had to prove it to save my job."

"You and I both know that less than half the drinks I have in here I get charged for. Receipts can be doctored. How many did he have? Honestly."

"I don't have to take this shit from you. You might be able to push other people around but not me. Do you think I want to do this, wear this for a living? I went to school to teach kids. I love kids. Do you know what that pays? Dick. So I have to babysit big kids who can't handle their liquor."

"Were you babysitting Jake that night? He must have been pretty wrecked. Bad choice of words, but you get it."

"I'm telling you he wasn't though. I'm being straight with you. I even told the cops the same thing. It was busy that night, as it is every night. The big spenders from Wayland weren't in because they were all headed to the event, but the Barstone crowd was here in full force. I was supposed to go to the event as well, I managed to get an invite through Jake, ironically. I was working alone when he got the phone call and asked for his check. It was busy but I know what I poured him. When he went to the bathroom, I switched out my drawer for the girl that replaced me so I could go home and freshen up. I never saw him leave, but he did because after I came out of the office when my drawer was counted, he was already gone and somebody else was in his seat. He had two beers. Full stop. End of story." She began to tear up.

"You seem wicked sure. To me, it all looks suspect. There is no way he got more drinks from someone else? Shots? Did you two do one together? Sometimes you do that with us. He ran a woman off the fuckin' road, Jenna. He was blitzed. So much so that he can't remember anything after leaving this very bar. He had Brady in the car. You say you love kids, you could have helped him kill his kid, Jenna. Talk to me here."

She was crying so hard at that point that she was having difficulty breathing. "You don't think I beat myself up about that every day? Feel guilty? Maybe he drank somewhere else before here. Or after. I don't know but I know damn-well what he had here."

"If that is true then why do you feel guilty? Seems like you didn't do anything wrong, so why would you feel guilty about anything?"

"I don't know what you want me to say, Deni."

"Start with the truth and we can move on from there."

"I *am* telling you the truth. I don't know how to say it any other way. If this is an old interrogation technique you need a refresher, because you've lost your touch. If you can't tell that I am telling the truth then the issue is you, not me."

"The whole truth. From the beginning. There is something you are not telling me, and that could be the thing thats not sitting right with me." He tried to look into her eyes; but those big, beautiful, green eyes were looking at her lap, and drizzling like small waterfalls.

10

"HEY HONEY I'M HOME. Where are you?" Jacob yelled to his wife as he entered the house from the side door to the garage.

"In the kitchen babe. You're home early," Anna said.

He took off his suit jacket and shoes, putting them in the entryway closet. "Your message said you wanted to actually see me before bed time tonight, so here I - hey, what is all of this?"

He had made his way to the large kitchen and smaller, less formal dining room. The small, round table was set formally, however; with candles, fine china, and an open, breathing bottle of 1997 *Josephs Phelps Insignia*, Cabernet Sauvignon from Napa Valley. It was Jacob's favorite. It was ridiculously expensive, but he felt it was worth every penny.

"I haven't seen you, truly seen you, other than the bedroom for a while. I thought a nice dinner at home and an actual conversation — not just 'we have to get pregnant' sex in the middle of the night when you get home — might be good for a change. You like?" She looked fantastic. Her natural, slightly strawberry-blonde hair always looked nice; but she had it highlighted and loosely curled, flowing over her shoulders. Her slate-blue eyes, bright and beautiful as ever, sparkled in the candlelight. Anna was wearing a formfitting tank dress with her cooking apron covering it. The apron hardly had any detritus from the magic she performed over the stove top. She was a beautiful woman. Always had been. Stop traffic stunning. She was posing in front of Jacob in the dim lighting which silhouetted her lean, athletic body. He thought himself the luckiest man on the planet.

"Wow. Yes, I like."

She unbuttoned his necktie, "Welcome home."

He could smell her sweet perfume as he lowered his head, kissed her lips.

"Slow down there speed-racer. We'll get there, I'd like to get through dinner first. Like I said, you know, have a conversation. It's almost ready." She turned to retreat into the kitchen. "Nice suit by the way, is it new?"

He grabbed her waist, pulling her back to him. "Yes, and it is about to get wrinkled in a ball on the floor."

"Stop. I went through a lot of trouble. While you're pulling off my apron is sexy....oh boy really sexy, I really do want to talk for a change."

"So talk. And make it dirty." He was gently nibbling on her ear, which was her weakness.

325

"Aaaaaaaaah....all this work for nothing. You are so not making this easy."

He smoothly lifted her on top of the small table, slid the china to the only available space, taking note of the open bottle of vintage wine, but only in passing.

"You should know by now babe, I'm very easy."

After their lovemaking, they spooned naked on the couch in the nearby living room. Their heavy breaths slowed into the afterglow. They maintained a great sex life since their first time together. It had gotten better over time, never boring like they had heard their friends warn. They had mixed it up; passionate, animalistic, makeup. All good. Great, in point of fact. The silent post-coitus purring was broken by Anna.

"I hope dinner is salvageable, I'll bet you've worked up an appetite."

"I'm starving but I don't have any desire to move."

"One of us is going to have to move to get you your wine."

"I'm happy where I am."

"Did you stop by Sully's on the way home? Insignia is your favorite. A '97. It was hard to find and its open."

"I'll drink it, if it didn't break when we were on the table. I just want to be here for a while. This is nice."

"Mmmm. It is. We aren't going to have many more quiet nights like this." She moved his hand to her stomach, hand over his, interlocked. "It is still rather early, and we've had so many false starts, but the doc likes our chances this time."

He slid the other elbow to prop himself up, looking into her beautiful, glowing face. "Really? Is that what she said? When did you go? Why didn't you tell me?"

"Like I said, we've had way too many setbacks to let you get excited for nothing."

"We're in this together, babe. You should have let me know when you knew. I feel terrible that you had to worry with this alone. How long?"

"Just a couple of months, but she said there doesn't seem to be any 'chromosomal anomalies' this time. This is the furthest we have made it so she is confident."

"Please don't get mad, but should we get our hopes up? I don't want to go through any of that business again. For your sake."

"Are you saying that you don't want kids now, Jacob? We talked about this and I - "

" — ssshhhhh. No, I am not saying that. You know I want to have kids with you, I know you know that. I just saw a piece of you die every time we've had a setback. Its like a knife in my heart every time I see you hurt. I love you, I don't want to get our hopes up for a big let down again. Its too far to fall, thats all I'm saying."

She kissed him on the mouth, rolling on top of him. "You're going to be a dad, so get used to it pal."

"I'm gonna be a dad?"

"You are going to be the greatest dad. It's going to be perfect this time you'll see. Now lets have dinner. Did we break the plates?"

✳✳✳✳✳✳

Shooting up from his bed, he just missed hitting his head on the bottom of the top bunk. Grantes stared at the dreary walls so close to him. His celly was above him, snoring, presumably having his own dreams. They had worked so hard for everything they had built, he and Anna, and it was steadily being disassembled. He did not yet know why Anna had not been at the courthouse that morning, nor did he know why she was not answering the phone at the prearranged times he attempted to call her. But Grantes was wide awake, forced to linger over the events of the day and the dream. Sleep would not return to him.

11

WARREN DENNIHAN WAS AN ENIGMATIC MAN with countless connections that he had made throughout the many incarnations of his life and careers. He was Boston born and bred, having grown up in a rough neighborhood of crooks in South Boston. *Southie* was a borough with a very bad rap; but it is well deserved, as it was an exclusively Irish, self-isolated community, and had an inordinate number of crimes which went largely unsolved.

As kids, Warren and his neighborhood friends would boost car radios for extra cash, and in some cases the entire car surrounding it. He learned when he was quite young, however, that those petty crimes were cause for added attention from authorities. And these small indiscretions were ones the bigger crime syndicates didn't appreciate. They didn't give a shit what he and his friends did as long as they didn't shit where they ate. They could have anything they wanted as long as they stayed clear of the neighborhood, that was for higher up the food chain. The big dogs ate alone.

He would get his offers to join those higher orders a few years later, but managed to steer clear of that life. In the meantime, the cops pretty much left him alone. His thefts, gun possessions, and what-not were Mickey Mouse compared to the organized crime, murders, armed robberies, drugs, hookers, money laundering, and extortion, to name the top few. The Police were too busy.

Deni managed to have his juvenile record expunged, but retained contact and respect from all the associates, family, and friends from his old neighborhood. There was an unspoken contract between them; they would continue to be useful resources, as they had been countless times, while he stayed clear of the crime in his old stomping grounds. He had become, of all things, a cop. They harbored no ill-will when he found work outside of Southie, good for him. They held their collective breath when they learned that he went into the academy, but after a few conversations he was able to maneuver through his maneuvers.

The Police Academy accepted him despite coming from Southie, more likely because of it. Early on they had asked him if he wanted to become an undercover detective in that part of Boston. He literally laughed out loud at them when the subject was first broached. He knew everyone down there, they knew he went into the academy, not even the most idiotic of the idiots would let him get involved in a crime with them.

Once they realized their mistake, which took the bureaucrats until nearly the end of his training, he was relegated to state highway duty. As punishment for getting one over on them, he sat in a cruiser all day catching speeders traveling east and west on the Massachusetts Turnpike, Interstate 90. He saw no value in that job whatsoever. He was a tax collector. He spent each shift filling the state coffers with money collected from the issuance of tickets and fines. These poor commuters were already taxed to use that stretch of road in the form of exorbitantly high tolls. The Pike would be backed up for miles in either direction, in part because of those toll booths, each and every day. Whenever a small bit of traffic would open up, commuters would try to take advantage by speeding up to make up for the lost time. A cluster of vehicles would travel ten or fifteen miles per hour over the limit, and Trooper Dennihan would be there to punish them. He felt dirty.

It took a couple of years, but he would in the end manage to make Detective Junior Grade in Boston. The honeymoon ended quickly, however. The political bullshit ran high in the big city. The job was not about how well you performed, how well you detected, it was about how good you looked doing it. It was also about the time that young kids with college degrees in criminology or some such nonsense were taking over for the 'uneducated' veterans. He had just gotten to the detective squad and he was already being forced out.

So he decided to take on a few side jobs the last year before he left the Staties. He worked part-time for a local private investigator, which was highly frowned upon, but he didn't care. With all that he knew, all the shady deals not on the books by his fellow officers, he was safe from any internal exposure. He would never have revealed any of those secrets or deals, but they didn't know that, which further ingratiated him to the corrupt. They would also eventually prove useful.

Deni also made a few bucks as a Mixed Martial Arts fighter. He had been a scrapper all of his life, starting from his old neighborhood, why not get paid for it? He didn't relish hurting people, but sometimes people needed a good beating. And it wasn't like he was going against unwilling participants. If he didn't hurt them, he was going to be hurt. He won more than he lost but he didn't want to go on the circuit like his younger pal Kenny Florian. He still practiced his Brazilian Jiu-Jitsu daily, but not for money. Well, not in a direct way. In his current line of work, it had come in handy more times than he could count.

As a private investigator, he was extremely successful because of his work ethic, street smarts, contacts, and most definitely his toughness. Though he was wiry, he was as strong and intimidating as they come. He was covered in tattoos from collarbone to thighs, completing his bad-boy image, though he had built credit with a diverse group of people. Journalists, crooks, and cops alike could see him coming from a mile away. Some would run while others were eager for the visit.

Warren had met a couple of attorneys from southern New Hampshire on a case during his moonlighting days, and had occasionally been on the payroll since. They had helped to extricate him from the legal excrement that was piled shoulder-high from time to time in his past, and he had reciprocated, getting them out of jams. They were his friends, in some cases closer than his childhood buddies, and he trusted them with his life. And now, JG was counting on him for his.

✴✴✴✴✴✴

Interstate 495 was a circuitous route around the main artery of 93, which runs south through Boston. Southbound commuters looking to circumvent the heavy traffic into the city, used 495 to steer west of the metropolis. Fifteen miles west of the city is exactly where Warren needed to be. This was called the Metro-west area of Boston and he was virtually at the junction of the Mass Pike and 495. The New England Emergency Services Information headquarters, or NEESI, was in all likelihood plunked there for lack of better place to locate it.

NEESI is the center for the communication, coordination, and storage of all 911 emergency phone calls. Each public phone company, cable bundler, and cell phone carrier must satisfy a minimum set of requirements for the handling and management of emergency phone calls. Though AT&T was instrumental in the invention of 911 with the FCC in 1968, the carriers no longer handle the calls themselves like they used to, all calls are connected to a regional administrator. There is a live person, of course, nobody wants to speak with an automated computer on the other end of the phone when they are in dire need, but that live person is not likely to be close to you. They relay the information to local authorities who respond locally. For New England States, the FCC regulates NEESI for all the emergency phone calls, which is located in Newton, Massachusetts for some reason. Home of Doug Flutie and Fig Newtons.

In 2011, the Federal Government made it illegal to broadcast; publish; or make public any 911 phone call in an effort to encourage anonymous tipsters, without fear of reprisal. What most people don't know is that every call can be traced using technology like GPS and geolocators for all VIOP lines. So while the spy movies show the ability to trace these calls may be somewhat true, laws are in place to protect the callers.

Warren was aware that he had no legal right to investigate the anonymous 911 call which reported a drunk driver, who ran a woman off the road in southern New Hampshire, that late summer night. He was also aware the woman that he was going to try to persuade to give him this illegal access, was his former scorned lover.

"You got fat," Althea said.

"Hello to you too. I'll take the high road. You look good." The truth was she had always been super-curvy, and she had gotten more so since last he had seen her. She was not built to be model thin, nor was she that day.

"I knew you would come back to me, less than a year after you dump me and your back already. Well you're not going to get back in that easy, Mr. Man."

"If I was crawlin' back, I wouldn't do it at your work Althea."

"Yeah I know, I'm squeezing your plums. Where is your sense of humor? You only call when you want something, so what do you want."

Her office was nondescript with all sorts of techie gadgets and screens. She sat down behind her desk, leaving Deni to stand before her with hat in hand. As if.

"I called you yesterday to tell you what I need, so how long are you gonna try and make me squirm? I drove all the way down here because you said you might be able to do something for me, if not 'totally hook me up'. Are you gonna help me out or not?"

He was not normally attracted to voluptuous women, preferring the more athletically built. He took painstaking care of his body, other than alcohol. He was lean and muscular, and he was attracted to women who were as well. But there was something about this crazy chick that kept him intrigued, and yet drove him nuts at the same time. Crazy was what he was attracted to. He had a thing for psychos.

"Keep quiet and close my door. You're gonna get me fired. You said I look good, right?"

"Yeah, you look good, Al."

"I love it when you call me Al. Can I squeeze your plums for real? We can just lock the door — "

" — maybe some other time. I'm here for the 911 call, that's all. I thought I made that clear yesterday when I - "

" - I got the message yesterday, asshole. I was just hoping to see you. I look good though right? Come over to this side of the desk and tell me that."

"Where are all the big spools of tape spinning with all the phone calls on them like they show on TV?"

"It's a good thing you're pretty, because TV is killing your brain. Read a book or something, this is the digital age. Its all on computers. Binary. Ones and zeros."

"It's the digital age and your talkin' to me about books. Funny. Anyway, this cat and mouse game is fun and everything but JG is depending on me here, so are you gonna play games or help me out? It didn't work out between us but that doesn't mean you should punish my friends. You remember JG right? The lawyer guy in New Hampshire? We had dinner with him and his wife that time."

"I remember. It's gotta be cold in here for all the computer equipment, why don't you come over here and warm me up?"

"*Althea.*"

"It's on my computer. You have to come over to my side of the desk if you want your information. Your choice. Do you want it or not?"

He went around her desk and was looking over her shoulder at both of her large monitors.

"Don't get any ideas, lover-boy."

He rolled his eyes behind her back. "So what are we looking at? I'm old school. I have trouble with my iPhone."

" I know just listen."

She played the recording with a click of a mouse.

> EMS: "911, this call is recorded, what is your emergency?"
>
> CALLER: "There is a bad accident on Wayland Country Club Road, by the big bend. It looks bad."

The female caller's voice didn't seem nervous, nor shrieking like that of someone who had just witnessed a horrific accident. She could have been ordering a pizza.

Warren was looking at the screen on the left which was indicating the various sound bars, they rose and fell based upon the specific pitch, bass, treble, decibels, dynamics, and the like. What struck him was that the bars for the caller were not rising very much, any of them. The caller was basically monotone, though the voices were coming out of some fancy speakers he had never heard of called Magicos.

> EMS: "Are you hurt miss?"
>
> CALLER: "No, no, I'm not involved. I just saw it happen."
>
> EMS: "How many cars are involved, miss?
>
> CALLER: "One. Well, two. The car that is totaled and the one that took off."
>
> EMS: "Emergency personel are on the way. Did you see the other vehicle? The one that left the scene?"

332

CALLER: "Of course. It was a black Volvo XC90 SUV. New Hampshire plates." She then recited the number matter of factly.

EMS: "Did you see which direction the Volvo went?"

CALLER:: "There is only one direction that the thing could have gone." This was the first time that the caller had any emotion in her voice.

EMS: "OK, can you see the victim?"

CALLER: "I can see where the victim is supposed to be. Like I said it's bad. She's dead."

EMS: "Did you get her pulse? Do you have medical training? Are you certain she is dead?"

CALLER: "I'm not going anywhere near that car. But there is no way she could have survived that crash.

EMS: "OK. What is your name and where are you at the sight? There will be someone on the scene within a few seconds."

CALLER: click.

"The caller was way too calm. Don't you think? You must hear a million of these calls," Deni said as he straightened, standing fully erect.

"You hear all kinds, but yeah she was totally calm. Especially when she knew the woman was dead."

"How did she know she was dead? She never went near the car. I saw pictures of the wreck, and I admit that it looked really bad. But still."

"The wreck must have been bad enough where she just knew."

"If she saw the whole thing happen, like she says, there was always a chance she could have been alive. I mean, she had no way of knowing without going up to the car that the woman was decapitated."

"Maybe she didn't want to see all the blood and guts."

"I don't think so. Have you ever driven by a wreck on the side of the road? Slows traffic to a stop because everybody has to see the damage. Everybody wants to see, or to help, or be a hero. She knew the woman was dead. Wait a sec."

"What? You have that look. That totally, super sexy look you get when you think you figured something out that nobody else knows," Althea said. Her eyes were taking him in again.

"How did she know it was a *she*?"

"The caller?"

"Yeah, the caller. Who else? She said the woman was dead. Played it off like nobody could have possibly survived the crash and wasn't going anywhere near the car. But she knew it was a chick."

"Interesting, but what does that prove?"

"Well nothing, but it's weird right?"

"I think you are desperate to help your friend and are reaching."

He looked onto the right screen where the caller's phone number and location was pulled up. He began to write it down when Althea stopped him.

"Hey you can't do that. I'm sorry, but my neck is out just letting you listen to the call. The cops can get it with a warrant, but it's anonymous, so they aren't likely to get authorization. Additionally, it's from a burner phone."

"Additionally? Who says that?"

"Smart people."

"Whatever. Anyways, you said that phone number is from a burner? Who bought it, who is it registered to?"

"I can't tell you even if I knew."

"Whattaya mean? You don't know? All this equipment and you aren't tellin' me shit." He was playing to her sense of IT superiority. She was an information junky and her skills with technology were extraordinary. Whatever NEESI was paying her, her talents were wasted.

334

"It is an *unregistered* burner phone. It's still legal to go out and buy a disposable phone without putting any of your personal information on it, especially if you pay in cash. Drug dealers would be out of business if they couldn't do that. You can't trace a phone that gets thrown away and that isn't connected to the dealer in the first place."

"Come on Al. You don't find this weird? Mysterious lady, who buys a burner phone, an unregistered burner phone like you just said, sees the whole thing but doesn't help? She never even goes near the car but knows it is a woman, and conveniently makes JG's vehicle and plate number?"

"It's not that odd. I'm sorry, but people are paranoid. Especially in New Hampshire. They think the Government is tapping their phones, tracking their movements so they get untraceable phones. She wants to be a good Samaritan, but she can't stand blood. Maybe she saw more than she needed to from a distance, and that is how she knew it was a female. It is all explainable. I know you want to help, but the call isn't gonna be it I'm afraid."

"Will you give me a copy of the call? And the phone number and who sold it to her?"

"Ugh. You are going to be the death of me. Its illegal and can't be used in court, so why do you need it?"

"I have a hunch. And I'm desperate. Come on, Al. I know you wanna."

She paused for ten-seconds, then pulled out a pink memory stick that said *Susan B. Komen* on it in small print. She had already had it inserted into the USB drive. She handed it to him and said, "you owe me dinner. Not just Wendy's but like, an actual date."

"You got it."

"Verizon."

"What?"

"Verizon is the carrier, so my bet is that this Samaritan bought it at a Verizon store or kiosk."

"Thanks. You look great by the way," Deni said as he dashed out of her office.

"Call me."

12

THE CORRECTIONS PORTION OF THE NAME Wayland County House of Corrections was designated such, in large part, because of the programs it offered the inmates housed there. The programs included trades like culinary, print pressing or counseling programs like parenting, substance abuse, and anger management. Considering the prison's unemployment and recidivism rates, only those who had a sense of humor or were defending their jobs could argue that these programs had any positive affect whatsoever. Federal money was doled out by the fistful to the States who opted to build institutions with these programs to curb rising incarceration rates. WCHOC was one of these county run, federally funded, maximum security institutions.

The Sheriff mandated that these program rosters remain full at all times in order to fleece the Federal Government for every dollar he could. If an inmate didn't have a high school diploma or equivalent, they got a GED whether they earned it or not. Federal monies came into the prison for every equivalency test passed. Cha-ching. If the inmate didn't have a job lined up upon his release, they earned a trade, but only one of the two trades offered. Cha-ching. And if any portion of the alleged or convicted crime involved substance abuse, well they received counseling for it. Cha-ching. Keep those dollars flowing, the system is working fine in Wayland County.

Grantes had received higher degrees from prestigious schools, was a successful attorney, and a business owner. He had not yet been convicted, but he was being housed in the Sheriff's institution. The Sheriff wasn't maximizing any federal tax dollars on Grantes's back, and so he was perplexed as to what to do with him. Attaining a GED was out, he had a trade, and his own business, so no money could be garnered there. Grantes was a father, and was alleged to have operated a vehicle under the influence of alcohol, so he would be made to take parenting classes and alcohol abuse treatment. Inmate #437261 was going to earn his keep one way or another.

The federal money was contingent upon the prison adhering to federal incarceration guidelines; such as twenty hour lock-ins, and the size of the cell that two men would spend locked into said cell. With four total hours for recreational time dispersed in intervals throughout the day, *rec time* meant; showering, eating, lawyer visits, seeing the nurse, exercise, phone calls, and any programs that were assigned. Grantes was mandated to be enrolled in three hours of programming, which meant he had one hour per day to eat, exercise, shower, call someone on his pre-approval sheet, and get an aspirin if he had a headache. His sanity was not part of his rehabilitation.

His every day was scheduled exactly the same. A routine was deemed an important element in correcting behavior. Grantes started every day with the loud clang of the opening of the metal door to his cell at 6:00 AM for chow, closing again with the same sound at 6:10 with him back inside of it. The door would open and close many more times throughout the day so he could; go to parenting class, lock-in, substance group therapy, lock-in, 11:00 AM chow, lock-in, self-help, lock-in, SAP (Spousal Advocate Program), lock-in, 5:00 PM chow, lock-in, one hour of rec to do whatever he had to do like shower or call Anna, then lock-in again until 6:00 AM the next day where he would do it all over again.

His parenting class was a counselor-led group with a preset agenda and course workbook. Grantes hadn't the faintest idea whom had written the course workbook, but he did surmise that it was written for those whom had difficulty with reading and writing in the English language.

Alphonse, the parenting counselor, was a megalomaniac, African-American man who was clearly not in the top of his field, and despised calling upon Grantes in class. He avoided the inmate at all costs as he had been embarrassed by him in the past. This suited Grantes just fine. Every so often, however, he would be forced to include the inmate in the discussion to avoid the appearance of favoritism, but always did so with trepidation. Alphonse would speak to the group standing in the front of the seated half-circle to further assert his dominance over the flock.

".... and wouldn't you agree, Mr. Grantes?" Alphonse said at the end of a monotonous monologue.

"Most likely not, but I can't say for certain as I wasn't really paying attention to you."

"We were discussing the likelihood that children of criminals tend to become criminals themselves. I was inquiring as to your thoughts, as you seemed to be lost in your own thoughts. Also, as an attorney, or former attorney, whichever the case may be, you are in a unique position to agree with that assessment."

"Cheery, that. You must be a glass-is-half-full kinda guy. You're trying to sound smart but I'm not buying. No, I do not agree. If the father is in prison, he would have little, if any, influence over his — "

" — if you you were to look at — "

" — I wasn't finished. You asked my opinion then you interrupted me, which is disingenuous. 'A man expects his son to be as good a man as he *meant* to be' - Franklin Clark. I am sure you knew that."

"No, I didn't know that. But I prefer the Bible which says — "

" — 'He who brings up, not he who begets, is the father.' There thats from the bible, now do you feel better? It isn't genetic, its environmental. And even that is just a statistic. You are statistically more apt to become a criminal if you live in an area where there is high crime, but that doesn't automatically mean that if you live in say, Barstone, that you are going to be here at one point or another. What are you trying to feed these people? Hopelessness?"

"I was trying to illustrate that they need to break the cycle of crime."

"I know what you are trying to do, Alphonse. You assume that because these guys are here, that their fathers were criminals also. You are only interested in kicking a man when he is already at his lowest point. It's not enough that he is here, in this horrible place. No, he has to be made to wonder how his kids are doing in his absence; only to be told that it doesn't matter one bit, because his kid is going to wind up here anyway. And he will probably have to listen to you tell him the same bullshit story you're spilling out right now. You must feel great at the end of your day."

"I don't appreciate your tone, inmate. The fact is that unless you are willing to change your behavior, the cycle will continue." He was losing the group of men, losing his stature as the authority figure of the group. He embarked in this dialogue to open up a non-participating inmate, a quiet one, but he was getting embarrassed again.

"You want us, oh wait, that last comment was to me directly wasn't it? You want me to change into what you consider to be a good parent. No parent is perfect, even you. Besides, how do any of us know that you're not a junkbox, or that your kid is? Is your kid some deviant destined to be here? You spend a lot of your life here, so what does that mean? What would you say to your kid if he were sitting here? That in all likelihood his kid, your grandson, is going to be sitting here no matter what he does?"

"Maybe we should move onto the exercises in your workbooks." He turned to everyone else in the group. "Open your workbooks and quietly complete the next two exercises." He lowered to say in Grantes's ear, "another outburst like that one and I will have you lugged for insolence and inciting a riot."

"The trouble is, Alphonse, you called on me. You don't like me and you don't like my opinions. You think you know me because of my circumstance, but you don't know me or anybody else here. And you won't unless you speak to them like they are human. We aren't animals in a zoo. If you want respect, you'll have to give some."

"You can't win, Grantes. You will never win. Not in this place, and not over me. No matter what you do or what you say, I get to walk out that door at five o'clock. And you stay here to rot. Society doesn't want you, so they send you here. This is your life and you better get used to it."

Instead of concentrating on the workbook, as he was instructed, Grantes thought back to when he first became a parent. He remembered it like it was yesterday, though he was four years removed.

******

The large flatscreen was tuned to football, as it was every Sunday during every season, with the surround sound blaring. Anna was standing in front of the couch with her oversized #12 New England Patriots jersey, filling it out more like a linebacker than the quarterback the uniform represented. She was nine months pregnant, and while she couldn't experience this football season the way she had in the past, she was enjoying listening to the helmets smash, bones crunch, feeling the hits as the bass kicked with a high fidelity that would make George Lucas proud.

"Baby, can you pleeeeeeaaaaase explain to me why they have such a hard time playing against Miami? The Dolphins suck, they always suck and yet we play like shit against them every time." She said 'we' like she was on the roster.

From the kitchen he shouted back to her. Neither one of them able to hear the other with the sounds of football turned up so loud. He was putting the finishing touches on a platter of boneless chicken wings.

"I honestly don't know, hun. The Pats always have to make things interesting. They can't just decisively beat the crap out of them, they have to keep you guessing." He walked back into the entertainment room with the large platter in one hand, and a bottle of Stone IPA in the other. His wife was standing in the middle of the room with her eyes glued to the enormous TV.

"Thanks babe. These better be spicy. They say spice helps induce labor and I'm ready for him to be out." She took the entire platter out of his hand, leaving him only the beer. He sat down in the recliner to her left.

"They're tossed in *Sriracha*, they are going to be spicy. Is that vat of ranch dressing going to be enough for you?"

"Fuck you, I'm hungry. I'll trade you. You carry your son around for a while and see how it feels." She was shoveling the wings into her mouth without looking away from the game. He was laughing despite being left to go hungry. He struggled to understand exactly what she had said between the mouthful of food and volume, but he was able to glean the gist.

"You look amazing in that jersey. Who needs 3-D when I've got that big #12 popping towards me?"

"Get off that couch, I'm gonna kick your ass. It's a good thing you are the most attractive shithead I have ever seen." She turned her face but not her eyes as she leaned down to kiss her husband. The kiss smeared hot sauce all over his face, matching hers. She licked the sauce off her thumb before grabbing another wing with her dripping hand.

"How are they, good? I like mine."

"Delicious. You are a master chef — oh honey, I'm sorry. Do you want one?

"Ha. No, you eat them. You look like you're enjoying yourself. I think the whole thing is a wive's tale anyway; but if you think spicy chicken will help, I'm here for you."

"Thank you. I love you."

"I love you too, although you might be bigger than the blimp that is floating over Gillette Stadium right now." And he did love her, with all of his being.

"When I get back to fighting weight, we are gonna wrestle, and not the naked kind, my friend. Now shut up so I can watch the game, we're on the 20."

They remained silent for a couple of minutes. Jacob found it odd that there was no reaction when the Patriots had to settle for a field goal, even more odd that she muted the TV right before the kick. Muting the television during a football game was forbidden.

"Babe, how many beers have you had?"

"I just started my third, why? You said it didn't bother you if I had a couple even though you can't. Are you gonna start in on me — "

" — shut up, I don't care about that. It's go-time."

"Go-time?" He was slow on the uptake.

"The wings worked, *go-time* you fool."

"Oh. Oh God, lets go."

"Call the hospital on the way, they need to have the game on when I get there. I'm serious."

"Yeah, yeah hun. Let's just get over there and we will worry about the game when we get there. They're gonna think we are nuts." He grabbed the prepared baby bag and his wife, stuffed both into the car. "No shit, the spicy wings did work," he said to himself as he made his way around the car to pack himself into the driver's seat.

******

The walk back to Grantes's cell was not long in terms of distance, but it was long in that it took a lot of time and was always an adventure. The rooms that held all the programming were in a separate area of the prison. He would make bets with himself, taking the over/under on how many times he would be pat-down or asked to see his ID. Just for some kind of fun. He thought the entire charade was inefficient, but soon realized that it was less about efficiency and more about the appearance of insurmountable security. Much like the security in airports, the armed guards, TSA, police, and security were all in place to create an atmosphere of impenetrable order.

He stopped by the COs desk when he returned to the pod. The desk which was known as the *bubble* because an inmate was not allowed within the imaginary forcefield around the desk, much like the game that kids play. Grantes asked if he could get some extra rec time so that he could use the library, but of course the request was denied. No reason was given. He had a couple of hours before the next evolution in his reprogramming and wanted to investigate some case law instead of being unproductive in his cell.

340

As the solid door loudly slid open, the acrid smell of burning paper and smoke billowed out at him. Loder yelled at him to close the door, as if he had control over it. His celly was smoking what appeared to be a cigarette, which was contraband. Grantes was trying to decide whether to go into the cell or stay out of it, when the door started to close. He went in.

"What the hell are you doing? You're gonna get us both lugged," Grantes said.

"Chew-ports, bro. I'm making smokes. You want one?"

"No. And it's not fantastic that I'm gonna be just as screwed as you when you get caught. Jesus-H, that stuff smells terrible. You are putting me in a spot here, Loder."

"You're not gonna snitch. But you are gonna block that window and keep flushing the toilet."

"The COs aren't gonna buy that one of us is taking a shit. It smells awful but it smells like burnt-awful, not shit-awful."

"Just shut up and keep flushing."

"How the hell do you make cigarettes in here anyway? You fly in some tobacco? It's not like they will let you receive that in the mail."

"The COs chew tobacco."

"What? And they just give it to you?"

"No, one of the guys in the pod cleans at night, so he saves their spit cups. I dry it out and then roll it up in paper I rip out of the library books. See? Who says readin' ain't useful."

"That is absolutely disgusting. Fucking gross. And I don't think this is what they are striving for with the library books. No wonder half the books I try to read are missing pages." He watched and flushed again when a thought crossed his mind. "Hey, how do you light those things, they don't allow us to have fire, let alone a lighter where we can make our own."

"Two batteries and a bread tie."

"You're shitting me."

"Nope."

"Loder, if you would just use your powers for good instead of evil, you could make something of yourself."

"My genius only works in here. Besides, other guys are just as smart if not smarter. Prison is full of MacGyver-types, I saw a guy the other day trying to sell speakers for the radio."

"Which brings us to back to the cigarettes. You either gotta sell them all today before cell searches tonight, or you have to cop to it if they find them. I'm having a hard enough time fighting off the charges I have, let alone pick up more. I'm not gonna snitch, but I won't cop to it either."

"Fair enough. For a lawyer, you ain't have bad Grantes."

"Gee, thanks."

Unfortunately, Loder, #437254, was very likely to be caught. Cell searches were at least daily, sometimes more if they were suspicious of a certain inmate. But the real danger was in the other smokers on the pod. The COs would find them in someone's cell during a search, and that someone would cut a deal to get out of the additional charge, and the additional time that the charge would bring. One of the worst things a man can be in prison is a snitch, but it happened every day. Someone would rat to save their skin, and everyone would know. A guy can't fart in prison without the entire prison population knowing. The rat would be hunted and beaten without mercy, take a trip to HSU, then spend the remainder of his stay in Protective Custody. Once you checked in there, you had better hope that you never run into another inmate on this stay or the next. Word gets around. A PC is the worst thing a man can be, just above a rat, and then a skinner although it's close. The prison protects a PC, hence the name, as much as possible by segregating them. But then, for some absurd reason, they give them a special color jumpsuit so they stand out a mile away. That is why they get themselves cornered by another inmate, and why those guys get killed.

Cigarettes were just one of the many commodities traded on the pods. The prison was not the NYSE, but the methods for successful trade negotiations were just as intricate. Economics courses could be taught on the supply and demand formulae used to compile price analysis and forecasting for the prison exchange system. Every day; pharmaceuticals, narcotics, hooch, smokes, hardcore mags, and the like were smuggled or manufactured in prison. If the inmate was a known quantity, hot, he has a seemingly inculpable cohort store and distribute the contraband. The value of the commodity is based upon availability, risk, and going rate of sale on the outside. Payment is then made in one of a myriad of methods.

One such method is in the form of outside trade. A phone call is made to someone who is on the pre-approved phone list on the outside, as calls can go out but never come in. All calls are recorded which makes necessary a highly elaborate code for communicating logistics, dollar amount, the recipient, their contact information, et cetera. The outside person then makes the appropriate calls and connections, the money transferred. The inmate then calls back his contact on the outside at a designated time to ensure that all funds have been exchanged, where it is then given to a baby-momma to hold, use, or send back to the prison in form of a money order through the mail to be deposited into his account.

The prison store, or canteen, is set up for inmates to buy various items from that account. Everything from sneakers and clothing, to radios and foodstuffs are sold at up to three hundred percent over the three hundred percent markup a retailer sells them for on the street. This is yet another way the prison makes money on the backs of the downtrodden.

Canteen is another way goods and services are exchanged because, without cash, canteen items are the same as cash. The value of each item is like money in the bank, or the pocket if prisoners were allowed to have pockets.

Prisoners can pay bills from their account, not just buy canteen items. Child support, alimony, and court fines are also the usual reasons for an inmate to send out a money order from a case manager. Once that money order leaves the prison, it is as good as laundered.

Grantes wanted no part of this system, no part of the cigarette distribution company currently being run out of his cell. The triangle trade was very lucrative for the professional inmate, which Grantes did not consider himself to be. His extra rec time was denied and he was, therefore, relegated to the lock-in with his celly. He couldn't tell anyone, nor could he escape. So he waited for his next dose of therapy or reprogramming, all the while his mind was still racing about the past.

******

The funeral of Norman Craig was a lavish affair. Jacob thought it gauche to have such extravagance for an event as somber. The enormous church to which his in-laws gave astronomical sums of money, though rarely (if ever) attended, was packed beyond capacity. The crowd spilled out onto the front lawn, onto the street, and down the block. The death of an Investment, Insurance, and Banking Mogul such as Craig Investment Group, CIG, brought the finest people out of the woodwork. Hundreds of America's biggest players (and some of the World's) had come out to pay their final respects. Jacob wondered how many were Norman's friends, and how many were sycophants. When Sheikh Hamdan of Dubai was in attendance, it made Jacob wonder just how rich Norman was.

Craig's battle with esophageal cancer was a short one. Jacob had thought that his father in-law could overcome any obstacle, that there was nothing in the world that could best him. This particular ailment, however, was terminal in statistically every case, regardless of wealth or power. What began as a sore throat, for which true movers and shakers have no time, became five months of torturous misery. For the family, the defeat was pronounced almost overnight. For the epitome of a mainstay, both familial and in commerce, it was an excruciating reminder that there are some things even the most influential can't control.

The pillar would never get to meet his grandson. Jacob and Anna had tried to conceive for years while Norman was alive, without success. When Brady finally became a reality, Jacob suggested that he be named after his deceased grandfather. The idea was immediately shot down, Anna would not hear of it, and Olivia was in exile then. After her father's death, Anna became isolated from her mother. What exactly had happened between them in the days that followed Norman's passing wouldn't be discovered until much later, but the mere mention of his name, or Olivia's for that matter, was deemed too painful, and would cause volcanic tirades.

Mrs. Craig was presumed alive and well, her whereabouts however, were unknown. She was financially one of the most secure and was most likely spending it in her golden years.

Jacob missed her terribly. The passing of his own parents, the death of his father in-law, and the isolation from Olivia was heartbreaking.

Olivia had disappeared and had been unheard of until a letter arrived at the law office years later.

✳✳✳✳✳✳

JG had taken a few weeks off after Brady was born. Ryan had covered the workload happily, keeping his partner apprised or seeking his advice only in the most dire of circumstances.

Upon his return to the office, amidst the immense stack of messages, to-do's, and mail; Angie had set aside an urgent, certified letter. It was a large, thick manilla envelope void of a return address.

"Welcome back, JG. We have several well-wishes, gifts, a ton of mail for you to go through, and this one marked 'urgent and confidential'. No return address and sent by currier, so I was curious about it. I almost opened it but thought better of it. If it's rigged with a device, I want no part of it. What mysterious person did you piss off? Do you want some coffee, by the way?"

"Thanks Ang. Yes on the coffee, but if we could take it down a notch please until I get caught up that would be great. Maybe you should switch to decaf."

"Ha ha. It's just good to have you back, and we have so much to go over, and I am curious about the package. I left it on top of your pile."

"Ang. Please, huh? It's like trying to take a sip of water through a fire hose with you right now. I'll be in my office." He closed the door behind him only to have it opened again thirty-seconds later.

"Here is your coffee. Sorry to come at you right when you walked in the door."

"Thanks, Ang. Sorry to tear into you. I'm not getting any sleep. I love that little guy but he never sleeps. Is that normal? Everybody says its normal, but not sleeping for this long doesn't seem normal to me."

"He never sleeps?"

"Well sometimes, but not for very long stretches."

"Yeah, that's normal."

He was behind his desk, took a sip of his coffee which, truthfully, Angie fixed better than his wife. "I gotta be honest with you, it was tough to leave the house today. My head is not really in it."

"I don't blame you. I'll hold your calls and leave you to it."

"Ang?"

"Yes."

"Thanks for all your help in holding it all together over here. I couldn't have spent all that time with Anna and Brady without you and Ry. I appreciate it."

"Anytime. You know that," she said as she closed the door behind her.

They were likely just as exhausted as he was. They had each been putting in fifteen plus hours per day, six days a week while he was taking maternity leave. They had lives of their own, albeit together, and had set them aside for the good of the firm. They needed the income more than JG did. But any critique about Ryan sliding into a free partnership could be quieted, he had worked his ass off.

He decided to inspect the mysterious package first. It was on the top of his pile anyway. The document sized envelope was uber-sealed, requiring him having to rip apart the outer envelope to retrieve the contents. No bomb. No anthrax. The thick stack of documents were typed, the top sheet a congratulations of the birth of his son, Brady. Whomever it was knew him and knew him well enough to know he was now a father. On the double, he rescanned the envelope, but still no clues.

The dawn broke in the next few paragraphs on the first page. The sender spoke about how sad it was that she could not be there for the birth of her only grandson. How she wanted more than anything to be a part of all of their lives. She apologized for being persona non grata, for her part in it anyway. She begged for continued anonymity and wished to take the opportunity to share the reasons she had been alienated. She further hoped that after laying all her cards on the table, that some sort of forgiveness and reunion would take place in the foreseeable future.

"She must be dying. Why else is she getting her house in order?" he said to himself. He went on to read the rest of the documents, which told of the day the earth shattered and swallowed Olivia Craig.

******

The meeting with Cecil Brand, the Craig family finance manager and board member of CIG, took place less than a week after Norman Craig had passed on. The meeting that took place after Craig's death was not unexpected but the result was very much so. Brand was a slight, weaselly looking gentleman. Frail-thin, beady eyes behind oversized oval glasses which rested on an aquiline nose; Cecil was as irksome to look at as his voice was to hear. Olivia and Anna would have to deal with him in order to sort out the nuances of the Will.

345

"I'm sorry we have to meet under these circumstances, Olivia. Anna, it has been too long," Cecil said.

"Your condolences are appreciated as are your years of service to my husband and our family. My daughter and I, if it is not too much trouble or crass Cecil, would like to take care of the business at hand without fetter, so that we may be free to grieve."

"Yes, of course. Once I've explained everything, you both will simply need to sign the documents. You don't even need to read them if you would prefer, though I see Anna has dived right into them."

Each of the women had been given a small binder of documents as they took their seats. Olivia had not so much as looked at hers.

"I'm sorry, Cecil, was I not supposed to read these? There has to be seventy-five or a hundred pages here," Anna said.

"Well, the Craig Estates and Holdings are extensive and complicated. Given how vast and diversified his assets are, it has been painstaking work to sort it all out. Much less to organize it in one small binder. I've been responsible for his personal financial well-being for years and I assure you that — "

" — my father was an investment mogul, I'm sure he was able to manage his own checkbook just fine."

"Anna, there is no need to be hostile toward Cecil. He was just trying to make a complicated situation less so, isn't that right Mr. Brand?" Olivia was ever the diplomat.

"Yes. Quite right and well said. So as I was saying, he was extraordinarily wealthy and while this may look complicated, since the numbers are so large, there should be no need to quibble or a few dollars, pounds, or euros."

"You mean Norman *and* Olivia's, don't you? You said 'he was wealthy' but you meant *they*, correct?"

"I apologize for her, Cecil. She has taken her father's death very hard. Though he was home so rarely, Norman and Anna were very close."

"Please don't apologize for me mom, like I'm not in the room. Cecil, I'm sorry. I don't really want to be here. Daddy gave me everything I've ever wanted and I hate that he is gone. I loved him very much, as I'm sure you can imagine. Mom worked just as hard as he did, though she just did it at home. So all of this is hers, I'm not sure why it takes all of these documents to sign over what is already hers."

"Right. Well that was a bit insensitive of me. I'm sure this is a very trying time for both of you. It certainly is for me. The reason for the lengthy legal documentation before you, is that it is far more complicated than just signing everything over to Olivia. There are many more beneficiaries."

"I'm getting a headache. How can there be many beneficiaries to Daddy's personal finances? CIG, of course, but personal should just be Mom, Me and maybe Jacob."

346

"Yes, well, if you look in the appendices in the back of the binder you have, you will see that it is not quite as simple as all of that, I am sad to say. There are vast sums, spread out all over the world, and — "

" — hold on please. Who are all of these people? I've never heard of any of these people. Aveda something or other, and — "

" — as I said, your father was quite wealthy and wanted to ensure that certain people of his acquaintance were well taken care of with the various homes, portfolios, trusts, accounts and stock holdings." Cecil was speaking to Anna, who had been questioning him much more than he had hoped, but was looking at Olivia for some help.

"What say we just have him tell us what monies and things are directly bequeathed to us, Anna? You don't want to be here any more than I do, so let poor Cecil just cut to the chase and we can sign whatever it is we must. How would that be?"

"Well, no I don't want to be here at all. But since I am, and since the man whom has been entrusted to manage yours and Daddy's money seems to be giving us the run-around about that money, I think I would like him to take the time to explain. So please, Cecil, please explain it to me. Since you need my signature, which you are not going to get until I get some answers. How would *that* be?"

Cecil was cornered, and the weasel didn't like to be cornered, but he was nothing even close to a fighter. He had backed out of every fight he had ever been involved in. And this was turning into an all-out brawl.

"There is the contingent of future heirs, so those are listed," he said after some thought.

"What am I stupid? I can see that. But everyone on the beneficiary list has money set aside for future heirs. So, for the last time and before I call an attorney, Mr. Brand, who are all of these people? In English. No more run-around, no more vagaries. Answers or I call a lawyer."

He looked to Olivia, who was looking at her lap. "Maybe you and your mother would be more comfortable using my conference room, to uh....collect yourselves."

"You know who these people are Mom?"

"Maybe we should take some time to, as Cecil put it, collect ourselves."

The two women were shown into a side, private conference room off of Brand's office. Once they were inside, he closed the door and bravely ran away from the situation. Olivia gracefully took a seat at the end of the conference table. Anna remained standing.

"Okay Mom, what gives? Who are these people and why doesn't anyone want to tell me?"

"Please have a seat dear so we can discuss this rationally and civilly."

"I'm fine where I am."

"Stop being stubborn and please sit down so I can explain."

"Explain what, Mom? Did Daddy have some distant relatives that I didn't know about? I know about Uncle Robert but Daddy despised him, and he is gay so future heirs is kind of a stretch. I don't see his name in here anyway."

"Would you like some water or something, dear?"

"Mom. Quit stalling."

"Your father was a complicated man. Generous but complicated."

"So these are charity cases? No wonder they have some exotic names."

"No, no. They aren't charity cases, dear, they are …. your half siblings."

"My what? My half siblings?" She did sit down just then. Hard.

"Your father traveled all over the world on business, sometimes he stayed extensively — "

" — hold on, hold on, hold on. Stop for a minute. Are you trying to tell me that Daddy had other families?"

"Well, not in so many words, but he was the father to other people yes."

"Like a father? Or he donated sperm?"

"I don't believe that I follow you, dear."

"Forget it. It doesn't even matter. Was this before he was married to you? No, wait, that doesn't make any sense, you two married after college, right? Tell me that is true."

"That is true. So no, not before we were married."

"And you knew about this?"

"Yes."

"How long? How old are they? How long have you known?"

"I was suspicious for some time, years ago. I found out what was going on many years ago. Fairly early on, in fact."

"What the fuck, Mom?"

"Please calm down dear. There is no need for vulgar language."

"You just told me that my father was a lying, cheating motherfucker, and you're worried about my language?"

"Please calm down."

"So Dad. Norman. Was touring the fucking world, spreading his seed like a landscaper, and you let him?"

"I didn't let him, he did it. I chose to keep our family intact."

"So my life is a big scam. My entire life. You allowed me to think we were a happy family. To bring Jacob into our happy family, which it turns out is just a big joke? I thought we were the luckiest people on earth, Mom. We had money, we were happy, we loved each other. A big fucking lie. It was all for show."

"It isn't a scam, nor a lie, dear. It's not as if I had a career. I did it to protect you. To protect us."

"Oh fuck that, Mom. It's betrayal. I love Jacob with all of my heart, but do you think for one minute that if I found out that he was cheating on me that I would stick around?"

There were a few moments of silence, which seemed like an eternity, as Anna tried to keep her composure, tried not to weep. She had to be strong. She was losing it, tears rolled down her cheeks, her hands trembling. Any attempt to touch Anna, was rebuffed.

Olivia said after a time, "What was I supposed to do?"

"What do you do? What do you mean what do you do?" She stood up, bent over to within an inch of Olivia. "You take me and you leave the son-of-a-bitch. You don't take shit then ask for another helping. You pick up whatever dignity you have, and with your child you leave. You take him for every dollar that he is worth. You leave him penniless, that's what you do." She stood upright again, wiped her tears on her shirtsleeves. Spittle had formed on the sides of her mouth. "Jacob will know nothing about this. You betrayed me, and you betrayed him too."

"So you do see why I kept the secret?"

"Am I really your daughter?"

"What Anna? Of course you are my daughter, how can you say that?"

"I can't believe we have the same genes."

"Anna, I love you. Please sit down so we can talk about this."

"You love me? Love is not lying to someone. Love means you don't betray. You don't really love me, and you cannot expect me to love someone who has done what you have done."

"Stop it, Anna. What are you saying?"

"What am I saying? Here is what I'm saying. I'm saying that you clearly do not know what love means. I'm saying that you decided to cover this all up and betray those people you say you love. I'm saying you are as guilty as he is, that you made your choice and that now you have to live with it. I'm saying that you make whatever excuses you need to, continue to cover up whatever you need to, but you disappear. You stay away from me and you stay away from Jacob. Live with that." Anna walked out of the conference room and never looked back.

※※※※※

Mrs Craig wrote that she would do anything to take it all back. Do anything to get her family back. She would do it all differently. All of it. If only she could have back what she was so desperate to save from the beginning.

She wrote how much she longed to see her only grandson. She assured Jacob that she loved him with all her heart though she had never met him. Her heart was breaking in exile, but there was nothing she could do about that. This was not her choice, only that she was being punished for a choice she had once made.

'Please keep this between us, Jacob. I just wanted you to know what happened and how I feel about you, and of course Anna. It has been too long and life is too short. I wanted you to

349

know why I had to move away and why I am still away. I sincerely hope that someday you can find it in your heart to forgive me and that we will be able to reunite. I would love to meet my grandson. In the meantime, please take care of him and yourselves. Love always, Olivia.'

13

THE RESIDENCE OF ROMAN AND CHAMILLE DESTRIER was a sprawling English manorial style home, if you could call a building that large a home. There were many wealthy homes in Wayland, each trying to be more majestic than the next. The Destrier estate, however, was the most stately north of Newport, Rhode Island. In fact, it was fashioned after a mansion owned by the Vanderbilts, then later the Dukes, known as *Rough Point* in Newport. There was nothing rough about it. It was set far back from the main road and gate, consisting of the main house, a guest house, housing for the help, and even a house for the boat located on the man-made pond.

Roman Destrier was bred from an upper-middle class family. He was an up and coming young financial mind when Norman Craig recruited him from Duke University (which is where Roman fell in love with *Rough Point,* which was owned more recently by James Buchanan Duke, the benefactor of Duke University). Roman began his career with CIG under Norman's tutelage, moving on to head his own financial division, and in the end his own conglomerate.

Chamille had gone to Wellesley College where she had met Anna at a social event for future business women which took place at Boston University. They became fast friends. Chamille had made the trip up to New Hampshire on several occasions. She too was from money, and of course the Craigs approved of Anna's friendship with her. Norman would introduce Chamille to the hot young talent he was grooming, Roman Destrier.

Soon after they married, Roman was heading his own international finance division for CIG, which made him wealthy, but never home. He would stay at one of their numerous homes, flats or an exclusive hotel somewhere on the globe, but not often in New Hampshire. Once he left CIG, the situation became worse as they were married in name only. Chamille saw her husband with such rare occasion she would forget what he looked or sounded like. They rarely spoke, and when they did it was as if they were strangers.

Chamille was bored in her corner of New England. With hired help doing any and all daily household duties, she involved herself in everyone else's life, chiefly Anna's. Chamille knew Roman strayed with other women, no man can go without being intimate for as long as she and her husband did. She had to make appointments with her own husband through one of his female personal assistants. She was bitter and lonely but at least she was rich. Immensely so.

Ryan put the car in park after stopping at the Destrier front gate, his driver window steadily receding into the door. He pushed the button on the security system to gain access, or speak to someone who could. The voice on the other side of the mechanism spoke in Queen's English.

"Good Morning. How may I help?

"Ryan Wells to see Chamille Destrier."

"Very good. Do you have an appointment, sir?"

"No, I don't. If you could please just let her know I am here."

"I beg pardon, but she is quite busy. May I be of some assistance in scheduling an appointment for a future call?"

"She knows me. If you could please just tell her that I am here, I only need a couple minutes of her time."

"I'm not quite certain that she is currently on the grounds Mr. Wells. I could confirm, but it may take a bit of time. Are you able to hold, or should we reschedule?"

"I'll wait."

"Very good, sir."

He waited for ten minutes but it seemed like ten weeks. The window was still down so he could hear the gentlemen when he came back on the line. He was freezing even with the heat blasting. He contemplated hitting the call button on the machine again, but kept telling himself, "twenty more seconds. If the guy doesn't come back in twenty-seconds, then I'll push the button". But twenty-seconds came and went and he would tell himself the same thing all over again. Had the fruity Englishman forgotten about him?

"Mr. Wells, are you still there?"

"Yes, still here."

"Mrs. Destrier will see you. Please follow the drive to the roundabout. Park to the side, if you please, by the car park. I shall meet you at the main door."

"Thank you." After his window was back up, he said to himself, "what a production." The drive, as it was called, was really a long road which was lined with tall, thin, perfectly shaped, isosceles triangular trees of unknown name or origin; evenly spaced every fifteen yards, on both sides. The car park was a small, covered parking area. He parked his car where he was told, was about to lock it and thought better of it. The car was in the safest place on the planet. His new Audi was nice, but it was not the Bentley nor the Maserati he was parked between. It was winter. *These cars should not be exposed to salted, frost-heaved roads of New Hampshire*, he thought.

A dark-skinned man met him at the door. It was the same person that matched the voice from the gate. "Mr. Wells. Welcome. Please follow me to the sitting room, Mrs. Destrier will be with you at her earliest convenience. May I get you a refreshment of some sort?

"Do you know how to make an Alabama Mudslinger?"

"I'm sure we have someone on staff who could make that for you, sir."

"Forget it. If you don't know how to make it then don't bother. Thanks anyway." He didn't really want one, didn't even know what was in it. Everything was just so stuffy. He thought of the most outlandish beverage he could think of at that morning hour, just to get a laugh or a reaction from the stiff. He failed.

"Very good, sir. Please wait here."

He sat on one of the two matching, very white, very plush sofas. In looking around the room, he predicted that the knick-knacks were worth more than everything he and Angie owned, in total. Who would think that all of this was located in southern New Hampshire? If a person had this kind of money, who would decide to live in the cold Northeast? "Wow, who knew?"

"Who knew what, Ryan?"

"Chamille. Nothing, nothing. I was just talking to myself." She wore long, flowing chestnut hair, deep-brown eyes and porcelain yet tanned skin. Hollywood had come to New Hampshire. She reminded Ryan of Angelina Jolie, though he wondered which was more wealthy. "Thank you for seeing me on such short notice, I hope I am not disturbing you this morning."

"No bother, though I am a bit surprised to see you. Pleasantly so, but still."

"Yeah, ten in the morning unannounced is probably impolite in your circles. But this is important."

"Well then, by all means." She sat on the other white sofa, opposite his but not before removing her suit jacket, revealing her transparent, lace camisole. That was all she was wearing on her upper body, which meant there was nothing left to the imagination. Her plastic surgeon was top-tier. "Were you offered a refreshment? I have Arnold Palmers on the way, would you like one?"

"I'm not sure what that is, but sure," he said. He was thankful for the distraction as the tray of lemonade and iced tea was delivered. If she noticed his leers, she didn't show it.

"So, what is so urgent Ryan?"

"When was the last time you've seen Anna?"

"Anna?"

"Anna Grantes, your best friend."

"Anna Grantes is my best friend? I was unaware, but it has been some time. Why, did she say that I am her best friend?"

"Come on now, Chamille. You two are practically inseparable. You did the charity event together this year."

"Yes, she is a very good friend, but a best friend? I'm not sure. What is this about?"

"She is missing. Her and Brady."

"Oh my. What do you mean missing?"

"Do you know where they are?"

"You mean other than her home?"

"They are not home. When was the last time you spoke to her?"

353

"About a week or so ago, I suppose. On the phone. I would have to check on the exact day. Maybe she took a trip with her son. You know, to get away from all the chaos. I was thinking of doing the same. Winter can be so dreary." She leaned to take a sip of her concoction, her spaghetti strap fell down off her shoulder. It was only one of two very small strings holding up her top.

"Do you know where she would go? She emptied the house."

"Wow. That does seem ominous, doesn't it? Have you contacted the authorities?"

"I wasn't sure how long she had been gone, so I couldn't file a missing persons until I knew. Plus all her and the kid's stuff is gone, which makes it look like she left of her own volition. Nothing illegal about that. But with this trial it is the worst possible time for her to, uh, take a vacation. As you put it."

"I'm not so sure she has been happy as of late."

"Of course not. I'm sure it has been very difficult with JG in prison."

"Before that. Are you faithful to your wife, Ryan?"

"What? Yes, why?"

"That's sexy. Ever been tempted?"

"What does this have to do with Anna and Brady being missing?"

"I was talking about you. And Me, but mostly you."

"Listen, Chamille, I've heard the rumors. I don't know if they are true, and it is none of my business. But if your marriage is one of convenience, that is yours to carry. There is not going to be a you and me other than friendship. I love my wife, she loves me. We might not be rich, and we are probably very boring. I'm not even sure how we fit into some of the same social circles, to be honest, but I'm not here socially. I'm here because my friend is about to lose his life, his freedom. And now it seems he has lost his family as well."

"Nice speech. Kinda sexy."

"Can we focus on why she was unhappy before JG went into prison? Why you think that anyway? Please?"

"She was always looking for someone to look after Brady. More so than usual, she seemed preoccupied."

"Didn't they have a babysitter? Why call on you? You don't have any kids, correct?"

"No children, no. I don't want to ruin my body with having to go through pregnancy. The thought of adoption crosses my mind occasionally, but then passes."

"So why did they use you?"

"I'm not so sure they were using their childcare anymore. I certainly didn't take care of the child, one of my staffers is really great with children. She used to be an au pair with another family. I'm friendly with Anna, she needed help one day, and it continued beyond that one time."

"Was she involved in some project or something?"

"I really don't know. She just needed someone to watch Brady quite a lot. She would disappear for a while, much like now I suppose."

"You say you haven't spoken with her in about a week, would she just takeoff for a week or so, leave Brady with you?"

"No, of course not, just for a few days sometimes. Maybe she took Brady because she was going to be gone longer."

"So I'm back where I started. Where did she go and why?"

"And I've already answered you. I'm afraid that I am out of time to speak with you."

"I'm sorry to have taken up your time, but if I could just speak with the maid or au pair or whatever for a few minutes, I will be on my way."

"I'm afraid I won't be able to help you there either. She no longer works for me."

"What? She doesn't work here anymore? Why?"

"I'm not sure that she was interested in all of this excitement."

"As usual I have no idea what you are talking about."

"It seems I am boring you as much as you are me. Good day, Ryan."

As if listening for his queue, the Englishman entered to put an end to the question and non-answer period. "Nigel will show you out. In the future, it is considered polite to have an appointment when calling on someone. Ten in the morning is still considered an inconvenient time," Chamille said as she left the large sitting room.

Ryan could not help but review the entire interaction in his mind, repeatedly as he returned to his car and drove out past the main gate. *What the fuck just happened?*

14

AFTER THE FIRST WEEK IN THE INVESTIGATION had passed, Ryan had asked Warren to meet him at Sully's Tavern to discuss the progress, or lack of it. There were twenty-one more days left before the trial and they needed a break. They needed some evidence to counter all the charges that would prove to be the end of JG. Unless Ryan had it wrong, they still had none. It was time to regroup.

Deni was more than happy to meet there. He wanted to see Jenna again, maybe mend a fence, without a doubt — flirt. He had arrived twenty minutes early, knowing that the 3:00 PM meet time would be a good time to see her, as it was before the start of the happy-hour crowd. He found a spot at the front bar, where there were just a few customers, which was unusual. Jenna looked great, which was usual.

Ryan was running late. He had called just before Warren's entrance, which gave him all the time he needed to chat up the beauty. She would be finished for the day soon, but not before being literally trapped behind the bar conversing with him. He made his way to the bar where he was all but alone with her.

"You again. What now?" Jenna said.

"Is it me or have service standards fallen a bit? I'm meeting someone here and they are runnin' late. Can I get an Irish Whiskey?"

"Do you have a preference?"

The top shelf alcohol was on the top shelf, of course, but at Sully's it was so the male patrons could get a good look at the posteriors of those serving it. Maybe that was why the stuff was so bloody expensive.

"Redbreast 12 year. Please."

"Going expensive today, what's the occasion? Good news with Jake?"

She made her way up a small ladder, reaching for the bottle located on one of the high, glass shelves. Whether it was her normal posture or she was so accustomed to posing for those that order expensive drinks, her butt was positioned for viewing. Deni was leering and he was not ashamed of it.

"More money means a bigger tip for you, right? I came to make peace, or to get a piece. Or both."

356

She came back down behind the bar and poured his drink. "Very funny. Here you go. I get off soon so if you can settle up with me before, that would be great."

"Yeah, I was hoping you could join us when you get done. I'll buy, of course."

"Another interrogation? I think I'll pass, thanks."

"No interrogation, just a chat with me and Ry. Friendly. We used to be friendly when we came in here."

"Friendly. Not familiar, Deni. I'm not going to sleep with you, ever. It is never going to happen no matter how many expensive drinks you buy or how many times you stare at my ass and chest. You think I don't know why people make me reach up for the good stuff?"

"I'm not tryin' to fight here, Jenna. You are a smoke show, we both know that, but all I want is to just sit and talk with ya. I'm not askin' for your hand in marriage, I'm askin' you to sit and have a drink with Ryan and me. No threesome, unless you're into it."

"All right asshole, but it will cost you."

"The threesome?"

"I'm regretting this already. Now pay me before I cash out."

He handed her the money, which was three times too much.

"Keep the change."

"That's a good start on the apology, thanks. Now go find a booth."

Ryan came into the bar and hurriedly made his way to Warren, who was making his way toward a booth with what was left of his drink.

"Hey, thanks for coming over. Sorry I'm late. I just can't keep up with everything at the office without JG. I'm swamped."

"Course I'd be here. Time is creepin' away on us here, kid."

"I need to grab a drink and warm up, it's freezing outside."

"You walk over?"

"The office is down the street, Deni. I'm not going to find another parking spot closer than the one I have." They sat down in a high-backed, round booth on the opposing ends of the horseshoe. "What are you drinking, Scotch or your usual Whiskey?"

"Irish Whiskey and I'm going exclusive today. Redbreast. Wanna try it? It's good."

"I'll stick with Scotch, thanks. Since you're so high-end today, I'll go big also. Truth is, I need a drink and we need a break."

"Go big or go home."

The server arrived, also scantily clad, showing more leg than chest which was hard to do without being naked. "Afternoon, boys. I see one of you has already started, so what can I get you? Happy Hour hasn't started yet but I can see about getting you appetizers at half off. Or is it all liquid today?"

357

"Lagavulin for me, and my friend here is drinking Redbreast."

"OKAY. I'll make sure to keep an eye on you boys."

"Keep 'em comin'," Deni said.

As the server left to fetch the expensive liquors, Jenna arrived with her filled martini glass already in hand. Deni slid over to the middle of the booth, leaving his spot for her on the end. She had changed into a tight, long-sleeved sweater to cover her black work garb.

"That was fast," Deni said. "What are you drinkin'?"

"You made quite the impression your last time here, Deni. The guy you nearly beat up is counting my drawer for me. I'm drinking a Cucumber Tea-ni with Belvedere. I told you, you were going to pay."

"Do I even want to ask what is in it?"

"Belvedere Vodka, yellow Chartreuse, Sencha green tea syrup, fresh cucumbers and a little lemon. Want a sip?"

"No thanks, and I'm sorry I asked. With all that stuff in it though, how can you taste the alcohol? What is the point of buyin' good booze if you aren't gonna taste it anyway?"

"The point is that you cornered me the other day, made me uncomfortable, and you are extending an olive branch, which is going to cost you. That is the point. And I don't want a hangover. Any more questions?"

"Yes but nothing to do with booze."

The server arrived with the expensive libations, giving the gents winks and smiles. Ryan was thankful for the interruption as he was feeling a bit awkward watching the other two at the table verbally spar.

"What happened the last time you were here, Deni?" Ryan asked.

"It was nothin', Ry. No big deal." To Jenna, "tell the big man that I said thanks for helpin' out."

"I will. It will have to be soon though, my days here are numbered." She immediately regretted the last statement. It was obvious on her face that she had revealed more than she had wanted to. *Maybe expensive booze is like a truth serum*, she thought.

"Oh yeah? Gettin' outta Dodge?"

"I'm not sure what you mean, but yes I'm leaving here. With all the events as of late, and our last talk. I'm not getting any younger and I don't want to be shaking my ass, slinging drinks for the rest of my life. Maybe I'll go back to school."

"Your last talk? I'm sorry to be behind in this conversation but what happened the last time you two were here?" Ryan hated the fact that he was so lost.

"Warren kindly pointed out the last time he was here that the reason that Jake is in this fix, is because I over-served him. But I didn't. But I do feel responsible for some reason."

"Well good for you, Jenna. It's gonna be tough to give up all the money you make here though, yeah? The place is always packed, so you must do pretty well. It seems sorta all-of-a-sudden to me."

"I thought you said that you weren't going to interrogate me again, Deni? I've been thinking about leaving Sully's for quite a while. I've come into some money, and I have some money saved. I told you before, I want to teach. I love kids, not big kids. I don't want to be doing this at forty, even if they allowed me to. The girls they are hiring are younger and bustier and have more 'junk in the trunk' by the day."

"You don't even look close to forty, you're beautiful, and you can thank your surgeon for me. He did and an amazing job. I'd like to shake his hand." Stick the jab, then flirt. That was Deni's plan.

Ryan sat idly by, watching the sparring. He was growing tired of the game after a long day at work and an even longer week. He thought the two of them would strategize, the reason for the meeting, but it was obvious that his friend had a hunch and was going with it. Ryan was just the there for the ride at the moment; he was so far behind the curve, he couldn't even play good-cop. He was going to be the audience while sipping, letting him work his magic, even if the audience could see the magic trick a mile away.

"Funny. You're quite the joke-teller. I'm all-real Mr. Funny Guy. I have to take this shit all day, but I'm not working, so if this is the way the conversation is going to go, then thanks for the drink and I'll be leaving now."

"I'm sorry, I didn't mean to offend you. I thought I was giving you a compliment," Ryan said.

"It's that type of chauvinistic bullshit that is getting out of hand. The unofficial uniform keeps getting smaller and smaller here, which the veterans like me keep going along with because if we don't, we lose shifts to the new girls. The smaller the outfit and the more we show, the guys think they can touch and be lewd, especially when they're all boozed up. Women come here because it's swanky and there are plenty of geared-up men with money. I've been fed up for a while, this is the final straw."

There was something else that was going on, Warren knew it. He had made a living being able to read people, and while she was sincere in what she was saying it was not the complete truth. He wanted more light on JG's last night here, something wasn't right and he wanted to get to the bottom of it. This meeting for social drinking was just an excuse to get there, only he wasn't getting anywhere. The eager server came back over toward the booth but before she had arrived, Ryan had nodded that they wanted another round.

"So with all the rubbin' and grindin', your dance card must be full."

"Fuck You, Deni. What is your deal? I don't date the guys that come in here and you know it. How many times have you tried? A million?"

"What about JG, er, uh, Jake?"

"What about him?"

"You tell me. I've seen the way you look at him. And you are right, nobody gets those kinda looks from you. You blame yourself for his present situation, that's why you're sittin' here. Whether that guilt is justified or not is what I'm trying to find out. That guilt is the real reason you are leavin' this bar, I think."

The new round of drinks arrived. Jenna's drink looked similar but not exactly the same color. This interruption was unwelcomed by Deni as the pause gave Jenna just enough time to regroup.

"I was close with Jake, Brady, and his wife. I babysat for them. To say that what happened hasn't affected me would be a lie."

Ryan said, "I thought Chamille Destrier's housekeeper was Brady's babysitter?"

"I'm not sure what you mean, but I picked Brady up from Jake's wife all the time."

"Did you ever pick him up at Chamille's estate?" It was Ryan's turn to interrogate.

"No, I don't thinks so."

"You would definitely know if you had been to that place. It's a palatial mansion owned by her best friend."

"Then, no I haven't. He was always with Jake or his wife when I picked him up."

Deni said, "Anna. His wife's name is Anna. You keep saying 'Jake's wife' but her name is Anna. And she is missing. She took the boy and left."

"What? Where did she go?"

"The definition of missing is we don't know. But you didn't ask why? You asked where, but not why. Is that because you know why?" Deni had hit the jackpot.

"I know what she thinks," Jenna said after a long pause and long pull from her first Cucumber Tea-ni, draining it.

"What does she think?"

"That Jake and I were having an affair. That we were in love."

"Is she right?"

"Do I love him? Yes. Do I love that little boy? Yes. But he is married, and I don't know if Jake loves me."

"Oh my God. How long were you two seeing each other?" Ryan asked. He couldn't just sit there anymore. "I feel like I've just been punched in the stomach."

"I just said, we weren't. I said I know what she thinks. I only saw him here. Well, at first I only saw him here. Then I started to see him around town here and there. I started to babysit because his wife was doing more stuff outside the house, or at night, or whatever, and he started coming in here more and more .... what can I say? I fell in love with him. But I never did anything about it."

"How do you know what she thinks? Did you get to know her also? Did you talk with her regularly?" Ryan was no longer a spectator, he needed answers.

360

While Ryan was back on the warpath, Warren swallowed the last of his whiskey, waved his hand ordering another round. It was now happy hour and the bar was busy, but the server spied him easily as if she had eyes in the back of her head.

"After that time maybe a year and half or so ago in the park, I think she was suspicious. Then I would run into her, or see her in the distance looking at me trying to be sneaky. Phone calls started after that. That is how I know what she thinks," Jenna said.

Ryan looked at Deni then back at Jenna. "I'm a little slow, I think. It may be that I'm half in the bag, but I need someone to start from the beginning. Phone calls? The park? I am officially lost."

She looked around the table, slugged back the rest of her second martini and told her version of the story.

******

"Careful of the swings, Brady." Jacob was yelling toward his son. At three years old, his motor skills, among his others, were advanced. And motor he did. The little man was fast.

Brady loved going to the park. He liked playing in the sand well enough; he liked the merry-go-round more, as long as the bigger kids weren't spinning on it at mach-3. But what Brady loved the most were the swing sets.

The recreational park was an expansive property that was annexed by the town of Wayland, but as it was located directly behind the Wayland Country Club, the plot was generously and gorgeously maintained by the landscapers and the maintenance crew of the exclusive club. The sandbox was filled with the soft, white sand that filled the bunkers of the golf course, which made it much more fun to be in. The slides and amusement equipment always looked freshly painted, gleamed like stainless steel kitchen appliances, or was replaced for new. The tennis courts were not as top shelf as in the club, but were used by the high school for tournaments as they were far nicer than the school's. The skate park within the park was rid of the graffiti that decorated it on a regular basis, which made it less hip but well groomed. The jogger and bike path meandered around the man-made body of water and grass that was like a soft, green carpet. The warm, late spring sun was the only accoutrement not controlled by the wealthy club. The less fortunate could go to the recreational park and fantasize about being an affluent member of society while they stared out at their benefactors from a distance.

As per usual, Brady was getting too close to the older kids playing on the swings. They were competing with each other to see which had the acumen to swing high enough to launch themselves over the top of the crossbar to the other side, and presumably around again. He was fascinated, not realizing the danger he was in if he were to be struck by the feet of one of the swingers.

"We will go on the swings a little later after the big kids are finished, little man," Jacob said as he lifted his son from under his armpits. He tossed him into the air a few times, which was another activity he thoroughly enjoyed.

"Higher. Higher," Brady said. He laughed and egged on his father for more. This was distracting him as he was being moved away from the swings.

A female jogger was approaching them on the jogger and bike path. She was removing her earbuds which was blaring the latest Christina Aguilera dance tune.

"Hey there, hunks."

Jake set his son down when he realized it was Jenna who had now stopped and was trying to catch her breath. She was fashionably dressed for either jogging or Yoga, and looked ravishing despite her exertions. She wore her hair back in a long ponytail; a pink jog bra, accentuating her ample top, gray capris spandex pants which started from her hips which exposed her rock-hard abs, buttocks, and shapely legs.

"Uh, hey Jenna. How are you? Fancy meeting you here. Nice sneakers."

"Nice running into you guys. Ha ha. This handsome guy keeping you busy? Chip off the old block, he has your eyes."

"He keeps me busy for sure. Brady, can you say hello to Jenna please?"

"Hi."

"Just the boys out playing today?" She was speaking to Jake but Brady answered.

"Yep."

"You mean yes, right Brady?"

"Yes."

"My wife is in a meeting at the club." He pointed toward the distant clubhouse. "She is coordinating the big charity event again this year, so we have been on our own a lot in the last couple of weeks."

"Oh yeah? Do I get an invite?"

"You want to hang out with us?"

"Of course, but I meant the event, silly. I need an excuse to squeeze into a slinky dress. I bet you clean up in a tux, you are always in suits when I see you. This is a nice change."

He was dressed in a Foo Fighters t-shirt and jogging pants, though he would be doing no jogging on that day.

"I can see about an invitation for you, plus one. I'll ask the wife. As for me, no tux I'm afraid. Brady and I will be on our own that night too, most likely."

"Bummer. I would have liked to see you in a tux. But if you need a babysitter, just let me know. Seriously, I love kids."

"Hitting the pavement today?"

"You know it. The miles keep the body fit and trim." She posed for him, accentuating her phenomenal figure.

"Well it's working. Maybe a little overtime. Maybe I should start running again."

"You look great to me, but it's a date. We can set it up next time I see you at Sully's. Keep me in mind for babysitting also." She began to jog in place, placing one of her earbuds back into her ear. "Well, I gotta run. Ha ha again. I need to keep that heart-rate up, though it did just skip a beat. Bye boys." She replaced her other earbud and continued her run down the path. When she had covered fifteen yards, she turned back around, and ran backwards while taking in a last look. When she had gotten her fill, she righted herself, continuing her jog while leaving Jacob and Brady staring at her ponytail swinging from side to side.

"Bye," Brady said with a wave.

"That might be trouble, little man."

"Who was that?"

Jacob turned with a start to see his wife next to him. "Oh hey, Anna."

"Mommy."

"Who was that?" she said again.

"Oh, just a bartender at Sully's Tavern. Jenna. You're out of your meeting early."

"So that is why you spend so much time and money at that bar." She lifted Brady up into her arms, who then gave his mother a big hug. "Yes, I got out as early as I could so I could spend as much time as possible with my guys. I think this year's event is going to consume even more time than we had originally discussed."

"Its good for you. You need to get out and use your talents, babe."

"It seems like it might be good for you too. I agree with you by the way."

"Great. What? You agree with what?" He leaned in to kiss his wife, but she stopped him by using her free hand to grab his chin.

"She is trouble," she said. She stared into his eyes.

He thought it an inopportune time to tell his wife that he had found a new babysitter for their son.

******

"So that was the first time that I had seen Jake outside the bar," Jenna said. She sat back in the booth, reminiscing like it was yesterday. "I saw her coming from a mile away, which is why I took off. She didn't like me from the start."

"She? You mean Anna? Why can't you say her name?" Deni stared at her, waiting for an answer. He never received one.

"How do you know that?" Ryan said. He was starting to treat her differently. Like a home-wrecker.

"Like I said, I saw her. I hadn't met her at that point but she was staring me down from afar. I just knew, so I took off. Also, Jake told me the next time he came into the bar. He said that running together and the babysitting offer sounded great but it might make his wife feel

363

uncomfortable. I told him that I understood but that it might make her feel better if we were to get to know one another. That I should meet her."

"So you couldn't leave well enough alone. You couldn't take no for an answer. You had to keep pressing."

"He agreed. He thought it was a good idea. He brought her and Brady in and had lunch in that booth right over there soon after." She pointed to an identical booth in another corner in the same room, then continued.

"I offered to babysit again right in front of her because I was told that she was going to be busy with the event committee. She said that she would think about it and back to me, but either way she would get me a free invitation. She kept pressing to get the name of my nonexistent boyfriend to add to the invitation. I repeatedly told her that I did not have a boyfriend to which she kept saying stuff like she 'didn't believe that a beautiful girl like me didn't have at least one man on the hook, but she could fix me up with someone if I wanted'. After that I saw her sometimes when I would pick up Brady. She was never friendly. And I saw Jake all the time. If I wasn't running with him, I was babysitting for him. Or he came to see me here."

"What do you mean 'never friendly'? She gave you her kid 'all the time'," Deni said.

"Let's put it this way, if looks could kill, I would have been a chalk outline at a murder scene whenever she laid eyes on me. I get the feeling that the child care thing was mostly Jake's idea. Then the phone calls started."

Yet another round of drinks had arrived. During the story they had multiple libations, the three of them were getting well-lubed. Warren was maintaining the best; while Jenna was loose and chatty, Ryan was getting angrier by the Scotch.

"What did you expect? You were moving in on her family. These are my best friends and while I'm not a violent person, I'm tempted to commit a felonious act right here in this bar."

"Is that what I was doing Ryan? Do you honestly think I would intentionally do anything to hurt them? I fell in love, God forgive me." She began to cry. She was trying with all her might not to lose control in her place of work, but emotion combined with alcohol overcame.

Ryan's anger began to dissipate in slight, and he was struggling with his movement toward sympathy. Warren, ever calloused, appeared indifferent and remaining unbiased in the investigation. A technique he was well accustomed to. He pushed on despite her tears.

"So let me see if I have this straight. You didn't want to hurt him or his family, but you moved in on them like you were stormin' Normandy. With your looks and charm, you invaded not only the marriage but formed a relationship with their kid. I don't understand how you don't see that as a problem. His wife hates you, but you don't give a shit because that works in your favor. Actually, I take that back, maybe you did give a shit. You realize he is not going to leave his wife, and you care so much that you get him cocked at the bar, and give him his keys. Only you omit some of the drinks, or you doctor the check so it looks like all is on the up and up. He goes off and instead of getting killed himself, he kills some poor lady, but you're not done yet.

You're still pissed about all of the phone calls and evil looks. So you figure two can play at that game. So you call her. Or you say or do something to Anna which makes her take Brady and vanish. You scared her so she took her son and ran for safety. Which is what you wanted from the start, her out of the way. You're not crazy in love, toots, you're cookin' a pet rabbit in a pot on the stove kinda crazy, lady. Tell me I ain't right."

That was all Jenna could take. The alcohol and the verbal attack was beyond what she could bear. She bolted from the booth, covering her mouth as she cried her way out of the bar.

"I think that was my answer, Ry. So I think we got the story. Now how do we help our boy?"

"Honestly, if we could prove any of what you just said, or heard her say? Not much."

"Whattaya mean? She just basically said that she got him all banged up and that she is a nutty, jealous bitch. She wanted the family and the picket fence and she couldn't stand the fact that she couldn't get it. So she went after the wife and kid."

"That and the fact that he still got in his car, picked up Brady and ran somebody off the road. Correct me if I'm wrong here, but she didn't *say* that any of what you just said is what happened. If it is true, which is a big if, and if we could get proof, because she certainly isn't going to go on the record and admit it, *might* be mitigating. But at the end of the day, he still did it. I say we add it to the fact that this poor lady shouldn't have been in the country to be on the road in the first place and call it the 'perfect storm of OUIs'. It was all of the above that created this whole conflagration."

"What if we had proof? Get a few years off?"

"I must be drunk. I just told you, maybe. But I don't think so. It's worth a try. Alas, we don't have any proof. So what is your point?"

"Look up in the corners, Ry. Cameras. Closed Circuit TV cameras for security. Maybe it prevents a bartender from stealing, maybe not. But I bet he had more than two beers."

"That was how long ago, Deni? Never gonna happen. In all likelihood, it has been long recorded over by now. If it was significant, the ADA would have it into evidence already."

"It's worth a try. Besides I've got a feeling about this. Plus the 911 mystery."

"Yeah what happened with that?"

"I don't have a name. But who buys a throwaway phone and doesn't provide a name or information on it? Drug dealers and people who don't wanna be traced. Nobody legit that's for sure. Janey Do-Good, doin' a solid on a burner phone, is botherin' me. So I got the kiosk in a mall up Nashua way that sold it to her. Cash of course. The cameras here give me an idea of how to see who bought it."

"Again, Deni, I hate to be a glass is half-empty kinda guy, but this was over six months ago. That tape has probably long gone by now."

"You say half-empty or half-full, I say there's always room for whiskey. My contact says that CCTV isn't tape anymore. It is all binary. Digital. Ones and zeroes. There is this thing called a cloud, stores like millions and millions of stuff. Nobody needs to worry about storage space anymore, so everything is saved."

"I have another mystery which you can solve then, Mr. Room for Whiskey. The Destrier servant, or au pair, or whatever. She disappeared. She was the one who babysat Brady the night of the accident, she was the one who put him in the back seat of the car without a word. She is gone too."

"I thought Busty Galore just said that she was the babysitter, before she ran off."

"You are getting drunk too, huh? Deni, she just told you that she was going to the charity event. Remember? Slinky dress .... not gonna miss it?"

"Oh yeah, right. She was feeding him drinks and was on her way out to go change and then go. Did she ever go? Maybe there is more to her than slinky dresses and slingin' drinks."

"Maybe, but too many people are disappearing, don't you think? Anna and Brady, the maid? It's unsettling."

"Add to that a female voice on a 911 call, a burner phone, and possible infidelity. At a minimum Anna thought there was. Maybe the wrong person was killed."

"OK. I'm definitely buzzed, if not completely drunk. Where does that leave us? Our working theory is that Anna leaves with Brady because she is getting muscled by the bartender about having an affair with JG? That Jenna intentionally got him all banged up to kill him because she couldn't have him? But he didn't die, so she threatens to make it right by killing Anna and the boy. Speaking of which, what about Brady? JG was going to pick up Brady, what did he ever do?" Ryan was in the weeds. He was fighting through the fog, trying to keep up with all the various revelations.

"I don't know all the specifics yet, but I think it was Jenna on the 911 call. She followed him outta here that night. Now I follow up with the cameras here and the kiosk where the phone was sold. I go see if I can find this housekeeper or whatever and put a trace on Anna and Brady. All that in three weeks. I'd ask for the tape tonight but I'm cocked."

"If you go to the Destriers, be warned that Chamille is rich but she is also completely nuts. Bored, horny, and nuts."

"Good. So am I."

15

WARREN WAS CONCERNED. He was hungover and concerned. He was trying to piece together a thought, any thought, through the fog. Nothing was clear except for the thumping pain in his brain and the thick wool sweater he must have eaten at some point the previous night. The meeting with Ryan over a vat of Irish Whiskey had left him with more questions than he had answers at present. A situation which he needed to correct. He was also left with the question of why he had spent so much money on alcohol that was supposed to reduce, if not eliminate, hangovers.

The biggest of all the concerns in his haze was why people in this case were disappearing. He had worked many cases throughout the years, people vanished when things were too heated around them. In every case they had something to hide. They never intentionally left a forwarding address; however, there were always clues left behind which could lead to them being found. Anna and Brady had left. That much was clear. He would need to get back over to the house for a more thorough inspection, for a clue as to where and why. The maid was gone too. Odd, that. Maybe she was afraid of Immigration coming down on her? The Destriers had resources to protect her, of that he was sure. So why was that protection deemed insufficient? He would have to go talk to the rich, crazy lady.

This was supposed to be a drunken crash that led to an unfortunate death. He was going to try to help his friend by finding some evidence that said it was less his fault, but under every rock he turned over there was another oddity which created more questions. It was turning out that this crash might not be his fault. Nobody had forced the beer to his lips. But while he was drunk, he was a pawn in a game which JG didn't know he was a part of. That maybe he was the one that was supposed to be dead on the side of the road.

Finding Anna was a priority. She would shed some light on this Jenna thing. She would help him right? Hell hath no fury …. so maybe not. But why did she leave now? Six months after the accident and the arrest, she decides to leave? He wondered what had changed. Jenna. Was Jenna muscling Anna out of town? Why? And why now?

He decided to go over the house again, to find a clue as to JG's family's whereabouts. The psyche of an inmate is simultaneously fragile and volatile. Warren knew this all too well from his time as an trooper. A prisoner's mind wanders night and day, having all the time in the world to think and rethink every detail, of every happenstance.

Once the decision was made, he rolled out of bed and fought off an inhuman bout of vertigo. He shook off the cobwebs as best he could, then padded into the kitchen to make coffee. The shower helped, but with coffee finally ready, that helped more. By the time the Escalade was warmed up and he was backing out of his short driveway, he was as right as rain. Which was funny because it was raining. Freezing rain.

Though the weather was bad, the drive wouldn't take long. It never took long from his house in New Hampshire. He grew up on the South end of Boston, a rough neighborhood which was no comparison to his neighborhood in Barstone. He could afford better, but he liked the fringe. It was close to JG and Ryan's law practice, so when he worked with them, or needed to be in New Hampshire, he stayed there. When he worked in Boston, he stayed at his place there.

He stayed in South Boston with less frequency as of late. His neighborhood was being gentrified, his community was being forced out. The yuppies had moved in and more were taking over. The Young Urban Professionals had started to buy up the triple-decker properties, converting them into upscale apartments. These new property owners demanded more police to keep these residences safe. These more affluent homeowners and tenants also had a taste for finer dining, clothing, and such. This brought businesses that the locals were unaccustomed to. Slowly but surely, the locals were being pushed out and Southie was becoming less like Southie.

The drive and lock-picking took a grand total of eighteen minutes. Upon his entry, he noticed that nothing had been touched since his last walk-through. Who moves but leaves all the furniture? Those that want to vanish in a hurry, he told himself. But why now, after six months was what was eating at him.

He toured the house again, going through drawers, closets and found nothing. She was thorough, he had to give Anna that. He went through the kitchen and out into the garage.

"I must be seeing double," he said to himself. Appearing before him were the two identical black Volvo SUVs. "His and hers, how cute." He walked around the first vehicle closest to the kitchen door. It was spotless. Hanging from the rafters on a piece of string was a pink tennis ball at the end of it, touching the windshield. Deni had seen this trick before; designed to give the driver a perfect reference point to drive into the garage with greater ease, leaving enough room around it. The pink tennis ball led him to believe that the vehicle closest to the house was Anna's. Chivalry isn't quite dead. He checked the driver door to see if it was locked. It would make little difference if it was, but it was not.

He opened the door and peered inside. It was immaculate. The soft, tan leather smelled new. Nothing in the console. The child carseat was in the back. He tried to get into the driver seat to reach across and check the glove box but the seat was far too close to the steering wheel for him to fit. He felt for a lever under the seat to move it back but there wasn't one. He then found the numbered, electronic buttons which adjusted the seat in every position. He pushed one of the numbers.

368

Everything moved. The driver seat moved back to a comfortable position, lumbar support included. The steering wheel moved into a different position, the rear and side-view mirrors adjusted for the new seat position as well. Presets. He pushed the number one on the panel, which moved everything back to the original position, where everything was compact. He was being crushed like the trash compactor on Star Wars only without the liquid sludge. He quickly pressed the number two before the movement was complete, which relocated everything back into the comfortable position. The other preset numbers did nothing.

He next opened the glove box, which was barren except for the owner's manual. No insurance card or registration. The vehicle was picked clean. She either kept a very clean car or it was cleaned for a purpose. He leaned back to see if there was anything in the back that was forgotten, that too was clean. Wherever she was traveling in the days before her departure, he thought, she didn't go by car. That car anyway. Or it was professionally detailed.

He gave up on Anna's rig and moved over to what he assumed was JG's side of the garage. No hanging tennis ball, pink or otherwise. He checked to see if this one was unlocked. It was also. He attempted to climb in and was crushed as he was in the first SUV. Surprised and uncomfortable, he pushed the number two button to move the seat but nothing moved. He pressed number one and all the movement began as it had in Anna's. He was again comfortable yet the thought struck him that made him ill at ease. Both cars were set for a shorter person.

He looked into the back of this vehicle to see the very same child carseat. On the floor was the refuse of a child. The ejected DVD in the player was *Despicable Me* and various action figures were peering out of the pocket on the back of the front passenger seat.

Baffled, he opened the glovebox and found that this Volvo was indeed registered to Jacob Grantes. He extracted himself from the SUV to inspect the exterior. This was the car that was involved in the crash. The damage remained ever-present along with the dirt and grime.

If ever there were two opposites, these once identical XC90s illustrated the definition. What confused Deni was, except for the outer damage, all evidence led to opposing owners. JG's vehicle indicated that it belonged to Anna, and vice versa. Both vehicles were adjusted for for a shorter person, presumably Anna. The presets, however, indicated the correct SUV was on the appropriate side of the garage.

Warren drew out his iPhone from his pocket, pressing the screen to call Ryan.

"What's up Deni? I'm due back in court any minute."

"Nice greeting, how are you?

"Hungover and busy, you?"

"Hungover and confused. How tall is Anna?"

"Five foot six or seven, I think. Why?"

"JG is like six feet, right?"

"Yeah, six-one. Get to the point."

"Anna and JG had identical rides."

369

"You must be hungover. We went over this already. After his parents were in a fatal car crash he always insisted on safety. Found the safest SUV on the market when Brady was born, and bought two of them. So what?"

"Anna drove both cars."

"Again, so what? They were married. I'm a little slow, what are you driving at?"

"I'm not sure what I'm driving at, mister bad-pun. Except the last person to drive each one of these vehicles was Anna. And that adds yet another question to the growing list."

16

RYAN WAS A BUSY MAN in those days. He truly was, or at least that is what he told himself. This was the excuse for not going to see JG in prison. He was busy with cases, keeping the practice running; court appearances were aplenty along with constructing a logical defense in JG's case, which seemed to an increasing extent like an insurmountable task. That is why he kept away. It was not because he had no good news at all, nor the whereabouts of his vanished wife and child.

Try as he might, he could no longer avoid JG. Ryan's cell phone, work phone, and house phone were all incessantly ringing from the same institution. Angie was told that she was not to accept any call when that number popped up on the caller ID, under any circumstances. His best friend was trying to get in touch with him to find out what was happening. He knew JG wasn't getting through to his wife, that number was disconnected. That was in all likelihood driving him insane. Not to get an answer from his best friend and lawyer was probably making him psychotic. It was not fair of Ryan, but he just couldn't face him.

Ryan was successful in procuring a private room at the prison in order for the two of them to speak at long last. He had told the Deputy Sheriff that there had been a death in the family and he had to tell his client, that privacy was essential. As if by miracle they had complied, setting aside not only the room but eliminated a time limit as well. The sole stipulation was that body searches take place. Inmate Grantes was used to them, Ryan was not.

Nerve racking minute after minute passed as he sat in the closet-like prison conference room waiting for his friend and client to arrive. When Grantes eventually did appear in the doorway, shackled at the wrists and ankles, Ryan was shocked at how disheveled he looked. Uneasiness became guilt as the once striking eyes of his friend stared into his. Prison was aging him, the week without communication had done immense damage. That damage was evident not only in his appearance but how he was carrying himself as well. Grantes was a broken man, the blind could see it.

Once he was unshackled and the correctional officers had left the room, Ryan leaned toward his friend on the other side of the table. "Hey buddy. How are you holding up? You don't look so good."

"Gee, I wonder why?"

"I'm sorry I haven't come to visit you. I've been busy with the practice, your defense, my life. I'm sorry. I'm trying."

"Too busy to answer the fucking phone, Ry? Any phone? I'm sitting in a cell wondering what the hell is happening, and I can't get in touch with anyone. Nobody."

"Deni isn't answering his — "

" — fuck you, Ryan. He isn't on my pin sheet and you are avoiding the point. And me. Why?"

The phone system at the WCHOC had been outsourced to a private contract. That business made an immense profit off of people who are already at rock bottom. Phone calls are not allowed in to an inmate. The prison set up a limited number of phone numbers per inmate which are designated on a pin sheet. The numbers on the sheet are then vetted to ensure that prisoners were not calling other wanted felons or those whom had restraining orders filed upon that inmate. Once the numbers are approved, the recipient of the outgoing phone call needed to activate that number by setting up an account. This required money. To add money to the account required a fee. Every call made out on the phone was assessed a connection fee. Each minute while on the phone cost money from the time the recipient picks up the phone. The entire enterprise was an expensive, elaborate scam endorsed by the county.

"I've been working on this case, with Deni, to try to bring you some good news."

"So you've been avoiding me because you don't have any."

"No, I don't. In Fact, that is why I am here in person instead of answering your phone call. I have some very troubling news."

"Anna? Brady? What happened?"

"What makes you say that, JG?"

"The phone is either shut off or there is no money on it. We have money so I am guessing that it is shut off. But either way it's not good. There is a reason, and all I do is think about what it could be."

"What reasons have you come up with?"

"Reasons she is not putting money on the phone or that it's shut off? All I can come up with is that she is upset with me. I'm not sure why now, but she must be. She was here with me saying, 'it will be all right, babe' and 'we will get through this together,' for six months. Then she is a no-show at court and I can't get in touch with her on the phone and she doesn't come to visit. I keep thinking that there is another guy, but she wouldn't do that. She wouldn't do that, would she Ry?"

"No. Well, I don't think so."

"Then?"

"That's just it, I don't know. All I can tell you is what I suspect and what it looks like."

"Just out with it. What happened?"

"They are missing."

"Missing? What do you mean missing?"

"I filled out a missing persons report on Anna and Brady but no hits, which is what I sort of figured when I filed it. We went to the house and it looks like they moved out. Gone, vanished. She left all the furniture, both the cars. She took everything personal though like clothes, and Brady's toys, jewelry. But it's all gone. I've been checking the accounts you had, the money."

"Money, what do you mean the money?"

"Well, it looks like she has been getting her ducks in a row for a while. It appears that she has been using all of her Dad's old contacts and been syphoning money into accounts without your name on them. She was the executor on Brady's trust money, so she leveraged that as well. She left you with a house, a couple of cars, and our practice, but that's pretty much it. It may be that she had a nudge, getting pressure to leave. We don't know that part for sure, but we're working on it. Maybe she thought you wouldn't need a ton of money, given your current situation."

He let that information sink in for a few minutes. They sat in silence.

"What we need to do now is focus on a defense for you."

"But why now, Ry?"

"Because you are looking at a long time in prison, that is why."

"No, why did she leave now? No notice, no goodbye, no reason? I can't believe it. There has to be someone else."

"I know what you meant, but dwelling on it doesn't help you get out of prison."

"This is my wife and child, Ryan. What am I going to get out of prison to?"

"She may have left for someone else because she thinks that you already did. Or she might have been scared off."

"What the hell are you talking about?"

"Jenna. Talk to me about Jenna."

"Jenna? The Babysitter?"

"Yes. And I noticed you didn't say, 'Jenna, the bartender?' by the way. Which is what you probably should have said."

"Jenna was our babysitter and yes, she was also a bartender. Never mind what I 'should have said', is that what you think? That I had an affair with Jenna? Is that what Anna thinks? Is that what you told her?"

"I didn't tell her anything, JG. I'm late to the party and everyone is hammered. I'm just trying to catch up here. Deni and I talked with her. Jenna."

"Yeah, so. What did she say?"

"She said enough. She said that she was in love with you and that besides being the babysitter, she went running with you. Often and alone. She didn't say that you two were balls-deep or anything, but then she really didn't have to did she?"

"Did she say that we had an affair?"

"In those words, no. But the way she — "

" — because we didn't."

"Well did you know she is bat-shit crazy about you? And maybe just crazy altogether?"

"Maybe. Yeah, I knew. I know. Not about being completely nuts, but about me. Yeah."

"And you saw her everyday anyway?"

"Yes, but not for the reason you think."

"Does it matter what reason I think? I mean seriously. What should I think, buddy?"

"You should think that Anna was consumed with her charity event. You should think that she was distant and growing more so. She was going through something but not with me. She was out more than she was home. I didn't want to pry, or to be controlling, so I let her work out her shit. I spent time with a pretty girl, Ry. She was good to Brady, and if you were my true friend, you would know that I would never cheat on my wife."

"I am your friend. I will always be, no matter what. If you say it, I believe you. But the real question isn't what I think, it's what did Anna think?"

"So you think she suspected that I was having an affair all this time, and used my crash as an opportunity to leave me? That over the last six months she has been getting herself situated? At my worst is when she decided to do this? When I need her the most is when she abandons all we had?"

"I'm saying that I don't know for sure. At least so far. I think she may have suspected, but Jenna had been shoving it in her face. But that's not the point. The point is that she is gone. We are working to find her, but that is something you are going to have to work on once you get out of here, and it can't consume you in the meantime. Getting you out of here is the number one priority."

"Easy for you to say."

"That was not easy, nor is anything else I have to say today."

"There's more? Jesus Christ, Ry. I don't think I can take any more bad news. Maybe you were right to stay away."

"We really don't have a defense for you thus far. We have less than three weeks to go before the trial and we might be able to piece together some mitigating circumstances, but nothing open and shut."

"What have you come up with?"

"We know the 911 call came from a burner phone. We know it was a female caller that didn't want to be traced, because she paid for the phone in cash with no address or contact information. The now infamous Jenna most likely served you way more than two drinks. Warren thinks that she was the one who bought the phone, followed you and called in the accident. As of today, I think maybe she is the one that maybe forced you and the lady off the road. Maybe she finally realized that you were never going to leave Anna, or that she was jealous of what you have, or had. And she is the reason that Anna has run off. You say that you didn't have an affair

374

with her, but she may not have received that memo, and she snapped. We are working to piece together evidence to corroborate all of this theory."

"But even if you do, I was still drunk and as a result still on the hook for the chain of events that took place once the OUI happened."

"Correct. We will try to get La Fontagne to go for a reduction, but I'm not confident."

"Lovely."

"At least you are off the hook for child endangerment. So once your out you won't have to deal with someone supervising you with Brady."

"Which will be great if we can find him."

"Deni is on it. Sooner or later he'll find them."

"Why didn't the Destrier maid make any attempt to stop me from driving?"

"That is a good question. I would love to ask her, but she is in all probability deported or something. She's gone. Disappeared. She may not have known you were drunk anyway. Her initial statement, through Chamille Destrier, was that she never even spoke to you. That you never left the car."

"You're kidding."

"Nope. My guess is that the crash happens, cops start asking questions, and that brings light on the fact that the good housekeeper is illegal — not so good for the Destriers. So they fire her, but not before providing more babysitting services. The entire thing is weird but we're digging. If she is around, or if Chamille knows where she is, we'll find out. She is cuckoo for coco puffs by the way."

"I know. She has gotten worse over the years. Thanks. So at this point we go for the vic, right. Did she have a legal driver's license? If so, how can an illegal immigrant get a valid license? It pains me, but it looks like that is our only option. Two wrongs don't make it right, but an OUI is better than going down with whole sha-bang."

"If that flies, then that gets you a reduced sentence and out of football numbers. That might be all we've got at this point, and it's a long shot. In the meantime; we see how many drinks you really did have from the cameras, find the maid and see why she didn't intervene, then we see about the 911 call and see where that leads. Deni is pretty confident that Jenni is behind this entire thing though."

"Swell."

Ryan left the conference room and the prison without mentioning the mystery surrounding the SUVs. Since Warren had mentioned it a few days ago, he had been thinking about what it could mean. Subsequent conversations with him had not shed any light on it. He was not sure why he didn't bring it up. If someone else drove the car, when? It had to be since the accident and not related to it. But if it had been untouched since and could be proven, then someone else had driven the car, not JG. But was that possible? *No, that didn't seem possible with all of the evidence*, he thought. Still...

17

IF RYAN WAS BUSY, Warren was to the point of being overwhelmed. He had many avenues to investigate and an impossibly short time to complete them. He needed to; acquire the surveillance video from Sully's, reconnoiter Jenna and her movements, track down who had purchased the burner phone, find the Destrier maid, and in his spare time put a trace on Anna and Brady. All in about two weeks. No sweat.

He went back to Sully's at 10:00 AM on a Monday, as was discussed between he and the owner as the best time to meet. It wasn't busy. It wasn't busy because it was an hour prior to opening for lunch service, not because it was a Monday, or that it was too early in the day. The front door was unlocked so Warren walked right in. A large man was behind the bar counting money from an open cash register. Over his shoulder and without a look, he said, "we're not open yet, we open in an hour." He continued to count without losing his place.

"Good 'cuz I need your full attention." Deni had arrived at the bar but did not sit down, he simply leaned on it with both elbows on the countertop.

When the large man turned to face the intruder, his annoyance softened once he determined whom was in need of his attention.

"It's Marty, right? We had an appointment. I don't think we've officially met but we spoke on the phone. I'm Warren Dennihan." He stuck his hand out over the bar-top toward the man behind it who was at least twice his size. Marty made no move to reciprocate.

"Oh yeah. I forgot you were coming in today. You had some questions about Jenna over-serving somebody, right?"

"Well, yes, it's a little more complicated than that, but yes."

"Funny, we get that a lot. People can't handle their booze so it's the bar's fault they got in trouble. Nobody takes personal responsibility anymore, everybody wants to sue everybo — "

" — this isn't about you getting sued, this is about me getting information about what exactly happened on a night six months ago."

"Oh, now I see. This is about that lawyer who hit and run that woman. You should have said something when we were on the phone. I don't believe I can help you."

"Can't or won't?"

"Pick one. The cops came in already, asked a bunch of questions including which guests were in that night. Not good for business."

"It doesn't seem to me that it affected business at all, I come in all the time and the place is packed."

"Whatever. Look, I'm busy. Whattaya say we cut to the chase. You ask me a question, and I tell you I don't know. Maybe after a couple of go-arounds you finally figure out that a guy came in and got hammered; that I'm not going to say or do anything to get my ass or my business in a sling, then you leave. So go ahead and show yourself out."

"And I'm here to tell you, or show you if I have to, that I'm not leaving until I'm fully satisfied that I have all of the information I can get from you on that night. We can do this the nice and easy way, where you get on with opening up for the day, or we can do this the hard way where shit gets broke. Maybe even you get broke. You may be bigger, but I guarantee you are gonna know you've been in a fight."

"What do you want from me? I'm almost never here, and I am for sure never here at night. I come in every morning or so and count money or make change when a manager or supervisor needs a day off. Like today."

"I want a copy of the check from that night, just like the one you gave to the police. I want a copy of the security footage from the CCTV from that night. I want to know about Jenna, good employee or bad, anything in her personnel file. That, for starters, is what I want from you."

"Personnel file? What do you think this is? We don't have a Human Resources Department, man. If somebody fucks up, they get canned or we cut her shifts. Pretty simple. Besides, she doesn't work here anymore. She *was* a great kid until she decided not to show up ever again. No phone call or nothing. Her phone is shut off too. Never even came to get her tips or her last paycheck."

"That sounds unusual. She said something about quitting the other night when we were in here, but not getting money that she is owed?"

"Whattaya gonna do, right? She isn't the first to no-call, no-show; and despite my prayers, she isn't gonna be the last."

"We can come back to that. How about a copy of the check from that night."

"You got a warrant?"

"I'm not a cop, so no. But I used to be one, and I can make life difficult for you with a phone call or two. Still want to see a warrant?"

Marty looked around the bar, then at the floor as he thought about his options. He was beginning to understand that he didn't have any.

"What day did you want?"

Warren gave him the date of the charity event, the date of the crash and the approximate time that he was in. Around 7 to 8:00 PM.

"Do you know where the guy sat, or any other information? There are, like, a ton of checks to go through."

378

"He sat at the bar, Jenna served him. If it makes it easier, we can look at the CCTV footage first so you can see where he was sitting."

"You want footage from six months ago? Ha. We keep that for two weeks, then the drive is recorded over with the new footage. If nothing happens, we don't save it."

"But something did happen. You remembered the event when I brought it up. The cops were in here, you mean to tell me that you didn't save that footage?"

"Maybe. I'll have to check. Maybe the cops have it. Did you ask them?"

"I know for a fact that they don't have it, because the prosecutor didn't include that in the evidence package they have against the guy I work for. So I guess you are gonna have to look."

"Let me make a phone call, maybe my General Manager knows where it is."

"You're not a real hands-on kinda owner, are you?"

"I've got other businesses. I can't do it all."

"I see that."

Marty left to go into the office. He seemed to be in there for a long time while Deni was hanging around in the open but not opened restaurant and bar. He thought it odd that the owner would leave a stranger in his establishment with still uncounted money out in the open, expensive bottles of alcohol, and an unlocked front door. He also thought this guy was not much of an owner, he was not much of a businessman, and overall he was unimpressed by the overall intelligence of Marty. When he returned after a bit, the big man looked as if he was thoroughly confused, which Deni thought about right.

"I have good news and bad news. The good news is here is the receipt I printed out of MICROS, our sales system. The bad news is that according to my GM, the footage was saved to a drive that is no longer in the office."

"What kinda game are you runnin' on me here, guy? You *had* the footage saved, but it's now conveniently missing?"

"You are more than welcome to come back to the office and look for yourself. My GM is on his way in. He isn't happy about it, since he closed last night and didn't get home until 4:00 AM. But he sounded concerned enough to make the trip."

"So help me, if this is a scam there are going to be beat'ns. Who else has access to the office, and wherever it was located in the office?"

"I honestly don't know. Like I said, I'm not usually here during hours of operation. I say we wait for him to arrive and we can all go in there together."

Marty had been finishing opening the place while Deni waited. Attractive females were also arriving about that time, presumably to start their shifts. The bar was officially opening. A lunch crowd was beginning to come in as well. Some for an honest lunch, some for a liquid one. A tall, lanky gentlemen entered through the back door looking haggard and disheveled. He made

379

no idle talk, no introductions; he plowed through any and all that tried to make contact with him. He heismaned through the office door like if it didn't open, he would just go through it. Warren spied him from where he was sitting at the bar waiting, and made his way back to the office to join who he assumed was the General Manager. Marty was nowhere to be immediately seen.

When Deni arrived inside the office he saw that Marty was already in the office, having a conversation with his manager. They both looked at the investigator with extreme caution, unsure of what violence he was capable of.

"What's the verdict, gents?"

The skinny one chimed in first. "It was here, it has been here since the day after the accident happened. I mean the Barstone and Wayland communities aren't that big, so when something big happens, everybody hears about it. It made the news. I knew he was having drinks here before the accident, so I purposely saved it. It's not here. It has been in the same spot for six months and now it's not here. I was waiting for the police or somebody to want it, but nobody ever asked."

"Well somebody wanted it, since you're sayin' it's gone."

"Even so, it isn't here."

"So make me another copy. Go back and pull it up, or whatever you do to get it."

"Our system doesn't work that way. It records over itself to save hard drive space. If you don't save and store something specific within two weeks, it is gone. We saved it, but since that flash drive is gone, the information is gone. That is what I am afraid to tell you, but that is what I'm telling you. The footage is gone."

"I have a friend that says that today all digital stuff is stored in a cloud, or on a cloud, or something about a cloud. Internet or something, right?"

"Well that is kind of, sort of, true. Except we don't have ADT, or LifeShield, or somebody like that off-site managing our system. Ours is a cheapo, self-contained system that isn't connected to the internet or anything. So no Cloud. That drive was what you needed, and it's gone."

"So what was on the footage? Did you see it?"

"Specifically? No. It was six months ago. It was a crowded bar."

"So nobody who works here knows what was on the drive that sat in this office for six months. And that drive, conveniently, is gone."

"It's not convenient, but yes it's gone."

"And so is Jenna. The girl who, according to this sheet of paper with the receipt on it, was the bartender who 'only served him two beers'. So you boys are tryin' to sell me on the fact that not only is the drive gone, but so is the employee? Both just disappeared?"

"You don't think Jenna took it do you? It's just a coincidence."

"Neither one of you are too smart, huh? There is no such thing as a coincidence. I came in a couple of weeks or so ago and had a chat with her. Then my lawyer friend and I came in the other night and for a follow-up. She stormed outta here crying that night. Mr. Marty or Sully or whatever here, says that she didn't show up, nor did she call, nor did she come to get her money that was owed to her since then. Now we find out that the footage, which in all likelihood shows that she over-served the guy that was in a car crash, a crash which left one person dead, is also missing. And neither of you are putting two and two together huh?"

"I admit, it does seem like they disappeared at the same time. Roughly."

"There are way too many things disappearing around here."

"Excuse me?" the tall man said, glancing at the stoic owner.

"Nothing. That is what I've got. A big fat nothing," Deni said as he walked out of the office and out of Sully's Tavern.

✹✹✹✹✹✹

Back in his car, Warren was angry. He wasn't ah-shucks-and-fiddlesticks angry, he was I-want-to-kill-something-with-my-bare-hands angry. This case had turned on its ear. This was no longer a situation where the stars had aligned and bad things happen to good people. This was something sinister. There was evil taking place. Someone had an agenda, and that agenda was to bury Jacob Grantes.

In Deni's business, he had investigated many cases where people covered their tracks to hide evidence. He was used to being smarter than those trying to cover-up their misdeeds. What he wasn't used to were the seemingly separate entities all conspiring to form a black hole that vaporized evidence. Why make something disappear unless there was something to hide. Were all of these bits going to the same place? Were all the people? Was there one big rock that, if uncovered, would provide; the maid, the 911 caller A.K.A Jenna, the CCTV footage, Anna and Brady? Cover-ups were one thing, this was something else.

Everywhere he turned, one more thing was added to the list of things he had to find. He was almost afraid to continue moving forward for fear of the next thing vanishing as well. Anger was helpful to him in certain situations, this was not one of them. He had to keep his cool. He was more determined than ever to uncover the truth behind the crash. JG had no memory of the night after leaving the bar, where he insisted, and the receipt provided proof, that he only had two beers. Now everything and everyone surrounding it had vanished. He had to pick away at his list, and do it fast. First on the list was the housekeeper.

He started the car and without allowing it to warm up, he headed toward the Destrier residence. Ryan had been there, but it was now his turn. He was in no mood for nut-jobs, but his threshold for much of anything was low. The servant was an important piece. She was the last person to see JG before the crash and was probably forced to disappear. Ryan had said there were separate living quarters for the Destrier help, he wanted to comb through that home. There, he would likely find the clue as to her whereabouts. In his experience, those from another country who had spent time, money, energy, and at great personal risk to get into this Country, didn't just leave unless they were forced to in shackles. Once they had become accustomed to the land of dreams, they didn't just leave without a fight. Especially when those back in their native land were counting on the money being sent back there.

Warren Dennihan arrived at the Destrier Estate, he pushed the white button to open the iron gate in front of him. The place was secure, he thought, as the button didn't open the gate but instead produced a British voice.

"Good Morning. How may I help?"

Warren looked at his watch, confirming the time on his dash, assessing that it was technically still morning but only by three minutes.

"Open the gate."

"Do you have some business here, or an appointment, sir?"

"Yeah. Open the gate."

"If I might have your name sir, so I may check the calendar."

"Warren Open-tha-Gate. I'm sure I'm on the calendar. Seriously, open the gate."

"I'm afraid you will need to be more specific regarding your business here, sir."

Warren was already on fire, and he was getting more annoyed with the voice emanating from the security box outside the gate. More so with every word. He had always found the male British accent to be a combination of being uppity and gay. He realized it was not necessarily true that they all felt superior to Americans, nor that they were all homosexuals, but that voice bothered him just the same.

"I need to speak with either Roman or Chamille Destrier. It is an emergency. Open the gate."

"Do you have an appointment, Mr. Warren?"

"How many emergencies have appointments? And it's not Mr. Warren, It's just Warren. Now open the gate or I'm coming through it looking for you."

There was a brief pause before the accent said, "please park your truck off in the service parking area, off to the side of the property, out of view." He said it in a way that suggested he was driving a disgusting garbage truck instead of an Escalade.

Then the gate opened.

Warren looked at the speaker next to the white button he had pushed, seeing a tiny camera which would normally go unnoticed he suspected. He smiled to himself and said, "can't go anywhere without bein' on TV anymore. Let's see if this one disappeared."

Once inside the estate, down the long road lined with trees, he parked his car where he was told. Even the help had decent rides, he thought. He walked up to the door, a dark-skinned man was waiting for him.

He was welcomed, for lack of a better word, by the man whose voice he recognized from the speaker. "I do hope that your rather large auto is parked out of sight."

"Easy there, guy. Don't get your turban in a twist."

382

"I beg your pardon. I demand to know what emergency has occurred to warrant such a presence without prior notice."

"What are you Indian? British accent kinda threw me off at the gate, there. Are you legal? Your papers in order?"

"I've had quite enough of your vulgar behaviour, I would like you to leave straight away."

"Its fine, Nigel. I believe I know what this is about." Chamille Destrier descended the wide, spiraled staircase. More like gracefully floated down it. "You may leave us, but please have some beverages sent into the sitting room." She turned to Deni as she arrived at the bottom of the stairs. "Would a Bloody Mary be acceptable to you?"

Warren was not easily impressed, nor easily at a loss for a witty retort in any situation, but he was mesmerized by the tanned beauty that had floated toward him. "Sure." That was all he could come up with.

She was wearing a key lime green silk dress with what Warren gathered to be nothing underneath. Her dark eyes were demure, yet penetrated him as if assessing his soul. The dress had a high slit that revealed her long dark legs as she negotiated her way through the house to the sitting room. She already had the air of Angelina Jolie, the slit up the dress was too much. Yet her appearance was elegantly exotic.

Chamille had gently cupped Deni's elbow urging him toward the sitting room. "Right this way. We can take refreshment in comfort, I hope."

Gathering himself out of stunned silence, while taking in the luxury of the room, he managed to recover his wit and charm. "In this dump? I guess we'll have to make do. So where is Brad Pitt and the million African kids?" He plopped himself on the plush, white-silk sofa, spreading his arms along the back.

She laughed as though that was the first time she had ever been compared to Angelina. His guess is that she secretly wanted to be her. "He is very, very away." She sat in the matching sofa opposite him, crossing her exposed legs. "What brings your delightful personality into my otherwise dreary day? Jacob? Or is it Anna and Brady?"

The accoutrements for their Bloody Marys arrived via the servant on a large serving tray doubling as a lazy Susan. The clear vodka in one carafe was resting inside a bowl on a bed of crushed ice; the premixed tomato concoction was in another, separate vessel. Lining the rest of the setup were; celery, shrimp, olives, limes, lemons, chili powder, Tabasco, more ice, and empty crystal highball glasses. The assemblage commandeered half of the glass coffee table between them.

"Ah yes. Here we are. That will be all. Thank you." The server was dismissed.

"I'm here about the housekeeper that babysat Brady. The one that I am told has disappeared."

"That damned housekeeper is getting more action than I am, lately." She leaned forward to assemble a cocktail, the plunging neckline to her dress fell loose exposing her entire top, giving

383

Warren a birds-eye view without fetter. His first impression of her lack of undergarments under the silk dress was correct, she was indeed naked under the very thin garment.

"I hope you like it spicy, I know I do," she said.

"What is that a navel piercing?" The big, pink elephant in the room was not going to leave without being discussed. It was not Deni's style. He tried to look as though it was blasé, as if he was not thoroughly turned-on, but he was unsuccessful. The black widow had him in her web.

She pretended to be embarrassed, changed her position to eliminate his vantage point. She mocked a sheepish laugh.

"Hmmmmm. You like to get right down to business, don't you? Here is your drink. You see, I can be servile if the mood strikes."

"Thanks. Speaking of business, I really do need to find that maid that you fired. Time is kinda of the essence. I could also use any records you might have from that night, like a time card and what-not. I'd love to see her room too." He took a sip of his drink, it was the best Bloody Mary he had ever tasted.

She seductively ate a shrimp off of the rim of her cocktail, staring at her prey as she did so. "Are you always so aggressive?"

"I get what I want, if that is what you're asking. I like to do things the easy way, but most people have to do things the hard way. I was kinda hoping that you being a smart, rich lady, that you would be above all that shit. I can see that you like to play games. You're bored, I get that. But I'm leavin' here with what I came to get, plain and simple. But listen, if you wanna do this the hard way, I'm game."

"I am all for doing this the haaaahhd way," she said, imitating his thick accent. "I always get what I want, also. It's just a matter of time. You intrigue me. You want something from me, and I know, without a shadow of a doubt, that I want something from you. I don't get too many bad-boys kicking in my door. You scared poor Nigel, but you don't scare me. Quite the opposite in fact."

To Chamille, Warren was ruggedly handsome, tall, and leanly muscular. His scars added to his bad-boy charm. He was also incredibly wrong and sinful for her, which made him perfect. She left her couch and sat on his lap, straddling him. He made no bid to protest.

"I'll give you everything you want, after you give me every single thing that I want."

She unbuttoned his Oxford shirt, which he almost never wore, and pulled it down to his waist, which essentially handcuffed him. His exposed torso uncovered a tattoo-laden tapestry which would normally be hidden if he had worn a short-sleeved shirt. Her eyes filled as she took him in. Her smile grew, the art was adding to her wantonness.

"Oh, you *are* a bad-boy." She slid off his lap and grabbed his belt, helping him to his feet.

"This is probably a very bad idea, lady." He slipped out of the shirt that tethered his hands.

"Cammy. Call me Cammy." She kissed him hard on the mouth, then neck and chiseled chest.

384

Warren gently pushed her away from him, she stood staring at him less than an arm's length away. He clutched her dress at the bottom of the plunged neckline and in one quick pull, tore the thin, silky dress off of her body; then threw it on the floor in ruins, while she stood before him, naked.

The two of them didn't make love, they ravaged each other in hot, animalistic, carnal sex. They devoured one another without any sensual romance, but in a raw, sweaty, lustful fuck. It was if it was a consensual rape. She dominated him, then he reciprocated. They were one another's personal plaything, using up the other until spent. And they spent each other over, and over again. They both found release multiple times until they were sweaty and exhausted like they had been marooned in the hot desert.

Depleted, thirsty, and dripping with sweat, they lay next to each other on the floor of the library, three rooms away from whence they started. They both panted heavily, letting each other enjoy their respective euphoric states in silence.

After a lengthy period of time, he caught his breath while remaining naked on the floor. Next to him was the sweaty but otherwise perfect, tanned woman. Deni broke the silence. "Hey Cam."

"Yes?"

"I really do need all those things I mentioned earlier. Also can I get the video footage from the outside security gate from that night?"

"Don't ruin this moment, honey. I'm wet in every possible way and enjoying every second of it."

"Cam."

"If you do that to me again in a few minutes, I swear on everything that I love, I will do anything you want. Including sign this house over to you." She rolled over on top of him and began to kiss him again. "We have to do this again."

"Cam."

She continued to re-seduce him. A desperate ploy to continue their very adult activities.

"Cam."

"I know, I know." She got up off of the floor and padded naked into the recesses of the enormous mansion.

Deni watched her leave, then return with a towel. She tossed it at him and left the room again. Nigel entered within seconds of her second departure with all of his various pieces of clothing that had been strewn from room to room during their activities. He stood staring at Warren, making the awkward moment that much more so. *Maybe he is gay*, Warren thought.

385

Nigel finally broke the silence. "MISSES Destrier will meet you in the sitting room in a short time. I will bring you some water once you have dressed. Would you care for sparkling or flat?"

"Huh?"

"The water. Would you like it with bubbles or not, sir?"

"Not."

Nigel turned and left the room after setting the clothes on a reading table.

"You never said if you were legal." Deni tried to salvage some dignity in the situation. The truth was he didn't care where Nigel was from, nor if he was in the United States legally. He was just breaking his balls. He didn't like being the recessive person in any interaction. He had just been used and discarded like a disposable toy, he was not going to be made to feel that way by the help.

Once he started to dress, he realized why he was being stared at. The tattoos. He was used to them, and when he was clothed, even in a T-shirt and shorts, nobody was the wiser. But standing there naked, he could see where it would be a sight. Maybe even off-putting.

Other than the awkwardness between he and Nigel, he felt great. He was going to get what he had come for, and he had a great time in accomplishing the task.

He made his way into the sitting room after he was fully attired. The Bloody Mary bar was replaced by a coffee tray. The last thing he needed was to be more dehydrated. He hoped that Nigel would keep his promise, and that water was in fact on the way. It was.

The assistant, after a long period, did enter the sitting room. "Apologies for the tardiness of your water. I was unavoidably detained in fetching it. It seems that Mrs. Destrier will not be able to revisit you today, as her, ehm, exertions this afternoon have exhausted her." He handed Deni a bottle of Tasmanian Rainwater, which he assumed was just expensive tap water that someone bottled. "She apologises for not being able to rejoin you, but wanted me to thank you for your, ehm, business. She said that she very much looks forward to future transactions with you." He placed a large envelope on the end of the giant, glass coffee table which literally had coffee set up on it. "These are yours to use with discretion. While all of Mrs. Destrier's relationships are important, and would never betray, I reckon that your relationship with her has been elevated rather apace, wouldn't you agree?"

"I'm not sure what you mean by that, guy, but I'm not the one hidin' her secrets and fetchin' her coffee." He picked up the envelope, peered inside. There were a few documents and computer memory stick. "Seems a little light on info here, Nige. Pardon the expression, but, what the fuck? Also I need you to show me where the house cleaner's room is, or was, or whatever."

"All the information that you seek is contained in that folder. I am to inform you that there will be no tour of the staff quarters today, but should you seek to come back, Mrs. Destrier will with pleasure, ehm, see you again." He turned and opened his right arm as if to show him the

386

way to the door. "Your presence here today has been and should remain discrete. If there is nothing further, the door is this way."

Back in his car, he emptied the contents of the envelope onto the front passenger seat. While he let his car warm up, he looked over the few documents that were before him. The first document had an address and directions on it that appeared that it had been printed from GOOGLE Maps. In the margin was large, feminine handwriting, "her last known address, family I think. We must do it again, and I hope soon. Cam." Below her name was a large lipstick kiss.

The address was in Brighton, Massachusetts, a borough of Boston. This area was well-known for college students as well as a significant Russian and Brazilian presence. The address was two hours south with traffic and Warren had other stops to make in New Hampshire. Brighton would have to wait a day or two.

******

The cell phone that was used to make the 911 phone call was sold at a Verizon kiosk that sat in the middle of a large mall off of Interstate 293 in Nashua, New Hampshire. It took some doing, but after a few phone calls to Verizon, he determined the phone was sold out of inventory there. Interstate 293 was a loop that diverted traffic off the main artery of Interstate 93. Inside that loop was a huge mall, located just off the highway.

Nashua was not far from Wayland, nor was it very far north of Boston, in distance. The amount of time the trip took depended upon traffic, to a large extent, which was a gamble at any hour. Many commuters worked in Boston but called Nashua home. New Hampshire houses were less expensive in comparison, the taxes were far less, and the politics slanted much more to the right than the Commonwealth State to the South. The commuter rail, or purple line, made it that much more convenient for those that chose not to fight the traffic on the main artery.

The only downside to living in New Hampshire and working in Massachusetts is the traffic. Getting into and out of the Hub of New England during rush hours made the commute a daily stress-test. Those that opposed taking the train did so because the stops were frequent, times could be a bit unreliable, and the parking structures were an open invitation for thieves. So those avoiding the train, also tried to avoid the heavy traffic times of rush hours, which became popular with many commuters, making those hours less clear. Most hours of the day on 93 were a headache, full-stop. And the loop of 293 was no picnic either.

Despite all of this, people still made the daily adventure south, because of the greater earning potential. Property values in New Hampshire started to rise, and therefore businesses began to adopt Boston pricing. Designer stores, factory outlets, and large malls all catered to the sophisticated metropolitan tastes in the sleeper towns of southern New Hampshire. So did the drug dealers, all of whom needed burner phones.

The kiosk in the mall was a legitimate business. Those shopping for a cell phone could purchase an iPhone, Blackberry, Samsung, Droid or the like, succumbing to the monthly service plans associated with all the data requirements those phones demand. Those looking for a phone that is untraceable, can buy those legally as well. There are a myriad of reasons to have a throwaway phone. Prepaying eliminates the required service fees or contracts, and the customer can simply pay as they go. Lack of credit, or bad credit, eliminates eligibility for said expensive monthly service plans, at any rate. Some consumers are not technologically savvy, therefore do not need all the bells and whistles of a smart-phone. Or they could be a drug dealer, call-girl, pimp or other felon that is on the run, and need to be untraceable which are less legitimate, all.

Warren walked around the kiosk twice without being asked by the nerdy kid behind the counter if he needed any help. The pimple-faced kid, with a very long black tie, a shirt three sizes too big, and pants below his ass-cheeks stood behind the counter, and was too busy typing away on his phone to offer anyone any help. The white man-boy could not have been twenty-one yet. He looked to be a cross between a nerd from the *Big Bang Theory* and a wannabe thug. The name tag he wore said his name was Slice, but that was not likely to be the name his mother had given him.

"How can I, like, help you? We have the latest and greatest of all the phones. The prices marked are negotiable if you commit to a two-year contract." The entirety of his spiel was performed without looking up from his smartphone.

"What if I don't wanna commit to a plan?" While doing laps around the kiosk, he was scoping out the cameras that were strategically placed to maximize coverage. He could see no blind spots where the security would fail to pick up anyone looking at the phones.

"Oh, so you want a prepaid. A go-phone."

"Yep."

"Well we got lots of goes, bro. All depends on how many minutes you need." This kid was a salesman through and through. His dialect went from nerdy wannabe to a young punk gangsta. This little chameleon was a hustler in the making, a used car salesman had nothing on this kid.

"Yeah well, I don't really need to make many calls with it."

"I see." He turned around and retrieved a phone, placed on the plexiglass counter between them. The phone was packaged in a hard, clear-plastic, sealed case. "You still burn minutes when your guys call you. Here is our cheapest burner, man. How many you need?"

"None."

"Man, are you wasting my time?"

"I don't see anyone else in need of help, you do work here, right? I need to see who bought this phone." He handed the kid a piece of paper with the date and serial number of the phone used to make the 911 call."

"What is this? I can't just give you someone's information. I'll get fired." Punk and gangsta had left the building. "Also I only have access to it if it is a Verizon phone and it was sold here, I don't have access to information about other — "

" — lucky for you it was sold here, which means it's a Verizon prepaid phone."

"Look, I can get into a lot of trouble. People get those phones for a reason. If you have a problem with some dude who is moving in on your territory, leave me out of it. Seriously."

Deni quickly snatched the kid's necktie, pulling his face to the glass counter which held the more expensive phones inside. "Let me put it another way. You are gonna do whatever it is you do in your little computer there, and you are going to tell me who bought that phone. You are not *going* to get in trouble. I *am* trouble, and I am right here."

"Alright, alright, alright." He was let go to begin typing and searching in his computer. In between searches, he tucked his tie into his shirt so his assailant wouldn't be able to use it to hurt him again.

"This is totally surreal."

"What?"

"It means — "

" — I know what it means, and it's overused. Just get to work kid."

He went back to work and when he was finished, he looked at Deni with a look of pure fear. He backed himself as far away from Warren as he could. "Ah, man. No name or address. The dude paid in cash. Please don't hurt me, there really isn't anything I can do. I'm sorry."

"You're gonna be if you don't get creative."

"Look it's not illegal, you know. You don't have to give your information on a prepaid. It could have been a gift. Look, they paid cash so that's the end of the road."

"You can give me a list of the phone calls made into and out of that phone."

"I could except there was only one. It was to 911. Go kill someone there."

"What about your cameras here?" He pointed at the cameras above them.

"What about them? Are you a cop or something? I mean, you can't just assault people even if you are the police. Don't you have to have a warrant?" He looked around the mall for a passersby that might be able to help him. The would-be witnesses showed no interest and walked right on past. "Yeah you aren't a cop, but maybe I should call them. Or security. Or my manager."

"Why does everyone have to do things the hard way? Listen kid, all I want you to do is tell me who bought this phone. You can get the shit kicked out of you in front of security or your boss or whoever you want to call, but if you don't figure out a way to give me what I want, you are going to get hurt. I mean hurt like you have never been before. I will break both your arms so bad, you won't even be able to think about jerkin' off again. So stop jerkin' me off and get busy."

"I don't know if I can get it. Seriously. I don't want to get hurt, but I don't think I can get it either. All the data is stored off-site and this phone was bought a long time ago, mister."

"What do you mean off-site. I was told by a friend of mine that all of these new fangled systems store all the information on a cloud or The Cloud or some internet thing."

"Yeah, your friend is right. That is what I mean by off-site. And that is what I mean by I can't get it. It's all password protected. They don't let people like me just have access to their security videos."

"Who has the password to get into it?"

"My boss. Good luck getting it out of him, but be my guest. If you beat him up though, I would love to watch."

"He won't give you the password over the phone if you call him?"

"No way. But if he was the one that set it, I might be able to figure out what his password is. He is a dog-lover and he has this sick man-crush on his little pug. It's gross."

"So you think his password is pug or pug related? Go ahead and try it."

He typed on the wireless keyboard with a grin on his face as he watched the computer screen in front of him.

"Ha, whattaya know? Fifth try," the kid said after twenty-seconds or so. "Lovepug. What a sicko."

"How did you get it? Never mind. So you are in? You got it?"

"Yeah, yeah. Hold on. This is really cool, by the way."

There were a couple of twenty-somethings that were browsing the phones, whether they were actually interested in making a purchase was anyone's guess, but they were completely ignored by Slice or whatever his name was.

"Got it," he said, at long last. " I just need something to store this onto."

Deni reached into his pocket and pulled out the memory stick that he had been given earlier by Cammy. "If you store stuff on this, will it erase what is already on it?"

"Your not much of a computer guy are you?"

"That beat'n isn't still out of the question, kid."

"Sorry, sorry. No. As long is there enough space on it, it will just add it to the stuff already on it. Just give it to me and you can be on your way." He inserted the disk and was storing the footage. While he was waiting, he said, "You know it's funny, I thought you were looking for a dude. I think I remember this lady, she had all kinds of questions, kinda like you. Only she wasn't violent."

"What lady? *The* lady? What are you talking about? Let me see that."

He turned the screen so Deni could see the multiple angles. The kid pressed a button and it turned into a single view, a view of the person who bought the 911 burner phone.

"This lady. If it's the same one I'm thinking of." He looked at the sheet of paper that he had originally been given with the date and serial number on it. "Yeah, that's my associate number. I sold it to her. I thought it was funny at the time because she was so not the type to buy a burner phone, but she kept asking about it being traced and stuff."

He handed the memory stick and the paper to Deni when it was finished saving. "Gotcha. I recognize her, too," Deni said. He grabbed it and ran off, out of the mall. "Your welcome. What an asshole. Not even a tip."

18

THE CITY OF BRIGHTON, MASSACHUSETTS is notable but not for the size, nor because it is a wealthy borough of Boston. When tourists flock to a New England city, Brighton is not usually a point of interest on their travel map. The exit, off of any of the major arteries into the area, doesn't even warrant its own sign. The exit shares a sign that reads: Allston/Brighton/Brookline. The tiny city within the city is noteworthy because it sits between Boston University and Boston College. It is also a haven for a large immigrant population from both Russia and Brazil.

The concentrated center for Russian Jews sits on the western side of Brighton, where the Orthodoxes have lived for generations. Within the enclave are shoulder-to-shoulder, rundown townhouses where the college students attending Boston College reside; those buildings being converted to apartments which are owned by said Russian Hasidic Jews. It was odd that the Jesuit College was nestled on the borders of this community in Brighton and Chestnut Hill, which was another concentration of a less orthodox, but a more affluent Jewish people.

On the opposing end of Brighton, in the East, there sits another devoutly religious community of Brazilians. This area is made up of the same style of rundown apartment buildings. Those residents not only live there without proper documentation, but generally live outside of the number allowed by fire code, and without landlord approval. In some cases, a dozen inhabitants would dwell in a single studio apartment. One of the more legal, or at least with the best paperwork, would score an apartment, which precipitated the phone calls and letters to others who would, in the end, fill the dwelling beyond legal capacity. They obviously don't do this for the comfort but for the sustainability. Under-the-table salaries are low, requiring many earners per apartment in order to afford it. And to be able to send a substantial portion of their incomes back to their homes in Brazil.

This Eastern part of Brighton is not a secret, the prideful inhabitants are brazen in flaunting their native flag throughout the community. It was in this concentrated area that the maid, Marina, formerly in the employ of the Destriers, now lived.

Warren made the trip down to Boston the morning following his tryst at the mansion, and the kiosk discovery in Nashua. He took care of a few things with his business and investigator that worked for him there, and slept in his three-decker in Southie. On Wednesday, he drove into Brighton on Commonwealth Avenue, which should have taken very little time if he could have taken a direct, traffic-free route. But in Boston, that was impossible. He was not able to take a direct route from Southie, with all the one-way streets and such. The traffic was as heavy as it always was. By the time he arrived at the address given to him by Cammy, he was sick of being in his car, sick of traffic, sick of looking for a parking space, and irritable was an understatement. He was in no mood for the shrugging of shoulders and the feigning of language issues by the people who responded as he knocked on doors.

Apartment number two may have been the mailing address, but the hidden side door where Warren would find Marina after a number of attempts, was not the physical address. From what he could ascertain from the number of unmarked doors, all answered by non-English speaking people, Warren guessed that seven apartments made up apartment number two, on the 1600 block of Commonwealth Avenue.

"Marina?"

"Sim. é você a policia?" (Yes? Are you the police?)

"Uh. Shit. I thought you would speak English. No English?"

"Yes, who are you?" The short, thick woman gave him a skeptical look, wondering who the intruder was. Her eyes gave the impression that she had decided that he was not the police, yet the visitor before her was very unusual.

"I'm Warren Dennihan. Mrs. Destrier sent me." He hoped the lie would go unchecked. Cam had more or less given him the address after using him for sex, but she certainly hadn't sent him there. He was hoping to ease his way into the apartment, which was not happening.

"Eu não penso assim, eh, I don't think so. Go away, please," She said but made no effort to close the door. "She no send you, whoever you are, no trouble para mim."

"I'm here about Jacob Grantes. I need your help. Please."

"I cannot help. I very sorry. Nenhum problema para mim." With that, she decided to close the door, which she would have done had Deni not wedged his foot on the bottom of the door to prevent her.

"Did you know the woman who died in the crash? She was from Brazil also." It was a long shot, that the two women had met.

"Sim. Yes, she was my cousin. I very angry that she die, e, I no help man who kill her." Brazilians use familial terms like cousin differently than Americans. Warren was aware of these loose cultural differences but not the exact relation between the two, if in fact there was one. Certainly the two knew of or about one another, which was all he wanted to know.

"I'm sorry. I understand. But something is very wrong about what happened, which I think is why you were fired. That is what I want to talk to you about. Can I come in?"

"No. I meet you at café. Fifteen minute." She pointed toward a Brazilian coffee shop on the next block, behind him. "Você não pode entrar."

"Are you hiding something from me, Marina? If I go over there, are you going to meet me there, or are you gonna run away?"

"No, I meet you. I promise. Eu prometo. Fifteen minute."

393

"I'm not going to hurt you, we are just gonna talk. Don't run away, that is only going to make me mad."

"Sim, sim. I meet you."

The café was in fact an internet café. It was either Brazilian owned, or the owner was a marketing genius. Brazilian flags, soccer balls, and pictures of famous World Cup victories were covering the walls, all while tanned beauties served coffee. If the locals had computers, they didn't use them. Every computer was being used while the small two-top tables were mostly free.

Deni hadn't dashed right over from the maid's apartment, instead he waited for her to leave so he could follow her. He wasn't entirely sure she wasn't going to run, despite her promise. Once he was certain she was on her way to the café, he then jetted over as quick as he could get over there.

He arrived within seconds before her arrival, still panting in fact, from the run over from his car. She ordered a concoction in Portuguese, which he doubled and paid for. It turned out to be delicious. Once they found a suitable table, he started with some light conversation.

"What is this? It's phenomenal."

"Cafezinho."

"Yeah, you'll have to write that down for me."

She gave no response, nor did she make any attempt to write down the name of the espresso drink. She just stared at him in bewilderment.

"So how long have you worked, or, did you work for the Destriers?"

"Many year."

"Look, I know you don't really wanna talk to me, but this is important. Maybe I can help you get your job back. If you help me."

"Why I help you. Por que?"

"Because while Arelia's death was tragic, someone is hiding what really happened. The truth is not complete. If Jacob really did kill her, he will pay for it in prison. But if someone else helped him or had a hand in it, they should pay too, right? I think you know something. You know that something isn't right, and that is why you were fired."

"I fired because I not legal here."

"Is that what Cam, er, Mrs. Destrier told you?"

"She tell me nothing. Nigel do it."

"OK. What did Nigel say? Listen, I don't like him either, so feel free to talk shit."

"He tell me to pack my room and leave. If I make trouble, it will be bad for me. Eu não o quero ser ruim para mim. I cannot have trouble."

"So she paid you to go away because she knew you knew something, and were in no position to put up a stink?"

394

"Que?"

"Never mind. How much did she pay you?"

"She still pay me. Every week. Cash. I save so I go back to Brazil rich. I like here, but minha familia es home."

"Wait. She still pays you even though you don't work there anymore? You don't think that is wicked weird?"

"Week - ed?"

"Weird. Very weird. You don't think that paying you without work is very weird?"

"Sim. Yes. But I get money to no work, they tell me no question but just hide. You here mean I must go home now."

"Who gives you the cash? How?"

"Nigel give me Sábados, eh, Saturday." She took a sip of her drink while looking out onto Market Street, which runs perpendicular to Commonwealth Avenue. She seemed very nervous.

"When were you told to go?"

"That night. They help me pack. But sometime they call me back to look after child."

"Who are they? Mrs. Destrier wasn't there that night. Right? Wasn't she at the charity event?"

"Sim. Nigel and other. Drive me here. Mr. Destrier and Mrs. Destrier both go to party. Sra. Grantes pick up Brady, I go to bed. I wake up by Nigel say 'you go but we pay'. I cannot have trouble, so I go. Next day, I find out Arelia tem morreu. Is very sad for me. I surprise you find me. I want no troubles. Sometime I go back with Nigel, then he bring me here. You here is no good for me."

"Wait, you're all over the place. Sra. Grantes. That means misses, woman, right? Mother?" Deni was frantic in his digging for the memory stick out of his black, leather jacket. The memory stick that was given to him by Chamille Destrier, through Nigel.

"Sim, yes."

He got up from the table they were sitting at, grabbed Marina gently by the wrist, bringing her with him to an already occupied computer terminal. "That is why you are here in Brighton, why they are still paying you. That sneaky minx." He commandeered an extra, empty chair from a table next to the terminal, telling Marina to sit in it. He then handed the twenty-something guy using the computer forty dollars while pulling him out of his chair at the terminal.

"Hey que?" There was complete shock on his face and because of the surprise, posed little physical resistance at being ousted from his spot at the computer.

"Beat it, kid. Kick rocks." He turned to Marina and said, "how do you say go away in Brazilian?"

"Portuguese. People seja de Brazil. Speak Portuguese."

"Whatever. I don't need a lesson, I need this kid to fuck off."

395

She looked at the young man and said, "Você deve partir ou você está indo ser dano por este homem. Please."

The young man turned and walked to the coffee counter.

Warren plugged the memory stick into the USB port on the processing unit of the Acer computer. He hoped there wasn't going to be any compatibility issues on what was clearly and older model computer. He was no computer genius, any problems would require someone more tech savvy than he.

Fortunately, the bell that sounded when he inserted the wand indicated that at least it recognized the device. The window that popped up looked like a small TV, with remote control features lining the bottom of the image. He began to fast-forward the video footage from the Destrier security gate, by clicking the double-right arrow. He hadn't had to wait but a heartbeat before clicking the double-vertical lines. The image was paused in front of them.

He looked over to Marina and said, "Sra. Grantes. When she picked up Brady?"

"Sim. Of course. I tell you this, I no liar." She looked outright confused, not understanding what the image meant. Not that Deni really knew what it meant either.

"*You* are not. But wasn't Mrs. Grantes supposed to be at the charity event, er, the party? Why was she picking up Brady when she was supposed be five miles away?

"Eu não compreendo. eu não sei. I don't know, senhor."

Just then, the disrespected twenty-something male was back with a wary, petite, female café manager in tow. She was there to bring some weight to the situation, despite her size, but anyone could see that her heart wasn't in it.

"Well ain't you the brave one? Bring a shorty over to fight your battles? Grow a pair of balls, guy." He stripped the two twenty dollar bills still in the adolescent's hand, pulled the memory stick out of the drive. "All yours chief." He looked at the manager who was speaking softly to Marina. "No sense of humor," he said to her as he pointed with his thumb at the kid. He handed the forty dollars to the manager with a wink.

✳✳✳✳✳✳

Deni's mind was turning as fast as the tires of his car on the highway as he returned north. He was making progress, but what was he learning? If JG didn't pick up Brady, and Anna did, then what else in this story isn't accurate? Was Anna at the charity event at all? If Chamille was covering for her, why stop now? How was Jenna involved, other than serving him the alcohol in the first place? Were all of these women working together? That seemed far-fetched.

The fact that Anna was hiding something, and was hidden herself for that matter, was disconcerting to say the least. Jenna had disappeared with the CCTV footage. Why? He thought these women despised one another, at least that was the impression Jenna had given him. Maybe that is why JG was bellying up to the bar in the first place, he knew he didn't have to pick up Brady. So why does he think that he did? Why was everyone saying that he did? How did Brady get up to his room? Anna? Jenna? His mind wouldn't stop.

Warren had wanted to track down Jenna the moment he learned that she had taken off, now it seemed imperative. Time was running out for JG and there were far too many unanswered questions. He needed to find this girl, and make her fill in the missing pieces, conclusively, once and for all. He had doubts that she would be there, but he would again have to sift through her home for clues.

It was illegal to make phone calls on a cell phone while driving unless using a handsfree device. Warren didn't have such a gadget, though if he had the wherewithal, his Escalade probably had the capability for handsfree communication. Either way he wasn't using it, nor did he give a shit. He was calling a contact, a New Hampshire Statie he had known for many years.

He wanted the last known address for one Jennifer Beaumont, Jenna. His contact hated when Deni would call him, using him for these types of crusades. Though he complained, he always came through. The conversation was short, if not curt. There was no breaking of balls, no 'you can't keep doing this', he just gave him Jenna's name and what she looked like and his contact spit back everything but her shoe size. Sometimes it paid to be a former cop. Fortified with her address, he continued his drive to it.

She was a Barstonian. He parked in her driveway, the VW *Passat* that was registered to her, according to his contact, was not.

He knocked on her door with a set of three raps. One set. Then the second. After the ninth knock there was still no movement. Also no surprise. Plan B was really Plan A anyway. Time for the pins.

Personal shame was beginning to form at the loss of his touch at picking locks. It took him three minutes to break into Jenna's place. Which was about as much time as he spent inside once the door was opened.

Upon his entrance, he had obtained all the information he had expected. He might as well have been a prospective renter, or homebuyer, or inspecting it to see about a security deposit. The place was empty. Empty empty. The garbage had been removed, so he wasn't able to rummage through it. She even took the ice cube trays.

"Who takes the ice cube trays?" he asked the empty room. "OK, Deni. Think this through old boy. She hates the job but makes great money at it. She says she is gonna leave so she can go back to school, or some shit. We break her balls a bit, she cries and takes off. At some point she has to go back to get the CCTV footage, then bails. She knows she has to leave town, cuz I'm onto her like a fat kid on cake. Where do you go? Family. Nah, this chick is smart. She ain't goin' somewhere obvious.

"So where did you go, Jenna? And why? You doin' this for Anna? By lookin' at this dump you lived pretty sparse. So all of a sudden you've got money. Cammy. That crazy nympho is payin' the bills. But why give me the maid and the video if she is involved?

"I gotta talk to Ryan. This is gettin' outta control." He closed the door behind him. The empty walls were not talking back, so it was not much of a conversation. He needed some light shed on this, at least another perspective. Ryan would help. He would have to.

He made a phone call to Ryan as he backed out of the driveway, again breaking the law. And again, he didn't give a shit.

19

PROGRESS, BE IT NOUN OR VERB, is defined as *'advancement, moving forward, development, growth or improvement in condition, space, or time'*. While JG was progressing in the forward movement of time, moving closer toward the trial, he was regressing physically and mentally. The regression was progressing, if you can call it that, with quick and drastic results.

A prisoner has nothing but time. Time to think, rethink, and dwell on every event that has ever taken place in his life. Be it significant or not is of no matter. Time is their enemy and so is their own brain. The insignificant becomes monumental once it festers over time. The thoughts eat away at the host like a cancer. An event that is already significant, metastasizes to the point of subjugating the host.

Grantes was no longer a confident yet mild-mannered attorney. He was an abandoned, caged animal. What had kept him going all of this time was the love of his wife and child. The many phone calls and letters he had received and sent had been his life blood. They were the white blood cells that were attacking those cancerous thoughts that destroyed men. The knowledge that he had Anna's love and support throughout his turmoil made the day to day abhorrence of incarceration tolerable. But barely. The absence of his family had decayed his driving force into nothingness.

The downward spiral began with the trivial event of being cut off in chow-line. Which was less about food than the cutter disrespecting the cuttee. The 5:00 PM dinner chow began like every other over the course of his six previous months. The cells open with the loud clang and slide of the solid steel door, everyone on the pod lines up in their best, Bob Barker jumpsuit, ID pinned to the collar. Once the line is formed, inmates would sneak to rearrange themselves in that line in order to eat with whom they like. The trays of food are handed to the men just before taking their seat in the order that they were lined up in. The wrong person cut in front of Grantes, on the wrong day, at the wrong time.

"What the fuck?" The outburst was not discreet. The cutter, it turned out, just wanted to eat with Grantes's cellmate, Loder (why was an entirely different question, nobody should have to eat with such a Neanderthal). Grantes was handed his plastic tray at the time of the outburst, which was the worker-bee inmate's mistake. The cover was quickly removed and the remainder of the untouched food was shot-putted at the offending inmate in front of him.

The correctional officers had watched this all unfold, expecting the disruption or worse after the vocal outburst, and immediately responded to eliminate the possibility of any retribution.

"Grantes. That's a seventy-two," said the CO. He made sure it was loud enough for the entire pod, both tiers to hear. The officer came out from behind the bubble, pulled him out of chow line, and led him back to his cell. Supper was over for him.

A seventy-two is the number of consecutive hours to be locked into the cell without being let out. No rec time. No shower. Nothing but cell time for seventy-two straight hours. At least he wasn't lugged down to the hole. Yet. The toilet had definitely flushed, and he was circling the bowl, but he had not gone down the drain quite yet.

While locked in, he was consumed with thoughts regarding the whereabouts of his wife and son. Even more than usual since he learned of their disappearance. His trial was imminent, his family had vanished. Ryan had no news. Unless he took a deal, which would keep him where he was for the next five and a half years, he would be facing football numbers in the same prison.

He wanted to speak to Anna. *Maybe about football,* he thought. He would lose his license to practice law. Brady would make a great lawyer, someday. *Where in the hell are they?* He was losing his mind.

The next event took place the following morning. It is hard to get into trouble while locked in your cell with no contact except with your celly, but he managed. The following morning, Grantes was not allowed to go to his mandatory AA meeting, because of his lock-in. Missing a meeting means a loss of rec according to the Sheriff's rules. This meant that a ticket would need to be served to him in his cell. This also meant that the first time he could come out of his cell after his seventy-two hour lock-in, he would not be allowed to. This was only day one of his three, so with all the meetings he would miss, he was going to get at least one additional day added to his lock-in, which would then lead to more unattended programming. Frustrated, he decided to sucker-punch his cellmate when the ticket was slid under his door by the CO. It was right in front of the officer, so there was no way to get away with it or to deny it.

Loder, inmate #437254, would not suffer one quick punch to the face, he would suffer twenty-seven more. At least that was the number written on his new charge of assault. He would now face another day in court, for another felonious act. He was able to beat his cellmate, hitting him as many times as he had, because the COs needed to get the lug team into the pod, the rest of the pod locked-in or on their knee, before the cell door would be opened. All things considered, they responded rather quickly. The Vegas-style camera coverage, covered every angle of the pod except for the inside of each cell. The twenty-eight total punches could not be proved or disproved, but Loder's face was all that was really needed to know that an assault had taken place.

The lug team, all six of them, invaded the cell (only two of them could actually fit inside the small cell, why they always bring six officers to diffuse these situations when all the other inmates

400

were locked down, was a mystery to him), taking shots of their own until he submitted. He was beaten, shackled at the wrists and ankles, and lugged to solitary confinement.

The Hole is a long row of single cells juxtaposed along each side. If the two-man cells in the pods were considered tiny, the singles in The Hole were microscopic. Upon arrival, his ankles were unlocked. Grantes was then inserted into the cell, back to the door, while the slot in the solid door was unlocked and opened. He then backed up against the re-closed door so his wrist cuffs could be removed.

He was given a one hour cool-down period before an officer in a white uniform shirt with a single metal bar on his collar arrived. The lieutenant was in a short-sleeved shirt and was jostling a huge set of keys on a ring while holding some documents. The food slash cuff-up slot was reopened, and a chair was then placed next to the door for him by a subordinate.

"Grantes. Come to the door so we can chat please." He said it without any detectable emotion. "If you are gonna be nice, I won't cuff you up. If you reach through the slot we are gonna have problems. Understand?"

"Yes."

"All right, well, you've got yourself into a serious situation here," said the lieutenant. He flicked the documents with his middle finger. "But you already know that don't you? You're a smart guy, a smart guy who just did something supremely stupid. Why? What's going on?"

Grantes knew to remain silent, and he did.

"Talk to me. I'm trying to help you. Loder is in HSU, broken jaw, broken orbital bone, he's pretty beat up. You did that to him. What did he do to you?"

Silence.

"Well he must have done something. Or did you take it out on him for the ticket?"

Stoic reticence.

"You're not giving me much to work with here, you must want this charge. We can make the charge go away if you help me, help you."

"Out of the kindness of your heart, you want to erase this? What, I just go back to my cell? That'd look good."

"Oh, you can speak. Maybe you go back up there, maybe you don't. Just tell me what happened."

"Off the record?"

"Nothing is ever off the record. You're an attorney, you know when you talk to the police all bets are off."

"You are not the police. You are a CO, a babysitter."

"I'm a lieutenant, wise-guy. The same rules apply, and I'm trying to help you."

"Then you are going to be having a one-way conversation."

"Hypothetically. Hypothetically, what happened?"

"Hypothetically, lock-ins mean missed meetings. Missed meetings mean more lock-ins. The Hole breaks the cycle. Hypothetically."

"Uh huh. Look, Loder is a low-life, a professional inmate. He gets his face rearranged Picasso-style, I don't lose a bit of sleep. But you are not a pro. You are a civilian, and you can help yourself."

"I'm accused of vehicular manslaughter. The trial is a week and a half from now, solitary seems good to me."

"The Hole means no visits, two showers a week, and no rec. You don't want that, trust me. Let me help you out. How about a single cell back up on your pod?"

"For free? What do you want from me?"

"Information."

"About?"

"Anything. Just general information. I'll give you my card here, which will work from the phone on the pod, without being on your pin sheet. You see or hear something, you call that number and leave a message. Simple as that."

"So you want me to be a rat," Grantes said. It wasn't a question.

"I take care of this, you take care of us."

"There are no secrets in this place. Doesn't matter which pod you put me on. Besides, how long do you think I would last if you just put me back up there the same day I get lugged with no celly? I'd get a buck-fifty within my first hour. Or is that your plan?"

A buck-fifty is what is given to a rat by another inmate. It refers to the one hundred fifty stitches it requires to sew up the slice made to the man's face. It is specifically done to the face so everyone who comes in contact with that inmate knows that he is a rat.

"You spend three days down here, for the sake of appearances. We give you a job up there so you basically have free reign, contact visits whenever you want. Life could be really good. Everything stays in place when you come back after sentencing."

"What if I win?"

The lieutenant laughed but there was no humor in it. "There is no way you are not coming back here."

"I'll give it some thought and get back to you. I'll leave a message."

"No, wise-guy. You'll decide right now. I'll make sure Loder doesn't want to testify, though he probably wouldn't anyway. He will be relocated to a different pod, so you won't even see him again. You tell me now what it's gonna be, if you accept, you go back up there in three days."

"If I get found out? What then?"

"We PC you."

"Protective Custody, how lovely."

"Then don't get found out."

"What a deal."

20

THE TRIAL WAS DRAWING EVER NEARER, the time provided by Judge McCaglia was over half-used. With only a week and a half to go, there was still too much to learn, too much to do, and the minutes were ticking off on the proverbial bomb. Warren had called Ryan to set up another meeting, only it took a few days to arrange, and it was not at a bar this time. This was no time for a drunk, a hangover, or the like; time was a-wasting and this was a time for action. They just needed a direction. They needed a plan.

With Ryan's busy schedule, they would meet at the law office. Ryan was backed up on his other cases and was drowning in work. His twenty-hour days were wearing on his relationship with his wife Angie as well. They saw each other at the office, but they had agreed a long time ago that work was work, and home was home.

Paperwork and assorted law books were stacked on top of file folders which were stacked on top of every hard surface. It looked like a scene from *hoarders*, with piles and piles of organized chaos. Ryan was diligent in his work behind one such pile on his desk but remained unseen.

"Ry? You in here?"

He stood up, revealing himself from the chin up behind his current heap. "Yeah, right here. Just move a pile and have a seat."

"I love what you have done with the place. Who's your designer?"

"Sorry, Deni. I'm swamped."

"I see. It looks like an Office Max threw up in here."

"Hey, stop breakin' balls. JG had cases, one of which is on appeal scheduled this week, on top of all of my work. I'm trying to keep this place going and help him get out of this jam at the same time. I get enough ball-breaking at home, I don't need the extra help. There is a system to all of this believe it or not."

"Yeah, I can tell. Get into JG mode, kid. I need help sortin' this out. You told me when we started this that I was supposed to find stuff to help lessen his sentence; dig up some dirt on the vic. I haven't even gotten into the vic yet because for every rock I turn over, all I get is more rocks. I haven't had the time, and my gut tells me it's a dead end anyway. Somethin' is wicked odd here, though. And I got way more questions than answers, with only ten days to go."

"I'm sorry I haven't been more helpful, but like I said — "

" — you got a computer under all this? It would be a lot easier to show you rather than have to explain. Besides that, I don't know what I'd be explaining. I have no idea how all this fits together, but it's wicked fucked up, Ry."

"Questions are good, Deni. Questions inject reasonable doubt. Reasonable doubt in a trial is our best friend. My computer is buried, here is my laptop. Give me a sec while it boots up."

When it booted up, the bells and whistles that indicated he had email were going off. Out of habit, he opened it and glanced at them. Most of them could wait, but one caught his eye.

"Huh. Deni, look at this."

He made his way around the debris, looked over Ryan's shoulder to see an email that said:

Subject: About Jacob Grantes. Urgent.

"You recognize the address, Ry?"

"No." He then opened the email, which revealed a long, complicated web address. "Should I open it? What if it's a virus, or a prank, or something?"

"Click it."

Ryan clicked on the blue, underlined address and a video panel appeared on his screen. After a few seconds of blank screen, a dark bar room appeared in black and white. It was busy with people moving about the small screen. It was virtually indecipherable what they were seeing. The picture was grainy in addition to busy.

"Can you make it bigger? I can't see shit," Deni said.

Ryan maximized the video screen to fill his laptop screen. The picture was still grayscaled and blurry with distorted pixels, but the overall image was a little easier to interpret."

"That's Sully's isn't it?" Ryan was staring at the video in squinted disbelief.

"It sure is, kid. It's hard to tell but I think that's our boy sittin' at the bar."

They looked at each other and said at the same time, "the surveillance video."

"The missin' CCTV video," Deni added.

"It's not missing, Deni. It's right here." Ryan was still unaware that both Jenna and the video were in the wind.

"That's one of the things I was gonna talk to you about. Jenna took the video from Sully's and then vanished. She never went back. But here it is. Why did she steal it, if what she said was true, that she only served him two Stones? And then here it is emailed to you? Why disappear with it and then send it to you?"

"Jenna is gone?"

404

They were speaking while watching the video. The person who looked like JG, likely was JG, had just received a call on his cell phone which he answered. The phone call was short, he hung up and then left his bar stool.

"This is probably when Jenna said he left to go to the bathroom. And yes, she's gone, Ry. Cleaned out her place. Took the fuckin' ice cube trays. Who does that?"

"Whoa, whoa, whoa. Who is that?" Ryan pointed to a woman with her back to the camera. She had a white, adjustable cap on with a long ponytail pulled through the opening in the back. It was impossible to tell what color her hair was, as the picture was in black and white but it certainly seemed light in color. The petite woman was moving like greased lightning toward the empty bar stool, and the unattended beer on the bar top.

"Do we have another angle on that? I'd love to see this chicks face," Deni said.

"No this is it. What in holy hell? Did she just put something in his beer? Look, her hand goes right over it, but I can't tell."

"That is why you never leave your drink. If ya do, this is what happens. If ya don't wanna bring your drink to the head, you should at least put a coaster over it so it's harder to mess with on the sly," Deni explained.

Ryan rewound and played that section of the video over and over again. It was impossible to tell who the female was, or if she did in fact doctor the unattended beer. He hit pause at the exact moment her hand was over the pint glass.

"Is that Jenna? Hair color seems light for Jenna, but I don't see her behind the bar. She was working that night and this is when she said she was finished for the night. She headed over to the charity event from here, right?"

"Yeah, she did. But there is more to this than just that. Why would she send you the video of her juicin' his juice?"

"How do you know she sent this?"

"The owner and manager said that the disk that this video was stored on, was in the same spot in the office for six months. It was in a desk drawer or somethin'. Then, just when Jenna quits without notice, she shuts off her phone, moves, and the video is gone too. Who else has it? If she didn't send it, who did?"

"OK, fair enough. So let's say she sent it. If that is her in the video, why would she send it?"

"Either she is thumbin' her nose at us, or that ain't her. She might be involved though, and dimin' out the person who did."

"Why would she rat someone out?"

"She took off, which means she is scared. You heard her say she was leavin'. She came into money or somethin' and screwed. It doesn't look like her on video, but it is next to impossible to tell. Unless she wore a wig, or died her hair lighter, then died it back …. which seems less likely. Plus … "

405

"Plus what, Deni?"

"Plus, Anna wasn't at the charity event that night. At least not all night. She picked up Brady from the Destriers, which means she couldn't be in two places at one time."

"Wow. You're sure? No doubts?"

"I've got the video from the gate right here, and I found the maid who confirmed it. She said she told people, but nobody listened. They pushed her out because of what she could say. I think Cammy, er, Cam .... Chamille is involved."

"Holy shit, you've been busy. Chamille Destrier; rich as all hell, Chamille Destrier, who I just heard you call Cammy by the way, is involved? How? Why? She's completely nuts, right?"

"I'm not sure exactly how, but she had to cover for Anna that night. There is no way the planner of the event leaves the big party without someone noticing unless she has cover. Cam was at the event, so the doser wasn't her. And the maid. She got rid of the maid and sat on this gate footage. They are really good friends, right?"

"Yes, great friends for years. But that means that you think Anna is in this too," Ryan said.

"I don't like thinkin' that way but, ok, maybe she is. Two weird things with her besides her vanishing."

"She wasn't at the event all night like she said she was, that's one. Which is a pretty good trick, because I was there with Ang and we had no idea she wasn't there all night. I would have testified under oath, given her an alibi, if she would have asked."

"That woulda been good."

"Yeah well, why would anybody accuse of her of anything? This seemed like a pretty simple case from the jump."

"Yeah well, it gets weirder, Ry."

"There was more? I'm missing something, what is another one?"

"She bought the burner phone."

"What? No way. She made the 911 call? I don't believe it." Ryan was shaking his head.

"I'm not sayin' she made the call, I'm sayin' she bought the phone. With cash. And she didn't activate any personal information when she activated the phone. Why go all the way to Nashua to buy an anonymous burner phone? There are plenty of places to buy one right here in Wayland."

"So what are we saying? I'm stunned. What does all of this mean? One of these, or all of these ladies, dump something into his drink so he would drive off the road and kill himself? And instead he kills some poor lady? Is that what we are saying? Are we saying that JG is *innocent* in all of this?"

"What I'm saying is that after seein' that email, that I think there is a strong possibility that someone dropped Rohypnol in JG's drink. He was given a Ruphie. The date-rape drug. It kinda makes sense now that you look at it. He can't remember anything, it takes fifteen minutes or so to work, kinda puts it all in perspective. I'm saying that Anna calls him while he is at the bar, or

406

somebody does, and says 'go home and put on a tux, muffin, Brady is covered. Come to the party.' Jenna, or somebody, waits for the poor prick to use the head and slips him the Mickey."

"I didn't think that it was legal to buy Rohypnol in the U.S., they took it off the market didn't they? Does it show up on a breathalyzer test?"

"It's not legal, but it's easy to get because it's still prescribed as a Valium substitute in countries like Brazil. And no, it doesn't show up on most tests. Nobody even thinks to test for it on guys, because nobody gives the date rape drug to a dude. At least usually."

"There is no way it is still in his system, and you can't tell from the video for sure, if that is what happened. How do we prove it?"

"I thought you said that reasonable doubt was our friend? We're runnin' out of time but I think we can shove this up that fat-fuck-prosecutor's ass. What are you thinkin'?" Deni was beginning to feel under-appreciated.

"I'm thinking that we don't have authentication, that we don't know for sure that is what happened and we most definitely can't prove it," Ryan said.

"She wasn't blessing the beer in the name of the Lord, Ry. She wasn't just waving her hand over it. She did something to the drink."

"Nevertheless, I'm thinking that I would like to have this conversation with Anna, or with Jenna, and find out if Chamille Destrier is financing this project and why. You're right, we don't have much time so where do we go from here?"

"If I go back to Cammy's, that's an all-day event and we don't have the time. Plus she will just deny it. She's bored and this is probably just some kinda game for her. Jenna, we find Jenna."

"What about Anna? If she is mixed up in this, we are going to need to find her. Poor Brady."

"Yeah, I get it. Poor Brady. We will get to Anna, but she has resources, and she will be tough to find. Jenna, she ain't got shit. She just came into money because somebody is payin' her bills, and she was the last to leave town so the trail is more fresh. I find her and maybe she rolls over on the others."

"OK, I'm with you. Sounds reasonable. You called the other day asking about the cars, what's up with that? You said Anna drove the SUV last?"

"Yeah, it looks that way. I still don't know where that fits in, but yeah. Did they impound the car to run tests on it, so she had to drive it home?"

"No, it was parked and the police ran their tests where it was. I'll double check, but I'm pretty sure that it didn't move."

"Then she drove it. After he did or something, but the seats were, like, on top of the steering wheel. The back seat was a mess like Brady had a play date back there. A DVD and the whole nine. The only thing missing was the bouncy room."

"So she used that SUV after the accident. Why? She had an identical one that wasn't in an accident."

"I'm not sure, Ry. That's why I called you. If I get the chance I'll ask her. Here, take these videos and the address of the maid. All the evidence you will need. One thing is for sure, buddy. In this day and age — everyone is on video, all the time. You can't escape it."

21

THE USUAL CONNECTIONS AND METHODS were not working for Deni. Whomever was financing Jenna's clandestine operation and new home, was very good and had more resources than he could muster. Which said a lot. Deni knew a lot of people. And she most certainly had to have help, he thought. She may have made a very good income from her tip jar, but to dump one life for another is expensive.

People move all the time. They hire movers, buy boxes, a moving truck, all of which costs money. People who move out of one area and into another need to switch bank accounts, get new jobs, and otherwise leave a trail for someone to follow. Should that someone be interested in following said trail. But Jenna had not left one.

She was alone and must have moved in the middle of the night. No friends to help her move, nobody to confide in, nobody to keep her new location a secret. He checked. Professional movers must have come in the middle of the night, quietly moved all of Jenna's belongings to her new location. But there was no sign of it. No tire marks left from a big moving truck, and the neighbors looked befuddled when asked about the move. She was apparently in the place one day, and without a sound or trace, was gone the next. Along with the ice cube trays.

The house she lived in was rented. The owner of the property said that she was paid through the end of the year. When asked if she always paid her rent in advance, the landlord said, "she said she would be traveling a lot for work and wanted to make sure the lease was taken care of."

Warren asked the landlord if he was aware the place was completely empty, that the place could easily be re-rented to someone else at that moment. He said, "I wasn't aware but people can live anyway they wanted to, with furniture or not. It's illegal to double-dip on the rent, so I won't rent it out again until the lease is up. I'm fine with it. She is probably just traveling, like she said." In other words, he was no help whatsoever.

The Post Office had no change of address form on file, he had one of his contacts look into it for him. She therefore no longer needed to receive mail. People were admittedly using snail-mail with less frequency, going green or whatever. But no mail, no change of address? That was intentional.

He looked into her finances extensively, diving in like a forensic accountant though he didn't have the degree. The VW Passat that should have been parked in her driveway was leased

409

through Volkswagen Financial Services. The car was paid off in full the month prior. This was further evidence that there was planning involved. And money.

A look at her other bank accounts and credit reports divulged no leads either. She didn't apply for any new credit cards in her new life; no new apartment lease, no major purchases, no new bank account. Her old credit cards were paid off and closed. She had cash and she was well funded.

All of this digging took time. Phone calls were made, contacts returning those calls with anything but answers. Visits were made, which meant travel throughout New England. Time was ticking away. Days were used up with nothing to show for it other than added miles to an already limping Cadillac *Escalade*.

He had an idea who had the deep pockets, but he was still unsure why. The three women seemed an odd trio. Chamille and Anna had been friends for years, since college. Both women were rich, but Mrs. Destrier was ridiculously so. Anna's only plausible motive for being involved in this was that she thought she was being cheated on by her husband. The woman with whom he was believed to be having an affair was the third woman in this odd team, an affair which Jenna denied. Chamille was Anna's friend and would help her through this time, though her views on adultery were obviously a bit more enlightened. *So where does Jenna fit in? Did Anna and Cammy hatch this scheme, setting Jenna up to be the fall-guy? The patsy? If so, why were they financing her new life?* All of these thoughts were rattling about his brain, yet his gray-matter was not manifesting any answers.

Deni had spent days on all of this, reviewing these questions again and again. There was only a week left before the trial and he was in the dark. He would have to suck it up and pay Mrs. Destrier another visit. While the exercise would be fun, he didn't want to be played. He would have to go in there blind and hope she would be willing to spill her guts about what the hell was going on in this case. Was the original plan to kill JG, but the plan went haywire? The plan was to make it look like an accident, but the wrong person had the accident? If Cammy was involved, why would she admit to this scheme? The rich bitch had lawyers, of that he was sure.

There was only one way to find out, he thought. He headed over there on a crisp, early Saturday morning. He was hoping to catch Chamille off-guard with the early hour, though he knew he would be made to wait until she had her coffee and was awake. Nigel would make sure of it.

The gate was closed, of course, but the white button on the security system was there and waiting.

"Good Morning, Sir. Are you aware that it is not yet 8:00 AM? A bit of an early time to call, yes?"

"I need to see Cam, er, Mrs. Destrier. It is an emergency."

"Yes, well, you seem to be experiencing many emergencies with regard to Mrs. Destrier as of late. You said as much the last time you were here, and it was decidedly not an emergency."

"Just ask her if she will see me. It really isn't up to you, Nige, is it?"

"I believe it bloody-well is, sir. It is my job to ensure that her schedule is kept and that undesirables are kept at bay." The nancy-boy's dander was up.

"Why don't you ask her what she desires, Nige. You said yourself on my last trip here that I've been elevated or whatever. So go ask her how desirable I am."

"My name is Nigel, not whatever basterdisation you might come up with on a whim."

"Sorry, Nige. Just go and tell her that I need to see her again. You can stick around for the show if ya want."

"I'm not going to even dignify. I cannot speak to her right now, nor would I even If I could. She is on holiday. She will be for some time. Now please go."

"It's not a holiday. Oh shit, you mean on vacation."

"And the dawn breaks. She is not here, nor will she be in the immediate future."

"Where did she go?"

"I'm afraid I cannot say. Would you like to schedule an appointment for when she returns?"

"Uh, yeah, yeah. I would like to *shed-yule*," Deni said. "What date are we looking at for her return?"

"If you will leave me your contact information, I will be in touch with a date and time when she returns. I can queue you up at that time, though I'm afraid I cannot be more specific just now."

"Never mind. Hey, Nige?"

"Yes?"

"You better hope I never see you out on the streets."

"Very good, sir. You will do what you must, and I will do the same. Good day." With that, the other end went dead.

Deni sat at the gate for a while in thought, his warm Escalade idling. He had finally gotten a rise out of the English Bloke, which made him happy. But as far as the investigation was going, he was at a loss. That didn't make him happy. Anna, gone. Jenna, gone. Cammy, now gone. Were they all in the same place? They were probably sitting on a beach somewhere, at a bar with a straw roof, drinking some exotic drink together, having a laugh. Job well-done ladies. You didn't kill him, but you killed him.

22

THE MONDAY BEFORE THE TRIAL; Ryan amassed all his courage, compiled all the information Warren had uncovered, coming up with a succinct presentation, and headed to the WCHOC. With exactly one week remaining before the big show, he needed to let his friend and client know where they were with his case. Most of what they had was supposition. Would it amount to reasonable doubt in the eyes of a jury? Not likely. Who would believe that a wealthy woman suspected her husband of sleeping around, so she conspired to kill him, making it look like an accident. In that plan, an innocent bystander was killed. This is the stuff in movies. Or books. This stuff didn't happen in stuffy Wayland, New Hampshire.

The case-law Ryan looked up concerning illegal immigrants obtaining driver's licenses, and the motor vehicle infractions surrounding it, was murky at best. Whether a person whom had questionable immigration status should be able to have a license was debatable, but if they had a valid license was the crux of the issue. In this case, Arelia Diaz did have a valid license. The Department of Motor Vehicles works their own agenda, with their own timetable. End of story. If it was proven that Jacob Grantes was indeed too impaired to drive, then who was on the road was of little consequence. Two wrongs didn't make a right, and if he hadn't killed this poor woman, he could have killed another innocent. This was not an avenue for defense that they could win. It was depraved indifference, either way. It wouldn't even affect sentencing if, or likely when, he was convicted.

The usual drill at the prison of x-raying the briefcase, the metal detectors, and pat-downs took place, only there was an unusual and excruciatingly long wait in the conference room. Ryan asked several times where his client was, had even called ahead so they could have JG waiting for him. Instead, it was Ryan who was waiting. And waiting. This was not the same long wait. Something was wrong. As the second hour approached, Ryan was freaking out. He was about to get up and complain for the umpteenth time, and likely ignored for the umpteenth time, when Grantes was pushed into the room.

"Oh, thank God you're ok. I was getting nervous. Nobody would tell me anything. I didn't think the prison was that big. What the hell is going on?"

"It's nice to see you, too. Been waiting long?"

"Yes, like two hours. It was pretty irritating, then upsetting because I thought something happened to you."

"You poor baby. I have to go through this shit every fucking day, Ry."

"Hey JG - let's not go there. I'm glad you're ok, ok? I'm here to tell you where we are and what we are going with. We go back to court next Monday, so we need to discuss our options. It's not good. It's not horrible, but it's not very good either. You look like shit, no offense. You need anything?"

"I need many things, Ry." He sat back in his chair, drained.

"Like what? I'm here to help you in any way I can."

"I just got out of The Hole. I need a bath, some daylight, some exercise. What I need is to get the fuck out of here." He leaned back forward, putting his head in his hands. After a long pause, he continued. "Do have an Attorney of Record form, or a Client Agreement form on you?"

"Of course, why?"

"I need as many copies as you have."

Ryan dug into his briefcase, retrieving his only two copies. He also withdrew a manilla envelope pre-stamped with a red 'confidential' on it. He then put the documents inside the envelope and handed it to JG.

"Grabbing a few new clients while you're here?"

"Just surviving, man."

"We are going to put our best foot forward to get you out of here. Just hang in there."

"Am I getting out of here, Ry? I mean really. Give it to me straight."

"It's all smoke and mirrors, but yes, that is still the goal. We are going to prove that; yes, you were banged up, but that it was not your fault. New evidence shows that you were induced, and we prove that you did do all the things that you were accused of, but that you had help."

"I'm listening. Start from the beginning. Who helped and how?"

"We are going with your wife set all of this up, because she thought you were having an affair. She used her friend Chamille Destrier to help finance this entire project off the books, and Jenna is involved in this somehow also. We are going to say that the three of them conspired to, and this is where it gets tough for you to hear …. they conspired to kill you. They slipped you a drug, we are going to say Rohypnol because the amnesia symptoms are very much like the date-rape drug, and hoped you drove off the road and killed yourself. Instead, you almost hit the woman who died, did hit a tree and then slept it off at home."

"A jury is going to wonder why my wife set up a plan to kill her son along with me. I picked up Brady, he was in the back seat when all of this happened."

"No, he was not. We have proof that you never saw Brady that night. You, in fact, received a phone call telling you not to go get him at the bar before you were Ruphied. You don't remember that though, right?"

"No, not at all. I remember most of what happened at the bar, leaving was a blur."

"Yeah well, we have your cell records. We also have a video showing that somebody, probably Jenna, drugged you at Sully's, so it's no wonder you don't remember. Anna picked up

413

Brady from Chamille's, and then dropped him off at your house so he was there when the police arrived."

"I thought she was at the charity event?"

"Chamille covered for her. She left and came back, nobody knew the difference."

"Hmm. If I was supposed to go off the road and kill myself, how was she going to explain Brady being home alone? This doesn't make sense even to me."

"That's the point. Brady was never going to be in any danger. Jenna was the babysitter, right? She followed you out of the bar and ran you off the road before you would have picked him up, even if you hadn't received the phone call telling you not to. She said that she was going to the event, but she never did. That part is a little wonky but explainable, we'll have to prove she was never there. I certainly don't remember seeing her there. Anyway, all hell breaks lose, then they scramble with a quick Plan B because you don't die. Some innocent bystander does. This is proven because they tried to hide the housekeeper that knew you didn't pick the boy up. The 911 call diming you out was from a phone bought by Anna at a mall in Nashua. She probably gave it to Jenna to make the call, or made the call herself."

"I can't believe it. Jenna seemed so sweet. I thought she genuinely cared about Brady, she was so good with him."

"We spoke with her and she seemed really into you as well. But facts are facts. Remember, this wasn't about Brady, it was about you. She's gone. Anna's gone, they're all gone. They are probably someplace tropical enjoying the shit out of themselves. Anna, we believe, paid her to get close to you. The whole thing was fake."

"No way, Ry. Now I know you're full of shit. Anna has an extremely low threshold for cheating. Her dad was big cheater. He had multiple kids, with multiple women. There is no way she set me up with someone to cheat with, and I didn't. Jenna had nothing to do with this. At least she isn't working with Anna. No way in hell."

"She's gone, buddy. She fled in the middle of the night. Planned to leave, she told us about it. Me and Deni. She steals the CCTV footage from the bar where she works, which shows you getting drugged, then leaves without even picking up the money that is owed to her. She has cash and she is using it to stay hidden. Who do you think is financing her? Probably Anna. Or Chamille. Or both. But any way you slice it, she looks guilty as sin."

"If she is missing, it's because she is dead. I'm telling you, there is no way that Anna partners up with a woman who she thinks that I had an affair with. I know the woman. She would kill her, maybe, but she is not going to buddy up with her. That's dead. No way."

"You know her so well, huh? She tried to kill you. Did you see that coming?"

"Because she thought I was cheating. I understand it. She is crazy and wrong, but I understand it. Jenna I don't understand, maybe she was played also. But I am telling you that you have it wrong if you think Anna and Jenna are in this together. I will go along to see what we

414

can do about getting me out of here, but there is no way. I guarantee we are going to find a body. Sooner or later someone is going to uncover a body, and it is going to be poor Jenna."

"There is one last piece that we cannot figure out, that we don't know how it fits. It's small but it is bugging Deni, and it's also bugging me. The SUV you used as a bumper-car off a tree hasn't moved since the police went over it when you were arrested. Documented, I checked and rechecked. But all the presets for the seats and mirrors were set up for Anna. Or at least a short person, but who else would drive your car? Jenna?"

"So she drove the car last? Is that what you are saying?"

"Either she did or someone short. But it seems more like it was her. Jenna is taller than Anna by a few inches. Anna's SUV has all the same presets, so she drove both vehicles last. What if she picked up Brady in your SUV?"

"Then how did I get home?"

"I don't know, like I said, I can't figure it out. But, and I'm just spit-balling here, what if you drove Anna's SUV home? They match, how would you know the difference?"

"You don't think I would be able to tell my own vehicle over my wife's, Ryan?"

"I don't know. You were pretty out of it, and it is the exact same car. The presets are just a touch of a button. One button and everything including the radio station is set for you. Is it plausible? Can we use it in court? I don't know, but it's worth a try."

"So I don't get in any wreck, is what you are saying. I'm banged up but I make it home, alone, and pass out with my own son upstairs? I don't remember much from that night, no matter how much I rack my brain. So I would say sure, why not? She would have had to switch car keys also. She would have had to change them out between my leaving for work and then driving home after the bar. Presets alone aren't going to impress a jury."

"Good point. I just thought of all this right now, as we were talking, so I haven't discussed it with Deni yet, but I will. Look, I'm not going to sugar coat it. This what we are going with, in the hopes that a jury will buy it. But I wouldn't hold out too much hope that you walk away from this free and clear. Like I keep saying, that is still the goal. But a lady is dead and somebody has to pay for that. Deni is trying to locate the people we are claiming are responsible for it, but without a little more than smoke and mirrors it's going to be tough to win. Finger-pointing is a long shot anyway, but without an actual person that the jury can see, to point at? The entire exercise becomes academic."

"I get it. I've done this before. I'm just not used to this end of things, though I'm getting there."

"Mull this all over and get your head around it before Monday."

"Look, we have to sell it but it doesn't mean I have to believe it."

"Of course not, JG. But Jesus, it helps."

23

WHILE RYAN WAS TRYING TO LIFT THE SPIRITS of his friend, Warren was calling upon another one of his friends. This friend was of the female persuasion. Again. He needed access to computer skills that he did not possess. The website and email came from someplace, someone either wanting to help JG out or send the investigation off-course. None of the people he had been looking for were coming to the surface. His last hope was tracking down the web address. He knew just the person, with just the skill set required for the job. Her phone was picked up on the second ring.

"Althea. It's Deni. What are you doing?"

"No plans, why. Are you in Boston? I can barely hear you."

"In the car, on my way to you."

"Now? It's 11:00 AM. I work nine to five, you know that. What is this? I don't see you for forever then you darken my doorstep twice in a month. What do you need this time?"

"Nothin'. I just wanna see you." He was not a smooth guy, but he was going to need to be smooth here.

"On a Monday morning out of the blue? Why am I not buying this? At any rate, a little warning would have been nice. I'm at work, I look a mess. I work behind a computer all day, there is no reason to get dolled up."

"Bail outta work. We can spend the whole day together. I want to thank you for your help the other day."

"I feel a cold coming on. Do you remember where I live?"

"Yeah, you're in the same spot?"

"Same one. The complex in Natick. Give me a couple of hours and I'll get into something clingy."

"Cool."

The drive wouldn't take the two hours Althea was looking for, and he wasn't planning on giving them to her either. He had one week before the trial, and neither he nor Ryan were satisfied with where the investigation was at this point. Too many pieces were missing, too many people were missing. He was flying south on the interstate, never one to follow the rules, nor the speed limit.

Deni was back in Natick, Massachusetts, and Althea's apartment complex was exactly like a million others spackled about the Country. The brick building was five floors high, nondescript with a large parking lot, outdoor swimming pool, which was set on the side of the building, hidden by a fence. It was nothing fancy, it was just located in Natick. That and the name of the place gave justification for higher-than-market value pricing. 'The Bluff at the Edgewater' sounded the part, but was not.

Though requested to meet at this illustrious apartment complex in two hours, he was on-location in a mere one hour twenty-five minutes. Warren dilly-dallied. The knock on the door went unanswered after several attempts. He was about to retrieve his iPhone out of his pocket to call her when he heard the chain rattling on the other side of the door. She opened it in a huff as she stood before him soaking wet, wrapped in a thirsty towel. The ends of her hair strands had droplets clinging to them like dewfall.

"I said a couple of hours, I am nowhere near ready. I just got here myself a few minutes ago."

He didn't respond, he pushed through the open door which closed itself much like a hotel door. Althea's frustration melted away almost as soon as he walked through the door. She put on a big smile, her eyes big with excitement as well.

"Well at least give me a few minutes to put on my face and get dressed. What are we doing anyway? I don't know what to wear."

She padded down the short hallway to the bedroom they had both shared for many nights, once upon a time. She had been in love with him back then, was still in love with him if she was being honest with herself. There was something about his rugged good looks and his ubermanliness. Even when he was a cop, he reeked of Southie bad-boy. His lean, muscular, tattoo-cloaked body turned her on the way no other had before or since.

"I thought we could get somethin' to eat, for starters. You hungry?"

"I could eat. Grab a seat on the couch, I'll be out in a few."

Deni had no intention of waiting in the living room. The smell of Indian or some other ethnic food was wafting in from another apartment, and was making him sick to his stomach. He wouldn't have waited there anyway, but that was the excuse he was going to use to go into the bedroom. Smooth.

He knew his former lover's idea of getting dressed and given that the encounter wasn't planned, she would turn her entire wardrobe inside out until the perfect outfit was created. He didn't have the time, nor the patience.

He followed her into the bedroom, stopping at the threshold, leaning on the doorjamb.

"It stinks out there. How can you live next to these people?"

He startled her as she was drying her hair and body in the mirror, not noticing his presence. She covered her naked body. She spoke to him with her back turned, but spying him in the mirror.

"Hey. A little privacy please. You've always complained about the neighbors and you've always dealt with it before. You're a tough guy, tough it out."

He walked into the room, approached behind her, and started to kiss her on the base of the neck from behind.

"Ah hell. We aren't going anywhere are we? This is a booty-call." She turned to face him, the towel dropped to the floor. They had been in this very room many a night before, she had spent many a night in it fantasizing about him since. Though she had not envisioned it quite like this.

"After," he said. He whispered in her ear, one hand on her lower back and the other pulling the wet hair from her eyes.

"Take your time," she whispered back.

Afterward, Althea was using Deni's right bicep as a pillow. Deni was staring at the ceiling, Althea was staring at him.

"Was that the only reason you pulled me out of work today? Or was there something else? She covered herself with the wrinkled sheet that was miraculously still on the bed, the way women who are suddenly embarrassed or uncomfortable will cover themselves. "I should have known when you called. You know I had a ton of stuff to do at work today."

"Are you complaining? You said call anytime."

"No, I'm not complaining. I just thought we were going on a real date. I was looking forward to it."

"What, for like, the hour after I called?"

"No, asshole. For, *like*, the entire time since we broke up."

"I'll take you out, we will do somethin' fun. I'm just wicked busy with a case right now."

"Same case as the 911 call? Your friend?"

"Yeah and I could use your advice. Well, your expertise."

"Ah-ha. I knew it. You needed my help, and why not get a piece of ass in the bargain? You are a complete asshole."

"I came for the help. You were naked, I got caught up. Just think of all the shit I will owe you when we do go out."

"You better know you are taking me someplace nice. Not *Legal Sea Foods*, someplace really nice. And don't even think about *Capital Grille,* either."

"What about *Abe and Louis?*"

"Getting closer, but I'm talking places like *Mistral,* or *Clio,* or *Radius.* I mean celebrity chef expensive. Somewhere Downtown. Someplace super expensive with wine and the works."

"Deal. Now can you look at my computer problem? We get this done and we can go have lunch someplace. And, no, it won't count as the date I owe you."

"Go wait in the living room while I get dressed. For real this time. Plug your nose or whatever, but I'll be out in a minute. Just so you are aware that I am aware, this is like extortion or something. Using sex for favors is illegal. As a former cop you should know this."

"So turn me in."

******

Althea is a woman with many talents. Warren was thinking this as he was driving away from Natick, without having lunch as promised, but fortified with information. *She was wasting her gifts with computers,* he thought, working in the IT department at NEESI was beneath her. He had no idea what skills were required of a truly great hacker, but was sure that Althea possessed them.

He had explained that the email containing the CCTV footage from Sully's Tavern was crucial evidence; that just like the 911 call, the sender wished to remain anonymous, a detail in which he could not abide.

She understood his dilemma and was willing to help him, but was struggling with helping a drunk driver. She loved her bad-boy; but because of her work, she had heard and seen the devastation from so many drunk drivers that she was reluctant to help. Once it was explained, even if inaccurate, that he was drugged and set up, she sat down at her computer and hammered away at the keys.

"In theory, you can determine a physical address from an IP address. But it's not always that simple. If the person is emphatic about staying well-cloaked, they could spoof the IP address or may be behind a proxy. If they were that clever, it will be much more difficult," she had said.

"I don't know what any of that means. Can you give me the physical address or not?"

She explained that the email was like a footprint. And that all web addresses, and emails, leave these footprints. She further explained that when people use software to eliminate those footprints, you have to be able to decode and deactivate that software. She spouted off more of what he thought to be gibberish while she typed furiously on her computer.

At one point, while Deni helped himself to a drink from her kitchen, she said that she was inside the sending computer, or at least that is what he understood her to say. She was enjoying her work. He sat back down and watched her delve into someone's computer, maybe their life. If it was illegal, he didn't care. Nor did she, apparently.

After what turned out to be relatively short work, she sat back in her chair, turning toward him, grinning like the cat that swallowed the canary. She had his information. She was clever and they both knew it.

419

He called Ryan from his Escalade, while he negotiated his way east on the Mass Pike.

"Ry, these bitches are startin' to piss me off. I think I found them though."

"What are you talking about, Deni? I've heard that tone in your voice before and you're scaring me. This is the second time today I've nearly had a heart attack. JG is — "

" — I'm on my way to the airport. I gotta catch a flight outta Logan as soon as I can."

"What? Slow down. We only have a week, *this* week. Where are you going?"

"I'm not taking a fuckin' vacation, guy. I'm going to Charleston."

"Wait, what? If you're in Boston, why are you flying to Charlestown?"

"NO. Not Charlestown, Charleston. South Carolina."

"You're accent makes that an easy mistake, Deni, don't get pissy. What's up in Charleston?"

"I found them. Those bitches are probably all laughin' and pushin' each other in the bushes, making fun of us. But I got 'em now. We caught them."

"I hope you can. Like I was saying, JG is cracking up. He spends his time in Solitary, then comes out and wants to take clients in prison. We're losing him."

"One thing at a time. Let's get him outta prison before we commit him to a rubber room."

He then explained that he had a contact that helped him locate the address in South Carolina from the email sent to him. He left out whom the information had come from, which was not at all unusual. In fact, it was the norm.

"Just keep in mind that the video was helpful. I'm not sure what game they are playing, but without that video we would still be in the dark. I'm not sure if they are sinners or saints."

"I'll keep you posted."

"Do that. And let me know if I can help."

Warren didn't reply, he just hung up. He sincerely hoped that the two hour flight would help to calm him down.

24

OF COURSE THE LAST AVAILABLE SEAT, on the first flight out of Logan for Charleston, South Carolina, was in first-class. Even the Irish hate that bastard Murphy. And his laws. The outrageous price pulled on a nerve of Warren's and there were too few remaining. He was already heated and hoping the flight would dissipate his rage, but it was not to be. The first available flight was a red-eye that night, which would put him in Charleston in the early morning on Tuesday. And yet another nerve snapped when he came to the realization of just how far first-class had sunk. The airlines had not been stellar at hiding their cutbacks, for what he presumed were for financial reasons. Coach was little more than being packed in a cattle-car like rush hour on the subway. First-class was demoted to what was once just coach.

He was thankful that the drinks were still 'free', so he was determined to get his thirteen hundred dollars worth. Slowly, he began to relax as the alcohol numbed his few remaining nerve strands. There used to be a flight attendant dedicated to those who paid the high price to sit in first-class, but that must have been another cutback. The two working this flight were spread thinly throughout the entire plane, and given the hour of the flight, were hoping for it to be a relaxing one. Deni's repeated calls for more alcohol were met with looks of concern and frustration, but no other exchange.

Upon arrival in Charleston, he made his way to the car rental agencies. He had no luggage, so he made his way cheetah-quick from the jetway to rental area. There were 'very few cars left available', which meant he had to pay yet another surcharge. He got on a bus which transferred him to the Budget parking lot with only four cars left in it, or at least only four cars they were going to show him. The four cars ranged from tiny tin-can to a Flintstone-mobile. After some discussion with both the security guard at the parking lot and the bus driver, he was brought back to the rental desk by the same bus. Discussion meaning he did a lot of yelling and the two Budget employees listened. The last nerve snapped.

When he arrived back at the rental desk in the terminal, Warren dragged the man behind the rental desk by the lapels, over the desk to customer side.

"I need a real fuckin' car. Not a Prius, not a leaf, not a battery operated go-cart, I need a real car. Something that will get out of its own way. When I let go of you, don't even think about chargin' me any extra money, don't get on a phone and call a supervisor, no faces with some hemmin' n hawin'. I want you to put me back on that bus, and when I arrive back on that lot, there had better be a real car waiting. Nod like you understand, cuz if I have to come back here? The kinda day I've had? I'll probably kill you."

Southern hospitality had it's finest hour. His second visit to the rental parking lot was quicker, friendlier, and a black Dodge *Charger* was waiting for him. This was a car that could get out if its own way, it would just have to do it with a six cylinder engine versus an eight. The bus driver didn't stick around for an encore performance. Deni wasted no time getting into the car and driving away. He had spent enough time in or between airports. The security gate was wide open before Deni approached it, the guard had had his fill as well.

The GPS on his phone directed him off of Interstate 95 and onto Route 17, which traversed the Ashley River draw bridge, through a nondescript and all but evacuated area, before he came upon the historic and beautiful downtown. The cobblestone streets were lined with shoulder-to-shoulder Georgian townhouses throughout the peninsula, block after block. These historic landmarks nestled in with Louis Vuitton class storefronts, were surrounded by ocean and restored cannons. It was an absolutely gorgeous city, he thought. Every other building was a postcard, every third a modern retailer or restaurant in a historic building.

While the Bostonians egged on the American Civil War, with their antislavery movement, the first shots of it were fired on Fort Sumter right there in Charleston. Warren found it funny that this little war was also started in the North and would end here in the South; as he stared at a plaque stuck to the side of a cannon on Murray Boulevard, in White Point Gardens. The city was immaculately clean, which was unlike Boston. On the other end of the spectrum if truth be told. In fact, by comparison, Boston was a dumpster fire. The only thing they had in common was lack of parking.

He was forced to park in a metered spot with a two-hour maximum. He was unsure if the meter-maids chalked the tires like they did in Boston, to penalize those who feed the meter. Nor did he know the going rate for a parking ticket in the South, but he knew he was going to find out. It was a rental anyway, he thought, try to find me.

The parking spot was a fair walk from where he wanted to stake out. The meters were along Murray Boulevard, which was fixed between the ocean and the park, he needed to be a few blocks inland. He would not be able to reconnoiter from the comfort and confines of his rental vehicle, he would have to sweat out the heat on foot. West of the gardens were all of the historic mansions overlooking the bay. Somewhere in that cobblestone maze was the address he sought.

Since he would be on foot, and he had no luggage, he was forced to buy some clothing from the shops. Only he had to wait for the shops to open. The trip was already breaking the bank, all being charged onto his magic plastic square. Charge it please and thank you. The overpriced couture in The Marketplace on King Street was the icing on the cake. His extravaganza ended with him sporting a Callaway Golf hat, Maui Jim sunglasses, a pink Lacoste alligator shirt (because the gorgeous saleswoman with her southern drawl said he looked hot in it), multicolored shorts from Benetton, and his tan shoes from Aldo. He hated the way he looked with all of his being, but he needed to be unrecognizable, and with this outfit he was. He thought he looked like a metrosexual tourist.

After his shopping spree, he walked through the maze of cobblestone streets between the historical mansion-turned-condos. Later, rather than sooner, he found the address with the help of the GPS on his iPhone. The ornate, wrought-iron gate was locked though he could see the gardened walkway beyond it. Set between two, four-storied townhouses, the flora was old-world gorgeous complete with ivy hugging the side of the buildings. The courtyard was painstakingly manicured and elegantly perfumed. He studied the property for a short while, though there was no movement.

"You must be my twelve o'clock." The woman behind him took him by surprise. She, too, had a sweet southern drawl. She was equally manicured, yet casual in her designer business dress. The forty-ish blonde eyed him from head to toe, while he was trying to assess the situation. The pause was almost to a point of awkwardness.

"I'm Faye. The realtor? I spotted you as I was walking down the street, only you're on the wrong side of it, sweetie. The unit for sale is on the other side of the street." She immediately stuck her hand out.

"Oh, right. I know …. I was just checkin' out the neighborhood."

"You're accent is …. well I guess I didn't pick it up on the phone. It's very intense. Where are y'all from?"

"My mom."

"You're funny. Right this way, hun. You'll just love Rainbow Row. This property is bright yellow, and as we discussed on the phone, completely restored to keep it's historic beauty, yet updated. Not that it will need it, but any further renovating would require city approval because it is a historic landmark, as are all of these homes."

"Rainbow Row?" He didn't hear anything after Rainbow Row. He thought she was referring to his outfit, which was very colorful. "What are you sayin' lady?"

"All of these houses along East Bay Street are various pastel colors, it's known as Rainbow Row. What did you think I meant?"

"Oh. I thought you meant somethin' else."

The showing, and the woman would prove to be a pain in the ass. He had to extricate himself from the situation without suspicion while maintaining a surveillance position on the house across the street. There was no activity there as of yet, but there was no telling what could happen while he was being dragged around what, in truth, was an amazing property. He took extra long pauses at the windows at the front of the house he was supposed to be interested in buying, so he could continue to investigate the inactivity on the other side of the street. Faye must have taken note, for after the third such pause she mentioned the view.

"If you're interested in the view, the estate has a three hundred sixty degree view from the well-appointed roof deck. Would you like to see it?" As if she didn't know.

"Absolutely."

"Usually I would save the best for last, but I can see that you are interested in the breathtaking scenery." They made their way up a wide staircase, opened the oak door onto a massive roof. She was right, the view was breathtaking.

To the East, a mostly unimpeded view of the Atlantic Ocean; only the roof of another historical mansion, the roof of the gazebo in the park, and the tree-line of the park itself marginally obstructed the any portion of the view. The trees and other horticulture made the deck oasis like a prized trophy hoisted toward the sky. Like a small heaven shot up toward that which it emulated.

To the North, were the roofs of the estates on the other side of East Bay Street. Warren leaned on the marble rail facing his prey and was disappointed at the lack of observation he would be afforded from that vantage point. The courtyard on the other side of the gate was well hidden for privacy behind the canopy of trees. Only the bird's-eye view of the cobblestone in front of the residence could be studied from where he stood. He was about to turn away, and back to the annoying real estate woman to tell her that the tour was over; when in the panorama, he spied someone walking down the street, toward them on foot. He was some two hundred or so yards away and above, but even at that scalene angle he knew who it was. He would recognize the pedestrian anywhere.

"Well, ok Faye. Thank you very much. I've seen all that I need to, I have your number and we'll be in touch."

She must have responded, but he didn't hear it. He bolted down the stairs, taking two and three at a time until reaching the bottom floor. If the front door had been locked he would have burst through it like the Kool-aid guy from the commercials. Fortunately it wasn't.

As he was rushing off the property, a bearded man he hadn't seen from above was just outside the door with a briefcase in his hand. This must have been Faye's real appointment. Deni almost ran him over but dodged him in a nick of time. "You're gonna love it, it's fuckin' beautiful."

Once he was beyond the bearded man, he slowed and began to catch his breath as the woman was approaching him not fifteen yards down the street and closing. He was blocking the entrance, the wrought-iron gate, and there was no place to go or hide.

He waved with his hand while he panted. "Hey Jenna."

25

INMATE GRANTES WAS ENJOYING HIS TIME back on the pod. Enjoying may be bit of a stretch, but he wasn't in The Hole. All the while, he had time to think and rethink the events leading him to what was his current situation. And his mind was running riot. Fortified with the knowledge, even if just theory, that things concerning his case were starting to work in his favor. He thought of all of the possibilities. Where once there was complete darkness, now there was at least some point of light off in the distance ahead. A penlight amidst a dark forest, but a light nonetheless. When a man is in prison, that man clings to any hope he can. That hope, however small, is what keeps him sane and alive.

There were questions on the block when he returned from his three days in solitary confinement. When an inmate caves in another's face, a mere three days in The Hole tends to pose some questions. None of them good. Was he a rat? Who did he know? Who did he blow? The Sheriff? All were plied to him, all went unanswered. Instead, he made illegal copies of the form given to him by Ryan and stuffed them under every steel door on the block. Both tiers.

They had given him a job on the block, one that gave him access to the counselor's office, which had a copy machine. That cleaning job, as disgusting as it was, also helped to occupy his days which freed him from being in his cell twenty hours a day. He had freedom to move about the pod, under the guise of having to clean it.

It was the Thursday before his trial, during afternoon rec time, that the Ellis alarm blared at near-deafening volume. That alarm dictated that if you were outside your cell, you were to get on a knee or your face. A dozen COs and two German Shepherds poured into the pod like SS troops in full riot gear. Shouts of "get down on your face" and "get the fuck down" and "eat the floor asshole" were shouted over and over, and over the sound of the Ellis alarm. All inmates complied one way or another. The invasion took less than ten-seconds and those who were too frozen in shock to understand the commands were beaten until they figured it out. It was prison, for some it took a while, and they had to learn stuff the hard way.

The officers knew whom they wanted in advance, but there would be a cleanup of fish big and small. Dirty urines had come back on twelve of the last eighteen they had sampled. Nine had been sampled on Wednesday morning, nine Wednesday night just like they had on every other day before. These last twelve dirties had come back testing positive for Seboxolan.

425

Seboxolan is an opioid, or more commonly called a narcotic. Big Pharma came up with a drug to cure those who are addicted to drugs. How nice of them. It is prescribed by doctors as an opiate blocker for patients who suffer from addiction to substances like heroine and crack. The fact that doctors who prescribe it often received kick-backs from the pharmaceutical companies who developed it, means that it is very often over prescribed. The drug was developed to deaden the receptors in the brain by filling it with a small amount of a mixed opiate. Those who are not on heroine or crack, can misuse Seboxolan as a primary opiate as it is not blocking anything, but filled the receptors in the brain by overdosing them. It gets into the blood stream faster by crushing and snorting it, rather than taking it in the proper pill form. These pills are snuck into the prison, usually in someone's rectum.

Twelve dirties within twenty-four hours meant that the Sheriff had a problem. The fact that the prison was rife with the drug was bad for him. Twelve dirties meant a shakedown.

Anything that was in a cell was thrown out of it and into the main part of the pod, used for eating and rec time. But not before being stomped on, shredded, and dog-chewed. Anyone unwittingly walking onto the pod would think there was a riot. Both tiers were destroyed. Paper, wool, insulation from the pillows and mattresses were floating in the air like feathers looking for a place to land. Inmates were buried, face down under the detritus.

Fifty-nine of the one hundred twenty-two men on the pod were lugged that Wednesday. It was heard about and talked about all over the prison, not just on that block. That day would henceforth be called by the prisoners Seboxo-gate.

Charges and indictments were being handed out like playing cards, so Grantes's favorite buddy, the lieutenant, came a calling. The ruse that Grantes had a visit was used to get him off the block, and became a hour-long interrogation.

"Where were you on this one Grantes?"

"On the block. You know that. You guys keep records of where I am at all hours of the day, don't you?"

"What are you a wise-guy now? Don't toy with me, I'm in no mood. I gave you a good deal, kept you from catching more charges. Now you play possum while drugs are rampant right under your nose?"

"Maybe they don't trust me yet."

"Maybe you should start making more of an effort. You dropped the ball big-time inmate."

Grantes sat there in quiet thought at the last comment. The Lieutenant paced back and forth in the room while the supposed informant sat quietly watching him. It was like he was a spectator at a tennis match.

"Well?" The lieutenant finally broke the silence.

"Well what?"

"Well, what do you have to say for yourself?"

"I don't have anything to say. My piss is clean."

"Why didn't you use the phone number I gave you on the card to drop a dime?"

"I didn't need to. You busted the twelve for dirty urines and what, sixty more? What do you need me for?"

"Where did it come from? Who had it and distributed it? Did it go to other pods? That kind of intel. That is what I need you for."

"I can't say."

"What do you mean you can't say?"

"I mean that I am literally not allowed to say, even if I know. Which I'm not admitting to either."

"I can make your life a living hell here smart-guy. What kinda game are you playing?"

"I'm not playing any game. I *can't* because of privilege, and you can't hurt me because it is illegal under reciprocity."

"What the hell are you talking about, Grantes? You're not a lawyer anymore."

"I haven't been disbarred yet, number one. I'm innocent until proven guilty in our system, a concept this prison is unfamiliar with. Second, I have one hundred and twenty-two signed agreements which make them believe that I am their attorney. It is their belief that makes any of their statements protected under the constitution. If I 'dropped a dime', as you call it, I *would* be disbarred. I'm sorry I couldn't be of any help to you."

"So you fucked me. Are you admitting to that? You are a useless piece of shit and I can't wait until you are here for good. Time is your enemy, asshole. Too bad for you, I'm not going anywhere."

"I'm not admitting to anything other than being caught up in the middle of a terrible situation. Seboxolan is no joke."

"No, it isn't. We don't have it on the Med Carts here, so we know nobody cheeked it. It had to have come in up someone's ass. When we find out who and when, I am going to make sure that the entire prison pop thinks we found out through you."

"Make me out to be a rat? Good luck with that. By the way, if I get shived; I'm suing the prison, the Sheriff, and you personally for the threat you just gave me."

"Get out of my face!"

"Go back to my clients? All one hundred twenty-two of them or just the sixty you busted?"

"Go back to your cell, asshole."

"Back to my single cell? Ouch. You're a real hard-ass, lieutenant." He got up and made his way to the conference room door. Another CO was there to collect him and bring him to his pod.

"You're ass is mine, Grantes. Sooner or later, I'm gonna nail your ass to the wall."

26

THE SHOCK ON JENNA'S FACE disappeared about as quickly as the big, shit-eating grin on Warren's. Which is to say, it took a hot minute. Both stood in the middle of the cobblestone street, speechless in the early afternoon sun. Deni was catching his breath, Jenna was stunned. Both stood and silently eyed one another.

She was wearing a light blue, high on the thigh sundress, and she looked as stunning as she was stunned. In her right hand was a large, brown paper bag with handles, which had a large logo from an expensive restaurant, Circa 1886, on the side. Her other hand was on her hip.

"Nice of you to bring me lunch. How'd you know I was starvin'? Where are the rest of the girls?"

"If I'd have known you were coming, I would have ordered you something," she said. Once she wrapped her head around the situation, getting her bearings, she continued. "What other girls?"

"Come on now, Jen. The jig is up. I know what you and Chamille and Anna have been up to. It's all over. Now let's go inside so we can get out of the sun."

"I don't think you're a cop anymore, are you Deni? You can't just barge your way inside someone's home. I'm certain you don't have a warrant in that very colorful outfit of yours."

"It's been a long couple of days, I'm not in the mood to fuck around. It wasn't easy to find you, I'll give you that."

"You're smarter than I gave you credit for, I'll give *you* that. Look, Deni, I don't know what you think you know, but from that last little comment, it's pretty clear you don't know a damn thing. Which is disappointing, quite frankly."

They reached the gate, she unlocked and opened it, and they walked into the courtyard together.

"Who's place is this, yours? You had a come-up, huh?"

"You don't know? You came all this way, I thought you had it figured out? Wow, maybe you're not as smart as I gave you credit for."

The perfumed smell of the flora in the courtyard was intoxicating, or maybe it was Jenna. Maybe both. But if heaven had a smell, Warren thought that was it. But he needed to stay focused, needed to be ready for what was on the other side of that door. The three women had planned, and schemed to bring about the death of JG, and were successful in killing a woman. He was here to call them on it.

428

They went through the front door and the interior was elegant. There was no other way for him to describe it. The antique furniture was plentiful but not gaudy. The pastel colors of the painted walls reminded him of a picture he had once seen of a mansion in the Garden District of New Orleans. What the Destrier home was to New England, this place was to the Southeast.

Jenna had left him in the dust. In his taking in all the appointments, he had lost his bead on the girl. She was somewhere in the confines of the amazing home, while he stood there taking it all in. He heard voices, all feminine, he cautiously headed toward them. He was not allowed to carry a gun on the plane, so he didn't have one. He wasn't sure if he needed one with a house full of rich women, but he sure wanted one just the same. Better to be safe than sorry, and he was hoping that he wouldn't be. If they were getting ready to eat, there were probably knives. Physical strength was not going to be an issue. Three women with sharp knives might prove to be a bit of a struggle.

He zig-zagged into the mansion from the foyer through the parlor, a right past the sunroom which overlooked the garden in the courtyard. He took a left past a formal dining room, the voices getting closer. He could only discern two voices, but there may have been more. He smelled food, the contents of the paper bag must have been opened. Whatever it was, it smelled phenomenal. He just then realized that he had not eaten since early the day before and was starving. When he took another left into an enormous kitchen, he spotted Jenna. And an older woman.

The elderly woman was sitting at a small table off to the side, a low breakfast counter. She was very well maintained. So well put together in fact, that it was nearly impossible to pinpoint the lady's age. Not a reddish-blonde hair was out of place. Wrinkles about her face were either well-hidden or permanently removed, nor was there a wrinkle on her attire. Most of her body was hidden by the table, but her face and torso suggested she was slim. She was watching him with an elegant grace.

"Mr. Dennihan. I'm embarrassed to say that I was not expecting you today. Won't you please come in, just the same."

"I'm embarrassed to say I don't know who you are." He looked over at Jenna, but she was looking at her feet, leaning against a counter closer to the massive kitchen.

"Of course. How rude of me, please for give me. I'm Olivia Craig. We've never met but I have heard quite a lot about you." There was more silence as Olivia let the information set in, it seemed to be taking a while for Deni to process the information. "Not what you were expecting?"

"Uh. No."

"I'm rather glad you're here, Mr. Dennihan. I believe we need to catch up. We are overdue, I should think."

"What are we, old friends? What the .... what's going on here?"

429

"Jennifer, maybe we should take lunch in the dining room. Would you be so kind as to set it up for us? There should be plenty for a third plate." She then turned to Warren and said, "Circa is not open for lunch, but I know the owners and the chef. He prepares us a beautiful lunch on occasion. You are in for a treat, the grilled quail and the foie gras au poivre are an absolute delight."

"I don't even know what you just said."

"Mr. - "

" - Call me Deni, or Warren. But only after you tell me what the fu …. eh …. sorry. What is going on here?"

"Very well, Warren. You may call me Olivia. With that out of the way, Warren, would you please join us for lunch?"

"Olivia Craig. As in Anna's mother. The one who has been dead for — "

" — excuse me for interrupting, but I am clearly not dead. I am Anna's estranged mother. She will no longer have anything to do with me, but I am alive and well, thank you. But I shall explain all of this over lunch. Right this way."

They moved into one of the rooms Deni had passed on the way into the house, a formal dining room. Jenna had put the finishing touches on the table, setting up a proper lunch from the takeout she had fetched. A bottle was in her hand.

"Would you care for some?" The southern hospitality thing had worn off on Jenna. She was pouring Chateau de Beaucastel Chateauneuf du Pape Blanc into the proper Ridel glassware.

"If it has alcohol in it, make it a double."

"It's french white wine. 2004. We were going to pair it with our lunch. In other words, it's not Whiskey."

"Whatever, it'll do. Now will someone please tell me what is going on? JG, or Jake as you call him Jenna, is going to trial on Monday and you two are playin' games down here like southern bells. I can't tell if you are friend or foe."

"Please calm down Warren. We are here to help. We don't under normal circumstances break bread with mortal enemies. Do you?" Olivia was as dainty and elegant as every rumor he had heard.

"Not normally, but people are funny, and these aren't normal circumstances are they? Where is your daughter?"

"We have been tracking her through her banks, with some help from Olivia's banking contacts," Jenna said.

"We? What, are you two a comedy team now? Or do you work for Olivia? Who else are you two tracking?"

"We have an arrangement, Deni. The specifics aren't important and are none of your business. Let's just say that Olivia has Jake's best interests in mind, as do I. And I trust her."

"Is that why you sent Ryan the video?"

"That is precisely why I asked Jennifer to, retrieve shall we say, the footage. She had firsthand knowledge that Jacob was not as inebriated as he was accused of being."

"And you contacted her, because you knew that something was not right?" He asked Olivia.

"I have been in contact with Jennifer for some time, yes. My daughter may have asked me to stay out of her life, but do you honestly think I would not keep watch over her, over my son-in-law, over my only grandson? My deceased husband was a man of means, bequeathing me a fortune. What good is any of it without family?"

"So Jenna, you weren't working with Cam and Anna to try to kill JG?"

"Jesus no. Excuse me, Olivia. No. And who is *Cam?*"

"I think he is referring to Chamille Destrier, Anna's close friend. Is that right, Warren? How do you suppose Chamille is involved with this?"

"I thought you were watching from afar? I'm tryin' to piece this all together and you two are sittin' down here spyin' on everyone. I thought you had all the answers."

"Do you honestly think that if I had all the answers that I would sit idly by and watch this tragedy? I have watched with as close an eye as I am able. This is a family that I am not supposed to be a part of. You did you know that, yes? Jennifer has sent me pictures of my grandson in secret, or has tried to as often as possible. I let Jacob know a long time ago that I didn't abandon my family. Anna forced me away because of her father's infidelities, and her belief that I was complicit. That knowledge has done so much damage to my daughter."

"And she thought Jenna here was bangin', excuse me, having an affair with her husband. So she sees red, and plots with Cammy to kill her husband. I find it a little bit weird that she chooses to be friends with a woman who is as loose as an alley-cat, but what do I know?"

"Yes, she thought that Jake and I were seeing each other, but she was distancing herself more and more. The entire thing is ironic. Not weird, Deni, ironic," Jenna said.

"What is this that I am eating? I am not sure if I like it because I am starving, or because it is some culinary masterpiece. It's wicked pretty, I'll give ya that."

"Since you didn't understand Olivia when she said it before, foie gras is duck liver. It's served on a rosemary and lemon biscuit with a blackberry .... you don't really care do you? Yes, it is a culinary masterpiece."

"So why are you two playing The Wizard of Oz down here, Olivia? All this behind the curtain stuff? Your daughter — "

" — excuse me for interrupting you again. But before you go any further, Warren, I need to clarify that I will not help you in further destroying my daughter. My objective is to preserve my family. I will not see Anna incarcerated, nor can I tolerate Jacob being imprisoned."

"So where have you been for the past six months? JG has been rotting in a cell all this time, and it seems less likely that he belongs there. I guess it is better than being dead though."

"I couldn't extricate him from that dreadful prison, unfortunately, no matter how I tried. As for Anna. Frankly, I have no excuses, nor do I have comment. I hesitated as long as possible in forwarding what little information I had that, compromises shall we say, my daughter."

"Maybe you can try to help in her defense at trial, lady, but she used Cammy as an alibi. And she called JG at the bar and told him not to pick up Brady. She Ruphied him and let him think that he endangered their son when he lived through the accident. He was supposed to die on that trip but another woman died instead."

"I find it incredibly hard to believe that she wanted Jacob dead."

"Believe what you want, Olivia, it happened. If it wasn't Jenna, then it was his wife. Your daughter."

"It seems hard to argue. I will say, Olivia, that she hated me. And she took it out on her husband and son. I can't help but feel somewhat responsible."

"That is nonsense, Jennifer. My daughter had problems, and while you certainly didn't help, you did nothing wrong and you most definitely didn't cause them."

"Olivia, do you know where your daughter is?"

"Warren, I am willing to help clear Jacob of the charges against him. I think I have demonstrated that. But I repeat, I will not help you destroy my daughter. She may have problems, and she may need help, but I will not see her go to prison for the rest of her life. I still love her though she wants nothing to do with me. She is still my daughter."

"She's goin' down one way or another. You seem like a sweet old lady, but you got this all wrong. Do you want her dragging Brady along from place to place hiding from justice? She is on the run, and she is always gonna be on the run. She may have money and she may be able to get away with it for while, but in the end there will come a time where she will be caught. Brady has a right to be with his dad. He didn't do anything wrong, yet he's not going to be able to play with just any kid, go to just any school, because his mom is a fugitive. She is a bad lady and it ain't your fault. But it will be your fault if Brady gets all messed up in the process. If you know where she is, you can put an end to it. He deserves a better life and he belongs with his dad."

Olivia began to tear up. She was as graceful and as sophisticated as she could be about her emotions, but she was losing the struggle for strength. She pushed the plate holding her culinary masterpiece away from her, untouched. Deni watched her for a few moments while she tried to regain her composure. He felt for her. He admired her.

Jenna was not so demure. She had once again lost control of her emotions, using the guise of clearing the lunch plates to excuse herself from the room. Deni knew where her loyalties lied. Whatever arrangement she and Olivia had, he knew that Jenna would walk away from it if it meant helping Jake and Brady. If the guilt trip on Olivia failed, he would have a strong backup plan.

"San Diego," Olivia whispered after a short time. She composed herself, dabbing the corners of her eyes, then looked into Warren's. "They are in San Diego, California."

"With Cammy?"

"I don't believe so, why do you ask?"

"You said, 'they'."

Jenna returned to the dining room and took her seat at the table. After draining her glass of expensive white wine, she replenished all three glasses. She seemed to be the only one measurably consuming it.

Deni said, "Cam helps your daughter, then me, then goes missing."

"She helped you because I told her to, Warren."

"Excuse me? *You* told her to help me?"

"Yes. How do you suppose you came about the address of the missing Destrier staff-member, and the security footage from the gate?"

"I, uh, earned it."

"Yes, I'm sure you did. However, I have some rather embarrassing information about her, that she would like to never see the light of day. When Jennifer spoke of your interest in any involvement she may have had, I reached out to her. I told her she needed to provide you with any information to help Jacob. I was unaware that she had anything to do with this except to provide childcare. And now you say she provided coverage for Anna at the event. I take it you believe she has more to do with this than that?"

He was still having trouble with the fact that he hadn't needed to sleep with Chamille in order to retrieve the information. That she was told to.

"I'm not sure anymore. But she did take off. I thought Jenna was involved too, but it looks like I was wrong about her also," Deni said.

"No offense, Warren, but it seems that while you may be good at your profession, you have missed the mark quite often in this case."

"And it's buggin' the …. it's really buggin' me." He took a long pull of his wine, though he didn't enjoy it as much as he reckoned he was supposed to. "Olivia, I'm gonna need an address in San Diego. I'm catchin' the next flight outta Charleston."

"Jennifer and I will go with you."

"No way. She is gonna be cornered, and cornered people do crazy things. It may get ugly."

"That is precisely why we are going to go, to bring some cool-headedness to this very upsetting situation. I will not see Anna get hurt. Brady cannot be exposed to any of this either. He is my only grandson and his protection is paramount. I'll have a private jet waiting when we arrive at the airport."

"I'm going with you to San Diego?" Jenna looked genuinely confused.

"Private jet?" So did Deni.

433

27

IT TOOK ALL OF THREE HOURS TO GET ORGANIZED, packed, and onto the parked plane at Charleston International Airport. The executive area for private jets was segregated from the major carrier area, though it did share runways since the entire airport had just two of them. They were chauffeured to the parked jet in an area near what looked like a hangar used by the United States Air force; which it may have, since they owned and operated the airport.

The silver Landrover pulled up to a gold 2007 Embraer Legacy *600 SN 1002* executive jet, currently worth between fourteen and fifteen million dollars, which was significantly less than when it was new. They were led from the SUV, up the stairs, and inside the luxurious aircraft. Everything on the inside was white leather, gold trim, and wood. The pillows on the jet sofa were nicer than Deni's actual sofa in his home.

"Jesus Olivia, how rich are you? You have this thing in case you want a quick flight? No *Travelocity* for you huh? I don't think I could afford the fuel."

"It is not my personal jet, Warren. I simply have access to it whenever I should need a flight."

"If by access you mean your friends, I gotta get myself some better friends."

Fortunately, Deni did not have to unload the luggage from the SUV and load it into wherever the stuff was being stored on the jet, as they prepared for takeoff. There was a crew for that. He was unsure if these people required a tip, nor how much the going-rate was, but he knew it was likely to be more than he had in his wallet. Olivia would have to take care of that as well. Besides, she was the one who had packed like she was leaving forever. She had Jenna do some shopping for Brady, so he would have things to wear and play with on the return. Olivia seemed to be more optimistic than he was.

Warren had what he had on his body, which is what he had bought at the overpriced marketplace that morning. He had shoved his clothes he wore on the red-eye down to Charleston into the back of his rented Dodge Charger, which was still parked in the metered spot by the water. He had remembered about the car once they were in the air, mentioning the dilemma to Olivia. With one phone call, she said that it was taken care of. He had alluded to his clothing situation while telling the rental car story, and she had said that would be taken care of as well. He really did need to get better friends, he thought.

He had never traveled in such luxury. Olivia, as always, was elegant and nonplussed. It was as if she hailed a cab, one that would take her twenty-five hundred miles. A very expensive cab ride indeed.

The captain and crew could not have been more affable, nor more accommodating. With the kind of money being shelled out for this little excursion, he thought, why shouldn't they be. No question was too trivial, no food or beverage request off-limits. He wondered who was really paying the bill for it. She said access, which meant friend or friends. He wondered if for rich people, asking to borrow their super-fancy jet was like a normal person asking to borrow their friend's row-boat for the weekend.

The novelty of the idea that the three of them were off to San Diego, on a private jet, to confront and convince Anna, had worn off. Warren thought it stupid to bring the woman whom Anna believed was sleeping with the husband she tried to kill along for the ride. Not to mention the mother she had thrown into exile. If their company was supposed to bring tranquility, he felt that they were going about it the wrong way. When he broached the subject with Olivia, she justified the decision by saying that she would be able to talk some sense into her daughter and that Jennifer would calm Brady, as she had never met the boy and was a grandma that he probably didn't know existed. Those may have been fair points if there was any chance in hell that Anna would listen to a woman she hated, and if they would be able to get anywhere near Brady. Anna was bound to put up a fight. And that fight was going to be an all-out war, which was Deni's big fear. Separating that momma from her cub means the claws would be out. And teeth.

He was, without question, exhausted. He had virtually no sleep on the red-eye to get down to South Carolina, and had no sleep since. The plush seats were wide and comfortable, easily able to recline if so inclined. But he had calls to make. He needed to call Ryan, only Olivia was across the aisle. He moved toward the sofa with the nice pillows, but Jenna was lounging there. So he made his phone calls from the confines and privacy of the toilet. A fancy toilet, but he was calling from a toilet nonetheless.

Ryan began the thousand-mile conversation by giving Deni the riot act. Things like, "what in the name of Christ are you doing, Deni?" and "you're going where?" and "unless she confesses, how does this help us?" were all screamed out of the phone, heard even over the dull hissing of the plane.

It took a while to calm Ryan down. Deni told him that this *did* help JG because they were going to bring back Brady before Anna realized the jig was up and took off again. That if Anna did take off, justice for the victim may never be done. They would attempt to get a confession, but even without one, anything she said might be helpful to JG. He wasn't a cop any longer, and didn't play by nor subscribe to many rules, but Anna had gotten his Irish up. He was going to bring her down.

His next phone call was to a contact in Boston, who gave him the phone number of a retired ex-cop in San Diego he could reach out to. Nobody who lived in San Diego was originally from San Diego, his contact had said. He was also told that if he needed a liaison with the police out there, he should contact the fellow in San Diego who was not originally from there. Deni wanted a weapon not a liaison, but that wasn't being offered, so he wouldn't have one. He was also unsure if Anna would come in peace or if police would be needed, but he was thankful for the information. They may have to extradite her, if she was unwilling to come back to New Hampshire. He also hoped that the plane would be able to be borrowed for the flight back to New England. He was ruined for commercial flying ever again.

The rest of the four hour and forty-five minute flight was uneventful. Warren slept, trying to catch up from close to forty hours without it. With the three-hour time difference, they just made the 11:00 PM curfew for what they consider a stage three aircraft. The planes land so close to downtown and the residential homes in San Diego, that a curfew was put into place in 1989. No planes, other than emergency aircraft, were allowed to takeoff or land before 6:00 AM or after 11:00 PM, unless the aircraft falls below the designated decibel level. Microphones were put into place and fines were assessed. When one lives in paradise, it cannot be noisy.

Another chauffeured car, this time a Mercedes *M-class,* picked them up at Lindbergh Field. They drove on North Harbor Drive, hugging the ocean toward downtown San Diego. It was late and they were going to deal with Anna in the morning. They took the left onto 5th Avenue and were dropped off at the *Taj,* a super luxury hotel that jetted up from the asphalt, past the palm trees, toward the sky. The enormous convention center, made famous by Comic-Con, was across the street and would have blocked their view of the ocean had they not been in the penthouse suite. Warren was too tired to comment on the extravagance, Olivia too unfazed to care, and Jenna said nothing in either case. They all retired to their respective rooms in the suite. It had been a long day, they would need their rest for the trying day to follow.

The five-star hotel would have gotten seven stars if the ratings went that high. Part of the reason for the high rating was the amenities, for sure, but their service was superfluous. The wake-up calls were not executed with a callous phone call from the lobby or a concierge, they were done in person. At least they were for guests in the penthouse suite. Warren hadn't asked or expected one, but he received one anyway. He forgot to thank Olivia. The nice, young man who entered the suite the following morning, who had knocked on Warren's individual door, was almost punched in the throat. This was not the young man's first wake-up call, or he had been warned, and so he was fortified with coffee and breakfast. Warren let him live.

The city of Poway, California, is a posh community spread out in the center of San Diego County. Because the various neighborhoods are sprinkled about the mountainous area, upper middle-class communities abutted the grossly affluent. Poway is consistently in the top twenty-five most expensive places to live in the United States, and it doesn't have a beach. One traveling through the 'City in the Country' can determine with ease which community is which by the existence of a very large forbidding gate. Or lack thereof.

The journey out of downtown toward the Poway address was a relatively short one, if one could fly there. The California Freeway system didn't allow for an easy hop or a direct route. Instead, the wide 15 north was a long stretch of freeway that should have been called a parkway. No matter how many lanes, they were always congested and slow-moving. Part of the 'sun-tax' was to put up with traffic. Paradise at any cost.

One hour and twenty-five minutes after departure, still stuck in traffic, Warren was ready to kill something. He would soon get the chance.

Olivia's desperation to calm her travel companion became more desperate with each slowly passing mile. Jenna was keen to help for a while, but as his Irish went into full swing, she backed off. She had witnessed Deni's physical abilities when he didn't want to hurt someone, the amount of potential violence concerned her when he was actually angry. Olivia was not backing down, her daughter and grandson were on the other end of this trip. She needed a calm and collected Warren Dennihan.

The final arrival at their destination necessitated a celebration. What they did instead was stare at yet another seemingly insurmountable gate.

"Ah, another fuckin' gate. What's this world comin' to when you can't stalk someone, or sneak up on someone easily?"

"You're language, Warren. Please. I thought you were able to circumvent these types of obstacles."

"If you mean, can I get around the gate? Then yes, it's just a pain in the …. well it's a pain. And it eliminates the element of surprise. Usually." He got out of the Mercedes, going around the front of the vehicle, in order to confer with the chauffeur. Once the conference was over, the SUV backed into an inconspicuous parking spot a couple of hundred yards down the road, but still in view. Warren hid in the manicured shrubbery which lined the massive gate.

The wait was a long one. The sun was getting hotter and the sweat dripped from places on his body he was not sure could sweat. They were well inland of the Pacific Ocean and there was a noticeable lack of a coastal breeze. The sun continued to beat down on the mountainous desert-like region, which heated even the shade. His iPhone rang. He removed it from the pocket of his new cargo shorts to find that sweat had saturated his screen.

"Olivia?" At least the phone still worked.

"Warren, what exactly are we waiting for? Let's just alert them to our presence and discuss this like adults."

"At least you are in air conditioning. I'm sweating my — "

The timing was perfect, albeit a little late, for the gate began to recess sideways into itself. He was not sure how much longer he would be able to hold off Olivia, but he was thankful not to have to find out. The gate was opening for the vehicle that was departing from the premises. The Jaguar F-type *V8 S* jetted away from the drive in the opposite direction from the Mercedes on a stakeout. The top was down on the salsa red convertible sports car, music loud, and the woman behind the wheel was gone with the same quickness in which she had arrived.

" — we're in Olivia. Hold on."

Warren slipped out of the shrubs and through the closing gate before it re-locked.

"Was that Anna in that car? I couldn't tell," Olivia said.

"I don't think so, but who knows?"

"So how was that helpful? We don't know if she is in the house, and Jennifer and I are still out here while you are in there. I will not sit idly by while you — "

" — easy, easy. You think I'm impatient. Brady wasn't in the car, that's definite. So either way we're leaving with him. Just have your guy pull up to the gate."

The chauffeur pulled the car up to the gate, spying Warren on the other side of it, doing jumping-jacks, waving, and running from side to side in the driveway.

"Jennifer, he's lost his mind."

"I think he is reopening the gate for us. At least I think he thinks he can reopen it."

The motion detector finally did its job, sensing the flailing and reopening the gate for the others. The driver pulled up to where Warren was; allowed him to crawl into the air-conditioned backseat, but the ride was not long enough to cool him down. The Spanish-influenced stucco building ahead of them had many front-facing windows. If anyone was watching from any of those windows, his jumping jacks and sweat-soaked clothing were for nothing.

Jenna took a jab at him. "That was cute, but what's the rest of your plan?"

"I'm wingin' it. I'm kinda surprised it's worked out this well so far, if truth be told."

"This is trespassing, I'm sure you are aware of that Warren. You are drenched with sweat and I don't know which is worse, your sight or smell. Maybe I should go to the door and discuss things with Anna."

"Yeah, that'd be pissah. The banished mother travels cross-country to confront her daughter and grab her grandkid, what could go wrong? Besides, we don't even know for sure if she is even in there."

"Your sarcasm is unappreciated, I am simply trying to help."

"Just stay in the car, both of you. Please. Just give me a sec and we will see what happens." He got out of the car, back into the heat. He made his way to the front door along the stone walkway.

The first set of knocks on the door with a doorbell follow-up went unanswered. As did the second set. Deni was beginning to wonder if anybody was home at all.

438

When the door did open, just prior to his third attempt, a house opened the door to the house. The mammoth man stood in the doorway, filling it. He wasn't mammoth-fat, he was over three hundred pounds of pure muscle.

"Oh shit."

"Who are you and how did you get in here?" He was as unfriendly as he was intimidating.

"I'm with the Jehovah's Witnesses. Is the lady of the house available to discuss the coming of our Lord and Savior? I'm here to save her from eternal damnation." Deni then realized with whom he was speaking.

"Hey, aren't you Vinny Mahlrhone? The Tackle from the Chargers? Fancy meetin' you here. I'm a big fan, we could use you on the Patriots," he continued

"Yeah, thanks. Who the hell are you, again? Reporters aren't allowed here."

"Holy shit! Get rid of him." Deni heard the female voice shout from behind the giant. She then sounded like she took off in a full run after her command.

If he hadn't been able to be a professional football player, Vinny would have made a phenomenal goalie. Deni couldn't see a thing past him in the doorway, so he didn't know for sure whom had yelled from inside the house, but he had a very good guess.

"Ah - ha. There's the lady of the house." His move to get past the All-Pro Tackle was unsuccessful, the gigantic mass that was Vinny didn't budge an inch. Instead, Deni was grabbed by the collar like a football dummy and pushed back onto the middle of the lawn with ease.

"You have to go now." He wasn't asking.

When he was set down on the lawn and given the ability to gather himself, Deni brushed the wrinkles out of his shirt. He was trying to be as non-threatening as possible when he spoke.

"I gotta talk to Anna, the lady of the house. I'd rather do this the easy way, Vin. You're still in good shape after the Chargers terrible season, by the way. You don't spend too many marches at Disneyland though, do you?"

"So this isn't random. What do you want?"

"It's between me and her. You are caught in a bad situation, and so am I. I just wanna talk with her."

"She just said that she don't want company, bro. Whatever this is, you aren't welcome here."

"I get that. But we came a very long way, and we aren't gonna leave without speaking with her. So maybe you could help convince her. What are you, her bodyguard? Kinda a big fall from professional football player to personal protection isn't it?"

"Fuck you buddy. This is my house, and *I* want you to leave. I don't want to hurt you, I don't need the headache, but I will if I have to, bro. You're trespassing."

"I don't wanna do this the hard way either, Vin. But I will warn you, you might beat the shit outta me, but you are definitely gonna know you've been in a fight. Nobody is *that* big. Think of your career. Just let me talk to her."

Meanwhile, Olivia and Jenna had already exited the SUV with stealth and entered the house behind the preoccupied football tackle. His back was still to his home, as he was ridding himself of the trash that was on his front lawn. Warren had seen their sneaky entrance and was finished stalling. He continued before Vinny could respond.

"I'm going in there Vin. Neither of us want the trouble a fight will cause. I'm not gonna hurt her, I'm just gonna talk."

"Not happening, bro."

Deni made a move to get passed him, but getting past a professional football player was all but impossible. Vincent made a move to grab him, with the same collar grab he had used two minutes prior, but failed as his elbows were pushed together in a clean sweep. With his right foot, Deni used the exposed right side of his aggressor, in order for him to step on the big right knee. This last made an audible cracking sound that made exactly as much damage as the horrifying sound indicated. The hyperextended knee looked like it belonged on an ostrich instead of a human. At the same time as Vinny's knee was being shattered, using his left fist, Deni punched the Adam's apple in the center of the man's huge neck. He was able to achieve a downward motion from his perch on the man's knee, further forcing Vinny toward the lawn.

Mahlrhone may have been choking and have a permanently destroyed knee but he was not finished, and managed to snatch Deni's right leg with his long, muscular arm. He was used to working through intense pain during games, his hold on the much smaller leg was like a vice-grip. Deni was being pulled into the huge chest for a crushing bear-hug. He went to work on the man's face with his elbows on his way toward the behemoth. Left, right, left, right. Elbow after elbow was drawing blood from the mangled face. Blood was gushing from what was left of the nose, eyes and mouth. Pain was making the powerful tackle squeeze his prey with more pressure rather than less. Deni was being squeezed like a rodent wrapped in a serpent.

The sound of crushed bone was now emanating from Deni, as his ribs were snapping like pretzel rods. This made the continued elbows to his attacker's face excruciating but he continued as it was necessary for his survival.

Deni was able to find purchase on the lawn, as Vinny was kneeling on his only good knee. He tried to leverage away from the Tackle, but elbow after elbow he remained unsuccessful. The bloody meat that was once a face, remained very determined to squeeze the life from Deni. Both falling to the ground, Deni using his position on top to lean on Vinny's massive neck.

At last, the hold on Deni was released and they both laid on the front lawn, bleeding and gurgling. Both trying to attain oxygen. The entire fight was over in a little more than a minute, but the damage would last much longer.

"It's a good thing you're not on the Pats, now that I think on it Vin. You're not that tough." He said this through the pain of his broken ribs, which made the pain worse. He struggled to get up to go into the house as Vinny continued to lie on the lush, green lawn now sprayed with blood and broken teeth. "I'm goin' inside, you just stay right here big-boy."

440

Vinny didn't respond.

Inside the house, Olivia and Jenna spread out, moving about the house looking for Anna. They were on opposing ends of the large home calling after her. "Anna? We just want to talk to you." Each of them getting no response at first, and not hearing each other either. Jenna had gone around to the back side of the house, spying the nonplussed yellow Lab in the back yard, chewing on a toy. Olivia had taken the front part of the house. As they circled around one another, they heard from a distant part of the house not yet covered by either woman, "Get the fuck out, I'm calling the police."

Olivia said, "I don't think that would be a good idea, dear." She knew her daughter's voice and knew she was just ahead of her in one of the rooms to come. What she didn't know was what she was going to do about it. Or if her grandson was here. "We know what has happened, Anna, and we know your part in it. Let's not make this any worse than it already is. It's very upsetting to everyone, but think of Brady. Just come out so we can have the lawyers sort it out." She slowly moved up a small flight of stairs, large windows to her left, and several rooms were to her right.

"I don't want anything from you. Just get the fuck out," Anna said from one of the rooms. Olivia was close. Jenna was somewhere else in the house, of no use at the moment.

"Where is Brady? He doesn't need to be exposed to any of this."

Anna didn't respond but Olivia had narrowed the search to the room in front of her as the shouting seemed to come from that door. She turned the doorknob with caution, opening the door. It was a weight room, and the mirrored room appeared to be devoid of humans though filled with exercise equipment. Olivia was wrong, nobody was in the large room, as she heard mumbled voices, one being a child's, deeper into the house to her left. She closed the door and continued in that direction.

"This is ridiculous, Anna. Just come out so we can speak like adults. Nobody needs to be hurt any more than they already have been."

"I already killed one woman, what makes you think I won't kill you?" The voice was still closer and could only be in one of two rooms remaining down that hall.

"You would kill your own mother, Anna? I cannot believe that. I'm sure you didn't kill her on purpose, accidents happen. Let's not make this any worse."

"Keep coming closer, bitch, and you'll see just how fucking bad it can get." The shout was on the other side of the door that Olivia was now in front of. Again, she cautiously turned the knob and opened the door. The mechanism was silent, as were the hinges, as the door slowly creeped open. Olivia peered into the room with apprehension as the door moved open inch by slow inch. The back wall was painted like a football gridiron, a small boy sat on the floor in front of it visibly frightened.

441

The Taylor Made *R1* driver swung out of nowhere, on a bearing toward the right side of Olivia's skull. Anna was on the other side of the door, swinging the golf club like a Louisville Slugger baseball bat. The swing and the eventual contact with the club face to her temple would shatter any chance at life beyond that moment.

In that last millisecond before coming into contact with Olivia's skull, the door swung completely open. Warren had come rushing through, taking the full impact of the club on his left shoulder which dislocated it in all of an instant. The thud made from the contact simultaneously fractured the humeral head (the ball going into the glenoid, or the socket), and vibrated the club out of Anna's grip. The sound that howled out of Deni's mouth was as awful as the sound of the impact itself. He fell to his knees in yet more agony.

The vibrating club flew away and the utter shock on Anna's face did not last long. She dove across the room to her son, now crying in a ball on the floor. Jenna was now behind Olivia and Deni, she had made her way to the large room that was getting rather crowded. Anna, seeing all of these people before her, clutched the sobbing child, putting him between her and the intruders.

"Just leave us the fuck alone." It was a last and final effort. One that was in vain and she knew it. She knew everyone in the room. Deni was like a relentless dog. There was no way he was going to be 'live and let live' about this situation, injured or not.

"You busted my arm Anna. Was that really necessary?" He was trying to keep both his temper and his language in check. The child was upset and could easily be more so if the circumstances were to degenerate further. "Olivia, talk some sense into your daughter before I really lose my temper." He was plainly in the throes of immense physical pain.

Olivia was almost catatonic. She was looking at Deni in horror, seeing that while his pain was debilitating, the blow from her daughter was meant to, and would have, put an end to her life. She too sat down harshly on the floor.

Jenna took the reins. "Brady, do you remember me? It's Jenna. I don't know if you remember Warren, he is kinda like your uncle. And this is your Grandma. You have never met her, but she loves you very much. We are here to bring you back to see your Dad. Do you want to go see your Dad?"

"Just leave us alone. Haven't you done enough damage?" Anna was a mess. What was once a beautiful woman was now a psychotic, angry, sobbing mess.

"I didn't do anything wrong, you just think I did. If you would have had a conversation, maybe ask a few questions, none of this would have happened."

"What was I supposed to do? Just sit quietly by while you, you fucking cunt, come in and ruin my family? And her. Look, even now she won't say anything. Look at 'poor old mom the martyr'. Never. I would never let him get away with it."

"No matter what you think of me, your husband doesn't deserve to rot in prison for the rest of his life. He didn't do anything wrong."

442

"When he dove into bed with you, whore, he deserved to die. But that would have been too easy for him. He needed to suffer. It's too bad the monkey-woman had to die, but better her than me."

Deni was reading between the lines while suffering from his injuries. How he was able to concentrate on anything else was a mystery, but he interjected.

"Anna, if you didn't try to kill JG, then what happened that night?"

"And everybody thinks you're the clever one, Deni. JG needed to suffer, he wasn't supposed to die, he was supposed to live with the fact that he killed someone else. He killed me Deni. He doesn't know what he did to us. We could have had a great life."

"He didn't do anything, Anna. You can keep saying it as many times as you want, but he didn't cheat. You did all of this for nothing. *You* ruined what could have been a great life. And that woman, the monkey-woman you called her, what did she do to you?"

"This twat and my husband have you all fooled huh? Well not me. The dead woman may have been innocent, she may have been my half-sister. Who knows. That was just a lucky bonus I guess. It could have been anybody coming down that road that night, but all the people of quality were at the charity event."

"How did you get outta there, Anna?"

"Chamille covered for me. Nobody knew the difference. How'd you know I wasn't there?"

"There are cameras everywhere these days. Saw you buy the burner phone, saw you drop the drugs into JG's beer, and saw you pick up Brady." While she was talking he wanted to put the last piece of the puzzle together, the presets on the twin Volvos. "And you forgot to reset the presets on the Volvos."

"Can't think of everything I guess. The drugs didn't work as fast as I had thought but they worked enough. He didn't realize he was in the wrong car, dumb shit."

"So if we get his keys out of property at the prison, is it going to be your key on his ring?"

"I switched them back when I dropped off Brady. I'm not an idiot."

"That's debatable."

"Hey Deni? Go fuck yourself!"

Brady had eased his way away from his mother, hiding by his bed next to Olivia. Anna, with all the chaos and interrogation was unaware that her son was no longer in front of her.

"So he made it home safely in your SUV, while you put a dinger in his. You really sold the story, Anna. Too bad you did it all for nothing. No matter what you think, JG didn't cheat. The more you thought it, the more you stayed away. The more you stayed away, the more time he spent with Jenna, here. And around and around it went."

"We are friends, Anna, that is it. There is nothing else going on," Jenna said.

"You moved in on my fucking family, I should have killed you too."

443

"Well, I don't think there is anything more to say to you." She turned to Brady and Olivia. "We should get him out of here, the rest of this is going to get even uglier." Olivia was in agreement and they made their way out into the hallway.

Anna realized that she no longer had Brady and began to freak out. Deni hoped his attempts to subdue her would not be physical. He was in no condition to move, let alone get into another physical confrontation. The police were on their way, maybe they had arrived. He hoped for the latter.

"We have some things for you in the car, Brady. It is going to be a long trip back to see your Dad." Jenna was trying to ease the young boy through the next set of hurdles, as this was a traumatic day, indeed.

"Is Uncle Deni going to hurt Mommy?"

"No, no. They just need to talk about some things while we go see your Dad."

"Mommy says that Daddy is gone." He looked over Jenna's shoulder at Olivia and said, "she said my Gramma was in heaven too."

Olivia's tears began to gently roll down her cheeks. She squatted down in front of him, grabbing his little hands as they had stopped at the top of the stairs.

"Well, I'm meeting you for the first time, sweetheart. For me this is very much like heaven." She pulled him into her chest to hug him and he didn't resist. His little arms wrapped around her neck in a tight hug. He gave great hugs.

When the embrace was finished, he held on to his Grandmother's hand while they descended the stairs. "Mommy said some bad words."

"Yes honey. Your Mommy has been a bad girl."

444

28

THE FLIGHT WAS THANKFULLY QUIET. Warren was unaccustomed to babysitting, nor was he used to traveling with a child. He was becoming very fond of private jets, however. How he would fly commercial again in the future was beyond him. His pain was being steadily diminished, however slight, by the unlimited amount of alcohol that was being supplied to him by the helpful flight attendants. He was falling in love with one of them.

Olivia had stayed behind in Poway. She wanted to be there to help sort out her daughter, though she was told without equivocation, and on repeated occasion, that she was not wanted there. Anna had killed a woman by staging it to look like a deadly OUI crash. Premeditated murder was going to be a great deal of work to sort out. He thought if he were in Anna's situation, he would take any help offered to him.

Arranging for Brady to go back to Wayland with Deni and Jenna also took some doing. Anna was losing everything in one fell swoop, her freedom was bad, but losing her child was the backbreaker. In the end, she was left with no choice, but that did not stop her from trying.

Olivia had finally met the Grandson she so desperately longed to hold. She hugged him repeatedly and at length, commenting on how good his hugs felt. Letting him out of her sight so quickly after meeting him was almost as torturous for her as it was for her daughter. But duty called, as it had so many times before.

Deni and Jenna had been chauffeured off of the property before the police had arrived. He had communicated with his retired contact on the trip toward downtown. He was notified then that the police were on their way to clean up the mess he had made. He didn't mention the mess his body was in, nor the amount of excruciating pain. Anna was in enough trouble.

The questions to Uncle Deni were fielded by Jenna on the ride back to the San Diego International Airport. He was in too much pain to deal with the youngster, even when he wasn't speaking with his contact on his cell. But only when all of Brady's questions were satisfied did he board the plane. He was a smart kid, smarter at almost five years old than people gave him credit.

Mercifully, the long flight into Manchester, New Hampshire was all but silent. Brady and Jenna slept while Deni drank away the pain. They were flying into Manchester because it was closer to Wayland than Logan Airport in Boston. It was a small airport, Southwest Airlines was the only major carrier out of it, but they had a private jet, so they could fly into almost any airport they wanted.

Olivia had arranged for a driver to pick them up as they didn't have a vehicle in Manchester to drive. They could have rented one, but Jenna was preoccupied with Brady. And Warren was in no condition to drive. To say that he was hammered would have been an understatement. He needed more help out of the plane and into the car than Brady, who was still half asleep. Jenna was left to babysit two children. Luckily she was used to it.

It was almost midnight, eastern standard time, but Warren called Ryan anyway. He could have called from the plane, which would have made more sense, but he was too busy getting drunk. It was technically Sunday, the day before the trial. It was fortuitous for them that Ryan was not asleep, as he was unable to as of late.

"Deni, what's going on? Where are you?"

"In the car."

"Wonderful, where is the car? I'm kinda losing it here."

"Almost at your place. Jenna and Me. And Brady." The slurring speech added to his already thick Boston accent was almost undecipherable.

"You're in New Hampshire? You sound hammered."

"That's cuz I am."

"That's terrific. You're not driving are you? Please tell me after all that has happened that you are not driving."

"I'm not driving. Ha ha. Be there in a couple of minutes."

"I'll put some coffee on."

"Coffee ain't gonna help, Ry."

"That's what I'm afraid of."

Ryan was not prepared for what poured through his door. What was planned to be a long day of preparation became an even longer day of interrogation and nursing. Jenna was not able to help carry Deni, as she was carrying a comatose Brady into a guest bedroom. It took both the driver and Ryan to carry a drunk, war-beaten Warren into the house. The jarring of his wounded body roused him in brief, intermittently, the pain cutting through the inebriation.

In one of the brief bits of coherence, he was able to articulate that he needed to vomit. Or urinate. Or maybe both. It was far too mumbled to interpret. Ryan asked the driver how he had gotten to this level of intoxication. To which he was told that he needed to ask the other woman in the car, but his guess was the mini bar in the back of the car. They propped him up as close to the toilet as they could in the downstairs bathroom.

After some time, Jenna came downstairs, after tucking the boy in. The driver had been tipped and coffee poured but Deni had still not resurfaced from his bodily functions in the bathroom.

"What the hell happened, Jenna?"

446

"He's drunk, isn't it obvious? He should go to the hospital, which he has been told repeatedly. He is killing his pain with alcohol."

"What's wrong with him?"

"We don't know for sure, because he won't seek medical attention, but he has some broken ribs and his shoulder is shattered in all probability."

"Again …. what happened? I'm supposed to go to trial in a little over thirty hours and nobody has called to tell me what is going on."

Jenna spent the next hour explaining everything that had happened in Charleston, which he knew from Deni's call while he was on the plane to California. He waited patiently and without interruption until she started explaining what had happened in San Diego. She was stopped only a few times to answer some of Ryan's questions. The big questions were toward the end; asking if any of the conversation was recorded, or if the San Diego Police had a statement from Anna. Both went largely unanswered.

"I don't know, Ryan. I don't think it was recorded, but she did admit to killing that woman. She switched vehicles and because they were the same and the fact that Jake was drugged, he didn't notice. She switched the cars back to their correct parking spots in the garage when she went home to put Brady to bed. Not resetting the presets was a mistake."

"Well, do we have a contact person at the police department?"

"Deni does. He had one all set up before we even got out there."

"Speaking of Deni, it's been over an hour. I've been so wrapped up in the story I forgot he's in the bathroom. I gotta check on him."

When he opened the door, Warren was face down on the tile floor. Ryan panicked, thinking he choked on his own vomit or worse. Had he given himself alcohol poisoning? He lifted his friend's head, the tile marks lined his cheeks. He had a pulse but a faint one. He called out to Jenna.

"Jenna call 911. He needs to go to the hospital."

"He won't go quietly."

"He's passed out, if he is going to go, this is the time. You go with him, I need to work and be here to explain when my wife gets up."

✴✴✴✴✴✴

When Deni did wake up at the hospital, he was pissed off. He was pissed at Anna, pissed at Mahlrhone, and pissed at his nurses who woke him up every hour on the hour. Jenna was allowed to go into his room to visit him, but only after a long wait and some cockamamie story she told about being his sister. He was in a foul mood and in a lot of pain. His head hurt but not as much as his ribs and shoulder.

447

She was told exactly what she expected to hear, that he had broken three ribs, bruised others, and that the ball in his shoulder was fractured. Debris had to be removed from the arm socket and fluid removed. It was going to be a long recovery for her 'brother'.

She asked him who the contact was in San Diego, and that Ryan desperately needed it in order to offer proof. Extradition would not take place in the time that they needed, so he was going to need an official statement. Deni told her, but only after a rambling complaint about his morphine drip dosage being 'bullsh'. Which she interpreted as not being enough.

She then called Ryan. The sound on the other end of the phone when she relayed the information, was as if she had just told him that he had won the lottery.

29

THE REMAINDER OF SUNDAY WAS like a fast-moving yet foggy dream. Ryan was making phone calls to San Diego to acquire statements and possible extradition dates, and to La Fontagne who was not happy to have his Sunday ruined. The day flew by. Angie was a Godsend looking after Brady, and she was even good about asking him some questions. Brady would never take the stand, but a statement could be used to broker a deal. A plan was formed and documents created. Ryan had one shot at avoiding a trial, which he wanted to avoid because trials were always a gamble. He needed to convince the ADA that they had the wrong man.

Ryan arrived at the courthouse fifty-five minutes prior to first call on Monday, which was ten minutes before he was supposed to meet Jabba. La Fontagne was aware of the new developments, but Ryan still had a dog and pony show that he needed to present in one of the conference rooms. He and the ADA didn't exactly get along with one another. He needed a presentation that moved beyond personalities and forced the prosecutor's hand. He was also aware that La Fontagne could continue on with a trial simply out of spite.

It wasn't long before the enormous prosecutor was spotted in the building, and not much longer after that, he was in the conference room.

"Okay Wells, what do you want to do here?"

"Hi, how are you? I'm fine, thank you. Nice manners."

"You called this meeting, I'm still happy to go to trial. You are long on supposition and little on evidence, unless something has changed since you phoned yesterday. Most of what you have cannot be authenticated."

"Well a lot has changed. I am sorry for having bothered you on a Sunday, but I didn't want to ambush you in front of the judge today, who hates you by the way. "

"You called this meeting, I don't have to sit here and take your abuse."

"I told you what happened yesterday, but today I have a statement from a San Diego Police Sargent. I also have a signed statement from your boss, the District Attorney, stating that he intends to extradite her back at a minimum for questioning. It's probable that formal charges will be made. I also have a statement from their son, who is only four years old. I would like to keep him from testifying in court if possible, but I will put him on the stand if I have to. She did it.

Premeditated. That, added to all the video footage that I emailed over to you, my client is never going back to WCHOC. He never should have been remanded to begin with."

"Nice speech."

"And your response?"

"Nothing you have said proves he wasn't drunk. Two beers may have put him over 0.08 BAC."

"Are you fucking kidding Jab, er, Pierce? What do you have against Jacob Grantes? He has been incarcerated for six months for crimes he didn't commit, now you want to move forward on a crime that he may have been guilty of, but you can't prove? It is not illegal to drink and then drive. It is illegal to drink over the legal limit then drive. You would have to prove he was over the limit."

"I need a win out of this. He pleads to OUI - first offense, he gets time served with no after care or treatment. He pleads but he is free and clear. This has been sitting on the books for six months, I need something here."

"You are going to get his wife, Anna, after she is shipped back."

"Uh huh. And do you think that she is going to be convicted? She is rich with all sorts of contacts and influence in this area. Who is going to convict her?"

"You thought you were going to convict JG, my client. It's the same family, same influence."

"You think that you were the only phone call I received about this case yesterday? Olivia Craig and friends are on the case."

"Look, that is up to you. I thought no special favors and that? You can't make my client pay for the fact that the right one might go free."

"Are you going to bring the offer to your client or not?"

"Drop it to careless and negligent operation, misdemeanor. No fine, time served. That is my counteroffer," Ryan said.

"Grossly negligent operation, first offense, which is still a misdemeanor. He keeps his ability to practice law. No fine, time served. Final. Green sheet it right now or we go to trial. We're out of time."

"Fine, deal. Now if we can get the judge to accept it."

"That's a big if, Mr. Wells."

******

JG had been moved from the Wayland County House of Corrections over to the courthouse for his trial. He was sitting in the large holding tank in the bowels of the building in shackles, and

450

impatient in his waiting for his friend and lawyer. He knew Judge McCaglia, he also knew that she held her court punctually. There was no clock in the tank, there wasn't a clock in view either. But 9:00 AM had come and gone.

At 11:00 AM on Monday morning, he was cooling his heels in the basement of the courthouse he was supposed to be in two hours prior. Something was wrong. The cacophony of irritating noises and conversation from the myriad other inmates or prospects were beyond aggravating. He called to the CO keeping watch over them over and over again, but the guard was very good at ignoring Grantes and the others. No word. No notion as to what the holdup was.

By lunch break, JG was nearly out of his mind. Had he not been shackled, he may have assaulted one of the ignorant wretches he was housed with, just to get one or more of the COs to pay attention to him. The lunch that they were fed consisted of; a half-full (or half empty depending on one's outlook on things) paper cup of Gatorade, and a paper-thin hamburger from the less-than-a-dollar menu, from a less-than-good fast food joint.

Grantes immediately threw the burger-like food substance back at the CO who gave it to him. The food bounced off the solid jail door and onto the floor with an essence of urine. Now that he had the man's attention, he wanted to use it to his advantage.

"I wanna see my lawyer."

"Join the club," the CO said. He turned and walked the other direction like nothing happened.

A hungry inmate picked the burger wrapped in paper off the urine-soaked, concrete floor, inspecting the outside of the packaging. Normally, it would be beyond belief that nobody was disgusted by the action. Nor were they when he ate it after unwrapping it. But Grantes hadn't even noticed, he shuffled back to the bench and sat back down.

Midway through their makeshift picnic, Ryan came down to the solid jail door. He looked into the large tank, spotted his client and waited until he looked his way. They were unable to hear one another until the port in the door was opened. Ryan was lucky to have not heard what was shouted back at him by his friend. The CO that was so gifted at ignoring everyone on the planet, brought a chair over for Ryan to be more comfortable. The porthole was at face level for Ryan when he was seated. Grantes, of course, was not as fortunate and had to manage bending at the waist, contorting his face upward to see his lawyer, as squatting was not an option in the shackles. Privacy was not an option either.

"What the fuck, Ry?"

"Nice to see you too, pal. You look like shit, what's your secret?" He was smiling and joking which should have calmed JG down, but it didn't. In fact he only got more angry.

"Pardon me for not making tea, asshole, but down here niceties are a little hard to come by. Besides the fact that I was expecting you fucking hours ago — "

451

" — hey, hey, hey. Take it easy. No trial. Not today, not ever for you. That's what has taken so long. We are finalizing the paperwork to get you out of here. Give me another hour at the most and you are a free man."

"Oh thank God. Jesus Christ, tell me I'm not dreaming. What happened? How? Get me out of here, then."

"Listen, I'll explain everything in a little bit. You just have to hang in there for just a little while longer. It's been a long couple of days."

"It's been a very long six months, Ry. I wanna get out of here and piece my family back together."

"That's part of what I have to explain to you in a little while."

"Did something happen to Brady?"

"He has been through some shit, but he's fine. He's gonna be fine."

"He is all I really need."

30

THE WELCOME HOME GATHERING was impromptu and wasn't at Jacob's home, for what seemed to be obvious reasons. Too many memories and nothing left in it. But what a glorious homecoming it was. JG rode with Ryan to his friend's house, where Anna, Jenna, and Brady were anxiously awaiting their arrival. Warren was out of the hospital and present as well. Heavily medicated but present. Physically. He was not supposed to be mixing alcohol with painkillers but he was not-so-big on rules.

It was a warm, sunny day for March. The snow was beginning to melt but still present. They decided to eat in the sunroom but grill the food on the deck. It was perfect. Everyone was excited to be able to see him, make contact with him, but they were also cautious and gave him space. There were plenty of hugs to go around, some more important to him than others.

Jacob could not stop hugging his son, who's main interest after giving his Dad one of his incredible hugs, was to play Uncle Ryan's Playstation. Angie and Ryan's main objective was to get JG back in the office and help with the heavy workload, but they knew it would take some time. JG was not interested in that at all. Jenna's goals were to help Jake and Brady get settled back in. Deni was interested in partying, which the others were doing with much more moderation. But not JG. His favorite, Stone IPA, was ice cold in the cooler and went untouched. Nobody said a word about it, and nobody asked why.

Instead, they grilled steak tenderloins and Maine lobsters while filling him in on all the recent events. Everyone chiming in on their perspective of a truly fantastic story. How well the plan had almost worked was the big elephant in the room that nobody would touch or recognize. They did make quite clear who deserved the majority of the credit, at least Ryan did.

"None of it would have been possible without Olivia and Jenna. They were your guardian angels pretty much the entire time," Ryan said. "Olivia's exile made her network with some people who would keep track of you. Jenna was just one of her sources of information, but she was most valuable to her in the weeks leading up to the crash."

"I think I did my part." Warren was half in the bag.

"All of you did, and I can't thank you enough. I'll spend the rest of my life trying to repay you for saving it." JG was getting misty-eyed. He wasn't drinking so he could not use that as an excuse, not that any of them would make him give one.

They all hugged him again, letting him know that they would do it again if asked. And they knew he would do the same for them, if the situation was reversed. It wasn't said outright, but it didn't need to be. It was an emotional time for all but Deni.

Warren always tried to portray a rough exterior, never one to get too emotional. Handshakes were all he could muster from his calloused soul. But while he was all but numb, inside and out, his beat-up heart was glad.

"You're welcome, but I'll just take the cash," he said.

They all laughed because they knew what he meant.

EPILOGUE

GETTING RE-ACCLIMATED TO CIVILIAN LIFE took some time. Six months doesn't seem like a long time to most, under normal circumstances it flies by like a football season. But six months in prison can and did change Jacob Grantes. Large spaces and being outside was unsettling after being in confinement for all that time. Making decisions became a daunting task, for he was not allowed to make many in prison. He didn't like being approached from behind or have his back to a door. Moving fast in a car was disconcerting, and he consumed his meals incredibly fast as if someone was going to take his food away. He could not go back to his house, the house he and Anna had lived in. He could not go back to work.

Ryan and Angie pressed often, if not daily, to get him to come back to the office.

"It will feel so good for you to sit behind your desk," they said. "Just take some baby steps, or just come by and check it out for a couple of hours," they said other times. Anything to get him back, but none of it happened. He preferred to spend all of his waking hours with his son.

Six weeks went by. His house was on the market for about a minute, it was purchased by the third couple that inspected it. The closing on the house was still a few weeks away though he was renting a home in the meantime. Nothing fancy, just enough room for he and Brady. The phone would ring, he wouldn't answer it. Not unless it was Deni, but he didn't call often. Or Jenna. She had gone back to Charleston but checked in every day.

He thought about Anna, and how they had gone so wrong from something that had started out so right. They were in love back then. Or did he imagine that? It had seemed so real. Maybe it was his drinking. Maybe he was drinking so often because she wasn't around very much in the last year or so that they were together. And around and around his mind went. Another bad habit that would be hard to break. Why was she living with Vincent Mahlrhone out in San Diego? Was she seeing him before he went to jail. How long after he went there? He was depressed when he wasn't hanging out with Brady. Was that healthy? And what happened to Chamille Destrier? She was most likely naked on a beach with some poor cabana boy.

Ryan tracked JG and Brady down one day at the park. Like time hadn't passed, Brady was trying to play on the swings with the bigger kids, while the two adults talked. Ryan told JG about the latest with Anna, that she was finally back in New Hampshire after being extradited. That she refused any and all legal help that came from her mother. She would have a long, hard road ahead of her, and she was determined to do it without her help. Ryan said that he had made some inquiries to see how she was doing and she was not good. She didn't want to see him, nor anyone else for that matter. She didn't even want to see her own son.

Ryan said that Olivia contacted him because she had made so many attempts to phone Jacob, but there was no answer. Ryan said that he told her that he wasn't answering many phone calls, including his. She said that she would send some letters, but Ryan told her that he wasn't opening those either, but not to take offense. He said to JG that Olivia was desperate for a relationship and reminded him of her role in his freedom. He said that he understood and would contact her.

Ryan was concerned with his best friend's solitude. He was worried that he would not bounce back from the depression that he was obviously in. He and his wife had discussed an intervention, but decided to wait a few more weeks to see if the situation would correct itself.

Another week had passed, JG and Brady just happened to come by Ryan and Angie's house uninvited after supper. He said he needed to talk with Ryan, his partner. Angie was desperate in wanting to be apart of the discussion, but she took Brady which gave the two friends their privacy.

"I'm giving you the practice." JG just blurted it out.

"What? Just take your time, you'll — "

" — I'm done. I'm done here anyway. Too many memories. People look at me differently, they talk to me differently. I drive by the crash site every day." He paused while trying to gather himself. "I've repaired my finances after Anna. This is very hard, Ry, and I'm not sure where we will end up, but it's not going to be here in Wayland."

"You're scaring me. Maybe some counseling will help."

"I've had my fill of counseling in prison. Listen, I've thought about this and the practice is yours free and clear. Get another attorney if you want, get five. It's all up to you. I just need one favor."

"Anything. You know that."

"I know. You too. The money from the sale of my house, can you get it to the family of the woman who died?"

"What? All of it? It wasn't your fault. You didn't kill her."

"I've got some money, with Anna's situation being what it is, I will probably have access to more. She siphoned off a fortune in our assets that I will be getting back. I don't want the house or the money from it. That Brazilian woman is dead and I feel horrible about it. Have Deni find her family, take out his fee or whatever, and send the proceeds to them. Please. It will make me feel better. Will you do it for me?"

"Of course." Ryan gave his friend a very tight hug, not the one or two pat, manly hug which was their normal exchange. "This is kind of all-of-a-sudden. You have time."

"It's not sudden for me, I've had my time." They were still embraced, as if this was the last time that they would see each other. "Thank you both again. For your friendship."

They silently embraced each other for a time. All that they had shared, all that they had been through since they had known each other, was now being washed over them.

"Speaking of Deni, are you going to say goodbye to him?" They separated, Ryan looking into his friend's eyes.

"I tried but I cannot get in touch with him. He has not called or answered for weeks. He is not at his place in Barstone, either."

"Yeah there seems to be a lot of that going around. Last I knew he was being nursed back to health by this woman named Althea." They both laughed a much needed laugh.

"That sounds about right. Hey, listen. I'm not dying, so I'm sure we will be in touch. I need my son, and I need to say goodbye to Angie."

✳✳✳✳✳

The next morning, after the car was packed, the new Volvo (some things never change) departed the driveway of the rented house for the last time. They didn't stop in Wayland at all. Not for gas, not to go to the park, not for coffee nor breakfast. They would do all of those things, for they were in no rush. They would not do them anywhere near their former home. They were leaving and they were leaving for good. JG sincerely hoped that Brady would never remember any of the events that took place here. At least the bad ones.

"Where are we going Dad?" Brady asked from his child seat in the back of the car.

He considered the question for a moment before responding.

"To Grandma's house. And to see a friend."

scott wellinger

Venom

a warren dennihan novel

Venom

A warren dennihan novel

By Scott Wellinger

PROLOGUE

THE RED AND BLUE LIGHTS COULD BE SEEN long before reaching the building, or entering the complex for that matter. The road past the main gate leading up to the enormous pharmaceutical research facility was lined with trees and signage which enabled workers and visitors alike to navigate to the appropriate building within the compound. All of which were reflecting the flashing emergency lights from deep within facility.

The property took up nearly one thousand acres just outside of Downtown Charleston, South Carolina. The various buildings which held various research data were dropped sporadically about the premises. The half-blind could have found the building being sought because of all of the lights and commotion in the early morning darkness of 2:00 AM. No signage nor a GPS was needed. A vehicle was approaching the epicenter of activity at triple the posted speed limit of twenty-five miles per hour, as the driver was late to the party.

The sedan made the right turn hardly slowing down, as if it were on rails. The blaring music of Miranda Lambert's *Crazy Ex-girlfriend* could be heard, muffled from outside of the racing vehicle, which ricocheted through the corner. The car raced beyond the large parking lot toward the building to the very edge of the cordoned area designated as such with yellow police tape. The illuminated sign which read 'BIOGENESIS Pharmaceuticals Toxicology and Herpetology laboratories' was lost in the flashing lights of the Charleston Police cruisers, unmarked Homicide Detective vehicles, the Coroner's van, CSU vehicle, and BIOGENESIS security vehicles. The scene was a rave, only previously without music.

The lissome and attractive Homicide Detective, Carina Fischer, exited her air-conditioned vehicle as rushed as she had driven onto the site. She pulled aside the bottom, left, front corner of her blazer, revealing her Charleston homicide detective badge to the sweaty, flat-footed patrolman who was maintaining the perimeter. He lifted the yellow police tape for her.

She nodded to him and said in her Southern drawl, "BIOGENESIS. Isn't that the steroid company that — "

The officer interrupted her, which she hated. " — totally unrelated. I thought the same thing. Somebody is dead but it isn't A-Rod, unfortunately."

She paused on the other side of the police tape, staring the patrolman in the eye. It was hot and humid even without the sun, she wanted to go into the building, into air-conditioning. But not before setting the patrolman straight.

"Very funny. You'd think that they'd change their name. Nobody wants to be associated with assholes. Take me, for example. I'm a cop, but then so are you. Your Momma never taught you not to interrupt people when they were talkin'?"

The Patrolman didn't like to be dressed-down, especially by woman. Even if she was a superior.

"Aren't you a little late? Probably nothing left to investigate at this point. I'm sure you'll take all the credit though."

"What are y'all doing here? Issuin' parkin' tickets?"

She was in no mood for the usual red-neck, sexist crap that was dished out to her regularly. She was promoted because she was good at her job, if the lesser-achieving males have a problem with that then they can just get over it. At thirty-four, she had already accomplished more than the forty-something uniformed cop who was razzing her.

If he had a snappy comeback, he either didn't say it or she didn't hear it. She moved quickly toward the entrance to the building where more personnel were milling about. Their conversations were abruptly halted as she approached them, preferring to gossip and theorize about what transpired inside privately. Once she had reached the main lobby, she was informed that they were waiting for her on the third floor laboratory. The loiterers didn't say who 'they' were, but she didn't need them to. She knew who was waiting because she had taken the late-night phone call from the people requesting her presence.

The ornate yet understated lobby was surrounded by glass, a waterfall fell from the top floor down into the center of the reception area. The falling water hid the side-by-side elevators behind it. All of the appointments were made of glass, wood, stone and to a lesser extent steel, creating a very natural-looking habitat. The tall trees added to the organic effect.

Both of the semi-hidden elevators were being held on higher floors, so Carina decided to take the stairs. Her long legs allowed her to ascend the stairs two at a time despite being in heels. She reached the third floor long before either of the elevators made a bid to drop to the lobby to collect her. The emergency stairs deposited her in the small reception area of the lab on the third floor which was decorated with the same muted, natural colors used in the lobby. A gaggle of people occupied this area, including her boss, the man whom had called her cell at her home. The Captain of the Charleston, South Carolina Homicide Division, Bryan Simms did not look happy.

"Captain Simms, I got here as soon as I could. I wasn't aware that I was on rotation. My desk is full, Sir."

"I called you because it looks like your desk and this homicide are related. We have ourselves a very serious situation."

"Isn't murder always serious, Sir."

He broke free of his entourage, drawing Detective Carina Fischer out of the crowd with him.

"You can lay on that Southern charm can't you? What I'm saying is that we unofficially have a serial killer here in Charleston."

"This is related to my poison cases? Here?"

"I think it will make more sense once we go inside. But before we do, I need for you to know that we are trying to keep this out of the public for as long as we can. At least until we have an arrest. The last thing we need right now is to destroy our prime tourism season with a panic."

"Y'all know this is going to go viral, if it hasn't already. All the people millin' around? I had to get through a half-dozen news crews before I could even get through the main gate." Her Southern drawl was thick.

"They know there was an incident and that a third-shift lab worker is dead because of it, but they know nothing else."

"Then they already know more 'n me."

"Always a wise-ass, Detective. Why can't you act like a lady? You certainly look like one. I let you walk all over me because of your close-rate."

"You wanted to show me the scene, Sir?" She was tired. Tired after having worked all day and then being dragged out of her much needed rest. Tired of the same conversation with her boss.

Captain Simms had overcome some of the same obstacles that Carina had to overcome on her way up the ladder. He gave her a wide berth for that and other reasons. He shook his head and guided her into the secure lab.

A security ID badge had to be used no less than three times to get into the main part of the lab. Simms had been fortified with a magnetized security card, which he needed to slide through the electronic reader. Each time Carina and her boss stopped at another electronic gate-keeper, she noticed that in addition to needing a badge, the entrances were being surveilled by Closed Circuit Television cameras.

"Before you ask, the system that records the security footage for this floor has been disabled and the card that was used to access the lab was assigned to a member of the night cleaning crew. Only that cleaner hasn't worked here in three years."

"They can't all be easy I guess. How'd you know I was fixin' to ask you that?"

"I can read your mind."

They entered the lab which was filled with wall-to-wall laboratory machines. Other than the trays with test tubes resting on the large machine that presumably filled them, Carina hadn't a clue as to what all the equipment did. Along the perimeter of the lab were glass walls with doors leading to an assortment of desks and computers. They made their way to the back of the room where under the counter of a workstation, a slight man was dead on the floor. The amount of blood that was pooled on the floor could have filled a gallon milk jug. The man's lifeless eyes stared at their shoes, his arms folded in a way which indicated he was dead when he hit the floor. There was obviously no way that he could have been comfortable or tried to move once he had landed there. The Medical Examiner, Spencer, approached behind them to restate the facts that had already been relayed to Captain Simms.

"You cannot see from this angle, but this guy was hit rather hard on the back of the head. He was a tiny man. Judging by the damage, he was hit harder than what was needed to kill him."

The M.E. Squatted down under the counter and turned the victim's head so Carina could see the matted, blood-soaked hair. The victim had been struck with such force that the hair and skin on his head had been pulled away from his skull.

"Wow. This little man really pissed somebody off."

"But that's not the best part. It gets weird."

He set the victim's head back on the cold linoleum floor, which was now red from the pooled blood, and pointed to the lumbar portion of the small dead man's back. He lifted the wet lab coat with tweezers the size of salad tongs which revealed what was once a white Oxford shirt. It had already been untucked and lifted, the M.E. pulled it up again for Carina.

"Same bite marks as the other two vics," Carina said.

"Exactly the same from what I can see. I will remeasure and confirm when we get him back to the morgue, but it seems pretty clear that he was bitten just like the others. I'm just not sure which came first, the chicken or the egg. Either one would have done the trick."

"So he could have gotten bit, which would have made him bleed out, then slipped and hit his head on the counter or something, which would have made him bleed out. But either way he never had a chance?"

"There are no clues or marks to indicate that he struck his head on this counter, or any other counter in this lab. All the blood is right here." He pulled a pen out of his shirt pocket and pointed to the bite on the victim's back. The two holes were swollen and purple, still slowly leaking blood. "These are classic snake bites, just like your other two victims Detective. I'm no reptile expert, so it is impossible for me to pinpoint the exact species of snake, especially without finding it, but the bleed-out suggests it is in the Viper family. The colleague that I consulted with on your other two cases said that there are several types of Vipers who's venom has a vicious anti-coagulant component. Meaning that if you get bit, you don't stop bleeding until your dead. Like your victims."

"So where is the snake?"

"Just like the others. Not here," Captain Simms offered.

Spencer continued. "Also there is the issue of not having any bite marks from the lower dentary. If the victim was bitten, there has to be a top and a bottom of the jaw. We only see the top fangs. Granted those two fangs are what inject the venom, but without the bottom of the jaw for leverage? Again, I'm no snake expert but that seems quite odd to me."

"Do we have a time of death, Spence?" Carina was continuing to look over the body while the M.E. was speaking.

"The window is too big right now. The trouble with these killings is that there is normally Petechial Hemorrhaging, spots on the skin, which help us to determine T. O. D. The placement, number and size of the spots on the skin are tell-tale signs. The snake venom prohibits the blood from clogging, or even collecting. Like I said, all of the blood from the vic just flows out of the body instead of pooling. Rigor is another factor used to narrow it down, but lack of blood messes with rigor. I don't think we are going to get a very accurate time-frame unless we look at outside factors."

"Like?"

"Like a time reading on the magnetic badge reader. Data entries on the computer may help as well."

"Makes it hard to nail the bastard, darlin'? If I don't know when they were here, alibis are pretty loose."

"Just like the others, Detective, I will narrow it down the best I can."

"Thanks a bunch." She turned to her Captain. "Who else was here in the lab tonight?"

"Nobody. There was another technician working in another lab on the floor directly below this one. The blood got under the linoleum, soaked through, and started dripping on the lab below. His ID card doesn't allow access to this floor, so he had to call security. The guard saw this mess and called us."

"We have someone on the loose who over the last five weeks has killed three people by unleashing a snake. You say that the ID used to get in here has a high clearance status but hasn't been used in three years?"

"Correct."

"Ain't that lovely."

"It gets even weirder Fish," Simms said as we waved off Spencer, relieving him of his duties with them for the moment. "Carina, take a guess at what they research here."

1

THERE ARE SOME THINGS IN LIFE that you will never forget. Certain people, certain events, are stuck in your mind no matter how much time passes. A smell or a word can trigger those memories to come rushing back like they happened yesterday. I wonder if when I'm eighty, if I make it to eighty, I will still have the ability to recall with such clarity the events that have transpired over the course of my forty years on this planet.

As I sit here with a cup of coffee steaming in my hand, the aroma takes me back to the not-so-distant past. The case wasn't closed yesterday, nor the day before. In fact, it hasn't yet been six months, but this one will be burned into my brain for while. It ripped the heart out of me for good measure. It's not like I live a boring life. So the story that I am about to share with you sticks with me, not because it was one odd-ball story in an otherwise dreary existence. Nope, I have a very colorful past.

I was born in Boston, and raised in Southie. For those that have never watched one of the many Boston movies that have been recently made and become hugely popular, Southie is South Boston. It was, and still is to a lesser extent, a rough Irish neighborhood. Irish Mob that Irish cops don't want to mess with. Whitey Bulger was from there.

I made my way through it by boosting car radios. Maybe the occasional car. I still stay in contact with all of my old acquaintances, but most of them have been gentrified out of Southie. But that's another story.

I became a Boston State Police Trooper, which was very boring, but it happened so I'm giving you context. Sitting on the Mass Pike watching the daily commuters struggle through gridlock was like watching grass grow and plucking the odd weed. It sucked. But the powers-that-be had originally sent me through the Police Academy, after my juvie record was expunged, *because* of my questionable past. Meaning they wanted me to rat on my neighbors. They got pissed when they finally realized that it wasn't going to happen. But I had already been through the Academy at that point and passed with flying colors. So they stuck me on the Goddamned Pike.

My memory isn't the only long one, as it turned out. It took forever, but I finally made Detective. I don't know what you do for a living, or what your daily life entails, but I can tell you that it probably involves exponentially less bullsh than what I had to deal with. Politics is not my thing. I grew up in a very tough and very poor neighborhood, you call a spade a spade. Mind games and alliances a-la-*Survivor* would earn you a beating. Again, I wouldn't play ball, so everybody in the department knew I was never going to be promoted. I would retire a Detective Junior Grade, which would just be sad.

So I took on some odd-jobs to keep life exciting. One of which was MMA fighting. I was only an amateur, but I had offers to go Pro. Technically I was a welterweight (170 pounds), and lean one at that, but I would always cut weight and fight the lightweights. I won more fights than I lost by far. I grew up fighting. That's just what you did in Southie. Even the Homos fought, they would scratch the shit out of you. Problems were a lot easier to solve back then. Anyway, I trained with Kenny Florian and learned Brazilian Jiu-Jitsu. No, I'm not name-dropping. Again, I'm just giving you context. I still practice five or six days per week, as time permits. I don't get into the cage anymore, but the skills come in handy for my current career.

While with the Staties, I also took side jobs helping out some friends in Southern New Hampshire with Private Investigations. This would not have gone over well with my superiors, but everybody saw the writing on the wall and anything to grease the wheels of my departure was looked at kindly. I helped out my friends so often that I ended up going into business for myself. I was a licensed Private Detective in both New Hampshire and Massachusetts. I still am. Life is good now.

I helped out one of those friends in New Hampshire, a lawyer with his own firm, regularly. I saved his life at one point. He had an entirely new perspective on the prison experience.

We don't talk about that though. Not anymore. That was a hum-dinger too. The past is the past. We don't really talk at all anymore, since he moved to South Carolina.

Everybody always says that they will keep in touch when friends move, but they never do. JG and I were no different. Out of sight, out of mind. Life happens. We get busy and one day leads into a week, which leads into 'holy shit has it been that long?'.

I don't have that many true friends. I have a ton of contacts, acquaintances, people to whom I owe favors, people who owe me. But true friends that you can call on when the feces hits the proverbial fan, no matter how much time has passed? No. I ain't got many of them. So I was shocked and stunned when Jacob Grantes called me. Happy to hear from the guy, don't get me wrong, but I knew there was a reason. He needed a favor. Again.

It wasn't JG's ass in a sling this time, but he needed help nonetheless.

As I sit here drinking my Starbuck's Costa Rican blend, I'm not sure if I should have gone down to Charleston. Hindsight is twenty-twenty. You know who your friends are when they drop everything and come to your aid. So I went. But sometimes a friend in need is a pest. Especially when you don't get all of the facts right away.

"Deni! It's JG. Long time, no see. How are you?"

"Hey. How are you? How is Charleston? You're still in Charleston, right?"

"Yes, of course. I was trying to think of the last time that we spoke. It must have been when Olivia passed."

Olivia Craig was Jacob Grantes's mother-in-law. Well, ex-mother-in-law. But, again that is another story. She was Filthy rich. How she got that way is yet another story. I told you that I have a colorful past. I've got lots of stories, but I digress. I had worked with her on the case that freed her only next of kin, as it were, so she left me a decent nest egg. JG was the sole care-provider for her only grandson. Other than a few charities and a couple of other odds and ends, she left them everything.

"Yeah, must be. Sorry I couldn't make it down there. I kinda felt like a heel, especially since she left me money."

I was not expecting it or I would have gone. I really didn't know her that well. But I guess you go to those things for the loved ones that are still alive. I messed up.

"No worries. There were so many people at the funeral that I would have felt bad for not being able to spend much time with you anyway. Hey look, I'd love to catch up but I have some time constraints."

Here it comes.

"I need to speak with you in person. I need your help with something that is going on down here. What does your caseload look like?"

"I've got some things going, JG. I can't just book a flight and pop down to Charleston on a whim."

"Look, I know it's terrible to just call after so much time and needing a favor. But it's important. I have a case that is an absolute mess. I was hoping that I could talk it over with you. Just have you take a quick look. I need you buddy. Name your fee."

Now that my good friend is free and rich, he has become just like some of the people that I can't stand. Money buys them whatever they want. 'NO' doesn't mean 'NO' because everybody can be bought. Then again, I don't know what that says about me because I didn't hang up on him.

"Are you in trouble?"

"Me personally? No. But I have a colleague and friend down here that is being charged as a serial killer. Falsely."

"Jesus, how long have you been down there? You don't have an investigator?"

"I have a few that I use. But none of them are as good as you."

He was playing to my amazing skills as an investigator. He thought that could win me over.

"I can have a private jet waiting at Logan airport in two hours. Fly down here and listen to the situation. If you don't want to take a look at that point, I'll understand. What do you say?"

He thought he could get me to do whatever he wanted by writing me a blank check, complimenting me on my expertise, and flying me on a private jet.

He was right.

Damned my hubris.

2

I CAN TELL YOU FROM PAST EXPERIENCE that the *only* way to fly is on a private jet. Security, jet-lag, and ears popping cannot be avoided. But you don't have to deal with things like the four hundred pounder that tries to squeeze into coach like he was trying to get in a Yugo. They always pick the middle seat too, have you ever noticed that? You don't have to deal with all of the screaming children, lines at the tiny bathroom, rude flight attendants, baggage claims, and believe me I could go on. None of that. You are now free to roam about the cabin. Drink your fill. For an Irish cat like myself, that is *the* perk. It also may have been my downfall.

When I landed in Charleston, I was buzzed and feeling good. I seemed to be getting on well with the super-hot flight attendant. There was no mile-high club involved, not even a good make-out session, but I still felt the vibe.

I deplaned and JG had a car waiting for me. I'm not usually impressed by such things, but he had a Mercedes Benz *S63 AMG* parked with the door open and a driver waiting. I felt like a million bucks.

The last time I was in Charleston, South Carolina, I didn't have such a great time. I was on a case and chasing a runaway suspect. I was in no mood to appreciate how beautiful the area is. The area around the coast that is. Which is where JG lived. He lived in his ex-mother-in-law's house. It was huge and in the Historic district known as Rainbow Row. These four-storied mansions-turned-condos were juxtaposed along East Bay Street and were varying shades and colors in pastels, which is why it has the nickname. Of course JG and his son Brady were not in a condo. They owned the whole building, which ran one-block deep. Brady had to be the richest six year old ever.

The ride from the airport didn't take long. None of it really took long when you stop and think about it. I was sitting in his home on Rainbow Row on the same day that he had reached out to me.

469

"Deni, thanks for coming down. I wanted to meet here rather than at the firm. It is a little less formal."

I was happy about that. I didn't want to be around a ton of stiffs because I had added to my buzz by having another drink in the car. Which was stupid.

"Thanks."

"Uncle Deni!"

I turned and saw his son, Brady, running toward me for a hug. He seemed genuinely happy to see me. How he remembered me was a mystery. The kid was always smart, but my gut told me that he had been coached. 'Make the long lost guy I'm trying to persuade to help your dad feel warm and fuzzy,' JG probably had said to his son. Joke is on them. I already felt very warm and fuzzy.

"Hey kiddo. How are ya doin'?"

"Great. Will you be around later? I've got to go for my guitar lesson now."

Yep. He was coached.

"I'm not sure. I might be. Your dad and I have to discuss some stuff."

"Great. Well, I hope to see you when I get back."

I'll bet.

"Can I get you anything before we sit down?" JG was smiling. Everything was to plan thus far, I would imagine.

"You got any Irish Whiskey?" Stupid.

"Of course. Right this way."

We went into a room that could have been an upscale pub. Only it was in my friend's house. Oversized leather seats, dark oak, old looking books that lined shelves library-style. The bar was long and the shelves behind it were stocked. None of the stuff was Well. All of the various bottles of booze were call brands.

"You like Redbreast right?"

"You've got a good memory." I also noticed that he had only one lowball glass out on the bar. "Aren't you going to have any?"

"I don't really drink anymore."

"You have a bar in your house, but you don't drink anymore?"

"Not often. The bar is for entertaining. Besides, I need to be sharp to go over this case with you."

Buzzkill.

"But Deni, feel free," he continued as he handed me my three fingers of expensive twelve year old whiskey that I didn't really need. I felt silly drinking in front of my friend who was abstaining. But I drank it anyway. Partly out of nervousness. Partly because 'why stop now?'. We sat in our respective plush, riveted, leather sofa-chairs. JG began spelling it out for me.

"Deni, it has been a while so let me catch you up on what I have been doing, it will give you some perspective."

I nodded but said nothing. What was there to say?

"When I came down here after the fiasco in New Hampshire, I was not sure that I wanted to practice law anymore. I was able to, I just needed to take the bar exam down here. Jenna and I played house for a while, but my being home all the time was too much. She went back to school and she continually urged me to get out of my funk and do something with my life. I had no idea what to do, so I went through the motions and studied for the South Carolina Bar Exam at the university library that Jenna was going to. Are you with me? You look bored."

"I'm here." Get to the point JG.

"So anyway, I passed the bar, started and expanded my practice with the money that Olivia had left me. It is now the largest law firm in South Carolina. But all of that time that I spent at the university library, kindled a passion for teaching. So I met a few contacts and now I teach law at South Carolina University, School of Law. In my practice, I am really just a figurehead and take only the cases that truly intrigue me."

"Must be nice to have that option. Why am I here? You are super-rich and can get anybody you want to investigate whatever it is you need to investigate. Why me?"

"I'm getting there. So South Carolina University at Charleston is an enormous campus. It actually started as a medical school in 1824, which is now the South Carolina Medical University and Research Institute. The Law School and the Medical University are on the same campus. I met somebody there and became very good friends with her. She is the one who has been charged as a serial killer."

"*Her? She?* Here we go, JG. Again? What is it about you that is attracted to crazy killer chicks? Haven't we been down this road?"

"It's not what you are thinking, and she didn't kill anybody."

"What am I thinking?"

"That I cheated on Jenna with a women who is as psycho as my ex-wife."

"So where is Jenna in all of this?"

"She is no longer in 'all of this', as you put it, because of Sierra. The woman."

Is this guy for real? Clearly my choice in friends could be better. And sure as shit my decision to come down here was not a good one either. I need to drink less.

"I've had a few adult beverages, so please interrupt me if I have this wrong. Your life in New Hampshire was very close to be ruined while you were suspected of cheating on your ex-wife. You get out of that mess and move down here. You miraculously get beyond all that, start a new life and *actually do* cheat on the woman who you were suspected of having an affair with up North? This new woman, the woman down here, being the one who is presumably incarcerated after being charged as a serial killer? What the fuck Jacob?"

"Like I said, it's not what you think. My relationship with the accused, Sierra Byrne, was not .... consummated .... until after Jenna and I both realized that our relationship wasn't going anywhere. She was left with quite a sum of money from Olivia, she will be just fine.

"As far as Dr. Sierra Byrne, even if we weren't together she needs a proper defense. She is innocent. There have been three murders of people attached to the same research facility and/or university where she works. The first death was originally designated an accident. The second was suspicious, so they reopened the first because the deaths were similar. The third was ruled a homicide, no doubt. Three individual deaths with a cool-off period between, in this case over a five week span, is classified as Serial. They needed someone to pin down and quick. A serial killer on the loose in the beginning of summer, prime tourism season, would be murder on the city. Sierra has ties with both SCMU and the research facility funded by BIOGENESIS Pharmaceuticals. They have some circumstantial evidence that they are going to try to make stick."

"So why me?"

"It is getting political down here. Big Pharma, serial killer, government officials trying to save their precious city and tourism .... You aren't part of any of that. I need someone that I can completely trust. Someone who doesn't give a sweet shit about anything and someone without fear. I need to save the woman I love. I need my friend, Warren Dennihan."

"Need, need, need. Want, want, want. It's all you do. Nice speech though. How long did it take you to practice that?"

"A good-long while. Did it work?"

Shit.

3

THE FOLLOWING DAY WAS A REAL TREAT. I was hungover and without a toothbrush. I was also without a change of clothes. I really did think that I was going to be able to go back to Boston, even if I did look into the case. So I didn't bring a bag. I called my business partner in the Financial District of Boston so he would know where I was and that I was generating three times my usual rate down in Charleston. He was as unenthused as I was, apart from the money.

My wealthy friend gave me a credit card for my expenses. An Amex Centurion Card. The black one with no limit. JG said that I could blow it up if I wanted, he would pay my inflated fee and expenses. I wondered if I bought a Mercedes like the one that I rode there in the day before was considered an expense? I needed transportation. But am not about avarice. I needed clothes more.

For the second time in my life, I went shopping for clothes in Charleston. And for the second time in my life I was taken to the pee-patch. I don't really need designer clothes. I don't really *like* designer clothes. I was just in want of basic jeans, some t-shirts and maybe a jacket in case I need to look presentable. Not in Charleston. My non-skinny jeans were over $300. One pair. What happened to t-shirts under $20? I was looking in the wrong places, because there weren't any. The sport jacket was as expensive as my first car. The one I didn't steal.

After purchasing my new wardrobe and had finally caffeinated away my hangover, JG and I were ready to go over to Leath Correctional Institution for Women. This was the level Three facility that was currently housing Dr. Sierra Byrne. She had been denied bail, which was no shocker. After all, it's not like she was accused of breaking into a piggy bank. This lady was labeled a serial killer and put into protective custody. The ride was long one. Apparently the posh don't like to have their societal refuse too close them. Or to their tourists.

I found that odd because the tourists spend hard-earned money on the Haunted Jail Tour of Charleston by the hundreds. But what the hell do I know?

After going through the various gates inside the prison and my new wardrobe being patted down by the butch she-man Correctional Officer, we were led to a private meeting room. It was drab and concrete, but it was private.

Two different female COs tugged Sierra into the room. They took off her ankle chains; the cuffs on her wrists, however, remained in place. She sat down only after the officers left the room, and they only left after informing us that they would be waiting outside if they were needed.

She was a stunner. Very sinuous. Very tan. Or maybe she was milatto or milano or whatever you call those gorgeous women who have the perma-tan. Perfect skin. Her brown eyes were currently wearing the weight of the world in them, but stunning. I could see why JG had given up on what was, at the time, the most beautiful girl I had ever seen face-to-face.

"Jay, I am so glad to see you. It's only been a week and I have no idea how I am going to make it any longer."

"This is Warren Dennihan. Everybody calls him Deni. He is going to investigate your case. I wanted you to meet and maybe you can fill him in."

"Nice to meet you Deni. I wish it was under different circumstances. I have heard so much about you. I am not sure how much Jay has told you."

"I haven't told him much," JG interjected. "The information is privileged and I wanted to make sure that everybody was onboard before we delved into it too far."

"Well, there really isn't very far to go. I have no idea who did this, but I know it wasn't me."

My turn.

"So why do *you* think, that they think, that it *is* you?"

"You're accent is thick. Where are you from? New York?"

"Not a fuckin' chance. Boston. Southie, actually. But back to the point, why are you getting blamed?"

"Because I knew all of the victims in this case. The first was a doctoral candidate that was working directly under me. The second was a lead researcher at our lab at SCMU and the most recent was a lab worker at the BIOGENESIS lab. He ran tests at the pharmaceutical lab. We worked closely with them. I worked closely with all of them."

"BIOGENESIS? Isn't that the steroid company that — "

" — no, Deni. I could see how you would be confused but no. Steroids are not what we do."

"I'm a little behind. Maybe we can share with me what it is you do, exactly."

"I apologize. I thought that Jay might have covered that. I hold three PHDs in Toxin/Toxicology, Herpetology, and Bioengineering. I am also one of the leading experts in Venomology."

I had no idea what any of that meant except that this chick was fuckin' smart. How does one person get all that? Looks and brains? God is cruel.

"Yeah, let's pretend I am not as smart as you and just tell me what you do with all of them degrees and what-not."

"Of course. I teach Bioengineering, among other things, at SCMU. My erudite grad students actually do most of the teaching these days, as my workload is very rigorous. My doctoral candidates assist in the research that I oversee, which takes up most of my time. They benefit from cutting-edge research to complete their respective thesis, while we attract top minds to assist in the work."

"Pardon for interrupting, but did you say what that work is yet? Lots of big words and really just the one question I need answered."

She gave JG a look that I didn't like. I make my living at being able to read people and she just shot a look that told her lawyer that she was afraid that I am not smart enough to investigate a missing dog. Lets face it, I ain't no genius. But I am smarter than I let on. I do that on purpose. People underestimate me. I may not be the best speaker, have the biggest vocabulary, or even have a degree; but I am not dumb.

"Simply put, we create drugs. There are many chemicals found in nature that have a very specific purpose. We study those chemicals and develop synthetic drugs to cure illnesses that align with the original purpose. For example, have you heard of the Nano-bee?"

"Nano-bee? No, I don't think so."

"Ok, well the Nano-bee, just like other bees, sting people to protect their hive. Every bee sting injects a venom, but the Nano-bee is named such because they contain nano-particles in their venom which carry a toxin that has a specific purpose. That purpose is to effect the immune system of the recipient, which has been shown to attach itself to HIV. HIV, as I'm sure you know is the Human Immunodeficiency Virus which causes AIDS. A synthetic drug is currently being tested which was derived from Nano-bee venom that has very few side effects. That drug will cure HIV."

The excitement was back in her eyes. I could see that she loved her work. Curing AIDS. Pretty cool. 'What did you do today honey?' 'oh, nothin'. Just cured AIDS'. What did I do? I took pictures of a cheating wife last week. Who's cooler?

"So you think that these murders are bee-related?"

"No. Not specifically. That was just an example. We have many projects. I say *we*. The university is funded by a huge pharmaceutical company that has many projects. SCMU, the research institute, BIOGENESIS, and the World Toxin Bank work closely together because the work is mutually beneficial."

475

"Did we go over what the Toxin Bank place is yet?"

"No, probably not. The World Toxin Bank houses the largest collection of natural toxins on the globe. It is the only one of its kind. Think of it like a semi-public spice rack. Or a toxin library. When researchers are looking to analyze a specific toxin, they can obtain a sample from the WTB instead of having to obtain a live specimen from the field."

"Semi-public?"

"Yes. It can get a bit political. Those that contribute to the WTB supply get first priority, along with the largest financial contributors. There isn't an infinite supply, so it has to be parceled out fairly. And while the WTB has over 10,000 toxins on hand, there are an estimated 20,000,000 toxins. Of those 10,000, only about 1,000 are actually being studied at present. The goal is to eventually have a blueprint of every toxin. That is a far-off goal as you can see. In the meantime, the arrangement with the WTB is the best we can do to accommodate everyone."

"Obviously not everyone is pleased. Have the police looked into this World Toxin Bank?"

JG chimed in while fumbling through his files. "The investigating detective's name is Carina Fischer. I had another investigator, Eric Stubbs, look into her. She is a tenacious thing. She looks clean and is very good at her job. Except this time."

Lucky me.

"So our alternate theory is that someone doesn't like this research or WTB arrangement. Who might that be?"

"Take a number. I get threats every day, Jay will tell you. We get some at home .... "

I let it slide that she said *we* and *home* in the same sentence. Clearly JG and Brady were not the only ones living on Rainbow Row.

" .... PETA, other research facilities, other universities, other big drug companies and — "

" — Walk me through that."

"PETA? People for Ethical Treatment of Animals are — "

" — they think bees are pets?"

She looked at JG again. I couldn't quite read what that particular look meant. She probably just continued on thinking about how stupid I am.

"No. No, they don't think that bees are pets. Bees populations are dwindling, but frankly they don't really know what they are talking about. They think that we kill and do drug testing on animals. They make a big noise despite not having any facts."

"OK. What about other universities?"

"This research is very competitive. Drugs are big business and everyone tries to get a piece of the pie. Research brings in dollars. Universities love dollars. The quicker and better the research, the quicker the patents. The patents mean that only those drug companies can produce that drug for the length of the patent. When the patents run their course, generic companies get involved."

"So we have no shortage of people who could have killed these people. All we really know is that it has to be research related, and somebody who had access to all three of the victims."

"That's what makes the most sense."

What had I gotten myself into? This was going to be like trying to find a needle in a stack of needles. As it turns out, I *am* dumb.

I really should have asked more questions.

4

I NEEDED TO LEARN MORE ABOUT THE CRIMES. The latest crime scene was going to be the easiest to glean information from. Which, according to the reports I had attained from Jacob Grantes, meant that I needed to go to the lab. JG made some calls and arranged it for the following day. The lab was on hold until day three.

The rest of my night was free until then. The house was big enough where all of the occupants could be present but not seen or felt. If Brady came home that night, he didn't come to see me. He must have forgotten. Or he was tied up with his mates and stayed wherever he was. It seems like the last was a long-shot though, he was only six. But I am no parent, however. So what do I know about kids and curfews?

With the night free, I wanted to look up Jenna. JG's old girlfriend was a smoke-show. She used to work at this bar, Sully's, in Barstone, New Hampshire. It is conveniently located across the street from JG and his partner Ryan Wells's practice. I still work with Ryan on occasion, as he still has the practice, and I still go into Sully's but with less occasion because it's just not the same without Jenna.

I wanted to get in-touch with Jenna, though it was very much against 'guy code'. It was against the rules because I very much wanted to touch Jenna. You don't date your friend's exes. That is axiomatic. A steadfast rule. But I'm not much for rules. Odd for a former Mass State Police Detective, but I am paradoxical I'm told.

I am not going to say that I didn't try to find her. That would be a big fat lie. I called the old cell number I had for her. Disconnected. I hit up six dining establishments and bars looking for her. I asked everyone who paused to talk to me, and showed just as many people the picture that I had of her on my phone. Only one person said that she looked familiar. I knew the guy was full of shit, because let me tell ya — if you saw Jenna you would remember. She wouldn't just 'look familiar'. She tried to disappear on me once before, and I found her down here. Now that she was through with JG, she had vanished for good.

Could she have been behind this? Tossed aside for another attractive and wicked smart woman was a strong motive to frame said attractive and wicked smart woman. I had suspected her of some shady shit in the past, could she be involved this mess? I would keep it in mind. Or maybe I just had her in my mind and I wanted to find her. Don't judge.

The following day, day three, I went out to BIOGENESIS Pharmaceuticals to check out the lab. I had an appointment with the Director of Operations, the top dog over there. JG had classes that day, so I was on my own. I'm not sure if the driver had the day off, but the Mercedes *S63 AMG* was available for use. I put it through it's paces. That car was as fast as greased-lightning. German engineering at it's finest.

The GPS told me it was going to take 27 minutes to get to the compound. Over the Ashley River, onto Route 17, and North a few exits on Interstate 95, I weaved in and out of traffic. I made it just over fifteen minutes. It would have been faster but I sped past my exit and had to turn around.

The rent-a-cop at the main gate was busy with all of the commotion outside, so it took a minute to get to me. News crews and protesters were congesting the entire entrance. Once I had made it past them without running someone over, which is what I wanted to do, I was told to park in the parking lot off to the left and a Jarod Lynde, the Director of Operations himself, would be there shortly to transport me to the appropriate lab. I was early for my 10:00 AM appointment, so I was made to wait. I spent the time playing with the buttons and what-not in the *AMG*. I also found a cool music channel on SiriusXM, called *Lithium*. Old-school Seattle bands. Nobody makes Grunge anymore.

Jarod Lynde showed up in a golf cart. After introductions he drove about ten football fields over to the Toxicology and Herpetology Lab. The building was still cordoned off, but from whom I had no idea. The parking lot was empty.

"You will have to excuse the mess. We have been cleared to clean it up but with the lab shutdown, it has not been a top priority."

"You aren't getting back to business as usual?"

"Unfortunately no. We have some other …. internal issues that have occurred which has further disrupted what you would call, 'business as usual'."

"Like what?"

"I am afraid that is confidential."

"I am trying to help you find out who killed one of yours. Help me help you, guy."

"BIOGENESIS is a publicly held company under the umbrella of a much larger conglomerate. I simply enforce what has been directed from above me, who report to the

479

Board of Directors, who report to a Fortune 100 Corporation. Stock Prices are volatile, I am only allowed to say so much without lawyers present."

"Then what am I doing here? If you aren't going to answer any of my questions, why did you agree to meet with me? Jacob Grantes, the attorney that I work for, had this all set up like we would be able to work together."

Lynde parked the golf cart, ushering me inside the building after using his magnetic ID card to unlock the door. He led me into a conference room on the second floor, not a laboratory. He waved his hand indicating that he wanted me to sit in one of the chairs surrounding the conference table. I wanted to rip off his arm and shove it up his ass.

"We can chat here for a bit, where I will give you what information I can. You will have to sign some waivers and confidentiality agreements before I can let you see our Lab. Then, and only then, will you be able to tour the third or any other floor."

"Pretty cloak and dagger, wouldn't you say?"

"As I said, we have a very large company to protect."

"Can you elaborate? I'm a bit confused by that."

"What I am about to tell you is public record, so I can. BIOGENESIS is one of the top Pharmaceutical Research Corporations in the world. We have thousands of projects in which we design and manufacture innovative drugs for human illnesses. All of which are in various phases of the process by which a drug is available for sale by prescription. Our revenues last year were close to $100 million US dollars. We are but a cog in the wheel of our umbrella company, PROXER, which is currently *the* number one Pharmaceutical Company on the planet. With revenues of just under half a trillion US dollars last year, they are in the top 100 of *any* company in the world."

"Did you say *trillion*? Maybe medication could be a little more affordable if you greedy fucks would settle for making half-billions."

"I said revenue, not profits. Everybody thinks it is easy to generate these medications."

"You just drove me over here in a golf cart wearing a designer suit that probably costs a years worth of my salary, and you claim to be a low-level Director of Operations. Don't cry poverty, guy. Especially after you just said trillion. You'll make me cry."

"Your quips aside, do you have any idea how much money and research goes into creating a drug?"

"No, not really. But I'm guessing that is what you are going to share with me, instead of the information I came here for."

He ignored the slam, and went on with the *School House Rock* version of how research becomes a drug.

"There are currently forty-nine umbrella companies in the pharmaceutical and biotech industries that generate as low as tens of millions of US dollars per year. Everybody from

Bayer to Proctor & Gamble to AstraZeneca and many, many more are all competing for the next miracle drug. We are just the underling of one of these companies. They are all trying to hire the best researchers in the field, from the best universities, to advise them in their research and testing of potential drugs. I say potential drugs because there are millions of dollars that go into a potential medicine before it even gets to a test phase.

"A lab, like ourselves, generates promising data off of a theory. We then submit an Investigational New Drug, or IND application, to the Center for Drug Evaluation and Research. The CDER. Once the application takes effect, clinical trials can then begin. But that application can be stalled by the FDA on a 'clinical hold' for virtually any reason, which is usually political. Kickbacks usually take place to spin the wheels of progress. Clinical trials can last years depending upon the side effects, and the FDA is basically up our ass the entire time about; rules on reporting, specs, methods of analysis .... everything from packaging to distribution. These formulae are patented, but the trials could outlast the term of the patent, which makes the research free game for competitors. Any of these forty-nine huge companies, never mind the smaller ones like us, could swoop in and generate the same medicine with comparatively no research money shelled out. That is *if* the drug even makes it to that point. I can't tell you the number of 'promising data' theories that never make it to the local pharmacy. Millions and millions of dollars are spent with no return.

"We haven't even mentioned pilfering researchers from competing companies to steal research. It is highly illegal, but it is done. It's easier and more cost beneficial to pay a Piracy or Infringement settlement than shell out money for research. By the time our lawsuit gets into the Civil Courts, this lab will have been vacant for years."

Ah-ha. There was the slip.

"So that is what you meant by 'internal issues'? Somebody defected?"

"Oh. No. I was speaking hypothetically. We do need you to sign those confidentiality documents now, if you please."

He handed me a stack of papers with little adhesive arrow tabs pointing to where I needed to put my John Hancock. I didn't even read them, I just signed while I pressed Mr. Lynde.

"OK, so let's speak in hypotheticals. Hypothetically, if some people were to be eliminated from the equation and other key people were to be enticed to bring their expertise to a competing company, that would put and end to the research?"

"Hypothetically, yes. At a minimum it would set the research back decades. By that time the patent would expire, the drug could be released by a competitor, or never get made at all. Millions of dollars lost."

"And millions of people don't get a cure for what ails them. You were studying a cure for HIV correct?"

"No, that is not correct. Who told you that? We are well beyond hypotheticals now aren't we?"

"I must have been misinformed. I thought you were studying bee venom or something to cure HIV."

"You have been misinformed. But even if you were correct, I couldn't say," Lynde said. He was visibly uncomfortable.

"So whatever it was that you *were* researching, who would want to kill it? Or kill for it?"

"Are you kidding? We have thirteen buildings with independent projects all working simultaneously — "

" — I'm not asking about the twelve other buildings, I'm asking about this one. Unless there were murders in the other labs, I don't give a shit about 'em."

"Get in line. Did you see the crowd outside the main gate?"

"The news crews? They have somethin' to do with this?"

"Yes, Mr. Dennihan. The news crews. The news affiliates killed a lab worker and are barricading the complex. Are you mad?"

"Are you tryin' to piss me off? 'Cuz I'll beat the life outta ya in your Italian suit."

"I apologize. It's a trying time and I am on edge, as I'm sure you can imagine. The crowd outside would be there whether there was a legal incident or not. PETA is upset about animal cruelty, religious organizations are incensed about snake venom being the seed of Satan, Unions about outsourcing, fair wages and benefits, doctors, politicians, and God knows who else are outside those gates every day trying to interfere with our work."

"Did you say *snake venom*?"

That's not good.

The tour of the lab was fruitless. The body was gone but the outline of the lake of blood was still present. I didn't see any animals in the lab, and Lynde said that they never have any animals in the labs with the exception of lab mice on certain projects. He would not elaborate on what was going on in that lab, or what was being developed. With all of the equipment in that glass fortress, it could have been microprocessors for all I knew.

For every question I asked, he would respond with statements of confidentiality and me not being a cop. I love the classics, but every once in a while some new material is nice. I was getting nowhere and I was getting there slowly.

Since I was being chaperoned, there was no way to get into one of the other buildings to interview other people who may have known what was going on in the now defunct one. Especially cleaning crews. The report JG had given me said that the last ID card that was used to enter the lab belonged to a member of the cleaning crew three years prior.

I asked for a list of employees and that went over like a fart in church. Square one. The only thing that Lynde said to me, that was of any interest, was about a defector. I needed to know who that was. He also had a quick comment involving snakes. I was desperate to get that out of my mind. I have no interest in them whatsoever.

Outside the gate, I parked the *AMG* in line with all of the news vans. I decided to canvas the crowd. See what I could learn. The reporters and cameras were doing their own interviews and coverage, which gave me an idea of how to approach the protestors. Amidst the crowd was a tall female in a blazer that I spotted as a detective a mile away. She could not be in many crowds and go unnoticed. She had a Natalie Portman thing going on, only taller. She was five-nine or ten. The interview pad she was writing on, the badge, and bulge for her weapon was what made me add 'detective' to the other things that I was thinking about her. The closer I got, the more I liked.

I started doing interviews of my own, but kept her in the corner of my eye. *Let her come to me.* Which she eventually did.

What I learned in those interviews wasn't much. PETA went on about the rights of animals, but had no specific information about the case or the specific lab. A religious group prattled endlessly about the facility being an anathema of God, an abhorrence in the eyes of Christ that will bring about Armageddon. The End of Days were upon us.

Good. I'm more of a night guy anyway.

There was also a unionized group or something that disliked that BIOGENESIS used cheap labor and college students instead of paying a fair wage, but their hearts didn't seem into it. There was a small faction of them that supervised the picketing, while the minions apathetically went through the motions. I found that to be hypocritical, but about right.

"Are y'all at the eighty?"

Here she was. Just a matter of time. When I turned to face her, she was even more beautiful than from afar. Not like high-def TV where the closer the camera gets to the celebrity, the less attractive they become. Her Auburn hair had the slightest of red highlights, which accented the green in her hazel eyes. And that Southern drawl melted my soul. She was hell on heels.

"Uh. Excuse me?" And apparently my brain.

"Eighty Broad. Crimes Against Persons?"

"Oh. No. I'm with myself."

"Not a cop? Y'all a reporter?"

"No. Private Investigator. I'm Warren Dennihan. You can call me Deni. And you are?"

"Ah, Lord Almighty. Let me see some ID, hun."

I didn't remember that all Southern women say *hun, honey, darlin', handsome, sweetie* and the like. Even if they can't stand you. I thought she was keen on me. When I see a pretty girl, I do what I always do. I flirt.

"You can see anything you want."

"Just your ID will be fine." The way she said 'fine'? I was in lust. I broke out my driver's license and my Private Security and Investigation licenses for both Massachusetts and New Hampshire. I handed all three of them to her.

"You didn't say who you are." My Boston accent is strong. Wicked strong. As strong as her Southern drawl. She picked up on the accent, I'm sure. She definitely did when I said *are*, because they sound like *ah*. I generally don't pronounce *r*'s if they are in a word, and I add one if there isn't one. But my licenses proved what she already knew.

"Missin' a State in here aren't ya there loverboy? I knew y'all were a Yankee. That accent gives you away, darlin'. I'm Detective Fischer, and we got a problem."

"You're damned right we do. I hate the Yankees. I'm a Redsox fan."

"Great. Follow me." She handed me back my IDs, along with her business card and guided me to her unmarked sedan. With her perfectly shaped buttocks in front of me, I would have followed her anywhere. She stopped at her car and turned around to face me. An even better view.

"Just what are y'all doin' so far from home?"

"I'm looking into the death that occurred here. I work for the attorney Jacob Grantes. He's defending the accused, Dr. Sierra Byrne. I'm helping with the investigation."

"Shit. You're not helping me or anybody else, darlin'. Not even yourself. You can't investigate a damned thing down here. So unless you are down here buyin' souvenirs, you should pack yer shit and head on back to your Redsox."

Hot as a two-dollar pistol, curses, and feisty. I was ready to propose.

"Not a baseball fan, huh?"

"This is football country down here. Real men play contact sports."

She was killing me.

"But that's got nothin' to do with it," she said. "Things are different down here. I'm gonna cut you a break. Today. I'm gonna help you out and tell you somethin' that your fancy lawyer-boss should have told you. You need to be licensed in South Carolina. These out-of-state PSI licenses don't mean shit down here. Even if they did, PI's in my fine State do background checks, insurance scams, security, infidelity cases and such. No crimes. Cold cases maybe, but only if they are no longer being investigated. This one *is* being investigated. By me. Which means it sure as shit ain't cold. South Carolina Title 40, chapter 18. Might be good readin' on your plane ride home."

"So maybe I'll just get a license down here, beautiful."

"Typical. Yer cute but you don't listen for shit. You can't be anywhere near this case. I see you again anywhere but on one of our beaches, and I'll see you get locked up and fined ten grand. Am I gettin' through that perdy little head of yours now?"

OK. Maybe she didn't dig me.

5

I HAD, FOR ALL INTENTS AND PURPOSES, been kicked in the gift-bag. Detective Carina Fischer intrigued me. Lets face it, we're all friends here, she gave me chest pains. Read into that what you will. I licked my wounds and headed to SMCU. I needed a word with my employer. I raced over there and made it in thirteen minutes, or three songs and a news report on the Rock Station, 98.1 FM. God, I love that car.

Finding your way around a campus that size is a nightmare. Whomever was in charge of the look and feel of that university was far more interested in beauty than function. Flowers and cobblestones everywhere, but find a fucking sign. It took me longer to get to JG once I reached the campus than it did to get to the campus from BIOGENESIS. I eventually had to call him back and have him talk me through it. SCMU and the law school within the university were next to each other but did not occupy the same buildings. I was lost but he got me where I needed to be. Freshman must never get to class at that school.

He was in his office. He was supposed to be having his office hours, where students with issues could go in and talk about what they weren't understanding. But I put an end to that. The two cute undergrads and the gay kid had to screw. And they did.

"Deni, you can't talk to people like that down here. They pay tuition and have the right to come see me during posted office hours. You can't just run them off like that."

"Listen, I've had a tough morning because you've been less than forthcoming about what I am able to do down here. Lynde was useless and the hot-as-hell detective chick dressed me down. I'm down here doing you a favor and you feed me to the fuckin' wolves."

"I don't know what you mean by 'feed you to the wolves', but I thought that more doors would open up for you, yes. When I spoke with this Lynde, he gave me no indication that he would be uncooperative. I kinda knew Detective Fischer was a ball-buster, but I had no way of knowing that she would be there. You're a big-boy, I've never heard you whine like this."

486

"Yeah well, it doesn't matter. According to her, legally I can't do anything anyway."

"That's not exactly true. I have a fix for that."

The door opened without a knock and tall, blonde, mountain of a man came in through it. I've never been one to be intimidated by anybody. The bigger they are the harder they fall kinda thing. The fights that I have been in, I might not have won them all, but the sons-of-a-bitches knew they had been in a fight. I have literally gone toe to toe with a linebacker.

But this guy was diesel. Huge and muscular. I'm six feet tall, and he stood over me by three or four inches. Imagine if he had a neck? He would have been seven feet tall. We won't even get into how much wider than me he was. His nose had been broken a few times, so he looked the part. He stuck out his hand as he made his way toward me in the mid-sized office. I was thankful and apprehensive at the same time. Thankful that he was only trying to shake my hand, apprehensive because his hand was the size of an Easter ham. And the grip on my hand crushed like a vice.

"Deni, this is Eric Stubbs. He is an investigator at my law firm," JG said.

Eric had the softest voice I have ever heard. "Nice to meet you. I've heard quite a lot about you. It will be an honor to work with you."

"Excuse me? Work with me?" *What the fuck just happened?*

Eric obviously read the shock on my face, because he immediately removed his hand and looked to JG for guidance.

"Ah, yes. We were just getting to that, weren't we Deni? Have a seat gents." We both did.

How Eric fit in his chair is still a mystery.

"Deni, Mr. Stubbs here is licensed in the State of South Carolina and has formed relationships with many people in Charleston. He is down here what you are to New England. Eric is from Charleston and almost played professional football, which makes him a celebrity. He will be able to — "

" — OK, well then. You don't need me." I stood to leave but that big ham was back, this time on my shoulder strongly encouraging me to remain seated. Apparently this ride had not yet come to a complete stop.

"I'm sure you don't like to work with other people. I don't like partners much myself. But from what I have heard, I could learn a lot from you. I can help you with the locals," Eric said. I could not get over his voice. It was soft and tranquil. This guy had the look of an enormous polar bear, but sounded less than a teddy bear. Winnie-the-Pooh has a more grisly voice. I wonder what it took to make him mad. I would eventually find out.

"Listen Eric — "

" — call me Stubbs."

"Really? You *want* to be called Stubbs?" *Is this guy for real?*

487

"Deni," JG said, "it takes a minimum of thirty days for you to get your PSI license down here. You have to take an oath with the Attorney General or SLED. But you can be made a temporary employee of someone who is licensed without having to be registered. That would also get you your Conceal and Carry permit. It normally takes ten days but I greased the wheels and can have one for you tomorrow, once they determine that you have no outstanding warrants. They have a much more tolerant approach to guns down here."

"So I would work for Eri .... I mean Stubbs? Technically."

"Correct. Technically."

"But why go through all of this trouble? I am telling you Detective Fischer was as serious as a heart attack when she told me to back off. Not that I am a big stickler for rules but you seem to have a capable investigator, why pay me, uh, what you're paying me when I am not really going to be able to do shit?" I was not sure what Stubbs was being paid, but I would bet it was less than me.

"Because I need a result. And more importantly, Sierra needs that result. I need you on this, Deni. You have not failed in the past, at least not with me. No offense, Eric, because I need you on this also, but you aren't Deni. Not yet anyway."

"None taken," he whispered. If he was offended in any way, he didn't show it.

"All right. With that settled, lets move forward with the real meeting."

He didn't wait for me to orally agree to the new terms of the arrangement. But he didn't really have to, I suppose. He knew what he needed to say to get me to stay, and he said it. Like I said, sometimes a friend in need is a pest.

Stubbs unzipped his shoulder bag, which I didn't even realize he was carrying until that point. He retrieved a shoulder harness with a handgun holstered in it.

"I wasn't sure if you had a preference in your pistols, but I like the stopping power of a . 45 calibre. You?"

"You are speakin' my language big-boy. What have we got?"

"Taurus *PT1911 stainless.* The key lock has been taken off the hammer but other than that it is out of the box."

The gun was beautiful. And loaded. Eight in the magazine and one in the chamber. I liked the guy's style.

"Just make sure you keep a low profile with it until your Carry Permit comes tomorrow. My gift to you as a way of saying thanks for working with me. JG can handle the paperwork to make it all legit. It will be registered to you here in the State of South Carolina."

Correction. I loved the guy. Full-on man-crush.

But it was time to get down to business.

"Deni, why don't you fill us in on what you found out over at the lab," JG said.

"Not much really. I now know the process by which a drug comes on the market. Whether that is beneficial in our investigation or not, I don't know. It does means that there are a ton of people along the way that could halt the process if they had a problem with the drug or the company."

"Right," Stubbs said. "So why not do what you can to stop that part of the process if the end goal is to eliminate the drug? No need to kill anybody."

Smart too.

"Good point. And I don't even know what drug they were making over there. Very hush-hush. It seems Sierra's HIV theory isn't what they were cookin' up over there though. Lynde may have been lying, but I don't know for sure."

"She may have been using that as an example, Deni. That was probably one example of what bioengineers do. Or maybe that was just one drug among the many that they are researching. She has a confidentiality agreement in place, so she is not likely to divulge her actual projects. Nor will Lynde. But I will see if I can find out the exact nature of what was being tested at BIOGENESIS."

"It doesn't matter anymore, I don't think. Whatever it was, the game is over. That lab is as deserted as the Sahara. I guess they had a defector or two, so that really put the kibosh on it."

"That's where I might be able to help." It was Stubb's turn. He was studying his notes which he had also removed from his bag. "The number two guy over there Enrique Estabados, excuse me *Doctor* Enrique Estabados, went over to Nahash Pharmaceuticals, which is a subsidiary of Wyatt, the number two pharmaceutical company in the world. Anybody want to venture a guess as to the number one?"

"Ooh, ooh, pick me." I raised my hand like I was in a classroom. Seemed fitting considering I was in the office of a professor at a prestigious university.

"You …. in the corner." I loved that he played along.

"Ummmmmm, would that be PROXER?"

"Give the man a prize. And we all know that BIOGENESIS works under PROXER," he continued. He was coming out of his shell. Still soft-spoken but at least he had some personality in that immense body of his.

"That scallywag. Lynde said that they had some internal turmoil over there."

JG chimed in. "So he murders and sabotages to bring down BIOGENESIS as a way of getting at PROXER because he is a mole for Wyatt. You almost need a scorecard."

"I can help. Wyatt is winning." I was a quick study.

"By killing three people? Seems a bit strong doesn't it? I could see taking all of their trade secrets and giving them to Wyatt, but murder?"

"Stubbs, I just spoke with Lynde and he told me that these umbrella companies generate a half-trillion dollars in revenue. Each. I would kill for a burger right now, just sayin'."

489

"Let's go talk to Estabados then. I'll fill you in on the rest and buy you a burger on the way."

Did I mention that I love that guy?

6

I WASN'T SURE IF THE AMG WAS going to be safe in the parking lot at SCMU, so we took it instead of Stubb's ride over to Nahash Pharmaceuticals, a division of Wyatt. We needed to have a word with Dr. Enrique Estabados. Route 52 north runs out toward the 17 and Summerville, where Nahash was situated. I offered to let Stubbs drive since he was technically my boss, but he declined because he wanted to reference his notes when he was filling me in on the other details of the case. It suited me fine, because driving that car was a blast. That is, of course, until I got my speeding ticket.

I was half-tempted to see if I could outrun the pig, the car was under two tons and had 451 horses, so my thinking was that I have a shot. But I didn't know the roads that well and you can't outrun radio. I didn't give a shit about the ticket anyway, JG would pay the fine even if he didn't know it yet. And since I was out-of-State, no points were attached to my license. My fear in not wanting the ticket was that two unfriendly interactions with the local law in the same day might get noticed. And not in a good way.

Stubbs dropped the big bomb on me after we were through with the speeding ticket, thankfully. Because if I had heard the news before being messed with by the Charleston County Sheriff, I may have been charged with murder myself.

The first death in the three serial murders was a doctoral candidate that worked under Sierra. That much I knew. But I didn't know that she died in her home, having bled to death from a snake bite. *Snake - there it was again.* She kept a pet snake, so it was originally labeled an accidental death. Only later, upon further investigation, the lovely Carina Fischer and the M.E. determined that the snake bite wasn't consistent with *her* snake. But it wasn't until after the second murder, seventeen days later, that it was officially deemed a homicide.

Stubbs enlightened me on the second victim as well. He was the lead researcher at SCMU, which again I knew from the report. He was penultimately killed at a lab on campus, again by a fucking snake. Which I didn't know. He too bled to death, but he had a nasty whack to the side of the head to go along with it. It ripped the flesh, tearing the ear off completely. Again, it was originally labeled as accidental but this time suspicions were up. They had an entire lab full of snakes, spiders and the like, but all were accounted for in their cages. Add to those facts that the shattered orbital bone and ear that they couldn't pair with any other surface or instrument in the lab, was leading to the scratching the collective heads of the investigators. Detective Carina Fischer first and foremost. It was then that the first death was coupled with the second.

Lastly, the death of the skinny lad at BIOGENESIS. It didn't take much to kill this poor prick, according to my new friend. He had his source or sources but I didn't ask him to share them with me because if the situation was reversed, I wouldn't want him asking. Anyway, this kid was a third shift lab worker. All he did was run tests for a living. He also had a massive head trauma, sending shards of cranial bone into his brain and tore the skin and hair off the back of his skull. That alone would have done the trick, but the signature snake bite marks were present. He also bled out. Only there were no snakes in the lab. No snakes in that building.

Snakes. I fucking hate snakes.

We arrived at the main gate of Nahash at 3:30 PM. The guard working the booth was unimpressed. He was not about to let two private investigators in to the facility to question anybody. But we got in.

Apparently the way to get what you want in the South isn't to be sneaky or with beatings. Which sucks because that is what I am good at. Stubbs could have choked the life out of the guy without missing a bite of his burger. His size alone would raise some pulses. But he didn't.

No rent-a-cop wants to be doing what they were doing for work. They all take on-line classes or go to Kaplan to study Criminology or some such thing. And they end up here, or places just like it. They don't show that on the commercials. They want to be investigators, they want to be cops, they want to be anything other than a babysitter to a security gate. They make $12 an hour, they could give two shits about a $12 billion patent. Which was probably the catch twenty-two of why he wasn't promoted and why he was still a security guard, but I digress.

Stubbs offered him a way out. He gave him his business card and told him if he let us in, that we wouldn't cause any trouble and he would see about a position as an Investigator with JG's firm. He also asked him politely to not call anybody inside to warn of our presence. We needed the element of surprise, he said, which is a key element of investigating, which he was sure the guard knew.

No shit, it worked.

For the second time that day, I was inside a pharmaceutical research complex, and it looked almost exactly the same as the first. I wondered if inside all of the buildings were projected drugs for illnesses that people suffered from. And if so, how many of them were redundant? There were forty-nine parent companies with who knows how many sub-companies like the two I was in that day. There had to be two separate entities working diligently on curing the same illness.

Was it a function of keeping up with the GlaxoSmithKlines, or have we invented illnesses? I also wondered if we needed to invent new drugs to counteract the side effects of the drugs that were being invented in these buildings. I still wonder that, because I never received an answer.

We had no idea which building Dr. Enrique Estabados worked in. It wasn't like the Mall of America where we could just look at a directory. I think the guard who hoped to have another job the following Monday was supposed to tell us where to go, but we never told him who we were looking for.

We eventually found the Administrative Building. It was completely by accident because we were lost and had to turn around. But we stumbled upon it and thought it a logical place to start, even if it did ruin the element of surprise.

I must have been looking incredibly 'Metro' that day. I don't know if it was the designer clothes that I was forced to buy; or that I was made of lean muscle; or my dirty-blonde hair with a touch of gray; but I was definitely the receptionist's type. The gay male receptionist's type.

He was not into steroids and rugged good looks, which was my new friend Stubb's look. That would have been my preference. Nope, he was into the heavily tattoo'd and athletic type, which was me. All of my tattoos are covered as long as I am wearing a t-shirt and shorts, that was on purpose in case I needed to look respectable. I had taken my sport jacket off because it gets hot in the South during the summer months. The super-expensive t-shirt that I had on fit smaller than any other shirt I had ever purchased. I mean, a large is a large right? Who tries on clothes in a fitting room? But again, I digress.

So some of my tattoos, or at least enough of them, were able to be seen. Enough where he liked what he saw. I know this because that is what he commented on before we had reached his desk. He cat-called me from across the lobby.

"Hello, handsome. Are those tattoos all over your body or they popping out to see me? I would be more than happy to see more of them. How are you delicious?"

Yep. Full-on Liberace, ballerina, pirouette, butterflies and rainbows gay. So I played the role. I am a total whore, what can I say?

"Better now."

"What can I do you for? That accent of yours is so sexy, you just made my month." Two words. I said two words and everyone in a five mile radius knew that I was a foreigner. Well, Boston. Which in the South means that I am a foreigner.

"I'm looking for someone, I was hoping you might be able to help."

"Get rid of that slab of meat and I think you found him." I am pretty sure that he was referring to Stubbs, because he was sending him looks like daggers through his eyeballs. I was sincerely hoping that I wouldn't have to promise this guy anything. I wouldn't have lived up to any promise that I made, but I was still hoping I wouldn't have to make one just the same.

"Flattering. But I was looking for, excuse me, *we* were looking for Doctor Enrique Estabados. I lost track of which building he is in."

"Oh he isn't your type, honey. He might swing from both sides of the plate, who knows, but there is something about him that I just don't like."

"Unfortunately, we have to do some business with him, so there isn't much choice. I'll keep your comment about him our little secret though. Which building did you say he was in?"

"I didn't muffin, because he isn't here. He is out of town on business. Are you sure you have an appointment with him? Maybe I should just call — "

" — no reason to get other people involved. I don't want to disturb anyone. I lost the piece of paper with his address on it, I probably got the date wrong too." And that was the comment that sent his little pink antennae up. I never recovered. He must have hit a silent alarm or something because the storm troopers walked toward us calmly from several rooms. We were surrounded by Secret Service looking dudes.

Stubbs and I had hoped to have the element of surprise, and we turned out to be the ones surprised.

Our first instinct, mine at least, was to go a couple of rounds with the security boys, just to see what was up. Stubbs looked at me for guidance as they slowly approached us. I think they were wondering what the giant was capable of just as much as I was. But it was neither the time nor the place. Dr. Estabados was our only real lead, and he was out of town. We weren't going to find out where the slippery son-of-a-bitch was hiding by causing a scene, or getting beaten up, or arrested, or all of the above.

These well-dressed security personnel weren't cops. Not even close. While they may have looked like FBI or Secret Service, they were not well-trained. They didn't cuff us, nor did they take either one of our weapons. I was happy about that, because I had just received my *PT1911* and hadn't even had the chance to test it out yet. They also put us in the same room to question us. Rank amateurs.

The guy in charge tried to play the bad-cop role, but he was the only person in the room besides us. No good-cop. And nobody was backing him up. With two guys that individually could give the guy a viscous beating, that was a stupid move. I know what I was thinking of doing to the guy, and I am nowhere near as big as Stubbs.

He kept asking us where we were from, what we wanted, what we were doing there and why we wanted to see Dr. Estabados. Neither of us said a word. It's not like we were in Guantánamo Bay and being water-boarded. This guy put on a scowl and changed his voice from soft to ear-drum shattering loud, and he would occasionally hit the table with his open palm, but he was pretty harmless. The last time he smacked the table I think he hurt his hand, because he winced and never did it again.

I didn't look anywhere but straight ahead. Not at Stubbs, and not at my watch. So I can only guess that it was about a half-hour to forty minutes of that nonsense before the guy left the room. Maybe to bandage his hand. I don't know that either because he never came back. Someone else did and led us to an elevator and then a non-numbered floor that needed an ID badge to get to.

We then went into an office. And when I say 'an office', I mean the mother of all offices. You could have played hoops in that thing if you took out all of the furniture. It was a corner office facing Northeast, two of the adjoining walls were floor-to-ceiling windows. Those windows overlooked the trees of the Francis Marion National Forest to the right and Lake Moultrie to the left. We were well above the tree-line, so I would guess that we were at least ten floors up. I don't know what a space like that costs in Summerville, South Carolina, but you cannot buy a view like that in Somerville, Massachusetts.

The office was filled with fine furniture and fine books and fine knickknacks, but was void of humans other than me and Stubbs. We tried the door but we were locked in. I could think of worse places to be locked up, but trapped is not really my thing. I made my way over to the expansive desk to play with stuff but was thwarted by the man who was coming out of his private bathroom.

He wiped his hands on a towel and tossed it onto the floor of the bathroom from whence he came.

"Good evening gentlemen. It is almost five o'clock and I was planning on leaving for the day, then you two showed up."

"I think this is called prevening. Not evening." I looked to Stubbs who was trying not to laugh, then back at the mystery man. "Do you know what hour officially starts evening? I know it's not afternoon anymore. Happy Hour. Yeah, it's happy hour. Prevening or happy hour I believe is the preferred nomenclature. Either way, you must have a bar in this office."

"Very funny, Mr. ? — "

" - Abbott. Bud Abbott and this is my friend Lou Costello. We're a comedy team. You might have heard of us.

Stubbs looked at me and said in his sheepish voice, "But I wanna be Abbott. He was the tall one right?"

"I am not amused gentlemen. You are trespassing on a secure facility — "

" — it's really not that secure. You should really look into that. As you can see anybody can just walk right in here and meet some hot-shot in a big corner office. What are you the President of the company?" I was fishing, and the guy knew it, but he bit anyway. My guess is that he thought he had to give a little information to get a little.

"Whomever you are, this is not a laughing matter. We have a great relationship with the Charleston Sheriff's Department, and both the Summerville and Charleston Police Departments. A simple phone call can make both of your lives fairly miserable, I presume. I'm sure you don't want that, and I don't need the headache." *Yeah, I'm sure that's why you haven't already called the cops pal.* "My name is Rueben Feinstein. I am President and CEO of Nahash Pharmaceuticals."

"A subsidiary to Wyatt Pharmaceuticals," Stubbs said.

"Pharmaceuticals?" I said, "you must have something for my headache then, Rueb. Something without side effects though please. I don't want any anal leakage or anything."

"Yes, yes. Very funny. So I see that this is not an accident, you both being here. What can I do for you gentlemen?"

"You can tell us what you were stealing from BIOGENESIS, and where Dr. Estabados is. Yeah, let's start with those two things," I said.

"I think I need to know who you are before I get into denying any of your ridiculous accusations."

"My name is Warren Dennihan and this is Eric Stubbs. You can deny anything you want, but we know that Estabados was a double agent or mole or whatever. We can prove that he was on the books as an employee of BIOGENESIS, and your fabulous little friend at the front desk confirmed that he works here. I'm certainly no genius but it seems to me that something is askew. I wonder what the media would think? Whattaya think, Stubbs? Stuff like this goes very public, very quickly right?"

Stubbs didn't have a chance to answer.

"I don't believe you know half of what you think you do." He sat behind his desk and straightened out something on his pants, he was definitely picking at something while he thought about what to do or say. "I will only say that Nahash and BIOGENESIS compete rather vigorously in different areas because we are after some of the same things."

"How politically correct, Rueb. What the hell does that mean? What are you both after? And why did you have to kill three people to get it?"

What the hell? He was talking, so why not go for broke. In for a penny, in for a pound.

He was lost in thought for a few moments. Again, I can only assume that he was looking at damage control. Because what he told us was far more than what he should have.

Everyone around this case so far was talking about confidentiality — this, and trade secrets — that. This Estabado was all about stealing trade secrets and research. In terms of sound business decisions, telling two people who stormed into his offices, whom he had not vetted, was just stupid.

"Do you know what Nahash means?"

"Enlighten me. My vocab ain't what it used to be."

"It is Hebrew for serpent."

I shit you not, I looked at Stubbs and thought, *is this guy going to confess to ordering the murders of the victims?*

"A pharmaceutical company named after a snake in a religious language. No separation of Church and State for you guys, huh?"

"Did you know that snake venom is already being used as a drug for people with heart conditions?"

Stubbs and I looked at each other and we both shook our heads. He took that to mean 'no' because he continued.

"We hold the patent, and Wyatt currently has in distribution, a drug in pill form for those with high cholesterol and who are at risk of a heart attack. You may have heard of it."

"Fluxir? Flexor? Something like that right?"

"Yes. We - "

" — did *you* know that all three victims of the serial killer were either bitten by, or made to look like they were bitten by, snakes?"

"I assumed. The news coverage had been extensive. The accidental death that has now been linked to all three was originally blamed on an unruly sna — "

" — so why isn't anybody beat'n down your door?"

"I'm sure it is just a matter of time before they do. But I can assure you that we have nothing to do with these victims."

"So you're saying the snake thing is just a huge coincidence?"

"We don't keep snakes here at the lab or in any of our buildings. We hired Dr. Estabados because of his expertise at the World Toxin Bank."

497

"Refresh my memory on what that is again." I was playing stupid, keep him talking.

"SCMU campus houses a library which holds the most complete collection of samples of natural toxins in the world. Frogs, lizards, scorpions, eels, spiders, bees, pufferfish, snails, insects, even some mammals all secret venom for a myriad of reasons."

"And snakes." The second victim died at a lab at SCMU. This guy was an idiot.

"Yes, and snakes. We are only interested in snakes. BIOGENESIS studies snake venom to create synthetic compounds, just as we do. They also have theories on other types of toxins found in nature, which is why they have sponsored the World Toxin Bank at SCMU."

"If everything is so confidential, how do you know that? Estabados?"

"The WTB is available to researchers all over the world. For a price. We have been unable to attain the access that we need. For reasons of self-incrimination, let's just say that it is my job to know what my competitors, such as BIOGENESIS, do on a daily basis and leave it at that."

"So why try to get them out of the way? If only part of what they do is what your company is focused on, why not merge or something?"

"This is cutting edge science. There is room at the table for everyone. I don't want them out of the picture. What I want is access to the World Toxin Bank and to beat them to the cure of very specific ailments. There are over 100,000 animals on this planet that have evolved to produce venom, and every few generations, they mutate. Some venom changes with either the prey's or the secreting animal's diet. So you see, there are an infinite number of combinations, and an almost unlimited amount of research that can be executed."

"Executed. That's a good word, the appropriate one. You are basically saying that you have unlimited resources for poison."

"You have no idea what you are talking about. There is an enormous difference between a toxin and poison. Venom is a toxin. If venom were a poison, the secreting animal wouldn't be able to then eat their prey after they inject it. Venom is injected, a poison is ingested — "

" — you say tomato, I say — "

" — if you would let me finish, sir. Venom contains toxic proteins and short strings of amino acids called peptides. Because of the ever-changing mutations and diets, we can only estimate that there are about 20 million venom toxins. That we know of, or can fathom. The World Toxin Bank, which my competitor has in its hip pocket, so far has only about 10 thousand samples. So you do the math, who would have easier access to a toxin?"

"Estabados. How's my math?"

He looked away from us and fixed his gaze on the bank of windows in the corner of the room. He was lost in thought again. Probably trying to help me and the silent Stubbs understand what the hell he was talking about. I was starting to get lost. All I knew is what I had known when I was marched into this room, that Estabados was in neck-deep. My only reason for finishing the conversation was to see if Rueben was involved also.

He started talking again, but didn't bother to look at us.

"Those toxic proteins and peptides that I told you that are found in venom? Each one has a very specific purpose, and that is what makes venom such a wonderful substance." He turned to face us again, to bring home his point. "They all have varying molecules with varying targets, which is what makes the science so cutting edge. Don't you see? While one venom might target the nervous system which paralyzes the messages from nerves to muscles, another might eat cells, which makes tissues collapse. Yet another might clot blood which makes it thick so blood cannot move and stops the heart, while its counterpart in yet another strain can prevent blood from clotting. Depending on what you want to target, you can use venom to cure Multiple Sclerosis, Arthritis, Diabetes, Cancer, Alzheimer's, Parkinson's, Heart Disease .... you could isolate the target to the point of curing everything from Depression to Nicotine Addiction. The possibilities are endless."

"And you wanted all of those possibilities to yourself."

"NO. NO. NO. You are not understanding what I am telling you. Compared to BIOGENESIS, we are small potatoes. All of those facilities out there, that you pasted on your way into my building, are *waiting* for samples of venom so we can begin to create these miracle drugs. We have created only one so far, and the rest are on the drawing board. It will be years before any of what we do gets to a pharmacy, if the FDA lets us get there at all. Estabados is to help us with that. BIOGENESIS has access to the World Toxin Bank, we don't. BIOGENESIS is on the verge of some major breakthroughs; but as I told you, those comparatively comprise one cell, off of one fingernail, off an entire human being."

"So where is Estabados?"

"You *still* think Dr. Estabados had something to do with these deaths?"

"I think, from what you just told us, that your good Doctor was number two in a huge machine. And now he gets to be number one and in on the ground floor of what could be another huge machine. I think that he had, and maybe still does have ties to the World Toxin Bank. We have three deaths and somebody wrongly accused for them. He had motive, he had access, and now part of BIOGENESIS is shut down because of it. If you would like me to get the police involved, or the media, I would be happy to do so. Otherwise, tell me where Estabados is."

I knew he didn't want the police to be involved, otherwise they would have already been there to arrest us. There was more to this than meets the eye, and the Doctor was the key to it, I was sure.

He turned back to face the windows. The long, early summer day was coming to a close and sun was fading into sunset on the other side of the building. The forest trees were reflecting the reds and oranges, while the stars were trying to wake up for the night.

"Costa Rica. He is taking samples in Costa Rica."

7

THE TWO INVESTIGATORS HAD NO SOONER left the office of Rueben Feinstein and he was on his phone. While the two gentlemen could do nothing to him legally, they could still pose quite a threat to his enterprise.

The President and CEO of Nahash Pharmaceuticals had underlings still in the building that were at his beck and call. It was late, and most of the employees that worked at one or more of the buildings had gone home for the day. A cleaning crew or two may have been lingering but for the most part the entire complex was empty. Rueben, some security personnel, and Jeffery his assistant were all that were left in the Administrative Building.

"Jeffery, get me connected with Enrique on the secure satellite phone please."
"Is this with regard to the gentleman who was flirting with me earlier?"
"Jefferey, I don't have time for your nonsense. Just get Enrique on the line right now."
"Yes sir."

Rueben had always been fascinated with snakes. He had spent his first seven years in this world living with his parents in Brooklyn, New York. He grew up in a Jewish community, not devout, but they went to Temple every week. His father paid for good seats, until he was laid-off. The garment factory could not keep up with the rising costs of doing business in the City in the 1950s. What was once a thriving business that paid it's workers well, was the shell of a building being sold for the real estate value. But there were many jobs available in the South. Rueben's father had a line on a job in South Carolina, so off they went.

Generally speaking, people in the South don't like New Yorkers. That is somewhat true today, and it was definitely true in the late 50s. They didn't like Yankee accents or their sense of superiority, even if it was just a perception. Maybe it was just the remnants of the ideals that

501

the 'South Will Rise Again!'. Or maybe it was that not many people from New York were Baptist. The Feinsteins were definitely not Baptist.

Rueben had no friends. Not people anyway. He found a pet snake within his first week in his new home. It wasn't difficult, South Carolina was rife with them. Especially in the country. Going from Brooklyn, New York to the back woods of western South Carolina was a culture shock to say the least. Nobody liked him, and he didn't like them or their 'Sweet Jesus' ways. All Rueben had were his snakes.

"Dr. Estabados is on the secure line, Sir. The signal is five by five," Jeffery said through the speaker on Rueben's desk phone.

"Thank you Jeffery. You may go home for the night now."

"Thank you sir. Should we alert the security at the main gate about our earlier visitors?"

"I'll take care of that, thank you."

Rueben picked up his Iridium 9555 satellite phone to connect to the one just like it in another time zone. The hand held device looked like an expensive walkie talkie but had the capability of securely speaking to anyone on the planet via satellite versus a cell tower. The secure line could also send and retrieve data by connecting it to laptops and other gear.

"Enrique. How is the field?"

"I have collaborated with the locals and we have a team here. The lab is rudimentary but we can make do."

"Excellent. When do we start sampling and when can we get molecular data to our researchers here? I have ten buildings full of people with their thumbs up their asses."

"I have some more people that I need to hire in order to ease the process. These people are very touchy about their natural resources. Any time the locals, especially the Government, thinks that we are going to damage their ecosystem, they come out with guns ablaze. Literally.

"I have the skeleton of a security team which we have already used, but should have a full compliment that is fully operational by tomorrow. Two days, maybe three, and we can start analyzing samples."

"Have there been any problems with the locals so far?"

"No. We have been covert, but there is another, more urgent problem."

"What is it?"

"The other entities down here. We are not the only ones. I am working as quickly as I can to, how shall I say? .... eradicate them and relieve them of their data. But there are at least five universities down here at the behest of other companies that are sponsoring them. New Colorado State and the University of Florida have been eliminated from the competition as of today. But we still have the University of Delaware, University of Utah, and the University of

Chicago that are still an issue. Not to mention the Clodomiro Picado Research Institute and the religio-"

" — what have they learned?"

"I cannot say what the others have learned, but New Colorado and Florida have made significant strides in analyzing, among others, the Bothrops Asper. I was going over all of their data and it seems that not only are the aspers excitable, unpredictable, and unbelievably dangerous, but they reproduce faster than any other in their genus. Which makes their venom mutations occur exponentially faster. Their venom is a virtual kaleidoscope of peptides with ever-changing attack sites. We just need to fix the other problem that I was about to mention before it is too late."

"More problems? Other than the Goddamned researchers? Just get rid of them and clean it up. Accidents happen. It's the rainforest for Christ sake."

"I told you, I would take care of them. It's those religious nuts again. They are very well funded and very well organized. They have taken to air-dropping toxic mice into the field. I have no idea how they get through the very tight Government controls down here, but they are doing it."

"Air-dropping toxic mice? What the hell are talking about, Enrique?"

"I inspected one of the mice today. It's rather ingenious actually. They give the mice Acetaminophen, which is harmless to them, but is poisonous to the snake. They are killing off the snakes here like genocide."

"*What*? They give the mice Tylenol and what, just give them little parachutes or something?"

"Yes. Precisely. The little parachutes get caught in the trees, which makes them easy prey and an easy meal for our precious material. Once they are dead their venom is rendered useless to us. But at least they won't have headaches."

"This is not funny! Get on it Estabados! We cannot let them do this! Do whatever it is you have to do, but make sure you take care of it. And I mean quickly."

"Yes sir."

"Oh, and I almost forgot. The reason I called. Two investigators came looking for you today. They seemed fixated on the three murders here in Charleston. One of them, the smaller one, seemed very tenacious. The other one was a monster but he was quiet. If I were a betting man, I would say that they are coming down there to pay you a visit."

"Pay *me* a visit? How do they know that I am down here, sir?"

"I'm not sure. They might be with BIOGENESIS. Be on the look out. I will forward you the pictures from the security footage. If you see them, take care of them."

"I'm not sure I am going to be able to contain all of this .... collateral damage sir."

"Just take care of it." Rueben terminated the transmission before Enrique could respond. He then turned around to look out his windows, but there was no view. Night had befallen the forested backdrop. Everything was pitch black. He needed to think things through.

You wanted to be the number one guy? Welcome to the big leagues, son.

8

AFTER THE MEETING WITH RUEBEN FEINSTEIN, we headed back into downtown Charleston. Which, oddly, they call uptown. I again drove because Stubbs said that he wanted to jot down the conversation we had just had with the President and CEO of Nahash while it was still fresh in his mind. I was beginning to think that he didn't like to drive, because he seemed to have repeated excuses for not wanting to.

When he was finished, we called JG using the bluetooth interface technology of the *AMG*. He could hear both of us and we definitely heard him in perfect Dolby Digital 5.1 surround sound that was generated from the Harman Kardon *LOGIC7* entertainment system. Man, that car is sweet.

Stubbs informed JG that the Doctor that had defected over to Nahash was a prime suspect. Like his girlfriend and client, he too had access to the three victims. He also had the means, just like accused. But he had a motive, whereas Sierra Byrne did not.

Dr. Estabados had been an undercover spy, if you will. Informing Nahash on trade secrets, stealing information, maybe even samples from the World Toxin Bank. Not only did he not want to get caught, he wanted to get rich. Getting in on the ground floor of what could be billions of dollars was good for his wallet.

Dr. Byrne had no such interest. JG, our boss and her boyfriend, was filthy rich. She was the lead consultant or whatever to BIOGENESIS, and I was sure that she made a pretty penny as a tenured professor at SCMU. What possible reason would she have to kill colleagues that were working toward modern medical breakthroughs? None that we could think of. But that didn't stop Detective Fischer now did it?

Dr. Enrique Estabados was in Costa Rica, however, which made putting his feet to the fire all but impossible.

Or was it? JG told us that he would make the jet available to us. Stubbs was virtually dusting off his passport, but mine was back in Boston. Who brings a passport to South Carolina? It is definitely another world, but it's still in the same Country.

JG, of course, had a fix for that too. He had a company that he had used in the past that could get me a replacement passport within 24 hours. He would let us know in the morning what time the flight left.

I had never been to Costa Rica before. I didn't really have a deep desire to either. And I'm not sure why.

I dropped Stubbs off at SCMU, where we left his ride in favor of the *AMG*. He really was the Southern version of me. He drove the same Escalade that I drove back in Boston. I mentioned that I had the same ride back home. I also asked him why he didn't like to drive. He did love to drive, he said, but he found that sports sedans were a bit too confining for a man his size. He preferred his truck.

After a short conversation about the day to come, we bid each other a fond adieu. I think he might have wanted to go get a drink or something but I had other designs on the evening.

The night before, I tried to seek and destroy an old acquaintance of mine in Jennifer Beaumont. Jenna. I had failed. I couldn't even find her. At the time, she was the most beautiful woman I had ever met, in person. Inside and out. But that changed the following day, that day, when I met Detective Carina Fischer.

She told me to stay away from the case, but I felt that it was the right thing to do to inform her that she had arrested the wrong suspect. The wrong would-be serial killer. I insinuated as much earlier that day, but this time I had proof. Well, kinda. Plus I wanted to see about getting into her pants.

She hated me. Which meant that I wanted her all the more. She was hot, fiery, and confident. She knew sports and was not afraid to speak her piece. I was intrigued and I wanted her in the worst way.

When men really want something, they will go to great lengths to get it. Search everywhere to find it, even the dark recesses of their brain. I am no different. She had asked me earlier if I was with the 'eighty broad'. Which meant 80 Broad Street. I was on my way to pay her a visit. I didn't care that she told me to stay away from the case. Insinuating that I should also stay away from her.

I arrived at the Crimes Against Persons building of the Charleston Police Department on 80 Broad Street at about 9:00 PM. The old guy at the reception desk paid me no mind as he was much more interested in his *National Rifle Association* periodical. Which was fine by me. I was happy about the fact that he was preoccupied, I could not have cared less what he reads.

The vestibule on the way in told me where the Homicide Division was located, so I shuffled on past the man at the front desk that probably should have been retired. There was a man in shirtsleeves and a loosened necktie in an office off the left, and at one of the sea of desks in the middle of the room was Detective Fischer. She was slumped with her back to me under a desk lamp. I walked through the long room, weaving through the desk farm, approaching her from behind. In retrospect, it is unwise to approach someone that is armed from behind them.

"Wanna get a cup of coffee or a late supper?"

Her head shot up as she saw me come around to the right side of her desk from behind her. She had an empty chair there, so I occupied it.

"You." She paused and looked behind her and around the room. "It's a little late in the day for coffee and I don't know what a *supp-ah* is. What is that, some kinda sissy drink?"

"What? No. It's a meal."

"What'er y'all doin' here? And how did you know where to find me?"

"I came to see if I could have a chat with you. Maybe a meal."

"What, like a date? I don't date possible suspects."

"Suspect? What am I suspected of?"

"Nothin' yet, darlin'. But I told you to stay out of my way and here you are. I'm bettin' you will be."

"C'mon. What harm is it in having a friendly conversation? Think of the positive reviews your Board of Tourism will have."

"How do you know I'm not married?"

"No ring. And the way you were eye-fuckin' me earlier today, I just know. Plus if you were happy, you'd be home in bed with the guy. It's after nine."

"Yer pretty cocky, ain't ch'a? Whattaya wanna talk to me about anyways?"

"You'll have to buy me a drink first. I'm not that easy."

"Yeah, I'll bet."

She took me to what she called a 'honky tonk'. I think that is what she calls a bar, because that is what it was. They had whiskey, so I was happy.

To my surprise she had one too. We settled into a relatively quiet corner where I started the conversation and made my first mistake of the evening.

"A pretty girl like you should be a model or somethin'. How are you a cop?"

"If I had a nickel for every piece a shit with a red neck and a small dick that asked me that? I'd be a rich girl."

"I didn't mean anything by it. I was just thinkin' that it might be tough to be taken seriously, looking the way you do."

"In the beauty lies the struggle."

"What is that, Shakespeare?"

"Is playin' stupid an act, or are you really not very bright?"

"I make up for it in other ways. But back to you. People probably give you a hard time. More than they give other cops. Men."

"I can handle myself, darlin'. It doesn't take-'em long to figure out that you don't have to mess with a bull to get hurt with a horn. You Yankees all think that pretty Southern girls are fragile and lookin' for a man to take care of 'em. This is gonna be a short conversation if you don't get over that notion and right quick. Now enough about my looks, and lets get on with why you wanted to talk to me."

She may have said to ignore her looks, but I just couldn't. Her hazel eyes and pouty lips were not to be ignored. She had pulled back her auburn hair which displayed her long neck. She was tall and athletic, made taller by her high-heeled boots. Victoria's Secret models could eat their collective heart out.

"Have you ever heard of Nahash Pharmaceuticals, Carina?"

"My name is Carina. Not Carin-er, or whatever you just said."

"It's my accent, I know what your name is. Your accent is pretty thick also. Do you know of them or not?"

"Yes. They are out in Summerville. How have *you* heard of 'em?"

"Listen, I know you told me to stay away from this case, but there are things that you should know. Things that I am very sure that you don't."

"My end of the case is closed. I have my suspect locked up. The DA always wants more, but you can't bleed a stone. Hell he'd love it we could get a confession out of 'em all, but life ain't perfect. Your lawyer-friend may have gone to Harvard and all, but he's puttin' the wood to the suspect. So pardon me if I don't rush on over to side of innocent just yet."

"He went to BU."

"What?"

"You said Harvard, but he didn't go to Harvard."

"In that case never mind. Let me just call the DA and see about gettin' the good Doctor released. How could I have been so careless?"

"You're a ball-buster. I like it. But there is more that you don't know. And if this case is closed on your end, why were you interviewing the protestors?"

"You've got plenty a balls to bust, I'll give ya that. You come down here and think you can just muscle your way into this. That's why we don't like you Northerners, you think you're better'n us. You think you're smarter than us too. But you don't know shit about shit."

She paused to take a sip of her whiskey. By sip I mean she slung it back.

"Did you know that your good Doctor, Sierra Byrne, has a juvenile record. This ain't her first rodeo. People think that juvenile records are sealed, well not when you're suspected of a Class A Felony. That thing flies open even if it was expunged.

"Has she come up with an alibi yet? Cuz she didn't have one when we arrested her. She wasn't where she claimed to be. She said that she was with her attorney, your boss. But she wasn't. In fact, nobody could place Attorney Grantes where he said he was either. He has a verifiable alibi for the first two, so he gets a pass. For murder, not for bein' a bad judge of character. I'm guessin' from the expression on your face that you didn't know any of that."

I didn't. That definitely complicated getting Dr. Byrne off the hook quickly. Where had she been for all three murders? And why hadn't JG mentioned that fact?

I ordered us another round of drinks and told Carina what had transpired the rest of my day. I told her about how competitive Big Pharma is. How they all beg, borrow, and steal to get their hands into the best universities. The best researchers. The best possible data.

I told her about our visit with Rueben Feinstein and his obvious reluctance to contact the police even when his security had been breached. About Dr. Enrique Estabados, who was essentially a double agent working for Nahash, and how he had set BIOGENESIS back decades according to Jarod Lynde. That the lab was shut down.

"My heart bleeds for 'em. But what does that have to do with tha price of tea 'n China?" She slung back the rest of her second whiskey and winked at the nearby male bartender who had been eyeing her since the minute she walked in the joint. He didn't need to be told to pour another round. He probably spit in mine.

"What that has to do with China, is that Nahash needs access to the World Toxin Bank, which they don't have access to currently. They are struggling while SCMU and BIOGENESIS are getting rich. Dr. Estabados was the number two guy, so his name wasn't going on any of the research, success or fail. PROXER stock prices are already a car payment per share, so investing in them is pointless. But if he tanks BIOGENESIS and gets in on the ground floor with Nahash, which is backed by Wyatt Pharmaceuticals and could also be elevated to the number one spot. These three murders are worth millions, maybe billions. And that, girl, is a lot of tea."

"You're a little short on proof though, Warren."

"Deni. Call me Deni. And Estabados fled the Country. He is hiding in Costa Rica. Besides, you must have a serial killer psychological profiler or something in your department. Does Sierra Byrnes being a mass murderer fly?"

"You watch too much CSI. We don't make psychological profiles on every suspect, we certainly can't afford one on staff full-time. A female serial killer is rare, which is different from mass murder. Your Boston Marathon asshole was a mass murderer. He did a lot of damage at one time. A serial killer kills outta anger, the thrill, for attention, or for money."

"Exactly. Money. Sierra Banks doesn't need money, she is dating my friend. My boss. He is stupid rich."

"That was just one of the motivations. We have to study all the psychological modeling published by the FBI, its part of my job. But they all don't fall neatly into place. For every profile that fits dead on the nose, there are the outliers. Did you know the first female serial killer ever recorded was right here in Charleston?"

"No shit?"

"None. It was back in the early 1800s. Her name was Fisher, but spelled different from mine. Anyways, her and her husband owned a hotel here, poisoned their guests and snuck the bodies out through trap doors. I think there might even be a tour if your interested."

That was an interesting side note. I wasn't sure if she was getting drunk or what the point of telling me that was. She flagged the bartender with her beautiful eyes again, but the drinks were already made and on their way over to us on our server's tray. I know I was getting drunk.

"Are you drunk, or what's your point? You still haven't said why you were conducting interviews on a closed case."

"I was dottin' my eyes, sorta thang."

"And?"

"Try and keep up with me, darlin'. What I'm sayin' is that sometimes there's just a black widow. She gets messed up as a child and does shit where she gets a taste for killin'. Like your Dr. Byrne. Serial killers are always perceived to have a high IQ, but they are usually about average. Unlike the movies, most villains don't have advanced degrees. Ninety-three IQ I think is the average figure. And serial killers usually ain't female. But they don't always fit the mold. But of all female serial killers, over half of 'em use poison and are organized. That sound like anybody you know?"

Organized, used poison, and smart? Yeah. It sounded familiar.

510

I woke up the next morning with a huge hangover and a kitten had crawled into my mouth. It may have died in there. The bright light glared in from a window that I knew was not the one from my room at JG's house. It was on the wrong side of the bed for starters. I quickly realized that I was not alone in bed, either. I would recognize that head of hair anywhere.

Carina had her back to me sleeping, snoring in fact, on the other side of the bed. She slept in the fetal position, which if I hadn't been so hung-over I would have found adorable. I lifted the covers enough to realize that I was naked, and let my hands do some reconnaissance to find that she was also. But my hands were cold.

"Aaaah. Warm your hands up first." She turned to face me. How was it possible that she was just as hot the morning after a night of drinking as she was while roaming the streets?

"What happened last night?"

"You don't remember? It was a hoot'n a half."

"I'm a little hazy."

"Lightweight."

"What do you weight, like a hundred pounds? How were you not blitzed?"

"You handled yourself alright."

"Oh yeah?"

"I did most of the work, but you can make that up to me right now."

I didn't mind that job one bit.

I had managed to have sex before my morning coffee. Which was rare. This woman was not bashful or reserved, which for me was also rare. When she was through with me, she left the bed as naked as the day she was born. She didn't cover herself in a sheet or tell me to look away, she just got out of bed and let me watch her go into the bathroom. She didn't even close the door when she got into the shower.

I guess when you look like she does, you get used to people staring at you. She was by far the most beautiful and most interesting woman I had ever been with. She didn't care what people thought, which is also unlike any woman I had ever been with. Her slender and perfect body is forever burned into my brain.

My iPhone rang while Carina was showering. It was JG. He told me that because he didn't know until too late in the day yesterday that we had to go to Costa Rica, my passport wouldn't be ready today, but we would fly out at oh-dark-thirty the following morning. I told him that was good, because we needed to talk. Today. That he needed to make time for me. He told me to meet him at 1:00 PM at a cafe on campus, and that he would call Stubbs to make sure he was there also. I liked Stubbs, but if he knew about Dr. Byrne's past and didn't tell me, we were going to have problems. I don't care how big he is.

When she returned from the shower and dressed, she was all questions.

"Are you sick? Do you have Alopecia?"

"No. I was drunk but my memory is fine. Mostly."

"Alopecia not Amnesia. The not having any body-hair thang."

"Oh. That. It didn't seem to bother you too much."

"So are you trying to show off all of those tattoos or all of your scars?"

"Being hairless isn't a choice, it's a lifestyle."

"You don't have to tell me, darlin', I'm a woman. I spend half my life shavin' my legs. Between ladyscapin', sleep, and the job, my day is pretty full. I'm askin' why *you do* it."

"You have very long legs, I'm sure it takes a while."

"Are you gonna answer me or not?"

"It's not just one reason. I have many. I don't understand why all women don't like it. Who wants a mouth full of hair? Can we get off of this subject now, please? I have a headache."

"Sure. So what are y'all plannin' on doin' today? It better be nothin' to do with this case. Don't let last night and this mornin' fool ya. I will bust you for interferin' if I have to."

I thought it was oddly sexy that she was ball-breaker, but not that early in the morning and not with a hangover.

"I'm going to talk to the boys about what you told me last night. About Byrne's past."

"The boys?"

"JG and Stubbs. Eric Stubbs."

"Oh Eric! Now he's a sweetheart."

"You know him?"

"Everybody knows him. He's like a local celebrity. He only had two minutes of fame with the Atlanta Falcons, but he will always be famous in our hearts. Big 'ol teddy bear that one. Just don't make him mad. That boy is like a bruin in body-armor you get him mad."

"So you *really* know him."

"Not like that, but yes. We went on one date. But I never called him back. Poor thang. Since we're gettin' into pasts sorta after-the-fact, you got a girl back home?"

"Not really. I have an on and off kinda *thang* with this chick who is crazy about me."

Althea was her name but I didn't get into it with Carina. She loved me right, but loved me wrong at the same time. Every once in a while I would run into Althea while on a case. Or

512

I made sure to seek her out so that she could help me on a case. There was nobody on earth that could handle a computer better. Not that I knew personally anyway. We would always end up in the sack, which would lead us down the same old path. She is needy and I need space.

"Girl. Or woman. Not chick. We don't like to be called chicks. It comes from the word 'shiksa'. Which essentially means an outcast woman. It's not nice."

"Well, get over it. Because you are very hot chick. And that's a compliment."

"Very funny. I gotta go to work, so you gotta go. But I'll give you my number in case you wanna call me sometime."

"How about tonight?"

"Smotherin' me already? When do you go home?"

"When this case is over."

"I'll pretend that I didn't hear that."

9

I HAD DRUNKEN SEX ON THE FIRST DATE BEFORE, but I really liked it this time. It wasn't just because she was super-model hot. It wasn't that she was smart and obviously had a wealth of useless knowledge. It wasn't that she was superbly confident in herself and what she wanted. Or maybe it was. But there was something about that woman that I can't put into words that drove be me bat-shit crazy. Maybe it was her foul mouth. I know my language could use some cleaning.

I had to find my car. Well, not my car but the one that I was using. The *AMG* had been left on the street overnight and I had hoped that it would be all right. The application was automatically downloaded onto my iPhone when it was synched to the *AMG*, and fortunately is was right where I had last parked it. The map appearing on my iPhone allowed me to walk directly to the car, which surprisingly didn't take long. It turns out that if you leave your car in front of a police station overnight, nobody tows it or even touches it. I was relieved.

By the time I got back to JG's house, had some coffee and freshened up, it was about time to find the cafe. I remembered that nothing on that campus was marked, so it was going to take some time to find the place where I was supposed to meet JG and Stubbs. And it did take a long time. Even the map on my phone had a difficult time. Plenty of time to get there turned into I was late.

JG and Stubbs were already out at an outdoor table on the patio of the cafe when I got there. They didn't have any drinks or food yet, so I wasn't *that* late. Or the service was terrible.

I made my way over to them, but I was made to go through the cafe first from the inside instead of just going over or through the outside gate.

"Hey guys, sorry I'm late. JG, why is nothing on this campus marked? How does anybody find anything? How do these kids make it to class?"

"We figure it out. Let's get going because I don't have a lot of time, even less now."

He was testy today. The early summer sun was bright and beautiful. Most of the other tables were utilizing their umbrellas for shade, but we were not. I could feel my Irish skin getting a sunburn. The campus and the cafe were not busy, I assumed because it was summer and fewer students were taking classes in the summer. Either way we were out of earshot and eavesdroppers.

"I found out some things last night, and we have a lot to discuss. You two have been holdin' out on me. You might need to clear your calendars," I said.

"I'm not sure I like your tone, Warren."

"And I don't like being kept in the dark, Jacob."

"Gentlemen. Why don't we calm down and chat like civil people," Stubbs said. Odd that the big brawler was the voice of reason in this trio, but he was.

"I met with Carina last night and she told me that you provided an alibi for Dr. Byrne . An alibi which proved to be false. She said that nobody can account for her whereabouts on any of the nights the victims were murdered. She said that you weren't where you said you were, but they *can prove* that you were nowhere near the murders. Which then leaves me to wonder two things. One, you aren't guilty of murder, but you are covering them up, which is a crime. And two, did you have any part or know about this Stubbs?"

"No. What's going on JG?"

"She's Carina now huh?" JG said to me.

"I think that you are fixated on the wrong point here, kid."

"Listen, it's not what you think. I didn't kill anybody. Deni, you of all people should know that I would not risk my freedom unless absolutely necessary."

"I'm listening," I said.

"I was with Jenna the night of the third murder."

"Who?" Stubbs asked.

"His ex. Girlfriend not wife. It's a long story. I'll fill you in later."

"We had to discuss logistics. She has money and assets that were left to her from my ex-mother-in-law, and money and possessions from when we lived together. Our breakup was too painful for her, so she was moving out of Charleston. To Savannah, I think. Sierra is very smart and level-headed, but spending the night with Jenna, my ex-girlfriend whom she was jealous of, would not have been good. I knew that she was incapable of the heinous murders, so I covered for her. It was impulsive."

"Why was she jealous of your ex-girlfriend, JG?" Stubbs asked.

"Jenna has the type of conventional beauty that stops traffic. While Sierra is incredibly smart and stunningly beautiful, she was not able to get past Jenna's looks. It bothers her that her jealousy isn't rational, but deep-down she knows that things are over between Jenna and I. It would have upset her to know that I met with her that night."

JG had a point. I don't care how level-headed you are, Jenna incites attention and jealousy. It wasn't her goal or intent, but when you look like she does, it just happens. Flaxen hair and jade eyes on a body like that of Sophia Vergara. She gets noticed.

Dr. Sierra Byrne was also strikingly beautiful, albeit in less of an in-your-face kind of way. I have never succumbed to the whole jealousy thing, but in my business I have seen enough about the damage it does. Unfortunately some people lie and cheat. Spending your every waking moment of everyday wondering if your partner is one of those people, may just drive them to do so.

"Well she obviously knows that you were lyin', JG. She knows you weren't with her on the nights of the murders, and you told the police that she was with you on the night of the last one. Like you said, she is smart. Your credibility is takin' a bit of a beat'n here, kid."

"Another reason that we need to prove her innocence. In order to save my reputation, and my relationship with her, we need to extricate her from her current predicament."

"Did she say where she was on all of those nights? You covered for her — "

" — I covered for her on only *one* of the nights. My thinking was that if she had an alibi for one, she couldn't be a plausible suspect in all three. She said that she was doing research in the labs those nights. She teaches, has projects at SCMU, the World Toxin Bank, and at BIOGENESIS. She is very busy."

"Only I have looked into her schedule and calendars. All of those facilities are secure, you need one of her ID badges to get into her offices or any of the labs. They weren't used, which means unless she passed through without using an ID, she wasn't where she said that she was on any of the nights when she said that she was there," Stubbs explained.

"And what is the likelihood that she was able to access any of those facilities without an ID, Stubbs?" I already sorta knew that answer but I was driving a point home to my boss. The other one, not Stubbs.

"Nearly impossible. The murderer at BIOGENESIS used an ID badge from a former cleaning crew employee. I say former, because the person hadn't worked there in over three years. But they took out the CCTV footage. But that employee ID wouldn't be able to get into the SCMU lab or the first victim's house," he explained further.

"Lets walk through this one more time to see if we can find some holes," I said. "The widely respected Dr. Sierra Byrne is a busy woman. She teaches at SCMU, where she had undergrads and doctoral students. Where she also heads the research for biotoxins, herpetology and venomology for that university. Her school also houses the World Toxin Bank, which is the authority on live samples of toxins, including snake venom. That university and the bank therein are funded, in large part, by BIOGENESIS, which is a subsidiary of PROXER Pharmaceuticals, whom she consults with on several projects.

"The number two Big Pharma company is Wyatt, which owns Nahash. Nahash has their own doctor working covertly under Dr. Byrne, in order to steal the research. Three deaths happen, all related to SCMU. All fingers point to Sierra because she worked with these victims, is really the only person who has unique access to two of the three crime scenes and can circumnavigate those security protocols. She really has no motive, but she also has no alibi either.

"Meanwhile this prick Estabados, has left SCMU and is the number one guy over at Nahash Pharmaceuticals. He not only fled the university, but he fled to Costa Rica in order to attain their own samples to start their own library of toxins. Do I have this right, so far?"

"You missed the part where Dr. Enrique Estabados also had the same access privileges *and* he had motive," Stubbs said.

"Right. Does he have an alibi? Was he investigated and cleared?"

"I don't know. Maybe you can ask Carina."

"Funny. We also have to discuss, speaking of information that I got from Detective Fischer, the fact that Dr. Byrne has a juvenile record."

Stunned silence infected the table. I waited for the weight of my words to settle in the brains of my two bosses. The fact that the famous Dr. Byrne had a record was obviously news to both of these men.

"Not possible," JG said. "She would have never cleared the background checks necessary for either the university or BIOGENESIS. What did Detective Fischer say that she did?"

"Juvenile record probably didn't show up on a background check. So you didn't know about it?"

"No, but that doesn't mean that she is a serial killer. What did she do?"

"I don't know, but it has to be pretty bad. We are going to need to ask her."

"I will ask her, Deni. Not we," JG said.

"Fair enough. You have anything else for me? Stubbs, no? You, JG?"

JG didn't answer. He was lost in thought about hearing for the first time that his beloved had a juvenile record that was severe enough to be re-examined and inserted into this case.

"No, but I did research Costa Rica a little bit last night while you were busy with Detective Fischer," Stubbs said after another awkward silence that was palpable.

What did he mean by busy? What did he know? Those thoughts ran through my mind along with *I gotta remember to ask Carina if she is going to look into Estabados after our chat last night.*

517

Which is why I was only half-listening to Stubbs. Which meant that nobody was fully listening to Stubbs.

" …. Costa Rica is a big Country, we can't just take a flight over there and hope to stumble into Estabados. But there is one central but large area where many universities and research projects go because of the diverse animal populations and the rainforest."

"Wait, what did you say? Are we are going into a rainforest? Like with the wildlife and shit?"

"Yes. Exactly. Where did you think we were going? The rainforest is located in the Tilaran Mountains which has an active volcano." Stubbs shuffled through some papers and read while continuing, "The Reserva Biologica Bosque Nuboso Monteverde, in the province of Puntarenas, is a tourist mecca for the wildlife and flora. But the research universities are permitted by the Government set up camps high up in the hills and rainforest, away from the tourists and modern comforts. That is where we are likely to find Estabados."

"Yeah, fuck that. Have fun. Keep me posted and let me know what I can do for you back here."

"You're not afraid are you? From what JG has told me, you're not afraid of anything."

"I don't have a passport." That was the only thing I could come up with at that moment.

JG was out of his funk and corrected me," you do in less than twenty-four hours. You leave at 9:00 AM tomorrow."

I wanted to call Carina once I was finished with the meeting at the cafe. I say meeting instead of lunch, because once I was informed of my impending trip, I was no longer hungry. I just needed to calm down first. I was nearly at the point of a panic attack.

I really don't like flying. I should clarify, I don't mind flying now that I was getting used to private jets. What I didn't like was the probability of crashing. You never hear of anybody surviving a plane crash. 'The odds are better of getting in a car crash' people say. And the way

I drive it is more than likely, but I can and have survived a car crash. My thinking is that with every flight I keep pushing the probability that something will go wrong on the flight, and you cannot survive that shit.

Aside from the flying, I really don't like going to foreign countries. I don't speak the languages, I don't know the customs, and from my experience the food always sucks. I went to Ireland some time ago on a case. It's my homeland and I had been meaning to check it out anyway, so my thinking was that it would be great. But apparently I don't speak the same language they speak, the weather was horrible, and the food was worse. That shit they serve you on St. Patty's is not what they eat in Ireland. I did love the whiskey though. That was where I fell in love with Redbreast.

But the big reason I didn't want to go on this trip was the real likelihood that I would be around snakes. I cannot express into words my hatred and fear of snakes. I am afraid of an aggressive worm. People have tried to reason with me; tried to explain that not all snakes are dangerous; but when something can move faster than me without arms, legs, or wings; I scream like a girl at a Justin Bieber show. Only not because I'm over-the-moon happy. With snakes there was the very real prospect of me soiling myself. I was going to have to bring extra underwear.

"Carina. You got a minute?" I had already added her into my contacts into my iPhone. The picture that I used was not one that she would appreciate, as I took it that morning while she was walking around naked.

"For you? Maybe one."

"Can we meet?"

"Sorry sweetie, but I don't have time for that kinda meetin'."

"That's not really what I was thinking but I like where your heads at. Have you looked into Estabados?"

"I told you that this case is off my desk. Why would I look into a case that has a suspect in lock-up? And why are you looking into him? This is all fun and games but if you go harassin' good citizens we're gonna have a problem."

"I spoke with Grantes about what you said last night. While Byrne may not have an alibi, she doesn't have motive either. Nobody but you thinks she did this. She may have been doin' somethin' shady but she ain't a serial killer. Estabados had the same access and he had a motive. Does he have an alibi?"

"Your attorney-boss lied to me, he is lucky I am not charging him with obstruction. I still might, along with you for interferin' if you don't knock it off."

"Do you know if he has an alibi or not?"

"No. Once we settled on Byrne, we stopped lookin'."

"I'm asking you to look. Please. For me."

"Why don't you do it, sense you are so hell-bent on breakin' the rules."

"Since."

"What, darlin'?"

"Since, not sense. Since I like to break the rules, not sense."

"I know how to speak, you ass. It's my accent. Yours is pretty hard to understand, we've been through this."

"Good point. Are you going to look into this or not? I would do this myself but I'm flyin' to Costa Rica in the morning. Me 'n Stubbs are gonna find Estabados."

"Is that really smart? If, and I do mean if, in the unlikely even that he is your serial killer, which I'm not sayin' he is, isn't it kinda dangerous to be huntin' him down in a foreign country? Besides, even if you do find him, it's gonna take more 'n a lick and a promise to get him back here."

"I've got Stubbs. Besides I can take care of myself."

"And *I've* seen your scars."

"I'll be back in a couple of days, can you help me or not?"

"We can talk about it tonight. You are comin' over to see me tonight, correct?"

"With an invitation like that, how can I refuse?"

"Pick me up at the station around 9:00 PM," she said.

"I'll wear somethin' clingy."

That night was magic. I was not drunk and able to focus on what I was doing. I couldn't keep my hands off of her. She seemed to be having the same struggle.

If our sex was compared to a boxing match, we were in a title fight. Round after sweaty round we went. And not just toe-to-toe.

We broke for food at one point. And some water. I had never felt so good in my life.

I had to get up at 3:00 AM in order to get home, change, and pack a bag for my flight. By get up I mean that I had to get up out of bed, because I was definitely already awake.

So was Carina.

"Hey Irish. Are y'all gonna come back and see me?"

"That's the plan. Are you gonna help me out? Look into Estabados?"

"You sure know how to ruin a moment."

"We've just had about fifty moments."

"Speak for yourself."

"Really? All that moanin' and grindin' and you didn't have a good time?"

"I was fakin'," she said with a shit-eating grin on her face.

"Yeah right. Ball-buster." *Sexiest ball-buster on the planet,* I thought.

"I'll see what I can do. Off the record. Just make sure you bring that dick back here. I kinda like it. My toys just ain't gonna cut it like they used to."

She was nasty and I loved every minute of it.

"I'll do my best."

10

NOBODY SHOULD EVER SEE 3:00 AM unless they are still up doing whatever debauchery that led them to that late hour. Which is what I was doing. Getting on a plane, going to a foreign place in Central America, where there are copious amounts of creepy-crawlies like snakes that want a taste of the Irish, is not my idea of a good time. I wanted alcohol. Or a drug like Prozac. I should have been relaxed. I was until I got on the plane at 8:30. I needed sleep. I needed something to help me relax, because there was no way I was going to be able to sleep. I was going to hell on earth and I was doing it sober, elevating it to the ninth circle of hell.

With the two hour time difference, the flight took four hours. We landed at Juan Santamaria International Airport in Alajuela, Costa Rica at 1:00 PM local time. Getting through Customs and acquiring transportation required a quarter of the flight time. There was no shortage of locals looking to make money on the fare from the airport to Puntarenas. The two and a half hour drive was going to make someone's week.

We climbed into the gold 1994 Toyota *Previa* that looked like it had a million miles on it. Believe it or not, it was the best looking vehicle big enough for Stubbs, me, and all of the gear we had brought. The suspension rode like there wasn't any. I looked for a seat belt on the front passenger bench, but there was only the broken receptacle. I should have counted myself lucky, Stubbs said that he had neither end of the harness on his third-row bench behind me. Every bump along Route 1, the Pan American Highway, was a struggle between hitting our heads on the ceiling or having the seats jammed so far into us it was like an experiment in proctology. I had only been in the Country for an hour and a half at that point, and I had already had my fill.

The driver was friendly enough. He fancied himself a tour-bus driver, giving us the play by play of everything we drove past. All 136 kilometers of the drive. To be honest, I really just wanted him to shut the fuck up. I was tired and cranky. Crankier than usual. But Stubbs was eating it up. He couldn't get enough of why we had to go South in order to travel Northwest. I wished that I had taken the seats in the far back of the van since Stubbs was so interested in what the driver had to say. Stubbs kept asking him to repeat himself. I didn't want to hear it the first time, I certainly didn't need the encore.

The roads were supposed to be major highways but were narrow, long, and windy. Every vehicle traveling in the opposite direction of us was engaging us in a game of chicken, neither driver wanting to yield on the shoulder.

The next road was a major artery, Route 27, and it was no-mans land. You could have told me we were in the middle of nowhere and I would have believed you. Mountains were always surrounding us, no matter which way we turned.

It wasn't until we crossed the 721 and headed closer to Route 23, that the road resembled a normal road. It had lines on it, delineating actual lanes for traffic, and guardrails. We went through several roundabouts headed West to some degree but remained predominantly South. We were traveling further and further away from where I thought we should be headed according the map I had purchased. It wasn't until we hit the coastal waters and kept them on our left, that I began to believe we could possibly be headed in the right direction. We traveled the coast, which was beautiful, seemingly ad infinitum before we headed East again onto Route 606 and the desolation resumed. We bounced along the long and circuitous roads through hills and mountains like Tigger and Pooh, the driver practically giving the life history of every tree.

There were a few communities once we reached the 620, but we didn't stop at them. No bathroom breaks, no food, and worse yet no drink. I wanted to have my whits about me but the tedium was driving me crazy. You can only be thrown around the inside of a *Previa* for so long before you want to kill something.

Once we reached the Reserva Biologica Bosque Nuboso Monteverde, otherwise known as the Cloud Forest, we were officially in the mountains. Green, lush, tropics with a few rustic hotels and even fewer walking paths. It was getting on 4:00 PM and we needed to find a guide further into this forest. I hoped that it would get cooler under the arboreal canopy, it was 80 degrees and humid as it had rained earlier that morning. It was said to rain again later that day, as it did every day in the 'green' or rain season. We were there in the beginning of it. I was ecstatic.

We hung out in the makeshift parking area, where the talkative driver had dropped us off, for about forty minutes when we spied a man with a hiking pack and gear. He was headed toward one of the dilapidated vehicles in the area that constituted the small park and ride. I approached him because Stubbs said his size might scare off the Latino.

"Excuse me. Do you speak English?"
"sí. Yes, but my Spanish es better. ¿Usted no habla español?"

523

I understood the word español but not the language. I certainly didn't speak it. In Boston we have an influx of Brazilians, which means Portugese. They both might be Latin-based, but they are not the same. You take your life into your own hands if you insinuate anything different back home. I made that mistake only once. I have dealt with a few Brazilians, so I can maybe sorta pick out a few words of Portugese, but not fluent in any Latin language. I was also brought up Catholic, as you can imagine. The Catholic schools that I attended as a kid required that we learn Latin. It would help us with other languages they had said. They were full of shit. I wonder how many 'Our Fathers' you have to say when you lie your ass off to dozens of little kids?

"Uh, no Spanish para mí." OK, I knew that much, but that was it.

"How I help?"

"We need a guide to bring us deep into the rainforest. We need to find our scientist friends."

I thought he was giving me a puzzled look, but I soon realized that Stubbs had come up behind me. Unbelievably, Stubbs spoke fluent Spanish. This guy was full of surprises. He spoke gibberish which I later found out was a bullsh story about us being from one of the universities and had to relay some sensitive information about a research project.

The guy nodded and said that he was finished working and had the next few days off.

"Tengo los próximos días apagado del trabajo a pasar con mi familia. Usted puede encontrar algún otro para dirigirle."

Stubbs was mumbling the translation to me while he spoke. I nodded my head because I knew the language that everyone spoke.

"What is your name?" I was digging into my wallet. I had plenty of cash. US dollars. I made sure he saw every bill.

"Hector." He said four or five other names after that, I think. All I understood was Hector.

I took out five $100 bills and handed them to him. What I didn't realize was that the exchange rate was about five hundred to one. I had given Hector ₡249,250, which was more than he made in a month at his regular tour job. He was listening.

I told Stubbs to tell him that he would get the other half when we got to where we were going, and I would double the amount if he would ensure that we got back here safely. We would have to revise the story we told him. There was going to be one more coming back. I hoped Estabados wasn't charming.

The prospect of almost a million Costa Rican Colones was too much for him to pass up. And my thinking was that two grand was short money if we would get outta there alive.

He told Stubbs that he was going to need to stock up on a few supplies for the three of us to make the journey, which would only take about a day, one way. Especially if we used the vast number of canopy lines along way. I gave him more money to attain said supplies.

At 6:00 PM we were backpacking our way into the rainforest. Stubbs had gathered and purchased gear for us after he had left the cafe on the SCMU campus the day before. He had gone to an REI store or something. He liked to hunt, fish, hike, camp and the like. I did not. I especially didn't like it in a place almost a continent away. And the new hiking boots were already giving me blisters. I had packed a small bag also. It contained mostly underwear. That bag was shoved into my large pack that I was lugging into the jungle.

The only thing about this little adventure that made me feel even somewhat safe was that I had Stubbs there. He knew the language and his size would make someone think twice about fucking with us. And we were able to sneak our guns into the Country. Again, that was all thanks to Stubbs. He was a clever monkey.

"If anyone sees a snake, you have my permission to shoot it. Consider it carte blanche, actually. If anything pokes out at us, feel free." I was last in the line, behind Stubbs who was behind Hector.

Hector took umbrage to my remark. "Nuestra fauna es muy preciosa a nosotros. usted no tirará nada."

"What did he say?" I asked Stubbs.

"He says 'nobody is shooting anything.'." It seemed like he used a lot more words than the four words that were translated to me, but I didn't argue.

It began to rain again by the time we reached the second canopy line. The harnesses and clips were complicated to figure out at first, but once you get the hang of it they're not that bad. I still had Hector double-check mine on the second, third, and fourth canopies because we weren't using helmets and a fall would likely kill me. The lines were long and strung up between towers that took us over these large ravines and rock formations. We were literally at or above the tree line of the rainforest. The only thing above us were the peaks of the Tilaran Mountains and sky.

It was slow going for the first few hours. We were having to deal with the tourists who were out there finishing for the day after their own tour groups looking at the colorful butterflies, lizards, toucans, and other wildlife. Stubbs and I were on a mission, Hector had seen them a countless times before and just as anxious to complete this adventure so he could collect his money.

We broke at well after nightfall. Technically we were never in the light because of the forest. Our packs were set up with small, battery-powered LED lights so we could see one another without casting too much light for predators.

We eventually did stop for the night, setting up the perimeter lanterns, set up camp and ate our meals from a pouch. The MREs were better than the kind the military get, Hector said.

Or at least that is what I understood him to say. He and Stubbs got on really well. I became the third wheel.

Since Hector brought it up, I asked him about the Costa Rican Military over our fire and sack of supper. He said that Costa Rica didn't have a military per se. The military was disbanded around 1950. What used to be a Government Militia was now a security for hire. Meaning townships usually hire would-be soldiers to protect their own. *Great*, I thought, *a Country full of mercenaries.*

I didn't sleep a wink that night. I was exhausted, especially since I hadn't slept the night before, but sleep would not come. I was surrounded by the loudest quiet I had ever heard. Birds and Howler Monkeys are up all night looking for food. Hell only knows what the other sounds were.

While the raised, one-man tent kept the moisture and man-eating ants off of the floor of the tent and me, the brush that we cleared to do so dug into my back. I would definitely prefer the brush in my back over the ants. Most venom-producing ants use theirs to protect the nest, I was told. Costa Rican ants use theirs to subdue and eat their prey. *Awesome.* I didn't think that bugs liked the cold, but they liked it out there that night, cold be damned. The bugs were everywhere.

The morning light started to cut through the canopy, but I was already awake. It was almost 6:00 AM and I decided to get up and see about a breakfast MRE. I was famished. Those Meals might be Ready to Eat, but they aren't very big. I'm not a big guy, I was unsure how Stubbs had been satiated. Breakfast in a sack was sounding pretty good. I was mindful to be quiet, letting the others sleep until a more respectable hour. Careful with every movement, unzipping my one-man tent. Walking about the small area with stealth.

I was successful in my efforts until I saw my first snake in Costa Rica on a nearby limb. The sound that emanated from my mouth was issued from the depths of my very frightened soul. Loud? You could say that. A more accurate description would have been that I raised the dead.

I definitely raised the slumbered. Stubbs came out of his tent with his gun ready and Hector was yelling in Spanish. Stubbs would never tell me exactly what he said. My guess is that as bad as my language can get, he said things that were worse and were directed toward me. At first I felt bad. But after some thought I decided fuck them. Stubbs got me into this mess by not coming alone, and Hector was getting paid. And the snake was a deadly one.

Over breakfast, and while we picked up camp, I would learn that there are all sorts of things that are worse than snakes. And they all lived right there in that forest. Costa Rica is home to more than 500,000 species. 300,000 are insects. Of the 200,000 species that aren't insects, more than half of them I should be afraid of.

In Costa Rica, all spiders are venomous. The question is if the jaw is big enough to penetrate human skin, and if so is the venom virulent enough to do serious damage. The ones with thick webs give you a fighting chance because they can't see very well. They use their webs to snag their prey. The large ones can see or sense you with their furry motion receptors. They can and will leap at a moving target. The Brazilian Wandering spider is the deadliest. I wished that they had just stayed in Brazil.

It is the same story with the scorpions. Only there aren't any questions with scorpions. If you were to get stung that far out in the jungle, you are dead.

Then there are the Poison Dart Frogs, the Golden Toads, some 70 species of lizards. Hector didn't elaborate on which snakes would kill me. They all would in one way or another. If it didn't eat me, it would give me a heart attack from fear. Either way I was a dead man.

We began the day and the hike earlier than scheduled, and were making good time according to Hector. We were beyond tourists and covering a lot of ground. We were all drenched from the humidity that you could almost cut with a knife. And sweat. I can't speak for the other lads, but I was drenched to the point where my skin was wrinkling. Added to the fact that my blisters on my feet had popped and you get the idea of how uncomfortable I was.

We only stopped once in mid-morning because Stubbs was admiring the congregation of Scarlet Macaws. The large and very colorful bird has a parrot-like appearance with cobalt blue wing tips; bright yellow wing radius and scapula; and fire engine red skull, vertebrae, and furcula. Who knew that the enormous football player, outdoorsman was also a Spanish-speaking birdwatcher? Upon further review, he was nothing like me. The guy could get along with anyone.

Hector and Stubbs were chatting away in Spanish, and again I was left off to the side. They watched and pointed while I was on the look-out for anything that was interested in Irish-flavored meat. We restarted our trek after a bit where we reassembled in our assigned spots in the line. Stubbs told me over his shoulder what Hector was explaining to him about the birds, like I gave a shit.

But it seems that the Scarlet Macaw is a very popular bird for a pet, people paying over $1000 each for them. Their population is threatened primarily from this but also because of their mating rituals. They form a monogamous breeding pair and share the responsibility for raising their young, which takes about two years. They cannot keep up with their demand. I was having entrepreneurial designs of my own with these birds. So it turns out that maybe I did give a shit.

About two hours after the bird watching, we stopped for water and a granola bar. This tree-hugger hiking, nature, and granola bar shit was wearing on me. I don't even like Kashi commercials. But I was hungry so I ate it. The two guys with the International man-crush were chatting away when I heard noises and voices that were not from our party. I whistled to them to shut up, and they did.

We moved as quietly as possible toward the voices, off the path and deep into the brush. Approximately seventy yards in we spotted a clearing where an elaborate camp had been constructed of indigenous raw materials. They were a young lot, many of which sharing the same name on their t-shirts. The time for secrecy was over.

I popped up from my crouched position and made my way into the clearing to meet the students of the University of Chicago.

The change of clothes, especially the change of socks did wonders for my comfort and attitude. I had returned back to my usual level of surliness. They had better food than our MREs and treated us to an early supper. We sat around a set of rudimentary picnic tables. The mystery meat with rice and beans was delicious. The students were going native, they said, wanting to eat the same traditional cuisine as the people of the Country they occupied. I was informed that this meal was different from gallo pinto, the breakfast dish, because the rice and beans weren't mixed. I hoped for their sakes that they slept in their own tents because beans for every meal could create quite a stink.

They originally thought that we were tourists who had ventured deeper into the rainforest in the desire to gain a more authentic cultural experience. We didn't alter their perception until we were finished with the meal. Hector remained silent, per my request, for virtually the entire time we were in the camp.

"So how long have you been out here, uh, camping?" I knew they were researchers, it didn't take a rocket scientist to understand that these kids were scientists.

They gave each other looks, all eleven of them, as if to ascertain how much or how little to share. They were under confidentiality agreements also, I was sure.

"We have been out here for three months and have several more to go. We are biologists on a research grant," the Asian girl said. I never did get her name. It was Naomi or Nanami .... something like that.

"It must be quite a grant."

"We, like, can complete our thesis and earn our doctorate degrees when we have finished and compiled our work," another student said.

"I would ask you what you are studying, but I probably wouldn't understand it anyway. Biologists, you say?"

"Uh, well, yeah. Sorta. It's complicated and we don't want to bore you," the Asian girl said.

"Thanks. And you have been so kind to feed us. We are deep into the jungle here. We are very grateful, aren't we guys?"

Stubbs nodded and Hector missed his queue. Whatever. It was time to come clean anyway. This ruse was getting us nowhere. They were running out of lies for their clandestine operation, and I was tired of pretending to be people that they were already beginning to suspect were not genuine.

"We are not out this far by accident, as you might have guessed from us having a guide."

"It's really none of our business," the Asian girl said again. She must have been the group's spokesperson.

"I would say from the looks of your camp, that it is exactly the same business. Do you know a Dr. Enrique Estabados? Or know of him?"

They all looked at each other with shock and amazement. The Asian student returned her eye contact with me, unsure of how to proceed.

"You're joking right? *Everyone* knows who he is. He has been crucial in the advancement of the World Toxin Bank. He is one of the top three or four people in the world doing .... uh .... the work that he does."

"And you are all out here doing the same type of thing, right?"

Again the looks.

"Who are you exactly?"

"We work for colleagues of Dr. Estabados, we need to find him."

"There must be some mistake. I don't think he is out here in the rainforest. He wouldn't need to be out here with his work at the WTB. And he can offer grants to students to collect samples for him."

"But just for the sake of argument, if he was out here, do you know where he would be?"

"There are all sorts of researchers out here. We are spread out all over the rainforest. This is one of the most biodiverse places on the planet. *If* he is out here, he could be anywhere. But I don't think he is, with all of the groups out here, we run into each other sooner or later. Florida, Arizona, California, NCS .... sometimes it is by accident and other times they come looking specifically to see how far the competition's research has come."

"Does it ever get dangerous?"

"Supposedly. They all have hired security to make sure their research is secure, but we can't afford it with the money we were granted. I think we are the only team without security. Anyway, we think that we are in more danger from the wildlife than the other universities. We are researchers for crying out loud, not warriors."

"So if you guys run into trouble, what is the protocol?"

"We have a supply of antivenoms, but outside of that we have a satellite phone and flares. There are dozens of tour groups that are only a half a day or so away. If we were in trouble they would see the flare above the canopy and send help. Not that we have needed to yet. Are you saying that we are in trouble?"

"No, of course not. I was just wondering."

I hoped I wasn't lying to the kids.

11

AGAINST HER BETTER JUDGEMENT, DETECTIVE CARINA FISCHER began to investigate the background and alibis of one Dr. Enrique Estabados. She was sure it was a waste of time. Time that she had a shortage of. Her case load was full to the point of being overwhelmed. Why she was revisiting a case that was for all intents and purposes closed was beyond her. But it was her decision, nobody else's. This Yankee had asked her to look into Estabados and Nahash, but nobody was forcing her.

Carina had never been involved with people she encountered through her work. She would occasionally date guys she met at her gym. Randomly if a guy said a certain thing or looked a certain way at a bar, but that never worked out. She was still single in her mid thirties because she was busy with work and because she was choosy. All women have needs, so she would allow a man into her life every so often to fulfill them, then send him on his merry way. She had broken many hearts, and that was her burden to carry. There were all too many men willing to fulfill that need. So she was desperate to figure out why was she hung up on Deni?

And why was she doing his bidding? There was absolutely no reason to reopen this case. She wouldn't. Not officially. But she had to be sure. She was an incredibly good cop that wasn't taken seriously because of the way she looked. Sending the wrong serial killer to prison while the real threat remained at large would not look good on her resume. That is why she was looking into this Estabados, she convinced herself. Not Warren Dennihan.

She decided to start out with a trip over to Nahash Pharmaceuticals. If what Deni had said was true, there was an infiltration into BIOGENESIS and possibly more by Estabados at the behest of Rueben Feinstein. The juxtapositioning of the two adversarial companies was not likely to be ethically justifiable, probably not legal. Had they gone so far as to commit murder over trade secrets? Carina found it far-fetched but remotely possible. The feeling was more visceral than rational.

The detective was pleasantly surprised to see that she would not have to fight through a mob of media teams, picketers, or protesters as she had at BIOGENESIS. Her only opposition to driving right onto the expansive property was the security guard manning the gate from the sanctity of his booth. She drove up to it, rolled down her window, and flashed her badge.

"Do you have an appointment, officer?"

"Its detective and no. But I'm investigatin' multiple homicides so I don't need one."

The guard had been given the riot act about letting other recent unwelcome visitors into the complex. He was almost fired for it. The guard was not about to let anybody beyond the outer gate without an appointment.

"This facility does sensitive research, ma'am. Without an appointment I cannot grant you access. Unless you have a warrant."

"Let me walk you through what's gonna happen if I have to get a warrant. I will make a few phone calls, and nobody will get in or out until a judge signs a warrant and an officer brings it here along with a whole mess of other cops. Then this place will be shut down for days until we go over every single inch, of every building, located on this property. The media will somehow be alerted and then it will go public that there is a major investigation here, which is all tied up with Wyatt Pharmaceuticals. That drops the stock price and some eager little go-getter is going to do an exposé on Big Pharma, maybe even dig up some dirt on you in the process. All because you won't let a decorated detective speak informally to your boss, Rueben Feinstein. We makin' any headway on gettin' me that appointment?"

"Let me make a phone call." He picked up the phone inside the booth and spent the better part of two minutes speaking to someone who was going to ease his culpability in this mess. When he was finished, he hung up the phone and said that she had an appointment in two hours, at 11:30 AM. She was told that she could come back at that time.

"Yeah, that's not what I had in mind, sugar. I'll wait for my appointment. Right here. Nobody in or out."

"Then I'm afraid that I will have to have your vehicle towed in order to clear the gate."

Now she was really pissed.

"Anybody touches this car but me and I will shoot them. I'll call it self defense. Then I'll have you arrested for somethin' I haven't quite thought up yet, maybe reckless endangerment or obstruction, I'm not sure. Us cops are real good at makin' *somethin'* stick. Who's gonna hire a security guard with a felony record?"

"I'm just trying to do my job, ma'am. He said two hours, so that is what I'm going to do. I'm in enough trouble already."

"My advice is to open that gate and find a new job, sweetie."

You could visibly see the gears grinding in the guard's head trying to figure out what he was going to do. The thirty seconds it did take felt like an hour.

"The Admin building is the last building up on the end of this main road. Please tell him something about arresting me so I don't get fired."

Outside of Rueben Feinstein's office, Carina found herself a seat in a large anteroom. She was alone after being told by the very effeminate male receptionist in the lobby where to go. Her posterior had not yet warmed her seat when the bamboo door opened to reveal a man with salt and peppered hair.

"Detective. My schedule cleared up suddenly so I have a brief moment now if you would like."

Carina looked at her watch and feigned a look of being impressed.

"An hour and fifty minutes early? I'll consider myself lucky. You must be Mr. Feinstein."

"Rueben, Yes. And you are?"

"Detective Fischer."

"Do you have a first name?"

"Yes. But you can call me Detective or Detective Fischer."

"I see. Please have a seat."

"I'll stand. This won't take long, unless you make me mad."

"What is this concerning?"

"The three related and recent deaths."

"I'm not sure that I understand, Detective."

"Come on now, Reuben. No need to be coy. This ain't Detroit or Miami. This is Charleston. We don't have murderin' like other places. It happens, but not three related in five weeks. Surely you've seen the news. Surely you know that these victims are from the same circles that you find yourself in."

"They don't have anything to do with my company, I assure you."

"Well that's my point. Three deaths in your rival company, all of whom had hands-on knowledge of the same research that you and your company conduct. Then the number two guy over there comes over here to work, or was working here the entire time. Now doesn't that strike you as odd?"

"Maybe I should have my lawyers present. I don't think that I like what you are insinuating, Detective."

"I ain't insinuatin' anything, sir. I'm sayin' it outright. We can certainly make this more formal if ya like, but really I just want time records and such on your Dr. Enrique Estabados. I want to see his personnel file, so I can see when exactly he started working here. I'd also like to speak with him when we are through here." She knew Estabados was in Costa Rica, she just wanted to see Rueben's reaction. And she got one.

"I'm afraid what you're asking is impossible, Detective."

"Nothin's impossible sir. I just haven't motivated you. So let me see if I can fix that. See my job is to find and arrest murderers. And the people who pay those people to do their murderin'. In this case, that's exactly what I am beginnin' to think is goin' on here. I don't give a rats ass about you bein' a thief and stealing proprietary information. That's what Civil Courts are for. I care about the murder of three innocent people who were guilty of doin' no more 'n goin' to work and doin' their job.

"You puttin' up a fight is only makin' me want to dig into you more. You can think of me like a rapist. You can kick and scream all you want to, but in the end I'm gettin' my way."

"Well that is very myopic. And very strong talk for a pretty little girl like yourself. Did you come with any back-up, Detective, or did you bring only your rapier whit with you? It wasn't very smart for you to have come here alone."

She didn't notice that the room now had more than just the two people in it, else she would have retrieved her service weapon. There were several security personnel that had entered the corner penthouse office behind her.

"Miss Fischer. I thought bringing backup was standard procedure, axiomatic. At a minimum you should have given it earnest consideration. Unless you are here outside the scope of an official investigation. If that is the case, then I would surmise that nobody knows that you are here. I believe my security team will now have to sort you out."

Rueben nodded to his staff, who surrounded Carina.

12

IT RAINED AGAIN THAT AFTERNOON in the rainforest. Rain in the rainforest, go figure. But we had just dried off and had a change of clothes. It was frustrating being wet all of the time. We were either drenched from the rain, humidity that hung in the air, sweat, or all of the above.

We left the kids from the University of Chicago and told them to be careful. Eleven twenty-somethings in the middle of an inhospitable jungle; with other researchers in the general area; whom were sponsored by Big Pharma and whom wanted their data; were not odds stacked in their favor.

We trekked for a couple of hours, our bellies were full and we were more than hydrated. We seemed to be hiking through a thick mist of water. The flora dripped down onto us as we passed under it on the narrow path below. It was so humid, maybe the trees were sweating on us.

All-of-a-sudden, Hector stopped and raised his right hand signaling for us to do the same. He didn't have to tell us to shut up, it was inferred. A few brief moments went by and then he turned to signal us to crouch down. His hand had not yet been brought down to the level of his waist when we all heard it.

It was the sound like compressed air had sprung a short-lived leak, and that leak lasted but a fraction of a second. It had come from in front of us and off to the right. I returned my look back and left toward Hector who was then not crouched on the ground, but lying in the brush off to the left of the path. He had sprung his own leak.

The red that was painted on the surrounding vegetation were not blossoms, they were splatter from Hector's neck. The rain that was coming down could not wash away the crimson that was Jackson Pollocked all over the surrounding vegetation.

Stubbs was closer, he had front row seats in viewing what a high caliber projectile could do to someone's neck once it has gone through it. I didn't think that he was alive but I wanted to go check. I was stopped by Stubbs.

"Get the fuck down you idiot or you're gonna be next!"

He grabbed me and pulled me back to the hardened ground on the path. I was next to him, to his left looking directly at Hector who was motionless. His body was contorted around his backpack which was still attached to the corpse. Bloody meat was protruding out of his neck like an ultra-crimson wattle on a turkey's neck. Ants and other insects were already beginning to crawl on him, attaining their nourishment. The circle of life rainforest-style.

"Crawl into the shrubs off the path," Stubbs said. He pointed to the right and behind us, away from Hector.

"There is no need, my friends."

A Latin man was walking down the path, towards us with at least six armed men behind him. His accent was not thick, hardly any perceptible inflections. He could have been from Costa Rica just as likely as he could have been from Idaho.

"No need for you suffer the same fate as your friend. Toss your weapons away from you and toward me. Slowly."

We complied, but I was more reluctant than Stubbs. My brand new gun. I had never fired it. Gone.

One of the men behind the Latin man was dressed in camouflage and carrying a Barrett *M82 .50 BMG* sniper rifle. I no longer questioned what had done such horrific and final damage to our tour guide.

Our weapons had no sooner hit the ground, when another hit came. The words uttered by Stubbs were like those coming from a tape being played at too slow a speed.

"Behind you" had come too late.

Everything went black.

536

When I awoke, the back of my head and neck felt like it had been through a dull guillotine. The hit I took drew some blood, as it was now dried where it had dripped down my shoulders and chest. The throbbing was making me want to throw up.

I looked around to find Stubbs, he was still unconscious or at least pretending to be. Moving my eyes hurt bad enough, but moving my head to determine my surrounds brought on severe vertigo.

We weren't tied up. We were locked into a large timbered room with a dirt floor. Both of us were haphazardly deposited and left on the ground. My watch was missing so I had no idea what time it was. The only thing I knew for sure was that it was daylight. I could see low levels of light between the trees that were fashioned together to form our prison walls. The warps and knots were big enough to let in a small amount of light, but not a large enough spaces between to allow any view outside those walls.

I began to dig at the earth at the bottom of one wall with my hands to see if I could dig out of the prison. I heard a knocking on the timber on the other side of where my hands were. Then many knocks. The more I dug, the more attention I was getting from something on the other side of the wall. Before I could determine what it was, or dig a big enough hole underneath, a large thud came outside the main door to the front of the room.

The thud was followed by what sounded like a large piece of wood sliding on the other side of our prison door. That door opened and the Latino man from the path entered, again he was not alone with two armed men behind him.

The two thugs were holding Heckler and Koch *MP5A3* submachine guns. I'm not sure why they needed them, we were unarmed. The men were also of Latin descent, but their weapons indicated that they were likely from Mexico. I had traced one back on a previous case some years prior to Mexico, the *MP5A3* is the weapon of choice for cartels and military-types there.

"I see that you are awake. Your friend was not subdued quite as smoothly as you, it may take him some time to regain consciousness. My name is Dr. Enrique Estabados, but you probably know that already."

"If you are a doctor, then what the hell are you doing? Isn't it part of your oath or something to do no harm?"

"Ah, yes. That would be my preference. Alas, when it comes to medical research, it seems that if you do not strike first; you end up penniless, unknown, and useless."

"I don't get it. You had a good thing going over at BIOGENESIS, why kill those people and risk it all to go to a start-up like Nahash?"

"I didn't 'go over to Nahash'. I have always worked for Nahash. BIOGENESIS funded my work at the World Toxin Bank, and they refused to allow those venom samples to be studied by other factions. Namely Nahash, despite my employer's very generous donations. Very selfish of them."

"So you killed those people to shut down the project over there?"

"What are you talking about?"

"The three murders in Charleston. Seems a bit strong, even for a guy like you."

"I didn't kill anyone in Charleston. I left BIOGENESIS after I attained the necessary data for Nahash. There was no reason to kill anyone."

"So standing there with the guys behind you holding assault rifles, you are trying to tell me that your departure just happened to coincide with the deaths of three employees over there. You didn't hit my head that hard."

The look on his face was a mixture of puzzlement and anger. It was a good act, but I didn't really want to stick around for an encore.

"You can't keep us here. People know we're here and why."

"Oh, don't worry about me. I would worry more about yourself. You see, in this very unique ecosystem, your bodies will never be found. Accidents happen in the rainforest all of the time. Two American men trying to shakedown a research team in this vast land? Anything can happen."

"We have already made contact with people out here. How long do you think it will take for someone to figure out that after them, we ran into you?"

"You mean the college kids from the University of Chicago? How do you think we found you?"

He turned to leave with his rent-a-thugs but stopped short of the door.

"One more thing. If you continue to dig under that wall you find a most inhospitable creature waiting to attack you. There is a caged moat on the other side filled with Bothrops Aspers. Not only will you be trapped in yet another cage, but you will be trapped with hundreds of creatures that are hungry and will enjoy eating you. Good Day."

I didn't know what one of those things were, but I was sure that I was alright with not finding out.

13

NIGHTFALL CAME, OR IT BECAME DARK, in the part of the rainforest that we were in. Either way it was pitch black in the large prison. What I lacked in sight I also lacked in sound. Other than rain drops on the roof that was fifteen feet above us, and the movement of the creepy-crawlies on the other side of the wall, I couldn't hear shit. Neither could Stubbs.

He woke up after the dark had already come. He grumbled and groaned which is how I knew he was alive and awake. It took me some time to convince him that he wasn't blind. To be honest, I wasn't entirely sure that he wasn't. It was so dark in that cage that he could have been. Had I not seen what the room looked like during the day, I might have thought the same thing.

I explained to him the exchange Estabados and I had; and that if we could somehow manage to get beyond the things thumping on the walls at us, we still had armed soldier-types beyond them.

It was so quiet in there that our whispers were like we were shouting. Who knows who was listening, and for that matter who cares? We were going to die there unless we figured something out and quick.

There was another big thud followed by the same wood latch that had occurred before. It was a first for Stubbs so I was explaining that someone was coming to chat with us, maybe feed us, when the door opened.

Neither of us could see who was at the door. Whomever it was, they didn't speak, nor were they at the door very long. They threw something toward us and re-latched the door. We both thought it was food, and we were both hungry. We blindly crawled on the ground, feeling our way toward it.

He found it first. "It's a body. It's alive but must be knocked out like we were."

"Shit," I said. I went to lie back and had a pillow. I felt around and realized that there was another body deposited into the prison with us. This one was female, for sure because in attempting to feel a heartbeat I inadvertently felt up her breast. She too was unconscious. Thankfully. "There is another one. This one is a girl."

"Mine is a boy."

We both felt around to see if there was a third or more but we didn't feel any. More mouths to feed and no food. I wondered if they were going to starve us to death.

For the third night in a row I wasn't able to sleep. I was definitely exhausted, but the thought that I would soon be in a forever kind of sleep made me not want to.

I am what you would call a recovering Catholic. I was brought up very devout. But although I was Baptized, had my First Communion, and Confirmed, I never really lived according to the way I was told. In my Irish-Catholic neighborhood, nobody did. I stole shit and then went to church on Sunday to get my Jesus Biscuit. I still went to that same church in Southie for funerals, weddings, maybe the odd 'high holiday'. I feel like a hypocrite every time I enter the Cathedral of the Holy Cross, on Washington Street. When your Catholic, you are guilty for even thinking about a sin, never mind when you actually commit one.

But I ain't gonna kid ya, I prayed that night. I prayed like my Maker was in the room. Nobody knows for one hundred percent certainty what happens after you die. But I was one hundred percent certain that I was going to find out in short order. So I begged, I would deal with the hypocrisy if I lived.

The daylight began to seep through the slats of our wood walls. Little by little I could see the inside of the room. It didn't take my eyes long to adjust, they seemed to welcome light. The bodies that were thrown into our cell were those of the kids that we had seen the day prior. The kids from the University of Chicago. But there were only two of them.

I'm not sure if Stubbs was silently praying along with me through the night, but I was sure that he was wide awake. He was from the Bible belt, so my guess is that he had his own conversation.

"Mornin'," I said.

"Yeah great."

"Believe me, I was hoping to wake up to someone different on my last day alive too."

"We're not going to die today."

"Really? You've got an idea of how we are gonna to get outta here?"

"I do."

"You must be my guardian angel. I'm all ears."

"I've still got my knife in my boot. I don't have anything else in my pockets, but they didn't find the knife. You said that we can't go under the wall, so we go over it."

"I hate to be the pessimist here, Stubbs, but that has to be fifteen feet up."

"Look at it. It's just brush lashing. I'm the biggest person here so I'll be on the bottom and hoist you up. You grab the little Asian girl and send her through. Depending on how heavy the other kid is, he might be able to go up also. They go for help. If those guys come in we ambush them and take their weapons."

"If we go out, we go out with a bang …. kinda-thing."

"Right. And the kids go for help. They must have some way of communicating their data back to their labs. That's what they said yesterday right? Lets hope they can communicate that we need help in time."

"You're the boss. I like the plan. Lotta shit can go wrong with it, but I like it."

The young Asian college student was awake but pretending to sleep. "Why can't we go under the wall? Over seems much more difficult."

"Because they have some bother aspirins or creepy-crawly that eats people on the other side of the walls," I said.

"Bothrops Aspers?"

"Yeah, that's it."

"If that is the case then we have to get out of here soon. Over or whatever. Those are the most excitable and vicious type of snake in this region, arguably on the planet. They move with unbelievable quickness and their venom causes; hemoptysis, gastrointestinal bleeding, hematuria, impaired consciousness, spleen issues, and localized necrosis, which means that even if you had an antivenin at the ready, you would have to amputate the limb that they bit."

I froze.

I'm not sure where my fear of snakes was born, maybe when I was born. But it is a fear that has complete control over me.

The fear that I speak of is so pervasive, so deep, that it is all-consuming. Not a hundred mile an hour puck shot at your unprotected face kind of fear. Not that split-second before a car that is speeding toward you is about to hit you; and *if* your survive, your life as you know it is over, kind of fear. Not Freddy Krueger. The fear that I speak of is beyond rational. Beyond fight or flight. The fear stops all bodily function. I mean pant-wetting terror. There is no word or phrase to describe it. If you've never felt this level of fear, count yourself lucky.

"Oh fuck me. Snakes? This is not good. This is not good." I began to pace about the dirt floor. "I get it, they're bad-asses. Why the urgency?"

"We are studying them because their venom is so potent, attacking so many specific targets that affect so many different things, that they could be the key to curing vast numbers of varying diseases. Also their venom changes with diet, which means that their venom mutates. They reproduce exponentially faster than any other snake in this environment so mutations occur faster than we can identify them."

"Kid. Enough of the science lesson. I fuckin' hate snakes. Terrified, actually. Why the urgency?"

"If we are surrounded by them, and as fast as they reproduce, with us being the only source of food .... the only thing that *is* predictable is that they *will* find a way through these walls."

"Oh fuck me. I'm gonna lose my mind. Stubbs. What do we do?"

"Your friends are going to miss you, right? They are probably already on their way with help," Stubbs asked Naomi, Nanimi, or whatever the Asian girl's name was.

She sat up and her face was a big puffy mess. She had been slapped around and crying. "My colleagues are all dead. Samuel and I are the only two that weren't slaughtered. They were after our research and you two. Mostly you two."

"Us two? How did Estabados know we were here?" Stubbs was looking at me but asking the girl.

"Estabados? Dr. Estabados? No no. We were attacked by soldiers after you left."

"And they work for Estabados," I said.

Stubbs went over to the kid she had called Samuel and tried to wake him up. "Miss? Your friend didn't make it either. The smack to his head must have created a brain-bleed. Cerebral Hemorrhaging. He was alive when they brought you here last night, but he's dead now."

She began to cry again and convulse uncontrollably. I tried to console her but she shoved me off. "This is all your fault. Why did you have to come into our camp? We've been here for months without issue. Why do they want you? We are all going to die because of you."

"Listen kid. I'm sorry, but this isn't our fault. This guy killed people back in South Carolina, and he was going to find and kill you no matter if we were here or not. You said yourself he wanted your research. We have to get it together and get the fuck outta here before we join the rest of your friends."

She wiped her eyes and tried to compose herself. Stubbs handed her his Gerber *Air Ranger* knife and re-explained the plan.

".... and be careful because this thing is sharp. Razor sharp. Like lightsaber sharp. It is made of surgical steel and will take off one of your limbs as easily as those tree limbs above us."

She nodded like she understood. The time that it had taken Stubbs to go over the plan had given her much needed time to collect herself.

I went to the door and listened to see if I could hear anyone coming, but I couldn't hear anything. Besides, after hearing the kid tell us with wonderful detail what was on the other side of those walls, I didn't get too close.

"I can't hear shit. Let's just go."

Stubbs quickly hoisted me onto his shoulders like I was his pet hampster. He reached up and held the back of my pants while I stood on his shoulders and pulled the girl up. She helped by walking up the front of Stubbs. Once she was sitting on my shoulders she began to hack away at the brush above us. It was working rather quickly and we determined that it was already raining outside because the hole she cut was already soaking us with rainwater.

Maybe it was because everything was so quiet, but the escape attempt seemed to be making a lot of noise. Thankfully it took her less than five minutes to cut a hole just larger than she was to climb through.

"What's up there?" I asked.

"They have a camp set up like us. We are toward the back of it. I can't see the other side of the cell."

"You're really light, do you think the roof will hold you?"

"Yes, but I'm not sure about you. Definitely not the big guy."

"OK. Pull yourself up, then close the knife and drop it back down to us."

Stubbs objected. If you can get up there, you should go too. She will have a much better chance of getting out of here if she has help."

"No way pal. We're getting outta here together."

The girl wasn't going to wait while we decided, I was still talking with Stubbs when the knife hit the dirt by his feet. And just like that, she was gone.

"Well that solves that."

I came down off of his shoulders in time to hear the big thud. The prison door was about to be opened again. The second part of the plan was going into immediate effect.

We both quickly took positions behind where the door would open, as the wooden latch was being manipulated. It was time to do or die. Literally.

14

JACOB GRANTES PARKED HIS VOLVO *XC90* in the parking lot of the Leath Correctional Institution for women. As usual he tried to find a spot in the shade, under a tree perhaps, because the sun was ablaze. The early afternoons of early summer in Charleston, South Carolina are the hottest of the day. They can be the hottest of the year. But those were prime spaces long taken by mid-morning, let alone by the time he had arrived well after the noon hour.

He rode the Ford *Econoline* van from the booth in the parking lot up to the prison where he needed to check in. Regardless of visitor; family member, or attorney, there were protocols for check-in. He did so every time he came to see his client and girlfriend. He had done so when he brought Deni there just two days prior. In the ten days since Sierra Byrne had been incarcerated, there were not many that went by where he didn't visit.

"Attorney Jacob Grantes to see inmate Sierra Byrne."

It almost killed him to say it out loud. To announce, even to the guards, that the new love of his life was spending her days as he had once spent a six month span. He felt for her. He knew all-too-well what it was like inside the razor-wire. To be wrongly accused and treated like societal scum. The refuse that nobody wanted to live with or near.

He went inside a room where she was already waiting. It was unusual for her to be waiting for him, it was usually the other way around. He had called and set the appointment up in advance, which he had almost always done. The guards were either getting used to the visits or it was a slow day.

"Jay. Oh thank goodness. What's going on? Any progress?"

He sat down across from her. The beauty that was once outward, for the world to see, was now getting buried deep inside of her. He could see the toll this new life was taking on her.

"We have a lead. Deni and Stubbs are working on it."

"Who did it? Who killed those people?"

"Did you know that Dr. Enrique Estabados was working for Nahash the entire time he was working with you? While he was working for the WTB and BIOGENESIS?"

"What? Of course not. Are you sure?"

"Quite."

"That explains his frustration with the WTB not being open for some of the other research institutions that were requesting access. His ideas about intellectual property were almost Communistic. The current arrangement can get a bit political. The more invested an organization was in Toxicology, Herpetology, and Venomology as demonstrated by their research and large investments into the WTB, the more access they would get to the samples held there. With competition being what it is, not all facilities can afford to keep up with investment required to have the greatest access. Enrique believed that the cures to what ails all humans were but a few short years away if all would be allowed access to the research, regardless of contribution."

"Well that doesn't jibe with what we are seeing. His altruism seemed to end at the front door to Nahash. He is and has been the number one guy over there in Venomology. Specifically snake venom. The CEO over there — "

" — Rueben Feinstein. I know Rueben. He offered me almost double my salary to leave SCMU, BIOGENESIS and continue my research with Nahash. I told him it was pointless because my research was protected under confidentiality clauses. Also, I would no longer be able to teach, tenured or not. But he persisted and checked in on me regularly to see if I was happy with my decision. He seemed to be a snake in the grass himself."

"Right. So he was the one that ordered Estabados to, uh, appropriate the valuable research. They are also making a bid to send Wyatt to number one over PROXER Pharmaceuticals. You are smack in the middle of a huge business war in Big Pharma. We are going to continue to attain evidence against them, provide as much reasonable doubt as possible. But at the end of the day, these two organizations are worth hundreds of billions of dollars. If not a trillion. My entire firm is going to use all of our resources, but if they dig their feet in? We cannot keep up. Those poor victims may never get justice."

"Oh Jay. That's awful. Not to sound crass, but what will that mean for me?"

"That is one of the worst parts of all of this. The fact is that once we bring all of the evidence to bear, the DA may decide to settle for low hanging fruit instead of fighting Goliath without having the necessary resources. That low hanging fruit being you."

"Isn't that against the law? You can't morally prosecute someone you know didn't commit a crime because punishing the right one is inconvenient. Can you?" She began to cry.

"Morally or ethically? No. But legally? We would have to prove malicious prosecution, which means we would have to prove you were innocent at trial. You wouldn't be locked up in the first place if the jury found you innocent. Unfortunately its like I tell my students, the lady with the scales is not blind. She is peaking. The District Attorney is an elected position. He would rather have a fighting chance at putting someone away as a serial murder, than being outgunned and out matched, likely being embarrassed. He can't win reelection that way. If they lose prosecuting you, he blames the jury. If he gets embarrassed, the public can only blame him."

"This can't be happening." She was a sobbing mess. The ten days she had already spent in prison, the culmination of stress and anxiety now combined with the realization that it could continue for the rest of her life, was more than she could endure. "Will they seek the death penalty?"

"Probably. Yes. But we will fight that to the bitter end. That would be years of appeals."

"No. If I am found guilty, even though I'm not, I don't want to live like this."

"Let's not go there. We are nowhere near that yet. I was just outlining the very real possibilities. That is why I have my best man on it. Deni has never let me down. He saved me from the very situation that you face, once upon a time."

"I trust you. I trust your judgement in him."

"Good. Because we need to talk about that very thing," he said.

"Trust? I know."

"I lied to the police, which is a felony. I was not with you the night of the third murder, as you well know. I lied because I was corroborating your story that you told the police. Which was the same lie, the same felony.

"Whatever you tell me, it will not affect our relationship. But as your attorney, I need to know where you were," he continued.

"I didn't lie. I *was* with you. You just didn't know it."

"But that's impossible. I was with .... Jenna. You followed me to meet Jenna."

"You're ex."

"But why? It was over between us. I left her for you."

"Men don't leave a woman that looks like that. Not in my experience."

"Sierra. I love you. I was married to a beauty, she turned out be a tortured soul. I was with Jenna who was also beautiful, but we didn't truly match either. You are gorgeous inside and out. I love you, Brady loves you. You have nothing to be jealous or suspicious of."

"Yeah well .... my jealousy has come back to bite me in the ass."

"More than you know. If this goes to trial, we have to try and justify you lying to the police. Then we have to convince a jury that you are not lying to them."

546

Sierra shook her head and looked down at her hands that were cuffed and resting on the table between them.

"This hole just keeps getting deeper."

"You don't know the half of it. Your juvenile record. Care to enlighten me?"

"My juvenile record? How could anyone know? How do you know? Those records are supposed to be sealed. Expunged."

"Not when you are accused of being a serial killer. They look at all of that stuff."

"This can't be happening."

"It is, so you had better explain. I hate to ask, but I am going to find out sooner or later if this goes to trial. I found out from Deni, who got it from the investigating detective. The DA has it and is sitting on it. They will have to give it to me eventually, but it would be best if you tell me now. I don't want to be ambushed."

"I have worked so hard to put that all behind me. To leave it all in the closet. It was supposed to stay there. Isn't that what expunged means?"

"Yes. But as I said, those things never really go away. And it obviously ties in with your current situation, so please just tell me. No judgements, I promise."

"My mother had a live-in boyfriend after my parents divorced. He seemed so at first, but he was not a nice guy."

She looked into her hands that rested on the table between them. There was a long silence which JG let linger for some time.

"Go on."

"As I developed, he was more hands-on. Especially when my mother wasn't around. I kept trying to get away from him, spend as little time as possible alone with him. But one day it went too far."

"And?"

"And I stabbed the son-of-a-bitch. Calling 9-1-1 was the worst thing I could have done. Had he actually taken my virginity, I might have had a case. I can't tell you how many times that I look back and wish that he had died. But he didn't. And he claimed that I snapped and came at him with a knife. My own mother didn't believe me. Then it got really out of control."

"Worse than that?"

"Yes. I was really into science, still am obviously. I found biology fascinating at that time, and I was doing a lot of dissections. My biology teacher would allow me to do extra credit by getting me extra specimens. I was able to learn specialized biology on real frogs, cats, sheep brains .... whatever she could get her hands on."

"So what?"

"So they said that it was an unhealthy fascination with death and killing. That I was a disturbed kid and that is why I attacked my would-be stepfather."

"I'm so sorry Sierra. What happened then?"

"My biological father came to the rescue and saved me. My biology teacher helped as well, but the damage was done. I pled out and had to see a counselor, but that was the end of it. I had never been in any trouble, nor had I after that. I had the entire thing expunged, I didn't want it to follow me even though I was never actually convicted of anything."

"I see. You know why they want to bring that into evidence, don't you? They are going to look at your juvenile case, and use it as evidence that you had a fascination back then, carried it into the serial killing as an adult."

"How can they do that, Jay? I didn't do anything wrong then, and I didn't kill anyone now."

"They are profiling you. Serial murderers don't just get sick one day and run loose on a community. They start off young, usually killing pets. That is what they are going to use to put you away. Or worse, give you the needle."

"You believe me, don't you?"

"Of course I do."

"You will make a jury see that these are all just a series of unfortunate circumstances? That each one was unproven but all together look bad?"

"I'm going to try and make sure that it doesn't come to that. Juries are fickle. Unpredictable. If the State is allowed to use your past records, records that were supposed to be sealed? That hole that you mentioned will be too deep to come out of. That hole will be the death of you."

15

THE LATCH ON THE DOOR TO THE MAKESHIFT PRISON cell was lifted and set aside. Stubbs and I waited on the back side of the door, waiting to see who and how many would enter the room. At the last second before it opened, Stubbs unfolded his Gerber *Air Ranger* knife in preparation for battle. I was behind him, ready to reallocate any weapon I could from any or all of the men that would enter.

"Whatever happens," Stubbs whispered, "there's no way this ends but grimly."

The door opened and the first guard walked through, fixing his gaze on the corpse of Samuel, the student from Chicago. The second guard was walking through when Stubbs shoved the door, knocking Estabados onto the ground in the front corner of the cell. The two guards turned around but too late. I have never seen anyone move as quickly as Stubbs did at that moment. For someone his size, it was almost a miracle.

Stubbs threw his knife at the first guard who was turning around to see what the commotion was. The blade landed at the base of the surprised guard's neck. It lodged in the dimple where the neck meets the clavicle, above his chest. The blow rendered him incapacitated as he tried to free the knife from his trachea, but it had severed the vagus nerve. His heart was speeding up faster than the initial adrenaline shock. I was quick to relieve him of his weapon, the *MP5A3*.

Immediately after throwing his knife, Stubbs pulled the second guard towards him. He used one hand on the sentry's throat, and the other to snap his left elbow, using Stubb's right armpit as a lever to hyperextend it. The left hand was the man's gun hand, the weapon dropping to ground and behind the still slightly opened door. Weaponless, with a broken elbow and wrist, and being choked to death, the guard put up no further fight.

Estabados began to crawl from his corner toward the cracked door, hesitating presumably to decide whether or not to get the other *MP5A3* which lay at the base of Stubb's feet near the door.

His hesitation gave me enough time to go around Stubbs and put the barrel of my rifle on his left temple. All parties were subdued without a shot being fired which was our unspoken goal. We both found it unrealistic in our own minds at the time. I know I had my doubts.

"Not so fast *Doctor*. How many men are out there?"

He didn't speak.

"Deni, we gotta get outta here. Look in the corner. Snakes are about to breach." He had shoved the second guard toward that corner and was retrieving his knife.

"Take me with you. You cannot leave me in here. My work is too important."

"You are gonna pay for those deaths, that's why you're coming along."

Stubbs returned his knife to his boot, commandeered the second gun, and we shut the door behind us trapping the two guards.

Outside, the snakes were agitated. Either by us or by their exertions at getting inside the makeshift prison cell. By the time we had latched the door and raised the bridge over the moat to the cell, the guard was screaming.

I nearly shit my pants at the sight of them. There must have been thousands of snakes surrounding the cage from whence we came. The girl had told us that they were 'excitable and quick moving'. She undersold it. Those vipers were fuckin' hideous.

How I had managed to keep it together is still a mystery. The sight of a solitary common garter snake makes me catatonic. That was infinitely more horrifying. But I did hold it together and move away from there fast. Coming down the hill toward the main part of the camp, I was looking around to see if I could find the girl from Chicago. I didn't see her.

"Stubbs, do you see the girl?"

"No, but we are starting to attract attention. Put your gun to the Doctor's head and stay behind him. We gotta find a way outta here."

That is when the first shots were fired. The dirt and trees around us started to spit. We were being shot at from above, as the trajectory was toward the ground. Estabados had been hit. He was wailing and bleeding as I tried to drag him out of the line of fire, but using him as a shield. Stubbs ran around me, trying to lead the way. There was no way he could use either Estabados or me as a shield. He was larger than both of us combined.

Stubbs took the lead position, dragging us both behind him. Red spit from him and onto me as I lay a blanket of cover fire toward the militia firing at us. I thought of Carina and how she described Stubbs. "Don't make him mad," she said, "he's like a bruin in body armor." She was right.

I have no idea to this day how many I hit, or if I hit any at all. When my magazine was empty, which didn't take long, Stubbs tossed me his weapon from the front of our line. We were almost out of the clearing and into the deep rainforest again. I continued to fire blindly hoping to curtail the bullets being showered upon us. I stopped firing once all three of us were safely under the cover of the natural canopy.

"Keep moving. As fast as you can go," Stubbs yelled. He continued to lead us, but we were not on a path. It was raining so I could not see then sun, could not tell in which direction we were traveling.

I checked the clip to see how many rounds I had left. Four. Including the one in the chamber. I cursed myself for not thinking to check the guards for extra ammunition before leaving them in their death chamber.

We were beginning to slow down. Stubbs's heavy breathing could be heard above the nonsense that Estabados was jabbering.

I began to wonder if Stubbs was going to make it at all. He was lumbering, obviously losing steam. I knew he was hit, but from behind him I couldn't tell how badly. He stopped for a moment, forcing us to stop behind him. I was not sure if it was to regain his breath or strength, or if he needed to recalibrate his sense of direction. The seconds of waiting seemed like minutes.

Before I could ask him, the ground from underneath us gave way. All three of us fell and landed on the soft bottom of large pit dug into the earth. We were surrounded by the fallen brush that had covered the excavation. We were all laying at the bottom of that large hole dug into the earth, when I saw another horrifying sight.

It took me a few seconds to try and regain my composure, preventing myself from screaming in both fear and anger.

"Stubbs, you ok?"

"No, I'm hit pretty bad. You?" His voice was weak and garbled.

I began to take inventory. I touched a spot on my shoulder which hurt like hell. My hand came back crimson. "I think I got nicked, but I'll live."

"I've been shot also," the Doctor said.

"Who gives a fuck? Stubbs. Do you see where we are?"

He was looking around the pit, getting as misty and as emotional as I was. He was cursing and mumbling something, but I didn't quite make out what. We were lying at the bottom of a deep crater, on top of dozens of dead bodies. Corner to corner, tall dirt wall to wall, the floor of the pit was covered two and three corpses deep. The most recent was an Asian girl wearing a t-shirt from the University of Chicago.

16

JG WAS LEAVING THE LEATH CORRECTIONAL INSTITUTION for women, when he noticed the front page of the newspaper. He was waiting for his van ride back to the parking lot when he noticed the guard in the reception/waiting area reading the Charleston Post and Courier. On the front page, above the fold, was a picture of a striking woman with the heading:

Charleston Police Searching for Missing Detective

"Excuse me. May I see the front page please? The missing detective." He pointed toward the picture on the outside of the front section.   The female guard lowered the newspaper, looked at JG in his suit, and decided that it was a grantable request.

He read the article which gave him very few details.   The police were seeking information from anyone who has information as to her whereabouts. She was last seen at her desk in the precinct. Her issued police sedan had a GPS tracking device which led them to her car. The sedan was found behind an abandoned church, in a rarely used graveyard, down by the Atlantic Ocean. The police vehicle had been set on fire, however no human remains were detected. Both the graveyard and the coast had been searched, though a dive team was still combing the ocean floor. There was no evidence as to her disposition in her apartment, and neither her family nor her friends have heard from her. She had been missing for three days and foul play was suspected.

"Holy shit."
"Do you know her, Sir?" the guard asked.

"Yes. Sort of. She investigated the case that I am currently defending. I know more *of* her than know her personally."

"It's a crazy world we live in."

"For sure. How long before the van gets here? I have to go down to the precinct on Broad. I just might have some information that might be useful."

"It should be pulling up any minute."

When JG arrived at the Crimes Against Persons Department of the Charleston Police on 80 Broad Street, the place was abustle. Nobody was paying him any mind because they had their hands full. Charleston, South Carolina is a small city in comparison to the Los Angeleses, New Yorks, or even the Bostons of the United States. Homicides happen. People go missing. But to have serial murders and the detective who investigated them disappear, did not happen. Not in Charleston. Bigger cities, maybe. Movies and video games certainly. This was chaos.

JG spied the directory and identified where the Homicide Division was located. He made his way there, through the thickets of people, progressing slowly but surely. The sea of people were scattered about the sea of desks. There weren't enough seats for all of the parties having business there. It was a real grab-bag of characters. Police, suspects, witnesses, homeless, and others all piled into one area. None of it making any sense as all were screaming like it was the opening bell of the New York Stock Exchange.

There was one solitary man off to the side in his office. The African-American's shirtsleeves were rolled up, the knot in his tie loosely hanging below the top two, unfastened buttons of his shirt. He looked disheveled and if stress had a picture, that was it. The closed door was labeled 'Captain Simms'.

JG continued to fight the congestion, making his way to the door. He didn't knock, he just stepped inside the tiny office.

"I don't want to hear it. Somebody outside will take your statement. You'll have to wait in line like everyone else," the Captain said.

"Captain, I am Jacob Grantes. The attorney for Doctor Sierra Byrne. I am working the case that Detective Fischer worked, which implicated my client."

"Not a good time counselor. You barge in here wanting us to do what? Drop the case because the Detective has gone missing? The DA has the case, it is off of our desk. Now get the hell out of my office. I have a decorated cop that I need to find and my patience is wearing thin."

It looked like his patience had worn thin a long time ago, but JG left it alone.

"Captain, that is why I am here. I think I might be able to help in finding her."

He now had Captain Simms's full attention. He straightened up in his chair, began to button the top buttons on his shirt and straighten his tie.

"You know where she is? Is she alive? Did your client orchestrate her disappearance? I will have no truck with allowing her to take out one of my detectives. She is going to pay — "

" - CAPTAIN! My client had nothing to do with the deaths of those people at SCMU and BIOGENESIS, nor did she have anything to do with Detective Fischer's disappearance. In investigating who may have been involved in the killings as an alternate theory for the trial, we uncovered some very troubling information. That information was disclosed to your detective and now she is missing. You don't have to be a whiz to connect the dots. Will you hear me out? Before it is too late?"

Over the course of the next hour, JG went into detail about Nahash Pharmaceuticals and Rueben Feinstein. He set aside his legal obligations about lawyer-client privilege and confidentiality clauses and gave him all of the information. Two women's lives were at stake. Sierra in terms of her freedom and Carina in the very literal sense. Both men hoped it was not too late.

He told the Captain about the underbelly of Big Pharma. He told him about Dr. Enrique Estabados and his duplicity. He told him about everything that Stubbs and Deni had come up with, but were still lacking in hard evidence. JG divulged that his two investigators were currently in Costa Rica attempting to bring back Estabados who was there either hiding, conducting research, or both. He explained that without proof there was little legally that could be done but that his investigators were getting around the red-tape. He even confessed, off-the-record, about he and Sierra's false statements to the police.

There was some volleying back and forth. Mostly because the Captain had questions or needed clarification. But overall the conversation was civil and without interruption in spite of the commotion outside his office.

".... and you think that Rueben Feinstein has abducted, and possibly done worse, to Detective Fischer because she was re-examining this case."

"I don't know for sure if she was re-opening the case. You would know that better than I, she reports to you. What I do know is that Estabados is about a football field beyond being a suspect. I know that he worked for Feinstein at Nahash and that they are trying to move their parent company, Wyatt to the number one spot over PROXER. The two companies generate hundreds of billions of dollars annually, and people have killed for less. My investigators were

554

nosing around, that is how they found out about Estabados being in Costa Rica. They had been in contact with your detective, the same detective who was assigned the serial murders. If she started …. digging …. her …. nose …. "

JG's voice trailed off as he started to reassess all of the moving pieces. His face became pale and panic was apparent on his face. Captain Simms was trying to determine what had just happened.

"Counselor? What is it?"

"We have to get over to Nahash. Right now. I'm coming with you, end of story. I'll explain on the way."

17

THE CONVOY OF MARKED AND UNMARKED POLICE CRUISERS raced toward Summerville, South Carolina. The lead car was a Patrol Unit with two officers clearing traffic with lights and loud sirens. The regular traffic was moving aside in panic and yet thankful that the six police vehicles loaded with officers were not interested in them. No accidents were caused because of the disruption, but there were some close calls.

The officer in the passenger seat of the front vehicle shot out of the car before it had come to a complete stop when they approached the main gate of Nahash Pharmaceuticals. He drew his weapon and restrained the guard who occupied the booth. The policeman then opened the gate to the remaining five vehicles which could now race through. Only they didn't know where they were going.

"Which building is Rueben Feinstein in?" the officer demanded.

"Man, I should have listened to that other police lady. I need a new job."

"What other police lady?"

"The one that was here the other day. She wanted to see the boss too. Admin building is all the way down at the end of this main road."

The officer removed the guard from his post and deposited him into the back of the cruiser for further questioning as they all made their way to their destination.

There were twelve people in all that barged into the lobby of the Administrative Building, including eight patrolmen, two detectives, Captain Simms, and the attorney Jacob Grantes. The Receptionist, Jeffrey, was being overdramatic and feigning a heart attack. Whether he was actually under duress or if he was stalling for time was anyone's guess. Either way it didn't work. He too was placed in custody while the remainder of the troop ascended to the office of the CEO and President.

There were many men in dark suits a-la FBI or Secret Service, but all relinquished their weapons and stood aside. Highly paid security is trumped by a police team with an arrest warrant. At least it was in this case.

In the digital age, a warrant can be signed by a judge and scanned, then sent digitally to an arresting officer. There are several cases currently on appeal where a Judicial opinion is pending, so the police department has deemed not in best practice. It is still done, however, in exigent circumstances. In this case, Captain Simms had the arrest warrant on his iPad mini because time was a factor.

The arrest warrant also gives the police the right to search the property if they feel the object of the warrant is hidden inside. Captain Simms was able to convince a Judge that not only was Detective Fischer likely on Nahash Property but that Rueben Feinstein was complicit in her disappearance. There wasn't much in the way of hard proof, but Judges tend to air on the side of the police when one goes missing.

Rueben Feinstein was sitting as his desk on the telephone when the police burst into his office. Shock was not even the word for the look upon his face.

"…. what the!? I will have to call you back." He hung up the phone and stood. "What is the meaning of this?"

Captain Simms held up his tablet. "Rueben Feinstein, we have a warrant for your arrest for abduction and accessory to murder. Please place your hands on your head and slowly walk toward us from behind your desk. We have the right to search the entire complex for Detective Carina Fischer, but you can save us all some time and energy. Just tell us where she is."

He complied with the request, slowly coming from behind his desk with his hands on his head, but he protested the reason.

"There is a grave mistake officer."

"Captain."

"Captain, there has been a mistake. I have no idea what you are talking about. Murders? I have not abducted anyone. Your detective left here, at my insistence, two or three days ago. I am sure that my security surveillance can verify that."

"But you admit that she was here."

"Of course. I called the hotline to say as much when I saw that she was missing on the nightly news."

The Captain looked at JG and then at his officers. "Cuff him and set him down over there on the couch. We are going to get to the bottom of this."

He called the squad and had someone there listen to all of the messages that had come in on the hotline but hung up as he did not wish to wait. They would call him back.

"Do you have a place where we could look at your CCTV footage?"

"Of course, Sir. Any one of my security staff can bring it up on my computer screen or the television inside that cabinet. I would do it myself but I am a bit tied up at the moment," Rueben said.

JG was incensed. "Captain. You can't be seriously entertaining this madman. He has had three days to doctor the footage and get his story straight in case we came calling. He ordered the murders of three people, surely manipulating video footage is not beyond comprehension."

"Quiet counselor. You are here as a courtesy."

One of the suited security men was brought into the enormous corner office by one of the Charleston patrolmen. He then pushed some buttons onto the massive touch-screen hidden inside the cabinet that Rueben had pointed to. It took a few minutes but the footage of Detective Carina Fischer came up on a few of the smaller screens that were split onto the large one. The security man then pushed another button or two on the right task bar and only the smaller screens in which Carina appeared were displayed, the rest had disappeared from view.

All of them watched her as she entered the complex at the main gate, headed to the building and office in which they were all currently. She was agitated and speaking to them in body language as there was no sound. The security team assembled behind her and after some conversation she was escorted by them to her car in the parking lot. She was then seen exiting the complex in her car out of the main gate.

The entire length of the demonstration was played in real-time, the onlookers watched and were absorbed in it all. It was played again so each person could try to identify anything that might indicate tampering, but nothing was found.

"You see? She left here as she came. She was spouting off accusations and quips, just as you have. All of them unfounded," Rueben said.

Captain Simms looked around the office, paced it actually, while he thought. He looked at JG then at the floor, shaking his head.

"Mr. Feinstein, we are bringing you in for questioning as you may have knowledge of a number of unsolved felonies," he said to the room.

"I will read you your rights although you are not officially a suspect. We need to have a serious chat. The pause was palpable, then Simms continued.

"You have the right to remain silent, anything you say or do can .... "

Once all of the confusion was winding down in the penthouse office of the CEO and President of Nahash Pharmaceuticals, the officers made their way down to their respective vehicles. One by one they waited out in front of the building for the Captain and his guests. They had arrived in a convoy, they were leaving as one.

Many of them were milling about. The two who had led the team, who currently had the main-gate security guard in cuffs in the back of their patrol car, were questioning him. They took turns firing questions. They were not playing 'good cop, bad cop'. They were both aggressive.

"What did you mean earlier when you said that the detective told you to find another job?"

"That was the second time this week that someone told me to find a different job. I really want to. I hate this job," he said.

"Go on."

"These two private investigators came and told me they could get me one with them if I let them in. So I did. And got in deep shit for it. So when this detective chick came, I kinda gave her a hard time cuz I was already on a shit list. I hate the job, but I still need it."

"Yeah, Yeah. Then what?"

"So I let her in. And after I do, then these protesters start raising hell by the gate. It took me a while to try and get rid of them but they wouldn't leave until the detective came out," he continued.

"What do you mean?"

"These religious nuts said that what we were doing was an anomaly or — "

" — an anathema?"

"Sure. Whatever. One woman in particular. Said that Nahash was an abomination, against the will of God. I knew I needed to get rid of them, maybe I could get off the shit list. But they wouldn't budge. I stopped the police lady when she came out of the complex because I thought protesters had to have a permit or something to assemble. She said it wasn't her department but all of the God-fearers left right after she came through the gate."

"You're sure it went down like that? We didn't see that on the CCTV footage when she was leaving."

"Yeah, I'm sure. I was off to the side dealing with the assholes. They weren't on camera, so when she pulled up to where I was, she must have been off camera too."

The two patrolmen looked at each other then exited the car. They ran toward the entrance to the building where their Captain was walking out toward them.

They yelled to him in unison, "Captain .... "

18

THE THREE OF US WERE STANDING at the bottom of an earthen pit with dozens of dead bodies in the middle of the Costa Rican rainforest. The situation was dire and getting more so. It was nearly impossible to think. The people on top of whom we stood had lives and families and friends. Had. Until the man between Stubbs and I had come into contact with them. The smell could have gagged a maggot. I hadn't eaten anything since the day before or I would have vomited. The last meal was the one that was generously shared with us by some of the people we were now standing on. These poor people were rotting and the remains of the bottom layer were being attacked by hungry insects. The brush and twigs that we had fallen through had hidden the deep grave from large predators as well. So far.

The University of Chicago was not the only school represented in that mass grave. New Colorado State and the University of Florida had t-shirts attached to human remains as well. I could not hold a thought in my head. Seeing those young academics, whose entire lives were still ahead of them. Wanting to attach their names to something that would change the world. Big dreams all snuffed. Some of them now absently stared toward the sky they dreamed to. Or they were staring at me as I stood on top of them. Those images still haunt me.

There was no time to lament. I was nicked and bleeding, but would survive as long as we escaped the deep pit before hungry predators were alerted to our presence. But Stubbs was in bad shape. He had been hit four times, once in the lung. It had collapsed and he was spitting blood. He was a tough son-of-a-bitch, I had faith that he would pull through it. How many people could be hit that many times and continue standing, let alone continue running? If it weren't for being in the pit, he would probably still be running.

Then there was the very real possibility that the people who were shooting at us, the people whom worked for Estabados, the piece-of-shit with us at the bottom of the pit, would likely be on our tail looking for him. And us. Who wanted to bet that they knew where the bodies are buried?

I tried to climb up the dirt walls, through Stubbs's gurgling protestations, but I failed. Or as the college kids below us might have once said, epic fail. I could find no purchase to move up. Ten feet could have been a mile.

There had to be another way out. The girl from the University of Chicago that was imprisoned with us was on top of the pile of the hidden mass grave. She could not have been there more than twenty minutes before us. But there wasn't another way in or out. She had to have been dumped there minutes before we fell in, then the pit recovered to hide the pile of corpses. Which was also disconcerting.

"Stubbs. Give me your knife."

He was leaning against the wall of the pit. He slowly was able to pull the Gerber *Air Ranger* out of his boot and hand it to me. He must have been hit in the leg as well because the knife and sheath were soaked in blood. Some of the crimson slime may have been from the guard he had used the knife on in our escape from the cell, but there was just too much of it. We had escaped one cell where death was moments away, only to find ourselves in another.

I began to cut the fingertips off the corpses under us, careful to do so in an organized yet expedient fashion. I wanted one from each person with no exclusion yet no redundancy.

"Jes…. What are you …. doing?" Stubbs asked trying to catch any breath. I needed to get him out of there before he drowned in his own blood.

"I have to make sure these people get accounted for. This sick fuck killed them and he is going to pay for every one."

"How can you …. victimize the victims …. twice? Let them rest. Whole."

"They're already dead Stubbs. They ain't gonna mind. We're gonna be dead too if we don't finish this and get the fuck outta here."

"I didn't kill any of these people," Estabados said. He had been shot also, but I didn't care. I wanted him to live so he could pay for his crimes. I wanted him dead also. But a relatively quick death was too easy.

"Shut the fuck up. Your lies are doin' my head in."

I put the fingertips in the cargo pocket of my pants and continued to think of a way out.

"I never killed anyone. Los Militares did. I am here for the research. The samples."

I shoved the barrel of the *MP5A3* into his mouth, breaking a few of his front teeth. "I told you to shut the fuck up."

I only had four bullets left, but if I had to I would use one to expose his brains to the light. The more he denied killing these people, the less interested I was in seeing to his survival. I wanted him to pay, yes. But he was beginning to tip the scales.

Around the barrel of the gun he continued to speak. It was difficult to understand, but he said that he had never killed anyone in his life. Apparently having someone else do the actual killing got him off the hook for ordering them dead. I had never hated someone so vehemently, nor since. How he could lie, or fool himself into believing he was innocent, while standing on top of the remains of those he had put there, was beyond me.

Stubbs had managed to gain some strength somehow, some way, and leaned a couple of the bodies against a corner of the pit. He asked for his knife back from me. Not in words, as he was breathy and bleeding. He just stuck out his hand and waved his fingers towards himself. I got the point.

Stubbs then quickly carved out some notches into the dirt wall. The grooves were deep enough where the bottom of them would not collapse under weight. He then, slowly climbed on top of the stacked bodies and found footholds in the grooves he had carved. He motioned for me to go over to him quickly. I did and with every last bit of strength he flung me up onto him, onto his back. I was able to then climb higher, high enough to hold myself on the solid ground above with my arms and armpits. I kicked and pulled myself up like I was getting out of a swimming pool until I made safe landing above them. He had the gun and knife with him below.

"Go." His footholds collapsed in that instant, sending him back down on top of the bodies. He laid there on his back for a few seconds in obvious pain. He coughed and painted as he rolled over, trying to stand.

"You can't leave me here," Estabados shouted. "I know too much. My research. I didn't kill anyone — "

He probably would have kept on going, kept on lying. But Stubbs was having none of it. He reached over and with his knife cut out the doctor's tongue. Estabados was screaming out of his blood-soaked mouth, so Stubbs knocked him out with the gun stock. He looked up at me and waved me to go. He coughed again, spraying fresh blood of his own onto the bottom of the pit and walls. Falling down on one knee, he looked up and waved me off again.

Loud voices and the trampling of brush could be heard. The noisy stampede was making it's way toward us. We both knew what that meant, but neither of us were ready to admit it. I take that back, Stubbs knew what had to happen. I was the one who refused to believe the truth. The sounds of the men were no more than seventy-five meters away. In the time it took an army-for-hire to run about ninety yards, there would be no escape.

"I'm not just going to leave you here, Stubbs."

I looked around to see if there was an ambush point. Someplace for me to hide in order to think, come up with a plan. The grave was set in the middle of a spacious clearing. In the clearing, I would be a sitting duck. In the pit, Stubbs was a fish in a barrel.

He didn't respond or even make another motion for me to leave. He looked into my eyes, and in that ten seconds, I knew what had to happen. Just before he collapsed he communicated to me everything that I wanted to say to him. My eyes began to fill, trying to

563

convey it back, but there was no time. With those eyes he said the words that I have said back to him almost every day since.

I love you too Stubbs.

19

SOME TYPES OF CHURCHES ARE EASY TO FIND. In Boston, for example, at least one Catholic church is in every borough. In Charleston, South Carolina, if you are looking for a Baptist church, you can throw something over your shoulder and it will hit one. It is considered to be part of the Bible Belt, and *everybody* goes to one church or another. Also the Methodists, Pentecostals, and others. In Uptown Charleston alone there are 125 listed active and/or historical churches. On Sundays, even corporate chains like Target or Walmart don't bother opening their doors until after the noon hour. No point. They wouldn't be able to get employees to work, nor customers to sell things to.

Other types of congregations are not as easy, even in the South. The protesters outside of Nahash Pharmaceuticals, according to the guard watching their main gate, were Christian Scientists. In South Carolina, this religion is a minority. These organizations don't advertise and run the churches like a business. Most of the organized religions in the South are for-profit yet have the benefits of being a religion, like not having to pay taxes. These were not mega-churches like the Born-Agains or the Later-Day Saints build. These were small, private congregations that didn't evangelize. Which made them difficult to find.

JG listened to the Nahash security guard intently as the retold the story of his and Detective Fischer's interaction with the group. He also thought that the man would say anything to keep himself and his boss out of prison. He kept his opinion to himself, however.

Captain Simms was also listening. Of the hundreds of possible leads into the disappearance of Detective Fischer, which were only a small fraction of what was coming into the department either in person or on the hotline, Nahash was the most promising. Now that he had definitive proof that she was at the facility and had left of her own volition, the guard before him became the most promising lead.

The guard, the receptionist Jeffrey, and the CEO Rueben Feinstein were all put into the back of separate vehicles and taken to Broad for questioning. They would be put into separate rooms and would simultaneously be asked to retell their versions of the events that transpired three days prior. The interviewers would then confer to see if the stories meshed and reinterviewed. The entire time they would be watched through one-way glass and recorded.

Jacob Grantes went back to the police station with the convoy, but was no longer allowed access to the investigation. He would be called if and when it was determined that his client was wrongly accused and incarcerated. He was to go home, or back to his office, or to just plain go away. Which he did.

The attorney, however, would not simply go quietly into the good night. Not only was he a zealous advocate for his client, but that client was the woman he planned to marry. He was not going to allow Sierra to spend one moment longer in prison if he could help it. He needed some proof. Something tangible that could not be ignored. He needed his investigator. Either one of them. He wondered how they were making out.

The first round of interviews in the interrogation rooms at 80 Broad were calm and collected. The three had been split up and were asked to retell their stories. They were more statements than they were actual interviews. There were less interruptions, for sure.

Once those statements were collected, the subjects were given some caffeine to raise their already elevated heart rates while the statements were compared. Any deviation in the events would then be picked apart during the follow-ups. The real interviews.

There were always variances from story to story. No two people ever told a story the exact same way, even if they were telling the truth. It is human nature to incorporate perception and experiences into a story. Some embellish, some have an agenda even if inadvertent. The police use those small variances to pick away at the pill in the proverbial sweater until there was nothing left but a ball of yarn. That was how you sweat someone. Interrogation 101.

But these three told the exact same story. Every detail.

"Mr. Feinstein," Captain Simms said. He was going to handle the CEO personally. He walked back into the interrogation room and sat across from the head of Nahash. "We have a problem, Sir. Your statement does not match the ones we have collected from your subordinates. Would you care to go through the statement again?"

"That is impossible."

"Why is it impossible? Were the statements rehearsed?"

"Of course not. Don't be ridiculous. Facts are facts."

"Yes. But as I just said, yours doesn't match. Some of the parts of these statements can't be 'facts', as you say, because they wouldn't know what happened if they weren't present. You for example. Part of your statement discusses things that supposedly happened when Detective Fischer was entering and leaving the Complex. How could you know what happened at the main gate? You said that you were cozy in your office. Was that true?"

"When it was made public that she was missing, I knew that she was here and sought out the information from my staff. What is this really about, Captain?"

"Why was Detective Fischer at your facility questioning you in the first place?"

"It's already in my statement. She believed that I was somehow involved in the recent deaths related to SCMU and BIOGENESIS. I told her, as I've told you, that her allegations were preposterous."

"It does seem a little coincidental, doesn't it? And I don't believe in coincidence. Three people are murdered by a poison that you conduct experiments on. Those three people conduct the same or similar research for a rival pharmaceutical company. One of the main people associated with the school and that company has left that company and now works for you. The police woman who was investigating those 'coincidences' is now missing, and has been for three days following a visit to you. Either you stepped into a perfect storm of shit, or you at a minimum have information that you have not shared about these events."

"I'd like to call my attorneys now."

"You're not a suspect, you don't need an attorney. This is just a conversation. I think you have more information that you have shared with us so far."

"You've read me my rights, which means that any statement I make or have made up to this point is admissible. You are now saying that you doubt the veracity of those statements. I would like to call my legal team."

He was correct.

567

GAME OVER.

While the interrogations were taking place, two young detectives from the convoy broke off and went back to the scene of the burned police car. They were told to quietly look into the religious protester angle, and to start with the area down by the water where Carina's car had been torched.

The car had long since been gone-over by the forensics team. They had examined the vehicle, running tests on anything and everything that had been found. Which was not much. The car had been incinerated. They had come up empty. Time was running out, and everyone knew it. Three days and no trace of their decorated detective was meaning that the likelihood of her being alive, if and when they found her, was increasingly slim.

They walked down to the water and spoke with the man in charge of the dive team. He told them that his team had found all sorts of detritus in the waters on an abandoned shore behind an abandoned church. None of it relevant. The divers were working in shifts, combing the water in a grid pattern. They had even found a gun in the water, but it was so old and the wood stock so rotten that there was no way the weapon had been fired recently.

They asked what type of church the abandoned building was up on the hill, just inland of the abandoned shore. The Dive Commander told them that he thought he heard someone say that it was once a Christian Science Congregation, but not to quote him.

The two gave each other a knowing look. That was the second time that day that they had heard the name of that organization. First at the Nahash Administrative Building, where the guard from the main entrance had said the protesters were from. And for the second time then. This was either connected or an elaborate frame-job.   Neither of the two patrolmen were detectives, but then you really didn't need to be.

One of the two young policeman asked, "Has anyone been inside that building to see if there are any clues?"

"What do you think, that none of us have ever investigated a crime scene before? You two flat-foots come out here to save the day? Of course. A team went in there as soon as we found her car. It's boarded up tighter than a drum. Nothing inside but cobwebs."

20

I DIDN'T WANT TO LEAVE STUBBS. I didn't want to leave Estabados in that pit either, but not for the reason you might think. I was officially beyond pissed off and I wanted him dead. With the armed mercenaries that were now arriving at that hole in the earth full of corpses, they would pull their boss out to safety. Dr. Enrique Estabados would live another day, he wouldn't be able to tell any more lies, however. Nor fess up to the truth.

I hoped that Stubbs would hide behind Estabados, maybe play dead. Find a way to survive. I am from Boston, there is always hope. Where I am from, the remarkable happens at the last second. I wanted my friend to pull off that miracle.

I had found the path we had come into the deep jungle on, and I was following it back. I was not stupid enough to be on the path itself, because there might be others following me or lying in wait. I was running as fast as I could through the very thick brush off to the right side of it.

I was not running long before I heard the shots. It was like a muffled bag of popcorn in the microwave. A burst of suppressed air that were not kernels. Those pops were gunfire. The same type of sound that I had heard when our guide Hector was shot. Only this time there were many more. Instead of a Barrett *M82* or some other sniper rifle, these shots were from the *MP5s*. I had left Stubbs with only four rounds, no way to defend himself in the pit. I hoped he saved one for Estabados.

It was difficult to see where I was going. Partly because no matter how much I tried to man-up, I knew that my new friend was dead. I had left him there to die. The other reason was that under the canopy and off the path, there was even less light. And yet another reason was that the cobwebs were many and mammoth. The silky webs were strong, as if made of nylon nautical rope. I could only imagine the size of the spiders that occupied such webs. In one such web that I was able to avoid, I spotted a small bird struggling to free itself.

I don't know if I had read it someplace; or if the driver or Hector told me, but I wasn't as concerned about the spiders in the webs. They catch in webs because they can't see. It was the large furry ones that use their fur to sense their prey. They can jump onto a moving target. I wasn't afraid, not like I am of snakes. But concerned. All spiders are venomous, it is a question of if the jaw is strong enough to puncture skin and if the venom is deadly enough. Every female I have ever met is afraid of the things, and for good reason.

I was still in the same jungle, with the same number of creepy-crawlies that could kill me. But I was now alone. I was left to my own devices to get out of that hell. I am not much of a naturalist, but I am a survivor. Scorpions, lizards, Brazilian wandering spiders, among others, were all concerning.

My major fear was the snakes. If snakes had a sense of smell, I was a dead man walking. I was sweating like a pregnant nun and hadn't showered since Charleston. I saw what those fuckers could do in the enclosed moat outside the cell walls. 'Pit Viper', my ass. Bothrops Aspers were the product of hell. If one of those things got ahold of me, it was all over but the crying.

I came upon the makeshift lab of the University of Chicago, a bit further down the path and to the left. I was somewhat familiar with the layout as we had spent some time there eating lunch and changing. The place was a mess. Walls caved in, equipment destroyed. I stopped and reconnoitered the area to see if the camp was being watched. It didn't appear to be. Yet.

I wanted to see if they had a phone of some sort. Stubbs had made a good point. They had to be able to communicate their results and findings somehow. I needed to communicate with anyone who could help and as quickly as possible.

They had a satellite phone in one of the tents, but it had been destroyed. Estabados's men were smart, unfortunately.

In my search I found some dehydrated beef. I think it was beef. I didn't really taste it, I was starving. I didn't hydrate it even. I used the bottled water to hydrate myself. I ate it like it was jerky, tearing at it like a Viking.

I continued to search the camp for anything that I might need for the rest of my journey. I didn't want to spend too much time there, anybody with a brain knew I would go back the way I came in an effort to make my way home. I found their flare gun and a first aid kit. The nick in my shoulder turned out to be a bit more than a nick. I cleaned that up with antiseptic, bandaged it, and kept searching.

I finally found a trunk that was under one of the kids' bunks. He or she had backup parts for some of the equipment. Those kids knew that things could go bump in the night, especially in the rainforest, and packed backups. In the haste of destroying everything, the mercenaries had missed one trunk. I am the least tech-savvy person anywhere on the planet.

It's not like I opened a trunk and it was like a hardware store or a Radio Shack. The labels were technical and there weren't any instructions. I just found parts that looked like the ones damaged and dangling from the satellite phone and I got the hell out of there.

There was a small backpack thankfully, so I filled it with water, some more dehydrated stuff of various types, some dry socks, the flare gun, a knife, a lantern, the broken satellite phone, the spare parts, and the solar charger for the sat-phone. I wasn't entirely sure if the charger was for the phone, if the charger would work with the thin sunlight coming through the canopy, or even if the damn thing worked. But I took it anyway. Time was up, I had to get outta there.

I ran like a bat out of hell, sprinting down the main path because I needed to make up for lost time. My thinking was that if the gunmen were tracking me and had not yet made it to the Chicago lab, then they wouldn't be further down the path. I was betting the lot, because if I ran into any resistance I was a goner.

Well after nightfall, I made my way off the path toward a spot to rest. I hadn't slept in days and I was exhausted, but I knew that there would be no sleep. Only a short rest. I had never watched *Survivor* or Bear Gryll's *Man vs. Wild* but vowed to if I could get out of there alive. The only things I knew about the outdoors were the things I learned from Hector and Stubbs. Which wasn't much. I really should have paid more attention. I really should learn to speak Spanish.

I used the knife from the Chicago camp to cut a little clearing, using some of the brush to make myself a place to sit but the majority to set up a small perimeter. If someone came upon me in the night, I would hear them as they snapped the twigs as they crossed the brush.

Using a couple of huge green leaves, each one could have covered my body, I was able to make a clean spot. The lamp was plenty of light to make sure that while I was taking limbs off of trees, I didn't cut anything that something gnarly was living on.

I covered the brush for my seat with one leaf, and used the other for my lap to work on rebuilding the satellite phone. I hoped it was going to be as simple as square peg, square hole, round peg, round hole. I didn't have many tools, just the bits that folded out of the knife.

The next order of business was to change my socks. Nothing dampens your spirits like damp feet. I wished I hadn't seen them. The parts of the feet that weren't blistered were damp, wrinkled sheets of skin that could peel off. The under sides of my toes were raw meat. Tender doesn't describe how much they hurt. Dry socks made it tolerable because no first aid was fixing that mess.

Next some food. More dehydrated jerky and water, I didn't want to spend the time to soak the mystery meat. Rehydrating it may have brought back the flavor. Since I didn't know what it was, I certainly didn't want to taste it.

The ingenious people at REDARC came up with a lantern that is bright, rechargeable from solar energy, yet generates light that will generate solar energy. The REDARC solar charger worked, thankfully, and was storing energy from the light given off by the lantern. The lantern could then be recharged from the solar charger. A circle of reusable energy. I would have to remember to send them a kind email.

No matter how much light, the reassembly of the phone was slow-going. Fatigue and frustration were taking over. I've never been accused of being patient. My Irish is up anyway, even when I'm supposedly calm. But that was just about the worst day ever, so I was on def-con 5. Or 1. Whichever the really pissed-off one is. Throwing the phone against a tree rendering it unfixable was a strong possibility. Not a smart idea, but a possibility.

Eventually the phone was put back together, though some of the parts were still hanging from it, and a green light indicated that it was charging. We would see if it would actually transmit once it was charged.

Then I heard them. It was impossible to tell how long it had been, since it was dark and I was without a watch. I had dozed off for a bit as well.

Either there was a stampede of moose coming toward me, which I found unlikely in Costa Rica, or the mercenaries had found me. I doused the light and stuffed everything in the backpack as I crawled into the thick. I couldn't see what, but there were things crawling on me as I crawled deeper into their world. Screaming was not an option. The path was no longer an option. Getting back home, dead or alive, might not be an option either.

21

THE CALL CAME IN ON JACOB GRANTES'S CELL PHONE at 1:22 AM. His phone roused him from his intermittent sleep. He was worried about Sierra. He was worried about his investigators whom he had not heard from in going on four days. He had not had a sound sleep in as many days. But he was experiencing some much needed rest.

"Hello?"

"Is this Jacob Grantes, the attorney in Charleston, South Carolina?"

"Yes, it is." He sat up and threw his legs off of the side of his bed. "Who is this? And do you realize what time it is?"

"It is almost 1:30 AM, yes. It is 12:30 AM here in Chicago. I understand that it is an inconvenient hour, Sir, but I received a disturbing phone call and I was told to contact you. Now."

He was wide awake now. What was going on in Chicago that would necessitate an urgent call in the middle of the night from a stranger?

"I'm listening."

"My name is Dr. Damien Pierce. I am the Dean of Toxicology and Herpetology at the University of Chicago. I have a research team on assignment in the Monteverde region of the Costa Rican rainforest."

JG was at full attention. His heart sank, yet was racing. His mind was moving faster still.

"Go on Doctor. I have some investigators there as well, is that what this is about?"

"In part. The satellite phone that I received the call from was how my team communicated with me and sent me critical data. Your man is in possession of that device which gives credence to what he is saying."

"Yes, Doctor. Please don't take offense, but get to the point. I can vouch for him."

Jacob was unsure which of 'his men' he was vouching for, but either way he wanted the doctor to cut to the chase.

"It seems that my team, as well as other research teams have been .... " Pierce trailed off.

"Your team has been what? What has happened?"

"Annihilated."

"Did you say annihilated? As in killed? All of them?"

"The transmission was not good, and there was a very heavy accent, but it was clear enough. It seems that the respected Dr. Enrique Estabados, of the World Toxin Bank is responsible for the massacre of several research institutions down there. Not individuals, institutions. I made him repeat it for clarity.

"Your man is also in grave danger. He needs help getting out of there before he befalls the same fate. He was being pursued when he called. He also says he can prove every word of what he has said. Then the transmission was abruptly disconnected. I am beside myself."

"What was the name of the man that called you?"

"He said his name is Warren Dennihan. He said that I was to call you immediately."

"Very good. You did the right thing. Did he say anything else? I have two men down there."

"He did not. But he did say that failure to call you or to respond would mean, and I'm paraphrasing because his language was quite vulgar, ... it would mean certain death."

" .... I understand that it is almost 2:00 AM, but I needed to speak with you urgently," JG said into his phone.

"How did you even get this number?" Captain Simms was enraged. His wife was awake and probably his kids.

"Your guy at Broad. That's not important. What *is* important is that we have proof that Feinstein and Estabados are not only serial murderers but mass murders as well. You cannot let them go free."

"Slow down. What the hell are you talking about?"

"I just received a call from a Dean at the University of Chicago. They have, or should I say *had*, a research team down in Costa Rica. As you know, my investigators went down there to find Estabados for the three murders here. It turns out that Nahash has been killing people

575

from all over the Country, maybe even the world, trying to steal research and wipe out any competition. My guys are in trouble down there."

"Feinstein, the guard, and the fairy are being held, but they won't be for long. Feinstein came down with the thunder as soon as we started sniffing too close. Team of lawyers. We had enough for warrants which means we can hold him for twenty-four hours, Forty-eight tops, before we have to present to a Grand Jury. You know what that means."

"It means that we have to get my boys back with proof before that hearing. Has it been scheduled yet? I am going to need help Captain."

"If what you're saying is true, this is above my pay grade. We will have to get the FBI involved. They don't play well with locals. They will box us out of the investigation. Finding Carina at that point will be an exercise in futility. They are not going to let him walk or go easy, even if it does mean finding a cop. If we don't have the ability to cut him a deal, I don't know if we will ever find her."

"Do you honestly still think she is alive, Captain?"

"She is until we know for sure. If we call in the FBI, we won't know. We might never know. She's one of mine, counselor."

"If we don't get my boys out, we have no proof and possibly more dead to add to the total."

There was silence on the phone. Both men were thinking of how best to proceed. At that hour of the morning, without coffee, it was taking a bit longer than usual. The consequences of their decisions required that they think their decisions through.

"Let me make a few phone calls and I will call you back."

"No way, Captain. Make your calls, but I want to meet you at Broad. One hour. Don't make me go around you."

"And don't you threaten me, Grantes .... Goddammit .... I'll be there, counselor."

JG was waiting in Captain Simms's office within the hour. The precinct at 80 Broad was busy for that hour of the morning, but not as busy as the last time he had visited. He was led to the office, Simms had called ahead to alert his team that the attorney would be calling.

Fortified with a cup of decent coffee, unlike the cliché about bad police station coffee, while he waited. But not for long.

Simms walked in with a large gentleman in pressed jeans, Oxford shirt and sweater-vest. His saddle-tan loafers were the ones with tassels. He was introduced as only 'a contact with the FBI'.

"Counselor. This is off the record and off the books, so the less you know the better. My friend here will see through the red tape in getting your investigators out of Costa Rica."

"Thank you, Sir. What do I need to do?"

The man spoke with an even keel, almost monotoned. "I am told that you are a man of means. My suggestion would be to arrange for a flight out of there as soon as possible."

"Done. I have a plane already in the air and on the way. We should have no problem in terms of flight paperwork with Customs, the same plane was used to bring them into the Country."

"You would think, but that is not the case. The American Consulate has begun to put pressure on the Costa Rican Government to assist in getting your boys out of there. Once they get out of the rainforest, the next step is getting the Customs officials to stamp them out of there. No stamp will only light up some flares with our TSA and Homeland Security when they arrive here. The genie will be out of the bottle at that point, and I will disassociate myself with any of this."

"Understood. How long will all of this take?"

"From what I understand from the Consulate General, it will take longer to find your guys. The rainforest is massive and obviously well-covered."

"At the risk of sounding greedy, what are we going to do about Dr. Sierra Byrne, Rueben Feinstein, Dr. Estabados, and company?," he asked the two gentlemen. It was directed more at Simms but the FBI man answered.

"Officially? Nothing."

Captain Simms interjected. "We hold them until your boys get back. All four of them. Dr. Byrne included. Hopefully within twenty-four hours we get them back here with enough evidence to put pressure on them. Getting a confession is the goal, but short of that we need to know what they have done with Detective Fischer. With the body count as high as it is, taking the death penalty off the table is our only leverage."

"What are the chances that your investigators will have Dr. Estabados in custody?" The FBI man had an agenda, but JG was unclear as to what it was.

"I only know what I have told you. They went after him and they have uncovered atrocities, but whether they have apprehended him is uncertain. What is the end-game? Use Estabados as leverage?"

"Any deal made by the Charleston Police would not have any effect on charges brought forth by a Federal Prosecutor," Mr. FBI said.

577

"Ah. I see. So you are vying for jurisdiction because of the Costa Rican victims being from several US States. Whatever promises or deals are made, are null and void when the Feds take over in prosecuting the case? That sets a pretty bad precedent. And Captain Simms? You're OK with walking away from these serial murders? There are three dead in your own backyard."

"The greater good, Counselor. Mass murder trumps serial murder in this case. The Charleston victims will get justice, whomever tries their case. I want my detective back and in one piece. I'd pony up the courthouse if I had to."

"And if she's not? If she is not in one piece? You'd bet the farm for nothing."

"We're not thinking along those lines. I just can't think along those lines."

22

THE SUN HAD JUST RISEN, THE STREAMS OF LIGHT were slipping past the canopy over my head. I welcomed those rays. They created warmth from the bone-chill the night had provided. The illumination provided me with some vision, however slight. I had no idea where I was, only that I was still stuck in the middle of the Costa Rican rainforest.

No matter which direction I turned, everything looked exactly the same. The thick brush, huge trees, the cacophony of sounds emanating from creatures that surrounded me, all worked in unison to create complete disorientation. The only thing I knew for sure was that it was about 6:00 AM. I had noticed back when I had a watch what time the sun came up in the early green season of the rainforest.

And that I was alive. I knew that also. Beaten up but alive. For now.

I had climbed a tree after escaping my pursuers the night before. I used the elevation to wait out the night and make my phone call on the precariously held together satellite phone. I was just a precariously balanced on a large tree branch. It was neither comfortable nor settling in any way. It had been dark and I knew not what was in the tree I had climbed. Sometimes you just have to make the best decision that you can and hope for the best.

If I wasn't fumbling to ensure my elevated balance, I was fumbling with the satellite phone. The call needed to be made. I didn't know if I should juggle the dangling parts or to just let them hang. The connection was bad but the call went through to the last number that had been dialed before I came into possession of it.

The Dean from the University of Chicago was going to help me get out of here. I was not big on trust, when you get burned as often as I've been, you get skittish to say the least. But I had to trust someone. I hoped that help would be in time.

Climbing up into a tree was a risk. Snakes, monkeys, scorpions, spiders, lizards, and all the other things that I wanted to avoid were in the trees. I needed to make the phone call and was uncertain if height would help, I still don't know if it helped. All I know is that the call went through. I had to repeat myself constantly. I had to mumble so the mercenaries that were chasing me didn't hear me. The connection was bad also. The professor kept saying something about my accent and not understanding me as well.

Going up into the tree wasn't as much trouble as coming down from it. Coming out of it would expose me if the mercenaries came calling. I decided to wait out the night up there. Fewer things wanted a taste of me in the tree, at least thus far. I would be exposed to hungry things at or below ground level. I would be an all-you-can-eat buffet by morning.

If being alone, lost in the middle of the jungle wasn't bad enough, you can add severe exhaustion to the list. I hadn't slept in days other than a brief doze. It's not like Vegas where you can go for days partying and gambling without rest. I didn't have Red Bull and purified oxygen pumped at me to keep me awake. I had run and sweat and hidden for days without slumber. I had more running to do if I was going to get out of there alive.

I waited until the sun gave me more than just a few rays before I began to move from my perch. I wanted to see if either predators or pursuers were waiting me out, I spied none. Left, right, front, back, I had no idea where the path was positioned in relation to me. I needed to find it. Not to walk on, that was too risky. I needed it to gain orientation. The way out was that path, but it could also lead to my death.

Blindly, I picked a direction. I knew that the tree that I had climbed was in front of me when I crawled into it the night before, which meant that there were three of the four possible directions to choose from. I made sure to stay in that direction, keeping the sun to my left. South was the best I could guess. I really should have listened more to the driver in the Toyota *Previa*.

The usual morning rain began. The heavy raindrops hitting the leaves was loud, drowning the plants and animals as well as all other sound. The team that was following me chose that moment to attack. I didn't hear any shots fired, but I saw the tree bark and heavy brush around me spit into the air.

I ran.

Without precision, I zig-zagged back and forth but kept the same general direction, expending every ounce of energy I had left in the tank. Looking back, I must have looked like Forrest Gump running out of the jungle in Vietnam. Only without a weapon. I ran with knees to my chest and heels to my butt, pumping away.

They were moving in on me. As fast as I could go, they had the great equalizer. Automatic weapons.

Miraculously, I came to the path. It was both a blessing and a curse. A blessing because I could make much better time running from my pursuers. I no longer had to hurdle over bushes, fallen trees, rocks, and other obstacles. A curse because the path was only a little larger than a single person wide. No zigging. No zagging. I was lined up for the kill.

When I heard the helicopter, I knew I was doomed. The canopy would provide great cover, but I was on the path. Eventually I would come to the gorges and ravines. The only way to cross was on the zip-lines. I would literally be a dangling target for whomever was in that helicopter. If I could even make it that far.

My lungs burned as I continued to run as fast as I could, trying relentlessly to get as far ahead of the team that chased me. I was in excellent shape. I worked out five or six days a week, sparring and training in Brazilian Jiu-Jitsu. But that wasn't running with a pack on my back. It wasn't days without sleep and undernourishment. I was spent.

The first of the rivers came quicker than I had thought. I was closer to the parking lot where Stubbs and I had met Hector than I had expected. Behind me, They were closing in. Above me, the chopper was thumping and circling. How they knew where I was, I didn't know at the time. If I crossed, I was dead. If I didn't, I was dead.

There was a shed near the tower where one end of the canopy line was attached. I kicked in the door and found the necessary harnesses and clips. I strapped on a body harness and clipped the carabiner to it.

I waited in the shed for the helicopter to circle toward me and pass over head before I climbed the tower. I clipped the carabiner to the trolley, gave it a hard pull to ensure I was clipped in and ran off the ledge to allow myself the momentum of a running start. I let the velocity take me as far down the line as it would take me, then hand over hand I pulled. The chopper was coming back.

The thumping of the rotors was getting louder from behind me. I was not yet even half-way across the line. That was the first of several that I remember we had crossed going into the rainforest. If I made it across this one, there were more to come. My chances of eluding them through all of the zip-lines were between slim and none. I needed to get rid of their air support.

I hung there, trying to get access to my backpack. That must have been a sight. I was able to finagle one arm out of the pack, giving myself just enough of an angle to unzip the bag and retrieve the flare gun.

The thumping grew ever louder and the flow of air was swaying me as I dangled like meat on a hook. I was officially spotted as the chopper came from behind me, circling fifty yards ahead of me for the return pass.

A Sikorsky *H-34* helicopter was coming directly toward me. I timed my swaying to squeeze the trigger of the flare gun as the aircraft came at me. The pilot pulled up, seeing it with plenty of time. As it circled again, the big blunt nose moved away from me, exposing the side view of the chopper. It said US MARINES on the tail. I was being attacked by the *US fucking Marines?* Impossible. They had not fired a single shot at that point.

But I was being shot at. The team that was chasing me from the ground began to open fire. That was when the Marines came back around and laid one long round of fire toward the

581

mercenaries. I was being *saved* by the helicopter, not pursued. I had shot a flare at the people who were trying to get me out of the rainforest.

Either the ground team had had enough at that point, or were reassessing how to retrieve me off of the zip-line. Regardless, they stopped firing shots at me.

The *H-34* opened it's big side door as it steadied above me. A rope line was dropped. It took some doing to grab the line, tie it into my harness and secure myself to safety, but it worked. I was reeled into the big bird and we circled out of the immediate area.

I was home-free. Or was I?

23

BEING QUESTIONED BY THE UNITED STATES CONSULATE GENERAL, surrounded by Marines, is not my idea of a great time. The United States Embassy is not someplace I ever care to visit again. But it sure beats the shit out of being shot at in the middle of the jungle.

I was able to call JG, to inform him that I had been extracted. I didn't get into too many details, didn't tell him that I shot a flare at my rescuers. I also didn't mention Stubbs. All I said was that there was ample evidence of murder. We had bitten off more than we could chew in going down there, Estabados had an army which was funded by Feinstein. He would not be going back with us.

The Consulate General had used his considerable influence to covertly utilize a small team of United States Marines, which were stationed in Costa Rica on a mission to stave off the drug cartels in nearby Colombia. They had utilized the GPS tracking device in the sat-phone that I had repaired to hone in on my exact location for the rescue. The mission to get me out was a success, only there wasn't an official mission. It was documented as a training exercise. I was thankful that my government footed the bill for my rescue, even if they didn't know it.

While I was being patched up, stitched up, hydrated and fed, I asked if they would go in for Stubbs. It would take a ground team, but we had to see if he was ok. They were not too keen on heading into the rainforest to fight an off-the-books war. I told them about the other research teams that the Chicago kids told me were also down there. They were also in grave danger if not already dead. Bureaucratic red tape meant that they would not go back in. At least not yet.

I was brought back to the airport in a US Diplomat car. They walked me through to Customs where I was told not to speak. For once I followed the rules and did as I was instructed. Before long, relatively speaking, I was back on JG's private plane and flying home.

I am pretty sure that I am not welcome back in Costa Rica. I am very sure that I don't ever want to go back to Costa Rica.

I was very thankful to be alive, but once the plane was in the air I slept like the dead. Both of the flight attendants tried to wake me once we were cleared to land in Charleston, but I wasn't able to be risen from my coma until well after the doors opened. The *AMG* and my driver were waiting on the tarmac.

I was surprised that JG wasn't at the airport to meet me. Had he told me that he would not be there for my arrival and I had forgotten? My state of mind was groggy to say the least. In either case, I was to meet him at the precinct on 80 Broad. I tried to argue that I needed a shower but there was no arguing. The main reason I didn't want to go there immediately was that I didn't want Carina to see me that way. I was a mess. I had slept about four hours in as many days. I had not showered since the last time I was in Charleston, which meant that I reeked. The pocket full of fingers in my cargo pants didn't help the stench situation.

When I arrived at 80 Broad, I was treated more like a perp than a PI. I had sweat through the clothes I had been wearing for days and unbelievably still damp. Pile on the dirt and I didn't really blame them for giving me the stink-eye. I stunk. I looked like someone who had done something dirty. Or I was homeless. Or both.

They brought me to the Homicide Division and JG was waiting there for me with another man in shirtsleeves. More staring at me. I was beginning to feel self conscious. Thankfully I didn't see Carina there yet.

JG led me into the office of the man that I had not as yet officially met.

"Deni. I'm so glad you're home. I would give you a hug but …. well, you get it right? You look terrible. And you smell worse."

"Yeah. I'm tired and I need a shower."

"This is Captain Simms. He is personally handling this Nahash thing. As well as a more pressing matter. Where is Stubbs?"

"Thank you for your help in getting me out of that hell-hole, Captain. My name is …. "

" …. I know what your name is." He shook my hand.

JG was tired of introductions. "Deni. Where is Stubbs?"

"You had better have a seat."

"Oh my God. What happened, Deni?" He did take a seat, and so did I. Simms was the last to get off his feet behind his desk.

"I have been trying to think positively about the possibility that he might still be alive. But the more I think about it, the less likely that it makes sense that they would keep him alive. They probably would have killed us both already if we hadn't escaped. To keep him alive with all that he knows …. "

"You're rambling, Deni. What happened?"

"I don't know how much the Captain knows."

"I am up to speed. I hope that I know as much as the counselor. There have been several developments while you were surviving the wild."

"We were trying to escape the prison that they have built in their camp. Estabados and his army for hire. They have it built for the other camps that they invade. If there are prisoners, they keep them there. These kids from Chicago. One never left the cell, the other died trying to escape. And we would have too. They are well-armed these mercenaries. We fell into this giant mass-grave. Dozens of kids in there. They all went down there to advance themselves and medicine, and they wound up in a pile of corpses buried in a pit .... "

The words were pouring out of me in rant. Emotion was pouring out with those words. I don't know how much of it made sense in my first telling. They asked a ton of questions that I answered as quickly but as best I could. This went on for some time, back and forth.

Finally, I emptied my cargo pants pocket on Simms's desk, much to his horror. The fingers rolled around as I pulled the pocket inside-out.

"These are the people that were in the pit. Stubbs and Estabados were in that pit when I ran away. Stubbs had been shot several times, probably collapsed his lung. There was no way he could make it out, and without medical attention ...."

"So Dr. Estabados is still alive? Or is he dead also?" JG asked.

"Probably alive. His men were coming for him."

Simms was reaching for his phone that was on his desk. "I will call my contact to see about apprehending him for questioning — "

" — waste of time," I said. "He won't be answering any questions ever again. He would just deny it anyway. He denied killing any of those people, let alone the people here."

He put down the phone receiver. "Mr. Dennihan - "

" - Deni. Call me Deni."

"Deni. There have been some developments since you have been out of Country. They are denying any involvement in these developments, and seem to have some evidence to back up their claims. With this latest information, however, I feel that Rueben Feinstein may be responsible for the disappearance of our Detective Carina Fischer, along with the rest of these crimes."

My heart sunk.

"What? Carina .... Detective Fischer is missing?"

"Yes. My guess is that she also had a hunch about Feinstein, went down to Nahash to question him, which led to her disappearance. Do you have any information that could help us find her?"

"No. I had no idea .... I think she might have gone down there because I asked her to look into him."

"They have CCTV footage showing that she left the complex, but they are the ones with things to hide. They are blaming a religious group, or pointing the finger in their direction anyway. We have been looking at that angle, quietly, but come up with nothing."

"No. No. No. These fucks are involved. They can point all they want, but I've literally seen where the bodies are buried."

I got up from my chair to go to Nahash Pharmaceuticals. I had no idea how I was going to get there. Logic and calmness had left the building. Stubbs and now Carina? This was personal.

Captain Simms stood from behind his desk. "Where are you going, Deni?"

"Feinstein. He and I need to have a chat. Best you not be there. It will be violent."

"He is here. Held for questioning."

"Point the way and turn off the cameras."

"As much as I would love to do that very thing, we have to handle this by-the-book or he will walk at trial. He has three lawyers here, waiting to pounce on any violation of his rights. Now that I have more information and these, uh, prints .... " He looked down at his desk, at the fingers haphazardly strewn. "I will go back in there. You can watch from the one-way glass."

I hated the fact that he was right.

Captain Simms walked into Interrogation Room #2 on 80 Broad with a large evidence bag in hand. The newly acquired fingerprint evidence was quite literal and the digits would be used for shock value.

He wasn't sure how much information he was going to be able to extract from the suspect with this three lawyers sitting next to him, but this would be his last bite at the apple.

"Mr. Feinstein, I am sorry to have kept you and your attorneys waiting. We needed time to confirm your story."

"At $5000 an hour, take your time," Feinstein said.

"I told you that legal representation wasn't necessary, though your right, as you were not a suspect at that time. That has now changed. You have already signed the card with your Miranda rights on them. However if you would like, I can remind you of them?"

"That won't be necessary. I am aware of my rights."

"All right. I also need to inform you that this conversation is being recorded." Simms pointed to the microphones that were in the center of the table between them.

"Fine."

Simms then tossed the bag of fingers across the table, where it took Rueben some time to ascertain the contents.

"Those thirty-nine fingers represent the thirty-nine bodies that are currently dead and in a ditch in Central America. Costa Rica to be exact. Do you know who has built a research camp on the property where those bodies are located?"

"I have no idea."

"Nahash Pharmaceuticals."

"Impossible," he said. He shook his head but whom he was trying to convince was unclear.

"A Dr. Enrique Estabados is currently down there heading that team, is he not?"

A whispered conference occurred between the four men before one of the three attorneys spoke.

"We are advising our client not to comment on that. He can neither confirm nor deny where this Estabados is currently."

"Well advise your client this; we have proof that he works for Nahash, a company that is operated by your client, the CEO. This Estabados was working for BIOGENESIS while he was under the employ of Nahash which violates confidentiality agreements. Three people around SCMU and BIOGENESIS have been murdered, here in my city — "

" — which we understand that you have someone incarcerated for. Is that not correct, Captain?" The same attorney spoke, he was taking the lead. "Mr. Feinstein has said repeatedly that he has no knowledge of those, or any murders."

"Pardon me if I don't ooze with confidence over his word. The same person who we think is involved in those murders, at your client's behest, has fled the Country and is now killing everyone in his path and piling up the bodies."

"If you had proof that our client had anything to do with those or any murders, he would be under arrest and the DA would be here."

"I am trying to determine the whereabouts of my investigating detective. I believe that your client knows where she is and might be able to improve his position by ensuring her safe return before it is too late. *Then* I assure you, the DA will be here."

Feinstein had had enough. He was no longer listening to his attorneys.

"I have told you, ad infinitum, that I had nothing to do with those murders or the disappearance of your police woman."

"Mr. Feinstein. How much of a leap do you think it is going to take for a jury to look at thirty-nine bodies and convict you of the three here in Charleston? Add the cop who was looking into the case that has now vanished in their own backyard? The jury will eat it up. Your toast, Rueben. It is up to you for how long."

"But — "

" — oh I'm not finished. You don't need to answer that quite yet. I want you to know that this little game of yours is up. Finished. I want you to think long and hard about what is going to happen if you do not cooperate with us. The media is somehow going to get wind that the top people at Nahash are being investigated for all of these murders, abductions, and espionage and they are going to have a field day. It may have already gone viral, I can't be certain. How long do you think it is going to take before Wyatt, your parent company, is going to cut ties. Your on your own, Rueben. These lawyers at $5000 and hour are gone. You are alone. Here. With me. Care to revise your statement?"

Feinstein looked around the room, at his legal representatives who were trying to tell him to remain quiet. The thought of him being at less than square one was something he could not endure. His company would be gone. These lawyers who were telling him not to explain himself, would be gone.

"Listen to me, Captain. For the last time, *I had nothing to do with those murders at BIOGENESIS or your Detective Fischer.* As far as Estabados, I will only say that we had an arrangement that when things came to an end at his former employer, that a lucrative opportunity would be available to him at Nahash — "

" — except that he was working for you at the same time as BIOGENESIS and the WTB. You had to know. And you knew that this was a direct violation of his confidentiality — "

" — which could be dealt with in the courts. That is why I pay these men." He pointed to his attorneys.

"So why send him to Costa Rica?"

"What we do is very competitive. We have all sorts of barriers to our research there. The Government and their natural resources. Other institutions vying for specimens and data. Religious groups dropping poisonous mice, wiping out our specimens. The list goes on and on. I sent him down there to straighten it all out."

"And murder dozens of people."

"NO! I never said that. Those are your words not mine. Dr. Estabados said that he was making the makeshift lab in the rainforest more secure against marauders. He said nothing about killing. He said that we were the ones who were suffering losses."

"So you are trying to tell me that all of this is just your bad luck? That you are up to your eyeballs in felonies but that you are innocent in all of this?"

"Captain, I believe my client — "

" — be quiet," Rueben said to his attorney. "I'll answer. Captain, what I am saying is that we are always one step away from either being a hero or a villain. I never ordered anyone to be harmed in any way."

"'Show me a hero and I'll write you a tragedy.' That is F. Scott Fitzgerald."

"My point, despite your literary insertions, is that if what you are saying is true, that Dr. Estabado is involved in all of this, then he is doing it on his own."

"To what end?"

"I don't know. I find it hard to believe. If you are asking me if I wanted research and data from others, to be the first at finding miracle cures and increasing human life expectancy a decade or more, then I admit it. That is my mission, that is what I want. Killing and risking my entire life's work? My answer is no. So please, Captain, either arrest me or let me go do that work."

I stood there behind that glass, next to JG, listening to Feinstein. I wanted to kill him. How could he continue to lie? How could he look at the evidence bag full of forefingers, which represented the dead and heaped bodies in Costa Rica, and deny his involvement.

Estabados had done the same thing prior to him losing his ability to speak. When the walls are crumbling around you, deny, deny, deny. The prime directive from above.

Was it possible that Feinstein wasn't lying? I have conducted countless interviews as both a detective and as an investigator. He was a damned good liar, or he believed what he was saying. He had convinced himself that he was innocent.

In Costa Rica, surrounded by bodies and what could have been his final hour, Estabados denied killing anybody. He was lying. I had watched him witness shots being fired, listened to him threaten. He may not have done the actual slaying but he was guilty.

But what about the murders here in Charleston? What about Carina? Estabados was out of Country when Carina went missing.

I was tired. The lies were doing my head in. I racked my brain to see what was going on in Feinstein's. What had they both said that was in common? Other than that they were innocent and victims of circumstance.

I had to take my mind off of Costa Rica. We went there to get Estabados. What we found were more bodies, mine almost added to the pile. But while that was horrific, and I wanted justice for them, my focus had to remain on the three murders there. The disappearance of Carina was tied to those murders.

My mind went back to my visit at BIOGENESIS. I thought about our struggle to get through the main gate due to the media coverage and protestors. I thought about the questions regarding who could have done those terrible things and who could have known about venom testing? The list went on and on. Hate letters, emails, and phone calls came in daily. PETA, religious nuts, unions, other institutions trying to derail progress in favor of their own.

Then my mind went to Nahash. No media, no protestors. Why? Weren't they conducting the same research? The questions about their research led to the admission that most of the buildings were empty and waiting for samples. So essentially they were stealing research rather than conducting their own. Feinstein just admitted his guilt to that. There weren't any protestors because they weren't researching yet, nothing to protest. How did the protestors know that? No PETA, no religious nuts, no unions, no competition. Not yet.

Carina's disappearance was blamed on the Christian Scientist protestors out by the main gate. When did the protestors come calling? Why? Again with the blaming of religious zealots. That was the only common thread.

I had to investigate that angle. If nothing more than to eliminate them from the conversation. Something wasn't adding up. If Sierra Byrne didn't kill those people; and Feinstein was insisting that he, and to a lesser extent Estabados, didn't do it, then who did?

590

Sierra didn't abduct Carina, she was locked up. Estabados didn't grab her, he was in Central America. Feinstein was the common denominator, but my gut said that there was a piece missing. He pointed toward the Christian Scientists. But he would have pointed to anyone to get him out of his current predicament.

I left the viewing room of Interrogation Room #2. JG called to me as I was walking down the hall toward the exit.

"Deni. Where are you going?"

I stopped and turned around. "This is getting us nowhere. He's pissing me off and I want to kill him. But before I do, I need to get some answers."

"That's what we all want. So what now?"

"I need to take a shower and call my priest."

24

IT ISN'T VERY OFTEN IN A CITY LIKE BOSTON, MASSACHUSETTS that you can call your priest and get him on the phone right away. Even with the plummeting numbers of attendees at church these days due to things like; science, pedophilia, stance against abortion, stance against gays, and the constant begging for money, they always seem to be too busy. Especially at the Cathedral of the Holy Cross in the South End.

But I was the lost sheep. And Father Sean Donnelly had been my priest my entire life. The few times I had gone to church after my Confirmation, he would always try to get me to come back with more frequency. I would be there for a wedding, or more likely a funeral, and looking to get out of there as quickly as possible for the after-party. Father Donnelly would fight through the crowds, ignoring the devout to shake my hand. He would ask me how I've been, how long it had been since my last confession, invite me back to church, and speaking of which how much the church could use some of my money.

The Cathedral holds seventeen hundred people. Every time it would be the same speech, and every time I would tell him that my God is less judgmental, isn't short of cash, and certainly doesn't have time for a sinner like me.

So when I called him, he got his Catholic ass on the phone.

"Deni. How nice it is to hear from you. I was just headed to Mass General."

"Sorry to interrupt your evening, Father. I need some of your time. Can You talk?"

"I have a few minutes before I have to leave for the hospital. Is it urgent?"

"Yes, and it may take a little more than a few minutes."

"You could meet me down at the chapel in the hospital. We could talk there."

"Yeah, that'd be nice except I'm in Charleston."

"Charlestown isn't that far, I could even — "

" — no Father. Not Charlestown. Charleston. As in South Carolina."

"Oh. I see. Well, what is so urgent?"

"What do you know about Christian Scientists?"

"You're not thinking of converting are you? I have been your priest for your entire life. I Baptized you."

"No Father. I'm in a situation down here, and I need to know about them. Some wicked nasty stuff has happened and fingers are bein' pointed at these religious nuts."

"Well I take offense to the slanderous term 'religious nuts'. There are extremists in every group, religion is no exception."

"Do you know about them or not?"

"Yes, of course. While they are not Catholic, it is my job to know about all that use Christ's name to justify their beliefs. What do you wish to know?"

"What do they believe in? Would they commit murder to advance their cause?"

"I doubt it. The religion was formed here in Boston, believe it or not, in the late 1800s. Mary Baker Eddy I believe was their deviser. She was a very sickly woman her entire life, developing a belief system that stemmed from Plato."

"Plato? As in the Greek philosopher?"

"Yes, very good Deni. He believed that abstract entities were figments of the material world. This Eddy woman took that notion, saying that her illnesses, *all illness and death,* are illusions caused by mistaken beliefs. That spiritual reality is the only reality. Prayer can and will correct what medicine cannot. She named her religion Christian Science ironically. Her beliefs are neither Christ-like nor do they hold any place in science."

"So they don't believe in Jesus?"

"No, they do. They believe that mankind, like Jesus, was created in the likeness of God, which is not material but spiritual. They believe in the Holy Trinity, that people create the Holy Spirit. It is identified with the New Thought Movement. Which is to say that they use the same vocabulary as the Catholics, but they completely redefine the terms. Take Jesus's death, they believe his death was simply that he manifested his divine mind. Catholics believe that he had to undergo a physical and painful death in order to cleanse mankind of their sins and that he was the first mortal man to enter into paradise. Very different theology around the same event."

"So how do they explain traffic jams if nothing is real?"

"Funny, Deni. According to them, there is no heaven, no hell, no death. Simply another level of consciousness. In order to move beyond traffic jams, you have to manifest beyond it. The current level we are in, on earth, was created in 6 days which is definitely not the King James Version of the Bible. The snake was the first manifestation of evil that needed to be overcome. Which is why knowledge is bad, ergo medicine is bad."

"So they don't believe in medicine?"

"Exactly. No. But their faith has adapted. Contradictions always have to adapt. When children started to die because of their refusal to take medicine, the authorities forced them to adapt."

"Adapt how?"

"They were being taken to trial as their beliefs were considered criminal. I say contradiction because the founder, this Eddy woman, sued everyone and their brother. She was cunning and manipulative, which is not exactly in line with materials being figments of our imagination. The cult had to be a religion in order to collect monies without being taxed, and the only way to do that was to allow medicine in certain situations to keep the law at bay. There are even Christian Science nursing homes now. They have reinvented themselves, but only so far as it makes them profitable."

"Sounds like another religion that I know of."

"Warren? Did you call me to insult me and the Catholic faith or consult me?"

"So they do believe in medicine now."

"Again, only so far is it keeps any criminal proceedings off of their doorsteps. They are international, but the home base is still here in Boston. The Christian Science Monitor has won Pulitzer Prizes. The die hards, those that still follow Eddy's version of Christian Science, call themselves Platists. When those that weren't mentally able to heal themselves, like children and the old or with handicapped for example, they were allowed to take medicine. Because of that realignment there was a separation. That was back when Mark Twain took on Christian Science as a crusade. His daughter became a Christian Scientist and he wrote articles and books denouncing them as heretics."

"*The* Mark Twain?"

"Yes. While we were talking I went to my bookshelf here in the rectory. I am pulling up one quote that I have bookmarked. Let's see …. ah yes, here it is. 'From end to end of the Christian Science literature, not a single (material) thing in the world is conceded to be real. Except the dollar.' There is a Mary Baker Eddy Library here in Boston as well. Again I find that odd, since knowledge is supposed to be avoided as it gets in the way of spiritual reality with wisdom of the current one."

"So these Plato people, they kick it old school? No medicine? Snakes are the prime-root of all that is evil?"

"Yes. Precisely. But I have to say that snakes being the representation of all evil is not just a Christian Science thing. Every version of the bible, King James to the Book of Mormon, use the serpent as the physical manifestation of evil. Depending on which version of the Bible, the serpent is mentioned between seventy-three and eighty-eight times. None of them are positive. Each of those roughly eighty times represents evil or chaos."

594

"You're kinda givin' me the runaround here Father. I just want a yes or no. Is it possible that these Plato people would kill in order to prevent a medicine from being devised from snakes?"

"You didn't mention that part. That is what this is about?"

"Yes or no, Father."

"That is difficult to say. Yes, maybe. But they are but a small faction within the Christian Science community, from what I understand. Like I said, there are always extremists in every organization or group."

"So conducting research on snake venom, which is the root of all evil, to create medicines to cure people from various diseases would blow them the fu …. would really upset them? Do I have that right, Father?"

"In theory, yes. Please answer me. Is that what is going on down there?"

"How would I find out where Platists would congregate down here?"

"You have me there. I could go over to the Christian Science Headquarters here in Boston and informally ask them."

"No but thank you father. You've been very helpful. Don't go stirring up the snake pit."

"You're not going to answer me are you? When are you coming back to Boston? I would love to see you at mass."

"Yeah, I know you would. Thanks again. I'll be in touch." Then I hung up.

25

I CALLED JG TO LET HIM KNOW WHAT I HAD FOUND OUT. He didn't see the connection at first, I had to spell it out for him. I admit that it was a stretch. It seemed like a lot of trouble to go through to stop research that was being done all over the United States. It was a race to see who could research the most types of venom the quickest, in order to get the drugs on the market the quickest. Father Donnelly said that the Platists were all over the Country. International even. That being said, were they committing the same criminal acts in other States or Countries in the name of religion?

JG told me that the FBI was waiting in the wings to investigate this case. From what I had uncovered in Costa Rica, this had become a national mass murder spree that was being conducted on foreign soil. There was a Dean at the University of Chicago who was going public, getting the CPD involved in the crimes against the students there. This was a powder-keg, and I needed to stay low profile.

I secretly wanted the FBI to take over the case. There was no way that Captain Simms was going to be able to cut the necessary red tape to get Stubbs's body home and Estabados behind bars, if he was still alive. But that was out of my control. Despite my desire to get justice for my new friend, I had to get justice for those who were killed here in Charleston. I had to ensure that an innocent woman was not incarcerated for life or worse, given the needle. I also had to find Carina.

JG told me where the torched car was located, and the old abandoned church. The dive team was still out on the coastal waters near there, but they had basically lost hope. I headed out that way and was surprised to see such a desolate area right on the Atlantic Ocean. That nobody had dozed the area and developed it into hotels or luxury homes on the water was a complete shock. It was an abandoned mess with homeless squatters and meeting places for drug deals. Meanwhile, I was driving down there in a $75,000 Mercedes. In the back of my mind, as I parked the *AMG* just outside the police tape, I was wondering if JG had good car insurance.

I walked down behind the church, through the back parking lot, to the edge of the hill overlooking the shore. The car was torched all right. Carina's police sedan was incinerated. Melted plastic and tires, shattered glass. What wasn't burned was stolen. There wasn't a license plate even. You can't just put a burning rag in a gas tank to achieve this kind of damage. This thing was doused with something highly combustible and ignited from afar. The police sedan was the fuel for a large fire and explosion. Even in that neighborhood, somebody had to have noticed. The flames would have been tall.

Inside the car was more of the same. Nothing recognizable. The reason for torching a car to this degree was to ensure that there wasn't any trace evidence left for an investigation. Mission accomplished. I hadn't checked with the Charleston CSU, nor would I likely be allowed to, but I was sure that there would be no evidence available to find.

Down the hill, off the shore and into the water, the police boats and divers were combing the ocean floor. There must have been a lot of junk down there. Having to comb through what was relevant evidence and garbage was not a job I wanted. Especially since they obviously hadn't found any relevant evidence. JG would have told me if they had.

I waved to the dive team, who waved back though they probably had no idea who I was. The fact that I wasn't being sneaky inside the police perimeter hopefully allayed any suspicion that I was tampering or pilfering from the crime scene.

I headed back across the parking lot toward the abandoned building. How long it had been forsaken, was a bit of a mystery. By the look of it, the building had been neglected for some time. It had been condemned for safety reasons, but not torn down.

The church was boarded up, which would make it hard to get inside. I am a magician when it comes to picking locks. If It was a matter of just a deadbolt or two, it wouldn't have been a big deal. But the place was boarded up to keep vagrants and squatters out of it. JG said that police had been inside, so I needed to find how they went in.

The back door, facing the parking lot appeared to have been resealed recently. The plywood looked the same but the helical ridges were new, indicating they used new sheetrock screws used to hold the board in place. I didn't have a Phillips screwdriver or a drill. I gave the plywood my best kick but the stuff was thick. I could have kept kicking it, and eventually broken in, but not without attracting a lot of the wrong kind of attention.

Making my way around the outer edge of the wood, I moved my fingers to see if there was a gap to pry it away from the frame. Luckily whomever had refastened the wide-threaded screws had stripped the holes, affording me the ability to pry the left side of the board just wide enough to slip through.

The inside of the church was as black as the burned car in the parking lot. I couldn't see anything at all until I used the flashlight app on my iPhone, and even then it wasn't bright enough. I wandered around the place like a little blind mouse, while I displaced the real mice and critters that lived inside. A week ago, that place might have freaked me out. A lot had happened since then.

The little white-footed mice were running about all over the place. The church was rife with them. Which meant that I needed to cover my nose and mouth. When you live in a populated area like South Boston, you know these things will piss and shit everywhere which creates an airborne virus that will seriously mess you up, if not kill you. There was a famous landlord who became so for the wrong reasons and because of the fury bastards. He wanted to get rid of his dead-beat residents in order to gentrify. Try as he might, he could not get them to leave. They were poor and had no other place to go. He decided to populate his building with these mice in order to scare them off. It didn't scare them off and they also couldn't get rid of them. Instead the mice piss and feces made them so sick that two of the three kids died. He freed up the building but he is currently spending his time behind bars.

With my face covered, I moved about the mid-sized church looking for clues. Nothing on or around the pews. Nothing on or around the pulpit. After forty minutes I was discouraged and about to leave when I noticed that one of the hundreds of mice was bringing detritus to a nest. The nest was made of paper, stuffing from the knee-pads on the kneelers, tiny pieces of wood and plastic. The light green paper which was used as the base of the nest is what stood out. I scared off the critters so I could remove the paper, careful not to get the piss and shit all over me.

The light green paper was actually part of a flyer. Parts of it were chewed off or stained, but the gist of it was the notification that the congregation was moving. Calhoun Street. I took a picture of the partial flyer, as best as I could given the lighting and condition of the subject. I snapped several before I could accomplish one that was usable. The flashlight app uses the flash from my iPhone, which I needed to take the picture in the dark. Also you cannot use multiple apps at one time, even with my 5S. So I oscillated from complete dark to the flash for the photo, which I couldn't use because I couldn't see …. wash, rinse, repeat.

598

The relocated church was called The Church of Christ, Scientists. It was on the 100 block of Calhoun Street, near an Episcopal Church. Nobody had messed with the *AMG* while it was parked in the desolate neighborhood of the old church, thankfully. The drive was easy, just up East Bay and over onto Calhoun. I was rocking out to the Foo Fighters song *All My Life* as I made my way over to the church.

There was plenty of traffic on the street and plenty of parking. The front of the new facility could have been anything. My accountant could have used the place as his office. The only indication that this was not an office building was the large lettering above the entrance stating that it was a Church of Christ.

The door was unlocked, the lobby and overall decor of the building was sparse. The congregation area itself had neutral, beige walls with nothing on the walls. There was just the one pulpit in the front center of the room. No altar, no cross, no gold chalice. Just to the left of the pulpit was a bouquet of flowers and on the wall above, in all caps, were two quotations:

YE SHALL KNOW THE TRUTH AND THE TRUTH SHALL SET YOU FREE
CHRIST JESUS

DIVINE LOVE ALWAYS HAS MET AND ALWAYS WILL MEET EVERY HUMAN NEED
MARY BAKER EDDY

"Can I help you?"

I turned to see a white haired woman in what I guessed was her mid-sixties behind me.

"Yeah. Maybe. I would like to speak with the Pastor, or Reverend, or Priest, or whatever."

"That would be me. I'm Meredith Brown. You are?"

"Warren Dennihan. You can call me Deni. Do you have someplace we can talk?"

"About?"

This could go one of two ways, I thought. *I can play this straight and see how it shakes out, or I play a part and see if I can sneak the information I need.* Stubbs and Carina had taught me that I could get more by playing it straight down here. In Boston, It wouldn't have even crossed my mind.

"About things that I don't want the world to hear. Do you have a place where the acoustics aren't so good?"

"You're accent, it is very peculiar yet familiar."

"Boston. I get that a lot."

"That explains it. Right this way."

We went back to the lobby and into an office. It was a formal office, she sat behind a desk, me in a not-so-comfortable chair in front of her.

"That accent is more harsh, but it makes sense. Our Mother Church is in Boston."

"So I've heard. I'm gonna cut to the chase here, OK?"

"By all means. But we will have to make it short. I am hosting an online service in approximately forty minutes."

"How very modern of you. Prayer through a device that is only an illusion. My mind is blown."

"Are we here to discuss theology or did you have a point? 'Cutting to the chase' you called it."

"Your group here, this cult or religion or what-not, has been doing a lot of protesting outside of pharmaceutical research facilities. Right?"

"That would be not right. Incorrect."

"I've seen pictures, been there myself. I've seen the signs and people shouting about evil and against the will of God."

"And what makes you think these people are members of our congregation?"

"Because they said that they were Christian Scientists. It's also on their signs."

"Unfortunately there are several factions calling themselves that, but not necessarily true. What is this about? If it was us, which it most certainly was not, protesting is legal with the proper permits. Are you with the police?"

"I am working with the police, yes. So you are saying that you believe in modern medicine?"

"I am saying that like all religious groups, leaders must make accommodations to certain things to keep up with laws and/or current practices. Children and the elderly many need medicine in order to survive. We feel that prayer works best, if dire medicine isn't absolutely necessary. Blood transfusions are beyond that scope and the work of evil."

"Evil. Like snakes?"

"Snakes are representative of the mind's focus away from God. What is this really about Mr. Deni?"

"Just Deni. Three people have been murdered using snake venom. The same snake venom that is being used to create synthetic drugs to cure many different diseases that kill people by the millions. Outside of these research facilities are people with your belief system.

600

The Charleston Detective that was investigating those murders is now missing. She was last seen speaking with those protesters. You see how this all ties to your group?"

"Now I understand. This has been all over the news. I don't believe I can help you, and I certainly have nothing more to say. Good day." Meredith stood. I didn't.

"If I leave now, I'm coming back here with a team of people that are going to tear this place apart. A cop is missing. The more days that pass where she remains missing, the more desperate they are getting because her chances of being dead are increasing by the minute. They aren't going to be polite, they are gonna trash this place looking for a clue in finding her. You can sit back down and talk to me, or do it the hard way. You seem like a semi-reasonable person, so why choose the hard way?"

She sat back down.

"We are not protesting. We support the purists in beliefs, but not in practice. Our religion is about love, not destruction. It is against every fabric of our belief system that the root of all evil, the snake, could be the very thing to create a potion that makes pain go away. Not prayer, not spirituality. Don't you see? We are back in the Garden of Good and Evil, where the serpent is in the Tree of Knowledge. Are we going to go down that road again? The snake is offering us life, but what life? This world is not a reality."

"So you know who it is? The protestors, are they Platists? Your purists?"

"Yes. But they are less organized, in the formal sense. They have many numbers, they gather but not in buildings such as this one. They tithe and are active in various causes. They go to the retreats and conventions, but they do not congregate as formally as we do. Some of them have services online, like I am about to do. This minimizes the expense of having a building in many cases. Here in Charleston? If there is a chapel, I am unaware of it."

"So how do I get in touch with them?"

"You don't."

"How do they recruit new members?"

"By meeting someone. You aren't going to be able to track these people down. I'm not hiding them, they are a completely different group. It would be like Protestants and Catholics. They have the same basic beliefs, but a very different way of going about salvation."

"Do you have a name?"

"Specifically? No."

"You said that they go to your retreats and conventions, you must know somebody. If you are hiding something — "

" — I assure you that I am not hiding anything. If they are doing what they are doing, which I am not saying that they are, then they are doing it under the guise of my religion. I may want the same things, but this is harmful all the way around."

26

THE DAY WAS A TOTAL BUST. Night had fallen and I was no closer to finding Carina than I was yesterday when I was in another Country. Tomorrow morning would officially be the sixth day that she was missing. There were no ransom demands. Why keep her that long and then simply let her go? My only hope was that she was being used as leverage once the killers/kidnappers were caught. Leniency for the cop. But hope was fading.

At the current rate we would never find the bastards. That is, of course, if Feinstein was telling the truth. And that was a big if. Everything pointed toward Rueben and his beloved company Nahash Pharmaceuticals. Motive, opportunity, means. Add the massive body count in Costa Rica and you could get the needle ready, no need for a trial. But there was something about the story that wasn't adding up. Estabados denied the murders, but then he denied the murders of all of the researchers as well. Could these be separate cases? Could Estabados have been taking matters into his own hands in Central America, while others were sabotaging the research in Charleston?

The Platists seem to also have motive. In spades. But without finding them, there was no way to determine opportunity or means. There was no need for Feinstein to create more attention for himself by abducting a Charleston Homicide Detective. Stubbs and I had already been to see him, he knew we were circling the wagons. The protestors were the last to see her. The Platists. But why kidnap a cop? There would have to be several of them. Carina would not go quietly. Maybe they didn't know she was a cop. She was driving an unmarked car.

I called it a night and headed back to JG's house. He was up and about, maybe even waiting for me to arrive, though he never said.

"You're here. What did you find out?" He had a drink and handed me one. Redbreast 12 year Irish Whiskey. My favorite.

"Nothing. Less than nothing actually." I sipped my beverage. It was heaven. "This is delicious, thanks." I took another sip. "I have more questions now than I did at the start of the day."

"We're running out of time, Deni. Carina is the one running out of time."

He had hit me between the eyes and he knew it. I think he knew what my feelings were for her. He knew that her disappearance was probably eating me up. Nobody wanted to find her more than me. He didn't need to push me, I was already very motivated.

"I know, I know. I'm doin' the best I can. Tomorrow I see about punching some holes in Feinstein and his alibi. I was thinking that maybe the Estabados thing and the murders were separate. If I can isolate Rueb out of this, then that pretty much means that they are separate and I can move forward. Estabados couldn't have kidnapped Carina, he wasn't here. If he killed those researchers down there to protect Nahash, he may or may not have done it on his own. And the more I think about it, why kill the team at SCMU and BIOGENESIS if he had access to all the research? He could steal anything he wanted. Samples from the World Toxin Bank, data from any lab he had access to. Which was all of them. The only reason to knock them down was to take them out of the game."

"Right. But according to your theory, isn't that why he was annihilating the teams in the jungle?"

"Yes, but he didn't have access to their research. He can't just walk up to their lab in the middle of the rainforest and ask nicely. It's competitive. He had to destroy them to get their data. Here, he had the data at his fingertips. He went to work every day on the campus and as far as we can tell nobody at the university nor the lab knew that he was a spy for Nahash. No need to kill anyone. In fact, that would draw more attention. He had to step up his game and get out of there once people started getting killed. If anything, those murders did more harm for his cause than good."

"You're not suggesting that Dr. Estabados is innocent in all of this?"

"Fuck no. He needs to die. And I'm willing to arrange it. But he is gonna be the Feds' problem now."

"And Feinstein?"

"Maybe, maybe not. He is guilty of stealing research, and being a huge bag of douche, but a killer? I don't know yet. We need to see how he fits into this. Tear his life apart. Is he still in custody?"

"Yes. He has been charged on a number of lesser charges. He will be cooling his heels until he goes before the Grand Jury. Then they will make a motion for bail if there is an indictment. If not, then he goes free. You've got maybe two days before the jury convenes."

"Two days. I hope Carina can hold out that long."

"You think she is still alive?"

"I'm hoping. Jesus man. I'm hoping until there isn't any. I'm hoping that the bags of shit that have her are holding her in case they get caught. Use her to try and plead down to lesser charges in exchange for her alive. Otherwise there is no need to keep her alive and she is already dead."

"I'll go see Sierra tomorrow at the prison. I'll let her know what is going on and that we are trying to get her out."

"You go over there every day, don't you?"

"Of course. I love her, Deni."

"I get it. For the first time in my life, I get it."

"We have to get her out. This case has to be solved."

"This thing is a mess, JG. I know. I'm doin' my best. I'm sorry that I got dragged into this, but thankful at the same time. I never would have met Carina."

"I know you, Deni. You'll make it happen. For both of us."

"Stubbs. That poor prick. I knew him for only a few days and I miss him. I have never seen so many bodies in one spot, man. If this turns out to be as I think it is, ya know, separate? Then he died for nothin'."

"No Deni. He died uncovering those atrocities which may never have been discovered. And from what you have told me, he died saving you."

"Yeah. I don't need the reminder."

A silence came between us. I drained my drink, JG finished his. What he was drinking was not entirely clear to me. If it was alcohol, I knew he was enduring some shit. He didn't drink very often, he said. If he was drinking then, I didn't want to rub his nose in it.

"Do you want another one?"

"Yes, but I'm getting up early. I need to get some sleep."

"There is another bottle upstairs in your suite. If you can't sleep .... "

"My brain is fried and I'm exhausted. I'll sleep."

And I did.

604

27

MORNING BROKE AND I WAS UP AND REFRESHED. Feinstein. I gave myself the day to enter his life. Uncover every single skeleton, in every single closet. I was going to know if his bowel movements were regular by the end of the day.

In this day and age, most of what Investigators do is on the computer. You can dig up virtually whatever you want on someone by searching the web. If the person you are looking for ran track, there was a team picture on the internet. Somewhere, it was a matter of looking hard enough. Medical records are only private when the proper resources aren't available. I'm not saying it's ethical, but for the right price any information that you want to know about somebody is yours for the taking.

Only I suck at computers. I have people in Boston that do that sort of thing for me. One woman in particular. We have an on again, off again type of relationship. At that time it was off again.

She could hack into anything, I have seen her do it. She has a moral compass, so there are times that I have to figure things out without her. Progress with her help was always exponentially faster than without. I was a thousand miles away from her, there was no way that I would be able to persuade her to help me out over the phone. I am a more face-to-face kinda guy. Which means that I wouldn't be able to talk her into helping me without sleeping with her.

I needed a plan B.

After my shower I went downstairs and found that JG was home. Which was a surprise.

"I thought you were headed over to Leath to see Sierra today."

"I am. Brady had a slow start, which means he missed carpool. I drove him to school but missed my class over at SCMU. My TA is covering for me. I will go see Sierra this afternoon. I have the morning free."

"Perfect. Do you know anybody that is good with computers?"

605

"Of course. Attorneys have privileged information that has to remain confidential. Its kind of a job requirement. All of my staff at the firm have at least a computer and a tablet."

"I don't mean can they fill out a spreadsheet and download an iTune or whatever. I mean I need someone who can delve into someone's life electronically."

"Deni, I am a respected attorney. If you are asking me to aid in a cybercrime then — "

" — I'm asking you to point me in the direction of someone that can help me look into Rueben Feinstein. Computers ain't my thing."

"I can have you spend time with Harold, my IT guy at the firm. He is the Director of Information Technology for the largest law firm in South Carolina, he is not going to help you commit a crime. So nothing illegal, Deni. I mean it. For my sake also. I don't have plausible deniability if a hack is traced back to my law firm."

If you were told that you were meeting someone for the first time with the name Harold, you would probably have a picture in your head of what he would look like. If you were given a little more information and told that this guy is a Director of Information Technology, a fancy name for super-smart computer guy, that might further develop that picture in your head. It did for me. I was expecting a Poindexter. Maybe a pocket protector.

I need to reevaluate my stereotypes. This kid was a complete paradigm shift. Are all the cool kids IT geniuses now? Harold was in his mid twenties and could have been on the cover of GQ. If you pointed to this guy and said that he was a Calvin Klein underwear model or did cologne ads, *that* would have made sense. Tall, dark, and handsome has a name. And his name is Harold.

I entered the chilly, glassed-in room with computer equipment stacked like library shelves in the back half of the large space. The front half had only one desk, which belonged to the handsome kid approaching me with his hand out.

"You must be Deni." I shook his hand. Not wimpy or frail like I would have expected. The metrosexual in front of me was dressed casually in jeans and a trendy, long-sleeved shirt. I was trying to decide if I liked the hipster.

"Yeah. And you must be Harold. Do you go by Harold or Harry or — "

" — Harold. No nicknames please. JG told me to free up my day. He said that you have a project for me, and that with your reputation it might involve some things on the fringe of legalities. I am to insulate him from all of that, and make sure you get what you want. So. What do you want?"

Right down to business. I *did* like that.

"It seems that JG has told you a lot about me."

"He says that you are the best investigator he has ever worked with, but a complete dunce when it comes to computers. I can tell from your accent that you come from Boston."

"Right. Well, I've been summed up in two sentences. I am down here investigating the recent serial murders, and the abduction or worse of a local detective. I believe that they are connected. Where you come in is that I need someone to find out everything they can on a Rueben Feinstein. He is the CEO and President of Nahash Pharmaceuticals, which is a subsidiary company for Wyatt Pharmaceuticals."

"I've read about them online. What other information do you have on this guy? Social Security number? Home address? Middle name? .... "

"Nope, nope, and nope."

He sat down at his desk which had two monitors, side by side, each one was bigger than my TV at home. He kicked back in his chair, banging away on his wireless keyboard. There was a mouse up on his desk but he never seemed to use it. His fingers moved at lightning speed, jumping back and forth from window to window. If that was all that the kid did, I would have been impressed. I stood over his shoulder, which he didn't like.

"This will take a while. Why don't you give me your cell number and I will call you when I have all of the data compiled."

"You don't want me to stick around? You don't really know what information I am looking for. What if you have a question?"

"Then I will call you. I will get you everything. Bank accounts, the works. I'm completely fire-walled, so there will be no worries about it coming back to the firm. My job is to protect all of our client data and to protect our computers from being exposed. I am good at my job because I can't even key into our computers without the appropriate codes. Others are not as good as me."

"Thanks Harold."

"No worries. I'm just doing my job."

I was pleasantly surprised to have my day freed up. I was going to get all of the information I wanted, hopefully, without lifting a finger. It must be nice to have a big staff. I have one other investigator in my firm and another guy that I use to help with the heavy lifting on occasion. I have contacts and people that use me for favors, and I them, but I don't have a staff at my beck and call. It was nice.

Feinstein was in lock-up. I wanted to question him, or at least be in the room with Captain Simms when he did so I could throw a couple of questions out there. But I couldn't do that without the information that Pretty-boy Harry was getting me.

Nahash might be a source of information. I wondered if there still was a Nahash after recent events. I headed over there to see for myself.

Twelve minutes and no speeding ticket. I had found a station on Pandora for a band called Kings of Leon. I really did love that Mercedes. I was blasting the tune *Crawl* when I pulled up to the main gate.

The front gate was unattended, a pad lock was used to secure the gate. There were no protestors, nor any media crews. What I lack in prowess on a computer, I make up for with other skills. Say picking locks. That particular lock was not a good one. I manually opened the gate, drove through, manually closed the gate, and fake-locked it in less than three minutes. It took longer to move the car than open the lock. Anyone coming by would see the padlock. They would have to pull on the base of it to realize it was not fully latched.

I drove down to the Administration Building, which was also locked. There was a green light illuminated, indicating an alarm system to keep riffraff out. But that system is broken now.

The massive corner office of Rueben Feinstein looked like he was going to show up for work that day. Messages on his desk, computer sleeping, everything neat and tidy. That is of course until I was through with it. I didn't ransack the place, but I wasn't meticulous in my search either.

There were all kinds of files, none of it very telling. Projects that were about to be started. New Hire paperwork and Resumes for top people in their respective fields. Indecipherable data from research, which may or may not have been reallocated from the parties who conducted the research. I could not find anything that linked Rueb to the three murders or to Carina.

But I did find a satellite phone. It was a different kind than the one I pieced back together in the jungle, but I knew what I was looking at. The Iridium *9555* was staring at me. Taunting me.

I was tempted to call. I had to know if the great Doctor Enrique Estabados was alive. But if I called him, he wasn't going to be able to speak with me. There was not a waking moment that went by where Stubbs and his sacrifice for me didn't enter my mind. Tipping my hand might make everything down in Costa Rica a fire-sale. They would destroy every piece of evidence, move the bodies, and vanish before justice could be done.

The phone stared back at me for an eternity. There was no upside to making that call. But I had to know.

Using the menu button on the left, and the up — down arrows in the middle, I recalled the last transmission. Before I knew it I had pressed the green button above the 1 button. Slowly, I brought the receiver to my ear.

When the transmission was connected, the voice coming through the other end was like a knife in my chest. I wasn't sure what to make of it.

"Hello. Hello."
I thought I was dreaming. How could it be?
The sound repeated in my ear. A voice I will never forget as long as I live.
It was Stubbs.

28

THE ELECTRONIC INVESTIGATION INTO RUEBEN FEINSTEIN by the IT genius, Harold Dempsey, was going rather well. Extremely well rather. He traced the CEO back to his days as a child growing up in Brooklyn, New York, in the Garment District. In theory nobody was supposed to be able to look into the past of a child. In every society, children are considered sacrosanct. Off limits. In real life however, especially in the information age, it is impossible to shield their digital footprint.

Parents these days do their best to protect their children, but in the 50s who knew what was to come. Letting your kids out of your sight was de rigueur. You didn't track your child's every movement or scrutinize every friend like parents do now. Bullying was part of growing up. It was in the 50s, just as it was in the 90's. The PTA is now more involved than ever, but still cannot protect youngsters from the dissemination of digital information. Cell phones, Twitter, Instagram, and the like doesn't make life any easier.

Once Harold found out Rueben's full name from the public records of Wyatt Pharmaceuticals financial performance statements and prospectus, he was then able to view Feinstein's birth certificate. From there, he was able to retrieve his parent's information. Then he was able to access his parent's application for a social security number, which afforded Harold the ability to get that number from the secure Social Security Administration web files, which was called the Department of Health, Education & Welfare at the time of issuance.

Fortified with Rueben's social security number, the floodgates opened and he could access everything down to his shoe size.

At the age of seven, young Rueben was uprooted and his family moved to South Carolina. He apparently had little or no friends because Harold was able to see his library and zoo membership cards, which were used virtually ever day. Why someone had taken the time to put the information onto microfiche and then scanned into the digital world was anyone's guess, but there they were in plain sight. Rueben was always in the public library or at the Magnolia Reptile Zoo.

He graduated high school at sixteen, achieving his Bachelor's degree by nineteen from Clemson University. By the astounding age of twenty-seven, he had earned two Doctorate degrees in Ophiology and Herpetology. He was strait-laced, not even a parking ticket had been issued to him in that time.

Rueben was a financial supporter of his Jewish Temple, but there was no way to determine his attendance. He had never married. There were internal emails at Wyatt that speculated that he was gay. The people that reported to him during that time spent all kinds of company time and resources bashing their boss digitally. Apparently he didn't have any friends as an adult either.

Moving up through the ranks at Wyatt, Rueben was able to see first-hand how a pharmaceutical company should run. Shuffling through several documents, Harold was able to discern that the Board of Directors was allowing their star to branch out with his own subsidiary, his own pet project. Over the course of his almost thirty-five years with Wyatt, he had proven himself. Both he and the oligopic corporation had made millions, or more accurately, hundreds of millions.

Feinstein's millions were tied up in Nahash. He had been funding Enrique Estabados out of his personal finances for the past two years, wiring money directly into his minion's accounts.

Harold looked into Estabados's finances by dialing into his accounts. He was a shady character, this Estabados, funding all sorts of other shady characters from those accounts. If he was trying to hide it, he was doing a terrible job. The Doctor even converted some of his payments into CRC, Costa Rican money, prior to the transfer to ensure he was getting the best currency rates. Stingy and stupid.

Large payments were made by Estabados to a private security team, the Clodomiro Picado Research Institute who is the top global venom exporter, and various Costa Rican officials. All of the money being siphoned from Wyatt, who paid Rueben, who then paid Estabados, who then paid off whomever he had to with shadowy deals. Quite the operation. Most money-laundering passed around that many times would go undetected. It had. But it didn't take a forensic accountant to follow the cash. Millions of US dollars.

He then began to search into Wyatt, which was more difficult due to the encryption protocols. Harold searched through emails and what was thought to be secure documents trying to link knowledge of the money-laundering to someone high up the food chain at the conglomerate. He came up empty.

Prying into Nahash emails garnered no more insight. The monies were wired to Estabados as both salary payments and an operating budget. Enrique's salary was coming from Nahash Payroll, while his operating budget was coming directly from Feinstein.

While the movement of operating money was regular, there was nothing in terms of correspondence which would indicate that it was earmarked for specific expenditures. Rueben funded an operation to spy on and to reallocate data from BIOGENESIS. He asked unrealistically few questions about the money. It seemed as though Estabados had a blank check without any accountability. Either his lawyers told him not to ask in order to stay removed from any culpability, or he didn't want to know because he suspected.

The salary payments to Estabados from Nahash confirmed that he was working for both pharmaceutical companies simultaneously and had been for some time. There was no denying that, whether Feinstein was or not, Harold didn't know.

Other than a DUI, Rueben had kept his life clean of legal entanglements. Technically his record was spotless, because the inebriated driving was thrown out of court caused by a lack of evidence. The lack of evidence suspiciously coincided with a large donation to the arresting officer's child's football booster's club. Funny how paperwork can be conveniently lost, but the electronic trail never fully disappears.

Feinstein's social life consisted of trysts with expensive male escorts at a local five-star hotel, once per week. The orders were conducted online through a website. The same male escort was ordered every time. Rueben must be smitten. Harold wondered how Rueben would make this information disappear if it ever came to see the light of day.

Harold had seen enough. He picked up his phone and dialed. The call went to voicemail.

"Deni. Harold here. I picked and poked but it looks like other than a few relatively insignificant personal secrets, Rueben has made a conscious effort to look clean.

Nahash paid the doctor's salary, and Feinstein wrote a blank personal check for operating expenses. There is no denying that Estabados was a mole and they committed industrial espionage together. That is fact.

Feinstein was funding Estabados's operating expenses out of pocket, like I said. I'm no lawyer but it would seem that he did so because he knew that something nefarious was taking place. Why else keep it off the corporate books? I think that it will be very difficult for him to claim that he is completely innocent in this, whether he actually knew the day-to-day or not. I cannot find anything that indicates that he knew, in fact it seems clear he was diligent in not-knowing.

Beyond that, Estabados is a scumbag though. This message is probably going to get cut off so I'll fill you in fully and print you out a formal report if you would like when you come back. See you soon."

29

THE SATELLITE PHONE RESTED IN MY SWEATY HAND while I listened to Eric Stubbs call out through the tiny speaker on the satellite phone. My mind was racing as I tried to fathom all of the elements of how this had come to pass. The only way to describe the situation was to use a word that is overused, and misused, by today's youth. Surreal. I hate that word, but it is the only way to describe my shock.

I'm happy that he is alive, but how is he still alive? Where is he being held? How can I get him out? How does he have Estabados's satellite phone? Estabados was trying to proclaim his innocence, though he was lying, Stubbs cut out his tongue. Was that because Stubbs was involved? How many secrets did Stubbs have? Was he working for Feinstein the whole time? For Estabados?

All of these thoughts were running through my head. I felt like such an asshole. I believed that he was my friend, yet he had betrayed me. JG would probably be just as devastated. I don't have many friends. Even though I had only known him a few days, I trusted him. He saved my life. Or did he? *What was his end-game?*

"Hello? Is anybody there? I can't hear you." Stubbs voice was undeniable.

"Stubbs? What the fuck? What's going on? Where are you?"

"Deni? Thank God. You made it out of here. You have no idea how much I hoped you would be ok."

His voice was weak. If it was weak before he knew it was me on the phone, I didn't hear it. But it was weak then . I wondered if he was playing me again. Or still.

"So how long have you been working for Feinstein, Stubbs?"

"What? I don't have long, Deni so don't mess around. They kept me alive long enough to torture me, looking for you. I escaped again, but they are trailing me."

"What am I a fuckin' idiot Stubbs? What's the coverup? Whats your deal, guy?"

"My 'deal, guy' is that I'm gonna die very soon. Doesn't get much more of a final deal than that."

"Then how do you have Estabados's satellite phone?"

"I stole it when I escaped. Who memorizes phone numbers anymore? This is the last number that was logged into this phone. I've been trying to call this number but there hasn't been an answer. There are international codes, so I can't just dial 9-1-1. How do you have Feinstein's?"

"I'm in his office looking for evidence. Where are you?"

"I'm in the Caribbean on a beach, having a drink with a little umbrella in it. Where do you think I am? If I don't die from my wounds, they will kill me this time for sure."

He sounded weak and fading. He was coughing, just as he was the last time I had seen him. It sounded like all of the fight he had left in him was being directed toward me. It was either an Oscar-worthy performance or he was in trouble. He was one tough bastard to have survived up to this point. If, in fact, he was really in any trouble at all.

"Why did you cut out his tongue? What was he going to say, Stubbs? He denied killing all of those people."

"He is a scumbag liar, and he is still alive."

"Convince me, Stubbs."

"I don't have the time or strength, Deni. I should have killed him. This is going to be the last time we ever talk, you want to fight? You want to think of me as a liar? Don't get me and Estabados confused."

A few moments of silence elapsed. I was collecting my thoughts, Stubbs was collecting the last of his strength.

"I'll see about getting you some help as quick as I can. You hold on." I can't honestly tell you at that point if I believed him one hundred percent or if I was just playing along. I wanted to believe him.

"Forget that, Deni. I'm a dead man. Just use the coordinates on the phone's GPS tracker to find me. I'll hide in the jungle with the phone on me. Find my body. And I got back your gun, too. The 1911 I gave you? I'm dying, Deni. Don't let me rot here. You want your gun, you come get my body and bury me proper. Promise me."

I felt like a piece of shit. The guy saved my life and I doubted him. I still doubted him then if truth be told, but I have no concrete reason why. Maybe that is why I don't have many friends. My chest was aching again, listening to him die all over again, and knowing that just like the last time there was nothing I could do about it.

"Deni? You promise me. Believe me or not, don't let me rot here. Promise."

"I promise, Stubbs. I'll make sure you don't stay there."

"They're coming. Make these assholes pay. For me. Don't make this all be for nothing."

"Stubbs, I - " But he was gone.

Again.

I listened to my message from Harold on my iPhone as I left the Nahash complex. Feinstein was clean. Ish. It sounded like Estabados was running his own show on the side, only Rueben was paying the bills. Whether that made him guilty in the eyes of the law was for people like JG to figure out. Stubbs was dying or dead. One more added to the dozens down there already. Legally or not, in my view Estabados and Feinstein were responsible for it. Whether Stubbs was dirty or not, he didn't deserve to rot down there. Not like that.

Harold wanted to tell me in person what he had found, but it sounded like he hadn't found much of anything according to the message. Forensic accounting was not going to make sure that justice was done. He could tell me that over the phone.

"Harold. Thanks for getting back to me so soon. You work fast."

"You're welcome. Are you headed back this way?"

"No. I was headed over to have a chat with Feinstein in holding. Did you find anything that would help me with that?"

"Yes and no. He is mostly clean. He made sure of it. Estabados is running his own game, but I can't find one single piece of correspondence that would suggest that Rueben officially knows about it. It is all his money though."

"So where is the 'yes' part?"

"I have a report that I have created for you that I can email — "

" — why don't you just tell me. I'm not much good with technology."

"It's very simple. You have an iPhone, it can handle emails."

"I know it can handle emails, but the writing is so small. Just tell me."

"I'll still send it to you. Have someone at the precinct show you how to open it in an app so you can print it. Even a homeless person over there will be able to help you print an email. How are you so incompetent with — "

" — just get to the point, Harold. I need your shit like I need a full-body rash."

"Bottom line? Rueben is gay."

"So what? Who cares?"

"Well, he does. He doesn't want anyone to know otherwise he would be out in the open about it. Instead, he is paying just shy of $2000 a night for a suite at the Wentworth, then another $3000 per night for his male companion. I'm sure the room-service isn't the only tip. He shells it out every week."

"Great. So what? He doesn't want some random dude knowing him or where he lives."

"Yeah but he gets the same not-so-random dude every week."

"I see. So I use that information as leverage to see what other secrets he has been keeping? Do you have the man-whore's name?"

"It is in the report I just sent you. I dove into his life, Deni. Everything is on computers now. There are no secrets. He was worth, personally, before starting up Nahash, about half a billion dollars. His personal portfolio and monies have taken a beating since then. He keeps shelling out money but nothing is coming in. He is only showing a fraction of the money going out to his handlers at Wyatt. If the Board of Directors at Wyatt knew what was going on they would have cut ties long ago. Now that he is being investigated, I'm guessing they are looking to get as far away from him as possible."

"Has that gone public yet?"

"It's starting to get some attention, from what I'm seeing. But it hasn't gone viral yet."

"OK Harold. Nice work. I'll let JG know what a help you were."

"Thanks, but he knows. Good luck over there. I don't like this Estabados guy."

"Me neither."

The precinct at 80 Broad was abuzz as usual. The late afternoon or prevening was when the place was usually busy. Cops went out all day and corralled their prey, taking them back to the police station for questioning and/or processing. This day was no different.

I was in no mood for small-talk. It had been a long day and I had made no progress on the Charleston murders, nor on locating Carina. The only thing that was discovered for certain was that Stubbs was dead. Again.

Feinstein was the purse strings behind his and the other deaths, whether he knew it or not. He was going to pay one way or another. He would help bring down Estabados and sort out who the Charleston serial killer was or he would pay the hard way. In either case, he was going to be ruined both financially and professionally.

Captain Simms was in his office, which I was beginning to suspect was usual. I didn't knock, I opened his door and entered which was also a custom he hated.

"No need to knock. Just walk right in."

"I did. Thanks."

"What are you doing here?"

"I want to have a sit-down with Feinstein."

"I'm sure you would. This is a police station. You know …. for police. Last I checked you aren't one anymore, and never were down here. Even on the off-chance that he admits anything to you, you're not a cop."

"Exactly. I don't have to read him his rights because he's not speaking with the police. No lawyer necessary. You guys can have the tape rolling and watch from the other side of the glass."

"I don't think that is legal."

"It is if I tell him that he is being recorded. He is in a police station, and he is being recorded. No reasonable presumption of privacy. It will be legal. Any deals will have to come from you or your DA though."

"He's not going to get a pass. If we cut him a deal on the three murders here, the Federal Prosecutors are going to want him for the mass graves in Costa Rica."

"That is for you to work out. I want to find Carina, and so do you. He admits to anything or gives us more evidence that gets Sierra Byrne out of prison, that'll be a huge bonus."

"Why would he talk to you? We have been at him several times, he lawyers up and shuts up every time."

"I have uncovered some of his peccadilloes that he has worked very hard to keep in the closet."

"We moved him into holding. Give me fifteen minutes or so to get him up into an interview room and the machines set up."

"One more thing. Can you look at my phone and see about printing off this email?"

30

INTERVIEW ROOM #1 WAS EXACTLY LIKE EVERY POLICE INTERROGATION room that had ever been shown on TV or in movies. The mirrored wall with the equipment and observation room behind one side of the room; the one table in the middle of it; the painted and perforated sound panels that lined the remaining three walls; all clichéd but very real. The unoriginality of Hollywood came from somewhere.

I entered the room, where the haggard Rueben Feinstein was already alone, seated, and waiting. He wasn't handcuffed, nor did I want him to be. I wanted him to feel comfortable. As comfortable as possible in an interrogation room on a metal chair.

I took my seat opposite him, staring at him for a long while, and began my spiel.

"How ya doin' Rueb?"

"It's Rueben. What are you doing here? And where are my lawyers?"

"It's not that kinda interview. I'm not a cop, so you don't need your lawyers. Unless you want them. But why would you at a million dollars an hour?"

"Then I am not speaking to you."

"You don't have to if you don't want to. Your choice. I am just going to record your not speaking though, just so you know."

He nodded his head, indicating he understood but didn't care. I had a blue folder in my hand which I then placed on the table in front of me. It contained the attachments to the email that Harold had sent to my iPhone. I didn't open it just yet.

"Are you good with computers, Rueb?"

He didn't answer.

"I'm a genius when it comes to computers." So I lied. Who cares?

"They say that ethical people do the right thing even when nobody is watching. Trouble is that nowadays, everyone is always watchin', Rueb. Big Brother. CCTV cameras, computer footprints, cellphone trackers. So when you think nobody is watchin' …. turns out they are. You're not a very ethical guy, Rueb."

He was eying me but remained silent.

"You don't have to speak. I'm just lettin' you know what is going to be public information. As of this moment, most of what I am sayin' isn't known by very many people. But when your little gems, your little secrets come out? How long do you think it is going to take for Wyatt Pharmaceuticals to distance themselves from you? You are only about an inch away from going to prison for the rest of your life, at a minimum, maybe get the needle. I'm no cop, so I can't really save you from any of that shit, Rueb. But maybe you can help yourself here."

"There is nothing to save myself from. I have done nothing wrong."

"Have it your way. But we have evidence of bodies that have been buried near your research facility in Costa Rica. And you are about to have one more added to your list of murdered victims down there. My partner, Eric Stubbs, do you remember him?"

No answer.

"Well he has your satellite phone. Estabados has been doing some pretty horrible shit, Rueb."

"I have no knowledge of any of that. I am a — "

" — if it waddles and quacks, don't tell me it's a fuckin' hippo, Rueb."

"If he is working on his own agenda — "

" — you think you are going to separate yourself from him? You funded him. The money came out of your personal accounts. Legally, it looks like hired hits. Sponsored genocide."

After opening the folder, I took out the email attachments Harold sent me tracking Rueben's funds into Estabados's account. I showed the document to Feinstein, then went on.

"How much of a stretch is it going to be for a jury to connect the mass murders to the serial murders here in Charleston? Are you really going to stay hitched to Estabados's wagon? You are already in financial ruin, you're hemorrhaging money with nothing coming in. You have a large number of expenses, like most rich people I would imagine. But unlike most rich people you are paying for an expensive male prostitute every week, which adds up. Wyatt is about to cut you off like an amputated limb, so professionally you're just as fucked."

Feinstein's face was white. Whiter than usual. Cold sweat was beading on his forehead.

"Now, added to the all of the bodies you and your subordinate have racked up, you now have a missing detective. The same homicide detective that was investigating the serial murders here in Charleston. The serial murders that a jury is going to connect to you based on the mass murders that we can prove you funded in Costa Rica. Are you startin' to feel the weight on this? You're in some serious shit, guy."

"And you think that you can make it all go away?"

620

"You're not listening, Rueb. *I* can't make it disappear. But if you want the DA and the Feds to start seein' your side of things, you better start sharin' some information. Where is she?"

"I wish I knew. I have absolutely nothing to do with her disappearance."

"That is not bein' very helpful, chief."

"Listen to me. I funded Dr. Estabados for a result. Did I have my suspicions about how he was getting his results? I have no comment on that. But there is no way that he had anything to do with the murders here. I have been racking my brain thinking about this, he was otherwise engaged doing business for me at the times that the three people were killed here in Charleston. He was in Costa Rica, as you well know, when the detective was taken. All I wanted was to advance my research on medical solutions by synthesizing venom. I wanted to be the first to patent those solutions, ahead of the competition. I didn't want any of this to happen. I did not order it, nor did I want anyone in my employ to kill people or draw attention to us by abducting Detective Carina Fischer."

"Then who did, Rueb? It's in your best interest to start bein' more proactive here."

"Do you realize how many people are after this same research? How many people don't want this research to exist?"

"I'm gettin' that vibe, yeah."

"Do you remember all of the hand-wringing that occurred when cloning research was first introduced?"

"Yes. But you're not researching making human parts or a new human."

"No. But everywhere in history, snakes are bad. From Adam and Eve to Medusa to that stupid movie *Anaconda*. It takes a lot of undoing to assure the public that snakes will save the planet from the illnesses that plague them. That venom is the solution to a longer life."

"But it's not just snake venom that is being researched, guy. Scorpions, bees, spiders — "

" — but *we* are only after snake venom. Nahash. We get threats every day. And not just strongly worded emails. We have religious groups that drop poisonous mice onto snake populations to stave off our research. Do you know how damaging that is? These people are well funded and well organized. That was what I was counter-funding. In part. That is what I thought. And that is just one example."

He had me at religious group.

"Do you know anything about this religious group?"

"I had them looked into, yes. They are an Orthodox Christian Science group called Platists."

"And?"

"And what? Do you think that they are responsible for mass murder and the kidnapping a police officer?"

"Lets put our cards on the table, Rueb. You and I both know that .... "

621

Some of the pieces to the puzzle were starting to come together. There were still several key pieces missing, pieces that needed to be sorted out. Dr. Enrique Estabados went down to Costa Rica to save the precious snakes from being poisoned and ruining Nahash's chances at developing miracle drugs. Maybe steal some other research. The guys he hired with guns were supposedly there to protect the snakes and deal with any resistance to others sharing their knowledge. The pit full of university researchers wasn't directly on the land Estabados had carved out to do research, but it was nearby. His private stash.

He hadn't questioned us to find out who we were or what group we were with, he just assumed. Or he already knew. Feinstein probably told him we were coming. Estabados vehemently denied being responsible for the deaths of those people in the pit, up to his last word. Clearly he was lying. But was he protecting Rueben, Nahash, or himself.

Estabados was afraid of the religious zealots. One of the reasons for his army. But would a religious group kill all of those people? Or the people in Charleston?

" …. You were saying?"

"Say for one brief second that I believe that *you* are innocent. Estabados is a different story. I've seen that fuck in action, and my partner is dead because of him. But let's just say that the mass murderers, the serial murderers here, and the abduction of Detective Fischer aren't you, but are Estabados and/or this religious group. Why are they picketing and protesting outside of BIOGENESIS and not outside Nahash? You are conducting the same research, only on a smaller scale, correct?"

"We are more specialized, yes. They do picket and protest from time to time. The detective spoke with them as she was leaving our facility the day that she disappeared. Also, you must remember, we are not fully operational as of yet."

"OK. Apart from that, how do they have access to BIOGENESIS, SCMU, and the World Toxin Bank?"

"I would have no idea. I just know that Enrique would have no reason to commit murder. It would draw undo attention to Nahash, and he had already taken the necessary research. Hypothetically."

"But nobody at Nahash was killed. And I saw the bodies in Costa Rica for myself. He killed there, for sure."

"Not to sound callous, but if you put all of those people in Costa Rica aside, what are you left with? If your burgeoning theory is accurate, two birds with one stone. The zealots are destroying all research in Costa Rica, while they frame my company in taking down another."

"Your Estabados had one agenda, Platists with another?"

"He is not *mine*. Dr. Estabados simply worked for me."

"Worked huh? Already distancing yourself? Nice. So that's what you're going with, Rueb? Final answer? You hired Estabados to steal data, and he was a bit too much of a go-getter? Without your knowledge? That all of these are separate yet entangled entities?"

"Without legal representation, that is what I am willing to say at this point."

"So where do I find these Platists?"

"I have absolutely no idea."

"You had never met with any of them?"

"No, of course not. These nuts would just breach us with emails, voicemails, and such. They organized the occasional picket out by the main gate but they were never were able to circumvent our security. You and your friend were the only ones to do that."

"I'm going to need to go back to your office. I need to see if I can get a physical address from those emails. Did you save the voicemails? Maybe we can trace them from the phone calls."

"No. I didn't save them, nor any emails. They were annoying but crazy, I thought. I had no need to save them."

"That doesn't help your cause, Rueb. I'm not saying that I buy your bullsh, but I am gonna need more than your word. Some sorta proof. Carina's life is at stake here. Those dead bodies need justice. All of them. I think its pretty clear at this point that the woman who is currently incarcerated for all of this is innocent.

"And we are gonna need to get Estabados back here, Rueb. "

"Anything I can do to help."

Now he wants to help, I thought.

"Better late than never, I suppose."

31

THE MEETING THAT FOLLOWED THE INTERVIEW WITH RUEBEN Feinstein was nonproductive to say the least. Captain Simms had been watching the interview from the observation room on the other side of the mirror. He was unimpressed with me. He still believed that Feinstein and his international team were behind all of the bodies. The mass murders, the serial murders, the abduction and possibly worse of Detective Fischer. In truth, I wasn't completely sold either, but the pieces fit better with Estabados working his evil on his own in Central America; while the Platists worked their own brand of terror, here in Charleston.

What I needed to do was find these religious zealots. Once I found them I could ask them how they had access to BIOGENESIS, to the labs at SCMU, and to the World Toxin Bank. Access was the key to proving the case. Access was going to be the only piece that would get Dr. Byrne, JG's client and therefore my client, out of stir.

Nobody was going anywhere. Feinstein was still in lockup, and would be no matter how many lawyers or billable hours he had amassed. Dr. Byrne wasn't leaving the jug anytime soon either. Not without someone to take her place. Estabados was presumably still in Costa Rica, though the FBI was waiting in the wings if not already working to extradite him. And poor Carina. Heaven only knew her location. Heaven and whomever was holding her. I hoped that her situation had not changed for the worse.

I called Harold. The only lead in finding these people, to either prove or disprove my new theory, was to trace emails and the phone calls. I asked him if he could do that when they had been deleted. He said his expertise was in email, not phones, but yes he could. That an email, though deleted, could still be found.

I told him to meet me at Nahash. I gave him the address and raced the AMG over there. I am not sure why I sped there. There was nothing I could do besides wait for Harold. Maybe because the SiriusXM station was on Ozzy's Bone-yard and *Five Finger Death Punch* was blaring in my ears. I raced over there like my hair was on fire. My ears were.

So I waited in the parking lot for a few minutes. Harold had all the know-how. Except for the breaking-in part.

"Thanks for rushing right over here, Harold. An hour? Is that the best you could do?"

"I came as quickly as I could. I have other responsibilities you know. I also had to clear it with my boss."

"You're boss is my boss. Anyway, Rueben's office is right in here."

"Do you have any of his pass codes?"

"No. This is not really on the record, if you know what I mean. I'm not the police. I don't have a warrant."

We walked into the corner penthouse office together.

"That would be too easy. Wow, this is an amazing office. Look at the view."

Harold was taking too much time for my liking, looking out of the corner windows of the CEO's office.

"Yes, it is. Is that going to be a distraction?"

"No. Relax, will you?"

"Are forgetting that a woman is missing? A Charleston Homicide Detective? The longer she waits the less likely she has of being alive on the other end."

"Why would they kill her?"

"Because the people who have her have killed enough people where one more ain't gonna matter."

"And you think that these religious zealots would kill someone? Isn't that against their ethos?"

"Their what?"

"What they believe."

"They believe that medicine is evil. That everything in this physical world are illusions caused by a lack of religious belief."

"Yet they send emails?"

"According to what I've found out, the Platists are like the pure form of Christian Science. They kick it old school, but even in the old school they know how to play the system. They sued everyone and their brother back in the day. The lead lady, Eddy, won lots of cash in dozens of lawsuits. She outlived three husbands. Who outlives three husbands? These people are survivors."

All the while I was ranting about the Platists, Harold was typing away. He had managed to circumvent the security and privacy protocols, passwords and what-not. I'm not sure how

625

he did it, only that he did it. He was able to recreate the emails of hate that were originally sent to Rueben Feinstein. The printer was practically smoking from all of the emails that Harold was printing off. But no matter how many he went through, he kept at it. Which meant to me that he had not found what I wanted him to find. A physical address.

Eventually Harold sat back in what was Rueben's office chair.

"They were good. They spoofed the IP address."

"In English please."

"They cloaked the address from which they sent the emails. For people who say that this world is just an illusion, they sure know how to operate in it."

"Are you trying to say that they are better than you?"

"It's not a matter of better than me. They knew how to make it so that anybody with the knowledge of how IP addresses work, wouldn't be able to trace them. Its like saying that a criminal who knew to use gloves, thereby not leaving a fingerprint, is better than the cops. They didn't leave anything for me to find. They aren't better than me, they just knew not to leave anything behind."

"So how do we find them?"

"That's just it. We can't. This is the end of the road."

"C'mon guy. Make an effort. You're givin' up?"

"Didn't you say that they picket or protest or something? Follow them to wherever they are from where they are picketing."

"They don't need to anymore. BIOGENESIS has been set back decades, they aren't researching venom right now. Not snake venom anyway. Nahash is out of business. Did you see anybody on the way in? You like this office so much, you can probably have it."

"Funny."

"What about the phones? Voicemails?"

"That is not really my area of expertise, but walk through the logic. They went through all of the trouble of making sure that nobody could track an email. They hid their whereabouts with highly randomized code, and a ton of it, which spoofed their IP address. They took the time to create a denial-of-service attack — eh, never mind. They went through a lot of trouble, essentially to inundate the recipient. So that being said, you think that they are going to be foolish enough to allow a phone number to be traced? If we could access Nahash phone records, and if we could pinpoint which phone call left which voicemail, that have all been deleted by the way, do you think that it is going to be linked to a traceable phone?"

"You're kinda a Debbie Downer aren't ya? I'm not givin' up. I'm gonna find these fucks."

"Your dedication is both admirable and blind. The police haven't found her after more than a week of searching. She is one of their own. They have come up blank. This was a very good idea, I'll give you that. I am impressed that you thought of it to be honest. Printing an email from your phone was daunting, so a physical address from an IP is rather ingenious for a guy like you. But it is over. You are not going to find them, ergo you are not going to find her. I am really very sorry. When people don't want to be found they — "

" — they don't want to be found. Right. But what if they came to me?"

"I'm afraid you've lost me."

"Why chase them? Let them come to me."

"Uh huh. And why would they do that?"

"You have to make it worth their while."

32

SKY PHILLIPS READ THE WEDNESDAY MORNING EDITION of the Charleston Post and Courier at her kitchen table. The article that caught her attention was on the second page in the front section. It was impossible to ignore, it took up the entire page above and below the fold. There were no advertisements, though she looked to see if this article might be sponsored. She had seen many phony news articles that were actually advertisements, TV shows that were actually infomercials. The article had to be an advert. But there was no logo to be seen. The big headline read:

Local Lab Discovers Miracle Cures in Venom

The article went on to discuss how this had come to be. That scientists collaborating from South Carolina Medical University, the World Toxin Bank, and BIOGENESIS Pharmaceuticals, a division of PROXER Pharmaceuticals, have uncovered the mysteries of several forms of natural toxins found in the venom of snakes, scorpions, bees, lizards, spiders, frogs, eels, snails and some fish such as pufferfish. That in their natural state, many of these toxins were severely dangerous if not deadly to humans. The article also elaborated that each of these toxins targeted very specific bodily functions and those targets were the sights of many forms of human disease. The scientists were able to synthesize smaller doses using the peptides found in these toxins creating drugs such as Tetrodotoxin (TTX) from pufferfish for example. Heart Disease, Diabetes, Cancer, HIV, Hypertension, Alzheimer's, Parkinson's, Multiple Sclerosis and many many more were all going to be cured within a few short months after the respective testing was completed. It went on to tell the reader to then tell their doctor to prescribe them these various drugs.

Sky ripped the newspaper into shreds. The remaining larger portions were crumpled up into a ball. She threw the balled paper at her television which just happened to be airing an ad for Cialis. She screamed at the top of her lungs toward the ceiling above her.

She was a large woman. Not large as in obese, large as in just shy of six feet and muscular. She had the physique of a body-builder. As she screamed her veins swelled, filling them with blood and raising them on her skin. Her biceps were engorged as her fists were curled into balls ready for a brawl.

After her tantrum, Sky gathered herself, leaning on her kitchen table. Both hands were flat, her arms straight-locked, as he dropped her chin to her non-feminine chest. She hovered over the table as she tried to compose herself.

The news was beyond belief. Drugs were everywhere, both legal and illegal. She had been accused of steroid use on many occasion but had never dreamed of juicing. Her body was a temple. Her mind had created the reality of her musculature.

The human mind has become weak, she thought. *Nobody mentally overcomes. Why conquer with the mind when you can pop a pill?*

She paced around her small apartment, through her kitchenette, the living room, and back again. Her abode was antithetical to her body. Her mass filled the tiny space. The lack of furniture, only that which was absolutely necessary, was both by design and necessity.

The news was intolerable. The article was against everything that she had felt or believed in. She began to ponder her options, realizing that doing nothing was not one of those options. Sky also realized that she had very little time to act, according to the news report. If the reporter was accurate, the drugs had already been produced and were in testing trials. It would be no-time at all before Pandora was out of the box permanently.

She went back into her kitchenette, retrieving a prepaid cellphone from the basket on her counter which also housed her car keys. She dialed a number into the smart-phone and waited for the recipient to answer. Unfortunately, there was no answer. She was forced to leave a voicemail message.

"It's me, Sky. I am not sure where you are or why you aren't answering your phone but we have a problem. Pick up today's newspaper, second page. It seems our efforts have been in vain. We need to come up with a plan and quickly. It is time to escalate things. Call me back as soon as you get this message."

She ended the call, tossed the phone back into the basket from whence it came. She continued to think. Rack her brain, in fact, trying to devise a plan.

In times of crisis, Sky Phillips did two things. She exercised and she prayed. Not at the same time of course. Her workout of choice was not Yoga. While she was certain that her spirituality enhanced her physique, her mass was from lifting weights. She wanted more than anything to sweat out her anger. She needed to exert herself to the point of exhaustion. Then and only then could her mind be clear. To think. To pray.

But there was no time. She needed an answer from her Maker. She needed to find a path. A path into a murky land that had just been revealed to her. This newspaper article was the beginning of the end. Satan was before her.

She was a knight in the war against evil. She thought herself to be a modern day Joan of Arc. She would lead her army to banish this new threat against God.

Would God speak to her?

Then it happened. She found God's answer in her own mind's eye.

Sky reviewed the top of the article, spying the correspondent's name. She had to ascertain if the information was accurate. She needed to know where the trials were being conducted, where the supplies of these various drugs were located. Where they were being produced.

Lance Grober. The story was written by Lance Grober. Sky went to her kitchenette and opened her Dell *Latitude E6430* laptop. She opened the website for the Charleston Post and Courier, then clicked on the `Index` button on the right. The window that popped up listed all of the assorted sections of the daily paper and myriad contributors and bloggers, again on the right. She clicked on the link for `Lance Grober, News`. That led her to his profile picture and generic information, along with the archived stories that he had reported in reverse chronological order.

Next she opened Facebook and searched for the news writer. There were many Lance Grobers, but fortified with the Courier photo, she was able to match it to the Facebook profile picture. She clicked on him.

His Timeline opened, then she clicked `About`. Amazingly, his information was readily available. Work and Education. Relationship Status. He was married to a woman with whom he had a young daughter. Contact Information. Why this information was not private was a question she could ask him when they met.

Which was about to happen.

33

LANCE GROBER HAD AN ACTIVE LIFESTYLE. He was always on the go. His wife and young child had consumed more than half of every day, of every week. He was happily married to his college sweetheart, and his four year old daughter was the light of his life. His little girl. But there were always recitals, both dance and violin. The girl in the pretty pink tutu and the tiara demanded a lot of time and attention. His wife was a stay at home mom, so when Lance was home she desperately needed an adult. Her husband. Work was supposed to be his little escape.

Except the Charleston Post and Courier was a heartbeat away from bankruptcy. The paper couldn't compete with the alternative media of the digital age. Nobody read the newspaper anymore, and certainly didn't want to pay for it. Alternative sources for news was winning. So his editor was always on his ass, driving him to do more with less. More hours, less pay. More in depth research, no budget. Fifteen hour days weren't enough to put food on the table sometimes.

Grober was able to carve out one hour for himself in his busy life. One hour where he wasn't eating, sleeping, working, reading a bedtime story, or listening to one his wife wanted to tell him. That hour was for the gym. Planet Fitness to be precise. It was open twenty-four hours a day, seven days a week. His varying schedule would always be able to fit in one hour.

The writer was not a weight-lifter by any stretch. Going to the gym five days a week clearly meant that he was in good shape, but he was not big. Lance was toned. He would start with fifteen minutes of cardio on the elliptical machine or the treadmill, then spend the rest of his time on the Nautilus machines. His muscle tone was from band resistance, not free-weights.

On Wednesday evening, while some of his colleagues were checking out the local talent at a happy-hour, Lance was taking his personal hour. There were, of course, plans for the night. His wife had already phoned him and told him so. But not until after he was able to work out some of his stress, leaving the things that weighed on him outside of his home. Away from his wife and young daughter.

Large format fitness centers, like Planet Fitness, are fodder for meeting people. People of the opposite sex, or same sex in some cases, could use the motions and sweat to jump-start their libidos. For some, that was the only reason for going to the gym. Women would put on make-up, wear their most fashionable jog bra and tightest yoga pants, while men would use any excuse to lift their shirts to show off their six-pack abs.

Lance found the entire charade ridiculous but no better or worse than picking someone up in a bar. Women would be in their jewelry and accentuate their poses, men would show their best body-building pose in the mirror. It always seemed that the meat market was open. But not for him. He would simply put in his earbuds from his iPod and sweat out the day. No conversation, no lingering looks regardless of how benign.

Occasionally Lance would get a long look from an admirer. Not often, but on occasion. Women who liked the shy type. Sometimes men would look. But on that night he was getting overt stares from one person that seemed to be a combination of both. It was definitely a woman, but she had a more muscular body than he did. She took him in, long at length. She would do a dead-lift with an insane amount of weight, then stare at him while he used the various Nautilus machines. It was not subtle. Even when she looked toward the mirror, her eyes found him in the reflection.

He found it odd that this woman was spending so much energy looking at him. If one was to guess what her type would be, one might think either another woman or a male who was at a minimum as muscular as she. But her focus was on him. He began to feel self-conscious. He looked at himself, no stains. Nothing had fallen out of his shorts. He looked in the mirror. No buggers, nothing was in his teeth.

When his hour was up, he went into the locker room, as usual. He showered, again the norm. After changing and packing his gym-bag he exited the men's lockers back through the gym, heading toward the door to leave. The woman was still on his mind, because he looked for her in the dead-lift area. She was gone.

Lance made his way out the front door, the cute college girl working the front reception saying goodbye to him as left. He half-heartedly said goodbye back and walked toward his car in the parking lot to the side of the building.

He pressed the button on his key fob to unlock the car, then another to pop the trunk of his Ford *Fusion*. He always kept his gym bag containing is sweaty work-out clothes in the trunk, else his wife would complain about the stink in the car. He threw the bag into the trunk and was about to close it when he heard a footstep from the graveled parking lot. Someone was behind him.

Lance turned to see who had followed him to his car when there was a thud on the back of his head. The lights went out.

"You're awake." Sky was sitting in a chair opposite Lance, who was attached to his chair with plastic zip-ties.

Lance was slowly coming back into coherence. He recognized the muscular women from the gym through the fog as he came-to. She was wearing different clothing and seated across from him. The room they were in was filled with snakes behind glass. Every wall was filled floor-to-ceiling with glass cases which housed various types of snakes. The fluorescent lighting in the terrariums were designed and hidden to look like their natural habitat. Each partitioned case was marked with a brass plaque which he couldn't read from Grober's vantage point.

"Can you hear me Mr. Grober?"

"Where am I? Who are you?"

"Those questions can be answered in time. First I would like mine answered."

"My head is killing me." He looked down at himself as he tried to free his hands unsuccessfully. There was dried blood on his shirt.

"Yes, I'm sure it does. I wasn't sure how much of a hit to the head you could endure, so I was forced to hit you very hard. You need to move beyond the pain because I need you to answer some questions for me. Your cooperation will go a long way towards determining how this ends for you. If you lie or withhold the truth, you will pay for your sins. Your head will seem quite mild."

"Who are you?"

"That is really none of your concern."

"Don't hurt my family. What have you done with them?"

"Your family hasn't been touched. Yet. Your phone has been ringing incessantly, so I am sure that they are worried about you. I'm worried about you also. I'm worried that you are going to try and be a hero and not tell me what I want to know. That will be bad for you, Lance."

"What do you want to know?"

"I want to know about the article that was printed on page two of today's paper."

"The venom article?"

"Precisely."

"You could have just read the article in the paper, no need to hit me on the head."

633

"But you didn't report what I want to know in your article. Who is responsible for this atrocity?"

"Atrocity? These drugs will save millions of lives."

Sky rose from her chair and swung a punch to Lance's jaw. Blood and teeth sprayed from his mouth. He was almost knocked back into unconsciousness.

"I'm not asking for your opinion, I'm asking for information. Who is responsible for the discoveries?"

It took him some time to recover from the blow. The hit was not a slap, nor typical of a female's strike. It was not open-handed. It was not typical of a normal man's strike either. The woman was very strong. He spoke through the blood and broken teeth.

"Fuckin' bitch!"

She hit him again. The pain was excruciating.

Again he almost passed out from the pain.

"Many people. They have an entire team of people working there."

"Are they developing the drugs there? At BIOGENESIS? Or at SCMU?"

"SCMU. The data goes to BIOGEN but the trials are done at the Medical University. They have more equipment and doctors there in case there are complications or side effects."

"Do they create the medicines there?"

"Right now, no. Like I said, the data goes back to BIOGENESIS where they make the drug. The medication is then stored over at SCMU where it is administered for the trials. Until the formulae are finished being tweaked. Once the drugs go live, they will then be manufactured in bulk overseas. It was in the article. Why do you want to know all of this? You could have just called me. Or sent me an email."

"You wouldn't have taken me seriously or you would have said that your sources are confidential. Who is in charge of it all over there? Lynde?"

"Yes. He is overseeing it all. But the day to day is overseen by a team at SCMU. Look, I've answered all of your questions, can you please let me go now?"

"Unfortunately no. I can't let you leave here. Ever. This is going to be the last conversation you'll ever have, Lance."

"But I cooperated. You said — "

" — and you will have to forgive me. The spiritual reality is the only reality, this is all just a temporary illusion. There is too much at stake to let you interfere with my plans."

"I won't. Whatever your plans are, I'll stay out of it."

"I know you will."

Sky injected a syringe into Lance's neck. The plunger slowly sunk, pushing the contents into his vein. He struggled to free himself from the plastic binds and the chair but to no avail.

634

The more he struggled, the quicker his heart raced. The quicker his heart pumped the toxic blood throughout his body. His brain began to thicken.

"The snakes will digest you too slowly, Lance. If someone suspected you were inside them, and found you? I can't have that. You didn't leave me with much choice. I have to get rid of you. I'm thinking the best course is to cut you up and bury you. Someplace where nobody will find you. But don't worry, you won't be alone."

34

THE CAMPUS OF SOUTH CAROLINA MEDICAL UNIVERSITY is all but abandoned late at night. This was not a party school. Not at this end of the enormous campus.

Other colleges within the university had their fair share of partiers, undergrads gaining the full college experience. In those parts of the campus the occasional drunkard would stumble down the various paths toward their dorm, sorority, or fraternity. The paths along the green were always lit at night with solar lights and the blue emergency call stations every hundred yards.

But nobody stumbled home on the end of campus that housed the medical labs, the World Toxin Bank, the fellowship and professor offices. Those were serious students whom were well beyond binge drinking. Well beyond the late-night booty calls. Those were serious buildings where serious work was being done.

At 2:00 AM on Thursday morning, those paths along the medical green were dimly lit as usual. The odd security guard walked along the path but there was never anything to report. They preferred to work their respective shifts in the comfort of the air-conditioned buildings rather than walking the paths, especially in the humid summer nights, between the various structures. Even with recent events and the subsequent heightened security, there was little to report. In truth, there hadn't been anything to report on the grounds the nights the murders had taken place either.

Whomever had circumvented the security measures on those nights had been good. Nobody had seen anyone suspicious go into or out of any of the campus buildings. They were not well-marked at any rate, someone would have to know exactly where they are going in order to get around. Then once they were inside the unmarked building, they would need a magnetized ID card in order to attain access beyond the vestibule. Upon getting through the entrance, the magnetized ID would only get them entrance into the specific areas that the particular card had security clearance for.

636

The police had caught the person who had passed through all of those barriers anyway. The mentality from those having to make the decisions about paying the extra manpower for security was that there should be no extra manpower. 'Heightened' security was still quite lax.

The person dressed in head-to-toe, black clothing dodged from shrub to shrub down the path toward the medical testing labs. The brick building that stood at the end of the paved walkway was as dimly lit as the path leading to it. The spot-lights that shown onto the brick and ivy growing up the walls did little more than show that a building was present in the dark of night. The windows, all five floors of them, were on energy saving mode. Only every fourth fluorescent light inside was turned on. Just enough for the cleaning crews and limited security.

The trespasser snuck up to the building and moved along the perimeter of the building through the hedges and ivy. When they came to the drainage pipe on the back side of the building that ran up to the roof, they took one last look at ground-level to ensure that they were not being observed. The six inch diameter drainage pipe was used to climb up to the roof of the brick building. Because it was the back side of the building, and the pipe rose between windows, the intruder climbed in the darkness unseen. The items in the small backpack rustled on the back of the intruder as it was being hoisted toward the roof. It was the only sound which could be heard, and only by the person wearing the pack.

Once on the roof, which didn't take long, the burglar peered over the lip of the roof to take yet another look to see if they were being observed. No one could be seen. Five stories up afforded quite the view of that end of the campus. Not a person in sight. Not a sound except the breathing of the person on the roof.

The building's HVAC system was set up to ensure that the labs had the best heating and cooling to suit the needs of the technicians being housed there. It was also set up with a filtering system that negated lint and allergens from contaminating the laboratories. This was achieved by utilizing two sets of huge fans to draw and push air, sifting off the pollutants into an enormous filtration room. Maintenance had easy access to that room to change the dozens of filters inside it from the roof.

There was a plastic box on the outside of the room which contained a large lever. That lever shut down the entire HVAC and filtering system for the building. Deactivating that system would set off all sorts of bells, whistles, and alarms. They would be silent, but personnel would come calling. Turning off the system was not an option for the intruder.

Since the system was running at full strength that night, and would continue to be, goggles and a mask were needed in order to move through the room and bypass the fans through the conduit. The intruder retrieved those items from the back pack, as well as a pry bar to open the locked door to the filtration room.

Moving beyond the filtration room was easy. One just needed to pull down the coarse 40x40 filter, exposing the large ventilation ducts. The ducts were large enough for a small child to walk through standing upright. That is to say that an average size adult could crawl through it without fear of claustrophobia. For the intruder, it was tight but manageable.

The system utilized two sets of large, rectangular piping made of durable galvanized steel which ran juxtaposed to one another. While they were partners in both position and purpose on the system, they had opposing duties. One set of ductwork would have a set of fans to pull the air out of the rooms, pushing the air up to the filtration room, which the intruder had just breached. The now-filtered air would then be reclaimed and sent back into the building using the twin set of ducts which ran along side the first. The temperature of the reclaimed air was modified to suit the needs of the labs, the second fan pushing it back into the various rooms.

The infiltrator slithered along inside the pre-filtered ventilation ducts, pulling and squirming further into the building. The air and debris that was pulled from the rooms were being moved toward the filter room, which meant that the burglar was literally moving against the grain. Moving with significant speed, considering the circumstances, looking through every inlet vent as they passed, seventy yards had been accomplished until a decision needed to be made.

There was a vertical shaft that was very much like the HVAC spine of the building. That spine was comparable to the trunk of an enormous tree, the branches coming off the trunk to service all of the rooms in the building, including the four floors below the intruder. A decision was needed to be made to either continue along the ductwork above the fifth floor, or slide down the shaft to the lower floors.

It was decided to continue along the top level, therefore it became necessary to somehow go over the top of chasm and continue along the same shaft. This required significant strength and agility. Lying prostrate, they stretched across the opening with their torso, gripping the ledge of the ductwork on the opposite side. With nothing to grab a hold of, the elbows were utilized to attain hold on the sides of the duct, letting the waist and legs drop down into the vertical shaft. Then, using both feet against the sides of the vertical duct and immense upper-body strength, the intruder pulled their body up onto the other side of the shaft and continued on.

Another forty yards had been accomplished when through an inlet vent, the burglar spied a male technician in a lab coat. He was working on one of the machines, all lights and computers were turned on in that lab. This was not a night cleaner, this was real work being done at almost 3:00 AM. The intruder backed up in the ductwork, squirming in reverse in the same direction as the air and debris to be filtered.

Once the previous inlet vent was reached, they peered through that vent to ensure that the adjoining dimly lit lab was empty. It was. A Kobalt *OS683* multi-purpose hand tool was produced from the small back pack.   It was unfolded to produce pliers, then a Philips screwdriver was flipped out of it's recessed home. The four screws were removed, enabling the vent cover to be removed. Once removed, the burglar emerged from the shaft but only to the waist. The CCTV camera was spotted to the right of the ventilation duct, less than six feet away. The long pry bar that was used to enter the filtration room was then used to turn the camera over to the corner of the room. Satisfied that nothing in that room would be seen or recorded, the intruder dropped into the adjoining lab from the shaft.

35

I HAD NO IDEA WHAT THE HELL I WAS DOING IN THE LAB. I putzed with this, or fiddled with that. I didn't even know what some of the equipment did, let alone know how to operate the stuff. I looked into a microscope at nothing. I turned on an electrophoresis machine and put a spot plate on it, it seemed right. If the damn thing hadn't had a label and manufacturer on it, I wouldn't have even known that it was an electrophoresis machine. Whatever that was.

I opened a microcentrifuge and put something inside, hoping nothing would smoke or combust. I barely graduated high school, the only reason I passed chemistry was because I knew the teacher was cooking and distributing Meth. I got a B because nobody would believe that I had legitimately achieved an A.

Donning a white lab coat, I looked the part. That was the important thing. I also wanted to see about getting one with my name on it. When I found Carina we could play 'naughty doctor' or something fun with it. I hoped I would find her. If this didn't work, I was out of ideas.

Because of all of the sensitive equipment and because it was a university, I was not allowed to have gun. It was against SCMU lab rules, but more importantly it was against the law. SCMU was a State-funded school and schools of all kinds were off limits to weapons. Even with my conceal and carry permit. The fact that I didn't have a gun anymore, that Stubbs had it, didn't depreciate my desire to have one.

I continued to move around the lab as if I had a purpose, my only purpose was to play the waiting game. I was sure that the newspaper article would generate a move. Captain Simms knew a reporter from the Charleston Post and Courier who owed him a favor. He generated a falsified story that a Lance Grober would then write and push through his editor. The story was published and created more of a buzz than any of us realized.

The Associated Press picked up on it and ran with it. Bloomberg reported it. CNN. Even the Daily Show with Jon Stewart was planning on covering the story on Friday. It was already going viral.

I was on a short leash. If the ruse didn't work, a retraction was going to be made and Carina wouldn't be found. If it did work, then the headline was going to be about the serial murderer who was caught while destroying the lab in another attempt to destroy vital research. That destruction had set SCMU and BIOGENESIS back in their launch of these forthcoming drugs.

I heard the ID card access control system click behind me and the door to the lab opened. A mannish woman entered wearing her white lab coat and carrying a small back pack. She was a muscular girl.

"Good morning. I wasn't expecting anyone in the lab this early."

"Good morning. Uh, yeah. I had a few tests to run," I said. I didn't know what else to say. For obvious reasons there weren't many people privy to my presence, this lab tech was going to know I wasn't a researcher in about ten seconds.

Her ID card coiled back into the retractor that was fastened to her front belt loop. "I haven't seen you in this lab before, are you new?" She eyed me with suspicion and I didn't know what I was going to say.

"New here. I was transferred here to replace somebody that isn't here anymore." I hoped that somebody already hadn't filled that role, maybe this chick. If so, my jig was up.

"That's a great accent. Where are you from?"

"My mom. What's your name?"

"Sky. What's yours?" She went around the perimeter of the lab and found a desk with a computer on it. She squatted down and went inside her back pack.

I wasn't sure if I wanted to give her my real name. There was something about her that I didn't like. Her size for one. If she wasn't whom she was portraying to be, as I wasn't, then a physical altercation wouldn't be cut and dried. I'm not afraid of men, I've fought many that were bigger than me. But I don't hit women. Not hitting this one, however, would very likely get me hurt.

"I didn't hear you. What did you say your name was?" She stood up with a large pry-bar in one hand, a stick with some sort of fanged device on the end in the other hand. That device looked like an unhinged stapler on the end of a large rod.

"I didn't say. But it doesn't make much of a difference does it?"

"Not really, no. You should have turned down that transfer. Where is the data?" She was circling the long lab table that centered the room, the same table I was standing behind. I began circling away from her in the same counter-clockwise direction. I was slowly coming around toward the door to the lab.

"That door has been deactivated. The reader is broken, there is no escape."

"Then you aren't going anywhere either. Bad plan if you want the data, Sky."

"I'll go out the same way that I came in, through the vent." She looked up at the vent above my head, behind me."

I pointed to the camera. "Smile, your on TV."

"This is not my first time here. The camera isn't recording anything. You are completely isolated. Just tell me where the data is and I promise to make your death as quick and painless as possible."

I took off my lab coat and wrapped it around my arm. Sky was still circling, as was I.

"Where is she, Sky? Where is Detective Fischer?"

"That is the least of your concerns." The dawn broke and she began to realize that this might not be what it seems. I could tell by the look on her face. "You aren't a lab tech, are you?"

"You've got me there, fella. What gave me away."

"You aren't scared."

As I circled around, I came to where Sky had left her back pack. Without shifting my eyes for any length of time, I retrieved it and continued circling. I clutched the bag with my left hand, the same side that had the lab coat protecting my forearm. I rifled through it with my right hand trying to find a weapon. I found a blue, multipurpose hand tool which would have to work. This time I took my eyes off of Sky for too long.

She high-jumped up onto the elevated lab table and came running on top of it toward me. She was lightning-quick. You don't normally think that somebody that big would be that fast but she was. It must have been something in the water down there, because Stubbs had moved that quick in spite of his size.

I threw the tool at her as she swung the pry bar at me. I ducked in time for it to miss my head but it made contact with the back pack and glanced off of my slightly protected forearm. The bar was caught on the arm strap of the pack and I pulled it from her hand. She swung the stapler thing at me and missed. I was able to get a better view of the object fastened to the end of the rod as it swung past my face. It was a snake skull. The top of the skull and fangs were somehow adhered to where the bottom part of the snake's hinged jaw would normally be. It went by me too quickly for me to see anything else at that point.

The pry bar clanged off of the floor and under the table that Sky was standing on. I dove under it to retrieve it, and she jumped down off of the table toward me. She kicked my arm and the pack went flying away from me. It hurt like hell, the bitch was strong. I was able to grab the pry bar and swing it. I hit the side of her foot, but it was not with as much force as I

642

would have liked. Although the table was tall, I was not able to get enough motion on my swing.

She didn't yell or indicate any pain, but she did back off enough for me to roll out on the other side of the table.

Sky again jumped up on top of the table and came for me. I swung the pry bar with both hands like it was an axe, landing it on her arm. It was the same arm that carried her make-shift, snake skull weapon, which was flung through the air away from the fray. That did some damage though she never cried out in pain. I heard the bone in her elbow break. Unbothered, she threw a punch with her left.

I have fought many men, both in and out of the MMA ring. When I get hit hard, I get angrier and fight back. I don't fight women. I've pissed off enough where they slap me or scratch at me, but Sky didn't slap or scratch. She hit like a dude. And it hurt like a motherfucker. I was in pain and angry. She was no longer a woman to me.

"You fuckin' bitch! I'm gonna give you such a pinch!"

She was weaponless as she jumped off of the table and came towards me. I took another one-handed swing with the bar to her knee and connected again. That too did damage, and she again showed no sign that it affected her. She blocked my third attempt, hit my wrist, sending my weapon, the pry bar, flying out of reach.

Sky kicked me in the upper-leg, just missing my coin purse and neutering me. I punched her in the throat. She would not go down. I swiped her now bad leg out from under her by kicking it with mine and grappled her to the ground.

I made work on her face with my elbows. Pain did not seem to bother her. Or she wasn't feeling any. She struggled to get out from under me as I pinned her legs down by interlocking them with mine. I knelt while sitting on her pelvis. Every time she would sit up with her incredible abdominal strength, I would go back to work with my elbows to her face, drawing more blood.

She wouldn't give up. I needed to take away her air. That was the only way to submit her. I pushed her back down as she raised her upper-body toward me again and used my forearm with the unraveling lab coat on it to apply pressure to her throat. Her head was pinned down against the linoleum floor as I leaned in for all I was worth trying to cut off her air supply.

"Where is Carina? Where is Detective Fischer?" I asked over and over again. How I was expecting her to answer was stupidity.

Sky, in a final gasp and attempt at freeing herself, flung me off to the side and rolled away. It was unbelievable. That chick was unstoppable.

643

She rolled over to the snake-head weapon and retrieved it with her good arm. I was already moving toward her, the swing of the weapon just missed me. She was unable to stand because of her broken leg, but she was attacking from the floor. I jumped down onto her with my knee on her sternum. That definitely cracked. I jumped up and repeated the downward knee to the sternum. I finally got a scream out of her as the snake head came at me again.

Those fangs coming at me, scared the living hell out of me. It was a damned good thing that it was dead and not real. I blocked her final swing, removed the weapon from her hand, and out of pure frustration and anger I dug those fangs into her lower neck. I swung that thing so hard that the fangs were stuck in the meat where the neck meets the shoulder. I couldn't pull them loose.

Blood was everywhere.

Under the snake skull was a small plastic pouch.

"What's in the pouch, Sky? Venom?"

She looked at me and nodded her blood-soaked face and head.

"What kind? Maybe they have an anti-venom here." I moved away from her toward the desk. I dialed 9-1-1 from the lab phone but left the receiver on the desk, off the hook.

" .... No .... medicine .... "

"Where is Carina?"

Sky rolled her eyes then closed them. She might have been praying, maybe just thinking, but she was definitely dying.

The blood was free-flowing from her facial wounds, the fangs that dug into her neck were somewhat blocking the gushing from the two holes there. I have fought bleeders before, but the blood was gushing out of the cuts on her face as if they were major arteries. She was going to bleed to death unless help came quickly.

I looked around the lab and spotted a big red panic button. Use of that was pointless. We had evacuated the building assuming that the assassin would come. The rent-a-cop campus security would be useless. 9-1-1 was called but they were likely to be too late.

"C'mon Sky. Don't you want your conscience to be clean when you meet your maker in a couple minutes? Where is she?"

She did nothing but lay there and gurgle.

I kicked her in the ribs. Final thoughts on conscience cleaning were not working. I tried a different approach.

"Where the fuck is she, bitch?"

When blood began to run like a river out of her mouth I knew all was lost. My elbows had taken out some teeth, her gums and mouth were bleeding profusely. She wasn't going to tell me anything.

Her secret died with her.

36

IT TOOK MAINTENANCE, THE POLICE, AND PARAMEDICS ALMOST AN
HOUR to gain entrance to the lab slash death chamber. Sky wasn't kidding when she said that
she had disabled the security reader. She disabled the goddamned door.

I had plenty of time to go through the remaining contents of Sky's bag and everything on
her person. I scrutinized every item trying to determine where Carina might be.

She had brought the bare minimum. I wondered if she had military training. She knew
not to have identification on her. She transported only the tools that she needed for her
mission.

But she did have a smart-phone.

Sky's smart-phone was password protected. I called Harold, though it was not yet 5:00
AM. He was groggy to say the least. After some time he understood who was calling but not
completely why.

" .... what kind of phone is it Deni?"

"It says Motorola on it."

"Great. What kind of Motorola?"

"AT&T."

"Look all over it. It will say something else besides AT&T and Motorola on it."

"Atrix. Is that right?"

"Deni, phones really aren't my thing but I think those phones have a fingerprint security
feature on them. Unless it is the Atrix 2, you are going to need the person who owns the
phone."

"Ya know for not believin' that this world is a reality, these guys have some of the latest
toys this world had to offer, huh?"

645

"I don't know, Deni. It's really early in the morning and I'm half-asleep. All I know is that you need the person if the fingerprint function was activated."

"What if I have the person who owns the phone but they aren't, uh, awake?"

"I don't even want to know. I'm pretty sure those phones have multiple ways to get into them. We can only hope that the fingerprint feature was used, otherwise your done."

"So what do I do?"

"Is there a reader on the back of it, or is it just the screen on the front? I think there should be a little window at the top of phone on the back side of it."

"Yeah. There is."

"Now find the right finger. Well, the correct finger. Probably one of the index fingers. Depends on if the person was a lefty or a righty."

It took something like eight attempts on the two pointer-fingers, I lost count, but it eventually worked.

"I got it Harold. Thanks."

"Don't mention it. Really, Deni. Do not mention it."

"Hey don't go anywhere. Do you have a computer handy?"

"Gee, Deni, let's see. What do I do for a living? What are the chances that I would have a computer?"

"Don't piss me off. It's been a rough night and it's gonna be a tougher day. I'm in no mood."

"OK Mr. Sensitive. You woke me up and you expect not to get a little 'tude? What do you need?"

"I'm gonna go through this phone, and you need to let me know where the addresses are based on the phone numbers that I give you."

"So I guess I'm up for the day."

"Are you gonna help me or not? I'm trying to find a missing cop and people are either dead or not being helpful."

"OK, OK. Fire when ready."

Captain Simms was bullshit. I normally say bullsh, but his state was past the point of abbreviations, so I'll use the full word.

He was beyond pissed at me, took a run past furious, and was rounding the corner on mental. Another body and no closer to finding Detective Fischer. He had lied to the press to create this mess in an attempt to draw out yet another *suspected* serial killer. That suspect was now dead. That suspect was never questioned. There was a strong possibility that the wrong person was currently incarcerated, and would continue to be because of it. Simms had let an out-of-State private dick lead this little ploy and it had run riot. Because this had taken place on a State-funded university, the South Carolina State Bureau of Investigators were looking to take over the case and the FBI was waiting in the wings. In the words Simms used, I had created a "cluster-fuck of epic proportions".

I wanted to tell him that epic was over-used in today's vocabulary, but he was already unamused and definitely not a fan.

It took JG all he could do to keep me out of the hoosegow. I watched him promise Simms to keep me away from this case and that I was going to get out of his jurisdiction forthwith. Meaning I was to fly anywhere out of Charleston, preferably out of South Carolina. If not, I was going to jail.

Everybody involved knew that JG was lying when he promised that. I was in for a penny, in for a pound on this one. I wasn't flying anywhere. I wanted to see this through. For JG. For Sierra Byrne. For Stubbs. For Carina. Hell, for myself.

What I didn't say out loud, nor even admit to myself, was my ulterior motive for finding Carina. I thought I was in love with her. How that was possible, I'm not sure. I didn't know her that long. I don't even know for sure if it was love, but I had never felt that way about a woman before in my life. She was like a wicked-beautiful, female version of me. And I certainly love me.

I had been taken from SCMU to the police station at 80 Broad in the back of a cop car. JG had come to the police station to find out what was happening, and to ensure that I wouldn't be locked up. He was already having difficulty freeing one of his clients.

JG took me back over to SCMU to retrieve the *AMG*. I told him that I had one more card up my sleeve, thanks to Harold. If the address that he gave me turned out to be a dud, we were out of options. On the drive over, JG tried to talk me out of continuing.

"I have reasonable doubt on Sierra's case. At this point it seems clear enough, or at a minimum plausible, that this Sky Phillips was the nut-job that killed the three victims surrounding BIOGENESIS. We have the murder weapon, at least one of them. I am going to schedule a motion hearing to see about getting Sierra out of Leath. There is no way they can keep her incarcerated after what happened this morning.

"You have done your job, Deni. There is no reason to get yourself further into trouble down here. Forget the address, let the cops handle it from here," he said as a final thought.

"What about Stubbs?"

"The Feds are all over it. They are already cutting through the red-tape to see that justice is served for him. Whether that was Nahash or this other zealot, Sky, is of no concern to us anymore."

"Fuck you, pal. It matters to me. I almost died in that grown-over hell-hole and the only reason I ain't on top of the pile of bodies down there is because of Stubbs. I wanna know who tried to make me a corpse. Stubbs is dead because because we went down there. *You* sent us down to a snake-infested jungle, I'm not gonna let it be for nothin'."

"There is nothing I can do to keep you out of jail *when* you get caught in the middle of this investigation."

"So nobody finds Carina? Nobody figures out the truth?"

"Have faith in the police. I am pretty sure the SBI is taking over the South Carolina cases, including Detective Fischer. Listen, there is a line from a Denzel Washington movie, I forget which one, but he says, 'it's not about the truth, it's what you can prove.' Or something like that. Anyway, my point is the same. We may never find out exactly what happened, all we know is that Sierra is innocent, which is why I had you come down here."

He pulled up beside the Mercedes, just to the right of it lining up my passenger door to the *AMG*'s driver door. I opened my door but remained seated.

"Fine. Take me off the books. You're done payin' me. Can I borrow your car for a few days?"

"Deni. Don't do this."

"I heard you. Can I borrow it or not?"

"Yes, of course. But don't come back to the house tonight. I have Brady to think about. We can't harbor a possible felon."

I got up and slammed his car door shut.

"I wouldn't dream of it."

37

THE ADDRESS THAT HAROLD PROVIDED ME WAS NOT TECHNICALLY located in Charleston. It was just outside the city limits. I took the 52 out of downtown, or uptown as they call it there, to Algonquin Road. It wasn't an Indian Reservation or anything, it was in the cemetery district. Four cemeteries were set around a small pond. How many people were plotted there because of the Algonquin Indians was a question I would have liked to have answered, but I didn't have the time for a history lesson just then.

My destination was on the back side of the Magnolia Cemetery. This was the furthest out, the most desolate of the four, and it would make it that much easier to dump a body. Which made me nervous about Carina.

At the end of Algonquin Road there was a closed gate. The sign said 'Road Closed'. My choices were to take the right onto Huguenin or proceed on foot. To the left was a field with half a dozen silos behind it.   The brick wall on the corner of Huguenin and the gated remainder of Algonquin barricaded the Magnolia Cemetery.

I left the *AMG* parked in front of the gate, though it stuck out like a sore thumb.   I climbed over the chain-link fence and continued on foot down the closed road. The brick wall and the bone yard was to my right. The chain-link fence continued on my left separating me from the field. Further ahead down the road, to the very end, was a small building with a parking area. Beyond that building were a wooded area with the tops of more silos set behind it. I turned around to look behind me. Nobody was around. Two hundred yards I continued to the very end of the road. The sound of my foot falls were about as loud as anything that I have ever heard. Sneaking up on the building was not an option. Maybe that was the point they were trying to make. It was very loud and clear.

There was an old Ford *F-150* parked on the back side of the building. The noon sun had not come out to play for the day, clouds still lingered overhead though there was no rain. The day was warm, as they all are in the South as far as I could tell. I put my hand on the hood of the truck, I couldn't tell if the damn thing had been there ten minutes or ten years.

I squatted down beside the *F-150* and listened. I don't mean listen like you do when somebody is trying to tell you something, I mean I listened like I was blind and the only information coming in was from sound. Nothing. My breathing was louder than the light breeze. Time to go in.

There was what I assumed to be a front door that faced the parking lot, for lack of a better term. That door was locked. I moved to the right around the building toward the woods and found another entrance. That door was propped open with a door jam about five inches. Again, I was without a gun. I was in the gun-amnestied South and without a gun. Pathetic.

Peering in through the small opening, I spied a room that was dimly lit. There was a raised area to the right which I assumed was used as a pulpit. The rest of the room was used for seating. By the main entrance where the door was locked was a set of tall bookcases, filled with some type of literature. A man was in front of them with a book that he was perusing. He had a straight line of sight to me, but he was engrossed. I needed to get through the door, but the opening wasn't wide enough. I moved it open a bit so slip in but the hinges creaked and echoed throughout the small room.

The man was startled and turned to see whom was entering. He cared not to find out who I was, he decided to shoot first and ask questions later. My Brazilian Jiu-Jitsu was, nor is, any match for bullets. The first one ricocheted off the wood door frame near my face, shrapnel-slivers burned the right side of my face. I dove inside and under a pew, the bullets continued to fly.

It was hard to keep my right eye open. I don't know if the burning and stinging was from pieces of debris in my eye or blood. Maybe both, it was hard to tell at that point. I just knew that I was bleeding like a stuck-pig. I was getting very tired of being shot at with no way to shoot back.

There were no other rooms to hide in, my only shelter was the pews. The dark oak from the wooden benches was spraying like toothpicks at me. I crawled as fast as I could from one row to the next, trying to get closer to him. My only hope was when he went to reload his gun. I kept count as best I could, and he was at or beyond eight so I knew he didn't have a revolver. That meant that reloading was going to be exponentially quicker. I would have maybe a second to attack him while he changed clips and reloaded the chamber.

The shooter was moving toward me, waiting for me to pop up from behind one of the benches. We were both shortening the gap between us. He was about nine or ten feet away from me, on the other side of a pew, when it was my time to move. Whether he knew how close he was to me or not, I will never know. I just know that he immediately regretted following me, realizing that he did not have another clip on his person. I saw the look on his face when I popped up and dove on him. We both toppled over the back of one row of pews and onto another row. He was below me as I broke my fall with his body. Smashing his gun-hand against the hard floor with both my hands, I simultaneously drove my knee into the side of his ribcage.

With the gun skittering across the floor under the pews toward the front of the room, I moved to a side mount. It was difficult to get perpendicular to him between benches, but with the man struggling I was able to knee him to the end of the row. I neutralized my attacker with a shoulder-hold or Kata-gatame, meaning the arm and hand that used to be holding a gun was now pinned against his neck. I needed information about Carina so I didn't choke him out with an arm triangle, I just kept working the side of his body with my knees. Royce Gracie would have been proud.

"Where is Carina? Where is Detective Fischer?"

My attacker was not yet the submissive. He continued to take a beating in silence. Whatever mind thing Sky and this guy used, it worked to repress pain. I had been in several MMA fights where the guy would tap-out after suffering less. This particular guy was pissing me off.

"Where is she asshole?"

Nothing but groaning. I finished moving him out into the aisle by pushing him with my upper body and knee-strikes. Once in the aisle, I was able to have enough room for a Kimura. I grabbed his wrist with my hand on the same side, my opposite arm was put behind his arm. I cranked his arm away from him which put immense pressure on his shoulder and elbow joints. He would tell me what I wanted to know or I would have a new arm. His.

No Jedi-mind-trick can withstand an arm-bar. The scream that came out of the man was unlike any I had heard, and I had heard plenty in my day. I may have snapped the poor prick's arm, for all I know. I was pretty pissed.

"Talk to me! Where is she?"
" .... rrrrrrrrr. Let me go!"
"Not a fuckin' chance. Tell me where she is or I rip it off and beat you with it."
" ..... aaaaaaaaa. Not here anymore!"
"Where? I'm losin' my patience here, guy."
" .... nnnnnnnnnnn. Taken. Not here .... rrrrrrrr .... "
"Last chance. WHERE?"

651

He said nothing. Nothing usable anyway. He continued to groan and gasp, grumble and howl. This was getting me nowhere, so I choked him out. Once he passed-out I was able to drag him back into the entrance where he was originally reading a book.

I wanted to tie him up.

I wanted to see if he had another clip.

38

JACOB GRANTES'S IPHONE RANG TWICE BEFORE HE ANSWERED. The caller ID said that it was Warren. He was not entirely sure that he wanted to take the call.

"Hello?"

"JG. What are you doing?"

"I'm filing a motion to get Sierra out of Leath, like I told you about two hours ago. Dare I ask what you are doing?"

"Are attorney-client conversations over the phone privileged?"

"Yes, unless the conversation is taking place prior to or during the act of a crime. I take it back, I definitely don't want to know."

"I know where Carina *was*. She isn't here anymore, but the guy knows where she is. I think."

"Where are you?"

"Out behind a bone yard called Magnolia."

"I'll call Captain Simms and — "

" — no, no, no. If he shows up here right now it would not be good."

"The police can question him, Deni. They can …. they *can* question him, right? You didn't kill him?"

"He's not dead but he is takin' a nap. He had some rope in the back of his truck, so he is all tied up right now. The motherfucker shot at me."

"Are you all right?"

"I've got shit in my eye and I'm bleedin' like it's my job. But otherwise I'm fine."

"So what now? Should I prepare myself to bail you out when the phone call comes? Because I am pretty sure that bail will be denied to you at this point."

"No. My goal is to stay outta the hoosegow. Can you find out more about Sky Phillips?"

653

"Like what? Between the press and the information that I have compiled to provide in my motion, we know quite a lot about her."

"Where she lives, works, hangs out — stuff like that."

"The police have already cordoned off her home, Carina wasn't there but they are still searching for evidence."

"What else?"

"Her neighbors said that she was a recluse. Didn't really socialize, kept to herself. She was obviously a fitness-buff so they are looking into where she worked out."

"What about where she worked? Did she work at SCMU? She had an ID badge."

"It belonged to one of the victims, the first one. The victim that was killed in her home. It was never deactivated. Six weeks and three deaths later, they never deactivated it. Unbelievable."

"So where did she work?"

"I just had it here in front of me …. Magnolia Zoo."

"Let me guess. Reptile Park?"

"It doesn't say. Why would you guess that?"

"These assholes are full of contradictions."

"You think that they hid a decorated homicide detective in a public zoo?"

"I'll let you know."

"Are you awake yet?" I gave the man who shot at me a good whack to the head to wake him if he wasn't. He rustled a bit, realizing his situation. His situation being that he was tied to the front double-doors to the church-like building, those doors open outward toward the small parking area and the Magnolia Cemetery behind it. Anybody pulling on those doors to open them would pull the arms off of him. He was seated at the base of the doors, legs straight out towards me, arms stretched above his head.

654

"Do you know who I am?"

"No, and I wouldn't give a fuck if I had a pocket full. Let's get back to where we left off, you and I. Where is Carina Fischer?"

"Not here."

"Thank you Captain Obvious. I know she ain't here. I looked around this one-room palace while you took a nap. I want to know where she *is*." I picked up the tire iron which I had leaned against the bookshelf after I had removed it from the *F-150*. "The cops will be here eventually, they will collect you. In how many pieces is going to be the question."

"I don't know."

"I don't know either, that is up to you. How many things am I gonna have to break off of ya before you break and tell me where she is?"

"That's not what I meant. I don't know where she is."

"You would be smart not to mistake my calmness for patience. I've run out. Where is she?"

"I don't know what you are talking about."

"We will see, won't we?"

I swung the tire iron down on the inside of his right knee. The thud was mixed with a snapping sound. Everything after that was wailing.

"Fight it off with your mind. Isn't that what you do?" I shouted to him over his sobbing and blubbering. It lasted for what seemed like an eternity.

"I'm gettin' tired of your bullsh, here guy. She *was here,* you said so yourself. Did she leave here alive?"

"Yes. Yes, she was alive …. aaaaaaaaaaaaaah! Help!"

"You want another tickle? Stop screamin'. Where is she right now?"

He replied through gritted teeth, "I don't know."

"You better start guessin'. This is about to get really fuckin' painful for you, so you better make an effort here."

"They didn't tell me. I don't know."

"Who are *they?*"

He just looked at me. Looked through me really. I was tired of playing games. Carina's life was at stake, and this guy was the only person standing between me and finding her. I may have believed him not knowing where she was until he held out who had come to get her. He liked pain, obviously. I didn't mind dispensing it.

"Have it your way tough-guy."

The tire iron came down on the other knee. I gave it all I had on his left knee. It sounded like I had cut through a head of cabbage with a dull knife. You never get used to that sound. It is both gnarly and nauseating. It was grisly work but it was necessary.

The man tried to pull himself up with his tied arms as he screamed louder than my ears could take. Tears and spit and sweat were pouring out of his ghostly white face.

"Just tell me where she is and I will go away. I haven't even used the lever-end of this thing yet. I wonder what I can pry apart on you?"

He continued to wail and cry. I had found another clip for his Sig Sauer Pro *SP2022* in his truck, when I had found the rope and tire iron. I couldn't take the noises he was making, so I retrieved his 9 mm pistol from the floor under a pew and loaded it.

"I can make all of the pain go away very quickly, guy. Tell me where she is."

"I don't — "

" — don't sit there and tell me what you don't fuckin' know. You had better start tellin' me what you do know. Apparently you are still not motivated. You want pain? That's what you'll get."

I walked back toward him with the *SP2022* in my right hand, and the tire iron in my left. I placed the muzzle of the pistol on the inside of this hanging right wrist, pressing it between the ulna and the radius. I fired the weapon, sending a 9 mm projectile through his wrist. The screaming grew still more intense. Next, I put the Sig into my back pants pocket and switched the tire iron from my left hand to my right. Then I pushed the lever end into the hole that I had just made.

"If I send this lever through your wrist, I can't tell you how much it's gonna hurt. I can't tell you because I've never done this shit before. I'm makin' this up as I go along. Are you as curious as I am as to how much it's gonna fuckin' hurt? You might even pass out again. Tell me where she is asshole!"

"Nooooooooooo. Stooooooooop. Please, please, please. No. No more. The snake pit. I think the snake pit."

"At the Magnolia Zoo?"

"I think. They never told me."

"Because Sky worked there?"

"Yes. And the others."

"What others?"

"The other parishioners who work there …. access to snakes and the mice they eat." It did look like he was about to pass out again.

"What do you mean access to the snakes and the mice? Stay with me."

"Specimens need …. food." Then he was gone.

And so was I.

39

THE MAGNOLIA PLANTATION WAS VAST TO SAY THE VERY LEAST. The property consists of the Gardens, the main house, the train and boat tours, the historic buildings tour retelling the events *From Slavery to Freedom,* the wedding and events wing, and we haven't even mentioned the various areas of the Zoo and Nature Center.

The Zoo and Nature Center has a bird and peacock wing, swamp garden, safari animals, reptiles, and list goes on and on. Once I was inside, I understood how immense the place was. I could have had a three-day pass and not seen the entire place. They charged me $39.50 admission for the rest of one day, Thursday. I was not interested in the price of more as I was hoping that it wouldn't be necessary.

I called JG to let him know where I was going and what I had done. He asked surprisingly few questions. He simply said that he would let Captain Simms know about the man in the remote church building and the suspected whereabouts of Detective Carina Fischer.

The zoo was busy. Why the children were not in school or the parents at work in the middle of the week, I didn't know, nor do I now. What I do know is that I was moving at an entirely different pace than the families I was trying to Heisman through.

Deer exhibit. Who gives a shit? I have seen more as road-kill than were on display. Bobcats and birds of prey, no thank you. You can keep your peacocks too, though they had every color in the rainbow.

Forty-five minutes beyond the admission gate and I had finally come upon the Reptile Park and Alligator Amphitheater. 'CLOSED FOR RENOVATIONS' the sign said. They were sorry for the inconvenience, it also said. I'll bet.

I looked around before climbing the gate and running into the turtle building to ensure that I was not spotted. Only the safety lights were illuminated, but it was enough for me to see my way out the other side. I was stealth in moving from building to building, not wanting to be stopped or even seen. I ran through the lizard kingdom, out the other side then through the spider hall.

The spiders were all in their own individual terrariums. With the lights off, they might have been sleeping. I didn't stick around to find out. I had seen enough of them in their natural habitat, I didn't need to see them behind glass. It had the feel of a spider pet-shop. I continued to move through that building and then entered a new one, which was hell on earth.

The next building was engulfed by a swamp garden, which took me back to earlier in the week in Costa Rica. That was frightful enough. I guess they wanted to make this layout as authentic as possible. Bully for you, first rate. I raced through the swampy exterior and into the concrete building, which is where I nearly soiled myself. The building was filled, wall-to-wall with snakes.

There was glass between the serpents and I, but I had my fill in Central America. I hated them before, during, then, and I still do to this day. They terrify me more now than ever. They surrounded me. I don't know if they noticed me or not, but in my mind they were all trying to break through the glass trying to have a go at me. I have nightmares to this day.

There was a chair in the middle of the large observation room, but I didn't sit in it. I was curious about it but I didn't linger. All I wanted was out. The room was just as dark as the others, energy-saver safety lighting was the only illumination. Everywhere I turned was a fanged fucker looking for a meal. I managed to find the red exit sign on a far wall. Out the other side I went, my body still shivers just thinking about it.

Once outside, I was able to catch my breath and gather myself. I also saw where the renovations were taking place. Another tall fence where it looked like a foundation was being poured.

My heart sank. I hoped that what I was thinking was wrong. *They wouldn't kill somebody and bury them in the middle of a busy zoo would they?*

Nobody was around. No construction workers, no zoo workers. If there were cameras in this area of the park, nobody was watching them. I had free-reign and I didn't belong there, imagine what could be done if you worked there? Right under their noses.

I climbed the tall fence and looked around the construction zone. The renovation company had dug into the ground, made trusses where about a quarter of them were filled with concrete. They were going to build another exhibit right there. The sign said they were 'EXPANDING OUR KINGDOM'.

There was a trailer that was toward the back of the area where a foreman had set up his temporary office for the job. It was locked but that didn't stop me from breaking out my pins and getting inside. I'm not sure what I was expecting to find, but what I did find was a desk with filing cabinets and plans. Rummaging through it all produced no evidence. Whomever the foreman was, he or she hadn't updated any of the plans or the progress journal in several weeks. *Was construction put on hold?*

As I turned to leave, I saw a rack with a few hard-hats and safety-vests hung underneath them. Which gave me an idea.

If you have never operated a backhoe before, I can tell you that it's a friggin' blast. I had never sat in one before that day, let alone moved the giant bucket that is attached to the arm. It takes some getting used to.

The stabilizers were already in place on the JCB *4CX-17 Super*, all I needed to do was swing the cab around so the back-boom was above the concrete slab. Only I was swinging it the wrong way and it may have tore a huge hole in the side of the foreman's trailer. Oops.

I then pushed the lever that looked like a shifter on a manual transmission forward instead of back toward me. The bucket on the back-boom then went through the other side of the trailer instead of away from it. I corrected it and figured out how to swing it around so it was above the concrete foundation.

With the position of the bucket over the spot I wanted to dig, I then pushed the right control stick to the right to open the bucket for scooping, then lowered the main boom to engage the concrete. Pushing the left lever to lower the boom into the hard foundation, I pulled the right lever to drag the bucket into a scooping motion, then began rolling the bucket forward by moving the right control lever to the left. It sounds like I was smooth, but I wasn't. I did some serious damage to the nearby equipment and the poured foundation didn't come up easily. It took some time.

Finally I had attracted some attention. Outside the construction fence there were six people shouting at me to stop. Pleading with me actually. I pretended not to see them, I definitely didn't hear them. I kept at it for one more pass before one of the six produced keys to open the fence.

I stopped the boom and shut the *4CX-17 Super* down. The area was quiet. The small crowd was no longer yelling at me, they were pointing at the bucket at the end of the boom, the looks on their faces were ones of horror.

There was a navy-blue Converse *All-Star* sneaker sticking out of the bucket. It was attached to a leg wearing dirty denim jeans. The leg was protruding out of a concrete chunk of foundation that was dug out of one of the trusses. It looked like a concrete lollipop stuck out of the bucket of a backhoe. The lollipop stick was a denim leg and sneaker.

The fun was over.

Sometimes I hate being right.

40

ALMOST THE ENTIRE CHARLESTON HOMICIDE DIVISION AND EVERY CSU investigator arrived within a half-hour of digging a clothed leg and foot out of the newly poured foundation. Whatever cop wasn't at the Platist church behind the Magnolia Cemetery was now at the Magnolia Reptile Zoo . They had utilized a service road so as not to disturb the rest of the patrons who had paid admission that day. The fenced-in construction area was cordoned off with police tape. It was as if the durable construction barrier was an easily dismissed suggestion and the thin, plastic, yellow police tape was a demand. It was the velvet rope syndrome in plain use.

The denim leg and hipster sneaker that was found, was a detached and severed limb. The remaining concrete was broken off of the appendage, requiring the equivalent of an archeological dig to recover the rest of the body. The CSU did a preliminary examination of the leg, determining that it was recent and was removed from a body of a male. In other words, not Carina.

I was both relieved and discouraged. I had come to the zoo thinking that she was being held here. The reptile wing was closed for renovations making it a prime location for nefarious bidding. I didn't find Carina. Instead, part of a male corpse was discovered that was recently buried under newly poured concrete.

It was beginning to seem like I would never find her. Ideas for further investigation were absent from my brain.

The very dramatic and destructive act of using the heavy equipment to dig up the construction area was devised to attract attention. I wanted to tear down the Platist's playhouse and draw them out into the open. Let them know that it was over. I had the suspicion when I first came upon the construction site but I was hoping that there wouldn't be a body under the foundation. That is what I told myself at any rate.

JG was late in getting over to the site. He had been busy with court filings and heading over to Leath to tell Dr. Sierra Byrne the good news. The motion hearing the following day, on Friday morning, was the only formality in delaying her immediate release. She was going home an innocent woman.

When he arrived, I was already stuffed in the back of a police cruiser. Captain Simms was still extremely pissed-off. Thankful that he was going to have a murder solved, one that he didn't yet know existed, but displeased that I was still in his jurisdiction and causing so much damage was an understatement.

Had I been sitting on my handcuffs in the back of the cop car the entire time, I would have been displeased. But I had moved my hands down below my butt and looped my legs through, working my hands to the front, in my lap. While my hands were moving past my ass, I pushed my wallet out of my back pocket and onto the seat. My pins were located in there. It was much more difficult to pick the lock on the handcuffs, especially with my hands in them, but I was able to get free.

Simms and JG came to the cruiser, releasing me. I handed the Captain the police handcuffs. This didn't further ingratiate me. He was much more calm than when he had me put there, however.

"Any leads on who the leg belonged to?" I asked both men, but I had assumed that Captain Simms was in the better position to comment.

"We are still pulling parts of him out of dirt and concrete but we have a hit on the hand that we found."

"And?"

"And it is an ongoing investigation in which you are not apart of."

"So I lead you here, and you are giving me nothing back?"

"There is more than one person under there."

"Oh shit. Carina?"

Simms looked at his shoes. He said nothing but he didn't need to. I read my answer in his body language.

"Fuck …. Ah, shit. No question? Definitely her?" I could lie and say that tears weren't welling up in my eyes, that I didn't have a horrible knot in my throat, but I won't. It was the feeling that you get when you know something absolutely fucking horrible has happened; where you know the truth but nobody had proven it to you yet, so you hold hope when there really isn't any.

"It's her," Simms said. He was still looking at his shoes, probably for the same reason I was trying to hide my eyes.

"And there were others?"

662

"So far one other. The reporter I used to draw out Sky Phillips. Lance Grober. The leg. His wife had reported him missing but it hadn't been twenty-four hours yet, so they blew her off. How am I going to tell her that it was our scheme that got him killed?"

"It was my scheme. It's my fault."

"Yeah well, it doesn't really matter does it? You're not a cop and I made the phone call. We will be lucky if she doesn't sue the City."

"It worked though. I wouldn't have known for sure how to get at the Platists, known to go to the hidden church. Known to come here. He would still be missing."

"I'm sure that will be a big comfort. I'll have to remember that when I'm giving her the news that her husband was cut up into pieces."

"I'm just trying to — "

" — I know what you are trying to do. Did you know that you were almost killed by Detective Fischer's gun?"

"What? What are you talking about?"

"Those tears in your cheek and forehead were ricochets off the shots fired at you in the church, right? The statement you gave the officer on the phone said that you were fired upon."

"Yes .... "

"The weapon that you recovered from the, uh, suspect at the church? The one you gave me when I arrived? It was Carina's Sig."

"Holy shit. How were they going to explain that away? If they had killed me."

"Lord only knows. You would have been the next one buried down under the foundation I would bet. Carina would never be recovered, nor you for that matter."

"I lost track of how many times people have tried to kill me. This case alone. Speaking of which, what are we going to do about Feinstein, Estabados, and recovering Stubb's body?"

JG interjected. "That is out of Captain Simm's hands. Feds are involved. Whether they were involved in the mass murder in Costa Rica, or if it was the Platists, they're taking over."

"So we went down there for nothing?"

"No. If it weren't for you and Stubbs those bodies may have never been found. There would be no closure to any of those disappearances, no closure for the families of the victims," JG said.

"You'll have to pardon me if I don't feel like a fuckin' hero. Stubbs, Carina .... "

Simms said, "We will make sure that justice is done. For both of them."

"You're out. It's on the Feds now. Besides, there will never be enough justice."

"That's the best we can do, Deni."

"All the justice in the world won't mend a beat-up heart."

663

The walk back to JG's car was a long one. Not because it was far away, but because we took it slow. I was going to get a ride from him, down the service road, and over to the *AMG* in the main parking lot of Magnolia Zoo. JG wanted to talk, I really didn't.

"Are you all right?"

"I'm pretty far from OK. This entire trip, this entire case, has been a kick in tha dick."

"I know and I — "

" — no ya don't know. Stubbs, Carina .... "

I didn't finish my thought. I couldn't. I was emotional and I didn't want to talk about it. We walked for about thirty yards before JG decided he had something else to get off of his chest.

"Just listen to me. Please. You did what you were supposed to do. I've told you that. Your job was to uncover evidence that would exonerate Sierra, and you did that. Everything else that you've accomplished is over and above what was asked of you. The espionage, the mass murders in Costa Rica, the serial murders here in Charleston .... all will be solved because of you. Justice will be done because of your work. You should be proud of yourself."

"Save it, Jacob. Really. I appreciate that you are trying to cheer me up, but take a break from it. Please. Just give me a ride back to the car."

"And then what? What are you going to do from there, Deni?"

"Get drunk. I'm going to try and forget that all this shit ever happened to me and get absolutely polluted."

EPILOGUE

I STAYED IN CHARLESTON FOR A FEW MORE WEEKS. To some degree because I needed the rest. I couldn't go back to Boston and start on a new case. Not yet. I had a beat-up heart from a new friend that I had lost and a new lover that I was certain that I had loved and lost. I needed to see what was going to be done about them.

Venom was supposed to save millions of lives. The cures would prolong life, save relationships, allow new ones to form. Yet the pursuit had killed so many. Costa Rica. Charleston. Who knows where else. Those kids were so young, all they wanted was to make a difference. And they died in heap with indifference.

The serial murders surrounding BIOGENESIS, SCMU, and the World Toxin Bank were about inhibiting the discovery of new cures. How a religious group could take the lives of those who were vested in saving millions was beyond my belief system. Would the rest of the people involved ever be held accountable? JG had told me that they would, but I still had my doubts.

There was an investigation into the Platists. Captain Simms wanted to make sure that all parties involved in what had happened to the five victims including the reporter and Detective Fischer, were made to pay for their crimes. That was going to take some time.

One fact that had come to light, was that the reason Sky Phillips knew her way around campus was because she, and her cohorts at the Magnolia Zoo, were always on the campus. She was always delivering snakes or lab mice to the various labs spread out throughout SCMU. I found it odd that they would work so closely with the very being that was supposed to be the root-sum of all evil. But that group was filled with contradictions.

Rueben Feinstein was handed over to the Feds. The US Attorney' Office was putting together a case against him. The Federal Prosecutor was a real hard-ass, which was a good thing. In my mind though, Feinstein would eventually cut a deal. That slippery son-of-a-bitch would say or do anything to keep his ass out of jail. My guess is that he would testify against his minion, Estabados.

That same hard-ass prosecutor was instrumental in apprehending Dr. Enrique Estabados from the Costa Rican Government. The Doctor was also being housed in segregation at a Federal Prison. He probably had to put every lie he ever told henceforth in writing. Stubbs had made sure that he would never speak a lie again. I hoped that Feinstein and Estabados had adjoining cells.

The rumor was that it was going to be years before either Feinstein or Estabados were brought to justice. There would be a lengthy investigation, followed by a lengthy trial. I toasted myself that those two fuckers wouldn't be breathing free air any time soon, if ever again.

The funerals of Eric Stubbs and Detective Carina Fischer were held separately. Both were widely attended.

Carina's was first. Her body was local and less red tape surrounded her arrangements. She had the full 'gone but not forgotten' honor service. The City was at a complete standstill. All officers were in their starched uniforms and white gloves to pay their final respects. Her closed casket was topped with her peaked cap and white gloves. The procession and three-volley salute drew as many tears as there were people. After which I got fuckin' hammered.

Stubbs's took a bit more time. His funeral was held almost two weeks later, held at Saint Michael's on Broad Street. It is one of the largest churches in the Southeast and it wasn't nearly big enough. He was a local celebrity for his fifteen seconds as a professional football player. He was also loved by everyone who knew him. All of the press surrounding his death, in part to grease the wheels of his return home, had further moved him toward sainthood. Nothing happened in Charleston that day either. There had to be tens of thousands of people around the church and the cemetery. I almost killed something when we arrived at Magnolia Cemetery to bury him. The small make-shift Platist church off in the distance was mocking me. I drank myself to sleep that night also.

I was staying with JG, Sierra, and Brady for the first couple of days but the constant inebriation was too much for any of them. JG was not much of a drinker anymore. He had been once-upon-a-time, and still had a craft beer once in a blue moon, but had given it up for the most part just prior to leaving New Hampshire.

Sierra was grateful for her freedom but judgmental. Even in my state I could see her looking down her nose at me. I hardly knew her, so it was just as unfair of me to judge her.

Brady didn't like it either. That's what JG said anyway. I moved to a nice hotel, the penthouse suite, and I never had to pay the bill. I probably couldn't afford the cost of the mini-bar.

The day after Stubbs's funeral, I was summoned by Captain Simms. Meaning that police officers had come to collect me. I was again stuffed in the back of an unmarked cruiser and taxied to 80 Broad.

It was difficult to say if I was more hungover or drunk. Probably a mix of both. I was depressed. I wasn't working out, and I was hardly eating. All of my meals were liquid. The alcohol was not helping me out of it, but was pushing me further into it. I know that in retrospect, though at the time it seemed to heal what was ailing me.

The officers never told me why I was being dragged over to the police station. I was in no mood or condition to get into a confrontation, or even resist in any event. On the ride over I had convinced myself that I was being arrested for my involvement in the deaths of my friend and of Carina. If I had to do it all over again, I would have found a way to do it differently.

I was a mess, and those that witnessed the two officers helping me into the station probably thought I was a perp. For all I knew, I was. Captain Simms looked at me with pity and concern.

"Taking this kinda hard, aren't you? You didn't know either of them very well did you?"

"Stubbs is in a box instead of me. He made sure I got out of the jungle. That means something to me."

"And Detective Fischer?"

"You know damn well why I'm upset about her. I've never met a woman like her. Probably never will again."

"I have your gun. It was found on Stubbs but is registered to you here in South Carolina. Taurus *PT1911*. The Feds' ballistics team cleared it. None of the GSWs on the bodies down in Central America match this weapon."

"Stubbs gave me that gun."

"And in your current state, I will continue to keep it safe for you."

"What does that mean?"

"It means you are going to get dried out."

I was put in lock-up within the bowels of the police building, fortunately in my own cell. I slept for two days straight other than to take a piss. They offered food but I don't remember eating.

JG and Sierra had come to collect me after my rest in the jail. There was no bail to post, I wasn't being charged with anything. They had been called to come pick me up and it was hoped that they would encourage me to leave Charleston.

Captain Simms was happy to be rid of me, shook my hand, and I'm sure he hoped it would be for the last time. He had me sign for my property, including my gun. All things considered it was rather nice of him.

The ride to the hotel produced little conversation. The country song *I Will Never Forget You*, by that young girl who won on the show *The Voice*, Danielle Bradbery, was softly playing on the car radio. I was a little choked up. Don't judge me, listen to it.

While I was packing my things in the hotel room, JG sat on one of the plush chairs and spoke.

"You don't *have* to leave. Nobody is forcing you to. You could stay down here, I need a Lead Investigator."

"I have two homes, one in New Hampshire, one in South Boston, and a business up there. I can't just …. I can't stay here after everything that has happened, even if I wanted to."

"You have been. I'm not sure if you know how long you've been down here."

"What is this an intervention? I'm going home."

"No, it's not. And I thought you would say that. I just wanted you to know that I appreciate everything that you have done and all that you have endured. I'm sorry I got you into this mess."

Sierra came out of the bathroom or the other room of the suite.

"I'm not sure I'll ever be able to thank you enough, Warren."

"You can start by calling me Deni. And we don't ever have to bring this up again, if you ask me."

She nodded like she understood. JG gave me a 9x12 manilla envelope.

"You're pay. I think the check in there should cover you. Also the title to the Mercedes AMG. I'll take care of the rest of the expenses on the credit card I gave you."

"*Oh yeah.* You probably want that back."

"It had crossed my mind."

"Listen, about the car. You don't have to — "

" — its the least I can do. Besides, its best if you don't fly home with a pistol. I had the Mercedes detailed, pulled anything that was mine out of it. The valet has it when you check out." He tossed the valet chip at me.

"Will you say goodbye to Brady for me?"

"Sure will. He wants a pet snake, and he wants to name it Deni."

"You're shitting me."

I had a sixteen hour drive ahead of me up to Boston. I headed out that night. I'd had enough sleep to get me there without a lengthy stop, but I would if I felt like it. I was in no rush. I think JG gave me the car because he knew I wouldn't drink and drive. Drinking and flying was another story.

I got on Interstate 95 and headed North. I left Charleston, South Carolina behind me. The memory of the events that took place there, however, leaving those behind is another story.

668

AUTHOR'S NOTES
AND ACKNOWLEDGEMENTS

The previous work is one of fiction, any resemblance to specific and true incidents is purely coincidental. Some of the places, laws, crimes, procedures and the prison experiences are based upon real research, however. They were used to add a legitimate feel to a completely fabricated story. Without the help of the people and entities listed below, this book at worst doesn't get written, at best isn't nearly as rich and believable.

There is no such university as SCMU that I am aware of, though there are many educational and research facilities that this fictitious place emulates. There is no venom library there, obviously, but the World Toxin Bank does exist and is helmed by Zoltan Takacs. He left the University of Chicago to collect "blueprints for toxin libraries". This library holds all the liquid gold secreted from animals the world over, and is used to research and create synthetic drugs. The research is real, the cures are also very real and/or just a step or two away from being in your medicine cabinet. The creepy-crawlies that scare us out of our minds, fodder for horror movies and halloween , are the very things that will cure what ails us. Very poetic I think.

The faction of Christian Science which I named Platists in this novel, are not real per se. In every legitimate group, there are always the outliers that take themselves a bit too seriously. While these particular outliers are not named Platists, they do exist. The old adage "there is one in every crowd" came from someplace. Or places. This debatable cult or religion is no exception. The beliefs and the history of Christian Science have been tweaked a bit to suit the needs of the story, but generally hold true. It was not my intention to impugn any religion or cult, but merely use the facts to enrich a story. Many thanks to the Mary Baker Eddy Library in Boston, MA, for their hospitality despite not agreeing with one single thing that I said. I would encourage any and all to read not only the works that I cited, but others as well to form your own opinion. The Christian Science Monitor has won seven Pulitzer Prizes from 1950-2002. Many thanks to them for speaking with me, and they too are located in Boston, MA.

I would like to thank the people of Costa Rica, especially the fine folks at Clodomiro Picado Institute, the Serpentario Monteverde Costa Rica, the Corcovado National Park, The

Monteverde Cloud Forest Reserve, the HUGE pharmaceutical company and research universities they sponsor (which will remain unnamed per their request) for your unbelievable hospitality. Your patience throughout all of my questions and incessant screams for safety amidst the snakes is the stuff of sainthood.

To my friends, family and acquaintances who are a part of this novel in spirit. I hope that you can see yourselves in some of the characters, as I drew upon the nuances of your characters that make you who you are, to make mine come alive. Thank you for being a part of my life and part of the fabric of this work.

Finally, but most importantly, I would like to take the time to thank those that spoke to me in "hypotheticals" or "off the record". You risked your livelihood to speak to me about your expertise and your organizations. Be it the FBI or the Big Pharma Company that shall go unnamed, I thank you with all of my being. I am just a guy trying to spin a good yarn. Without your insights into the mind of a serial killer, policies and procedures, drug procedures and legislation, and many many other topics, this is little yarn never gets spun. If you enjoyed this book, it is largely because of them.

Thanks for your time and I hope you enjoyed the read.

-sw-

REFERENCES

Apitherapy (http://www.cancer.org/docroot/ETO/content/ETO_5_3XApitherapy.asp?sitearea=ETO). From American Cancer Society.

Bartol, Curt R.; Anne M. Bartol. (2004). *Introduction To Forensic Psychology: Research and Application.*

Bates, Ernest Sutherland and Dittmore, John V. *Mary Baker Eddy: The Truth and the Tradition.* A.A. Knopf, 1932.

Bellwald, A.M. *Christian Science and the Catholic Faith* (http://archive.org/details/ christianscience00belluoft). The MacMillan Company, 1922.

Bradeb, Charles S. *Spirits in Rebellion: The Rise and Development of New Thought.* Southern Methodist University Press, 1963.

British Medical Journal. "Mark Twain on Christian Science" (http:// www.ncbi.nlm.nih.gov/pmc/articles/PMC2412999/?page=7), 2(2025), October 21, 1899.

Camfield, Gragg. *The Oxford Companion to Mark Twain.* Oxford University Press, 2003.

Cather, Willa and Milmine, Georgine. *The Life of Mary Baker G. Eddy and the History of Christian Science* (http://www.unz.org/Pub/MilmineGeorgine-1909). Doubleday 1909, latest edition University of Nebraska Press, 1993.

Censo Nacional 2011 (http://www.inec.go.cr/Web/Home/pagPrincipal.aspx)

Clodomiro Picado Institute. Costa Rica. Various Interviews.

College of Agriculture and Life Sciences. University of Arizona. Various interviews.

Commonwealth vs. David R. Twitchell (http://masscases.com/cases/sjc/ 416/416mass114.html), decision of the 1993 appeal.

Corcovado National Park. Costa Rica. Guided tour.

Eddy, Mary Baker. *Historical Sketch of Christian Science Mind-healing,* 1888.

Eddy, Mary Baker. *Miscellaneous Writings,* 1897.

Fox, James Alan; Jack Levin (2005). *Extreme Killing: Understanding Serial and Mass Murder.*

Gardner, Martin. **"Mind Over Matter"** (http://articles.latimes.com/1999/aug/22/books/bk-2412), *Los Angeles Times,* August 22, 1999.

Holland, Jennifer S. **"Venom"**, *National Geographic,* February 2013 (p. 68-83).

Kaplan, Fred. *The Singular Mark Twain: A Biography.* Anchor, 2005.

Multiple Sclerosis Society, *Bee Venom Study* (http://www.mssociety.ca/en/research/CAT980602.htm)

Organization for Tropical Studies. (http://www.ots.duke.edu/)

Quimby, Phineas Parkhurst. *The Complete Collected Works of Dr. Phineas Parkhurst Quimby.* Seed of Life Publishing, 2009, first published 1921.

Serpentario Monteverde Costa Rica. Costa Rica. Various Interviews.

South Carolina Code of Laws, Unannotated (current through end of 2013 session). *South Carolina Legislature,* Title 40, chapter 18, sections 20-372.

The Monteverde Cloud Forest Reserve. Costa Rica. Various Interviews and guided tours.

Twain, Mark. *Christian Science* (http://www.gutenberg.org/ebooks/3187), 1907

Vitello, Paul. **"Christian Science Church Seeks Truce With Modern Medicine"** (http://www.nytimes.com/2010/03/24/nyregion/24heal.html), *The New York Times,* March 23, 2010

ABOUT THE
AUTHOR

Photo ©2013 WWPGroup

Scott Wellinger is a well-traveled writer and novelist. He has ghost-written many articles, scripts, and essays as well as under pseudo names. His Scott Wellinger novels feature, among others, the fictitious private investigations of Warren Dennihan. A native of New England, he was born in Vermont and was educated in Boston, Massachusetts. He holds a Master's Degree in Applied Economics and when he is not traveling, he is on a golf course.